Although J.R.R. Tolkien is well-known for *The Hobbit*, *The Lord of the Rings* and *The Silmarillion*, the material which laid the groundwork for what must be the most fully realised sub-creation ever to spring from a single imagination was begun many years before the publication of *The Hobbit*, and indeed Tolkien continued to work upon its completion until his death in 1973.

In one of the single largest works of 'literary archaeology' ever undertaken, J.R.R. Tolkien's son and literary executor, Christopher Tolkien, edited the vast collection of manuscripts together with maps and illustrations and these were posthumously published in twelve volumes as *The History of Middle-earth*.

Christopher Tolkien also compiled a very detailed and thorough index for each of these books. This companion edition to the twelve-volume *History* now brings together all of the indexes in one place, together with their introductory notes, and provides the reader with an invaluable source book to all the peoples, places and other significant entries from *The Silmarillion* and *The Lord of the Rings* which appear in *The History of Middle-earth*.

Works by J.R.R. Tolkien

THE HOBBIT
LEAF BY NIGGLE
ON FAIRY-STORIES
FARMER GILES OF HAM
THE HOMECOMING OF BEORHTNOTH
THE LORD OF THE RINGS
THE ADVENTURES OF TOM BOMBADIL
THE ROAD GOES EVER ON (WITH DONALD SWANN)
SMITH OF WOOTTON MAJOR

Works published posthumously

SIR GAWAIN AND THE GREEN KNIGHT, PEARL AND SIR ORFEO*
THE FATHER CHRISTMAS LETTERS
THE SILMARILLION*
PICTURES BY J.R.R. TOLKIEN*
UNFINISHED TALES*
THE LETTERS OF J.R.R. TOLKIEN*
FINN AND HENGEST
MR BLISS
THE MONSTERS AND THE CRITICS & OTHER ESSAYS*
ROVERANDOM
THE CHILDREN OF HÚRIN*
THE LEGEND OF SIGURD AND GUDRÚN*
THE FALL OF ARTHUR*
BEOWULF: A TRANSLATION AND COMMENTARY*
THE STORY OF KULLERVO
THE LAY OF AOTROU AND ITROUN
BEREN AND LÚTHIEN*
THE FALL OF GONDOLIN*
THE NATURE OF MIDDLE-EARTH
THE FALL OF NÚMENOR

The History of Middle-earth – by Christopher Tolkien

I THE BOOK OF LOST TALES, PART ONE
II THE BOOK OF LOST TALES, PART TWO
III THE LAYS OF BELERIAND
IV THE SHAPING OF MIDDLE-EARTH
V THE LOST ROAD AND OTHER WRITINGS
VI THE RETURN OF THE SHADOW
VII THE TREASON OF ISENGARD
VIII THE WAR OF THE RING
IX SAURON DEFEATED
X MORGOTH'S RING
XI THE WAR OF THE JEWELS
XII THE PEOPLES OF MIDDLE-EARTH

* Edited by Christopher Tolkien

THE HISTORY OF
MIDDLE-EARTH
INDEX

CHRISTOPHER TOLKIEN

HarperCollins*Publishers*

HarperCollins*Publishers* Ltd
1 London Bridge Street
London SE1 9GF

HarperCollins*Publishers*
Macken House, 39/40 Mayor Street Upper
Dublin 1, D01 C9W8, Ireland

www.tolkien.co.uk
www.tolkienestate.com

A Paperback Original 2002
19

First published in Great Britain by HarperCollins*Publishers* 2002

All material previously published in the following books:
The Book of Lost Tales I first published in Great Britain by George Allen &
Unwin 1983; *The Book of Lost Tales II* first published in Great Britain by George
Allen & Unwin 1984; *The Lays of Beleriand* first published in Great Britain by
George Allen & Unwin 1985; *The Shaping of Middle-earth* first published in Great
Britain by George Allen & Unwin 1986; *The Lost Road and other writings* first
published in Great Britain by Unwin Hyman 1987; *The Return of the Shadow*
first published in Great Britain by Unwin Hyman 1988; *The Treason of Isengard*
first published in Great Britain by Unwin Hyman 1989; *The War of the Ring* first
published in Great Britain by Unwin Hyman 1990; *Sauron Defeated* first published
in Great Britain by HarperCollins*Publishers* 1992; *Morgoth's Ring* first published
in Great Britain by HarperCollins*Publishers* 1993; *The War of the Jewels* first
published in Great Britain by HarperCollins*Publishers* 1994; *The Peoples of
Middle-earth* first published in Great Britain by HarperCollins*Publishers* 1996

Copyright © The Tolkien Estate Limited and C.R. Tolkien 1983, 1984, 1985,
1986, 1987, 1988, 1989, 1990, 1992, 1993, 1994, and 1996

This edition copyright © HarperCollins*Publishers* 2002

ISBN 978-0-00-713743-5

Printed and bound in the UK using
100% renewable electricity at CPI Group (UK) Ltd

MIX
Paper | Supporting
responsible forestry
FSC
www.fsc.org
FSC™ C007454

NOTE

This book has been compiled from the various indexes contained in the twelve volumes of *The History of Middle-earth*. It provides the reader with a single A–Z listing of all the peoples, places and other significant entries that Christopher Tolkien compiled in his original indexes.

For ease of reference, there is a separate listing for any entry which appears in more than one of the twelve volumes, e.g. see '*Ainur*'. The reference codes are explained as follows:

I	The Book of Lost Tales, Part One
II	The Book of Lost Tales, Part Two
III	The Lays of Beleriand
IV	The Shaping of Middle-earth
V	The Lost Road
VI	The Return of the Shadow
VII	The Treason of Isengard
VIII	The War of the Ring
IXa	Sauron Defeated – The End of the Third Age
IXb	Sauron Defeated – The Notion Club Papers and The Drowning of Anadûnê
X	Morgoth's Ring
XI	The War of the Jewels
XII	The Peoples of Middle-earth

In addition to the various indexes, the accompanying prefaratory notes by Christopher Tolkien are also included, which provide further information on the nature and content of the lists of entries.

INDEX

Notes on the index of The History of Middle-earth vol. 1 –
The Book of Lost Tales Part I

This index provides (in intention) complete page-references to all entries
with the exception of *Eldar/Elves*, *Gods/Valar*, and *Valinor*; the entries
include the rejected name-forms given in the Notes, but the Appendix
on Names is not covered.

Occasionally references are given to pages where a person or place
is not actually named, as 'the door-ward' p. 46 under *Rúmil*. References
are given to mentions of Tales that will appear in Part II, but not to
mentions of those in this book. The explanatory statements are kept
very brief, and names defined in the Index to *The Silmarillion* are not
as a rule explained here.

Notes on the index of The History of Middle-earth vol. 2 –
The Book of Lost Tales Part II

This index is made on the same basis as that to Part I, but selected references are given in rather more cases, and the individual *Lost Tales* are not included. In view of the large number of names that appear in Part II fairly full cross-references are provided to associated names (earlier and later forms, equivalents in different languages, etc.). As in the index to Part I, the more important names occurring in *The Silmarillion* are not given explanatory definitions; and references sometimes include passages where the person or place is not actually named.

Notes on the index of The History of Middle-earth vol. 3 –
The Lays of Beleriand

This index is made on the same lines as those to *The Book of Lost Tales* Parts I and II, and like them it is intended to provide (with only a few exceptions) complete references to all entries, and includes occasional references to passages where the person or place is not actually named. The note on the submission of the *Lay of Leithian* and *The Silmarillion* in 1937 is not indexed.

Notes on the index of The History of Middle-earth vol. 4 – *The Shaping of Middle-earth*

This Index, like those of the previous volumes, attempts both to provide an almost complete register and to give some indication of the inter-relations of names for the same places, persons, and events; but from the nature of this book the range of such variation is here particularly large, and some names appear in complicated relations (and several languages), so that inconsistency in the arrangement of the material has been hard to avoid.

In general, Modern English names are not given separate entries when they occur solely in association with an Elvish name, but are included under the latter.

Page-references include the occurrences of names in Ælfwine's works in Old English ('O.E.'), but these are not distinguished as such unless the name has a distinctive Old English form; and in such cases the Old English name is not given a separate entry, but included under the original name (as *Elfethýð* under *Alqualondë*).

Names that occur on the first 'Silmarillion' map and its Eastward and Westward extensions are not referenced to the reproductions them-selves, but those on the *Ambarkanta* maps and diagrams are (including the emended names that are noticed on the facing pages, as *Silma* > *Ilma* > *Ilmen*): all these references are preceded by an asterisk.

References to the published *Silmarillion* are not included, and those to the individual tales of *The Book of Lost Tales* are collected under the entry *Lost Tales*.

So many variant arrangements of capitalisation and hyphenation are found in compound names in the texts (as *Sarn–athrad*, *Sarn-Athrad*, *Sarn Athrad*) that I have adopted a single form for the purposes of the Index.

The vast array of forms contained in Part III of this book constitutes
a problem in respect of the Index. In the first place, a large number of
names found in the *Etymologies* do not occur elsewhere in the book, and
in many cases names are registered in greatly varying forms according to
the divergent phonetic development in the different languages. In the
second place, discussion of the history of names and the isolation of
their elements makes the distinction between 'name' and 'common
word' unreal; for the purposes of this 'etymological dictionary' *Alqualondë* illustrates *alqua* 'swan' and *londë* 'harbour-entrance, roads'. But
to list alphabetically even a proportion of these Elvish 'common words'
in Part III would be preposterous, since (quite apart from the practical
consideration of length) it would mean rewriting the 'dictionary' in
such a way as to conceal the historical relation between words which
it is the object of the work to display.

I have in fact excluded the whole content of the Etymologies from
normal representation in the Index, but I have attempted to assist reference to them in the following ways. (1) In the page-references to names
that do occur elsewhere in the book I include also pages in the *Etymologies* where these names are explained – all such references being
printed in *italics*. As a general rule I restrict these references to actual
occurrence in the *Etymologies* of the name in question, but I have
departed from this rule where it seemed useful to provide a reference
to an element in a name that only appears in the *Etymologies* as a
'common word' (e.g. *nyárë* 'tale, saga, history' under *Eldanyárë*). (2)
Where the *Etymologies* give names for persons, peoples, or places that
are different from those found elsewhere in the book these are mentioned in the Index but not given separate entries; e.g. the Noldorin
names *Mirion* and *Núron* are given under *Silmarils* and *Ulmo*. By these
means, the great majority of names in the *Etymologies* are at least
indicated in the Index. But beyond this, the many curiosities of the
work – such as the structure of the Valinorian year and the names of

the days in the Valinorian 'week', or the etymology of *cram* – emerge only from the study of it.

From the large number of names that occur in or in association with *The Lost Road* I have excluded some of the more casual and insignificant. References are not given for names on the tables accompanying the *Lhammas* or on the reproductions of the second Map.

As before, I have adopted a single form of capitalisation and hyphenation for the purposes of the Index.

Notes on the index of The History of Middle-earth vol. 6 –
The Return of the Shadow

This Index is made on the same lines as those of the previous volumes, but the extreme fluidity of names in this case, especially among the hobbits, has proved taxing, as a glance at the entries under *Took* will show. The complexity of the matter to be indexed scarcely allows of a consistent presentation.

Certain names appear constantly throughout the book, and where possible I have reduced the more intimidating blocks of references by using the word *passim* to mean that a name is missing only from a single page here and there in a long series.

Forms are standardized, and no account is taken of the innumerable variants in capitalization, hyphenation, and separation of elements that occur in the texts.

Names appearing in the reproduction of pages from the original manuscripts are not indexed.

Notes on the index of The History of Middle-earth vol. 7 –
The Treason of Isengard

As in the Index to *The Return of the Shadow*, I have slightly reduced the number of page-references in the case of names that occur very frequently by using the word *passim* to mean that the name is missing only from a single page here and there in a long series otherwise unbroken.

The very large number of names occurring in this book that were soon rejected and replaced are nearly all given separate cross-references to a primary name; exceptions are cases where such a name falls in immediate proximity to the primary name (thus whereas *Dolamarth* is entered separately from *Amon Amarth*, *Amarthon* is not), and certain purely experimental names (such as the rejected names for *Amon Hen/ Amon Lhaw*). Names in *Errantry* are all entered under *Errantry*.

Names appearing on the redrawn maps, on the reproductions of pages from texts of *The Lord of the Rings*, and on the manuscript pages at the end of the *Appendix on Runes*, are not indexed.

Notes on the index of The History of Middle-earth vol. 8 –
The War of The Ring

In this book the variables are so many that the arrangement of the index, if it is to be more than a simple list of forms, becomes to some degree a matter of choice; for on the one hand there was a great deal of alteration and substitution among the names themselves, while on the other their application changed as the narrative, and the geography, changed. Thus for example the *Stone of Erech* was originally a *palantír*, but when it became a stone brought from Númenor the *palantír* (or *Stone*) of Erech was for a time still present; *Kirith Ungol* and *Minas Morghul* (*Morgul*) were several times shifted in relation to each other; and the Lord of Westfold was in succession *Trumbold*, *Heorulf* (*Herulf*), *Nothelm*, *Heorulf*, *Erkenwald*, *Erkenbrand*, while *Westfold* was originally *Westmarch* and the original *Westfold* was a region in the west of the Misty Mountains. I hope at any rate that my attempt will be found accurate and serviceable for all the inconsistencies of presentation.

With constantly recurring names I have used the device employed in *The Return of the Shadow* and *The Treason of Isengard* whereby the word *passim* means that in a long run of references no more than one page here and there happens not to carry that name. Names occurring on the maps and on the pages reproduced from the original manuscripts are not indexed, and only exceptionally those in chapter-titles. Under the entry *Old English* are collected only special instances, and not of course the very large number of names in Rohan that are in fact Old English.

Notes on the first index of The History of Middle-earth vol. 9 –
Sauron Defeated
To Part One *The End of the Third Age*

This first index is made with the same degree of fullness as those to the previous volumes dealing with the history of the writing of *The Lord of the Rings*. As before, names are mostly given in a 'standard' form; and certain names are not indexed: those occurring in the titles of chapters etc.; those of the recipients of letters; and those appearing in the reproductions of manuscript pages. The word *passim* is again used to mean that in a long run of references there is a page here and there where the name does not occur.

Notes on second index of The History of Middle-earth vol. 9 –
Sauron Defeated
To Part Two *The Notion Club Papers* and
Part Three *The Drowning of Anadûnê*

In view of the great array of names occurring in these two parts of the book this second index is a little more restricted in scope than the first, especially in the reduction or omission of explanatory identification in many cases, and to some extent in the amount of cross-reference to related names. A number of names occurring in the Notes to Part Two that are casual and insignificant outside the immediate context have been omitted, but very few from the actual texts of the Papers. Inevitably the choice between omission and inclusion in such cases is rather arbitrary. In the case of names from the works of C. S. Lewis and from Michael Ramer's accounts of his experiences their provenance is indicated by '[Lewis]' and '[Ramer]', often without further explanation.

The exclusions mentioned in the note to Index I are made here also; and names are similarly given in 'standard' form, especially in the matter of accents and marks of length: thus the circumflex is generally used in Adunaic names.

Members of the Notion Club are included under the surname, and references include the initials of members and pages on which the person speaks but is not named. All names of streets, colleges and other buildings in Oxford are collected under the entry *Oxford*. O.E. = Old English.

Many names and groups of names have given exceptional difficulty in organisation and presentation, for there are here not only several languages, changing forms within the languages, rejections and replacements of names, but also shifting identities and intended uncertainty of reference.

Notes on the index of The History of Middle-earth vol. 10 –
Morgoth's Ring

In this book certain names appear very frequently indeed throughout –
in the most extreme cases, *Valar* and *Melkor*, the number of reverences
is well over half the number of pages in the book. Such great blocks
of numbers must be of doubtful utility, but I have in fact included all
references in the index, apart from the occasional use as in previous
volumes of the word *passim* to cover a long run of references from
which only a single page is missing here and there. In some cases, as
in *Melkor, Elves*, I have in addition listed references to certain central
and recurrent topics. On pp. 470–1 will be found an appendix to the
index in which I have collected separately the large number of words
(many of them specialised terms) in the Elvish languages that occur in
the book.

Names occurring in the titles of chapters and other headings are not
normally indexed, nor are the names of the recipients of letters; and
individual 'Lost Tales' are not given separate entries.

Star-names

The names of the stars and constellations that appear on p. 160 are
mostly left unidentified in the index, despite much that has been written
on the subject since the publication of *The Silmarillion*; and this is a
convenient place to refer to a matter that I neglected to mention in the
text of the book. This concerns an isolated manuscript page preserved
with the texts of *The Lord of the Rings* at Marquette University; and
I am very grateful to Mr Charles B. Elston of Marquette for his help
on this question.

One side of this page carries primary drafting for a passage in Chapter
3 (*Of the Coming of the Elves*) of the *Quenta Silmarillion* (§§18a–19),
and the other a second draft for the same passage, which though very
roughly written almost reaches the text printed on pp. 159–60. I have
noticed (p. 158) that in the case of Chapter 3 my father himself made
a new text, intervening between the revision carried out on the old

pre-*Lord of the Rings* texts and the amanuensis typescript LQ 1; it was in that version of the chapter ('Text A') that the new material in §18a–19 entered (see p. 166, §19). The place of the Marquette page is thus very clearly defined; as drafting for the passage in Text A it belongs to the 1951 revision of *The Silmarillion*.

In the second, all but final, draft my father is seen in the act of devising the names of the constellations, with various experimental forms before those that appear in the final text were reached; but he set down the names of the stars without any hesitation, thus: *Karnil, Luinil, Nénar, Lumbar, Alkarinque, Elemmire*. Above *Karnil* he wrote 'M', above *Lumbar* 'S', above *Alkarinque* 'Jup', and above *Elemmire* again 'M'. No letter stands above *Luinil*, but above *Nénar* there is an 'N' which was struck out (Mr Elston informs me that this 'N' is perfectly clear in the original and that no other interpretation is possible).

Now if *Alkarinque* is Jupiter, then a great red star named *Karnil* and marked with 'M' must be Mars (cf. Michael Ramer's name *Karan* for Mars, IX.220) – which in turn leads to the identification of *Lumbar* ('S') with Saturn, and *Elemmire* ('M') with Mercury. In an article by Jorge Quiñonez and Ned Raggett, *Nólë i Meneldilo, Lore of the Astronomer*, published in the periodical *Vinyar Tengwar* no.12 (July 1990), the authors concluded that my father originally intended *Nénar* ('N') for the planet Neptune, but transferred the identification to *Luinil*, *Nénar* thus becoming Uranus. The six names, therefore, are the Elvish names of the planets other than Venus (*Eärendil*); and this conclusion appears to be no mere ingenious deduction but to derive from my father's own clear indications.

Nonetheless, I find it so extraordinary as to be altogether incredible. It is to be remembered that the six names appear in the context of the making by Varda of 'new stars *and brighter* against the coming of the First-born': they must be the names of very conspicuous objects in the heavens of Arda. That Mars and Jupiter, if not Saturn, should appear among them would seem inevitable, seeing that in my father's astronomical myth the planets were never distinguished from the 'fixed stars'; but how is it to be thought that *Nénar* and *Luinil*, self-evidently the names of great lights in the region of Ilmen, should refer to Uranus and Neptune, faint and minute among 'the innumerable stars', the one barely visible to the naked eye, and the other not at all? Reference in this connection to the extraordinary powers of sight possessed by the Elves is beside the point: because from the astronomical myth as presented in the *Annals of Aman* and in the first post-*Lord of the Rings* revision

of the *Quenta Silmarillion* the entire conceptual basis of the astronomy by which the remote planets of the Solar System were discoverable must of very nature be absent. But what then is to be said of the letter 'N' written above the name *Nénar*?

It seems to me quite possible that the six names existed before the writing of the draft page now at Marquette, even if they were never written down, and further, that some of them did not possess specific identifications with our names – though *Karnil* was surely always Mars, and *Alkarinque* no doubt Jupiter. On this hypothesis, I could well imagine (it would not be uncharacteristic) that as he reflected on these names my father amused himself by extending the list to include all the planets (with the exception of the Evening Star – and Pluto!), and whimsically, as one might say, with a sense both of appropriateness (associating the stem *nen-* 'water' with the sea-god) and essential inappropriateness, wrote in the N of Neptune above *Nénar*.

This is not of course offered as a formal and precise proposal in explanation of this extremely puzzling fact, but it does seem to me that something on these lines is very much more probable than that he seriously intended the name *Nénar* to signify the planet Neptune.

Notes on the index of The History of Middle-earth vol. 11 –
The War of the Jewels

As in the Index to *The Return of the Shadow*, I have slightly reduced the number of page-references in the case of names that occur very frequently by using the word *passim* to mean that the name is missing only from a single page here and there in a long series otherwise unbroken.

The very large number of names occurring in this book that were soon rejected and replaced are nearly all given separate cross-references to a primary name; exceptions are cases where such a name falls in immediate proximity to the primary name (thus whereas *Dolamarth* is entered separately from *Amon Amarth*, *Amarthon* is not), and certain purely experimental names (such as the rejected names for *Amon Hen/ Amon Lhaw*). Names in *Errantry* are all entered under *Errantry*.

Names appearing on the redrawn maps, on the reproductions of pages from texts of *The Lord of the Rings*, and on the manuscript pages at the end of the *Appendix on Runes*, are not indexed.

Notes on the index of The History of Middle-earth vol. 12 –
The Peoples of Middle-earth

The very great number of names occurring in this book, and the frequency of reference in many cases, would require an index much larger than those of the previous volumes if the same pattern were followed; and I have therefore reduced it by omitting three categories of names. Each of these is concentrated in a small part of the book, and in the case of the second and third it seems to me that, even apart from considerations of overall length, the utility of detailing alphabetically such complex material is very doubtful.

(1) *Hobbit names*. The number of names of individual Hobbits, including all the recorded changes, is so large (about 370) that I have restricted the references to the entry *Hobbit-families*. Here all the family-names are listed, with references to every page (including all the genealogical tables) where the name of the family, or of any member of the family, occurs. Exceptions to this are Bilbo and Frodo Baggins, Sam Gamgee, Meriadoc Brandybuck, and Peregrin Took, who are entered separately in the index on account of the large number of references to them.

(2) *The Calendars*. All page-references for the names of the *months* and the *days of the week* in the different languages are collected under those entries. Under *Calendars* are listed the entries in the index concerning the matter of Chapter IV, and references to the Elvish names and terms are given under *Calendars* and *Seasons*

(3) *The Common Speech*. References are given under *Common Speech* and *Hobbit families* to all pages where 'true' names (supposed to underlie the 'translated' names) appear, these being only exceptionally included in the index.

The entries *Second Age*, *Third Age* and *Shire-reckoning* do not include simple references to dates. Some names spelt with initial C in

The Lord of the Rings will be found under *K*: *Calimehtar, Calimmacil, Calmacil, Castamir, Cemendur, Cirith Ungol, Ciryaher (Ciryahir), Ciryandil.*

Abari (XI) See *Avari*.

Abarzâyan (IXb) The Land of Gift. 378, 388, 396. (Replaced by Yôzâyan.)

Abonnen (XI) See *Apanónar*.

Abrazân (IXb) Lowdham's Adunaic name for Jeremy. 252, 290. See *Voronwë* (2).

Adan (XI) See *Edain*.

Adanel (X) Sister of Hador Lórindol; a 'Wise-woman'. 305-7, 309, 313, 328, 344-5; *Tale of Adanel* 344-9, 354, 360

Adanel (XI) 'Wise-woman' of the People of Marach. 230-1, 233-5

Adrahil (XII) Twenty-first Prince of Dol Amroth. 32, 36, 206, 220-1, 223, 240; earlier *Agrahil* 220

Adrahil of Dol Amroth (VIII) 340

Adûnâi (IXb) Men of Westernesse. 305, 312, 361-6, 368, 371-5, 379, 385-6, 388, 438. See *Adûnâim*.

Adûnaic (V) 75, 149

Adûnaic (VIII) 161

Adunaic (IXb) 147-8. 241, 246-8, 259, 284, 286, 288, 290, 292, 304, 306, 309-13, 340, 356, 375-6, 379, 387-90, 397, 406, 413-39 (Lowdham's *Report*), 439-40; Lowdham's *Language B* or *Númenórean B* 238-41, 247-8, 305-6, 309, 379

    Adunaic (IXb) Adunaic cited (including single words and stems) 240-1, 247-8, 250-1, 288, 290, 305-6, 377; 413-39 (the language described)

Adûnaic (X) 4, 7, 28, 42

Adûnaic (XI) 390, 402, 419

Adûnaic (XII) 31-2, 34, 55, 63-5, 75, 79, 140, 146, 155, 157-8, 314-15, 317, 320, 330, 364-5, 368-72, 376. See *Númenórean*.

Adûnâim (IXb) Men of Westernesse (replaced *Adûnai* in narrative). 240, 312, 375, 382, 388, 391-2, 394, 413, 426, 433

Adûni; Adûnar, Andúnar (XII) See *Common Speech*.

Adurant, River (IV) 135, 189, 230, 331, 335

Adurant, River (V) 128, 263, 268, 305–6, *349*

Adurant, River (VII) In Ossiriand. 271

Adurant, River (XI) In Ossiriand. 13, *185, 191, 195

Adventures of Tom Bombadil, The (I) 27, 32, 204

Aegnor (X) Son of Finarfin (=Finrod (1)). 177, 323–4, (325–6), 327, 335, 357; *Ægnor* 197; earlier form *Egnor* 113, 121, 125–6, 177, 182, 195–7, 327–8. See *Aikanár*.

Aegnor (XII) Son of Finarfin. 346–7, 350; other names *Aikanáro* 346–7, 363, *Ambaráto (Amrod)* 347

Ælfhâm (II) Old English) 'Elfhome'. 301–2. See *Eldaros*.

Ælfhâm (IV) (Old English) 'Elfhome'. 257. See *Eldaros*.

Ælfheah (II) (Old English) Companion of Ælfwine; called 'the fatherless'. 315–16, 320, 323, 330, 332–4. (Replaced *Gelimer*.)

Ælfred of Wessex (II) (language of) 301

Ælfwinas (IXb) See *Elf-friends*.

Ælfwine (I) 'Elf-friend', later name for Eriol. 24, 49, 107, 234; the tale of *Ælfwine of England* (I) 24, 134.

Ælfwine (II) (Old English) 'Elf-friend'. 278, 300–5, 307–11, 313–23, 325, 327, 329–34. 'The *Ælfwine* story' 300, 303, 305, 310–12, 323, 326. See *Eldairon, Lúthien* (1).

Ælfwine (III) 28, 87, 140, 154, 182

Ælfwine (IV) (Old English) 'Elf-friend'. 42, 76, 205–6, 209, 257–8, 263, 274, 281, 284, 290, 292, 327, 337–8; the tale of *Ælfwine of England* 199–200, 208. On the relation of *Ælfwine* to Eriol see 206.

Ælfwine (V) Ælfwine the Mariner. 7, 21, 44, 53, 55, 78–81, 83–5, 87, 98, 100, 102–4, 120, 156, 164, 167, 201, 203–4, 240, 243, 275, 299, 334, 412; called *Widlást* 'Far-travelled' 44, 55, 203; his wife 85; the tale of *Ælfwine of England* 85, 104; *Song of Ælfwine* (poem) 100–4, 203. Other Englishmen named *Ælfwine* 38, 55 = Alboin Errol 44; =Alboin the Lombard 38, 55, 91

Ælfwine (IXb) Ælfwine the Mariner *(Eriol)*. 244, (269–70), 271–3, (274–5), 276–80, 285, 287–8, 292–4; called *Wídlást* 'Far-travelled' 244, 280, 285; his mother 270, 293; the tale of *Ælfwine of England* 280; *The Song of Ælfwine* 280

Ælfwine (IXb) Other Englishmen named *Ælfwine* 236, 243; =Elendil 258; =Alboin the Lombard 236, 276; Lowdham's first name (changed to *Alwin*) 234, 236; the name itself 235, 242

Ælfwine (X) Ælfwine of England, the Mariner. 5, 8, 11–12, 14–17,

22, 25–6, 30, 35–6, 40, 42, 65, 110, 121, 123–4, 127–8, 130, 136, 143, 153–4, (157), 160, 163, 166, 168, 175–6, 179, 185, 192, 195, 198, 200, 202, 208–9, 225, 231–2, 257, 271, 326. See *Eriol*.

Ælfwine (XI) 192–3, 206, 311–12, 314–15

Ælfwine (XII) 142–3, 153, 156–9, 395–403; named *Elendil* 401, 403

Aelin-uial (II) 'Meres of Twilight'. 217, 249. (Replaced *Umbothmuilin*, the Pools of Twilight.)

Aelin-uial (V) 'Lakes of Twilight'. 262, 268, 349, 362, 369, 400 (also *Lhîn Uial* 374). See *Hithliniath, Meres of Twilight, Umboth Muilin*.

Aelinuial (VII) 'Lakes of Twilight'. 292

Aelin-uial (XI) 194. See *Hithliniath, Urmboth Muilin, Twilight Meres*.

Aeluin (III) See *Tarn Aeluin*.

Aeluin (X) Tarn Aeluin, lake on Dorthonion. 325

Aeluin (XI) See *Tarn-aeluin*.

Aerandir (IV) Companion of Earendel. 197

Aerandir (XI) Companion of Eärendil on his voyages; earlier form *Airandir*. 246

Aerin (XI) Wife of Brodda. 145; earlier form *Airin*. 88, 90, 145–6

Æsc (I) (Old English) 245. See *Askr*.

Æthelwëard the Chronicler (V) 92

Africa (IV) 258

Africa (IXb) 185

Afros (II) River in Tol Eressëa, joining the Gruir at the bridge of Tavrobel (see 288). 284, 287

Afros, River (V) In Tol-eressëa, joining the Gruir at Tavrobel. 413

Afterborn, The (V) Men. 63–4

After-born, The (XI) Men. 386–7. See *Apanónar*.

Aftercomers (X) Men. 111–12, 121, 130. See *Followers, Hildi*.

Afterworld, The (XII) 243, 246

Agaldor (V) Chieftain of a people in the North-west of Middle-earth. 11–12, 78–9

Agar, Hills of Agar (XII) The town and land of Tal-elmar. 423–6, 428, 432–5, 437

Agarwaen (II) 'Blood-stained', name given to himself by Túrin in Nargothrond. 128

Agarwaen (III) 'Blood-stained', name given by Túrin to himself in Nargothrond. 92

Agarwaen (XI) 'Blood-stained', name taken by Túrin in Nargothrond. 138, 142. See *Iarwaeth*.

4

Agathor (XI) Father of Manthor of Brethil. 270

Aglahad (XII) Nineteenth Prince of Dol Amroth. 223

Aglarond (VIII) 28, 76–8, 399; *Caves of Splendour* 76–7; *Glittering Caves* 28, 77; *Caves of Helm's Deep, the Caves* 26–8, 297. The *palantír* of Aglarond 76–8, 399

Aglarrâma (IXb) 'Castle of the Sea', the ship of Ar-Pharazôn. 372, 385. See *Andalóke, Alcarondas.*

Aglarrâma (XII) The ship of Ar-Pharazôn. 156. See *Alkarondas.*

Aglon, Gorge of (III) Between Taur-na-Fuin and Himling (Himring). 227, 235, 263, 272, 274, 310–11, 313, 361

Aglon, Gorge of (IV) Between Taur-na-Fuin and Himling. 103, 106, 114, 119, 173, 219, 233, 316; *Pass of Aglon* 330, 335

Aglon, Pass of (V) 127, 145, 265, 283; *Gorge of Aglon* 264, 311; *348, 370*

Aglon, Pass of (XI) 38, 49, 53, 77 *(Gorge of)*, 188, 326, 329, 338; *Aglond* 188, 328–9, 332, 338; *Aglon(d* *183, 188. On the two forms see 338.

Aiglir Angrin (III) The Iron Mountains. 49. (Replaced *Angorodin*, replaced by *Eiglir Engrin.*)

Aiglir Angrin (IV) The Iron Mountains. 220. See *Angeryd, Angorodin, Angrin Aiglir, Eiglir Engrin, Ered Engrin.*

Aikanár (X) 'Sharp-flame', Aegnor son of Finarfin. 323–4

Aikanáro (XII) See *Aegnor.*

Ailios (I) Earlier name of Gilfanon. 197–8, 204, 220–2, 227, 229–31

Ailios (II) Earlier name of Gilfanon. 69–70, 144–5, 221–2, 228, 242–3, 256, 284, 294

Ainairos (I) Elf of Alqaluntë 208, 222. (Replaced *Oivárin.*)

Ainimor (V) 'The Wise' (cf. 215), a name of the Noldor. 403

Ainulindalë (I) 49, 60–3 See *Music of the Ainur.*

Ainulindalë (II) 219. See *Music of the Ainur.*

Ainulindalë (IV) 253

Ainulindalë (VII) The Music of the Ainur. 455

Ainulindalë (IXb) 280

Ainulindalë (X) (not as title) 66, 74, 110, 409. See *Music of the Ainur.*

Ainulindalë (XI) 3, 406; *the First History* 406

Ainur (I) (Singular *Ainu*; plural *Ainu* 52, 60–1.) 52–7, 59–63, 66–7, 102, 105, 147, 150–1, 154–5, 219, 225; *Ainu Melko* 147, 150. See *Music of the Ainur.*

Ainur (II) Singular *Ainu* 15, 32, 36, 113, 177, 198; *Ainu Melko* 15, 18, 33; *Ainu of Evil* 22. Plural *Ainu* 202, 264 *Ainur* 151–2, 165,

174, 197, 202, 204, 218–19. See *Gar Ainion, Music of the Ainur, Valar*.

Ainur (IV) 253. See *Music of the Ainur*.

Ainur (V) 156–66, 204, 217, *350*; singular *Ainu* 159. See *Music of the Ainur*.

Ainur (X) (not including *Music of the Ainur*) 8–14, 21, 23–8, 36–9, 41, 43, 49, 65–6, 105, 144–5, 149–50, 244, 253, 271, 336–8, 345, 352, 359, 376, 378–80, 384; singular *Ainu* 12; *the Holy Ones* 8, 12, 14, 42, 359

Ainur (XI) *Vision of the Ainur* 341; singular *Ainu* 399; *the Music* 341

Ainur (XII) (364); see *Music of the Ainur*.

Airandir (V) ('Sea-wanderer'), one of the companions of Eärendel on his voyages. 324

Airin (II) Wife of Brodda; called *Faiglindra, Firilanda*, 'of the long hair' (90, 93). 89–91, 93, 126–8. Later form *Aerin* 126–7

Airin (IV) Wife of Brodda. (30), 122, 126, 131, 183

Airin (V) Wife of Brodda. 316

Aiwenórë (IV) 'Bird-land', lower region of Vista. 236, 240–1, 242–3, 253; earlier form *Aiwenor* 240, *242–3

Aiyador (III) Name of Hithlum among Men. 29

Akallabêth (V) 7–9, 13, 20–2, 29–30, 32, 71, 75–7

Akallabêth (VIII) 169

Akallabêth (IXa) 59

Akallabêth (IXb) 'She that has fallen' (*Atalante*). 247, 312, 396, earlier *Akallabë* 375, 396. The work so titled 152, 340, 353, 356–7, 376–87, 389–96, 406–7

Akallabêth (X) 179

Akallabêth (XII) 'The Downfallen' (not as title of work). 157–8.

Alairë (XI) Vanyarin Elf, wife of Turgon. 323. See *Anairë, Elenwë*.

Alalminórë (I) 'Land of Elms', region of Tol Eressëa. 16, 25, 33, 36, 39, 41, 43, 94; *Alalminor* 40; the first part of the poem *The Trees of Kortirion* 39. See *Gar Lossion, Land of Elms*.

Alalminórë (II) 'Land of Elms', region of England (Warwickshire) and of Tol Eressëa. 292, 313, 324, 327

Alalminórë (V) 'Land of Elms' in Tol-eressea. 148, (*348, 367*)

Alamanyar (X) Elves of the Great March who never reached Aman (Sindar and Nandor). 163–4, 170–1, 173, 223, 232. (Replaced *Ekelli*, replaced by *Úmanyar*.)

Alatar (XII) One of the Blue Wizards. 385

Alatáriel (XII) See *Galadriel*.

Albarim (IXb) [Ramer] 221; *Albar-plays* 221. (Preceded *Enkeladim*.)

Albarth (XI) Precursor of Hunthor of Brethil. 153, 155–6, 164, 267; *Albard* 153. See *Torbarth, Gwerin*.

Albion (II) Used once of Luthany (England). 304

Alboin Errol (V) 36–53, 56–7, 75–7, 104, 180, 203, 243

Alboin the Lombard (V) 7, 37, 53–5; called Ælfwine 38, 55, 91

Alboin the Lombard (IXb) 284; *Album* 236; *Ælfwine* 236, 276

Alcarondas (IXb) 'Castle of the Sea', the ship of Ar-Pharazôn. 385

Aldalómë (VII) Fangorn. 420

Aldamir (XII) Twenty-third King of Gondor. 199, 214

Aldarion and Erendis (The Tale of) (IXb) 286, 379, 406

Aldarion and Erendis (XI) 232

Aldarion and Erendis (XII) (title of work). 141, 155, 351. See *Tar-Aldarion*.

Aldaron (I) Name of Oromë, 'king of forests'. 66, 79; *lord of forests* 71

Aldaron (IV) Name of Oromë. 79, 207, 209; O.E. *Wealdafréa* 207–8, *Béaming* 209. See *Tauros*.

Aldaron (V) Name of Oromë. 206, *357*, 404. See *Galaðon*.

Aldaron (X) Name of Oromë. 124, 146, 202. See *Tauron*.

Aldemanton (VII) See *Westermanton*.

Aldor (VIII) Third King of the Mark. 408

Aldor the Old (XII) Third King of Rohan. 271

Aldudénië (X) The Lament for the Trees, made by Elemmírë. 100, 105, 166, 288, 292

Alfion (IV) Gnomish form of *Alqualondë*. 250–1, 261, 277

Alfred, King (V) 38, 55, 80, 85; his son *Æthelwëard* 55; his grandsons *Ælfwine* 38, 55, and *Æthelwine* 55

Alfred, King (IXb) 236, 270–2, 293–4; *Ælfred* 271

Alkar (V) 'The Radiant', name of Melko. 63–4, 68, 72–5, 120

Alkarin (XII) 198, 212. See *Atanatar II*.

Alkarinquë (X) The planet Jupiter. 160, 166; *Alcarinquë* 166. See pp. 434–5.

Alkarondas (XII) The ship of Ar-Pharazôn. 156. See *Aglarrâma*.

Alkorin (V) =*Ilkorin*. 200, 349, *367*

All that is gold does not glitter (VII) 49–50, 52, 77–8, 80, 137, 146

Allen and Unwin (V) 8, 57, 73, 78, 97, 107, 293; *Stanley Unwin* 8, 98, 199

Allen and Unwin (VI) 11, 40, 43, 84, 108, 386

Alley of Roses (II) Street in Gondolin. 183

Allfather (IV) Ilúvatar. 78, 97, 206, 263, 292; O.E. *Ealfæder* 206, 281, 285, 293, *Allfeder* 291

All-father (V) 110, 156–7, 160, 204, 234; *the Father* 63, 72, 213, 232. See *Ilúvatar*.

Allfather (IXb) See *Ilúvatar*.

All-father (X) Ilúvatar. 8, 39; *Eru Allfather* 112

All-Hallows (I) 34, 38, 42

Alliance of Dwarves and Men (XII) 303–5.

Almain, Ocean of (I) The North Sea. 205–6

Almaren (I) 87, 110, 222

Almaren (IV) The first dwelling of the Valar in Arda. 42, 45

Almaren (X) First abode of the Valar in Arda, an island in a great lake. 7, 23, 32–3, 38, 52–4, 60–1, 133, 179; earlier form *Almar* 7, 18, 23, (25), 27, 38. Earlier names *Eccuilë* 22, *Eremar* 23. See *Great Lake*.

Almaren, Isle of (VI) 122

Almáriel (V) A girl in Númenor. 59, *357*

Almighty, The (IXb) 258, 290, 314, 316, 398, 401; O.E. *Ælmihtiga* 257–8, 313, 316–17; *Sanavaldo* 401

Alphabets (VII) 453–5

Alphros (XII) Twenty-fourth Prince of Dol Amroth. 221, 223

Alps (V) 92 ('the Welsh Mountains').

Alqaluntë (I) See *Kópas Alqaluntë*

Alqaluntë (IV) See *Kópas Alqaluntë*.

Alqarámë (II) 'Swanwing', Tuor's ship. 254, 265. See *Eärrámë*, *Swan-wing*.

Alqarámë (IV) 'Swanwing', Tuor's ship. 69. See *Eärámë*.

Alqualondë (I) 171, 223

Alqualondë (III) 136. See *Cópas Alqalunten*, *Kinslaying*, *Swanhaven*.

Alqualondë (IV) 10, 198, 261, 273, 287; *Alqalondë* 265–6, 276, 283; O.E. *Elfethýð* 282–3, 287, 341, *Ielfethýð* 283. See *Swanhaven*.

Alqualondë (V) (including references to the Battle of Alqualondë and the Kinslaying) 109, 113, 115, 119, 189, 224–6, 228, 236–9, 246, 286, 326, 334, *348*, *370* (Noldorin *Alfobas*, *Hobas in Elf 364*). See *Havens*.

Alqualondë (VII) 322; Noldorin *Alfobas* 322

Alqualondë (X) 87, 91, 93, 104, 115–18, 125–6, 128, 177–9, 183, 196, 283. See *Haven of the Swans*.

Alqualondë (XI) 19, 26, 43, 177

Alqualondë (XII) 362, 365, 380

Altariellë (X) Galadriel. 182

Aluin (I) Time, the oldest of the Ainur. 219, 222. (Replaced *Lúmin*.)

Alwin (IXb) Lowdham's first name (changed from *Ælfwine*): see 234, 236, 269, 284

Amaldor, Ammalas (VII) See *Amroth*.

Aman (I) 23, 26, 93, 135, 137, 196. See *Blessed Realm*.

Aman (II) 64, 266

Aman (III) 348, 357. See *Blessed Realm*.

Aman (IV) 43, 197, *250–1, 254, 258, 261

Aman (V) 21, 198, 338; *Mountains of Aman* 300

Amân (IXb) (1) Adunaic name of Manwë (many references are to *the land of Amân*). 357–61, 364, 369, 371–3, 376–7, 381–3, 385–6, 388, 390–1, 393–4, 407, 420, 435; *Mountain of Amân* (Taniquetil) 391.

   Amân (IXb) (2) *Aman*, the Blessed Realm. 312, 376, 393–4, 396

Aman (X) (1) Adûinaic name of Manwë. 7, 28. (2) The world, Eä (often *the Halls of Aman*) 7, 12, 14, 20, 22–3, 28–9, 30–1, 34, 37–8, 40, 44, 149–50, 156. (3) The Blessed Realm. 7, 33, 37–8, 48, 51, 54, 58, 61, 67, 73, 75, 78, 80–1, 84–7, 90, 92, 96, 103, 114, 116–18, 120, 125, 129, 132, 138, 155–6, 159, 161, 163, 170, 172, 174, 181–2, 190, 192, 204, 206, 211, 219, 221, 223, 236–42, 247–8, 253, 255, 257–8, 261–2, 268–71, 274–7, 279, 281–6, 289, 309–10, 339–41, 349, 358–9, 361–5, 370–1, 385–6, 388–9, 397, 401, 403, 405, 412, 420–1, 424–31; *Aman the Unshadowed* 240. See *Blessed Realm, Mountains of Aman*.

Aman (XI) 5–8, 16–17, 21, 24–6, 35–6, 40–2, 105–7, 121, 216, 323, 365, 370–6, 378–86, 392–3, 396–400, 403, 405, 407, 409, 420. *The Chronicle(s) of Aman* 5, 30, 105; *Mountains of Aman* 403 (see *Pelóri, Valinor*).

Aman (XII) 157, 312, 317, 325, 332–4, 341, 344, 346, 348–50, 357, 359, 361, 364, 371, 398, 401, 403–4. See *Blessed Realm*.

Amandil (V) Last lord of Andúnië, father of Elendil. 7, 57, 71

Amandil (XII) Father of Elendil. 156, 159–63, 165, 175, 183, 186–7, 191, 257. (Replaced *Valandil* (2).)

Amandil Father of Elendil. 356, 382, 384. See *Amardil, Arbazân, Aphanuzír*.

Amaneldi (XI) =*Amanyar*. 373

Amanyar (XI) '(Elves) of Aman'. 373–4, 381, 409; adjectivally *Amanya(r)* 381, 383, 411

Amardil Earlier name of Amandil. 346, 348–9, 352, 356, 382

Amareth (IXa) Transient name preceding *Arwen*. 66. See *Finduilas* (1).

Amárië (XI) Vanyarin Elf, beloved of Felagund. 44, 62, 67, 129–30, 243, 323

Amárië (XII) Vanya, beloved of Felagund. 318, 349

Amarth (XII) Doom. 365

Amatthânê (IXb) The Land of Gift. 361, 363–4, 370, 375, 378, 380–1, 385, 388, 390. (Replaced by *Zen'nabâr*.) *Amatthâni* 'Land or Realm of Aman' (420, 435), the Blessed Realm, 388, 391, 413, 420, 435

Ambar (IV) 'Earth'. 236, 240–1, 242–5, 247, 255–6

Ambar (V) 'Earth'. 11, 372

Ambar (X) 'Earth'. 28, 359, 382–3, 385; *Ambar-endya* 'Middle-earth' 76; *Ambar-metta* 359. See *Imbar*.

Ambar (XI) ('Habitation'), the Earth. 402, 420. See *Imbar*.

Ambaráto (XII) See *Aegnor*.

Ambar-endya (IV) 'Middle-earth'. 241, *242–3, 254–5. See *Endor*, *Pelmar*.

Ambarkanta (I) 'Shape of the World' (cosmological work). 86, 227

Ambarkanta (II) 'Shape of the World' (cosmological work). 325

Ambarkanta (V) 9, 11, 13, 20–1, 32, 56, 107–8, 121, 156, 165, 184, 207, 217, 225, 239, 243–5, 248, 257, 266–7, 270–1, 294, 302–3, 335

Ambarkanta (VIII) 167

Ambarkanta (IXb) 383

Ambarkanta (X) 22, 26, 28–9, 39, 63–4, 76–8, 88–90, 123, 126, 135–6, 157, 373

Ambarkanta (XI) 104–5, 109, 174

Ambarto (XII) See *Amrod*.

Ambarussa (XII) (1) Amras. 353, 355. (2) Name given to both the twin sons of Fëanor. 353–5 (see *Amros*). On the twins (*i·Wenyn* 353, *Gwenyn* 365) see 355, 366.

Amillo (I) Youngest of the great Valar, called also Omar. 67, 75, 80, 89, 93, 228

Amillo (II) Youngest of the great Valar, called also *Ómar*. 279

Amin (XII) See *Estel*.

Amlach (XI) Grandson of Marach, a leader of dissension in Estolad. 220–1, 227, 233–4

Amlach (XII) A leader of dissension in Estolad. 325

Amlaith of Fornost (XII) First King of Athedain. 193, 208, 228, 253

Amnon (I) Prophecy of Amnon, Amnon the Prophet. 172, 197

Amnon (II) 'the prophet'. 184. See I. 172.

Amnor (I) Strands of Amnor. 176, 197. (Replaced *Amnos*.)

Amnos (I) The beaching-place of the ship Mornië; the prophecies of Amnos. 167, 170, 172, 197. (Replaced *Emnon, Morniento*.)

Amon Amarth (VII) Mount Doom. 348. Earlier names *Amarthon, Dol-amarth* 343

Amon Amarth (XII) 176, 186. See *Mount Doom*.

Amon Carab (XI) See *Carabel*.

Amon Darthir (II) A peak in the range of Ered Wethrin. 126

Amon Darthir (XI) Mountain above Húrin's house in Dor-lómin. 181, *182

Amon Dengin (IV) Early name of the Mound of Slain on Dor-na-Fauglith. 146, 193, 312. See *Cûm-na-Dengin, Hill of Slain*.

Amon Dengin (V) 'The Hill of Slain'. 314, 322. See *Cûm-na-Dengin, Hauð-na-Dengin*.

Amon Dîn (VIII) The seventh beacon in Anórien. 233, 343–6, 350–1, 353–4, 404; *Dîn* 351–2. Earlier name *Amon Thorn* 232

Amon Dîn (IXa) The seventh beacon in Anórien. 61, 67

Amon Ereb (IV) 'The Lonely Hill' in East Beleriand. 313, 326

Amon Ereb (V) 'The Lonely Hill' in East Beleriand. 38, 56, 143, 153, 262–3, 283, *356*; described, 263

Amon Ereb (XI) 'The Lonely Hill' in East Beleriand. 16, 112, *185

Amon Ethir (II) 'Hill of Spies', east of Nargothrond. 128, 135. See *Hill of Spies*.

Amon Ethir (XI) 'The Hill of Spies' east of Nargothrond. 93–4, 149–50

Amon Garabel (XI) See *Carabel*.

Amon Gwareth (II) 'Hill of Watch' on which Gondolin was built. 158–60, 163, 166, 168, 171, 175–6, 178, 180, 189, 196, 207, 212. See *Hill of Watch*.

Amon Gwareth (IV) The hill of Gondolin. 34, 66, 137, 139–40, 144; *Hill of Watch(ing)* 34, 137, *Hill of Defence* 139; other references 65, 136

Amon Gwareth (V) The hill of Gondolin. 56

Amon Gwareth (XI) The hill of Gondolin. 200; *Amon Gwared* 200

Amon Hen (VII) 214, 318, 364, 370–6, 378–81, 385–8, 405, 413, 426–7; *Tirmindon* 364. Rejected names for Amon Hen/Amon Lhaw 387. Visions on Amon Hen 372–4, 379–81

Amon Hen (VIII) 20, 59, 72, 118, 128; *Amon Henn* 128

Amon Lhaw (VII) 318, 364, 373, 381, 387; *Larmindon* 364

Amon Lhaw (VIII) 72

Amon Obel (II) Hill in the Forest of Brethil. 135

Amon Obel (V) Hill in the Forest of Brethil. 412

Amon Obel (XI) Hill in the Forest of Brethil. 89, 92, 145, 151, 159, *182

Amon Rûdh (XI) 'The Bald Hill', abode of Mîm. 138, 187, 311, 313– 15. Discarded names *Carabel, Amon Carab,* ~ *Garabel,* ~ *Nardol,* ~ *Rhûg* 187

Amon Sûl (XII) Weathertop (most references are to the *palantir*). 176, 189, 191, 193–4, 208–10, 229–30, 245

Amon Thorn (VIII) See *Amon Dîn.*

Amon-Uilas (IV) Gnomish name of Taniquetil (see *Ialassë*). 81, 167, 209; later form *Amon Uilos* 167; O.E. *Sinsnáw, Sinsnæwen* 209

Amon Uilos (V) Noldorin name of Taniquetil (see *Oiolosse*). 209–10, 357–9, 379 (also *Guilos 358*); earlier form Amon *Uilas* 210

Amon Uilos (X) 154. See *Taniquetil.*

Amon Uilos (XI) Sindarin name of Oiolossë. 403. See *Ras-Arphain.*

Amoury (III) Unknown. 123

Amras (II) Son of Fëanor. 251. (Replaced *Díriel.*)

Amras (IV) Son of Fëanor. 69. (Replaced *Díriel.*)

Amras (XI) Later name of Díriel son of Fëanor. 197, 225, 240, 329

Amras (XII) Son of Fëanor, twin of Amrod. 352–3, 355, 366, 368; other names *Amros* 366, 368, *Telufinwë, Telvo* 353, 365, and see *Ambarussa.*

Amrath (VII) See *Andrath.*

Amrod (II) Son of Fëanor. 251. (Replaced *Damrod.*)

Amrod (IV) Son of Fëanor. 69. (Replaced *Damrod.*)

Amrod (XI) Later name of Damrod son of Fëanor. 197, 240, 329

Amrod (XII) Son of Fëanor, twin of Amras. 352–3; other names *Ambarto, Umbarto* 353–5, 366, *Pityafinwë, Pityo* 353, 365, and see *Ambarussa.*

Amrod and Amras (X) Later names of Damrod and Díriel. 177. On the death of one of the brothers at Losgar see 128.

Amros (XII) =*Ambarussa* as the name of both the twin sons of Fëanor. 367

Amroth (V) King of Beleriand after the Downfall of Númenor. 12, 18, 23, 31, 79. (Replaced by *Elendil*).

Amroth (VII) 223, 234, 239, 243. Earlier names *Ammalas* 223, 225– 6, 239, 243; *Amaldor* 223

Amroth (VIII) See *Dol Amroth.*

12

Amroth (IXa) (1) The Hill of Amroth in Lórien. (115), 124. (2) See *Dol Amroth*.

Amroth (XII) King of Lórien. 36, 65, 82, 206, 222–3, 294

Amrothos (XII) Third son of Imrahil of Dol Amroth. 221, 223

Anach (II) Pass leading down from Taur-nu-Fuin. 211

Anach, Pass of (XI) *183

Anadûnê (IXb) Westernesse, Númenor. 147, 240, 247, 361–3, 365–6, 369–76, 378–9, 385–6, 388–9, 391–2, 395–6, 407, 426, 428, 433; *Anadûn* 305, 375; *Anadûni* 311; *Anadunians* 429

Anairë (XI) (1) Vanyarin Elf, wife of Turgon. 323 (see *Alairë, Elenwë*). (2) Wife of Fingolfin. 323

Anairë (XII) Wife of Fingolfin. 344, 361, 363

Anar (V) The Sun (Quenya). 41, 56, 63, 72 (*Úr-anar*), 240–1, 243, 348, 374 (other names *Atyante, Eriant* 'Day-bringer' 348–9, *Ankalë* 362). Anor (Noldorin) 41, 56, 243, 348, 374 (*Anar*).

Anar (VI) One of the Dwarves who accompanied Bilbo from Bag End. 238, 240, 315

Anar (IXb) The Sun. 302, 306; *Anaur, Anor* 302–3, 306

Anar (X) (1) Of uncertain meaning (see 44): *Halls of Anar* 22–3, 40, 44, *Kingdom of Anar* 22, 41, 44. (2) The Sun. 40, 44, 130–2, 134, 136, 198, 377, 382 (*Fire-golden* 130, 198); *Anor* 44.

Anar (XI) The Sun. 401

Anardil (XII) Sixth King of Gondor. 197, 212

Anárion (VII) 119, 123, 126, 138, 144, 146; realm of 282; name of region 310, 318

Anárion (VIII) 149, 153, 168, 397; *sons of* 374–5; name of region 243–4, 252, 254–5, 266

Anárion (IXa) 15, 59

Anárion (IXb) 335, 387, 401

Anárion (X) Son of Elendil. 44

Anárion (XII) 32, 157, 169–70, 172, 176–7, 188, 191–2, 195, 197–8, 207–8, 210, 212, 218, 227, 232–3, 254, 257

Anárioni (XII) Heirs of Anárion. 196

Anarríma (X) Name of a constellation. 160

Anaxartaron Onyalië, Anaxartamel (XI) Titles of *Of the Ents and the Eagles*. 340–1

Anborn (VIII) (1) Father of Falborn (precursor of Faramir). 136, 170. (2) Ranger of Ithilien. 154, 164, 169 (replaced *Falborn* (2)).

Ancalagon (V) The Black Dragon. 144, 329, 348, 374

Ancalagon (XI) The Black Dragon. 346–7

Ancalagon (XII) The Black Dragon. 374–5

Ancalagon the Black (IV) Greatest of the winged dragons of Morgoth. 160, 203–4, 209, 309; O.E. *Anddraca* 209

Ancient Days (VI) 169, 179, 260, 358. See *Earliest Days, Elder Days. Anduin* 205, 410. See *Beleghir, Great River*.

Ancient Days (VII) 255, 259

Ancient Mariner (II) See *Man of the Sea*.

Andabund, Andrabonn (VIII) 'elephant'. 136, and see 139. See *Mûmak, Oliphaunt*.

Andafangar (XII) 321. See *Longbeards*.

Andalókë (IXb) 'Long Serpent', the ship of Tarkalion. 350. ['The Long Serpent' was the name of the great ship of Olaf Tryggvason King of Norway.] See *Aglarrâma*.

Anderson, Douglas (XII) 117

Ando Lómen (IV) The Door of Night. 237, 240–1, 243, 252

Andon (VII) See *Anduin*.

Andor (V) 'Land of Gift', Númenor. 19, 25, 65

Andor (XII) The Land of Gift, Númenor. 144; *the Gift* 144

Andóre (IXb) 'Land of Gift'. 241, 247, 305, 310, 343, 349, 356; *Andor* 315, 332, 356, 403

Andram (V) 'The Long Wall' running across Beleriand. 262–3, 268, 348, 382

Andram (XI) 'The Long Wall' across Beleriand. 15, *185, 190, 193, 195, 335

Andras, Cape (XI) The 'long cape' west of Brithombar. *184, 189, 379, 418

Andrast (XI) The 'long cape' in the west of Gondor. 189

Andrath (VII) Place near the Greenway. 79, 298, 306. Earlier form *Amrath* 69–72, 74, 79, 298, 306

Andreth (X) 'Wise-woman' of the House of Bëor. 303–28, 333–6, 338, 343–5, 349, 351–4, 357–9, 364–5, 390. See *Saelind*.

Andreth (XI) 'Wise-woman' of the House of Bëor. 227, 230–3. See *Saelin*.

Andreth (XII) 'Wise-woman' of the Edain. 325, 374–5, 419; other names *Saelon, Saelind* 419

Andróg (XI) Member of Túrin's outlaw-band. 311, 314–15

Andromeda (IXb) Constellation. 207

Andros (VIII) See *Cair Andros*.

Androth, caves of (XI) In the hills of Mithrim. 91

Anduin (IV) The Great River. 257

Anduin (V) The Great River. 33–4

Anduin (VII) 123–4, 138, 144, 151, 157, 207, 211, 213, 215, 218, 221, 231, 233, 236–8, 267, 269, 284, 287–8, 290–2, 295, 298–9, 304, 306–7, 311–13, 315–16, 318, 320, 323, 329–30, 339, 346, 351, 353, 355–6, 364–5, 368, 427, 435, 439; *Mouths* 307, 311, 382; *Vale (valley) of Anduin* 292, 322, 336. Earlier names *Beleghir* 122; *Sirvinya* 119, 122, 125, 299; *Andon* 298–9, 306. See *Ethir Anduin, Great River*.

Anduin (VIII) 73, 85, 95, 98, 100–2, 110, 125, 128, 131, 133–4, 146–7, 149, 157, 182, 218, 229–30, 235, 243, 266, 268, 270, 275, 288, 295, 330, 333, 340, 353, 356, 360–3, 369–70, 372, 374, 378, 391, 398, 405, 412–14, 419, 422, 426, 428–9, 433, 436, 438; *Mouths of* 213, 246, 255, 262–3, 276, 278, 293, 413–14; *Vale of* 291, 324. See *(The) Delta, Ethir Anduin, (The) Great River*.

Anduin (IXa) 16, 18, 22, 49, 65. See *Ethir Anduin, Great River*.

Anduin (X) 82, 89; *the River* 83; *the Great River of Wilderland* 89

Anduin (XI) 105–6, 110, 384; *Vale of Anduin* 110, 381, 410; *Mouths of Anduin* 13. See *Great River*.

Anduin (XII) (including *sources, vale(s), mouths* of Anduin; *Upper, Middle, Lower Anduin*) 10, 32, 34, 38, 49–50, 56–7, 65, 74–5, 122, 152, 167, 174–7, 183, 186, 192, 197–200, 204–7, 214, 229–30, 233, 235–6, 238, 242, 251, 258–9, 267, 272–3, 302–3, 311, 313, 316, 329, 371, 384, 411, 416, 422, 437; see *Great River*.

Andúnë (X) The West. 23

Andúnië (V) (1) 'Sunsetland', Númenor. 14, 19, 376. (2) The chief city of Númenor 19, 25, 29; *Lord of Andúnië* 71

Andúnië (IXb) Western haven in Númenor. 333, 340, 344, 351, 378, 380, 382; *Undúnië* 333, 340

Andúnië (XII) (chiefly in *Lord(s) of Andúnië*) 145, 152, 154, 156, 159–62, 164–5, 257

Andúril (VIII) 'Flame of the West', Aragorn's sword. 370. Replaced *Branding*; see also *Elendil*.

Andvari (IV) 187

Andvír (XI) Son of Andróg. 311, 314–15

Anfalas (VII) 310

Anfalas (VIII) Fief of Minas Tirith. 287, 289, 293; *Dor-Anfalas* 287, 293; *Langstrand* (VIII) 287, 293. See *Belfalas*.

Anfalas (XII) Fief of Gondor. 34

Anfangrim (XI) 'Longbeards', the Dwarves of Belegost. 322. See *Enfeng*.

Anfangrim (XII) 321, 383. See *Longbeards*.

Anfauglin (IV) 'Jaws of Thirst', name of Carcharoth. 115, 178; later form *Anfauglir* 178

Anfauglith (I) 243

Anfauglith (II) 57, 62. See *Dor-nu-Fauglith*.

Anfauglith (III) Another name of Dor-na-Fauglith. 273, 284

Anfauglith (IV) 59. See *Dor-na-Fauglith*.

Anfauglith (V) =*Dor-na-Fauglith*. 301

Anfauglith (XI) 'The Gasping Dust', name of Ardgalen after its desolation. 52, 55, 60, 63, 68, 70–3, 79, 85, 124–5, 131, 141, 167–8, 252. See *Dor-na-Fauglith*.

Angaino (I) 'The Oppressor', the great chain in which Melko was bound. 101, 103–5, 114; later form *Angainor* 111

Angainor (III) The great chain in which Morgoth was bound. 205, 208–10. Earlier forms *Angaino*, *Angainu* 209, *Engainor* 208

Angainor (IV) The great chain in which Morgoth was bound. 40, 45, 71, 157, 160, 168, 198

Angainor (V) The chain in which Morgoth was bound. 213, 329

Angainor (X) The chain with which Melkor was bound. 75, 161, 167, 391–3; earlier *Angaino*, *Angainus* 168

Angainor (XI) The chain with which Melkor was bound. 247

Angainu (II) The great chain in which Melko was bound. 19, 46; *Angaino* 68

Angali (II) Angles. 306

Angamandi (I) 'Hells of Iron.' 77, 90, 92, 198, 230, 238. See *Hells of Iron*.

Angamandi (II) 'Hells of Iron'. 13–14, 18, 21, 23, 29, 31–2, 34, 36, 43, 51, 56–8, 62, 68, 87, 94, 138, 223, 264, 280. See *Angband*, *Hells of Iron*.

Angamandi (III) Name of Angband in the *Lost Tales*. 282

Angamandi (IV) Name of Angband in the *Lost Tales*. 44, 53

Angaráto (XII) See *Angrod*.

Angband (I) 158–9, 198, 240–4; *Siege of Angband* 242

Angband (II) 35, 43–5, 51, 57, 61–2, 65–6, 68, 72, 77, 79, 124, 140, 142, 206, 211, 213, 238, 241; *Siege of Angband* 209. See *Angamandi*, *Hells of Iron*.

Angband (III) 7, 16, 32, 35, 49, 51, 53, 55, 69–70, 75, 87, 102, 107, 116, 126, 205, 209, 212, 220–1, 226, 231, 234, 244, 253, 257, 270–3, 279, (281–2), 283, 285, 289, 292–4, 298, 302, 304–7, 309, 314, 341, 348; described 294–6. *Siege of, Leaguer of, Ang-*

band (III) 55, 83–6, 171, 212–13, 221–2, 247. See *Hells of Iron*.

Angband (IV) 13, 17, 22–3, 25–8, 35–6, 44, 52, 54, 57–60, 67, (80, 84, 91), 93, 101–4, 106–7, 112–13, 115, 117–19, 123, 136, 138, 141, 144, 157–8, 160, 177–8, 180–3, 193, 209, 220, 223, *250–1, 257, 259–60, 269, 280, 282–3, 295, 299–303, 306, 309, 313–14, 322, 324, 327–30, 332–3, 336–8, 340; *Iron-hell* 13; O.E. *Irenhell* 209, 282–3, 338, *Engbend* 209. See *Halls of Iron, Siege of Angband*; and on relation to Utumno see 257, 259–60

Angband (V) 'The Hells of Iron'. 108, 118, 121, 125–7, 130–1, 133, 135–8, 141, 144, 148, 153, 177, 189, 210, 233, 238, 241, 249–59, 266, 273, 279–81, 284–6, 288, 297, 309, 311–12, 319–20, 329, 371 (also Quenya *Angamanda*), 412. See *Siege of Angband*.

Angband (VI) 182–3, 187, 218; *King of Angband* 183; *Halls of Iron* 182, 187; *Iron Halls* 183

Angband (IXa) 45

Angband (X) 67, 109–10, 124, (127), 131, 156, 167, 197, 284, 291, 295, 297–8, 306, 341, 350, 419, 421, 423; *the Siege of Angband* 305, 307, 324(-5), 328, 336, 357(-8); Quenya *Angamando* 350

Angband (XI) 15–18, 30–1, 35–7, 46, 50, 54–6, 60, 63, 68, 71–5, 77, 79, 82–4, 86, 97, 111, 113, 116, 118, 121, 124–5, 128, 131–2, 134, 137–8, 166–8, 196, 203, 252–3, 259, 263–4, 267, 275, 277, 284–5, 321, 329–30, 344–5, 347; *the Iron Prison* 15, *the hells of iron* 196; called *hell* 46. Later story of the origin of Angband 196, 344. *The Siege of Angband, the leaguer* 36, 38–9, 46, 52, 54, 116, 203, 216, 221, 329

Angband (XII) 302, 342, 358, 372

Angbor (VIII) Lord of Lamedon. 414, 419

Angbor (XI) The 'Doom-rock' in the Moot-ring in Brethil. 283, 290, 309; called *Halabor* 309; *the Stone* 283–4, 286, 290–2, 305, 309

Angel (IXb) Ancient home of the English. 273; *Angol* 274

Angelcynn (IV) (Old English) The English people. 206, 263, 284, 292; *Ongulcynn* 290

Angelcynn, Angolcynn (V) (Old English) The English people. 201, 203–4

Angelimir (XII) Twentieth Prince of Dol Amroth. 220–3; *Angelimar* (erroneous) 222

Angeln (I) 24

Angeln (II) 294

Angerthas (VI) 173, 467

Angerthas (VII) 452. See *Runes*.

Angerthas (XII) (Runes) 300; *Angerthas Moria* 319. See *Cirth*.

Angeryd (IV) The Iron Mountains. 220. See *Aiglir Angrin*.

Anglachel (XI) Beleg's sword (made by Eöl) that was reforged for Túrin. 321. See *Gurthang*.

Angle (VII) (of Lothlórien) 207, 213, 218, 221, 225, 231, 236–8, 241, 244–5, 256, 261, 268–9, 280–1, 287–8, 325. The meaning of *Angle* discussed 287–8; see *(The) Gore*.

Angle, The (VI) Land between the rivers Hoarwell and Loudwater. 202

Angle, The (XII) Land between Hoarwell and Loudwater. 66–7, 250

Angles (II) 306. See *Angali*.

Angles (V) 91; *South Angles* 86; *Angli* 92; (Old English) *Engle* 91

Angles (IXb) 276

Anglo-Saxon (IXb) (language) 151, 159, 220, 234–9, 242–3, 245, 255–6, 259, 279–82, 284–5, 291–2, 299, 301–4, 318. Other references under *Old English, English*.

Anglo-Saxon (X) 5, 30. See *Old English*.

Anglo-Saxon (XI) 141 *(Chronicle)*, 314 (verse). See *English*.

Anglo-Saxon(s) (I) 24. See *Old English* (references to the language).

Anglo-Saxon(s) (II) 266, 305, 309, 323

Anglo-Saxon(s) (V) 44, 46, 78, 81, 98; *Anglo-Saxon Chronicle* 80, 84, 124

Angmar (VI) 128

Angmar (VII) 37, 59

Angmar (VIII) 334, 369; *King of Angmar* 334

Angmar (XII) 9, 66–7, 189, 193–5, 201, 209–10, 217–18, 230, 232, 242, 254, 256, 258, 283

Angol (I) 'Ironcliffs', Gnomish name of Eriol and of his homeland. 24, 107

Angol (II) 'Ironcliffs', Gnomish name of Eriol and of his homeland. 290–2, 294

Angol (V) The ancient home of the English. 88, 91. Cf. *Old Anglia* 92

Angolcynn (II) (Old English) The English people. 291; *Angelcynn* 300. See *Engle, English*.

Angoloð (IV) See 174.

Angomaitë (XII) Corsair of Umbar. 199, 215, 231, 248; later *Angamaitë* 215. See also *Angrod*.

Angor (V) King of Númenor. 9, 15–16, 27, 75. (Replaced by *Tar-Kalion*.)

Angorodin (II) The Iron Mountains. 77, 140. See *Iron Mountains*.

Angorodin (III) Early name of the Iron Mountains. 49

18

Angorodin (IV) Earliest name of the Iron Mountains. 220. See *Aiglir Angrin*.

Angrenost (VII) Isengard. 420. Earlier name *Angrobel* 'Irongarth' 71–2, 130, 139

Angrenost (VIII) Isengard. 44, 72, 79; also *Angost* 44, 72, 79

Angrenost (XII) See *Isengard*.

Angrim (III) Father of Gorlim the Unhappy. 336, 349

Angrim (V) Father of Gorlim the Unhappy. 296–7

Angrin Aiglir (IV) The Iron Mountains. 220. See *Aiglir Angrin*.

Angrist (II) Curufin's knife, made by Telchar of Nogrod. 58

Angrist (V) Curufin's knife. 303

Angrobel (VII) See *Angrenost*.

Angrod (III) Son of Finrod/Finarfin, slain in the Battle of Sudden Flame. 80, 85, 138, 213, 222

Angrod (IV) Son of Finrod (1) =Finarfin. 46, 55, 88, 95, 103, 106, 169, 173–4, 176, 267, 271, 279, 295–6, 298, 310, 314, 318, 327–8; earlier form Anrod 15, 19, 46, 169; O.E. *Angel* 213

Angrod (V) Son of Finrod (1) =Finarfin. 116, 119, 127, 132, 145–6, 150, 223, 226, 234, 237–9, 264, 269, 276, 279, 281, *383*

Angrod (X) Son of Finarfin (=Finrod (1)). 113, 121, 125–6, 177, 182, 195–6, 328

Angrod (XI) Son of Finarfin (=Finrod (1)). 32–3, 38, 43, 52, 115, 119, 136, *183, 195

Angrod (XII) Son of Finarfin. 346–7, 350–1; other names *Angaráto*, *Angamaitë* 346–7, *Artanga* 346

Annael (II) Grey-elf of Mithrim, fosterfather of Tuor. 205

Annael (XI) Elf of Mithrim, fosterfather of Tuor. 79, 136–7.

Annals of Aman (IV) 262, 277, 294

Annals of Aman (V) 109

Annals of Aman (X) For the relation of the *Annals* to the *Quenta* tradition see 102, 191–2, 205, 283, 289–91

Annals of Aman (XII) 62, 79, 142, 147–8, 185, 190, 355, 359, 375, 388–9. *Annals of Beleriand* 375; see *Grey Annals*.

Annals of Beleriand (IV) References in *the Annals of Valinor*: 263, 270, 292; O.E. *Beleriandes géargetæl* 284, 290, ~ *géargesægen* 338

Annals of Beleriand (VI) 384, 412, 433

Annals of Beleriand (VIII) 169, 297

Annals of Beleriand (X) 3, 49, 102–3, 110, 123, 125, 127, 290, 306, and see *Grey Annals*.

Annals of Valinor (II) 300

Annals of Valinor (IV) See *Valinórelúmien.*

Annerchin (VI) Goblin Gate (in the Misty Mountains). 416, 432

Annerchion (VII) 'Goblin Gate'. 114

Annon Torath (VIII) See *Sern Aranath.*

Annon(-in-)Gelydh (XI) 'The Gate of the Noldor' in Dor-lómin. 181, *182

Annon-in-Gelydh (IV) The Gate of the Noldor. 174

Annúminas (VII) 122, 145, 304. See *Tarkilmar, Torfirion, Westermanton.*

Annúminas (IXa) Elendil's city on Lake Nenuial. 58 (the sceptre of Annúminas)

Annúminas (XII) 167, 169, 176, 191–3, 195, 208, 210, 228, 258, 268. See *Dunhirion, Tarkilion.*

Annúnaid (XII) See *Common Speech.*

Anor (V) The Sun. See *Anar.*

Anórien (VII) 310, 318

Anórien (VIII) 77, 141–2, 219, 231–4, 244, 253, 255, 262, 275, 318, 340, 343, 345–7, 353, 363–4, 373, 404, 415; *Anórien road*, see *Roads.*

Anórien (IXa) 49, 61

Anórien (X) 44

Anórien (XI) 187

Anórien (XII) 45, 315

Anrod (IV) See *Angrod.*

Antirion the Golden (IXb) City of the Númenóreans. 347, 356, 381, 384. See *Tar Kalimos.*

Aotrou and Itroun, Lay of (VII) 345

Apanónar (XI) 'The After-born', Men. 386–7, 403; Sindarin *Abonnen*, plural *Eboennin* 387

Aphadon (XI), plurals *Ephedyn, Aphadrim* 387. Sindarin rendering of *Hildor.* See *Echil.*

Aphanuzîr (IXb) Amandil. 389–90. (Replaced *Arbazân.*)

Appledore (VI) Family name in Bree. 137, 141

Arachon (XI) Father of Beldis the mother of Brandir the Lame. 231

Arad Dain (VI) See 432.

Aradan (XI) See *Malach.*

Arador (XII) Fourteenth Chieftain of the Ddnedain. 196, 211, 238, 258, 263, 268; former name *Arvoreg*(?) 211

Ar-Adûnakhôr (XII) Twentieth Ruler of Númenor. 154, 165, 312. See *Herundmen.*

Ar-Adûnakhôr, Ar-gimilzôr (V) Rulers of Númenor. 75

Arafain (VII) See *Keleborn.*

Arafinwë (X) Finarfin. 230, 238, 265. See *Ingalaurë*

Arafinwë (XII) See *Finarfin.*

Araglas (XII) Sixth Chieftain of the Dúnedain. 196, 211; former name *Arallas* 211

Aragorn (III) 124, 126, 269

Aragorn (VI) (1) Suggested name for Gandalf's horse. 351. (2) Aragorn son of Arathorn. 128, 176, 210, 367–9, 379, 387, 414, 430–2, 434–5, 437

Aragorn (VII) 6–7, 9, 15, 50–2, 63, 65, 77–84, 105, 111–13, 116, 120, 129–30, 135, 137, 146–8, 151, 157, 162–5, 168, 170–1, 176, 187, 196, 200, 203, 206–7, 210–12, 214, 216, 218, 222, 224–5, 227–8, 230–2, 235–6, 238–9, 243–4, 256, 258, 260, 262, 265, 276–8, 291, 293, 326, 358, 361–2, 364, 366, 381, 384–5, 390, ́392–404, 406–7, 424–31, 434–5, 437–9, 441–50. His ancestry and history 6–8, 116, 120–1, 147, 360–2; weds Eowyn 448; King of Gondor 448. See *Elfstone, Ingold, Tarkil, Trotter.*

Aragorn (VIII) 3–5, 10–15, 17–22, 24–6, 37–9, 42, 47, 49–50, 52, 54, 56–60, 65, 67, 69–70, 72, 74–5, 77–8, 80, 124, 126, 140–1, 146–7, 149, 165, 219, 226, 229–30, 235–68 *passim*, 272, 274–6, 281, 291, (294), 296–321 *passim*, 327, 329, 339, 359–64, 370, 372, 375, 378–80, (382), 385–431 *passim*, 437–8. His standard 302, 359–60, 363, 370, 389, 397, 399, 411, 415, 422, 424. See *Elessar, Thorongil, Trotter.*

Aragorn (IXa) 7, 10, 14–16, 18, 22, 47–9, 52, 54–9, 61–4, 67, 70–3, 117, 119, 121, 128, 135; called *Arathornsson* 117, 119, 121, 128, *Arathornion* 128

Aragorn (IXa) *King's messengers* 83; King's guard(s) 47–8; the King's letter to Samwise 117, 119–21, 125–8, 133; his coronation 55–6; his life-span 57

Aragorn (IXa) See *Elessar, Elfstone; Trotter, Strider.*

Aragorn (IXa) *The King* 46–51, 55–6, 61, 64–5, 67–9, 74, 76, 83, 91, 93, 111, 116–28, 133–4; *The Return of the King* 111; *King of Gondor* 48, 61, 117, ~ *and Arnor* 128–9, *aran Gondorar Arnor* 128–9, 135; *King of the West* 74; *Lord of the Westlands* 117, 128, *Hîr iMbair Annui* 129, 135.

Aragorn (IXb) 378

Aragorn (X) 211, 341, 359

Aragorn (XI) 130, 177, 369

Aragorn I (XII) Fifth Chieftain of the Dúnedain. 196, 211

Aragorn II (XII) 32, 42–3, 65, 70, 167, 196, 202, 206, 211, 220, 226, 238–43, 253–4, 258, 262–70, 364, 410, 419–20. See *Elessar*, *Thorongil*.

Aragost (XII) Eighth Chieftain of the Dúnedain. 196, 211; former name *Arandost* 211

Arahad I (XII) Seventh Chieftain of the Dúnedain. 196, 211

Arahad II (XII) Tenth Chieftain of the Dúnedain. 196, 211; former name *Arangar* 211

Arahail (XII) Second Chieftain of the Dúnedain. 196, 211; former name *Aranhantil* 211

Arakáno (XII) Son of Fingolfin. 345, 361–2; Sindarin form *Argon* 345, 361–2. See also *Fingolfin*.

Araman (I) 83, 93, 172–3

Araman (IV) 171, 173, *250–1, 260–1. (Replaced *Eruman*.)

Araman (X) Wasteland beneath the Pelóri and the Sea, north of Taniquetil. 108, 115, 117, 119, 123, 132, 134, 194, 198, 283, 291, 295. (Replaced *Eruman*.)

Araman (XI) Wasteland between the Pelóri and the Sea, north of Taniquetil. 175, 417. See *Eruman*.

Aramir (VII) See *Arathorn*.

Aran (VII) See *Keleborn*.

Aran Endór (X) 'King of Middle-earth' (Morgoth). 121, 126. See *Endor*, *Tarumbar*, *King of the World*.

Aran Isles (IXb) 267, 293

Aranarth (XII) First Chieftain of the Dúnedain. 196, 211, 232, 253

Aranel (XI) Name of Dior Thingol's Heir. 71, 133

Arantar (XII) Fifth King of Arnor. 192

Aranuir (XII) Third Chieftain of the Dúnedain. 196, 211; former name *Aranuil* 211

Araphant (XII) Fourteenth King of Arthedain. 195, 201, 209–10, 215–16, 232

Araphor (XII) Ninth King of Arthedain. 194, 209, 230; former name *Malvegil II* 209

Arassuil (XII) Eleventh Chieftain of the Dúnedain. 196, 211; earlier *Arasuil* 211

Aratan (XII) Second son of Isildur. 208. (Replaced *Eärnur* (1).)

Aratar (I) 62, 80

Aratar (IV) 166

Aratar (X) The High Ones of Arda. 203. See *(The) Great Ones*.

Aratar (XI) The Chiefs of the Valar. 399, 402 *('the Supreme')*, 406. See *Máhani, Varda.*

Aratar (XII) 'The Exalted', the chief Valar. 363

Arathorn (VI) Father of Aragorn. 176

Arathorn (VII) Father of Aragorn. 361–2, 392–3, 404, 443, 447, 449. Original name *Aramir* 7, 63; and see *Elfhelm, Ingrim, Kelegorn.*

Arathorn (VIII) Father of Aragorn. 15, 319

Arathorn (IXa) Father of Aragorn. 55. See *Aragorn.*

Arathorn I (XII) Twelfth Chieftain of the Dúnedain. 196, 211

Arathorn II (XII) Fifteenth Chieftain of the Dúnedain. 32, 196, 202, 211, 226, 238, 263–6

Araval (XII) Thirteenth King of Arthedain. 195, 209–10; former name *Arvallen* 209

Aravir (XII) Fourth Chieftain of the Dúnedain. 196, 211

Aravorn (XII) Ninth Chieftain of the Dúnedain. 196, 211

Araw (VIII) The Vala Oromë. 281, 292

Araw (X) Oromë. 124

Araw (XI) (Sindarin) Oromë. 400; *Arum* in Mithrim 400

Araw (XII) (Sindarin) Oromë. 204, 219, 358

Ar-Balkumagan (XII) Adûnaic name of Tar-Kiryatan. 151

Arbazân (IXb) Amandil. 365–7, 369–70, 374, 382–3, 389–90. (See *Aphanuzír.*)

Arbol, Field of (IXb) [Lewis] The Solar System. 213; *Fields of Arbol* 199–200, 204, *Arbol* (the Sun) 199, 203, 219

Arch of Heaven, the Arch (II) See *Heavenly Arch.*

Arch of Inwë (II) Western entry to the Place of the Well in Gondolin. 182

Archenfield (V) In Herefordshire. 80, 84; *Irchenfield* 83–4; Old English *Ircingafeld* 80

Archenfield (IXb) In Herefordshire. 269, 272, 293–4; O.E. *(æt) Ircenfelda* 272, 294, *Ircingafeld* 294

Archet (VI) Village of the Bree-land. 133, 165, 174, 332, 352, 354, 367

Archet (VII) In the Bree-land. 45

Archet (XII) Village of the Bree-land. 39, 81

Arciryas (XII) Brother of Narmakil II of Gondor. 216

Arcturus (I) 133, 200. See *Morwinyon.*

Arda (I) 80, 87, 110–11, 133, 199, 202

Arda (III) 138, 352

Arda (IV) *242–3, 253, 255, 261, 291

Arda (V) 164, 294, 299, 301–2, 338, *360*

Arda (VI) 122 (*the Spring of Arda*).

Arda (IXb) 246, 310, 312–13, 401, 405, 440

Arda (X) (including many references to *the Kingdom, Realm, of Arda*)
3, 7, 12, 15–17, 20, 22, 25–31, 34–5, 37–9, 41, 43–4, 48–71
passim, 74–5, 80, 87, 93, 97, 99–100, 105, 112, 114–15, 118,
120, 129–30, 132, 135–7, 144–5, 147, 151–4, 159, 161, 172,
179, 187, 201–3, 206–7, 209–10, 212, 215, 217–20, 222–8, 231–
5, 237, 240–55 *passim*, 258–60, 267–71, 275, 280–2, 284–6,
295, 304, 308–9, 311–22, 325–6, 331–43 *passim*, 349, 351–2,
354, 356–9, 361–5, 372–406 *passim*, 410, 416, 419, 424–31.

Arda (X) *King of Arda*, see *Manwë*; *Queen of Arda*, see *Varda*;
Girdle of Arda 115, 135. For *the Tale of Arda* see *(The) Great
Tale*; for *Arda Marred, Arda Unmarred*, etc. see *(The) Marring of
Arda*; for the later meaning of *Arda* see references under *Solar
System*; and see *(The) Earth, Rulers of Arda, Spring of Arda*.

Arda (XI) 10–11, 18, 24, 41, 69, 78, 204, 207, 216, 341, 346, 397,
401–2, (413), 419–21, 423; *Arda Marred, ~ Unmarred* 401; *Spring
of Arda* 106, *Second ~* 20, 27, 30

Arda (XII) 149–50, 157, 305, 323, 370–1, 380; *the Circles of Arda*
401

Ardamir (XI) Name of Eärendil. 235

Ardamir, Ardamírë (XII) Mother-name of Eärendil. 346, 348

Ard-galen (II) 62

Ard-galen (III) The great grassy northern plain, called after its desolation *Anfauglith* and *Dor-na-Fauglith*. 284

Ardgalen (XI) The great northern plain. 17, 36, 38, 46, 52, (111), 113–
14, 175, *183, 191, 195, 238. See *Bladorion*.

Arditi, Colombo (IXb) Member of the Notion Club. 159

Aredhel (II) Sister of Turgon, mother of Maeglin. 212. (Replaced *Isfin*.)

Aredhel (IV) Later name of Isfin, sister of Turgon. 193, 280

Aredhel (XI) 'Noble-elf' (318), sister of Turgon, wife of Eöl. 317–19,
322–3, 325–30, (333), 336; *the White Lady of the Noldor* 317.
See *Isfin, Írith, Feiniel*.

Arfanyarassë (XI) Taniquetil. 403, 416. See *Ras-Arphain*.

Arfaxed (VII) See *Shadowfax*.

Ar-Feiniel (XI) See *Feiniel*.

Ar-Feiniel (XII) Daughter of Fingolfin. 362. See *Írissë*.

Argeleb I (XII) Seventh King of Arthedain. 189, 194, 208–9, 230;
former name *Celebrindol* 209

Argeleb II (XII) Tenth King of Arthedain. 9, 15, 194, 209, 231, 254; former name *Arveleg* 209

Ar-Gimilzôr (IXb) Twenty-third King of Númenor. 381–2. See *Gimilzôr*.

Ar-Gimilzôr (XII) Twenty-third Ruler of Númenor. 154–5, 159

Argon (XII) See *Arakáno*.

Argonath (VIII) 132, 281, 291; *Pillars of the Kings* 132. See *Sarn Aran*, *Sern Aranath*; *Sarn Gebir* (1).

Argonath (XII), *Gates of, Pillars of* 198, 259

Argonath, Gates of (VII) 359–60, 362. Earlier names *Gates of (Sarn) Gebir* 359–60, 362; *Sern Aranath* 366. *Pillars of the Kings* 360–2, 387, 450

Argonui (XII) Thirteenth Chieftain of the Dúnedain. 196, 211

Ari the Learned (V) Icelandic historian. 81

Arien (I) 88

Árien (IV) The Sun-maiden. 99, 170–1. (Replaced *Úrien*.)

Arien (IXa) Aragorn's translation of *Daisy* (Gamgee). 117, 120–1. [Cf. *Arien* the Sun-maiden in *The Silmarillion*; *Daisy* > *Days's eye*, in origin probably a kenning for the Sun, transferred to the flower.] See *Erien*, *Eirien*.

Arien (X) The Sun-maiden. 130–4, 136–7, 198, 385, 405. Other, late names: *Áren* 376, *Ár(i)* 380, 385, *Ázië* 380, *Árië* 380–1, 386; Old English names *Dægred* 130, 136, *Dægbore* 198

Arien, Arien (V) The Sun-maiden. 240–4, *349*. (Replaced *Úrien*.)

Arkenstone (IV) 283

Arkenstone, The (VII) 160

Arkenstone, The (XII) 281

Arlisgion (II) 'Place of Reeds' above the mouths of Sirion. 153, 202, 217. See *Lisgardh*.

Ar-Melian (III) Melian. 347, 350. See *Tar-Melian*.

Armenelos (V) City of the Kings in Númenor. 30

Armenelos (IXb) City of the Númenóreans. 378

Armenelos (XII) City of the Kings in Númenor. 145–6, 148, 160–1, 164. *Arminalêth* (Adûnaic) 145, 147–8, 154, 164. See *Númenos*, *Tar Kalimos*.

Arminalêth, Ar-Minalêth (IXb) City of the Númenóreans. 257–8, 292, 363, 365–7, 369, 381, 384; called *the Golden* 367. (Replaced by *Armenelos*.)

Arminas (II) Noldorin Elf who with Gelmir guided Tuor through the

Gate of the Noldor and afterwards brought the warning of Ulmo to Nargothrond. 123, 125, 204

Arminas (III) Noldorin Elf who with Gelmir brought the warning of Ulmo to Nargothrond. 92

Arminas (XI) Noldorin Elf who with Gelmir (2), also called Faramir, came to Nargothrond with warning of its peril. 141–2, 256, 299

Arnach (VIII) See *Lossarnach*.

Arnen (VIII) See *Emyn Arnen*.

Arnor (V) Northern kingdom of the Númenóreans in Middle-earth. 7, 71

Arnor (VIII) 395. See *North Kingdom*.

Arnor (IXa) 56, 128–9, 135. See *Aragorn*.

Arnor (X) 370, 373

Arnor (XII) 66, 170–1, 176, 186, 189, 191–4, 196, 202, 208, 226–8, 230–1, 239, 243–4, 247, 253–4, 265–6, 269, 315. See *Arthedain*.

Arod (VI) (1) Suggested name for Gandalf's horse. 351. (2) Name of a horse of Rohan. 351

Arod (VII) 'Swift', Legolas' horse of Rohan. 402, 439. Earlier name *Whitelock* 402

Arod (VIII) Horse of Rohan. 78, 423

Arod (IXa) Horse of Rohan. 70, 72; Legolas's horse 120, 123. See *Hasufel*.

Aros (II) The river forded at Sarnathrod. 236–8, 251; identified with the river flowing past the caves of the Rodothlim, 236 (see 244 note 15).

Aros, River (IV) 222–4, 232, 330, 332, 334

Aros, River (V) 127–9, 260–2, 265, 277, 400

Aros, River (VII) In Beleriand. 292

Aros, River (XI) 15, 112, *183, *185, 188–90, 194, 222, 319, 324, 332–4, 337–8. *Ford(s) of Aros* *183, 188, 319, 324–6, (327), *331, 332–6, 338

Aros, River (XII) In Beleriand. 330

Arossiach (XI) The Fords of Aros. 326, 338

Arothir (XII) Son of Angrod; Father of Gil-galad. 346, 350–1, 358, 363–4; Quenya *Artaher* 346, 350–1. See *Orodreth*.

Ar-Pharazôn (IXb) (including references to *the King*) 247, 251, 290, 311–12, 363–72, 374–5, 381–6, 389–91, 407, 415, 428–9, 433, 435; *King Pharazôn* 428, 435. See *Tarkalion*.

Ar-Pharazôn (X) 397–8

Ar-Pharazôn, Pharazôn (XII) 149, 151, 153–7, 159–65, 175–8, 181–3, 186(-7), 262. See *Tar-Kalion*.

Arrow-elves (V) A name of the Teleri. 215

Arrow-elves (X) A name of the Teleri. 164

Arsiriand (III) Rejected name for Beleriand. 160

Artaher (XII) See *Arothir*.

Artamir (XII) Son of Ondohir King of Gondor. 201, 215, 232

Artanáro (XII) See *Gil-galad*.

Artanis (XII) See *Galadriel*.

Artanor (I) Region afterwards named Doriath. 175, 196, 240–1

Artanor (II) 'The Land Beyond', region afterwards named Doriath. 9, 13, 21, 30, 35, 37, 41, 43, 47,49, 52, 54, 56, 58–9, 61–5, 120–2, 127–9, 141–2, 223, 230–4, 236, 240, 243, 246, 248–51, 254, 276. See especially 61, and see *Doriath, Land(s) Beyond*. References to the protection of Artanor by the magic of the Queen: 9, 35–6, 43, 47–8, 63, 76, 122, 132, 137, 230–2, 249–50

Artanor (III) Early name of Doriath. 27, 87, 125, 147–8, 270

Artanor (IV) Name of Doriath in the *Lost Tales*. 7, 62–3, 189, 223

Arthad (III) One of the twelve companions of Barahir on Dorthonion. 335, 349

Arthad (XI) Companion of Barahir. 56, 126, 240; earlier *Arthod* 126, 240; erroneous *Arthrod* 240

Arthael (XII) See *Saelon*.

Arthedain (XII) (1) Earlier name of Arnor. 9, 167, 169, 171–2, 188, 207–8, 211; *Artheden* 167. (2) One of the divisions of earlier Arnor. 193–5, 227–8, 232, 254, 256, 328

Arthod (V) Companion of Barahir. 282

Arthórien (XI) Doriath between Aros and Celon. 112–13, *183, 189; *Arthórien*, name of Doriath, 189 (see *Garthúrian*).

Arthur, King (V) 95

Arthur, King (IXb) 192, 216, 227, 229, 283; *Arthurian legend, romances* 216, 228

Arthur, King (X) 366, 399; *Arthurian* 355, 365

Arthur, King (XII) 44

Arthurian legends (III) 160

Arthurson, John (IXb) Pseudonym of J. R. R. Tolkien. 303, 307, 309

Arûn (IXb) Original name of Mulkher (Morgoth). 357–8, 364, 367, 376, 383–4, 390; *Arûn-Mulkhêr* 367, 384. Replaced *Kheru*, 376

Arundel (IXb) (1) See *Lowdham, Alwin Arundel*. (2) In Sussex. 284

Árundil (IXb) Passing name for a son of Elendil. 401

Arval (II) An early name of Eöl. 220

Arvalin (I) Name interchangeable with *Eruman*, q.v. 19, 22, 32, 68, 70, 74, 76–7, 79, 82–3, 85, 87, 90–1, 93, 118, 125, 130–1, 145, 147, 155, 157–8, 167, 170, 188; *Arvalien* 148, 155; *Bay of Arvalin* 119, 122–3, 125

Arvalin (II) 286

Arvalin (IV) Region between the mountains and the sea south of Taniquetil. 16, 47, 91, 171, 239, 249–51, 257, 260–1, 265, 271, 277–8, 288. (Replaced by *Avathar*.)

Arvalin (V) Region south of Taniquetil. 114, 230, 242, 349

Arvalin (X) Wasteland between the Pelóri and the Sea, south of Taniquetil. 97–8, 105, 108, 132, 184, 190, 290–1. (Replaced by *Vastuman, Avathar*.)

Arvedui (VIII) 'Last King' of Arthedain. 311

Arvedui (XII) 'Last-king' of Arthedain. 190, 195, 201, 204, 208–10, 215–16, (225–6), 232, 248, 253–4, 256, 258, 328

Arvegil (XII) Eleventh King of Arthedain. 194, 209, 254

Arveleg I (XII) Eighth King of Arthedain. 189, 194, 209–10, 230; former name *Beleg II* 209

Arveleg II (XII) Twelfth King of Arthedain. 194, 209; former name *Argeleb* 209

Arvernien (VII) Coastlands west of Sirion. 99, 102–4

Arvernien (XI) High country west of Sirion's mouths. *184, 190

Arwen (VI) 213, 365

Arwen (VII) 83–4

Arwen (VIII) 302, 307, 370; *Lady of Rivendell* 307. See *Finduilas* (2).

Arwen (IXa) 59, 61, 66, 108, 110, 124–5; called *Undómiel* 59, 66, *Evenstar* 66–7; *the Queen* 66, 118, 127. The white jewel, her gift to Frodo, 67, 108–10; the choice of Arwen 66, 125. For earlier names of Elrond's daughter see *Finduilas* (1).

Arwen (X) 211

Arwen (XI) 71, 132, 369

Arwen (XII) Also *Undómiel, Evenstar*. 196, 202, 211, 234–5, 239–41, 243–4, 246–7, 249, 258, 262, 265–70, 349, 364–5. See *Finduilas* (2).

Aryador (I) 'Land of Shadow', name of Hisilómë among Men. 119, 138–9; poem *A Song of Aryador* 138–9

Aryador (II) 'Land of Shadow', name of Hisilómë among Men. 15, 42, 44, 50–1, 61, 70, 202, 249. See *Dor Lómin, Hisilómë, Hithlum, Land of Shadow(s), Mathusdor*.

Aryador (IV) Hithlum. 220

Ar-Zimrahil (IXb) Earlier name of Ar-Zimraphel. 373, 387. See *Tar-Ilien*.

Ar-Zimraphel (IXb) Queen of Ar-Pharazôn (*Tar-Miriel*). 387

Ar-Zimraphel (XII) Queen of Ar-Pharazôn. 154–5, 159; earlier *(Ar-)-Zimrahil* 155, 157, 159–62. See *Tar-Míriel*.

Âs (X) The Sun. 380–1; *Asa* 381

As I was sitting by the way (VI) 98

Ascar, River (IV) (33, 62), 133–5, 189, 209, 230, 232–3, 325, 331–2; variant form *Asgar* (IV) 209, 307, 325; O.E. *Bǽning* 209. See Rathlorion.

Ascar, River (V) 128–9, 141, 263, 265, 272, 274, 386

Ascar, River (XI) In Ossiriand. 13, *185, 206, 216, 221, 334–5, 337, 347–9; *Ford(s) of Ascar* 347–50, 352(-3); *Asgar* 336–7. See *Rathlóriel*.

Asfaloth (VI) Glorfindel's horse. 368

Asgil-Golamir (VIII) Lord of Anfalas. 287. (Replaced by *Golasgil*.)

Asgon (I) Earlier name of Lake Mithrim. 238–9, 241

Asgon (II) Earlier name of (Lake) Mithrim. 70, 88, 202, 204, 263. See *Mithrim*.

Asgon (IV) Earlier name of (Lake) Mithrim. 3, 8, 52

Asgon (XI) (also earlier *Asgorn*, see 301) Companion of Húrin after his release. 146, 253, 257–8, 261–7, 270–1, 278, 298, 300–1, 304, 306–7, 310, 355

Ash Mountains (VII) See *Ered Lithui*.

Ash Mountains (VIII) 268, 438. See *Ered Lithui*.

Ash Mountains (XII) 258

Asia (IXb) 398, 410

Askr (I) The first Man, in Scandinavian mythology. 245

Assariad (IV) Earlier name of Ossiriand. 133, 173, 179, 189, 224, 233

Astaldo (I) Name of Tulkas. 80

Astaldo (X) Name of Tulkas. 149. (Replaced *Poldórëa*.)

Atalantë (V) Númenor. 11 ('The Falling'), 12–13, 14 ('The Ruin'), 25 ('The Downfallen'), 30, 47, 354, 390; apparently referring to the chief city of Númenor 19, 29; *Atalanteans* 12. *Atalantë* 'Downfall' (=*Akallabêth*) 8

Atalante (IXb) 'The Downfallen' (*Akallabêth*). 247–9, 310–12, 315, 333, 353, 375, 396

Atalantë (XII) 'The Downfallen'. 157–8. See *Akallabêth*.

Atanamir (XII) See *Tar-Atanamtr*.

Atanatar I (XII) Tenth King of Gondor. 197

Atanatar II (XII) Sixteenth King of Gondor. 198–9, 212–14, 229, 231, 259–60; named *Alkarin* 198, 212

Atanatári (XI) 'Fathers of Men'. 39, 175; *Atanatardi* 174; *Atanatarni* 166, 174. *Atanatárion*, 'Legendarium of the Fathers of Men', 175

Atanatári (XII) 54, 62, and see 324–5. See *Fathers of Men*.

Atanatárion (X) 'Legendarium of the Fathers of Men'. 373

Atandil (X) 'Friend of the Atani', name of Finrod Felagund. 306, 349. See *Edennil*.

Atani (V) =*Edain*. 338

Atani (VIII) Edain, 'Fathers of Men'. 161

Atani (X) The Followers, Men; Western Men. 7, 30, 36, 39, 314, 317, 320–1, 323, 349, 352, 428. See *Edain*; *(The) Seekers*.

Atani (XI) 'The Second', Men. 31, 114, 174, 206, 219, 386–7, 403; *Atan* singular 386–7, 403. See *Edain*.

Atani (XII) Men of the Three Houses. 31, 34, 54, 63, 65, 173, 198, 306–8, 311–14, 317, 324–30, 339, 348, 357, 360, 364, 369–70, 372–3; *Atanni* 54, 62; *Atanic* 311, 364, 371; origin of the name 324–5. See *Edain*.

Athânâte, Athânâti (IXb) The Land of Gift. 305, 312, 375, 378. (Replaced by *Amatthânê*.)

athelas (III) Herb of healing. 269

Athelas (VI) Healing plant. 190, 197

Athelas (VII) Healing plant. 221

athelas (VIII) Healing plant. 17, 386, 394. See *Kingsfoil*.

Athelney (IXb) In Somerset. 293

Athenians (IXb) 289; *Solon the Athenian* 289

Athrabeth Finrod ah Andreth (XI) 226–8, 230, 233, 235, 418–19

Athrabeth Finrod ah Andreth (XII) 419

Athrad Daer (XI) 'The Great Ford', Sarn Athrad. 335; *Dhaer* 338. See *Harathrad, Sarn Athrad*, and next entry; also *Northern Ford*.

Athrad i-Nogoth, ~ i-Negyth (XI) 'Ford of the Dwarves', Sarn Athrad. 338

Athrasarn (IV) The Stony Ford. 223–4. See *Sarn Athra(d)*.

Atlantic (Ocean) (V) 45

Atlantic Ocean (I) 24

Atlantic Ocean (II) 261

Atlantic, The (IXb) 234, 246, 252

Atlantis (V) 7–10

Atlantis (IXb) 152, 204, 206, 221, 232, 249, 265, 281–2, 284, 289, 409–10, 412

Atlantis (XII) 158

Atlas (IXb) (1) The Titan, upholder of the heavens. 289; *daughter of Atlas* 249 (see *Calypso*). (2) First King of Atlantis. 289

Attalyar (XI) (Quenya) Petty-dwarves. 389

Attercops (VII) Spiders (in the poem *Errantry*). 86, 88, 108; (in *The Hobbit*) 106

Auden, W. H. (VI) 382

Audoin Errol (V) 45–7, 49–53, 56–7, (75), 77

Audoin the Lombard (V) 7, 37, 53–5; called *Eadwine* 55, 91

Audoin the Lombard (IXb) 284; *Auduin* 236; *Éadwine* 276

Aulë (I) 16, 48, 50, 56, 58, 60, 62, 66–71, 73–4, 76–80, 82, 90, 100–5, 111, 113–14, 117–18, 121–2, 124, 126–8, 133, 135, 137, 141–2, 145, 147–9, 152–4, 158–9, 176–7, 179–81, 183, 185–6, 189, 191–2, 195, 198, 201, 209–10, 212, 215, 217, 224. See *Talkamarda*.

Aulë (II) 19, 46, 174, 218, 269, 272

Aulë (III) 137, 139

Aulë (IV) 14, 50, 78, 87, 166, 207–8, 255, 263, 265, 267, 275, 277, 279, 285, 287, 291–3; O.E. *Cræftfréa* 208

Aulë (V) 11, 14, 24, 110, 113, 116, 120–2, 129, 146, 149, 159, 161–2, 165, 178, 190, 205, 214, 223, 225, 240, 243, 273, 278, 358 (other names *Gaul, Belegol, Martan(o), Barthan* 358, 372, 390). See especially 120, and on Aulë and the Dwarves see 129, 146, 149, 178, 190–1, 273, 277.

Aulë (IXb) 332

Aulë (X) 13–15, 19, 24–6, 31–5, 38, 40, 48–9, 52, 56, 60, 66–8, 92–3, 103–4, 107, 114, 120, 130, 144–5, 147, 151–3, 161, 163, 167–8, 176, 179–80, 201–2, 240–2, 244–5, 247, 253, 272, 276–7, 364, 372, 377, 382, 409, 411, 417; called *the Maker* 107, 120, *Friend of the Noldor* 19; *Friends of Aulë*, a name of the Noldor, 163. Aulë and the Dwarves 93, 104, 202, 409, 417

Aulë (XI) 10, 108, 203–5, 207, 210–15, 340–1, 399, 402; called *the Maker* 10. *Children of Aulë*, the Dwarves, 213. See *Mahal*.

Aulë (XII) 295, 322–3, 354, 366, 368, 383–4; *Aulendil, Aulendur* 'Servant of Aulë' 365–6; *Aulëonnar* 'Children of Aulë' 391. See *Návatar*.

Aulenossë (I) 'Kindred of Aulë', name given to the Noldoli who remained in Valinor. 176, 197–8; *Aulë's kindred* 16

Aulian (V) Languages of the Dwarves. 179, 197. See *Nauglian*.

Aur The Sun (Gnomish). 196

Auredhir (II) Son of Dior. 240–1, 251

Auredhir (IV) Son of Dior. 64

Aureldi, Auzeldi (XI) Elves who left Middle-earth for Aman; singular *Aurel, Auzel.* 363–4, 374; Telerin *Audel, Audelli* 364, 376. See *Oäreldi.*

Auron Tulkas (as Vala of the Sun). 376

Aurvandill (Aurvendill) (IXb) Old Norse name cognate with *Éarendel.* 301, 307–8; *Aurvandil's Toe*, star-name, 301, 308. Cognate names in other languages 237, 301, 307

Ausir (II) (1) 'The Wealthy', name of Dior. 240, 244, 251. (2) A boy of Mar Vanwa Tyaliéva. 5, 7–8, 40–2, 50, 59, 311

Avakúma (IV) The Outer Dark. 240–1, *242–3, 252. See *Kúma, Outer Dark, Void.*

Ava-kúma (V) The Outer Dark, the Void. 335, 349, 365 (other names Noldorin *Gaw, Belego* 358, *Gast, Belegast* 366, Quenya *Oiakúmi* 379). See *Outer Darkness, Void.*

Avalâi (IXb) Gods and Elves (see 353–4). 341, 344–9, 351–6, 376, 381, 387, 407. (Replaced *Balâi.*)

Avalê (IXb) 'Goddess'. 428

Avallon (V) Tol-eressëa. 24–9, 64–5, 73, 78, 334, 338, 349, 370. *Avallonë*, haven in Tol-eressëa 20, 29

Avallon (VI) Númenor. 215

Avallon (IXb) The Lonely Isle. 290, 313–15, 332, 334, 336, 354–5, 379, 386, 412

Avallon (XII) 144, 146–7, 173, 175–8, 185, 189, 191, 244. See *Eressëa.*

Avallondë (IXb) 'Haven of the Gods', land of the Avalâi (Balâi). 344, 351–2, 354–5, 379, 407. See *Avallôni.*

Avallónë (VIII) Haven in Tol Eressëa. 169

Avallónë (IXb) The Haven of the Eldar in Tol Eressëa. 380, 386, 393–6, 412; earlier form *'Avallon(de)'* 399, 403, 407, 411–13

Avallónë (X) (1) Tol Eressëa. 175, 179; *Avallon* 179. (2) Haven in Tol Eressëa. 179; *Avallon(de)* 180

Avallónë (XII) (1) Eressëa. 146–7, 157. (2) Haven in Eressëa. 144, 146–7, 157–8, 185

Avallôni (IXb) 'Haven of the Gods', land of the Avalôi(m). 241, 251, 257–8, 305, 309, 361, 372–3, 379, 385–6, 388, 391–2, 394, 407 (see especially 385–6)

Avallonian (IXb) Lowdham's name for Quenya. 241–2, 247, 249, 259, 288, 306, 309, 379, 413–20, 423, 432–4; Lowdham's *Language A* or *Númenórean A* 238–41, 247–8, 305–6, 309, 379. See *Eressëan*, *Nimrian*, *Quenya*.

Avallonian (X) Quenya. 136. See *Eressëan*.

Avalôi (IXb) The Valar. 305, 311, 357–8, 360–82 *passim*, 385–8, 407, 410–12; *Children of the Avalôi* 358, 376. See *Avalôim*.

Avalôim (IXb) The Valar (replaced *Avalôi* in narrative). 241, 247, 375, 382–3, 385, 387–9, 391, 407, 412

Avaltiri (IXb) The Faithful in Númenor. 347, 356

Avamanyar (XI) Elves who would not go to Aman (Avari). 370

Avari (I) 64

Avari (II) 131, 234

Avari (IV) 51

Avari (V) 'The Departing' 170, 183, 219, 344; in later sense 'The willing' 183, 198, 200, 214–15, 219, 344; 347–8 (also Noldorin *Efuir*, *Efyr*).

Avari (VIII) 'The Unwilling', Elves who would not join the Great March from Kuiviénen. (VIII) 158. *The Refusers* 157; *Wild Elves* 157

Avari (X) 'The Unwilling', Elves who refused the Great March, 82, 88, 109, 123, 130, 162–3, 169–70, 416

Avari (XI) Elves who refused the Great March. 12, 112, 173–4, 371–4, 376–8, 380–2, 384, 386, 408–10, 418, 420; singular *Avar* 371, 377; Telerin *Abari* 380. See *Avarin*, *Evair*.

Avari (XII) (and singular *Avar*) 29, 174, 312, 328, 401; *the Refusers* 312. See *East-elves*.

Avarin (XI) (languages) 381, 389–91, 410; Avarin forms cited 410

Avathar (I) 82, 157, 160

Avathar (IV) 'The Shadows', south of Taniquetil. 47. (Replaced *Arvalin*.)

Avathar (X) 'The Shadows', later name of Arvalin. 284, 286, 291, 295, 298. See *Vastuman*.

Avathar (XI) 'The Shadows', wasteland between the Pelóri and the Sea, south of Taniquetil. 404

Avon, River (II) 295–6

Avradî (IXb) Varda. 428. See *Gimilnitîr*.

Avranc (XI) Son of Dorlas of Brethil, enemy of Húrin and slayer of Manthor. 275–9, 284–90, 292–3, 296, 303–4, 308–9; rejected names *Farang*, *Faranc* 303, 306; late change to *Daruin* 309

Awakening of the Elves (XI) 105, 108, 207, 211, 342, 389; ~ *of the*

Quendi 37, 117, 406; legend of the Awakening (*Cuivienyarna*) 380, 382, 420–3

Axe-elves (X) (1) A name of the Nandor. 164, 171. (2) A name of the Sindar. 171

Axe-elves (XI) The Sindar. 109, 126

Azaghâl (IV) Lord of Belegost. 180–2

Azaghâl (XI) Lord of Belegost. 75, 143

Azanulbizâr (VI) Dwarvish name: Dimrill-dale. 465–6; 'Vale of Dim Streams' 466; *Azanûl* 466

Azanulbizâr (VII) Dimrill Dale. 143, 164, 166, 174; *Azanûl* 184

Azanulbizar (XII) 275; *Battle of* ~ (278)-9, 286–7. See *Dimrill Dale, Nanduhirion.*

Azog (VII) Orc, slayer of Thrór. 143, 156–7

Azog (XII) Orc of Moria, slayer of Thrór. 278, 284

Azores (IXb) 234

Azores (V) 80, 82

Azrubêl (IXb) Eärendil. 241, 305, 364, 375, 377, 388, 413, 427, 429, 433; earlier *Azrabêl* 359–60, 363, 366, 369–70, 375, 377, 388; *Azrabêlo* 365, 382, *Azrabêlôhin* 382, son of Azrabêl; the wife of Azrabêl 360. Earliest Adunaic name *Pharazîr* 305, 375

Azrubêl (XII) (Adûnaic) Eärendil. 373

Bablon (II) Gnomish form *of Babylon.* 196, 203, 214; *Babylon* 203, 214

Bad Uthwen (II) The Way of Escape into the plain of Gondolin. 189, 203; earlier *Bad Uswen, Bad Usbran* (II) 203. See *Way of Escape.*

Bag End (VI) 14–18, 20, 23, 26–7, 30–5, 38–40, 43, 45, 53, 74, 76–7, 85, 221–2, 228, 233–5, 237–8, 240–4, 247–8, 250–1, 254–5, 266, 268, 274–7, 280, 283–4, 288–9, 314–15, 318–19, 324, 374–6, 385, 398, 459, 466; *Bag End Underhill* 16, 30, 37, 39, 76, 138, 244, 247, 376

Bag End (VII) 8, 16, 20–1, 29–31, 52, 62, 71–2, 80, 337, 340

Bag End (VIII) 45, 96

Bag End (IXa) 3, 52, 79–80, 84–5, 88, 90–1, 93–4, 97–8, 100, 102–7, 112, 117, 121, 126, 132–3, 135.

Bag End (XII) 4, 48, 83, 87, 91–2, 113, 288–9; true Hobbit name 48, 83

Baggins (VII) (family name) 13, 25, 31, 37, 41, 43, 45–6, 48, 55, 62, 69, 71–2, 74

Baggins (VIII) Used by Gollum of Bilbo and Frodo. 111, 115

34

Baggins (IXa) (and *Bolger-Baggins*), *Bingo* 3, 37, 53

Baggins (IXa) 79, 108; *Bagginses* 111, 113

Baggins (X) See *Bilbo*, *Frodo*.

Baggins family, Bagginses (VI) 13–15, 17, 19, 22–3, 25, 27–8, 31, 34, 36, 54, 78, 96, 221–2, 234, 249–50, 254, 264, 279–80, 287, 289, 291–3, 313, 338, 357; *Baggins country* 279, 296

Baggins, Angelica (VI) 15, 17–18, 32, 35, 247

Baggins, ~ *Balbo* (VI) Bilbo's great-grandfather in LR. 249. (Replaced *Inigo Baggins* (2).)

Baggins, ~ *Bilbo* (VI) 11, 13–42, 46, 53, 56, 58–60, 62–3, 65, 69–70, 73–7, 79–87, 95–6, 103, 108–9, 122, 126, 128, 139, 144, 150, 154, 177, 194, 203–4, 207–8, 210, 212–13, 220–9, 233–56, 261–8, 271–2, 274–7, 280–4, 288–90, 292, 300, 305, 310–22, 330, 346, 357, 360, 365, 369–81 *passim*, 384–7, 391–406 *passim*, 412, 414, 417, 424, 429, 444, 459, 466. *Mad Baggins* 250; Bilbo's book, memoirs 13, 19, 29, 229, 240, 245, 288, 300, 305, 314–15, 371–2, 376–8, 380, 405; his marriage 17, 29, 36; Primula Brandybuck his wife 29, 42

Baggins, ~ *Bingo* (VI) (1) Son of Bilbo. 27–36, 40–3, 245, 267; origin of the name 28, 34. (2) Bilbo's cousin (see also under *Bolger*, *Bolger-Baggins*), son of Drogo Baggins. 221–5, 227–8, 233–302 *passim*, 305, 309; references after *Bingo* > *Frodo*, 315, 323–5, 330, 369, 371–3, 375, 377, 379–81, 391, 393. (2) Grandfather of Drogo. 247, 249 (replaced by *Largo Baggins*).

Baggins, ~ *Bungo* (VI) Bilbo's father. 13, 19, 25, 27, 35, 222, 247, 249, 316–17

Baggins, ~ *Dora* (VI) Frodo's aunt (in LR). 247, 249. (Replaced *Semolina Baggins*.)

Baggins, ~ *Drogo* (VI) Father of Bingo > Frodo. 26, 38, 221–2, 234, 244–5, 247, 249, 282, 316–17, 385, 400. (Replaced *Rollo Bolger*.)

Baggins, ~ *Faramond* (VI) Passing replacement of Frodo Baggins. 373, 409

Baggins, ~ *Folco* (VI) Passing replacement of Frodo Baggins. 371–3

Baggins, ~ *Fosco* (VI) Father of Drogo (in LR). 249. (Replaced *Togo Baggins*.)

Baggins, ~ *Frodo* (VI) (references in this book before the change Bingo > Frodo is reached) 30, 41, 66, 70–1, 107, 112–13, 120, 122–3, 126–7, 176, 193–4, 198, 204, 212–13, 220–4, 234, 241, 246, 250, 268, 272, 277, 280, 284, 287, 297; (after the change)

309, 311, 313–87 *passim*, 391–8, 400–1, 403, 406–24 *passim*, 427–31, 436, 438, 440–60 *passim*, 463, 467

Baggins, ~ *Inigo* (VI) (1) A contemporary of Bilbo's. 17, 35. (2) Bilbo's great-grandfather. 222, 247, 249

Baggins, ~ *Largo* (VI) Frodo's great-grandfather (in LR). 249. (Replaced *Bingo Baggins* (3).)

Baggins, ~ *Mungo* (VI) Bilbo's grandfather. 222, 247, 249

Baggins, ~ *Rosa* (VI) (1) Bilbo's aunt. 222, 224, 316–17. (2) Bilbo's cousin (in LR). 272

Baggins, ~ *Semolina* (VI) (1) Bilbo's aunt or cousin. 15, 18, 32, 35. (2) Drogo's sister, aunt of Bingo > Frodo. 247, 249. (Replaced by *Dora Baggins*.)

Baggins, ~ *Togo* (VI) Father of Drogo. 247, 249. (Replaced by *Fosco Baggins*.)

Baggins, Bilbo (VII) 5–8, 10, 15–16, 19–27, 29, 37–9, 43, 46, 62, 64–6, 81, 83–4, 95, 106, 110–11, 115–18, 126, 129–30, 137, 146–9, 152, 162–3, 165, 169, 173, 185, 188, 190, 192, 201, 212, 221, 260, 264, 287, 292, 451. His book(s) 5, 65, 83, 115; wrote *The Cat and the Fiddle* 64; his song at Rivendell 90 ff., 292; his mailcoat (*elf-mail*, *dwarf-mail*, etc.) 19, 137, 173, 185, 188, 218, 221, 331, 336, 353

Baggins, Bilbo (VIII) 45, 47, 49, 96, 115, 156, 194, 207, 219, 275, 357

Baggins, Bilbo (IXa) 47–8, 52–3, 64, 72, 74, 92, 109–14, 121–2, 132. His mailcoat, see *mithril*; his books of lore 64, 72, 111, and see *Red Book of Westmarch*.

Baggins, Bilbo (XII) 3–5, 7, 10–13, 15, 19, 25, 29, 36, 39–40, 43–4, 50, 54, 56, 58, 60, 69, 72, 86–7, 89–93, 99–101, 109–12, 123–4, 129, 131, 169, 220, 226, 238–9, 241, 243, 251, 255, 282–3, 288–9, 311, 327; his farewell party 85–7, 89, 94, 99, 102, 106, 118, 124, 131, 226, 241, 289; true Hobbit name 46, 50

Baggins, Bingo (VII) 31, 34, 59, 110, 122–3, 137, 158

Baggins, Drogo (VII) 193, 371

Baggins, Frodo (VII) 6–11, 13–16, 20–52 *passim*, 54, 56–7, 61–5, 68–9, 71–4, 76–7, 80–4, 105, 110, 112–15, 117, 122, 126–7, 129–30, 132, 134–5, 137, 139–40, 146–9, 151–2, 156–7, 161–2, 165, 168–9, 171–3, 178, 181, 185, 190, 192–8, 201, 207–54 *passim*, 258–60, 263–6, 268–9, 271, 275–6, 281, 283, 286–7, 321, 324–58 *passim*, 361, 363, 365–8, 371–81, 384–7, 389, 396, 398, 404–5, 407, 409, 411–13, 423, 426–8, 437–8, 440, 446,

451. His sword 10, 16, 115, 137, 173. See *Baggins*, *Dream of the Tower*.

Baggins, Frodo (VIII) 17, 45, 50, 77–8, 81, 85–152 *passim*, 154, 156, 161, 163–8, 171–8, 182–226 *passim*, 229–30, 233–4, 241, 256–7, 259, 262–3, 267, 270–2, 275–6, 286, 291, 294–5, 322, 326–7, 329, 339, 341–2, 360–2, 364, 398, 425, 430(-1), 438

Baggins, Frodo (IXa) 3–14, 18, 21–2, 24–5, 27, 29–53 *passim*, 56, 61–2, 64, 66, 70–114 *passim*, 121–3, 125, 129, 132, 135; *Frodo of the Nine Fingers* 44, 83, *Frodo of the Ring* 125; Old English *Fróda* 47. His character in the Scouring of the Shire 80, 93, 95, 103; his sicknesses after his return 108–10, 112; the Praise of Frodo and Sam at Kormallen 46–7, and at Edoras 62, 70–1

Baggins, Frodo (XII) 13, 19, 25, 36, 42, 50, 52, 60, 69, 86–92, 94–7, 100–1, 104–5, 109–11, 124, 166, 168, 226, 241–3, 255, 282, 288–9, 320, 326; *Frodo of the Nine Fingers* 242; true Hobbit name 50, 59

Bagshot Row (VI) 21, 26, 30, 35, 244, 276

Bagshot Row (VII) 29, 253

Bagshot Row (IXa) 88, 108; called *Ruffians' End* 108

Bain (VI) Son of Bard, King of Dale. 26, 210, 213, 369

Bain (VII) Son of Bard, King in Dale. 404

Bair am Yru (VII) Dwellings of the Galadrim. 243

Bair Nestad, Bair Nestedriu (VIII) See *Berin a Nestad*.

Balâi (IXb) Name replaced by *Avalâi*. 341–4, 353

Balan (XI) True name of Bëor. 218, 229, 231

Balar (X) *Bay of Balar* 84, (174); *Isle of Balar* 174

Balar (XI) Name of Ossë. 5, 104; origin of the name *Beleriand* 5, 104; *Bay of Balar* 6–7, 104, *184, 379; *Cape Balar* 104, 107, *184; *Isle of Balar* 5, 7–8, 11, 54, 80, 104, 107, 125, 136, *184, 345

Balar Bay of (IV) 258, 331, 335; Cape 225; *Isle of* 331, 335

Balar Bay of (V) 129, (221), 260, 267, 404; *Cape* 404–5, 407; *Isle of* 133, 143, 149–50, 153, 221, 225, 266, 288, 412; the name *Balar* 180, 192, 256, *350*

Balar, Isle and Bay of (III) 183

Balar, Isle of 209

Balcmeg (II) Orc slain by Tuor in Gondolin. 181

Baldor (VIII) Son of Brego (second King of the Mark). 315–16, 321, 407, 416, 421; *Bealdor* 321, 397, 405, 408, 421

Baldor (XII) Son of Brego King of Rohan. 236, 270–1

Baldr (VIII) Norse god (Balder). 369

Balin (VI) Dwarf, companion of Thorin Oakenshield. 15, 17, 210, 213, 217, 226, 369, 381, 391–2, 395, 397–400, 409, 412, 429, 443–4, 459–60, 467; *Lord of Moria* 443, 460, 467; *son of Burin* 443–4, 460, 467; *son of Fundin* 444, 460; Balin's tomb 443–4, 460–2, 467; *Balin's Book* 460, 467 (see *Mazarbul*).

Balin (VII) 82, 116–17, 141–2, 155, 158, 172, 190–2, 195, 200–1, 204, 247, 257, 456–9; *Balin Lord of Moria* 186, 191–2, 200, 458; his tomb 67, 161, 176, 190, 194, 379; inscription on the tomb 186, 452, 456–7

Balin (XII) Companion of Thorin Oakenshield. 240, 279–80, 293, 299–301, 320, 322

Balrog (XII) (the Balrog of Moria) 222, 233, 249, 275, 277–8, 286, 383; 379, 421. *Demon* 379–80, 390

Balrogs (I) 93, 161, 241, 250

Balrog(s) (II) 15, 34, 44, 67, 85, 156, 169–70, 174–6, 178–84, 180, 189, 193–4, 212–13, 216. Numbers of, 170, 179, 184, 213; described, 169, 181, 194, 212–13. See *Malkarauki*.

Balrog(s) (III) 7, 36–7, 70, 97–100, 102, 142, 281, 288, 296, 301, 303

Balrog(s) (IV) 12, 17, 22–3, 36–7, 39, 47, 52, 66, 82, 93, 101, 118–19, 142, 144–5, 147, 151, 157, 160, 173, 202, 209, 266, 268, 288, 295, 302, 307, 309, 314, 318, 321, 328, 338; origin of 295, 314, 328, 338; numbers of 302, 321–2; O.E. *Bealuwearg, Bealubróga* 209 (but *Balrogas* in the texts).

Balrog(s) (V) 114, 117, 122, 125, 137, 142, 144, 148, 152, 212, 216, 233, 238, 249, 256, 280, 282–3, 290, 298, 310–11, 314, 328, 336, *384* (also Quenya *Malarauko*), 404. See especially 148, 256, 336

Balrog(s) (VI) (VI) 187–8, 215, 462

Balrog(s) (VII) (almost all references are to the Balrog of Moria) 142, 186, 188–9, 197–200, 202–3, 206, 211, 236, 247, 257, 262–3, 354, 422, 430–1, 434, 441; the Balnog described 197, 199, 202

Balrogs (VIII) 372. See *Gothmog*.

Balrogs (X) 70, 75–6, 78–80, 109, 123, 159, 165, 203, 297–8, 391, 410–11, 414, 418; *Balrogath* (X) 79. See *Valaraukar*, and on their origin and number see especially 165 and 79–80.

Balrog(s) (XI) 18, 74–5, 110, 113–14, 134, 194, 415; number of 74, 134; etymology 415

Balthronding (III) The bow of Beleg. 17, 127; later form *Belthronding* 26, 127

Bamfurlong (IXa) (1) Village in the Eastfarthing (replaced by Whitfurrows). 107. (2) Maggot's farm. 107

Ban (III) Father of Blodrin the traitor. 48–9, 52. See *Bor*.

Ban (IV) Father of Blodrin the traitor. 28, 59, 123, 210, 304; O.E. *Bana* 210

Ban (V) Father of Blodrin. 138

Ban (XI) Father of Blodren. 82

Ban of the Valar (V) 20, 326, 334

Ban of the Valar (X) 340

Bandobras Took (IXa) See under *Took*.

Banks (VI) Hobbit family name. 137, 236. *Eglantine Banks* 297

Bansil (II) 'Fair-gleam', the Tree of Gondolin with silver blossom. 160, 184, 186, 203, 207, 214, 216; later form Banthil 203. See *Belthil*.

Bansil (III) The White Tree of Valinor (Silpion, Telperion). 5, 73, 81–2, 195, 219. (Replaced *by Belthil*.)

Bansil (IV) Gnomish name of the White Tree of Valinor. 81–2, 167, 209; O.E. *Béansil, Béansigel* 209. See *Belthil*.

Bansil (V) Gnomish name of the White Tree of Valinor. 211. (Replaced by *Belthil*.)

Bar Bëora (XI) The House of Bëor. 230

Bar Haleth (XI) Transient name replacing *Ephel Brandir*. 157, *182, 186

Barad Amroth (VIII) 409, 423–4; *Castle Amroth* 423. See *Dol Amroth*.

Barad Eithel (XI) Fortress of the Noldor at Eithel Sirion. 168

Barad Nimras (IV) The tower raised by Felagund on the cape west of Eglarest. 229, 335. See *Tindobel*.

Barad Nimras (XI) Tower on the cape west of Eglarest. *184, 190, 198; *Nimras* 198. (Replaced *Ingildon*.)

Barad-dûr (II) 67

Barad-dûr (VII) 177–8, 208–9, 213, 332, 334, 336–7, 341, 344, 371, 373. See *Dark Tower, (The) Eye*.

Barad-dûr (VIII) (in many instances spelt *Baraddur*) 64, 69–70, 72–3, 79–80, 119–20, 185, 189, 214, 219, 238, 241, 256, 362, 368, 403 *(Lord of)*, 433, 438–9; *Lieutenant of Barad-dûr* 419, 430–1. The *palantír* of Barad-dûr 80 *(Ithil-stone)*, 362, 404. See *Dark Tower*.

Barad-dûr (IXa) 5–11, 24, 29, 38, 40, 43. See *Dark Tower, (The) Eye*.

Barad-dûr (IXb) 382

Barad-dûr (X) 413

Barad-dûr (XII) 121, 129, 132–3, 153, 168–70, 174, 176–80, 182, 192, 206, 240, 243, 252, 265, 310, 323, 382. See *Dark Tower*.

Baragund (II) Father of Morwen. 139

Baragund (III) Nephew and companion of Barahir and father of Morwen. 335, 349

Baragund (IV) Father of Morwen. 209, 297–9, 311, 315–16, 319; wife of Baragund 299; O.E. *Beadohun* 209

Baragund (V) Father of Morwen, and cousin of Beren. 131, 133, 153, 289, 316, 328, *351*, 366

Baragund (XI) Father of Morwen. 51, 56, 61, (79), 162, (224), 230–2, 241–2, 268; his wife 126

Barahir (II) Father of Beren. 43, 51. (Replaced *Egnor*.)

Barahir (III) Father of Beren (son of Bëor, 198, 334, 348). 25, 153, 161, 163–7, 170–1, 188, 190–1, 193, 198, 201, 213–14, 216, 220, 242, 245, 247, 249, 334–5, 337–43, 345, 348–9, 351, 360

Barahir (IV) Father of Beren. 22–4, 54–5, 100, 104–6, 109, 179, 209, 226, 297–300, 315–19, 332–3; O.E. *Beadomær* 209

Barahir (V) Called 'the Bold'; father of Beren. 130–4, 146, 150–1, 275–6, 281–2, 289, 291–2, 296–7, 305, 307. 316, 328, *351*, *364*

Barahir (VI) Called 'the Bold', father of Beren. 182

Barahir (VII) 240

Barahir (VIII) (1) Father of Beren. 155. (2) Messenger from Minas Tirith to. 242, 244. See *Hirgon*.

Barahir (X) Father of Beren One-hand. 305–6, 328, 373

Barahir (XI) Father of Beren; originally son of Bëor, later son of Bregor. 49, 51–2, 56, 59, 61, 64(-5), 71, 126, *183, 217, 224, 229–32, 234, 240–2

Barahir (XII) (1) Father of Beren One-hand. 307. (2) Eighth Ruling Steward. 204

Baran (X) Elder son of Bëor the Old. 306–7

Baran (XI) Elder son of Bëor the Old. 218–19, 229–31, 334; called *Bëor the Young* 230–1

Baranduin (VII) 66, 131, 272, 289, 402, 416; *Baranduinen* 124; *Branduin* 61, 66, 144. Ephemeral name *Malevarn* 66. See *Brandy-wine*.

Baranduin, Bridge of (IXa) 117, 128; *(i) Varanduiniant* 129. See *Brandy-wine*.

Baranduin, River (V) The Brandywine. 345, *351*, (355)

Baranduin, River (XII) 9, 39–40, 54, 56, 67, 70, 72, 83, 86, 193–4, 196, 209, 225, 228, 231, 248; *Branduin* 67. See *Brandywine*, *Malevarn*.

Barangils (VII) Men of the Harad, Southrons. 313

Barangils (VIII) Men of the Harad, Southrons. 136

Baranor (VIII) Father of Berithil (Beregond). 282, 288

Baranor (XI) Son of Baran. 230–1

Barathil, Barithil (VIII) See *Berithil.*

Baravorn (IXa) Aragorn's translation of *Hamfast* (Gamgee). 121, 126, 129. (Replaced *Marthanc.*)

Barazinbar (VII) Caradras. 166, 174, 432; *Baraz* 174

Barazinbar (XII) 275. See *Caradras, Redhorn.*

Bard (VI) Called 'the Bowman', King of Dale. 26, 210, 213, 369

Bard (VII) King in Dale. 404

Bard of Esgaroth (XII) 239

Bardings (VII) Men of Dale. 296, 307, 404–5. See *Brandings.*

Bar-goll (XI) 'Hollow dwelling', translation of *Novrod* (Nogrod). 414

Bârim an-adûn (IXb) Lords of the West. 247, 251; *Bârun-adûnô* Lord of the West 311

Bar-in-Myl (XI) 'Home of the Gulls', cape south-west of Eglarest (replacing *Bar-in-Gwael* 418). 190, 379–80, 418. See *Ras Mewrim.*

Barren Hill (VIII) See *Death Down.*

Barren Land, The (V) 31–2

Barren Lands (VIII) Before the Morannon. 140

Barrow Downs (XII) 194, 208, 228. See *Tyrn Goerthaid.*

Barrow-downs (VI) (including references to *the Downs*) 107, 111–12, 115, 117–18, 121, 125–6, 192, 334, 349, 401

Barrow-downs (VII) (including references to *the Downs*) 11, 41, 73, 79, 402, 416

Barrow-downs (VIII) 209, 368

Barrow-downs (IXa) 29, 77

Barrowfield (IXa) At Edoras. 68, 73; *Barrow fields* 62, 73

Barrows (VII) 16; hobbits' swords from 16, 381

Barrow-wight(s) (VI) 42–3, 109–12, 115–19, 121, 125, 127, 129–30, 132, 160, 169, 198, 218, 226, 401, 414; relation to Black Riders 118–20, 401

Barrow-wights (VII) 152

Bath of the Setting Sun (IV) 49

Battle of (the) Green fields (XII) 8–11, 15, 211, 236

Battle of Bywater (XII) See *Bywater.*

Battle of Eglorest (V) 144, 153, 336

Battle of Eldorest (IV) (later > *Eglarest* > *Eglorest*). 309, 313, 326. See *Eldorest.*

Battle of Five Armies (VI) 77, 210, 263, 319, 429

Battle of Five Armies (VII) 22, 143, 157. Last battle of the War of the

Ring 208; *last battle of Gorgoroth* 211. At end of the last Alliance: *Battle of (the Field of) Gorgoroth* 444, 450; *Battle Plain* 310, 389, 450 (see *Dagorlad*).

Battle of Five Armies (XII) 239, 276–7, 288, 383

Battle of Palisor (I) See *Palisor.*

Battle of Sudden Fire (V) 132, 150, 258, 280–1, 289–91, 297; *the Sudden Fire* 147, 287. See *Dagor Húr-breged, Dagor Vregedúr, Third Battle.*

Battle of Sudden Flame (I) See *Dagor Bragollach.*

Battle of Sudden Flame (III) 83, 147, 171, 247, 284, 351; other references 55, 85, 221–2; described 212–13, 275

Battle of Sudden Flame (IV) (23), 53, (55, 105), 108, 173–4, 176, 179–80, 182, 226, 316–17, 334, 336; *Battle of Sudden Fire* 298, 315, 317–20. See *Dagor Bragollach, Dagor Hurbreged, Second, Third,* and *Fourth Battle.*

Battle of Sudden Flame (X) 306, 336, 357–8; *Dagor Bragollach* 306, 326

Battle of Sudden Flame (XI) The Fourth Battle of Beleriand (formerly the third). 52, 127, 134, 238, 241, 329; *the Sudden Flame* 53; earlier *of Sudden Fire* 124, 126, 238, ~ *of Fire* *183. See *Dagor Bragollach.*

Battle of Sudden Flame (XII) 350

Battle of the Gods (IV) (1) The first battle, when Morgoth was chained. 84, 86, 239, 257; *Battle of the Powers* 258; *War of the Gods* 250–1, 259–60. (2) The second battle, second war, at the end of the Elder Days. 239, 241; see *Last Battle* (1).

Battle of the Gods (V) (1) *The First Battle of the Gods,* when Melko was chained. 213, 217, 221; *War of the Gods* 112, 259, 270. (2) *The Last Battle of the Gods,* at the end of the Elder Days. 11. See *Great Battle, Last Battle.*

Battle of the Gods (XI) (when Melkor was chained) 207

Battle of the Haven (X) 119. See *Haven of the Swans.*

Battle of the Powers (I) 111

Battle of the Silent Pools (IV) 68, (71)

Battle of Unnumbered Tears (I) 230, 239–44. See *Nirnaeth Arnoediad.*

Battle of Unnumbered Tears (II) Called also the *Battle of Tears, of Uncounted Tears, of Lamentation,* and the *great battle.* 9–10, 17, 43–5, 65–6, 70, 73, 77, 83–4, 88, 91, 101, 120–1, 140, 142, 157, 198, 200, 208–9, 216, 218. See *Nieriltasinwa, Nínin-Udathriol.*

Battle of Unnumbered Tears (III) 6, 11, 23–6, 59, 83–6, 92, 96, 111,

137, 146–7, 274, 310; field of tears 80, 85, (111). See *Nínin Udathriol/Unothradin, Nirnaith Arnediad/Ornoth/Unoth.*

Battle of Unnumbered Tears (IV) 4–5, 26, 28, 32, 34–5, 53, 56–8, 60, 65, 67, 117, 126, 132–3, 136, 138, 141, 181–2, 188, 191–2, 220–2, 227, 229, 232, 301, 312, 315–16, 321, 323–4, 336. See *Nirnaith Arnediad, Third Battle.*

Battle of Unnumbered Tears (V) 256, 290, 295, 313–14, 322–3, 405; *Unnumbered Tears* 136, 310. See *Dagor Nirnaith, Nirnaith Arnediad, Nirnaith Dirnoth, Fourth Battle.*

Battle of Unnumbered Tears (VI) 12

Battle of Unnumbered Tears (IXa) 44

Battle of Unnumbered Tears (XI) The Fifth Battle of Beleriand (formerly the fourth). 28, 71, 121–2, 136–7, 165, 168–9, 174, *182, 236, 243, 245, 312, 314–16. See *Nírnaeth Arnoediad.*

Battle of Unnumbered Tears (XII) 419

Battle of Wrath and Thunder (IV) 157, 160; *War of Wrath* 199. See *Last Battle(s).*

Battle Plain (VIII) 85, (109), 111, (112). See Dagorlad.

Battle Plain (IXa) 7, 13

Battles (VII) *Great Battle* (at the end of the Elder Days) 122, 124, 247.

Battles (VIII) See *Fords of Isen, Great Battle, Homburg, Pelennor, Valar.*

Battles of the Gods (X) The First Battle of the Valar for the dominion of Arda 16, 25–7, 376, 380; *the Battle of the Gods* (when Melkor was chained) 161, 174, *the Great War of the Gods* 74, 78, called *the Third Battle* 378; *the Last Battle* (1) the final overthrow of Melkor 110, called *the Great Battle* 27, 203, (2) the battle 'at the end of days' 71, 76, 160, 166, 399

Battle-under-Stars (III) 87

Battle-under-Stars (IV) (52), 103, 172, 268, 274, 280, 283, 295, 328, 333. See *Dagor-os-Giliath, First Battle of Beleriand.*

Battle-under-Stars (V) 117, 239, 249, 255. See *Dagor-os-Giliath, First Battle.*

Battle-under-Stars (XI) The Second Battle of Beleriand (formerly the first). 17, 111, 113–14. See *Dagor-nuin-Giliath.*

Bauglir (III) (1) Earlier name for Blodrin the traitor. 48–9, 52. (2) Name of Morgoth (replaced *Belcha, Belegor, Melegor*). 6–8, 10, 16, 21–2, 28, 41, 49, 52, 57, 59–61, 64–6, 84, 96, 98, 100, 116–17, 135, 168, 170, 182, 196, 211, 230, 282, 286–7

Bauglir (IV) (in *Morgoth Bauglir*) 79, 99, 122, 139, 164, 209; trans-

lated *Black God Terrible* 79, *Dark Power Terrible* 164; O.E. *Bróga* 209, *Sweart-ós* 281, 283

Bauglir (V) Name of Morgoth. 206 ('the Constrainer'), 208, 246, 317, 332, 372

Bauglir (X) Name of Morgoth. 146 *(the Constrainer)*, 149, 151; *Baugron* 149, 151

Bauglir (XI) Name of Morgoth. 84

Bay of Balar (IV) See *Balar*.

Bay of Balar (V) See *Balar*.

Bay of Elfland (IV) *249, 257. See *Elfland*.

Bay of Elfland (V) 230, 232

Bay of Elvenhome (IV) 155, 198, 235 (replacing *Bay of Faërië*). See *Elvenhome*.

Bay of Elvenhome (V) 222, 224, 232, 243, 324, 334

Bay of Faërie (Faëry) (IV) 14, 38, 45, 87–8, 91, 150, 153, 155, 198, 200, *235, 250–1, 260; *shores of Faërie (Faëry)* 20, 40, 72, 98; (poem) 70

Bay of Faërie (V) 171

Bay of Faëry (I) 68, 83, 119, 125, 129, 134, 209–11. See *Faëry*.

Bay of Faëry (II) See *Faëry*.

Baynes, Pauline (III) (Map of Middle-earth) 26

Baynes, Pauline (V) Map of Middle-earth. 338

Beacons (VIII) In Anórien. 77, 141, 231–4, 256–7, 259–60, 262–4, 270–2, 275–6, 317, 344, 351–2, 354, 438

Bealdor (VIII) See *Baldor*.

Beardless Men (VI) See 434.

Bede (XII) 137

Bee of Azure (II) Sirius. 282; *Blue Bee* 281. See *Nielluin*.

Beechbone (VIII) Ent. 53

Belaurien (III) Rejected name for Beleriand. 160

Belaurin (II) Gnomish form of *Palúrien*. 281, 328; *Belawryn* 310

Belaurin (III) Gnomish form of Palúrien. 160

Belaurin (IV) Gnomish form of *Palúrien*. 40–1; *Ifan Belaurin* 12, 20, 43; *the Pine of Belaurin* 73, 75

Belcha (II) Gnomish name of Melko. *Belcha Morgoth* 44, 67

Belcha (III) Name of Morgoth (replaced by *Belegor, Melegor, Bauglir*). 21–3, 52

Belcha (IV) Gnomish form of Melko. 167. (Replaced by *Moeleg*.)

Beldir (XI) Son of Belen son of Bëor the Old. 230–1

44

Beldis (XI) Wife of Handir of Brethil, mother of Brandir the Lame. 231, 237–8, 268; earlier the daughter of Bregor 230

Belecthor I (XII) Fifteenth Ruling Steward. 205, 219

Belecthor II (XII) Twenty-first Ruling Steward. 205, 220, 238, 250

Beleg (II) 21, 47, 59, 62, 73, 76–83, 102, 118, 121–4, 141–2. Called 'wood-ranger', 'hunter', 'huntsman' 73, 76–7, 81, 123; a Noldo 78, 122–3; later surname *Cúthalion* 'Strongbow' 59, 62, 124

Beleg (III) 10–12, 16–17, 25–7, 30–51, 53–8, 60, 63–4, 76, 86, 89, 94, 110–12, 116–18, 127, 259, 311, 313–14; see especially 25–6, 127. In *The Children of Húrin* called *the Huntsman, the Hunter, the Bowman.* Túrin's elegy *The Bowman's Friendship* 64, 89, *Laer Cú Beleg*, the Song of the Great Bow, 89

Beleg (IV) 28–9, 59, 113–14, 117, 123–5, 172, 179–80, 183, 209, 220, 224, 304, 322; called *the Gnome* (28) and *the Bowman*; O.E. *Finboga* 209; his sword 125, 183–4, 304; Túrin's elegy *The Bowman's Friendship* 29, 124

Beleg (V) Called 'the Bowman'. 133, 138–9, 151, 256, 287, 291, 293, 308, 317–18, 320–2, 352

Beleg (VI) Called 'the Bowman', Elf of Doriath. 183

Beleg (XI) 'The Bowman', of Doriath. 56, 63, 81–3, 102, 126, 133, 138, 140, 160, 314, 352

Beleg (XII) (1) Beleg the Bowman. 404. (2) Second King of Arthedain. 193, 208

Belegaer (XII) The Great Sea. 363

Belegar (IV) The Great Sea. 210, *249–51, 285, 289, 310, 328, 333, 339; later form Belegaer 254; O.E. *Garsecg* 199, 208, 210, 285, 289, 339, *Ingársecg* 210, *250–1, 261, 285, 287, 289, *Widsǽ* 210. See *Great Sea(s), West(ern) Sea(s).*

Belegar (V) 'The Great Sea'. 14–15, 19, 126; *Belegaer* 19; *Belegoer* 349, 352 (Quenya *Alatairë* 348–9)

Beleghir (VI) Early name of the Great River. 410–11, 434

Beleghir (VII) See *Anduin.*

Belegor (III) Name of Morgoth (replacing *Belcha*, replaced by *Melegor*, *Bauglir*). 21

Belegor (XI) Son of Boron. 230–1

Belegorn (XII) Fourth Ruling Steward. 204, 219; former names *Bardhan, Belgorn* 219

Belegost (II) City of the Indrafang Dwarves. 230–1, 235, 244–8; *Ost Belegost* 244

Belegost (III) A city of the Dwarves. 44 (*black Belegost*), 306

Belegost (IV) 32, 62, 103, 116, 118, 132–3, 174–5, 180–2, 188–9, 210, 220–1, 232, 300, 331, 335–6; O.E. *Micelburg* 210

Belegost (V) 'Great Fortress'. 129, 134, 141, 274, 277–8, 303, 307, 319, 322, *352, 379*. See *Gabilgathol*.

Belegost (VII) Dwarf-city in Eredlindon. 301, 304

Belegost (X) City of the Dwarves in the Blue Mountains. 93

Belegost (XI) 'Great Fortress', city of the Dwarves in the Blue Mountains. 10, 45, 75, 108–9, 134, 143, 167, *183, 201–2, 205–6, 208–9, 215, 321, 329, 335, 347, 350, 352, 389, 408. See *Gabilgathol; Turosto; Great Fortress, Mickleburg*.

Belegost (XII) Dwarf-city in Ered Lindon. 185, 275, 322

Belegund (III) Nephew and companion of Barahir. 335, 349

Belegund (IV) Father of Rían. 297–9, 301, 311, 315–16, 319; wife of Belegund 299

Belegund (V) Father of Rian, and cousin of Beren. 131, 133, 136, 151, 282, 289, 316

Belegund (XI) Father of Rían the mother of Tuor. 51–2, 56, 71, (224), 230–2, 241–2; his wife 126

Belegûr, Belegurth (XII) (Sindarin) Melkor. 358; *Belegor* 358

Belemir (X) Husband of Adanel, grandson of Belen. 305–7

Belemir (XI) The husband of Adanel. 230–1, 233–4

Belen (X) Second son of Bëor the Old. 306

Belen (XI) Second son of Bëor the Old. 230–1

Beleriand (I) 51, 132, 240, 242–3

Beleriand (II) 64, 128, 205, 217, 245, 324; Drowning of Beleriand 251, 324

Beleriand (III) 83, 152, 155, 157–8, 160, 166, 168–9, 184–5, 195, 222, 226–7, 236, 243, 297, 304, 331, 333, 346. (Replaced *Broseliand*; for other rejected names see 160)

Beleriand (IV) 51, 53, 56, 77, 107–8, 115, 120, 122, 125–7, 131–2, 136, 138–9, 141, 157, 159–62, 174–5, 179, 187, 198–200, 224, *249–51, 257–8, 262, 264, 268, 271–2, 277–9, 286–8, 296–8, 301–3, 309–10, 317, 319–21, 324, 327–31, 333–6, 338–9; a Gnomish name 107–8, but ascribed to 'the language of Doriath' 174; other names 108, 174. See *Broseliand; East, West, Beleriand; Chronology of Beleriand*.

Beleriand (V) 18, 22–3, 28–35, 38, 56, 76–8, 112, 114, 117, 119, 122, 126, 128–31, 134–8, 144, 146, 153, 170–1, 174–84, 186–7, 189–91, 193–5, 197, 215, 219–23, 226, 238–9, 248–50, 252, 254, 256, 260–4, 267–9, 273–9, 281, 283–4, 286, 288–9, 291,

299, 307, 312, 317, 328, 330–1, 337, 344, 346, 404; the name 350, 404. See *East, South, West Beleriand, Ingolondë.*

Beleriand (VI) 215–16, 433; Runes of Beleriand 467

Beleriand (VII) 110, 122–4, 137, 239, 292, 454; *Beleriandic letters* 453, *languages* 454; runes of Beleriand 455–6

Beleriand (VIII) 155, 159, 161; see also 184, 187, and *Annals of Beleriand.*

Beleriand (IXb) 279, 331, 339, 406; *Annals of Beleriand* 280; *Men of Beleriand* 331; *Beleriandic* (language) 304, 308

Beleriand (X) 83, 85–6, 89–91, 93, 103–4, 106, 109–10, 127, 138, 164, 169–70, 172, 174–5, 177, 196, 217, 297, 304–5, 316, 325, 336, 340, 352, 370, 373, 403, 431; *East(ern) Beleriand* 84, 305; *Beleriandic* (not of language) 102, 106

Beleriand (XI) 5–9, 12–15, 19–33, 36–9, 42, 44–7, 49, 52, 54, 59–61, 64, 70, 77–80, 103–12, 116, 118–19, 121–4, 127–8, 132, 135–6, 160, 177, 186, 192, 197, 199–203, 206, 215–16, 218–20, 225–6, 228–9, 231–5, 241, 260, 283, 296, 304, 311, 313, 315, 322, 334, 337, 343–5, 360, 365, 373–81, 383–7, 389–90, 396–7, 400, 408–10, 418–19; *Belerian* 5, 104

Beleriand (XI) *East(ern) Beleriand* 7, 49, 53, 59, 127–8, *185, 189, 327, 330, 334, 377, 385, 388, 409; *West(ern)* ~ *182/184 193, 378–9; *Mid-Beleriand* *182/184, 190 (see *Methiriad*); *South* ~ *185, 191, 239; *Northern* ~ 7, *North Marches of* ~ 194.

Beleriand (XI) Origin and reference of the name 5, 104. *Lays of Beleriand* 103, 160, 311

Beleriand (XII) 73–6, 78, 146, 163, 174, 185, 223, 301–3, 305–7, 309–10, 313–14, 317, 319, 324–6, 328–9, 337, 339–41, 345–9, 357–8, 368, 372–4, 379, 385, 387, 389, 391–2, 400–2; *East Beleriand* 307

Beleriandic (V) (language) 41–2, 45, 180, 185, 192, 194, 243, 256, 343, 346

Beleriandic (XI) (of language) 22–4, 110; (with other reference) 107, 344

Belerion (II) Harbour in the west of Britain. 313–15, 317, 322, 324, 330–3

Belerion (IV) Harbour in the west of Britain (in the tale of *Ælfwine of England*). 200

Beleth (XI) Daughter of Bregolas. 230–2; earlier the daughter of Boron 230

Belfalas (VI) See 438.

Belfalas (VII) 310, 322, 382. *Bay of Belfalas* 119, 125, 144, 298–9, 356, 389, 435. Earlier name *Bay of Ramathor, Ramathir* 119, 125

Belfalas (VIII) (in different applications, see 293) 28, 41, 233, 236, 238, 252, 278, 287, 293–4, 372, 412, 437

Belfalas (XII) Fief of Gondor. 220–2; *Bay of Belfalas* 183, 313

Bell-Tinker (IXb) Oxford professor. 219–20

Belthil (III) The White Tree of Valinor (Silpion. Telperion). 5, 81–2, 192, 195, 210. (Replaced *Bansil*.)

Belthil (IV) Later form for *Bansil*. 167

Belthil (V) Gnomish name of the White Tree of Valinor (replacing *Bansil*); the White Tree of Gondolin. 210–1l, *350*, *385*, *392*

Belthil (X) Image of Telperion in Gondolin. 155

Belthil (XI) Image of Telperion in Gondolin. 200

Belthil (II) The Tree of Gondolin with silver flowers, made by Turgon. 207. See *Bansil*.

Belthronding (II) The bow of Beleg. 123

Belthronding (III) See *Balthronding*.

Benish Armon (VI) See 464.

Bennas (VII) The Angle of Lothlórien. 238, 241, 288

Benrodir (VIII) Prince of Anárion (?). 252, 255, 266

Bëor (I) 236

Bëor (III) Father of Barahir. 198, 334, 348; *Bëor's sons, Bëor's house* 187, 335, 348, 350–1

Bëor (VI) Father of Men. *Sons of Bëor* 331

Bëor (VII) (house of, people of) 455

Bëor (VIII) Father of Men. 157, 159

Bëor (IXb) 333

Bëor the Old (IV) (including references to the house, race, children, etc. of Bëor) 104–5, 109, 121, 158, 175, 179, 200, 202, 297–8, 311–12, 315, 317–18, 332–3; *Bëorians* 175, 316–17; the people described 297, 317

Bëor the Old (V) 130–1, 146, 149, 274–6, 279, 289, 296–7; called 'Father of Men' 130–1, and 'the Vassal' 274–5, 279, *352*; the sons, house, people of Bëor 18, 25, 64, 130–2, 135, 146, 179, 191, 275–6, 279, 281, 287, 291, 299, 310

Bëor the Old (X) 305–7, 327–8; *House of, People of, Bëor* 305–7, 327–8, 336, 349, 358

Bëor (the Old) (XI) 48–9, 51–2, 123, 206, 216–19, 224–6, 229–31, 240–1, 334; name signified 'Vassal' 206, 217, 226–7, 229, 'Ser-

vant' 218, 227; used as title of Bëor's successors 217, 229; see *Balan*.

Bëor (the Old) (XI) *House, People, Folk, Men of Bëor* 50–2, 61, 64, 77–8, 123–4, 126, 128, 161, *183, 217–21, 224, 226–34, 236–8, 240, 268, 270, 300, 406; *Bëorian(s)* 229, 236, 268; see *Bar Bëora*. Ancient tongue of 202, 217, 226–7, 270, 406; genealogical table 231

Bëor *(the Old)* (XII) 63, 146, 307–8, 325, 368, 370, 372–3; *House, Folk, People of Bëor* 294, 307–8, 311, 313, 326, 330, 368, 374–5; *Beorians* 326, 372–3; *Lesser Folk* 370, 373–4

Bëor the Young (XI) See *Baran*.

Beorhtnoth (VII) 106–7

Bëorian (XII) (language) 325, 330, 368–71, 376

Bëoring(s) (III) Men of the house of Bëor. 335, 348, 351

Beorn (I) (1) Uncle of Ottor Wǽfre (Eriol). 23. (2) The shape-changer, in *The Hobbit*. 23

Beorn (II) Uncle of Ottor Wǽfre (Eriol). 290–1, 294. See *Hasen of Isenóra*.

Beorn (VI) 387

Beorn (VII) 138, 248, 263, 287

Beorn (XII) 72; *Beornings* 34, 71, 272

Beornings (VII) 233, 248, 264, 289, 372, 390, 395

Beow (V) 'Barley', see 92, 94–5; changed to *Beowulf* 93–4

Beowulf (I) 23

Beowulf (II) 298, 323; J. R. R. Tolkien, *On Translating Beowulf*, 331

Beowulf (III) 127

Beowulf (IV) 208, 211–12

Beowulf (V) (the hero) 91, 94–5; (the poem) 92–4, 97

Beowulf (VII) 65, 442, 449

Beowulf (VIII) 266

Beowulf (IXb) (the poem) 145

Beowulf (X) 124

Bered Ondrath (VIII) The Causeway Towers. 340. See *Causeway*.

Bereg (XI) Son of Baranor, a leader of dissension in Estolad. 220–1, 227, 230–1

Bereg (XII) A leader of dissension in Estolad. 325

Beregar (XI) Father of Erendis of Númenor. 232

Beregond (VIII) Man of Minas Tirith. 276–7, 282–3, 288, 292, 325, 340. See *Berithil*.

Beregond (IXa) Man of Minas Tirith. 59. See *Berithil*.

Beregond (XII) (1) Twentieth Ruling Steward. 205–6, 220; former name *Baragond* 220. (2) Man of Minas Tirith, father of Bergil and Borlas. 411, 421

Berelach (XII) Son of Borlas of Pen-Arduin. 416–17, 421; rejected names *Berthil, Bergil* 421

Beren (I) 82, 90, 238, 240–1; also in references to the original Tale of (Beren and) Tinúviel, see *Tinúviel*.

Beren (II) 11–19, 21–31, 33–41, 43–5, 48–9, 52–63, 65–8, 71–3, 116, 123–4, 137, 139–40, 144–5, 215, 223, 231, 233–43, 246, 248–51, 259, 330. Called the *One-handed, of the One Hand* (see *Ermabwed, Elmavoitë*); *Beren of the Hills* 49; *huntsman of the Noldoli, of the woods* 13, 237. For Beren as Man or Elf see 52, 116, 139, 215, 248

Beren (III) 9, 12–13, 22, 25, 52, 61, 87–9, 104, 106–10, 112, 114, 120–2, 124–6, 136, 138; *passim* in *Lay of Leithian* and commentaries. Beren as Man or Elf 25, 124–5, 171; his second life 125–6. See *Ennabwed, Erchamion, Maglor* (1).

Beren (IV) 5, 22–6, 28, 33, 36, 39, 54–6, 62–4, 69, 71–2, 74, 100, 109–15, 120, 122, 133–4, 138, 143, 148, 150, 152, 177–9, 181, 187, 189–91, 196–7, 201–2, 221, 223, 230, 233, 277, 297, 299–301, 304, 307, 315–17, 325; *the geste of Beren and Lúthien* 300; Beren as Man or Elf, see 54.

Beren (V) 32, 128, 131, 133–5, 138, 141, 176, 187, 194, 247, 268, 282, 289, 291–9, 301–8, 313, 315–16, 318, 322–4, 335, 352, 405; the fate of Beren 303–6

Beren (VI) 179–84, 186–7, 197, 358; called *Camlost, Gamlost* 179, 186, *Erhamion* 183

Beren (VII) 58, 173, 271, 331

Beren (VIII) (1) Beren One-hand. 155, 159, 184, 187, 218. (2) Man of Minas Tirith, precursor of Berithil, Beregond. (276), 282–4, 286, 292–3

Beren (IXa) 13, 45

Beren (X) (1) Grandfather of Beren One-hand. 306. (2) 'One-hand'. 3, 123, 141, 228, 267, 305–6, 336, 340, 364, 371, 373, 408

Beren (XI) (1) Grandfather of Beren One-hand. 231, 233–4

Beren (XI) (2) 'One-hand'. 22, (50), 51, 56, 59, 61–71, 79, 83, 126, 129–32, *185, 195, 224, 228, 231–2, 234, 241–3, 247, 345–50, 353, 355–6. Called *the blessed* 65; and see *Camlost, Erchamion*.

Beren (XII) (1) Beren son of Barahir. 307, 326, 348–9, 368–9. (2) Nineteenth Ruling Steward. 205, 220, 248, 274

Bergil (VIII) Son of Berithil (Beregond). 287, 294, 388, 395, 415. See
   Gwinhir.

Bergil (XII) Son of Beregond (2); brother of Borlas (2). 421

Bergrisland (VII) See *Ettendales*.

Beril (IXa) Aragorn's translation of *Rose* (Gamgee). 117, 121.
   (Replaced by *Meril*.)

Beril (XI) Daughter of Boromir (2). 231

Berin a Nestad (VIII) The Houses of Healing. 379–80; *Bair Nestad,
   Bair Nestedriu, Edeb na Nestad* 380

Beringol (V) See *Peringol*.

Berithil (VIII) Man of Minas Tirith (replaced by *Beregond*). 288–9,
   294, 336, 338–40, 374–5, 377, 379–81, 388, 390–3, (415), 426.
   Also *Berethil* 324–6, 339; earlier *Barathil, Barithil* 287–8

Berithil (IXa) Man of Minas Tirith. 52, 59. (Replaced by *Beregond*.)

Bert (VI) One of the Trolls turned to stone. 193, 360

Beruthiel, Queen (VI) 454

Bethos (II) Chief of the Woodmen. 101–2, 106, 111, 130, 142; Bethos'
   wife (a Noldo) 101, 130

Bethos (IV) Chief of the Woodmen in the *Tale of Turambar*. 60, 185

Bidding of the Minstrel (IV) (poem) 70

Bidding of the Minstrel, The (II) (poem) 269–71; associated outline
   261–2, 265

Bideford (IXb) In Devon. 267

Bifur (VI) Dwarf, companion of Thorin Oakenshield. 210

Bifur (XII) Companion of Thorin Oakenshield. 279

Big Folk (IXa) Men (as seen by hobbits). 117, 126

Big Folk (XII) Men (as seen by Hobbits). 311

Big Folk, Big People (VI) Men (as seen by hobbits). 54–5, 66, 95, 121,
   132, 134, 150, 178, 197, 221, 253, 278–9, 294, 310–1l, 313, 408

Bilbo (X) 90, 365

Bilbo (XI) 190

Bilbo (XII) See *Baggins*.

Bilbo Baggins (III) 49, 159

Bilbo Baggins (V) 23, 294; *Bungo Baggins* his father 294

Bilbo Baggins (VI) See *Baggins*.

Bilbo Baggins (VII) See under *Baggins*.

Bilbo Baggins (VIII) See under *Baggins*.

Bilbo Baggins (IXa) See under *Baggins*.

Bill the pony (VI) 432. See *Ferny, Bill*.

Bill the pony (VII) See *Ferney, Bill*.

Bill the Pony (IXa) (52), 78

Bior (II) Man of the Ythlings who accompanied Ælfwine. 319, 321–2, 331–2, 334

Birthday Party (VI) See *Party*.

Bitter Hills (I) See *Iron Mountains*.

Bitter Hills (II) See *Iron Mountains*.

Bitter Hills (III) Name of the Iron Mountains in the *Lost Tales*. 29

Bitter Hills (IV) Early name of the Iron Mountains. 52

Black Captain (VIII) 330, 334, 336, 363, 367, 369, 387; *Fell Captain* 324. See *Angmar, Nazgûl, Wizard King*.

Black Captain (XII) Lord of the Ringwraiths. 207, 241–2

Black Country (VI) Mordor. 131, 216, 218; *Black Land* 129, 131

Black Country, The (V) Mordor. 29, 31, 33

Black Fleet (VIII) (including all references to the fleet after its capture) 275, 296, 359, 369–70, 372, 374–5, 378–80, 388, 390–3, 398–9, 415, 419, 428, 438; see also *Harad, Southrons*.

Black Foe, The (X) Morgoth. 120, 146, 194, 294; *the Black God* 146. See *(The) Enemy*.

Black Gate (VII) See *Morannon*.

Black Gate (IXa) 45, 55. See *Morannon*.

Black Gate (XII) 242, 271. See *Morannon*.

Black Gate(s) (VIII) (including references to *the Gate*). The Morannon; originally name of the pass into Mordor (see 122). 113, 118–19, 122–3, 126–7, 130, 134, 138, 173, 190, 219, 271, 275, 330, 361–4, 400, 416, 419, 430; *North Gate* 213; *Parley at the (Black) Gate* 361–2, 416–17, 419, 430–1. See *Ennyn Dûr, Gates of Mordor, Morannon*.

Black Gulf (VI) Moria. 429, 435, 437; *Black Pit* 435

Black Gulf, Black Pit (VII) See *Moria*.

Black Hand (VIII) 404

Black Land (VIII) Mordor. 403, 414

Black Land (IXa) 46. See *Mordor*.

Black Mountains (IV) The Iron Mountains. 328, 333, 340; O.E. *Sweartbeorgas* 338, 340. *The Black Mountain*, Thangorodrim, 295, 314, 333

Black Mountains (VI) Range south of the Misty Mountains. 410–11, 436, 440. See *Blue Mountains, South Mountains*.

Black Mountains (VII) (including references to *the mountains*) 124, 132, 137, 139, 144, 149, 169–70, 177, 225, 239, 241, 272, 282, 311, 316, 320, 322–3, 336, (373–4), 389, 395, 398, 433, 435, 446;

Mountains of the South 453; Elvish names *Ered Myrn, Eredvyrn, Mornvenniath* 124. Replaced by *White Mountains*.

Black Mountains (VIII) (including references to *the mountains*) 4, 8–10, 12–13, 22, 52, 56, 133, 137, 167. (Replaced by *White Mountains*.)

Black Númenóreans (VIII) 431

Black Plain (IV) Dor-na-Fauglith. 220, 223

Black Rider(s) (VIII) 177, 187 *(Rider)*, 275, 331, 337; *Fell Riders* 292, 294; *Black Horseman* 336

Black Rider(s) (IXa) 5–7

Black Riders (VI) (including references to *Riders, (black) horsemen, black men,* &c.) 44, 48, 54–5, 58, 60, 63–4, 66–7, 69–71, 73, 84, 87–91, 95–7, 100, 103–4, 106, 109, 118–20, 126, 129, 131, 151–5, 157–63, 171–6, 178, 185–6, 188–91, 194–9, 207–8, 211–13, 217–18, 221–5, 269, 272, 277–9, 281–2, 285, 287–8, 291–3, 295, 297, 301, 303, 324–6, 328, 336, 339–44, 347–50, 353–68 *passim*, 371–3, 381, 401, 408, 416, 462. See *Ring-wraiths, (the) Nine*.

Black Riders (VII) (also *Riders, black horsemen,* etc.) 6–7, 9, 11–14, 16–17, 29, 32–6, 40–1, 43–5, 47–9, 52–5, 57–8, 62–5, 68–79, 82, 105, 113, 130, 132–5, 138, 149, 151–2, 190, 208, 211–13, 215, 326, 335, 337, 341, 423; borne upon vultures, see *Vultures*. *King, Captain, Chief, of the Riders (the Nine)* 9, 13, (33–4), 69–72, 74, 116, 132–3, 135, 149; *Black Captain* 79. See *Nazgûl, (The) Nine, Ringwraiths, Wizards*.

Black Riders (XII) 241; *Lord of the Black Riders* 267

Black Sea (IV) 258

Black Speech (VIII) 20

Black Speech (X) 413

Black Speech (XI) 390

Black Speech (XII) 65, 83 (cited), 320

Black Sword (IV) Name of Túrin in Nargothrond. 29, 125, 184, 304; the sword itself 31, 40, 59, 73, 125, 130, 165, 183–4, 324. See *Gurtholfin, Mormakil*.

Black Sword, The (XI) Túrin. 83, 90, 97, 99, 101, 152, 158, 162, 256; *the Blacksword of the South* 90. See *Mormegil*.

Black Throne, The (IXb) (341), 342

Black Tower (VI) 218, 253. See *Dark Tower*.

Black Years (VII) 144

Black Years (XII) The Second Age. 166–8. See *Dark Years*.

Blacklocks (XII) One of the kindreds of the Dwarves. 301, 322

Blackroot, River (VII) (1) Earlier name of Silverlode, replacing *Redway*.
166–7, 174, 190–1, 207, 213, 215, 218, 220–2, 225, 230–1, 235,
237–8, 240–1, 287–8, 296, 306. (2) River of Gondor. 177, 187,
241, 298, 306, 310–11. On the transposition of the names see
235, 241; and see *Buzundush, Celebrant, Morthond*.

Blackroot, River (VIII) 265, 409; *Blackroot Vale, Vale of Blackroot*
243–4, 253, 287. See *Morthond*.

Blacksword (II) Name of Túrin among the Rodothlim (later Nargothrond). 84, 128. See *Mormagli, Mormakil, Mormegil*.

Blacksword (X) 217; the black sword of Túrin 76. See *Mormacil,
Túrin*.

Blackwater, River (VII) In Essex. 106; Old English *Panta* 106

Blackwell, Basil (IXb) Oxford bookseller. 153. See *Whitburn and
Thorns*.

Bladorinand (III) Rejected name for Beleriand. 160

Bladorion (IV) The great grassy northern plain (later *Ard-galen*) before
its desolation. 262, 268, 280, 296, 298, 316, 329–30, 334, 340

Bladorion (V) The great northern plain. 117, 127, 130, 132, 249, 254–
5, 259–60, 264, 280; *East Bladorion* 127

Bladorion (X) The great northern plain (*Ard-galen*). 328

Bladorion (XI) Earlier name of Ardgalen. 113–14, 175, 191, 195, 238

Bladorwen (III) 'The wide earth, Mother Earth', name of Paúrien. 160

Bladorwen (IV) 'The Wide Earth', a name of Yavanna. 280

Blanco (XII) Hobbit, first settler of the Shire, with his brother Marcho.
6, 17, 87. (Replaced *Cavallo*.)

Blasted Plain (III) Dor-na-Fauglith. 49, 55

Blessed Elves (V) A name of the Lindar. 215

Blessed Elves (X) A name of the Vanyar. 164

Blessed Realm (I) 173; *blessed realms* 182, 199. See *Aman*.

Blessed Realm (III) Aman. 334, 348, 358; *Blissful Realm (s)* 72, 93,
132

Blessed Realm (VI) 182–4, 187, 225, 364, 394, 398–9; *Blessed Realms*
187

Blessed Realm (VIII) 164

Blessed Realm (XII) 130, 144, 146, 305, 334, 337–8, 378–81, 386,
388. See *Aman*.

Blessed Realm(s) (II) 34, 82, 266

Blessed Realm(s) (IV) 89, 96, 236, 279, 331; *Blessed Land* 237; *Blissful
Realm* 97, 155, 157; *Noontide of the Blessed Realm* 264, 270,

272, O.E. *Godeðles (Valaríces) Middæg oþþe Héahþrymm* 281, 286

Blessed Realm(s) (V) 25, 30, 56, 64, 73, 129, 149, 222, 233, 236–8, 300, 304, 325; *Blissful Realm* 328; *Noontide of* 112, 227

Blessed Realm, The (IXb) 332–3, 342–5, 348, 354, 358, 360–2, 364, 368, 377, 379–80, 385–6, 388, 391, 407, 409. *A Great Land beyond the sun* 400, (412), 413, *the West Land* 401

Blessed Realm, The (X) 7, 19, 33, 37, 84, 118, 120, 134, 137, 163, 176, 180, 182, 186, 196, 237, 239, 255–6, 258, 274, 284, 286, 289, 400–3, 407, 426–8; *the Blessed Land* 94, *Land of the Blessed* 203; *the Noon (tide) of,* 81, 94, 183, 236, 255–6. See *Aman*.

Blessed Realm, The (XI) 6, 8, 106, 130, 175, 390; ~ *Realms* 39

Blickling Homilies (IXb) 285

Bliscarn (VI) Early name for Caradhras. 433, 438

Blodren (XI) Easterling who betrayed Túrin's lair in Dimbar. 82; earlier *Blodrin*, a Noldorin elf, 137

Blodrin (III) The Elf who betrayed Túrin's band (earlier named Bauglir). 31–3, 40, 48–9, 52

Blodrin (IV) The Noldo who betrayed Túrin's band. 28, 59, 123, 183, 210, 304, 322; O.E. *Blodwine* 210

Blodrin (V) The traitor in Túrin's band. 138

Blue Bee (II) See *Bee of Azure*.

Blue Elves (V) A name of the Teleri. 215

Blue Elves (X) A name of the Teleri. 164

Blue Mountains (III) Ered Luin. 160, 313; not named, 83, 156, 332

Blue Mountains (IV) 103–5, 108, 119, 122, 132–3, 175, 187, 189, 199, 224, 227, 230, 232–3, 239, *249, 255–6, 258–9, 296–7, 328, 331, 336–7; not named 53, 135, 157, 161, 198, 200, 301–2, 335. See *Eredlindon, Eredluin*.

Blue Mountains (V) 32, 34, 126, 128, 148, 175, 253–4, 258, 260, 262, 267, 273, 277, 337, 405, 407; not named 18, 22, 29, 33, 134–5, 146, 171, 176, 188, 194, 263, 274–7, 281. See especially 267, and see *Eredlindon, Eredluin, Luindirien, Lunoronti*.

Blue Mountains (VI) (1) Eredlindon. 466. (2) Range south of the Misty Mountains. 410–11, 436, 440. See *Black Mountains, South Mountains*.

Blue Mountains (VII) 124, 301, 455; *the Mountains* 123–4; *Mountains of Lune* 416. See *Eredlindon, Eredluin*.

Blue Mountains (X) 104, 307, 327; *the Mountains* 83, 93, 164, 307. See *Mountains of Lindon*.

Blue Mountains (XI) 5, 9, 45, 104, 108–9, 121, 123, 128, 179–80, 193, 201–3, 209, 229, 232, 385; *the mountains* 9, 12–14, 20, 45, 48, 59–60, 107, 109, 121, 127, 203, 206, 215–18, 221–2, 225, 296, 335–6, 350, 353, 377, 386, 408. See *Eryd Lindon, Eryd Luin.*

Blue Mountains (XII) (including *the Mountains*) 31, 173, 185, 279, 287, 301, 307, 313, 325, 328, 374. See *Ered Lindon, Ered Luin.*

Blue Wizards (XII) See *Wizards.*

Bob (VI) The ostler at Bree. 135, 164, 174, 345–7; also called Rob, 164, 174

bo-Dhuilin, bo-Dhrauthodavros, bo-Rimion (II) 'son of' Duilin, etc.; see the names. (*bo-* replaced *go-*).

Bodleian Library (VII) 107, 187

Bodleian Library (VIII) 193, 199, 221

Bodleian Library (IXa) 136

Bodruith (II) Lord of Belegost. 230–1, 234–5, 246–7

Bodruith (IV) Lord of Belegost in the *Tale of the Nauglafring.* 62

Boffin family (VI) 25, 31; *Boffinses* 13–14, 18, 23, 31; *Boffins* 22, 284, 304, 313, 385; *Boffin-country* 298; *Mr Boffin of Overhill* 254, 284

Boffin, Fosco (VI) Cousin of Bilbo; son of Jago Boffin. 317, 319, 386
   Boffin ~ *Hugo* (VI) Husband of Donnamira Took. 317–18, 386
   Boffin ~ *Jago* (VI) Son of Donnamira Took and Hugo Boffin. 317, 386
   Boffin ~ *Paladin* (VI) Father of Peregrin Boffin. 385–6
   Boffin ~ *Peregrin* (VI) Grandson of Donnamira Took; known in Bree as *Trotter.* 371, 373–4, 376, 384–7, 392–3, 395–6, 406, 412, 415, 422, 430–1; called *Perry* 393

Boffin (family) (VII) 31

Boffin, Folco (VII) 30–2

Boffin, Peregrin (VII) (1) Trotter. 7–8, 15, 19, 21, 31–2, 81, 83, 111. (2) Friend of Frodo Baggins. 8–9, 11–12, 16, 21, 30–2; called *Perry* 8, 11–12

Bofur (VI) Dwarf, companion of Thorin Oakenshield. 210

Bofur (XII) Companion of Thorin Oakenshield. 279

Boldog (III) Orc captain, leader of a raid into Doriath. 229, 235, 274, 288, 293, 310–13

Boldog (IV) Orc captain. 113, 179

Boldog (X) Orc-name. 418, 423; leader of a raid into Doriath 423
   Book of Lost Tales, the Lost Tales (including references to individual tales, not separately indexed) 26–7, 35, 61, 68, 77, 103,

105, 136–7, 142, 150, 158, 167–8, 171, 265–6, 291, 299, 371, 393, 406–7

Bolg (VII) Orc, son of Azog. 143, 157

Bolger (VII) (family) 31, 76, 161; ~ *Olo* 31; ~ *Odovacar* 20; ~ *Rollo* 20

Bolger, Bingo (VI) 31, 33, 49, 78, 96, 267, 284, 304

    Bolger (VI) ~ *Bolger, Bingo* (VI) Bingo Bolger-Baggins before his adoption by Bilbo. 36–7, 40

    Bolger (VI) ~ *Caramella* (VI) A relative of Bilbo's (formerly a Took, subsequently a Chubb). 32, 35, 38

    Bolger (VI) ~ *Fosco* (VI) Bingo's somnolent uncle. 38, 51, 65, 247

    Bolger (VI) ~ *Fredegar* (VI) Called *Fatty*. 112, 273, 275, 299, 301, 326, 373

    Bolger (VI) ~ *Hamilcar* (VI) 373. (Replaced by *Fredegar Bolger*.)

    Bolger (VI) ~ *Odo* (VI) (including all references to Odo both as Took and later as Bolger, see p. 267 note 3). 41–66; *passim*, 69–70, 74, 83, 88–104, 106, 109–10, 112–13, 115, 118, 125, 127–8, 130, 136–9, 141, 148, 155–6, 160–1, 163, 166–9, 171–2, 177, 185, 209, 221–2, 250–1, 267, 273, 275–80, 283–95 *passim*, 299–305, 316–18, 323–8, 330, 336–57 *passim*, 359, 361, 364–8, 371–5, 395–8, 409, 413. Called *Odo Took-Bolger* (VI) 316–17, 323; passes as 'Baggins' 339–41, 347, 352, 356, 366, 368, 375

    Bolger (VI) ~ On the history of 'Odo' see 221, 250, 273, 299–303, 323–4, 374–5, 396, 409

    Bolger (VI) ~ *Olo* (VI) (1) = Odo Bolger. 299–300. (2) Odo's father. 317

    Bolger (VI) ~ *Rollo* (VI) (1) Precursor of Drogo Baggins. 26, 37–8, 222, 234. (2) A friend of Bilbo's. 247

Bolger, Fredegar (VII) (also *Freddy*) 8, 30–2, 39, 54, 76

Bolger, Hamilcar (VII) (also *Ham*) 8–9, 11–14, 21, 30–3, 36, 39, 54–6, 58, 61, 68–72, 74–6, 78, 111, 136, 152

Bolger, Odo (VII) 6–8, 31–2, 36–7, 39–40, 42–3, 51, 53, 75, 82, 172; originally *Odo Took* 31

Bolger, Fredegar (IXa) 108, 110

Bolger-Baggins, Bingo (VI) (before he became Bingo Baggins (2)). 36–40, 45–106 *passim*, 109, 112–13, 115, 118–45 *passim*, 148–74 *passim*, 176, 179, 185–6, 188–99, 206–17, 219–23, 226, 233–4, 247, 267, 277, 284, 310, 327–8, 334, 336, 354, 362, 365–6, 369, 371–2, 375. On Bingo's sword see 128, 186, 190, 213–14

Bombadil (VI) See *Tom Bombadil*.

Bombadil (VII) See *Tom Bombadil*.

Bombadil (VIII) See *Tom Bombadil*.

Bombadil (IXa) See *Tom Bombadil*.

Bombur (VI) Dwarf, companion of Thorin Oakenshield. 210

Bombur (XII) Companion of Thorin Oakenshield. 279

Book of Lost Tales (IV) Written by Eriol (source of the *Quenta*). 76–7, 191

Book of Lost Tales (VI) 187, 437

Book of Lost Tales (VII) 242, 322; individual tales 95, 172

Book of Lost Tales (VIII) 372

Book of Lost Tales, The (IXb) 412; *the Lost Tales* 280; *the Book of Stories* (in Tol Eressëa) 279–80

Book of Lost Tales, The (XI) 121, 244–5, 424; *the Lost Tales* 130. *Gilfanon's Tale* 424; *Turambar and the Foalókë* 121, 141, 144, 152, 154–5, 160, 251, 300, 315, 352, 354–5; *The Fall of Gondolin* 120–1, 201, 302, 317–18, 320, 344; *The Nauglafring* 108, 201, 208–9, 346–7, 349, 352, 354–5

Book of Mazarbul (XII) See *Mazarbul*.

Book of the Kings (XII) 25, 191, 253; ~ *and Stewards* 255, 261

Bor (III) Father of Blodrin the traitor (briefly replaced *Ban*). 31–3, 40, 49, 52

Bor (IV) (1) Transient name for Ban, father of Blodrin the traitor. (2) Easterling who fought with his sons at the Battle of Unnumbered Tears. 121, 180, 300, 302, 320–1

Bor (V) (later *Bór*, see 147). Easterling, called 'the Faithful'. 134–5, 137, 147, 151, 179, 192, 287, 291, 308, 310–1l, 314, 353, 403

Bor (VI) Man of the Elder Days. 412

Bór (XI) A chieftain of the Easterlings, faithful to the Eldar. 61, 64, 70, 74, 128–9; his sons (unnamed) 74, 135

Bór the Easterling (XII) 419

Border Hills (VII) 268–9, 281, 313, 315–16. See *Emyn Rhain*.

Borin (XII) Brother of Dáin I. 276, 279, 288. (Replaced *Nár* (1).)

Borlach (XI) Son of Bór. 240. See *Boromir* (1).

Borlad (XI) Son of Bór. 240; earlier *Borlas* 61, 64, 128, 240

Borlas (V) Eldest son of Bor. 134, 287, 310, *353*, *357*, 403

Borlas (XII) (1) Son of Bór the Easterling, later *Borlad*. 419. (2) Borlas of Pen-Arduin. 409–18, 420–1.

Boromir (V) (1) Second son of Bor. 134, 151, 287, 310, *353*, *373*, 403. (2) Father of Bregor father of Barahir. 151

Boromir (VI) (1) Son of Bor, slain in the Battle of Unnumbered Tears. 412. (2) Man of Ond. 395, 398, 400, 403–4, 406, 408–11, 414–15, 417, 419, 424–7, 429–32, 436–7, 440, 447, 451, 457, 463; his horse 432

Boromir (VII) 110, 112–14, 116–17, 120–2, 125–9, 136, 138, 146–7, 151, 154, 159, 162, 165, 169–71, 175, 177, 192–4, 200, 203–18 *passim*, 224, 231, 239, 241, 243, 248, 254, 258, 263, 266, 268–75, 278–9, 281–2, 292–3, 311, 324–30, 345–6, 352–4, 357–60, 371–88 *passim*, 392–4, 397, 401, 406, 411–13, 429, 435, 437–8, 440, 445; Lament for Boromir 384, 388

Boromir (VIII) 20, 22, 58, 101, 135–6, 139, 144–52, 154, 156, 160, 162–3, 165–7, 169, 229, 262, 276, 281, 285, 292, 328, (330), 332–3, 339; *Highwarden of the White Tower* (VIII) 130; his horn 146–50, (165), 277, 281, 294

Boromir (X) Father of Andreth and Bregor. 306

Boromir (XI) (1) Son of Bór (replaced by *Borlach*). 61, 64, 128, 240.

Boromir (XI) (2) Son of Boron; fourth ruler of the House of Bëor. 224, 228–31, 240

Boromir (XII) (1) Eleventh Ruling Steward. 205, 219, 235. (2) Son of Denethor II. 32, 206–7, 219, 221, 240–2.

Boron (X) Father of Boromir. 306–7

Boron (XI) Third ruler of the House of Bëor. 224, 229–31

Borosaith (IV) 'Everhungry', name of Carcharoth. 115, 178

Borrow, D. N. (IXb) Oxford scholar interested in *The Notion Club Papers*. 156–8

Borthand (XI) Son of Bór. 61, 240; earlier *Borthandos* 61, 64, 128, 240

Borthandos (V) Youngest son of Bor. 134, 287, 310, *353*, *363*, 403

Borthendor (VI) See *Rohan*.

Boss, The (IXa) See *Sackville-Baggins, Cosimo*; subsequently the orc-man at Bag End 91–2, 94. (Replaced by *The Chief*).

Bosworth (Field), Battle of (IXb) 174, 214, 283

Bounders (VI) (of the Shire-borders) 254

Bounders (XII) Border-guards of the Shire. 6

Bowra, Maurice (VII) 90, 107

Bracegirdle (VI) Hobbit family name. 23, 25, 28, 31, 33, 284

Bracegirdle, Hugo (VI) 32, 35, 247

Bráglorin (I) A name of the Sun (Gnomish). 187

Bragollach, The (XI) See *Dagor Bragollach*.

Brand (VI) Son of Bain son of Bard, King of Dale. 210, 213, 220, 369, 398, 404

Brand (VII) King in Dale. 118, 404

Branding (VII) Aragorn's sword. 165, 201, 274, 276, 290, 393, 399, 429, (437). See *Elendil, Sword that was Broken.*

Branding (VIII) Aragorn's sword. 14–15, 19–20, 370, 372, 405, 418. (Replaced by *Andúril.*)

Brandings (VII) Men of Dale. 395, 404–5. See *Bardings.*

Brandir (II) 130–4. (Replaced *Tamar.*)

Brandir (XI) (1) Uncle of Brandir (2). 231, (237). (2) Brandir the Lame, son of Handir of Brethil. 89, 92, 96–7, 99–102, 148, 151–2, 155–61, 163–4, 231, 234, 237, 256–7, 263–70, 278, 285, 297, 299, 302–5, 309. See *Tamar.*

Brandir the Lame (IV) 129–30, 185, 305–6, 315, 317. (Replaced *Tamar.*)

Brandir the Lame (V) 140–1, 351, 354, 412

Brandon Hill (IXb) On the coast of Kerry. 267, 293

Brandor (VII) See *Tol Brandir.*

Branduin (VII) See *Baranduin.*

Brandy Hall (VI) 99, 101, 104, 245, 289, 304–5, 313, 386; *Master of the Hall* 301. See *Bucklebury.*

Brandy Hall (XII) 87, 103, 105–6

Brandybuck (VII) (family) 31, 152

Brandybuck (IXa) 79, 92

Brandybuck family, Brandybucks (VI) 22–5, 27, 29–31, 34–5, 37, 49, 78, 92, 95, 99–101, 104–6, 235, 241, 244, 267, 273, 275, 283, 289, 291, 296–8, 313, 318, 330, 332, 334

Brandybuck, Alaric (VI) Son of Gorboduc Brandybuck. 317

Brandybuck, ~ *Amalda* (VI) 35. (Replaced by *Primula Brandybuck.*)

Brandybuck, ~ *Athanaric* (VI) Son of Gorboduc Brandybuck. 317

Brandybuck, ~ *Bellissima* (VI) Daughter of Gorboduc Brandybuck. 317

Brandybuck, ~ *Bercilak* (VI) 273. (Replaced by *Lanorac Brandybuck.*)

Brandybuck, ~ *Caradoc* (VI) Father of Meriadoc. 251, 267, 301, 317. (Replaced by *Saradoc Brandybuck.*)

Brandybuck, ~ *Frodo* (VI) See 42–3, 45–6.

Brandybuck, ~ *Gorboduc* (VI) Grandfather of Bingo > Frodo. 37–8, 234, 244, 249, 317–18

Brandybuck, ~ *Lanorac* (VI) Cousin of Meriadoc and Bingo. 273, 275, 330

Brandybuck, ~ *Marmaduke* (VI) Earlier name for Meriadoc. 33, 35, 39, 42–3, 45–6, 49, 51, 65, 67, 76, 83, 89, 94, 98–104, 106, 108–13, 115, 123, 286, 302, 327

Brandybuck, ~ *Melilot* (VI) 315. (Replaced *Melissa Brandybuck*.)

Brandybuck, ~ *Melissa* (VI) 38, 101, 106, 315. (Replaced by *Melilot Brandybuck*.)

Brandybuck, ~ *Meriadoc* (VI) (including references to Merry) 33, 76, 83, 106, 114, 118, 120, 123–5, 127–30, 136, 141, 148, 159–61, 163–4, 169, 171–2, 174–5, 178, 184–5, 193, 195, 207, 209, 221–2, 241, 250–3, 267–8, 273, 275–6, 283, 288–9, 291–2, 295–303, 305, 314–17, 323–4, 326–30, 334, 341, 353–8, 361, 365–8, 370–1, 373–5, 395, 397–8, 406–10, 419, 423, 427, 429, 436, 446, 449, 451–2, 456, 459, 463, 465. (Replaced *Marmaduke Brandybuck*.)

Brandybuck, ~ *Orlando* (VI) 26, 35. (Replaced by *Prospero Brandybuck*.)

Brandybuck, ~ *Primula* (VI) 26, 29, 35, 37–8, 40, 42, 221, 234, 244, 247, 249, 267, 317–18, 386; as Bilbo's wife 29, 40

Brandybuck, ~ *Prospero* (VI) 24, 26, 32, 35. (Replaced *Orlando Brandybuck*, replaced by *Prospero Took*.)

Brandybuck, ~ *Roderick* (VI) =Rory Brandybuck. 317–18

Brandybuck, ~ *Rorimac* (VI) =Rory Brandybuck (in LR). 318

Brandybuck, ~ *Rory* (VI) Grandfather of Meriadoc; often called *Old Rory*. 25, 27, 32, 35, 38, 95, 101, 104, 237, 241, 267, 288, 296, 315, 318, 386, 393

Brandybuck, ~ *Saradoc 'Scattergold'* (VI) Father of Meriadoc (in LR). 106, 267, 301. (Replaced *Caradoc Brandybuck*.)

Brandybuck, ~ *Theodoric* (VI) Son of Gorboduc Brandybuck. 317

Brandybuck, Caradoc (VIII) Father of Meriadoc. 26, 35, 40–1

Brandybuck, Meriadoc (VII) (also *Merry*) 6, 8, 21, 30–2, 36, 41, 48, 52, 56–8, 68, 112–13, 115, 162, 164, 167, 171–2, 175, 193, 210–11, 214, 216, 226, 228, 231, 235, 250, 253, 264–5, 271, (272), 274–5, 279, 285–6, 328–30, 339, 344, 346–9, 352–3, 365, 375–8, 385–6, 397, 404, 408–9, 411–15, 417, 423, 426–7, 429, 434, 436–7, 448; his ponies 56, 71, 448

Brandybuck, Meriadoc (VIII) (also *Merry*) 3–4, 6–7, 26, 35–41, 43, 47–50, 52–61, 66–8, 78, 80, 229, 236, 238, 240–8, 252, 263–4, 274–6, 296–312 *passim*, 316–19, 321–2, 343, 345–53, 355–6,

359–60, 362, 366, 368, 375, 380, 384–7, 390, (392), 394, 396, 399, 403, 405–7, 410, 415, 417–19, 421, 423, 425, 430; his pony 238, 240, 299, 301, 318 (and see *Stybba*); his sword 49, 59, 368, 384

Brandybuck, Meriadoc or *Merry* (IXa) 7, 18, 22, 49, 51–2, 61–6, 68, 72–3, 76–7, 79–86, 88, 90, 92, 94–104, 107–11, 115–16, 123–4. Called *a Knight of the Riddermark* 61, 72; his horn 68, 98, 100–1

Brandybuck, Meriadoc (XII) *(Merry)* 7, 39, 49–50, 59, 69, 80–1, 83, 87, 95–7, 99, 102, 104–7, 109–11, 117, 261, 273, 283–4, 309; true Hobbit name 50, 59, 69, 81, 83; his title 102, 105; and see *Holdwine*.

Brandybuck, Rory (IXa) 71; 'Rorius' 62, 71

Brandywine Bridge (VI) 53, 56, 72, 100, 102–8, 132, 170–2, 275, 278, 280, 284, 286, 298, 338, 350

Brandywine Bridge (VII) (including references to *the Bridge*) 12–13, 57, 65, 68, 71–2

Brandywine Bridge (VIII) 309

Brandywine Bridge (XII) (9), 17, 93, 117, 258

Brandywine River (VI) (including references to *the River*) 29–30, 35, 37, 42, 52–3, 56, 58, 66, 72, 89, 92, 94, 96–7, 99–100, 103, 105–9, 112, 121, 236, 247, 280, 284, 286, 293, 298, 305, 312, 316, 324, 371, 376 *Bree* 107, 110, 121, 126, 129, 131–5, 138, 140–2, 144, 150, 153–7, 159–62, 164–7, 170–6, 198, 211, 214, 217, 222–3, 235, 269, 329, 331–3, 337–56 *passim*, 359, 367–8, 374–5, 387, 414, 430–1. On the people of Bree see 132–4, 223, 331, and see *Bree-folk*.

Brandywine, River (VII) (including references to *the River*) 13, 54, 68, 70, 124. See *Baranduin*.

Brandywine, River (IXa) 76–7, 100; *Brandywine Bridge* (including references to *the Bridge*) 77, 79–80, 103–4, 107, 117, 119–20, 126, 133–4. See *Baranduin*.

Brandywine, River (XII) 6, 9, 39–40, (48), 54, 67, 72, 86, 105, 225, 231, 235, 238, 313; history of the Hobbit name 39–40, 54, 72, 83–4

Breaking of the Fellowship (VIII) 22, 100–1, 142

Breca of the Brondings (V) In *Beowulf* 91

Bredhil the Blessed (III) See *Bridhil*.

Bree (VII) 7, 9–13, 33, 35–7, 40–5, 48–53, 55–6, 59, 62–3, 69–76,

79, 83, 105–6, 130, 132, 135, 152, 165, 173, 196, 244, 286, 291, 296, 448; *Bree-hill* 4l; *Bree-land* 45; *Breelanders* 69, 135

Bree (VIII) 38, 44, 52; *Bree-hill* 38; *Bree-folk* 38

Bree (IXa) 52, 64, 76–8, 80, 82, 104

Bree (XII) 9–10, 34, 39, 52, 56, 80–1, 119, 121–3, 125, 127, 129, 131, 193, 208, 225, 228, 230–1, 281, 287–8, 311, 327; *Bree-land* 248; *Bree-folk, Men of Bree,* &c. 10, 34, 39, 52, 70, 81, 123, 230; *the Old Home* 9–10

Bree-folk (VI) 132, 154–5, 159, 164, 223, 331, 351; *Bree-dialect* 137

Bree-hill (VI) 129–34, 165, 174, 223. See *Brill.*

Bree-land (VI) 133, 332, 342, 354–5; *Breelanders* 132

Bregalad (VII) Quickbeam the Ent. 419

Bregalad (VIII) Ent. 25–6, 30–1, 39–40, 42–3, 49, 53, 55. See *Quickbeam.*

Bregil (XI) Daughter of Bregor, grandmother of Brandir the Lame. 230–1, 268; earlier the daughter of Boromir 230

Brego (VII) Builder of the Golden Hall. Son of Brytta 435, 445; in LR son of Eorl the Young 440, 445

Brego (VIII) Second King of the Mark, son of Eorl. 244, 321, 397, 405, 407–8, 421; *Bregu* 315–16, 321. Originally grandson of Eorl 243–4, son of Brytta 244

Brego (XII) Second King of Rohan, son of Eorl the Young. 236, 270–1

Bregolas (III) Brother of Barahir and father of Baragund and Belegund. 335, 343, 349

Bregolas (IV) Brother of Barahir. 297–9, 312, 315–18, 332–3

Bregolas (V) Brother of Barahir. 130–3, 151, 281–2, 296–7, 352

Bregolas (X) Brother of Barahir. 306

Bregolas (XI) Brother of Barahir; originally son of Bëor, later son of Bregor. 49, 51–2, 56, 217, 224, 229–32, 240–1, 268

Bregor (III) (In the later legends) father of Barahir and Bregolas. 25

Bregor (V) Father of Bregolas and Barahir. 151

Bregor (X) Father of Bregolas and Barahir. 305–6

Bregor (XI) Fifth ruler of the House of Bëor. 224, 228–31, 240, 268

Bregu (III) (Old English) =‘Vala’. 127

Brendan, Saint (V) ‘The Navigator’. 80–2, 99–100

Brendan, Saint (IXb) 152, 261, 264–5, 270, 283, 292, 296, 299; *Abbot of Clonfert* 292; mediaeval works on 152, 265. *The Death of Saint Brendan* (poem) 261–4, 295; later version *Imram* 296–9

Brethil, Forest of (II) 125, 130, 132, 135, 141

Brethil, Forest of (III) 50, 309–10

Brethil, Forest of (IV) 115, 120, 178, 181, 226; *Men of Brethil* 181, Lords of Brethil 323

Brethil, Forest of (V) 134–5, 139–40, 146, 151, 261, 276, 287, 289, 291, 308, 317, *352 (Brethiliand)*, 376, 412; *Men of Brethil* 310, 313–14, 412

Brethil, Forest of (X) 374

Brethil, (Forest of) (XI) 47, 49–50, 56–8, 70, 72, 79, 84–5, 89, 92, 95–7, 101, 122–4, 126, 132, 139, 141, 144–5, 147, 157–8, (161)-2, 166, *182, 200, 223, 228, 231, 236, 238, 241, 244, 251, 254–8, 260–71, 273, 276, 278–9, 283, 285, 288–91, 296–310, 332, 355

  Brethil, (Forest of) (XI) *Men of Brethil* (XI) 74, 92, 97, 102, 127, 141, 147, 163, 168, 236, 241, 256–7, 263, 270, 286, 290, 305, and see *Woodmen. Folk of Brethil* 278, 287–9, 306–8; *the Folk* 278–81, 283–4, 286, 289, 293–4, 303–5, 309. *Folk-moot* 281, *the Moot* 282–6, 291–2, 294–5, 304; *Moot-ring* 282, 287, 289, 291, 305, 307, 309, *the Ring* 291–2, 295, 309; the Stone in the Moot-ring, see *Angbor. The Garth of the Graves* 295

  Brethil, (Forest of) (XI) Titles of the Chieftains of Brethil: *Lord* 262, 270, 299, 302; *Master* 262–3, 265–7, 270–1, 277–9, 304; *Warden* (see *Halad*) 267, 270, 304, 308–9; *Chieftain* (the final term) 148, 256, 263–4, 269, 271, 275–7, 279, 281, 287, 291, 293, 295, 297, 299, 303, 308–9, *Chief* 258. *Hall of the Chieftains* 263, 279, 292, 305–6, *Hall of the Haladin* 293; and see *Obel Halad*.

Bridge of Heaven (I) See *Ilweran*.

Bridge(s) of Ice (IV) 227, 238, 254. See *Grinding Ice*.

Bridgefields (VII) In the Eastfarthing. 33, 39

Bridgefields (XII) Region of the Shire. 93, 117

Bridhil (III) Gnomish name of Varda; called *Bridhil the Blessed, Bridhil Queen of Stars.* 135, 139, 169–70, 219, 233; changed to *Bredhil* 133–5, 139. See *Timbridhil; Elbereth*.

Bridhil (IV) Gnomish name of Varda. 12, 14, 19 (*Briðil*), 20, 43; *Bredhil* 43. See *Tim-Bridhil*.

Brill (VI) Village in Buckinghamshire ('Bree-hill'). 131

Brilthor, River (IV) 135, 189, 230, 331, 335

Brilthor, River (V) 128, 263, 372, 393

Brilthor, River (XI) In Ossiriand. 13, *185

Bristol Channel (V) 80

Britain (I) 23–4

Britain (II) 294, 301, 305, 309

64

Britain (IV) 39–40, 72, (81), 166, 199; *British Isles* 199. See *Leithien, Lúthien* (3).

Britain (V) 39, 92, 203

Britain (VI) 41. *British* (language) 131

Britain (IXb) 216, 229, 272, 280; O.E. *Brytenrice* 271

Brithiach (XI) Ford over Sirion at the northern edge of Brethil. 57, 127, *182, 186, 188, 222, 228, 261(-2), 267, 270–1, (273), 301, 303, 319, 324–5, 332–3, 335

Brithombar (I) 134

Brithombar (IV) The northern Haven of the Falas. 169, 227, 229, 271, 278, 290, 296, 305, 314, 324, 329, 331, 335

Brithombar (V) The northern Haven of the Falas. 114, 129, 140, 146, 152, 175, 180, 186, 192, 222, 225, 261, 265, 267, *353* (and the river *Brithon*), 407

Brithombar (X) The northern Haven of the Falas. 85, 175

Brithombar (XI) The northern Haven of the Falas. 8, 40, 80, 111, 117, *184, 197, 418; *Brithonbar* 380, 418 *Brithon, River* 80, *182

Brithon, River (IV) 227, 229

Brithonin (II) Invaders of Tol Eressëa. 294

British (Celtic) (XII) 81

British Isles (IXb) 255

British, The (V) (Celts) 81; *British Isles* 153

Brittany (II) 285

Brittany (III) 160

Brittany (V) 80

Broad Relic (IXb) See 277–8, 295

Broadbeams (XII) One of the kindreds of the Dwarves. 301, 322

Broceliande, Forest of (III) 160. See *Broseliand*.

Brockhouse (VI) Hobbit family name. 137, 236, 315

Brodda (II) Lord of men in Hisilómë. 89–90, 93, 126–8

Brodda (IV) 30, 122, 125, 127, 131, 183–4, 305, 322

Brodda (V) 140, 316, 353

Brodda (XI) Easterling in Hithlum, slain by Túrin. 88, 90, 145–6, 253, 257, 298, 300; *the Incomer* 90

Broken Sword, The (VII) See *Sword that was Broken*.

Broken Sword, The (VIII) 393

Bronwë (XI) Companion of Tuor. 90–1, 137, 146; *Bronweg* 137, 354. See *Voronwë*.

Bronweg (I) Gnomish form of Voronwë, 48, 52

Bronweg (II) Gnomish form of *Voronwë*. 144–5, 148–9, 156–7, 160, 197–8, 228, 256. See *Voronwë*.

Bronweg (III) Gnomish form of Voronwë, companion of Tuor. 148

Bronweg (IV) Gnomish form of *Voronwë*. 3, 35–6, 38, 67, 70, 141–2, 146–50, 193, 195–6, 204, 305; replaced *by Bronwë*, 146, 148

Bronweg (V) Tuor's companion on the journey to Gondolin (Quenya *Voronwë*). 140, *353, 398*

Brook of Glass (II) Near Tavrobel. 287

Broseliand (III) Earlier name of Beleriand. 152, 157–60, 169, 194–5, 232, 243, 304, 312, 315, 322; at first spelt *Broceliand* 158–62, 169

Broseliand (IV) 24, 54, 77, 103–5, 107–9, 115, 119, 122, 125, 131, 179, 200, 219, 224–7, 230, 233, 262, 322; *Broceliand* 224; the bounds of Broseliand 226–7. See *East Broseliand*.

Brósings, Necklace of the (IV) 212; *Brósingas* (O.E.), the sons of Fëanor, 212

Brown and green Elves of the wood (IV) 33, 62

Brown Elves (II) See *Green Elves*.

Brown Elves (X) A name of the Nandor. 164, 171

Brown Lands (VII) 316, 351, 364. See *Withered Wold*.

Brown, Mr. (VI) Assumed name of Frodo Took at Bree. 135–6, 140, 152

Brownhay (VII) Rhosgobel, home of Radagast. 164, 173

Bruathwir (III) Father of Feanor in the *Lost Tales*. 137, 139

Bruinen (VI) The river of Rivendell (Loudwater). 126, 192, 199–201, 204–5, 210; *Ford of Bruinen* 199, 367. See *Loudwater, River of Rivendell*.

Bruinen, Fords of (IXa) 75–6

Bruinen, River (VII) 17, 59, 65, 296, 299; *Ford of Bruinen* (including references to *the Ford*) 13–14, 16, 57, 61, 70, 113, 137, 172. See *Loudwater*.

Bruinen, River (XII) 56, 193, 208. See *Loudwater*.

Bruithwir (I) Father of Fëanor. 145–6, 148–9, 155–6, 158, 243; *Bruithwir go-Fëanor* 155 *Bruithwir go-Maidros* 146, 155

Bruithwir (IV) Father of Fëanor in the *Lost Tales*. 9. See *Felegron*.

Brunanburh, Battle of (V) (38), 55

Brytta (VII) Father of Brego. 435, 445; in LR eleventh King of Rohan 440

Brytta (VIII) Eleventh King of the Mark. 408; originally father of Brego, 244

Brytta (IXa) Eleventh King of the Mark. 72. See *Háma*; *Léofa*.

Brytta (XII) Eleventh King of Rohan. 274; earlier *Léof* 274

Bucca of the Marish (XII) First Shire-thain. 232, 248

Buck Hill (VI) The hill in which was Brandy Hall. 298, 304

Buckland (II) 328

Buckland (VI) (village; see 105) 29–30, 35, 37, 40, 46, 53, 55–6, 61, 65, 89, 92, 105–7; (region) 65, 67, 94, 100, 104–5, 107, 109, 160, 175, 244, 273, 275–6, 279–80, 283, 286, 288, 291, 298, 303, 323–4, 326, 366, 375, 392, 401; *Bucklanders* 100.

   Buckland (VI) Road to Buckland 46–7, 50, 66, 72, 89, 92, 97, 105, 107, 288, 291; road within Buckland 104, 106, 286, 298, 304; causeway road 105, 107, 286, 291; *North Gate* 304

Buckland (VII) 6, 11, 13, 30–1, 53–5, 68, 72, 135, 249; *Horn-call of Buckland* 54

Buckland (VIII) 26, 35

Buckland (IXa) 82, 106, 115; *Buck land Gate* 77; *Bucklanders* 82

Buckland (XII) 10, 17, 50, 57, 80, 99, 104–5, 112, 235, 255; *East March* 17, 112

Bucklebury (VI) 92, 97, 100–2, 105, 107, 221–3, 273, 275, 279, 283, 289, 292–3; *Bucklebury-by-the-River* 100, 105, *-beyond-the-River* 298; *Great Hole of Bucklebury* 234, 245, 386 (see *Brandy Hall*).

Bucklebury Ferry (VI) (including references to *the Ferry*) 107, 200, 286, 291–2, 294, 298, 300, 304, 325, 350

Bucklebury Ferry (VII) (including references to *the Ferry*) 13, 55, 70–1

Buckwood (VI) Original name of the Old Forest. 35

Budgeford (VII) In the Eastfarthing. 33, 39

Budgeford (XII) In Bridgefields. 88, 93, 96–7, 117

Buldar (XII) Father of Hazad Longbeard. 424–6, 429, 437; earlier *Tal-Bulda* 437

Bundu-shathûr (VII) One of the Mountains of Moria (Cloudyhead). 174; *Shathûr* 174. Earlier name *Udushinbar* 432

Burin (VII) (1) Son of Balin. 172, 204. (2) Father of Balin. 456–7

Burin Dwarf. (VI) (1) Son of Balin. 395, 397–8, 400, 409, 412, 4.44. (2) Father of Balin. 443–4, 460, 467 (see *Fundin*).

Burning Briar (III) Name of the constellation of the Great Bear. 167, 170, 251, 345, 349

Burning Briar (IV) The constellation of the Great Bear. 84, 168, 289; O.E. *Brynebrér* 286, 289

Burning Briar (V) The constellation of the Great Bear. 111, 212

Burning Briar (X) The constellation of the Great Bear. 160, 166

Burnt Land of the Sun (V) 32

Burrowes (VI) Hobbit family name. 18, 25, 31; *Burrows* 18; plural *Burroweses* 13–14, 17, 23, 31, *Burrowses* 22

Burrowes, Folco (VI) Lawyer. 33, 36

Burrowes, Folco (VI) ~ Orlando (VI) Friend of Bilbo's. 32, 36; spelt *Burrows* 247. (Replaced *Orlando Grubb*.)

Bury Underwood (VI) Early name of Buckland (as village). 35, 105. (Replaced *Wood Eaton*.)

Butler, Samuel (IXb) 213; *Erewhon* 172, 213

Butterbur, Barnabas (VI) 130, 133–41, 148–56, 158–60, 163–4, 172–3, 175, 329, 331–4, 338–43, 345–6, 349–50, 359, 431; called Barney 139, 159; later name *Barliman Butterbur* 130. (Replaced *Timothy Titus*.)

Butterbur, Barnabas (VII) 10, 34, 37, 40, 42–9, 51–2, 56, 62–3, 73, 77–8, 132, (134), 152, 448; *Barney* 47; later name *Barliman* 77

Butterbur, Barnabas (VIII) 39, 45; *Barliman* 45

Butterbur, Barnabas (IXa) 73, 76, 78; later name *Barliman* 78

Butterbur, Barnabas (XII) 51–2, 60, 70, *Barney* 52; later name *Barliman* 70; his true name 52, 60

Button, Jo (VI) Hobbit who saw a Tree-man beyond the North Moors. 254, 319, 386

Buzundush (VII) Dwarvish name of the Blackroot river (= Silverlode). 166–7, 241 *Bywater* 253

Bywater (VI) 13, 19–22, 29, 50, 101, 244–5, 249–50, 253, 278, 294; *Bywater Pool* 50, 72; *Bywater Road* 244

Bywater (IXa) 80–1, 87–9, 92, 94, 98–100, 106–8; *Bywater Pool* 41, 105; *Bywater Road* 88, 92, 107 (see *Roads*); *Battle of Bywater* 75, 93, 100–4, 108; *Battle Pits* 101

Bywater (XII) 114–16; *Battle of Bywater* 9

Byzantium (XII) 102

Cabad Amarth (XI) 'Leap of Doom'. 160. See *Cabed Naeramarth*.

Cabed Naeramarth (IV) Ravine in the Teiglin where Túrin and Nienor died. 199

Cabed Naeramarth (XI) (also earlier *Cabad ~*) 'Leap of Dreadful Doom', name of Cabed-en-Aras after Niënor's death. 100, 102, 160, 273–4, 296, 306

Cabed-en-Aras (II) 'The Deer's Leap', ravine in the Teiglin. 134–5

Cabed-en-Aras (XI) (also earlier *Cabad ~*) 'The Deer's Leap' (157),

deep gorge in the Taiglin. 98, 100, 102, 156–7, 159–60, 267, 299–300. Original name *Mengas Dûr* 156

Caergwâr, Caer Gwâr (II) Name of Kortirion in Welsh. 292, 307

Caerost on Kiril (VIII) 427, 437. (Replaced by *Calembel* (2).)

Caesar (V) 92; *Augustus Caesar* 96

Cair Andros (VIII) Island in Anduin. 340, 353, 356, 415, 431. Earlier names *Tol Varad* 326; *Men Falros* 326–7, 329–30; *Cairros* 340; *Andros* 340

Cair Andros (IXa) Island in Anduin. 49, 51–2, 55

Cair Andros (XII) Island in Anduin. 206, 371

Cairros (VIII) See *Cair Andros*.

Calacirian (VII) The Pass of Light. 98, 101; *Carakilian* 93, 95; *Kalakilya* 95

Calacirya (I) 'Pass of Light'. 135, 157, 171, 223

Calacirya (IV) The pass in the Mountains of Valinor. 169

Calaciryan (X) See *Kalakiryan*.

Calapendi (XI) See *Kalaquendi*.

Calaquendi (V) See *Kalaquendi*.

Calben (XI), plural *Celbin* Sindarin name derived from *Kalaquendi* (for the meaning see 376–7, 409). 362, 376–7, 408–9, 420

Calembel (VIII) (1) Lawn beneath Amon Hen (afterwards *Parth Galen*). 297, 301, 307. Other names *Calledin* 301; *Calembrith* 307. (2) Town in Lamedon. 419, 437 (see *Caerost*).

Calembel (VII) (1) Town in Lamedon. 388. (2) See *Calenbel*.

Calenard(h)on (VIII) Rohan as a province of Gondor. 168, 316, 321; *Calenardan* 168. Earlier names *Elenarda* 155, 167; *Kalenarda* 155, 167, *Kalinarda* 156, 168

Calenardhon (VII) Rohan as a province of Gondor. 450

Calenardhon (XII) Province of Gondor, afterwards Rohan. 273, 315; earlier spelling *Calenardon* 205, 219, 236, 272

Calenbel (VII) Lawn beneath Amon Hen (afterwards *Parth Galen*). 371, 382, 384, 388, 393–4, 401; *Calembel* 384, 387–8. Earlier names *Kelufain* 371, 377, 382, 388; *Forfain* 382

Calendars (XII) See *Days of the week, Months, Seasons; Moon, Sun; Old Year, New Year, Yule, Midyear('s) Day, Lithe, Overlithe; New Era*. For terms employed in the Eldarin calendar see 125–7, 131–2, 134–5, 137

Calendil, Calennel (VII) See *(The) Tongue*.

Calenhad (VIII) The second beacon in Anórien. 233, 344, 349

Calenhir, River (VII) In Gondor. 312

Calenhir, River (VIII) In Gondor. 436

Calledin (VIII) See *Calembel* (1).

Calypso (IXb) Daughter of Atlas. 249, 289; her isle Ogygia 289

Cambridge (IXb) 212, 284

Camelot (V) 95

Camelot (IXb) 229–30

Camelot (XII) 44

Camera, The (IXb) See *Oxford*.

Cameron, Alexander (IXb) Member of the Notion Club. 151, 160, 173–4, 211, 214, 245, 253, 260

Camlan, Battle of (IXb) 231, 283

Camlost (IV) 'Empty-handed', name of Beren. 317. (Replaced *Mablosgen*.)

Camlost (V) 'Empty-handed', name of Beren. 146, 301–2, *361*, 370, 405; *Gamlost* 301–2. See *Mablosgen, Mablost*.

Camlost (VI) 'Empty-handed'; see *Beren*.

Camlost (XI) 'Empty-handed', name of Beren. 51, 69, 247; *Gamlost* 231, 234

Cape Balar (V) See *Balar*.

Captains of the West (IXa) 43, 48, 51; *the Captains* 59

Carabel (XI) Also *Amon Carab* 'Hill of the Hat', *Amon Garabel*; names of Amon Rûdh. *182, 187

Carach Angren (IXa) 'Jaws of Iron', the Isenmouthe. 33

Caradhras (IXa) 70

Caradras (V) 'Redhorn', one of the Mountains of Mona. 345, *383*. See *Taragaer*.

Caradras (VI) (1) The Redhorn. 433, 435, 438; later form *Caradhras* 437, 440–1. For other names see 433. (2) The River Redway (later Silverlode). 433–4, 438, 462. For other names see 433.

Caradras (VII) 161, 164, 166, 169–71, 174, 188, 215, 247, 257, 296, 306, 367–8, 430; *Caradhras* 166–8, 174. See *Barazinbar, Redhorn, Ruddyhorn*.

Caradras (XII) 69. See *Barazinbar, Redhorn*.

Caradras dilthen (VI) The Little Redway, first name for Sirannon the Gate-stream of Moria. 462

Caragdar (XI) Precipice of Amon Gwareth from which Eöl was cast. 325. (Later form *Caragdûr*.)

Carakilian (VII) See *Calacirian*.

Carandrian (VIII) Ent ('a rowan-ent'). (54), 55

Caranthir (IV) Son of Fëanor. 69, 174, 320, 335, 337. (Replaced *Cranthir*.)

Caranthir (X) Son of Fëanor, called 'the Dark'. 128, 177, 181; earlier form *Cranthir* 112, 128, 177, 181

Caranthir (XI) Son of Fëanor. 115–16, 119, *183, 197, 215, 218, 221–2, 227, 240, 329, 352–3; *Carathir* 227; earlier form *Cranthir* 33, 43, 45–6, 53, 61, 64, 115, 119–21, 134, 197, 201, 203, 206, 215, 227, 240, 320, 348, 351

Caranthir (XII) Son of Fëanor. 318, 353; other names *Morifinwë*, *Moryo*, *Carnistir* 353

Caras Galadon (V) In Lothlórien. 345

Caras Galadon (VII) 233, 235, 242, 245–6, 249–50, 256, 258, 261, 265, 279, 285, 289, 354, 363, 367, 431; *Caras Galadhon* 235; *Caras* 367

Caras Galadon (XII) 36, 65, 82

Carcaras (II) See *Karkaras*.

Carcharoth (II) 58–9, 68; 'the Red Maw' 68

Carcharoth (III) The Wolf of Angband. 107, 119, 125, 151, 208, 289–94, 304, 307–9, 313, 362. Earlier forms *Karkaras* 125, 208, 294; *Carcaras* 125, 208; *Carcharas* 208, 210, 258, 271, 292–3, 310; *Carcharos* 292, 294, 305, 309, 312; *Carcharolch* 119, 125, 208; *Gargaroth* 292. *Knife-fang* 292–4; *the Red Maw* 289, 292, 294

Carcharoth (IV) 115, 177–8, 187, 300–1; earlier forms *Carcaras* 25 ('the Wolf-ward') *Carcharas* 112 ('Knife-fang'), 113–15. *The Wolf-hunt* 25, 62, 114

Carcharoth (V) The Wolf of Angband. 135, 293–4, 362

Carcharoth (XI) 63, 68–9, 131

Carchost (IXa) The eastward(?) of the Towers of the Teeth. 23

Cardolan (XII) One of the divisions of earlier Arnor. 193–5, 208–10, 228, 230

Carn Dûm (VI) The stronghold of the Witch-king of Angmar. 128

Carn Dûm (VII) 37

Carnbeleg (VI) Early name for Caradhras. 433, 438

Carndoom (VI) The Red Valley; early name for Dimrill-dale. 433. For other names see 433, and *Dunruin*.

Carnen, River (XII) The Redwater, flowing from the Iron Hills. 316

Carnil (X) See *Karnil*.

Caron-dûn (VI) The Red Valley; early name for Dimrill-dale. 419, 429, 433, 437; *Caron-doom* 433, 464. For other names see 433, and *Dunruin*.

Carpenter, Humphrey (I) *J. R. R. Tolkien, a Biography.* 32, 204, 221

Carpenter, Humphrey (II) 69; *J. R. R. Tolkien, A Biography,* 146, 267, 271, 273, 277, 300

Carpenter, Humphrey (III) 3, 315, 319, 363

Carpenter, Humphrey (IV) *Biography.* 214–15

Carpenter, Humphrey (V) *Biography.* 8, 53, 98

Carpenter, Humphrey (VI) *Biography.* 18, 28, 131, 214, 227

Carpenter, Humphrey (VII) *Biography* 66, 187; in *Letters* 90; *The Inklings* 106

Carpenter, Humphrey (IXb) *(The Inklings)* 150–1; *(Letters of J. R. R. Tolkien)* 153

Carpenter, Humphrey (XII) *Biography.* 409

Carrock (VII) Beorn's 'carrock' 287, 307; *the Great Carrock* (Tolondren) 268–9, 287

Carrock, The (VI) Great rock in the Anduin. 205, 438

Carrock, The (XII) Beorn's rock in Anduin. 38, 57

Casarrondo (XI) (Quenya) Khazad-dûm. 389, 397. Cf. *Kasari.*

Castle Amroth (VIII) See *Barad Amroth.*

Cat and the Fiddle, The (VI) 141–2, 145–7, 336

Cat and the Fiddle, The (VII) 40, (64)

Cataclysm, The (IV) (The Earth Made Round) 240, *246–7, 261

Cataclysm, The (IXb) 354, 385, 394, 396; O.E. *Midswípen* 242, 286–7; accounts of it 316, 336–7, 351, 372–3, 386

Cataclysm, The (X) 67. *The Catastrophe* 341

Causeway (VIII) From Osgiliath to the Pelennor Wall. 278, 330–1, 416; *Causeway Forts (Towers)* (VIII) 278, 330–1, 340, 342, 353–4, and see *Bered Ondrath.*

Causeway Forts (IXa) In the Pelennor Wall at the entrance of the road from Osgiliath. 18

Cavallo (XII) Earlier name of the Hobbit Blanco. 6, 9–10, 17, 86–7, 209, 225

Caves of Helm's Deep (VIII) See *Aglarond.*

Caves of the Forgotten (V) 27; Forgotten Caves 16, 27

Caves of the Forgotten (IXb) 336, 386

Celbin (XI) See *Calben.*

Celduin, River (XII) 330; erroneously *Celon* 316. See *(River) Running.*

Celebdil (VII) Silvertine. 174–5, 288, 306. Earlier name *Celebras, Kelebras (the White)* 174, 306, 431

Celebdil (IXa) One of the Mountains of Mona. 70. Earlier name *Celebras* 70, 72

Celeborn (V) 'Silver Tree', a name of the White Tree of Valinor; afterwards the Tree of Tol-eressëa. (V) 210–11

Celeborn (VII) See *Keleborn*.

Celeborn (VIII) 112

Celeborn (IXa) (1) 'Tree of silver', a name of the White Tree of Valinor. 58–9; *Keleborn* 59. Afterwards the Tree of Tol Eressëa, 58

Celeborn (IXa) (2) Lord of Lothlórien. 52, 64, 73, 115, 124–5, 133, 135; *Keleborn* 116, 133

Celeborn (X) (1) 'Tree of silver', a name of Telperion, and also of the White Tree of Eressëa. (X) 155, (176), 180. (2) Lord of Lothlórien. 128, 135

Celeborn (XI) 350, 353, 355

Celeborn (XII) (1) The White Tree of Eressëa. 148. (2) Lord of Lórien. 36–7, 79, 174, 222–3, 234, 317–19, 328, 348, 364, 385; *Teleporno* 347, 364

Celebrant (VI) The river Silverlode. 434

Celebrant, Field of (IXa) 72

Celebrant, Kelebrant (VII) 175, 235, 241, 288; *Field of Celebrant* 450. Earlier names *Celebrin, Celeb(rind)rath* 241. See *Silverlode* (2), *Kibil-nála*.

Celebrant, River (V) In Lothlórien. 344, *383*

Celebrant, River (XII) 198. *Field, Battle of Celebrant* 205, 219, 236, 271–2, 330; *Parth Celebrant* 330. See *Silverlode*.

Celebras (IXa) See *Celebdil*.

Celebras, Kelebras (VII) See *Celebdil*.

Celebrían (IXa) Daughter of Celeborn and Galadriel, wedded to Elrond. 58–9

Celebrían (XII) Wife of Elrond. 226, 234–6, 243, 247, 249, 264–6, 268, 348, 365

Celebrimbor (III) *Son of Curufin.* 274

Celebrimbor (V) Son of Curufin. 300, 345, *366*

Celebrimbor (VII) 188

Celebrimbor (XII) Great craftsman of Eregion. 179, 297, 317–19, 382; origin of the name 179, 317–18

Celebrimbor of Hollin (VI) 404, 449

Celebrin (VI) Early name of the Silverlode. 434

Celebrin, Cele(rind)rath (VII) See *Celebrant*.

Celebrindal (IV) 'Silverfoot'. See *Idril*.

Celebrindal (V) 'Silverfoot'. See *Idril*.

Celebrindon (IV) Silver Bowl. 313, 325. (Replaced by *Celebros*.)

Celebrindor (XII) Fifth King of Arthedain. 193, 208; former names *Celebrindol* 193, 208–9, *Celemenegil* (?) 208–9

Celebros (II) Stream in Brethil, tributary of the Teiglin. 130, 132–3, 135, 140

Celebros (IV) 'Foam-silver', 'Silver Foam', falls in the Taiglin (see *Silver Bowl*). 131, 185, 313, 325; later, *falls of Celebros* =falls in the tributary stream Celebros, 185–7, 222

Celebros (V) 'Silver Rain', falls in the Taiglin. 140, 152, *384–5*

Celebros (XI) (1) The Falls. 96, 151, 153; *the Falls of Silver-bowl* 151. See *Dimrost, Nen Girith*. (2) The name of the torrent (tributary of Taiglin). 151, 164, 186, 295

Celebros (XII) 'Silver-rain', waterfall in Brethil. 371–2

Celeg Aithorn (III) Mythological sword (lightning?) named in Beleg's 'whetting spell'. 45, 54

Celegorm (II) Son of Fëanor. 54, 56–7, 241, 250

Celegorm (III) (1) Transiently used =Thingol. 158–9, 171. (2) Son of Fëanor, called 'the fair'. 65, 80, 84–6, 91, 135–6, 151, 159, 169, 171, 182, 195, 198, 211, 213, 216, 218–22, 229, 236–40, 244–9, 256, 260, 263–5, 270–4, 283, 310–13, 358–9 (see especially 84–6, 171, 220–1, 247).

Celegorm (IV) (1) =Thingol. 5. (2) Son of Fëanor; called 'the Fair'. 15, 22–7, 46, 54–7, 64, 69, 88, 104, 106, 109–17, 120, 134, 169, 175–7, 179, 182, 191, 213, 225, 227, 267, 271, 279, 296, 298–301, 307, 318–21, 330, 334; *Celegorn* 120, 182; O.E. *Cynegrim Fægerfeax* 213

Celegorm (V) (and later *Celegorn*, see 226). Son of Fëanor, called 'the Fair' (see 299–300). 116, 119, 125, 127, 132–3, 135, 142, 145, 147, 150, 223, 225–6, 237, 265, 269, 283, 289–90, 296, 299–300, 308, *359, 366*; Old English *Cynegrim Fægerfeax* 300

Celegorm (X) Son of Fëanor, called 'the Fair'. 177, 179; earlier form *Celegorn* 112, 126, 128, 177, 179, 181

Celegorm (XI) Son of Fëanor. 47, 62, 122, 130–1, *183, 320, 324, 327–9, 332, 338, 346–50, 352; *Celegorn* 17, 53, 62–3, 65–7, 69, 113, 125, 130–2, 239, 242, 255, 351

Celegorm (XII) Son of Fëanor. 318, 352; *Celegorn* 373; other names *Turkafinwë, Turko* 352, *Tyelkormo* 353

Celegorn (VII) (1) Son of Fëanor; also *Celegorm*. 63. (2) Father of Aragorn; see *Kelegorn*.

Celepharn (XII) Fourth King of Arthedain. 193

Celon, River (IV) 223–4, 330–1, 334

Celon, River (V) 127, 260, 262, 265, 269, 285, *363*

Celon, River (XI) 6, 15, 53, 112, *183, 188–91, 218, 222, 320, 326, 332–4, 336–8. See *Limhir*.

Celon, River (XII) In Beleriand, tributary of Aros. 330. See *Celduin*.

Celos, River (VII) See *Kelos*.

Celos, River (VIII) See *Kelos*.

Celtic (V) 43, 91; *Celts* 92

Celtic (VII) 420

Celtic (IXb) 159, 216; *Old Celtic* 294

Celtic (XII) 46, 50, 80

Ceola (IXb) Companion of Ælfwine and Tréowine. 279

Céolwulf (IXb) (1) Father of Tréowine. 269, 273. (2) Preceded Tréowine as reciter of *King Sheave*. 294

Ceorl (VIII) Rider of Rohan. 4–5, 8(-9)

Cerin (Kerin) Amroth (VII) 233–6, 242, 245, 258; *Coron Amroth* 234

Cerin Amroth (XII) 240, 244; *Kerin ~* 265–6, 269

Chamber of Fire (IXa) See *Sammath Naur*.

Chambers, R. W. (III) 143

Change of the World (V) 202

Change of the World (X) 51, 132, 134, 136–7, 149, (179), 203, 397, 427

Charlemagne (II) 330

Chasm (of Ilmen) (X) See *Ilmen*.

Chasm of Ilmen (IV) See *Ilmen*.

Chasm of Ilmen (V) See *Ilmen*.

Chaucer, Geoffrey (III) 143–4

Chaucer, Geoffrey (VI) 382 (*The Reeve's Tale*).

Cheerless Lands (VII) East of Weathertop. 14

Cherwell, River (VI) 35

Chetwood (VI) 175, 332, 355

Chetwood (VII) 11, 296

Chetwood (XII) Forest of the Bree-land. 39, 81

Chief, The (IXa) See *Sackville-Baggins, Cosimo. Chief Shirriff*, see *(The) Shire*.

Chieftain(s) of the Dúnedain (XII) 188, 192–3, 195, 197, 202, 210–11, 215, 232, 238, 254, 263–4; *Lord(s) ~* 253, 263

Children (of the Cottage of Lost Play) (II) 284

Children of (the) Earth, of the World (X) 109, 124, 160, 163, 281, 299, *of Arda* 319, 382. *Elder Children, First(born) Children* 71,

120, 159, 286, 361; *Younger Children, Second (race of the) Children* 130, 299, 319, 356

Children of Aulë (XI) See *Aulë.*

Children of Eru (XI) 51, 63, 397, 403; see *Eruhíni. Children of Ilúvatar* 9, 30, 203, 213, 219, 224, 342, 345–6, 386. *The Children* 203–4, 210, 212, 341; *Elder* ~ 63, 83, *First* ~ 403; *Younger* - 30, 63, 83, *Second (race of the)* ~ 386, 403

Children of Eru, Children of Ilúvatar (X) (including many references to *the Children,* also *My Children,* etc.) 9, 11–12, 14–16, 18, 21–2, 24, 26, 28–9, 31, 36, 40, 50–1, 54, 71, 74, 79–81, 86, 95, 99, 107, 109, 127, 129–30, 144, 147, 159, 165, 185, 194, 201, 206, 211, 220–1, 240–2, 244–7, 255, 259, 268–70, 278, 282, 286, 289, 293, 308, 3 11–12, 315, 319–20, 336–8, 342, 345, 349–50, 356–8, 361–3, 375, 379, 382, 388, 400, 409, 412, 416, 420, 425, 427; *Children of God* 330, 356, 377, 379. See *Eruhíni, Mirrôanwi.*

Children of God (IXb) 249, 258, 312, 341, 354, 358, 389, 411 (see *Eruhil, Eruhîn*); O.E. *Godes bearn* 257.

Children of Húrin (III) (poem in rhyming couplets) 130

Children of Húrin (X) 76

Children of Húrin (XI) See *Húrin.*

Children of Ilúvatar (I) 57, 63, 80, 97, 115–17, 150, 179, 223, 235; *Ilúvatar's younger sons* 180; *Children of (the) Earth* 211, 225, 227; *Children of the World* 44, 117, 142, 220

Children of Ilúvatar (IV) 78, 84; *Elder* 84, 264 (O.E. *Þá yldran Ealfæderes bearn* 286), *Younger* 81, 98, 266. *Children of (the) Earth* 12, 84, 96, 235; *Younger* 20, 99. *Children of the World* 78, 134, 154; *Elder* 149, *Younger* 82, 163–4

Children of Ilúvatar (V) 63, 157, 159–65, 178, 204, 212–13, 216–17, 227, 232, 239, 273, 276; *Elder* 111, 212; *Younger* 111, 118, 178, 242; *Children of the Creator* 129, 146, 149. *Children of (the) Earth* 172, 212, 237. *Children of the World* 214, 325; *Younger* 245, 332

Children of Ilúvatar (XII) 325, 390; ~ *of Eru* 334, 364–5, 381, 413; ~ *of God* 420; *the Children* 357; *Elder Children of the World* 23, 77; *the Second Children* (Men) 391; *the Third Children* (Dwarves) 391. See *Eruhîn.*

Children of Ingwë (X) A name of the Vanyar. 164

Children of Lúthien (VI) The Half-elven. 395, 400, 413

Children of Melkor (X) 416. See *Melkorohíni.*

Children of the Gods (I) 145, 183, 189; *Children of the Valar* 63

76

Children of the Gods (II) 8 (*daughter of the Gods* 10, 43); *Children of the Valar* 216

Children of the Gods, of the Valar (IXb) 332, 377

Children of the Stars (IV) The Elves. 270, 276

Children of the Stars (V) The Elves. 111, 115, 183

Children of the Sun (V) Men. 118, 245

Children of the Valar (IV) (*Sons* > *Children* 160, 163), 263, 293; O.E. *Valabearn* 285, (293)

Children of the Valar (V) 110, 121, 186, 233, 329, 404; *Children of the Gods* 120, 162, 165. See *Sons of the Valar, Valarindi.*

Children of the Valar (X) 20, 34, 49, 59, 66, 69, 151–2; *Sons of the Valar* 133, 137, 152; *elder children of the World* 66. See *Valarindi.*

Children of the Valar (XI) See *Valar.*

Children of the Valar (XII) 143. See *Sons of the Valar.*

Children of the World (VI) 182

Chill Gulf (I) See *Qerkaringa.*

Christ (V) 82, 96

China (IXb) 197; *Chinese* 241, 306

Christ (IXb) 236, 285; *Christian* (myth) 410

Christianity (X) 354, 356; *Christian* (religion, belief, myth) 270, 355–6

Chronology (of composition) (XI) 3–4, 47, 57, 105–6, 117, 122, 127, 140–2, 144, 175, 187, 191, 207, 213–15, 229, 244, 258–9, 316, 322, 325, 338–42, 354, 359

Chronology (VI) (1) within the narrative. 160, 175, 193, 211, 219, 337–8, 355–6, 360, 362, 432, 434–6. (2) of writing (external dating).11, 40, 43–4, 108–10, 309, 369–70, 461

Chronology (VII) (1) Within the narrative. 10–15, 33, 36, 47, 49, 55–6, 61–3, 68–72, 77–80, 113, 115, 157–8, 163–5, 169, 172, 207, 215, 237, 253, 265, 344–5, 355–7, 361–2, 366–9, 393–4, 398–9, 401, 406–7, 419, 422–3, 425, 434, 438, 450. (2) Years of Middle-earth. 9. (3) Of composition (external dating). 8–9, 40, 67, 70, 79, 96, 261, 362, 379, 406–7, 419–20, 423, 425

Chronology (VIII) (1) Within the narrative. 3–7, 21–2, 25–6, 41–2, 53, 57–60, 70, 73, 80–1, 85–6, 93, 100–3, 118–20, 126, 129–30, 134–5, 139–43, 145–6, 150, 166, 178–80, 182, 226, 231, 237, 240, 245, 255–56, 259–60, 262–4, 270–6, 286–7, 291–2, 294–6, 299, 308–9, 311, 321–2, 324–5 (change of month), 327, 339, 341–4, 349, 355–6, 360–1, 397–9, 411–14, 426–9, 431–2. (2) Years of Middle-earth. 37–40, 45, 58, 309, 408, 424. (3) Of

composition (external dating). 40, 44, 59, 77–8, 80–1, 85–6, 100, 104, 121, 131, 144, 151, 183–4, 218, 226, 231–5, 250–1, 255, 274

Chronology (IXa) (1) Within the narrative. 7–11, 13–16, 18, 22, 25–6, 36, 43, 45–6, 49, 51, 57, 59–61, 69–70, 72–4, 76, 78, 87, 103–5, 109–10, 112, 117–19, 127–9, 133–4. (2) Years of Middle-earth (Shire-reckoning). 101, 107–9, 111–12, 114, 120–1, 129, 134–5. (3) Of composition (external dating). 7, 12–13, 129

Chronology (X) (1) within the narrative. 48, 306–7, 326–7, 357–8, 375, 378, 417, 420, 423. (2) of composition. 3, 6–7, 47, 60, 64, 66, 141–3, 18 1–2, 191, 199, 205, 233, 300, 304, 350, 352, 354, 360, 365, 370, 385, 389–90, 394, 409, 415, 421–2

Chronology (XII) (of composition: external dating) 3, 6–7, 14–16, 18, 28, 54, 61–2, 68, 119, 140–1, 148, 158, 163, 177, 188, 190, 222, 226, 246, 259, 293, 295, 318, 331, 350–1, 359, 367, 377, 395, 403, 409–10, 422

Chronology of Beleriand (IV) 319–20, 322–3, 327, 333, 336

Chronology of Beleriand (V) See especially 257–8

Chubb family, Chubbs (VI) 14, 18, 22–3, 25, 31, 33; Chubbses 13, 18

Chubb, Adamanta (VI) Wife of the Old Took. 317

   Chubb, ~ Caramella (VI) 38, 247, 315. (Replaced Caramella Bolger.)

   Chubb, ~ Cosimo (VI) A friend of Bilbo's. 33, 36, 38. (Replaced by Cosimo Hornblower.)

Cilthorn, Cilthoron (V) 'Cleft of Eagles'. 365, 392, 405; Cilthorondor 365, 392, 405. See Cristhorn.

Cinderion Hither Lands. (V) 405

Circles (of the world) (X) 13, 327, 355, 405; circles of time 40

Circles of the World (V) 304, 330

Circles of the World (XI) 213

Circles of the World, The (XII) 77, 150, 157, 257, 374–5, 381, 401; and see Arda.

Círdan (VI) 413

Círdan (VIII) 76, 78; Kirdan 77

Círdan (XI) (also Cirdan) 'The Shipwright'. 8–9, 11, 15–17, 21, 34, 39, 42, 60, 77, 80, 107, 116–18, 128, 135–6, 189, 197, 379–80, 384, 418

Círdan (XII) 145, 179, 194–5, 228, 232, 243, 281, 385–7, 392; called Círdan of Lune 195, 232; his original Telerin name Nowë 392

Círdan the Shipwright (I) 134

Círdan the Shipwright (IV) 169, 191, 334–5

Círdan the Shipwright (IXa) 67, 109

Círdan the Shipwright (X) 85, 90

Ciriáran (XII) See *Olwë*.

Ciril, River (VIII) See *Kiril*.

Cirion (XII) Twelfth Ruling Steward. 205, 219, 236, 272–3, 328; former name *Hador* 219; *Cirion and Eorl* (title of work) 293, 330; *Oath of ~* 328

Cirith Gorgor (VII) 321

Cirith Gorgor (VIII) See *Kirith Gorgor*.

Cirith Ninniach (II) 'Rainbow Cleft'. 204. See *Cris Ilbranteloth, Glorfalc, Teld Quing Ilon*.

Cirith Ninniach (IV) 'Rainbow Cleft'. 5, 193. See *Kirith Helvin*.

Cirith Ninniach (XI) 'Rainbow Cleft', at the head of the Firth of Drengist. 181, 256, 299; *Kirith ~* *182

Cirith Thoronath (II) 'Eagles' Cleft'. 213. See *Cristhorn*.

Cirith Ungol (VI) 382

Cirith Ungol, Stairs of (VII) (later sense) 214; see *Kirith Ungol*.

Cirth (XI) 14, 110, 396; singular *Certh* 396; Quenya *certa(r)* 396. See *Runes*.

Cirth (XII) (Runes) 22, 75–6, 81–2, 319; *Short Cirth of Dale and the Mark* 76, *Long Cirth of Moria* 76. See *Angerthas, Daeron, Runes*.

Ciryon (XII) Third son of Isildur. 208. (Replaced *Vëandur*.)

City of Present Sorrow, The (II) (poem) 295–8

City of Seven Names (II) Gondolin. 158

City of Stone (*Gondobar*) (II) Gondolin. 77, 157–8, 161. *City of the Dwellers in Stone* (*Gondothlimbar*), Gondolin. 158

City of Stone (III) (*Gondobar*), Gondolin. 145. *City of the Dwellers in Stone* (Gondothlimbar), Gondolin. 145

City of Stone (VI) City of the Land of Ond. 379–82. See *Stone-land*.

City of the Gods, The (I) (poem, earlier title *Kôr*). 136

City of the Gods, The (III) (poem) 94

Cleft of Eagles (II) In the Encircling Mountains about Gondolin. 168, 174, 189, 201; *Eagles' Cleft* 191, 196, 210, 213–14. See *Cristhorn*.

Cleft of Eagles (III) See *Cristhorn*.

Clonfert, Abbey of (V) In Galway. 81

Clonfert, Abbey of (IXb) In Galway. 267, 292

Cloud, The (IXb) In *The Death of St. Brendan*. 26 1–3, 296–8

Closed Door, The (VIII) Leading to the Tombs in Minas Tirith. (337–

8), 374, 377, 380, 382; *Steward's (Stewards') Door* 380. See *Fenn Fornen*.

Cloud of Unseeing (X) 377

Cloudyhead (VII) Fanuidhol. 174. Earlier name *Horn of Cloud* 174, 432

Clonfert, Abbey of (IXb) In Galway. 267, 292

Cloud, The (IXb) In *The Death of St. Brendan*. 261–3, 296–8

Clúain-ferta (IXb) Clonfert. 261, 264, 292, 296, 299

Cobas Haven (VII) Bay north of Dol Amroth. 312, 322

Cobas Haven (VIII) Bay north of Dol Amroth. 43 6–7

Cobas Haven (IXa) Bay north of Dol Amroth. 16–17; *Cobas* 15–16

Coldfells (XII) Region north of Rivendell. 263

Combe (VI) Village of the Bree-land. 132–3, 155, 157, 165–6, 174, 223, 332, 339, 354; *Combe-under-Bree* 236, 315

Combe (VII) In the Bree-land. 45

Combe (XII) Village of the Bree-land. 53, 81

Common Speech (VIII) 136, 144, 161–2, 356; *Common Tongue* 159–60, 162; *the ordinary language* 158–9

Common Speech (X) 422

Common Speech (XI) 337

Common Speech (VII) 223, 239–40, 244, 277, 294, 392; *Common Tongue* 244, 390; *Common Language* 244; *lingua franca* 424; *ordinary speech, language* 227, 244

Common Speech, Common Tongue (XII) 16–17, 20–2, 24, 28, 32–9, 41–5, 48–52, 54–5, 57–60, 63–5, 68, 70–4, 76, 78–9, 81–2, 120, 122, 128–9, 133, 203, 295–301, 311, 316, 319–21, 327, 332, 360. Other names: *Adûni* 316, *Andúnar, Adúnar* 32, *Annúnaid* 316, *Undúna* 55, *Yandúnë* 32; *Falathren* 32, 55; *Sóval Phárë* 32, 55; and see *Westnish, Westron*.

  Common Speech, Common Tongue (XII) Common Speech and related names and words (not 'translated') cited: 44–54, 58–61, 68–9, 76, 78, 81, 83–4; and see 299.

Common Tongue (IXa) 31; *Plain Language* 117, 126

Companions of Men (V) A name of the Noldor. 215

Companions of Men (X) A name of the Noldor. 164

Company (of the Ring) (VI) 406, 409, 411, 419, 430, 432, 435–7, 444–5, 461–2, 466

Company (of the Ring), The (VII) 67, 112–14, 161–72 passim, 176–80, 183, 188, 190, 192, 199, 201–2, 204, 208, 211–16, 218–19, 223–5, 227, 230–41 passim, 245, 247–8, 256–9, 265, 269–93

passim, 311, 315, 324–5, 327–30, 345–6, 350, 352, 355, 360–2, 365, 367–72, 375–6, 387, 397, 413, 426–7, 438–9, 445–6. Choosing of the Company 112–15, 161–5, 172–3

Company (of the Ring), The (VIII) 85–6, 93, 98, 100–1, 112, 142, 145, 147, 166–7, 276, 304–5, 346, 387; *Company of Nine* 285; *the Fellowship* 79, 241

Company (of the Ring), The (IXa) 48; *Companions of the Ring* 57

Company of the Ring (V) 345

Company of the Ring (XII) 242, 265

Constantinople (II) 330. See *Mikligarðr*.

Cópas (I) See *Kópas Alqaluntë*.

Cópas Alqalunten (II) 'Haven of the Swanships'. 82. See *Kópas, Swanhaven*.

Cópas Alqalunten (III) 'Haven of the Swanships'. 90. See *Alqualondë, Swanhaven*.

Côr (III) 21–2, 29, 73, 93, 98, 103, 118, 123, 132–3, 149, 219; *Kôr* 21–2, 24, 84, 93, 139–40, 149

Côr (IV) The hill on which the city of Tûn was built (see 45; the city itself 9, 13). 14, 18, 20–1, 37–8, 40, 45, 47, 72, 85, 87, 94, 100, 133, 149–50, 154, 159; *the Pass of Côr* 14, 16–17, 89, 91, 94, 98; O.E. *on munte Córe*, etc. 281, 283, 286. *Côr > Kôr* throughout the *Quenta*, 86, 89, 93, 97, 99–100, 135, 156; other occurrences of *Kôr* 4, 6, 45, 53, 68–72, 74, 171, 195–7, 204, 264, 274, 289, 292; *the Pass of Kôr* 50, 169

Cordof (IXa) Aragorn's translation *of Pippin* (Gamgee). 117, 126, 129

Cormallen (IXa) See *Kormallen*.

Corn-gods (IXb) 227. See *Sheaf*

Cornwall (IV) 214

Cornwall (V) 40, 42–3, 84–5

Cornwall (IXb) 266, 293; O.E. *Cornwealas* 293. See *Wales, Welsh*.

Corolairë (X) See *Korolairë*.

Corramas (VIII) See *Ramas Coren*.

Corsairs of Umbar (VIII) See *Umbar*.

Corsairs of Umbar (XII) 199–200, 203, 205, 214, 218, 220, 222, 231, 236, 242

Corthûn (III) 7, 21, 29, 103. See *Tûn*.

Cortirion (IV) City of the Elves in Tol Eressea. 41, 76, 165; *Kortirion* 42, 76, 78, 274

Cortirion (V) See *Kortirion*.

Cortirion (IXb) City of the Elves in Tol Eressëa. 280

Cosmology (X) (discussed) 3–6, 26–9, 37–9, 43, 62–4, 135–6, 157, 358, 369–74, 383

Cottage of Lost Play (I) (not including references to the Tale itself) and other names *(Cottage of the Children, of the Children of the Earth, of the Play of Sleep; House of Lost Play; House of Memory)* 14, 19–20, 27–8, 31–2, 62, 140, 189, 199, 211, 225, 230; poem(s) on the subject 27–31. See *Mar Vanwa Tyaliéva*.

Cottage of Lost Play (II) (not including references to the Tale) 7, 258, 292, 302, 326–7. See *Mar Vanwa Tyaliéva*.

Cottage of Lost Play (IV) 42, 76. (For references to the Tale see Lost Tales.) *Cranthir* (IV) Son of Fëanor, called 'the Dark'. 15, 22, 64, 88, 134, 191, 213, 300, 302, 307, 320–1, 331–2, 335, 337; O.E. *Colþegn Nihthelm* 213. (Replaced by *Caranthir*.)

Cotton, Farmer (IXa) 41, 84–8, 93–9, 102–3, 105, 107–8, (119); named *Jeremy* 84, *Tom* 105; his wife 84, 96–8, (128); his children 41, 84, 96–8; *Tom Cotton* the younger 96, 98–100; *Nick Cotton* 101; *the Cottons* 101

Cotton, Rose (IXa) See *Gamgee, Rose* (1).

Council of Elrond (VI) 216, 225, 363, 395–6, 399–401, 404–5, 407, 409–14, 437, 461

Council of Elrond (VII) 10, 14, 32, 37, 81, 110, 112–13, 116–17, 126, 129–30, 163, 172, 177, 255, 278, 311, 361, 439, 445–6

Council of Elrond (VIII) 149, 156

Crack of Doom (VIII) 190, 362

Crack(s) of Doom (VI) 265, 274, 323, 374, 379–80

Crack(s) of Doom (VII) 6, 28, 208

Cracks of Earth (VI) 82–3, 85, 126, 265

Cracks of Earth (IXa) 3. *Crack (of Doom)* 3, 5, 37

Cram (VI) 177, 186, 194, 357, 368

Cram (VII) 57, 271

Crandir (VI) The River Redway (later Silverlode). 432–3

Cranthir (III) Son of Fëanor, called 'the dark'. 65, 80, 86, 131, 135, 211; earlier form *Cranthor* 80, 86, 131

Cranthir (V) Son of Fëanor, called 'the Dark'. 125, 128–9, 132, 134, 137, 142, 223, 262, 265, 269, 273–4, 283, 287, 311, 362, 392

Cranthir (VI) Son of Fëanor. 466

Cranthir (VIII) Man of Minas Tirith. 233, 277. (Replaced by *Ingold*.)

Cranthir (X) See *Caranthir*.

Cranthir (XI) See *Caranthir*.

Cranthor (II) Son of Fëanor (later *Cranthir*). 241–2, 250

Creator, The (IXb) 316, 400; *the Maker* 290, 336; O.E. *Scyppend* 316

Creator, The (XI) 212

Crebain (VII) Crows seen over Hollin. 167

Crick (VI) Village of the Bree-land. 132, 140

Crickhollow (VI) 140, 174, 221, 273, 283, 299, 301, 303–4, 323, 326, 328, 336–8, 350–1, 366, 371–3, 375, 401, 413. See *Ringhay*.

Crickhollow (VII) 8–13, 16, 33, 35–6, 53–6, 64, 68–72, 74–6, 111, 135, 152, 173

Cris Ilbranteloth (II) 'Gully of the Rainbow Roof', by which Tuor came to the Sea (later *Cirith Ninniach*). 150, 202; *Ilbranteloth* 263. See *Glorfalc, Golden Cleft, Teld Quing Ilon.*

Cris Ilbranteloth (IV) 'Gully of the Rainbow Roof', early name of Cirith Ninniach. 193

Cris(s)aegrim (V) Mountains south of Gondolin. 290–1, 301

Crisaegrim (XI) Mountains south of Gondolin. 57, *194, 239, 260–1, 302, 325; *Crissaegrim* 193–4

Crist (IXb) Old English poem. 236, 285

Cris-caron (VI) The Red Pass. 419, 422, 429–31, 433–4, 438, 445; also *Cris Caron, Cris-carron, Criscarn* 433

Cris-caron (VII) Pass beneath Caradras. 176

Cris-Ilfing (IV) 'Rainbow-cleft'. 141, 146, 193. (Replaced by *Kirith Helvin*.)

Cristhorn (III) 'Eagles' Cleft' in the Encircling Mountains about Gondolin. 141–3; *Cleft of Eagles, gap of the Eagles,* 142–3

Cristhorn (IV) 'Eagles' Cleft' ('Eagle's Cleft' 145). 37, 66, 145–6, 194, 220, 308. (Replaced by *Kirith-thoronath*.)

Cristhorn (V) 'Cleft of Eagles'. 142, 365 (*Cristhoron*), 405. See *Cilthorn*.

Cristhorn (XII) 'Eagle-cleft', in the mountains about Gondolin; later name *Cirith Thoronath*. 379, 388

Cristhorn, Cris Thorn (II) 'Eagles' Cleft', in the Encircling Mountains about Gondolin. 174, 189, 191–3, 201, 203, 214, 216, 267. See *Cirith Thoronath, Cleft of Eagles.*

Crithosceleg (I) A name of the Moon (Gnomish). 192

Cross Roads (IXa) In Ithilien. 10, 18, 43

Crossings of Taiglin (XI) See *Taiglin*.

Crossings of Teiglin (II) 127, 130, 132

Cross-roads (VIII) In Ithilien (also *Cross ways*). 121, 125, 132–5, 171, 177–80, 182, 184, 295, 326, 342, 432; the broken statue 132,

134–5, 171, 177, 326 (names for this, 132) *Cyneferth* See *Dernhelm*.

Cú nan Eilch (IV) Unknown place. 9

Cúarthol (XI) See *Dor-Cúarthol*.

Cuilwarthien (IV) The Land of the Dead that Live. 133, 135, 179, 224 (replaced by *Gwerth-i-cuina*). *Land of (the) Cuilwarthin* 223–4, 230, 233. *i·Guilwarthon, i·Cuilwarthon* (in the *Lost Tales*) The Dead that Live Again, 179, 224

Cuilwarthon (II) See *I·Cuilwarthon*.

Cuinlimfin (III) Transient form replaced by Cuiviénen. 23, 29

Cuiviénen (I) 85, 131. See *Koivië-néni, Waters of Awakening*.

Cuiviénen (III) 18, 23, 347 *Waters of Awakening* 29, *Waking Water* 349. Original form *Koivië-Néni* 23

Cuiviénen (IV) 12, 44, 84, 86, 276; *Kuiviénen* 86, 239, *249, 256, 276; original form *Koivië-néni* 256. See *Water(s) of Awakening*.

Cuiviénen (VII) The Waters of Awakening. 184, 292

Cuiviénen (X) See *Kuiviénen*.

Cuiviénen (XI) The Waters of Awakening. 195, 382, 418, 423–4; *Kuiviénen* 5, 105, 117, 174; the waterfall of ~ 382, 418, 423–4. See *Koivië-néni*.

Cuivienyarna (XI) Legend of the Awakening of the Quendi. 420, 424 Curufin Son of Fëanor. 53–4, 62–3, 65–9, 115, 125, 131–2, *183, 239, 242, 255, 320, 324–9, *331, 332, 336, 338, 346–52

Culbone (IXb) In Somerset. 268

Cûm a Gumlaith, Cûm a Thegranaithos (I) 'Mound of the First Sorrow', tomb of Bruithwir Fëanor's father. 149

Cûm an-Idrisaith (II) 'The Mound of Avarice' in Artanor. 223, 251

Cûm an-Idrisaith (IV) The Mound of Avarice (in the *Tale of the Nauglafring*). 61, 189. See *Cûm-nan-Arasaith*.

Cûm-na-Dengin (IV) The Mound of Slain on Dor-na-Fauglith. 312. See *Amon Dengin*.

Cûm-na-Dengin (V) 147, 314, *365, 375*. See *Amon Dengin, Hauð-na-Dengin, Mound of Slain*.

Cûm-nan-Arasaith (IV) The Mound of Avarice (in the *Quenta*). 133, 189, 325. See *Cûm an-Idrisaith*.

Cunimund (V) King of the Gepids. 37, 54

Curufin (II) Son of Fëanor; called 'the Crafty'. 54, 56–8, 124, 241–2, 250

Curufin (III) Son of Fëanor, called 'the crafty'. 65, 80, 84–6, 91, 135, 151, 171, 211, 213, 216–18, 221, 223, 237, 239–42, 244–7, 260,

263–5, 270–4, 276, 303, 305–6, 313, 358–9; his horse 263–4, 269, 273, 275–6, 283–4; his knife (unnamed; later *Angrist*) 264, 272, 274, 303, 305–6, 309

Curufin (IV) Son of Fëanor, called 'the Crafty'. 15, 22–4, 26–7, 54–7, 64, 69, 88, 106, 109–12, 114–17, 120, 134, 176–7, 191, 213, 225, 227, 267, 271, 279, 296, 298–301, 307, 318–21, 330, 334; O.E. *Cyrefinn Fácensearo* 213; Curufin's knife (unnamed) 112–13, 178

Curufin (V) Son of Fëanor, called 'the Crafty'. 116, 119, 125, 127, 132–3, 135, 142, 147, 150, 223, 226, 237, 265, 269, 283, 290, 298, 300, 303, 313, *366*, *381*

Curufin (X) Son of Fëanor, called 'the Crafty'. 112, 126, 177

Curufin Son of Fëanor. (XII) 317–18, 352, 354–5, 358; his wife 317–18; other names *Kurufinwë*, *Kurvo* 352, *Atarinkë* 353

Curufinwë (X) Fëanor. 87, 91, 217, 230, 236, 263, 277; *Kurufinwë* 256

Curunír Saruman. (XII) 228–9, 233, 235, 249.

Cúthalion (II) See *Beleg*.

Cwén (I) Wife of Ottor Wǽfre (Eriol). (I) 24

Cwén (II) Wife of Ottor Wǽfre (Eriol). 290–1

Cynewulf (IXb) Author of the *Crist*. 285

Daedeloth (VII) (1) See *Ephel Dúath*. (2) *Dor-Daedeloth*, realm of Morgoth. 175

Daeron (III) See *Dairon*.

Daeron (of Doriath) (XII) (and earlier *Dairon*) 76, 297, 319; Alphabet, Runes of ~ 75–6, 297–8, 319, 321

Daeron (VII) See *Dairon*.

Daeron (X) Minstrel of Doriath. 106 ('loremaster of Thingol')

Dagmor (III) Beren's sword. 344, 350

Dagnir (III) One of the twelve companions of Barahir on Dorthonion. 335, 349

Dagnir (IV) Companion of Barahir on Taur-na-Danion. 311, 319. (Replaced *Dengar*.)

Dagnir (V) Companion of Barahir. 133, 282, 289

Dagnir (XI) Companion of Barahir. 56

Dagnir Glaurunga (XI) Title of Túrin. 103, 156; cf. *Túrin the bane (slayer) of Glaurung* 224, 291

Dagor Aglareb (IV) The Glorious Battle. 108, 174, 182, 314, 329, 334, 336, 340–1; O.E. *Hréþgúþ* 340–1. See *Second Battle of Beleriand*.

Dagor Aglareb (V) 127, 145, 254, 257–8, 348, 362. See *Glorious Battle, Second Battle.*

Dagor Aglareb (XI) 21, 25–6, 28, 36, 38, 116, 118, 199. See *Glorious Battle.*

Dagor Arnediad (XI) 22, 28. See *Nírnaeth Arnoediad.*

Dagor Bragollach (I) 'The Battle of Sudden Flame'. 242

Dagor Bragollach (III) 83. See *Battle of Sudden Flame.*

Dagor Bragollach (IV) The Battle of Sudden Flame. 53, 191. (Replaced *Dagor Hurbreged*.)

Dagor Bragollach (X) See *Battle of Sudden Flame.*

Dagor Bragollach (XI) 52, 121, 124, 127, 136, 238, 330; *the Bragollach* 59, 70, 73; old names *Dragor Húr-Breged* 124, *Dagor Vregedúr* 124, 238. See *Battle of Sudden Flame.*

Dagor Dagorath (IV) The final battle, foretold in prophecy. 73. See *Last Battle* (2).

Dagor Delothrin. (V) 'The Terrible Battle'. (355), 405. See *Great Battle. Dagor Húr-breged* 132, 147. See *Battle of Sudden Fire, Dagor Vregedúr, Third Battle.*

Dagor Hurbreged (IV) The Battle of Sudden Fire. 311, 317. (Replaced by *Dagor Bragollach*.)

Dagor Nirnaith (V) The Battle of Unnumbered Tears. 405 *Dagor-os-Giliath* 117, 119, 125, 145, 255; later form *Dagor-nuin-Giliath* (-nui-Ngiliath) 119, 145, 249, 255, 358, 378. See *Battle-under-Stars, First Battle.*

Dagor Vregedúr (V) 147, 280, 352, 396. See *Battle of Sudden Fire, Dagor Húr-breged, Third Battle.*

Dagor Bragollach (II) 'The Battle of Sudden Flame'. 209

Dagorlad (VII) Battle Plain. 310, 389, 438, 450. Earlier name *Dagras* 310, 389, 450

Dagorlad (VIII) 111–12, 256–7, 361. See *Battle Plain.*

Dagorlad (XII) The Battle Plain. 169, 176, 192, 200

Dagor-nuin-Giliath (XI) 17, 36, 113; ~ *nui-Ngiliath* 113. See *Battle-under-Stars.*

Dagor-os-Giliath (IV) The Battle-under-Stars. 262, 268, 280, 295, 310, 328, 333, 336, 338; O.E. *Tungolgúð* 282–3, 338, 340, *gefeoht under steorrum* 338. Later form *Dagor-nuin-Giliath* 280. See *First Battle of Beleriand.*

Daidelos, Daideloth (IV) See *Dor Daideloth.*

Daideloth (III) Early name of Dor-na-Fauglith. 49

Dailir (III) Beleg's arrow that never failed to be found and unharmed. 42, 45, 53, 55

Daimord (II) Son of Beren and Tinúviel (=Dior). 139, 259. See *Damrod* (1)

Dáin (Iron foot) (VII) 117–18, 141–3, 205; *Dáin of the Iron Hills* 143

Dáin (VI) King under the Mountain. 210, 226, 366, 391, 398–9, 414, 437

Dáin I (XII) Father of Thrór. 275–7, 279

Dáin II (Iron foot) (XII) 35, 237, 239, 250, 276–8, 281, 284, 286, 288, 383, 391

Dairon (II) Minstrel of Artanor, brother of Tinúviel. 10–13, 17–21, 30, 36–7, 43, 46–7, 49–50, 52, 59, 62, 65. Later from *Daeron* 52. See *Kapalen, Tifanto.*

Dairon (III) Minstrel of Thingol. 104–5, 108–10, 119, 124, 156, 174, 176, 179, 181–2, 185–8, 190–1, 195, 197–8, 200–1, 203–6, 209, 270, 310–11, 313, 333, 356; later form *Daeron* 196–7, 313, 353, 355

Dairon (IV) 113 ('the piper of Doriath').

Dairon (V) (and later *Daeron*) Minstrel of Doriath. 292, 295, 299–301, *354*

Dairon (VI) Minstrel of Doriath. 187–8

Dairon (VII) Minstrel of Doriath. 454; runic alphabet, songs of 453–5. Later form *Daeron* 186, 455 (runes of).

Dairon (XI) 13–14, 20, 26, 28, 34, 65–6, 69, 110, 116, 129; *Alphabet of Dairon* 110; later form *Daeron* 110. See *Runes.*

Dairuin (III) One of the twelve companions of Barahir on Dorthonion. 335, 349

Dairuin (V) Companion of Barahir. 282

Dairuin (XI) Companion of Barahir. 56

Dalath Dirnen (V) The Guarded Plain of Nargothrond. 299, *353, 394*; later form *Talath Dirnen* 299

Dalath Dirnen (XI) See *Talath Dirnen.*

Dale (VII) 83, 118, 248, 264, 296, 392, 404; runes of 200; Men of 395; language of, =Norse, 424.

Dale (VIII) 157; *tongue of Dale* 159

Dale (IXa) 68

Dale (VI) 14, 21, 24, 26, 30–1, 54–5, 65–6, 177, 210, 213, 220–1, 225, 369, 392, 398, 404, 412, 429; *Lord of Dale* 225; *Dale-men, Men of Dale* 54–5, 65–6, 177 (language), 221

Dale (XII) 21–3, 34–5, 38–9, 41, 53–4, 57, 60, 65, 70, 73, 75–6, 81, 122, 236–9, 319

Damrod (II) (1) Son of Beren and Tinúviel (Dior). 72, 139. (2) *Damrod the Gnome*, apparently a name of Beren's father (Egnor). 116, 139–40. (3) Son of Fëanor (later Amrod). 241–2, 251

Damrod (III) Son of Fëanor. 65, 135, 211

Damrod (IV) Son of Fëanor. 15, 22, 46, 69, 88, 133, 150, 152, 195, 213, 232, 308, 326, 331, 335 O.E. *Déormód* 213. (Replaced by Amrod.)

Damrod (V) Son of Fëanor, twin brother of Diriel (223). 125, 128, 132, 143, 223, 226, 262, 265, 269, 283, *375, 383*

Damrod (VIII) Ranger of Ithilien. 136, 139, 151, 431; the name 160

Damrod (XI) Son of Fëanor, twin-brother of Díriel. 39, 53, 197, 240, 329, 352. See *Amrod.*

Damrod and Díriel (X) Sons of Fëanor (twin brothers). 112, 128, 176, 181. See *Amrod and Amras.*

Dan (IV) Leader of those Noldoli who abandoned the Great March. 270–1, 277. (Replaced by *Lenwë.*)

Dan (V) Leader of the Danas. 112, 114, 175, 187, 215 (*Dân*), *353, 375*

Dân (X) Leader of the Nandor. 83, 89, 93, 163–4, 169. *The Host of Dân*, a name of the Nandor, 164. See *Nano.*

Dân (XI) First leader of the Danas; father of Denethor. 13, 111 *(Dan)*, 195, 418; *Host of Dân* 195. (Replaced by *Lenwë.*)

Danas (V) The Noldorin (Lindarin 188, 196) Elves who abandoned the Great March. 175 (and *Nanyar, Danyar*), 176, 178–9, 188–9, 196, 215, 218–19, *353* (also *Nanar, Danath*), *375*; *Dani* 188. Other names of the Danas 215. See *Danians, Green-elves, Leikvir, Pereldar.*

Danas (VI) Green-elves. 412

Danas (X) The people of Dân. 89, 169. See *Nandor.*

Danas (XI) The people of Dân, the Nandor. 118; *Danian Elves* 110

Danathrim, Danians (X) =*Danas.* 169

Danes (II) See *East Danes*; *Dani* 306

Danes, Danish (V) 80, 83–4, 93–7; *North-Danes, West-Danes* 86; *Sea-Danes* 91; *Spear-Danes* 92

Danes (IXb) 272–3, 277–8, 293; *Sea-danes* 276, 295. *Danish* 269, 293; O.E. *Denisc* 268; *Danish History* of Saxo 307

Danians (V) =*Danas*, and adjective *Danian*; also *Danian* as name of their language. 119, 122, 188–9, 191, 193–7, 200, 263, 268, 347

Danians (XII) Nandor. 75–6; *Danian Elves* 76; *Danas* 76, 364

Danians, Danian Elves (VII) Green-elves. 124, 454–5; *Danas* 454

Danigwethil (III) Gnomish name of Taniquetil. 22. See *Tain-Gwethil, Tengwethil*.

Danigwiel (II) A form of the Gnomish name of Taniquetil. 202

Danish peninsula (I) 24

Dant-ruin (VII) Falls in Anduin. 283, 285, 323, 366; *Dant-ruinel* 285, 316, 323, 328, 346, 366. See *Rhain Hills, Rhosfein, Rauros*.

Danuin (I) 'Day', child of Aluin 'Time'. 217–19, 222, 227; earlier forms *Danos, Dana*, 222

Danwaith (XI) The Nandor. 385; *Denwaith* 385

Dark Ages (IXb) (of Middle-earth) 344, 398, 403; *Dark Years* 362

Dark Ages (X) 304

Dark Ages (XII) 306

Dark Days, Darkness (VII) See *Great Dark(ness)*.

Dark Door, The (VIII) In the Dwimorberg, leading to the Paths of the Dead. (Including references to *the Door*) 313, 315–16, 319–21, 406–7, 420–1. See *Dead Men of Dunharrow*.

Dark Elves (I) 232–7, 244. See *Hisildi, Humarni, Kaliondi*.

Dark Elves (II) 64, 141

Dark Elves (III) 146; *Dark Elf* (Eöl) 147; *Dark-elvish* 239; *kindreds of the dark* 74

Dark-elves (IV) 4, 85, 99, 104–5, 107, 117, 120–2, 146, 158–9, 161–2, 176, 182, 200, 202, 232–3, 296, 301, 303, 316, 329–31, 334–5; with reference to Eöl 34, 136, 301; *Dark-elfin* 140 > *Dark-elven* 146; O.E. *deorcelfe* 288, 339. See *Ilkorins. Dark Land* See *Southland*.

Dark-elves (V) 29, 122, 126–9, 135–7, 146, 148–9, 176, 179, 181, 191, 197, 215, 219, 240, 246, 253, 256, 261, 265, 267, 273–5, 277, 281, 285–6, 307–8, 311, 316, 321, 330–1, 334, 405; *Dark-elvish* 269. See *Ilkorindi, Moreldar, Morimor, Moriqendi*.

Dark-elves (VI) 71

Dark-elves (X) 131, 169–70, 223, 236; *Elves of the Darkness* 163. See *Moriquendi, Wild Elves*.

Dark-elves (XI) 12, 39, 79, 107, 117–18, 136, 175, 179, 193–4, 197, 201, 203, 205, 207, 214, 216–17, 239, 320, 361, 376–7, 408; *Elves of the Dark* 8; *Dark-elf* (applied to Thingol) 33, 115, (to Eöl) 47–8, 320. *Dark-elven* 121, *Dark-elvish* 118, 209. See *Moriquendi.Dark Foe* (XI) Morgoth. 14; *Dark King* 220, 227;

    Dark Lord 15, 221, 252, 259, *Lord of the Dark* 220; *Dark Power*
    39; *Dark Throne* 272

Dark Elves (XII) 312; *Elves of Darkness* 312

Dark Kingdom (VI) Mordor. 208

Dark Land (V) 32

Dark Lands (IXb) Middle-earth. 400

Dark Lord (VI) 75, 86–7, 121–2, 127, 192–3, 196, 211–12, 224–7,
    253, 258, 260, 269–70, 272, 322, 329, 364, 381, 397–9, 401,
    403–4, 437–8; *Dark Master* 78, *the Master* 78–9, 81–2, 261, 398;
    Dark Power 78. See *(the) Lord, Lord of the Ring(s), Necromancer,*
    Sauron, Thû.

Dark Lord (VII) 6–7, 10, 82, 110, 118, 151, 153, 177, 252, 255, 265,
    332–3, 372, 418, 427, 434. See *(The) Lord.*

Dark Lord (VIII) 49, 72, 122, 125, 145–6, 156, 195, 331, 335, 376,
    380, 401, 403; *the Lord* 112, 380, 431. See *Sauron.*

Dark Lord (IXa) 32, 38. See *Sauron.*

Dark Lord (X) 224, 231, 284, 292, 411; *Dark Power* 124; and see
    Dark.

Dark Lord (XII) (references to Morgoth and Sauron) 31, 35, 65, 200,
    215, 245–6, 264, 306, 373, 382; *Dark Power* (Morgoth) 78

Dark Men (IXa) 15

Dark Men of Eilenach (VIII) See *Eilenach.*

Dark Men of the Mountains (VIII) See *Men of the Mountains.*

Darkness, the Dark (IXb) 223, 347, 367–8, 384, 398, *the Ancient*
    Darkness 367; *Lord, Power of Darkness* 335, 344, 358, 363, (367),
    383; *Nether Darkness* 344, 362

Dark Tower (VI) 81, 127, 131, 198, 209, 214, 217–18, 381–2. See
    Black Tower.

Dark Tower (VII) 136, 144, 178, 209, 213, 257, 299, 335, 337–8,
    343, 348, 397, 426–8; *the Tower* 216. See *Barad-dûr, (The) Eye.*

Dark Tower (VIII) 68, 71, 73, 77, 119, 124, 211, 268, 331, (360),
    430–1; *the first Dark Tower* 127

Dark Tower (IXa) 6, 9, 13, 22, 39, 55, 59, 83, 91; *the Tower* 38. See
    Barad-dûr.

Dark Tower (XII) 83, 173, 242, 265, 411, 419. See *Barad-dûr.*

Dark Years (VIII) 207, 215, 223, 236, 238, 246, 278, 350, 401; *the*
    Dark 257; *days of Darkness* 159

Dark Years (X) 413

Dark Years (XII) 32, 65, 74, 173–4, 178

Dark, (Great) Darkness (X) (with various and often indeterminate ref-

erence, as of the Void, of Melkor, of Middle-earth, of the Darkness behind and before Men) 20, 29, 37, 74, 100–1, 105, 108–10, 112, 120, 122–3, 146–7, 153, 159, 165, 179, 190, 194, 223, 231, 284, 288–9, 291, 294–5, 305, 307, 309–10, 313, 317–18, 320–1, 323, 325–6, 328, 344, 346–8, 351, 354, 361, 372, 377–9, 382–4, 389–90, 399, 401. *Eldest Dark(ness)* 63–4, 154, 157; *Outer Darkness* 17, 27, 105, 190, 193; *Lord of the Darkness* 309

Darkening of Valinor (X) See *Valinor*.

Darkness (out of Mordor), *Great Darkness* (VIII) (and other references, as *shade of Mordor*) 177–9, 182, 260, 262–3, 271, 274–5, 286, 289, 295, 317, 319, 322, 324–7, 330, 334, 341, 347, 350, 361, 368, 398–9, 403–4, 410–14, 419, 422, 427–9, 437

Dark(ness), *The* (XII) 182–3, 427, 436–7, *Nether Darkness* 149; *Men of ~* , *People of ~* 312, 435–6, *Servants of ~* 373

Darlas (XI) See *Dorlas*.

Daurin (I) A Gnome, slain by Melko in the attack on the Trees; also called *Tórin*. 153, 156, 160

Daruin (XII) see *Avranc*.

Dawnless Day (VIII) 179, 182, 295, 342, (412), 428–9; *Day without Dawn* 421

Day of Doom (IXb) 336, 386

Day of Dread (XI) The end of the Battle of Unnumbered Tears. 280

Days before Days (X) (before the Two Trees) 51, 58; *Days of Bliss* (in the Light of the Trees) 51, 56, 377

Days of Dearth (XII) 17

Days of Flight (VII) 257

Days of Flight (XII) 168, 174

Days of Gloaming (I) See *Lomendánar*.

Days of the week (XII) Hobbit names 123–5, 130, 137; Quenya names 130, 133, 138; Noldorin (Sindarin) names 125, 130, 138

Dead Marshes (VI) 401, 409, 413, 438

Dead Marshes (VII) 10, 111, 148, 208, 268, 283, 298–9, 306, 310, 321, 329–30, 346, (352); *Dead Marsh* 148

Dead Marshes (VIII) (including references to *the Marshes*) 85, 93, 104–5, 107, 109–12, 115, 118–20, 128, 136, 185, 270, 330, 430

Dead Marshes (XII) 201

Dead Men (of Dunharrow), *The Dead* (VIII) 267, 289, 310, 315–16, 319, 321, 406, 409, 411–14, 417–18, 426; *King of the Dead* 397, 414, 419, 425; *Gate of the Dead* 313, 418 (see *Dark Door*). See *Shadow Host*, *Paths of the Dead*, *Dunharrow*.

Dead that Live Again (IV) See *Cuilwarthien*.

Dead, The (IXa) 15. See *Paths of the Dead*.

Dead, The (X) (of Elves) 222, 226–7, 233–5, 255, 259–61, 362–5; (of Men) 365

Deadly Nightshade (III) Taur-na-Fuin. 34, 36, 48, 55, 63, 155, 227, 232, 254, 275, 279, 332; *Deadly Night* 227, 232; *Tangled Night* 232; *Forest of Night* 38, 55, 233–4

Deadly Nightshade (IV) Taur-na-Fuin. 103, 123, 211, 220, 223, 299. See *Gwath-Fuin-daidelos*.

Deadmen's Dike (IXa) Name of Fornost after its ruin. 76

Déagol (VI) Gollum's friend, finder of the Ring. 86. See *Dígol*.

Deagol (VII) (1) Gollum. 23; earlier form *Dígol* 23. (2) Gollum's friend. 23–4, 26–8, 38–9

Déagol (XII) 38, 53, 57, 81, 166, 168–9, 172, 225, 233, 247

Death (X) See entries *Elves*, *Men*.

Death Down (VIII) Below Helm's Deep. 40–1, 70; *Dead Down* 298; *Barren Hill* 41

Deathless Folk (IXb) 372; *Children of the Deathless Folk* 344, 354, 362, 377, 379–80, 388, *lesser ones of* ~ 344, 354; *the Deathless* 365

Deathless Land (IXb) 372–3, 385, 392–3; *Deathless Lands* 386. See *Undying Lands*.

Deathless Land (XII) 158

Deathless Lands (V) 21. Cf. *Undying Lands*.

Deathless, The (X) The Valar. 69

Death of Saint Brendan, The (IXb) See *(Saint) Brendan*.

Debatable Land (XI) South of Ivrin. *182

Deep Elves (X) A name of the Noldor. 163

Deep Heaven (IXb) [Lewis] Space. 213

Deep-elves (IV) The Noldoli. 13, 44, 85, 87; O.E. *déopelfe* 212, 283

Deep-elves (V) A name of the Noldor. 214, 403. See *Nurqendi*.

Deep-elves (I) Gnomes. 43

Deephallow (VI) Village in the Eastfarthing. 286, 296, 325

Deeping Coomb (VIII) (including many references to *the Coomb*, also spelt *Combe*) 10, 12–13, 17, 27, 29, 40, 42, 49, 54, 69–70, 72–3, 75, 78–9, 130, 140, 275, 291, 297–8, 300, 304–6

Deeping Stream (VIII) 19, 24, 47, 310

Deeping Wall (VIII) 11, 18, 21. See *Heorulfs Wall*.

Deeps of Time (X) 12–14, 16, 28, 40, 159, 384. See *Time*.

Deldúath (VII) (1) See *Ephel Dúath*. (2) Taur-na-Fuin. 175

Deldúwath (V) 'Deadly Nightshade', Taur-na-Fuin. 147, 282, *354–5*

(also *Taur-na-Delduath* 377). See *Fuin Daidelos*, *Gwathfuin-Daidelos*.

Deldúwath (XI) 'Deadly Nightshade', Taur-na-Fuin. 239

Delin (IV) Son of Gelmir. 6–8

Delta, The (VIII) Of Anduin. 252–5, 268. See *Anduin*, *Ethir Anduin*.

Delu-Morgoth (III) Form of Morgoth's name, of unknown meaning. 6–7, 21, 49, 102; *earlier* Delimorgoth 21, 49

Demon of Dark (IV) Morgoth. II

Denethor (IV) 277–8, 336. See *Denithor*.

Denethor (VII) (1) King of the Green-elves. 377, 454. (2) Lord of Minas Tirith. 291, 375–6, 381, 429; *Lament of Denethor* 384

Denethor (VIII) (including references to *the Lord (of the City)*) 146, 148, 151, 153, 165, 167, 231, 236, 253, 255, 257, 259–60, 262–3, 274–7, 281–4, 287–8, 292, 294, 316, 323–30, 332–40, 348, 353, 359–60, 363, 374–82, 385–6, 388–92, 400, 402–4; the name 159–60. *The Tower of Denethor* 77, 130, 278, 281, 288, 292

Denethor (IXa) 26; *the Lord (of Minas Tirith)* 22, 83

Denethor (X) Son of Dân; leader of the Green-elves. 93, 102, 104, 164, 169. Transient name *Enadar* 102

Denethor (XI) Leader of the Nandor into Beleriand. 4, 13, 15–16, 109–12, 195, 385, 412, 418–19; etymology 412; earlier *Denithor* 111

Denethor I (XII) Tenth Ruling Steward. 204–5, 219, 235, 249

Denethor II (XII) Twenty-sixth Ruling Steward. 32, 43, 68, 206–7, 220–1, 240–2, 258, 410

Dengar (IV) Companion of Barahir on Taur-na-Danion. 311, 319. (Replaced by *Dagnir*.)

Denilos (IV) Leader of the Green-elves; son of Dan. 271. (Replaced by *Denithor*.)

Denilos (V) Earlier form for *Denithor*, *Denethor*. 188

Denithor (IV) 271. (Replaced *Denilos*; replaced by *Denethor*.)

Denithor (V) (and later *Denethor*, see 188). Son of Dan; leader of the Green-elves. 112, 114, 119, 125, 128, 145, 148, 175–6, 186–8, 215, 263, 269, *353*. Other forms *Nanisáro*, *Daintáro*, *Dainthor* 188

Denmark (II) 323; *Danish peninsula* 294

Denmark (V) 95–6

Denweg (XI) Nandorin form of Lenwë. 385, 412. See *Lenwë*; *Dân*.

Déor (II) (1) Father of Ælfwine. 313–14, 323, 330, 334. (2) The Old English poem *Déor*, and Déor the Minstrel. 323

Déor (VIII) Seventh King of the Mark. 408

Déorwin(e) (VIII) Rider of Rohan. 352; called *the Marshal* 371

Derndingle (VII) Place of the Entmoot. 420. Ealier name *Dernslade* 420

Dernhelm (VIII) Name of Éowyn disguised. 349–50, 353, 357, 368, 372; *'a young kinsman of the king'* 369. Earlier names *Cyneferth* 348, 355; *Grimhelm* 347–9, 355, 369; *Derning* 349

Derufin (VIII) Son of Duinhir of Morthond Vale. 287, 370

Dervorin (VIII) Son of the Lord of Ringlo Vale. 287

Devil, The (IXb) 231, 314; O.E. *Déofol* 257, 313

Devon (V) 82–3

Devon (IXb) 267, 293; *Devenish* 'of Devon' 269, 293

Dhrauthodavros (II) In *bo-Dhrauthodavros* (changed from *go-Dhrauthodauros*) 'son of the weary forest', name given to himself by Túrin. 89. See *Rúsitaurion*.

Dhuilin (II) =*Duilin* (1) in prefixed (patronymic) forms.

Diarin (VI) See *Ilverin*.

Dicuil (V) Irish monk of the ninth century. 81

Dígol (VI) Gollum. 78, 86, 261

Dígol (VII) See *Deagol*.

Dimbar (II) 214

Dimbar (IV) Land between Sirion and Mindeb. 334

Dimbar (V) Land between Sirion and Mindeb. 261, 267, *354*.

Dimbar (VI) (1) Land between Sirion and Mindeb in the Elder Days. 432. (2) A region north of Rivendell. 432

Dimbar (XI) Land between Sirion and Mindeb. 57, 81–2, 137–8, 188, 193, 261, 266–7, 271, 278, 301–2; *Dimbard* *182–3, 186, 188

Dimgræf, Dimhale (VIII) Helm's Deep. 23; *Dimgraf's gate* 23; *Dimhale's Door, Dimmhealh* 23

Dimholt (VIII) Wood before the Dark Door of Dunharrow. 266, 313, 320–1. (Replaced *Firienholt*.)

Dimlint (IV) Unknown. 9

Dimrill Dale (VII) (1) Original sense, troll-country north of Rivendell. 10, 16, 58, 114; see *Entish Land(s)*. (2) Later sense (including references to *the Dale*) 10, 16, 143, 166, 191, 199–201, 203–4, 213, 215, 218–19, 225, 237–8, 253, 280, 286, 289, 372. See *Nanduhirion*.

Dimrill Dale (XII) 275; *Battle of ~* 237. See *Azanulbizar, Nanduhirion*.

Dimrill Gate (VII) East Gate of Moria. 183

Dimrill Stair (VII) (1) The pass beneath Caradras. 164, 166, 168, 171,

174, 224, 240; *Dimrill Pass* 164, *the Pass* 167–8. (2) Later sense, path from Dimrill Dale to the Pass. 164, 235

Dimrill Stair (IXa) The pass beneath Caradhras (see VII.164). 64

Dimrill-dale(s) (VI) (1) Troll-country north of Rivendell. 205, 360–1, 367–8, 415, 432; *Dimrill-lands* 360. See *Entish Lands, Hoardale, Tum Dincelon*. (2) In later sense, Nanduhirion. 432–3, 437, 459–60, 464–6

Dimrill-stair (VI) (1) Name of the pass beneath Caradhras (later the Red-horn Gate). 433–4; *Dimrill* 438. See *Pendrethdulur*. (2) Later sense, the descent from the pass on the eastern side. 433

Dimrost (II) The falls of Celebros in Brethil. 130

Dimrost (IV) 'The Rainy Stair', falls in the stream Celebros. 185–7

Dimrost (XI) 'The Rainy Stair', the falls in the stream Celebros. 151. See *Nen Girith*.

Dín (VIII) See *Amon Dín*.

Dinithel (?*Durithel*) (II) Son of Fëanor. 241, 245, 251. (Replaced ?*Mailweg* 241, 244–5). See *Díriel*.

Dinithel (?*Durithel*) (III) Earlier name of Díriel. 86

Dior (II) Son of Beren and Tirniviel, father of Elwing; called 'the Fair'. 139, 214–15, 240–1, 244, 246, 249, 251. See *Ausir* (1), *Daimor, Damrod* (1).

Dior (IV) Called 'Thingol's Heir'. 33, 35–9, 62, 64, 68–9, 101, 134–5, 137, 140, 143, 145, 148, 150, 152, 158, 161–2, 191, 301, 306–7, 325–7

Dior (V) Called 'the Beautiful' and 'Thingol's Heir' (see *375*). 135, 141–2, 178, 194, 306, 330, 332, 334, 403

Dior (VII) Thingol's Heir. 110, 136

Dior (VIII) Thingol's Heir. 297

Dior (XI) (often called *Dior Thingol's Heir*) 22, 71, 133, 23 1–2, 234, 257, 300, 346–51, 353; called *Half-elven* 257, and see *Aranel, Eluchil*.

Dior (XII) (1) Thingol's Heir. 223, 348–9, 368–9, 371–2; his sons 373. See *Eluchil*. (2) Ninth Ruling Steward. 204, 219, 235, 249

Dior the Fair (III) Son of Beren and Lúthien. 125, 137, 182

Dior Thingol's Heir (VI) 68

Dirgon (VIII) Messenger from Minas Tirith to Théoden. 316–17. See *Hirgon*.

Dirhael (XII) Grandfather of Aragorn II. 196, 238, 263; changed to *Dirhoel* 238, 263

Dírhaval (XI) Man of Dor-lómin, author of the *Narn i Chîn Húrin*. 312–15; *Dírhavel* 311–12, 315

Díriel (II) Son of Fëanor. 251. (Replaced *Dinithel/Durithel*; later *Amras*.)

Díriel (IV) Son of Fëanor. 15, 22, 46, 64, 69, 88, 133, 150, 152, 195, 213, 232, 308, 326, 331, 335; O.E. *Tirgeld* 213. (Replaced by Amras.)

Díriel (V) Son of Fëanor, twin brother of Damrod (223). 125, 128, 132, 143, 223, 226, 262, 265, 269, 283, 354, 359

Díriel (VIII) Ancient name used in Gondor. 161

Díriel (X) See *Damrod and Díriel*.

Díriel (XI) also *Diriel*) Son of Fëanor, twin-brother of Damrod. 39, 53, *183, 197, 225, 240, 329, 352; *Diriol* 218, 225, 227. See *Amras*.

Díriel (III) Son of Fëanor. 65, 86, 135, 211

Dís (XII) Sister of Thorin Oakenshield. 277, 285

Dispossessed, The (IV) The House of Fëanor. 212, 265, 277, 289, 295, 328; O.E. *Erfeloran (Ierfe-, Yrfe-)* 212, 277, 288–9, 338, 340

Dispossessed, The (V) The House of Fëanor. 114, 125, 252

Dispossessed, The (X) The House of Fëanor. 117

Dispossessed, The (XI) The House of Fëanor. 33, 177

Distances (VII) 57, 65, 165–6, 215, 220–1, 238, 282, 311, 344, 348–9, 356, 365, 389–90, 395, 417

Distances (VIII) 12, 27, 36, 42, 68, 78–9, 119, 123, 125, 128, 132–3, 145, 252, 257, 259, 267, 278, 283, 291–2, 294, 296–7, 308, 327, 330, 339–40, 343–4, 348, 352, 354–5, 361, 363–4, 370, 397–9, 411–12, 414–15, 422, 424

Distances (IXa) 10–11, 14–16, 33–6, 88, 92, 103–4

Distances (XI) 15, 89, 111, 145, 149, 158, 193, 295, 306, 332–3, 335

Dol Amroth (VII) 299, 310, 312

Dol Amroth (VIII) (including references to Imrahil as *Prince* or *Lord of Dol Amroth*) 252, 278, 287, 289, 294, 301, 306, 326, 331, 338, 340, 369, 386, 390, 415, 423–4; *Amroth* 372. See *Barad Amroth*.

Dol Amroth (IXa) 16; *the Prince of Dol Amroth* 61; *Amroth* 54

Dol Amroth (XII) 36, 206–7, 220–3, 240, 244, 329

Dol Baran (VIII) Last hill of the Misty Mountains (also *Dolbaran*). 72, 75, 79–81, 119–20, 129, 140, 142, 235, 270, 276, 320, 322, 342, 392

Dol Dúghol (VIII) 122. See *Dol Guldur*.

Dol Dúgol (VII) Dwelling of the Necromancer in Southern Mirkwood

(see 298). 178, 233–4, 242, 244, 296, 298, 306. Replaced by *Dol Dúghul* 244, 296, 306, 333, 351, 372; and that by *Dol Guldur* 292

Dol Dûgul (XII) See *Dol Guldur*.

Dol Guldur (VI) 85, 414

Dol Guldur (VII) See *Dol Dúgol*.

Dol Guldur (VIII) 122, 357–8

Dol Guldur (XII) Sauron's dwelling in Mirkwood. 193, 229, 234–5, 237, 239, 247, 249–50, 252, 276–7, 280, 283–4, 287–8, 311; former name *Dol Dûgul* 225, 247, *Dol Dúghul*, *Dol Dúgol* 247

Dolamarth (VII) See *Amon Amarth*.

Dolbaran (V) Southernmost height of the Misty Mountains. 345, 351

Dolbear, Rupert (IXb) Member of the Notion Club. (Including references to him by his nickname *Rufus*) 150–2, 159, 161, 169–73, 175, 178–9, 183–4, 187–8, 191, 211, 213–15, 219, 223, 228, 230–3, 245, 250, 253–5, 259–60, 266, 277, 283

Dolereb (VII) See *Erebor*.

Dolm, Mount (IV) Great height in the Blue Mountains. 232, 332, 336

Dolm, Mount (V) Great height in the Blue Mountains. 129, 146, 278, 412; later form *Dolmed* 146, 274, 278, 373, 376

Dolmed, Mount (IV) Later name of Mount Dolm. 232

Dolmed, Mount (VII) In the Blue Mountains. 301

Dolmed, Mount (XI) In the Blue Mountains. 10, 16, 75, 112, 134, 202, 206; *Mount Dolmeð* *183; earlier *Mount Dolm* 334

Dome of Valmar (XII) 371; *Dome of Varda* 376

Dome of Varda (X) 286, 292, 385–8, 390. See *Nur-menel*; and cf. *the domed halls of Varda* 67

Dominion of Men (X) 31, 68, 217, 327, 340–2, 404

Donegal (IXb) 293

Doom (X) 112, 160, 323–4, 336; *Doom of the Noldor*, see *Noldor*.

Doom of Mandos (IV) 50, 267, 273, 278–9, 293. See *Prophecy of Mandos*.

Doom of Mandos (V) 115, 123, 178, 247–8. See *Prophecy of the North*.

Doom of the Noldor (XI) 224 (see *Mandos*). *Doom of Men* 247

Doom-hill (X) (of the Valar) 259

Doom-ring (XI) (of the Valar) 399, 401. See *Máhanaxar*.

Doon-Caron, Dûn Caron (VI) The Red Valley; early name for Dimrilldale. 433. See *Carndoom, Caron-dûn*.

Door (of Night) (X) 27, 407

Door of Night (I) 215–17, 219, 221–2, 226–7. See *Moritarnon, Tarn Fui.*

Door of Night (II) 255, 259, 265, 268, 273, 325; *dragon-headed door(s)* 272–5; *mouth of night* 276

Door of Night (III) 149. See *Gates of Dread.*

Door of Night (IV) 40–1, 49, 70–1, 73, 75, 164, 203–4, 235, 238, 241, 252–3; *Door of (out of the) Timeless Night* 164–5, 237, 252. See *Ando Lómen.*

Door of Night (V) 20, 327, 332–3, 335

Door of Night (IXb) 292. *Door of Days* 292, 298

Dor Athro (II) 'The Land Beyond'. 41, 61. See *Artanor, Doriath, Land(s) Beyond.*

Dor Caranthir (VI) The land of C(a)ranthir son of Fëanor (Thargelion). 466

Dor Caranthir (XI) Thargelion. *183, 197–8; *Dor Cranthir* 198, *Dor Granthir* 197–8

Dor Daedeloth (II) The land of Morgoth. 328

Dor Daideloth (IV) The Land of Dread. 269, 272; replaced *(Dor-) Daidelos* *250–1, 259, 272; replaced by *Dor Daedeloth* 259. (*Daideloth, Dor-na-Dhaideloth* in other applications 259; cf. *Gwath-Fuin-daidelos.*)

Dor Dínen (XI) 'The Silent Land' between the upper waters of Esgalduin and Aros. *183, 188, 194, 338; *Dor Dhínen* 333, 338

Dor Edloth, Dor Us(g)wen (I) Earlier Gnomish names of Tol Eressëa. 21. (Replaced by *Dor Faidwen.*)

Dor Faidwen (I) 'Land of Release', Gnomish name of Tol Eressëa. 13, 21, 51

Dor Granthir (V) 'Land of Cranthir'. 265, 269, 405. See *Radhrost, Thargelion.*

Dor Haeron (XII) Land between Entwash and Isen. 273

Dor Lindon (XI) See *Lindon.*

Dor Lómin (I) 'Land of Shadow'. 112, 138, 240–1, 243. See *Hisilómë.*

Dor Lómin, Dor-lómin (II) 11, 43, 50–2, 61, 65–6, 71–2, 87, 120, 122, 126, 128, 149, 152–4, 202, 204, 215, 219, 250, 256, 279. See *Aiyador, Hisilómë, Hithlum, Land of Shadow(s), Mathusdor.*

Dor Tathrin (IV) See *Nan Tathrin.*

Dor-Anfalas (VIII) See *Anfalas.*

Dor-Cúarthol (III) 'Land of Bow and Helm', the country defended by Beleg and Túrin in the later legend. 50–1

Dor-Cúarthol (XI) 'The Land of Bow and Helm', defended by Túrin and Beleg from Amon Rûdh. 144, 314; *Cúarthol* 256

Dor-Daedeloth (XI) 'Land of Great Dread', the land of Morgoth. 18, 30–2, *183. See *Dor-na-Daerachas*.

Dor-Daedeloth (XII) The land of Morgoth. 362

Dor-Daideloth (V) (and later *Dor-Daedeloth*, see 256). 'Land of the Shadow of Dread', realm of Morgoth. 118, 120, 250, 256, *354–5* (*Daedhelos*); *Dor-na-Daideloth* 405

Dor-deloth (V) 'Land of Dread', realm of Morgoth. *355*, 405, 407

Dorgannas Iaur (XI) 'Account of the shapes of the lands of old'. 192; *Dorgannas* (XI) 195, 206. See *Torhir Ifant*.

Dori (VI) Dwarf, companion of Thorin Oakenshield. 210

Dori (XII) Companion of Thorin Oakenshield. 279

Doriath (I) 196, 240, 243. See *Artanor*.

Doriath (II) 41, 52–3, 57–8, 61, 64, 122, 126–8, 130, 137, 247, 250–1 *Doriath beyond Sirion (Nivrim)* 249. See *Artanor*, *Dor Athro*, *Land(s) Beyond*.

Doriath (III) 10, 16, 20, 22, 24–8, 30, 33–4, 50–1, 53, 76, 87, 93, 104, 106–7, 109–10, 114, 116, 126–7, 146–7, 155, 158, 170, 173, 183, 185, 188, 195–6, 198, 200–2, 209, 215–17, 227, 229, 235, 238–40, 244, 247, 261–3, 267–8, 271–4, 280–1, 283, 287–8, 310–14, 316, 331–2, 346, 352–3, 359; *Doriath beyond Sirion* 89; *the Dancer of Doriath* 9, 61, 88; *King of Doriath*, see *Thingol*. See *Artanor*, *Guarded Realm*, *Hidden Kingdom*, *Hidden People*.

Doriath (IV) 13, 21, 23–9, 33–5, 51, 55, 57–8, 60–4, 85, 100, 103, 103, 105–6, 108–14, 116–17, 119–20, 123, 125–8, 131–5, 137–8, 140, 148, 150–2, 159, 174 (language of), 176–8, 182–3, 185, 188–9, 191, 202, 210, 220–7, 230, 232, 271, 288, 296, 299–300, 303–7, 311–12, 314, 322–3, 325, 327–8, 330, 339; O.E. *Éaland*, etc. 210, but *Doriaþ* in the texts; bounds of Doriath 224. See *Artanor*.

Doriath (V) 114, 125–8, 133–5, 138–42, 151, 170, 175, 180, 183, 186–90, 192, 194–6, 215, 220, 246, 252–3, 259–63, 265–6, 273–4, 276–7, 281, 283, 285, 287, 289, 291–3, 295, 299, 305–8, 312, 317–18, 320, 322, 324, 331, 346, *358* ('Land of the Cave'), *376*, 404, 407 (other names *Eglador*, *Ardholen*, *Arthoren*, *Arthurian*, *Garthurian*, *358*, *360*, *393*). *Doriath beyond Sirion* 128, 261, 267 (see *Nivrim*). See *Hidden Kingdom*.

Doriath (VI) 180–3, 188, 216, 384

Doriath (VII) 110, 124, 331, 453–5; runes of Doriath 456–7

Doriath (VIII) 184, 187, 297

Doriath (X) 104, 164, 169, 171, 173, 374, 423

Doriath (XI) 5, 14, 16, 19, 21–7, 32–5, 39, 44, 50, 53, 56, 59, 62–
70, 72, 77, 79–81, 83, 85, 88–90, 93, 101–3, 107–8, 110–13,
116, 119, 121, 123, 127, 129, 132, 135–6, 138, 150–1, 175, 178,
180, 186, 189, 193–4, 197, 203, 218–19, 244, 254–6, 258, 281,
298, 301, 303, 310–13, 315, 318(-19), 321, 326, 328, 332–4,
345–56, 369–70, 378–9, 408–9; *Land of the Girdle* 16; *Dôr Iâth*
'Land of the Fence' 370, 378; *Guarded Kingdom, ~ Realm* 16, 21;
Hidden Kingdom 89, 102, 158, 161–2, 312; *Annals of Doriath* 4,
12, 104. See *Arthórien, Garthúrian, Eglador; Nivrim, Radhrim.*

Doriath (XII) 76, 174, 185, 301, 307, 319, 325, 337, 349, 360, 369,
372, 385, 392

Doriath beyond Sirion (IV) (127), 185, 224–5, (226, 330), 334

Doriathrin (V) The language of Doriath. 178, 188, 194, 256, 347, 405.
Many references to the language of Doriath are included under
Doriath.

Doriathrin (XI) (language) 22

Dorlas (II) Companion of Turambar in the attack on Glaurung. 132–
4

Dorlas (XI) Man of Brethil. 92, 96–8, 100, 147–8, 152–6, 163, 257,
275, 284, 288, 303–5, 309; his wife 101, 163; late change to
Darlas 309

Dor-lómen, Dor-lómin (V) 117, 249, 259, 261, 266, 367 (also
Lómendor, Dorlamren), 406; *Dor-lúmin* 406–7. On the changing
meaning of the name see 406.

Dorlómin (III) 8, 16, 24, 26, 29, 93, 104, 114, 116, 126, 148

Dor-lómin (IV) (also *Dor-lómen*) 4, 7, 22, 53, 58, 101, 182, 192–3,
210, 220–1, 230, 268; equated with *Hithlum* 22, 101, 221; 'Land
of Shadows' 4, 7, 22, 192, Land of Echoes' 193, 210; O.E. *Wóman-
land* 210. *Dragon (-helm) of Dor-lómin* 182

Dor-lómin (X) 119

Dor-lómin (XI) 49, 51, 56, 58, 61, 64, 78, 81–2, 85, 87–92, 102,
123–4, 126, 138, 145–6, 150, 166, 169, 176, 187, 223, 228, 234–
5, 256–7, 262–3, 265, 267, 284, 287, 289, 299–300, 302, 310–
11, 313, 344, 350; *Dor-Lómen* 181, *182, 202; *Lóminórë* 145

Dor-na-Daerachas (XI) Late substitution for *Dor-Daedeloth.* *183,
187, 338–9

Dor-na-Dhaideloth (II) (Battle of) 287; for the name see 328. See
Ladwen-na-Dhaideloth, Heath of the Sky-roof

Dor-na-Dhaideloth (III) 49

Dor-na-Fauglith (III) Name given to the great northern plain (*Ard-galen*) after its desolation in the Battle of Sudden Flame. 39, 41, 48–9, 55, 58, 87, 271, 275; see 284, and see *Anfauglith, Blasted Plain, Daideloth, Dor-na-Maiglos, Land of Thirst, Plains of Drouth, Thirsty Plain*.

Dor-na-Fauglith (IV) 26 ('Plain of Thirst'), 27, 29, 57–9, 101 ('Land of Thirst'), 119, 124, 157, 160, 172, 177, 180, 192, 220, 259, 298 ('Land of Gasping Thirst'), 301–2, 309. See *Anfauglith, Black Plain, Thirsty Plain*.

Dor-na-Fauglith (V) 132 ('Land of Gasping Thirst'), 136, 144, 280 ('Land of Thirst'), 291, 309–10, 328, *369, 381* ('thirsty sand'); *Fauglith* 289, 291, 301, 309, 314 *Anfauglith* 301

Dor-na-Fauglith (XI) Earlier name of Anfauglith. 124, *183, 23 8–9; *Dor-no-* ~ 238–9, *Dor-nu-* ~ 239, translated 'Land under Choking Ash' 240; *Fauglith* 128, 134

Dor-na-Maiglos (III) Earlier name of Dor-na-Fauglith. 49

Dornhoth (XI) 'The Thrawn Folk', the Dwarves. 388, 408

Dor-nu-Fauglith (II) 62. See *Anfauglith*.

Dor-tathrin (III) Another name of Nan-Tathrin, the Land of Willows. 89

Dorthonion (II) 'Land of Pines'. 62. See *Forest of Night, Taurfuin, Taur-nu-Fuin*.

Dorthonion (III) The great forested highlands afterwards called *Taur-na(nu)-Fuin*. 171, 335, 345, 350–1

Dorthonion (IV) 108, 173, 175, 211, 258. (Replaced *Taur-na-Danion*.)

Dorthonion (V) (and earlier *Dorthanion*, see 145). 'Land of Pines'. 145–6, 239, 254, 257, 260–1, 263–7, 269, 272 (its extent), 280–1, 283–4, 289–92, 296, 298, 392 (also *Dor-na-Thuin*), 405. See *Taur-na-Danion*.

Dorthonion (VII) 240, 420. See *Orod-na-Thôn*.

Dorthonion (X) 123, 323–4, 328

Dorthonion (XI) 6, 15, 17, 32, 38, 46, 49–52, 56, 58–9, 61, 64, 70, 104, 113, 132, 167–8, *183, 187–8, 193–4, 219, 224, 228–9, 238–9, 324

Dorthonion (XII) 68, 185, 350

Dorwinion (V) 334, 338

Dor-Winion, Dorwinion (III) A southern land from which wine was imported into the North. 11, 17, 22, 26, 112, 118, 127

Double Mirth (I) Great festival in Valinor. 143–4, 222. See *Samírien*.

Downfall of Númenor (XII) See *Númenor*.

Downfall, The (IXb) (Also *The Downfall (Fall) of Númenor, of Ana-dûnê*) 152, 217, 279–80, (282), 339, 353, *355*, 374, 390, 392, 394–5, 401, 404, 407–10, 414–15, 419, 433–4. *The Downfallen*, see *Atalante*.

Downs (VII) East of Entwash. 320, 391–2, 394, 398–9, 406. See *Barrow-downs*.

Downs (VIII) In the Eastemnet. 361; *Down-end* 361

Dragon(s) (VI) 19, 22, 29, 41, 78, 82–3, 227, 245, 260, 320, 379, 384, 399; referring to Smaug 77, 256, 319, 429; *dragon-gold*, *dragon-curse* 18, 43, 73, 233, 379, and cf. 42.

Dragon(s) (VII) 28, 170; referring to Smaug 22, 142, 160; *dragon-fire* 28

Dragon(s) (XI) (not including references to Glaurung) 46, 74, 302, 346; *dragon-gold* 347, 350; *fire-drakes* 46 (see *Urulókë*).

Dragon-helm (III) 13–14, 16, 26–7, 51, 114, 116–17, 126; *Helm of Hador* 27, *of Húrin* 114–15

Dragon-helm (IV) 118, 182–3; *Helm of Gumlin* 124

Dragon-helm (V) 293, 303, 314, 316, 320, 322; *the helm of Gumlin* 319–20; *Dragonhead of the North* 319; described 319

Dragon-helm (XI) *(of Galion, of Hador, of Dor-lómin)* 81–2, 85–7, 93, 135, 137–8, 140, 142–4, 255, 350

Dragons (II) Selected references (including *drakes, worms*): concerning dragons 85, 96–7, 125, 142–3; the 'dragons' that camë against Gondolin (called also *monsters, serpents, snakes*) 169–70, 172, 174, 176, 178–89, 195, 210, 213. See *Foalókë, Glorund*.

Dragons (IV) (not including references to *the Dragon* =Glómund) 30, 36, 39–40, 73 *(drakes)*, 118 *(Worms of Greed)*, 144, 157, 164, 194, 297, 307; winged dragons 160, 203, 309

Dragons (V) (not including references to Glómund) 24, 65, 130, 142, 332, *(lókë, lhûg* 370); *winged dragons* 144, 329, *(rámalókë* 370); *Black Dragon*, see *Ancalagon*.

Dragons (VIII) 217, 232

Dragons (XII) 72, 227, 252, 275; *drakes* 374. See *Ancalagon, Smaug*.

Drama of the Silver Tree (IXb) [Ramer] 206, 221

Drama, The (X) (of Arda, especially of the war against Melkor) 26, 329–30, 333, 335, 33 7–8, 375 (cf. also 349, 389)

Dramborleg (II) The axe of Tuor. 164, 181, 203, 213; rejected form *Drambor* 203

Draugluin (II) 55–8, 68

Draugluin (III) The great werewolf of the Wizard's Isle, slain by Huan. 205, 210, 252, 256, 258, 278, 282–3, 289–93; *Fearphantom Draugluin* 292

Draugluin (IV) 111

Draugluin (V) 134 ('the Werewolf'), 135, 151, (*354*)

Draugluin (XI) The werewolf. 67–8, 131

Dream of the Tower, Frodo's (VII) 11, 33–6, 56, 130. See *Western Tower.*

Drengist, (Firth of) (XI) 5–6, 8, 16–17, 38, 46, 60, 89, 107, 176, 181, *182, 197, 206

Drengist, Firth of (IV) 210–11, 230, 262, 268, 280, 354, 332, 336; O.E. *Nearufléot* 210

Drengist, Firth of (V) 117, 125, 130, 145, 249, 255, 258–9, 271, 274, 278, 412

Drengist, Firth of (X) 119–20, 122, 196, 295

Drengist, Firth of (XII) 354

Drowning of Anadûnë (XII) (title of work) 64, 140–5, 147, 149–50, 154–6, 158, 164, 171, 183, 374; (not as title) 157

Drowning of Anadûnê, The (X) (title) 5, 7, 22, 28, 179–80, 355

Drowning of Númenor, The (IXb) Title of the original text of *The Drowning of Anadûnê.* 341

Druadan Forest (VIII) 344, 352–3

Drúadan Forest (XII) 65

Druadan Forest, Forest of Druadan (IXa) 18, 22, 56, 67

Druedain (VIII) The Wild Men of the White Mountains. 352. See *Wild Men, Woses.*

Druedain (XI) 391

Drúedain (XII) Wild Men of the White Mountains. 293, 309, 324, 326

Drûgs (XII) Drúedain. 309–10, 314, 326

Drûn (III) Region north of Tarn Aeluin. 344, 350

Drûn (XI) Region north of Tarn-aeluin. *183, 187

Dry River (II) The entrance to Gondolin. 207

Dry River (IV) 66, 194

Dry River (XI) The entrance to Gondolin. *182, 271, 324

Duath (VII) See *Ephel Dúath.*

Dúath (VIII) See *Ephel Dúath.*

Du-finnion (VI) Elvish name of Trotter. 361, 392. See *Ethelion, Padathir, Rimbedir.*

Du-finnion (VII) Trotter. 61

Duil Rewinion (IV) The Hills of the Hunters. 225

Duil Rewinion (V) Old name of the Hills of the Hunters. 268. See
  Taur-na-Faroth.

Duil Rewinion (VII) Hills of the Hunters. 287

Duilas (VIII) See *Targon*.

Duilin (II) (1) Father of Flinding. 79, 119 with patronymic prefix go-
  > *bo-Dhuilin* 'son of Duilin' 78, 82, 119. (2) Lord of the people
  of the Swallow in Gondolin. 173, 175, 178, 203; rejected form
  Duliglin 203

Duilin (III) Father of Flinding, in the *Tale of Turambar*; with patronymic prefix *go-* > *bo-Dhuilin* 'son of Duilin'. 53. (Replaced by
  Fuilin.)

Duilin (VIII) Son of Duinhir of Morthond Vale. 287, 370

Duilin (XII) (1) A lord of Gondolin. 421. (2) Original name of the
  father of Gwindor of Nargothrond. 421. (3) Father of Saelon (1).
  421.

Duilwen, River (IV) 133, 135, 189, 230, 232–3

Duilwen, River (V) 128, 263, *355*, *359*

Duilwen, River (XI) In Ossiriand. 13, *185

Duin Daer (XI) The river Gelion. 336; *Duin Dhaer* 191, 336

Duin Morghul (VII) Stream in the Morgul Vale (in LR *Morgulduin*).
  312. Also named *Ithilduin* 312

Duin Morghul (VIII) Stream flowing through Imlad Morghul, formerly
  called *Ithilduin*. 436. See *Morgulduin*.

Duinhir (VIII) Lord of Morthond Vale. 287, 370–2

Dúnadan, The (VII) (of Aragorn). 83. *Dúnedain* 291. See *Tarkil*.

Dúnedain (VI) 294; *the Dúnadan* (Aragorn) 369

Dúnedain (VIII) 161–2, 310, 363, 369–70, 395, 411; *Dúnadan* 302,
  309; *Star of the Dúnedain* (299), 309. See *Kings of Men*.

Dúnedain (IXa) 52, 55–6

Dúnedain (IXb) 393; *Dúnedanic* 406

Dúnedain (X) 370, 373

Dúnedain (XI) 378, 386, 402. See *Núnatani*.

Dúnedain (XII) 31–4, 36, 38, 40, 55, 63, 68, 74, 119–20, 122–3, 125,
  127–31, 145–6, 149, 193–5, 213, 225, 227, 230, 232, 245, 253,
  258, 260, 263, 267, 324; *Dúnadan* 324; *Dúnedein* 31, 55. See also
  Chieftains of the Dúnedain.

Dúnedhil (XI) 'West-elves' (of Middle-earth). 378, 386

Dungalef (III) Riddling reversal of *Felagund* (replaced by *Hate*, 233).
  229, 233–4

Dungorthin (IV) See *Nan Dungorthin*.

Dungorthin, Dungortheb (III) See *Nan Dungorthin.*

Dungorthin, Dungortheb (V) See *Nan-dungorthin.*

Dunharrow (VII) 320, 447, 450–1. Earlier name *Dunberg* 447, 451

Dunharrow (IXa) 18, 136–7; *the Hold* 136–7

Dunharrow (XII) 53, 236, 271, 309

Dunharrow, the Hold (of Dunharrow) (VIII) 69–70, 72, 141, 235–59 passim, 262–3, 265, 267, 272–4, 289, 296–7, 299, 301, 303, 305, 307–9, 311–13, 315–16, 318, 320–2, 343, 345, 347, 351, 355–6, 386, 396, 405–7, 413, 416–19, 421–3, 426, 428–9. Also the name of the mountain at the head of Harrowdale (later *Starkhorn*) 235–7, (238), 240, 242, 257, 308; *the Lap of Dunharrow* 238, 241. Former men of Dunharrow 236, 238, 241–4, 246, 251, 265, 267, 315–16, and see *Dead Men of Dunharrow. From dark Dunharrow in the dim morning* 349, 355–6

Dúnhere (VIII) Rider of Rohan, chief of the men of Harrowdale. 316, 318, 355, 371

Dunhirion (XII) Rejected name of Annúminas. 167. See *Tarkilion.*

Dunland (VII) 167, 320

Dunland (VIII) Region in the west of the Misty Mountains, at first called *Westfold.* 22–3, 27, 40–1, 236, 249, 253; *tongue of Dunland* 21, 159; *Dunlanders* 52 (origin of), 242, 247, 253, 298; *Dunlendings* 321. See *Westfold* (1).

Dunland (IXa) 69, 74, 103, 107; *northern Dunland* 69; *Dunlanders* 93, *Dunlendings* (IXa) 69

Dunland (XII) 11, 34, 38, 65–7, 229, 250, 271, 279, 319, 329; *Dunlandish* (language) 38; *Dunlanders* 271; *Dunlendings* 34, 65, 205, 314, 329–30 (see *Gwathuirim*).

Dunruin (VI) The Red Valley; early name of Dimrill-dale. 454, 464

Durin (the Deathless) (XII) 173, 185, 237, 275–7, 279, 286, 304, 322, 324, 382–3; his awakening 301, 321–2. *Durin's Folk, House, Line, Race* 227, 233, 236–7, 275–6, 278, 281–6, 288

    Durin (the Deathless) (XII) Later kings named *Durin* 275, 284, 383–4; *Durin III* 275, 277, 279, 284, 286, > *Durin VI* 284, 383; *Durin VII and Last* 278–9, 383, 391

Durin (III) 316

Durin (V) 7

Durin (VI) 429, 437, 449, 451, 466; *Lord of Moria* 449; *Durin's race, clan* 391, 429; *Doors of Durin* 449, 463

Durin (VII) 141–2, 180, 183–5, 189, 220, 234; *Durin's folk, clan* 143,

156, 246; *axe* 191, 200; ~ *crown* 220; ~ *stone* 203, 219; ~ *tower* 430–1; ~ *bridge* 431

Durin (IXa) 122, 135

Durin (XI) 204, 207–8, 211–13; called *the Eldest* (of the Seven Fathers of the Dwarves) 208, 211–13

Durin's Bane (VII) 143, 185–6, 188–9, 202, 257

Durin's Bane (XII) 286

Durin's folk (VIII) 357

Durthang (IXa) Orc-hold in the mountains west of Udûn, originally a fortress of Gondor. 33–6

Duruchalm (I) Rejected name for Turuhalmë. 244

Dushgoi (VIII) Orc name of Minas Morghul. 216–18, 226; *Lord(s) of Dushgoi* 216–17

Dwalin (VI) Dwarf, companion of Thorin Oakenshield. 210

Dwalin (XII) Companion of Thorin Oakenshield. 279–80, 288

Dwarfmine (XI) Nogrod. 108, 201, 209

Dwarf-road (IV) 133, 189, 220–1, 224–5, 232, 332, 336

Dwarf-road(s) (XI) 121, *185, 189–90, 202, 206, 216, 218, 221, 321, 334–6; North road of the Dwarves *183, 189, 321, 334–6

Dwarrowdelf (VII) Moria. 166, 173, 183, 186

Dwarrowdelf (XI) Khazad-dûm (Moria). 201, 206, 209, 419 (also *Dwarrowmine*, *Dwarrowvault* 389, 419). See *Dwarfmine*.

Dwarrowdelf (XII) Moria. 24, 44, 58; Westron *Phuru-nargian* 44, 76, 78 (earlier forms 58).

Dwarves (I) 236–7, 267. See *Nauglath*.

Dwarves (II) (including *Dwarf-folk*) 68, 136, 223–30, 232, 234–9, 241, 243, 245–51, 283, 328; adjective *dwarven* 227, *dwarfen* 238. See especially 223–4, 247–8, and see *Indrafangs*, *Nauglath*, *Nauglafring*.

Dwarves (III) 32, 44, 52, 56, 111, 127, 161, 264, 306 (see especially 52, 306); *dwarfland* 115, 126; adjective *dwarfen* 44, elsewhere *dwarvish*. See *Longbeard Dwarves*.

Dwarves (IV) 24, 32–3, 54, 61–3, 103–4, 108, 112–13, 116, 123, 132–5, 174–5, 178, 180–1, 183, 187–90, 209, 221, 223–4, 293, 300–1, 306–7, 309, 311, 320, 325–6, 331–2, 335–6. See especially 104, 116, 174–5; and see *Nauglar*, *Nauglafring*, *Necklace of the Dwarves*; *Mîm*.

Dwarves (V) (also Dwarfs, see 277). 7, 23, 129, 134–5, 141, 144, 146–7, 149, 178–9, 190–1, 197, 256, 258, 265, 269, 273–4, 277–8, 286, 303, 307, 313, 405; *Dwarvish* 141, 178–9, 278, 303, 313. For

the origin and nature of the Dwarves see *Aulë*; for their languages (*Aulian, Nauglian*) see 178–9, 273. See *Nauglar, Naugrim*.

Dwarves (VI) Visitors to Hobbiton 20, 30–1, 36, 48, 63, 66, 101, 106, 149–50, 156, 160, 221, 234–5, 238, 246, 253, 315, 336; companions of Bilbo 203–4, 392, 398; Dwarves of Moria 173, 226, 391, 429, 437, 448, 458–9, 463; of the Lonely Mountain 31, 210, 226, 381, 391–2, 398–9, 411, 414, 429; other references 75, 79, 87, 117, 132, 140, 178, 243, 253, 294, 311, 313, 315, 348, 385, 429, and see *Hoards of the Dwarves, Rings of the Dwarves*.

Dwarves (VII) At Bag End 20–1; of the Blue Mountains 301; of the Lonely Mountain 117, 142, 155, 160, 424; of Moria 142, 156, 164, 166, 175, 179, 181, 183–6, 188, 218, 225, 247, 263, 304, 431, 455; other references 24, 114, 125, 142–3, 152, 158, 160, 162, 170, 181, 212, 227, 231, 257, 275. War of the Dwarves and the Orcs (Goblins) 142–3; *Western Dwarves* 455; *Dwarf-cities, Dwarf-road* 301; *Dwarf-door* (of Moria) 191, *Dwarf-doors* 187; language 117, 181, 185–6, 455; runes of the Dwarves 186, 200, 452–9. See *Seven Rings*.

Dwarves (VIII) (general references) 14, 37–8, 153, 217, 292, 294, 357–8, 411; *Dwarflord* 300, 305

Dwarves (IXa) 68, 119, 122–3

Dwarves (X) 93, 103–4, 202, 251, 409, 415, 418, 421. See *Naugrim, Nornwaith; Aulë*.

Dwarves (XI) (including many compounds as *Dwarf-kings, -knife, -mines, -speech, -women*, etc.) 9–12, 45, 59–60, 68, 71, 107–9, 113, 118, 120–1, 128, 132, 134, 138, 143, 167, 179, 189, 201–16, 239, 255, 280, 321–2, 324, 326–7, 329, 332, 334–6, 340–1, 345–53, 355, 359, 372, 387–91, 395, 397, 402, 408–9, 418–19; *Dwarfs* 202–3, 239

Dwarves (XI) Origin of the Dwarves 10, 108, 203, 210–13; Elvish names for 209, 214, 387–8; language (*aglâb* 395) 10, 108, 205, 207–9, 211–12, 395, 402, gesture-language (*iglishmêk*) 395, 402; Dwarf-cities and their names 108, 201–2, 205–6, 209, 389, 419; nature of the Dwarves 109, 203–7, 395. See *Fathers of, Necklace of, the Dwarves*.

Dwarves (XII) (and *Dwarf*; also many compounds, as *Dwarf-boots, -mines, -cities*) 4, 7–8, 10, 15, 21–4, 26, 31, 35–6, 44, 46, 54–6, 58, 60, 70–1, 73, 76, 81–2, 173–4, 184–5, 205, 220, 222–3, 227, 230, 233, 235–40, 244, 246, 249–50, 252, 261, 275–6, 278, 280–1, 283–5, 288, 295–8, 300–5, 310–11, 313, 316, 318–23, (324),

327-8, 351-2, 358, 382-4, 391. Names of the Dwarves 22, 35, 54, 60, 71, 73, 81, 296, 300, 304, 321-2

Dwarves (XII) *Dwarfs* 210, 217, 221; *Dwarf and Goblin War* 382; *Dwarf-city* 391, 466; *Dwarf-folk* 463; *Dwarf-gates* 444, 449; *Dwarf-home* 466; *Dwarf-kingdom* 210; *Dwarf-lords* 258, 269, 458, 465-6; *Dwarf-regions* 466; *Dwarf-writing* 443, Runes 460; Dwarf-names and language 246, 444, 451, 466

Dwarvish (VI) (of language) 465

Dwarvish (VII) 174, 191, 241, 455, 457; *dwarfish* 241; *dwawen* 104, the *Dwarven-door* of Moria 178, 204

Dwarvish (XI) (of language, names) 108, 179 *(Dwarfish)*, 180, 336, 391, 412, 414; (with other reference) 335-6, 355

Dwarvish (XII) (of language and writing) 44, 81, 279, 286, 297, 300, 304, 319, 324, 351-2; (with other reference) 301, 317, 383, 391; *Dwarfish* 351

Dweller in the Deep (III) See *Ulmo*.

Dweller in the Water (VI) 443-4; *Dweller in the Pool* 453; *the water-monster* 455

Dwellers in the West (IXb) See *(The) West*.

Dwimorberg (VIII) 266, 312-13, 315, 372, 406. See *Haunted Mountain*.

Dwimordene (VIII) Lothlórien. 372

Dyfed (V) South Wales. 80

Dyson, H. V. D. (IXb) 150-2

Eä (I) The Universe. 173, 199, 225 (the word of Ilúvatar bringing it into being 62, 225).

Eä (IV) The World. 279. See *Ilu*.

Eä (V) The World. 338. See *Ilu*.

Eä (IXb) The Universe. 312

Eä (X) 7, 31, 37-9, 44, 48-54, 56-8, 60-7, 76, 80, 88, 97-9, 105, 107, 114, 117, 121, 129, 135, 144, 148, 150, 153, 156, 159-60, 190, 193, 201, 220, 244, 252, 267, 270, 280, 311, 318, 321-2, 326, 330, 334, 336-8, 342, 352, 373-82, 384, 386-9, 397, 403, 425, 428. See *(The) Great Tale, (The) Universe*.

Eä (XI) 399, 402-3

Eä (XII) 396-7, 400-1

Éadgifu (II) (Old English) (1) Ælfwine's wife, Elf of Tol Eressëa. 290. See *Naimi*. (2) Déor's wife, mother of Ælfwine. 313-14, 323, 330-1.

108

Éadgifu (III) Mother of Ælfwine. 140

Eädwine (V) (1) Son of Ælfwine. 7, 55, 78–80, 83. (2) King of the Lombards, =*Audoin*. 55, 91. Other references 46, 53, 56

Éadwine (IXb) (1) Father of Ælfwine the Mariner. 244, 270, 285, 288. (2) Son of Ælfwine (in *The Lost Road*). 292. (3) =Audoin the Lombard. 276. (4) =Edwin Lowdham. 244. The name itself 235–6

Eagles (II) 58, 193, 211; King of Eagles, see *Ramandur, Sorontur, Thorndor*; *People of the Eagles*, see *Thornhoth*; *Eagles' Cleft*, see *Cleft of Eagles*; *Eagle-stream*, see *Thorn Sir*; the Eagle as emblem, 193, 267

Eagles (IV) (not including references to Thorndor King of Eagles) 23, 52, 102, 145, 173, 318; *Eagles' Cleft*, see *Cristhorn, Kirith-thoronath*.

Eagles (V) 12, 162, 251–2. See *Gwaewar, Landroval, Sorontur, Thorondor*; *Lords of the West*.

Eagles (VI) 416

Eagle(s) (VII) 75–6, 116, 130, 134, 139, 151, 389, 400–1; eagle seen far off 357, 361, 379–80, 385, 387–9, 396–7, 403, 425–6. See *Gwaewar*.

Eagle(s) (VIII) 219, 256, 361–2. See *Gwaihir*.

Eagles (IXa) 5, 7, 44, 55; *white eagle* 5. See *Gwaihir, Lhandroval, Meneldor, Thorondor*.

Eagle(s) (IXb) (All references are to the great clouds, and most to *The Eagles of the Lords (of the West), of the Powers, of Amân*) 231, 238, 246, 251, 266, 274, 277, 279, 281, 290, 350, 371, 391

Eagles (X) 185 *(of Manwë)*, 412; the nature of the Great Eagles 138, 251, 410–11. See *Gwaehir, Landroval, Sorontar, Thorondor*.

Eagles (XI) 55, 57–8, 63, 126–7, 170, 193, 198, 239, 272, 302, 341, the Great Eagles 272, the Eagles of Manwë 272; and see *Gwaihir, Lhandroval, Sorontar, Thorondor*.

Eagles (XII) 239

Eagles' Cleft (III) See *Cristhorn*.

Ealá Eárendel engla beorhtast ((II) poem) 266–9, 271, 277

Ealdor (VIII) The seneschal of Edoras. (256, 259), 267. (Replaced by *Galdor*.)

Eälótë (XII) Eärendil's ship. 143. See *Rothinzil, Vingilot*.

Eär (IV) The Sea. 241; the Western and Eastern Seas named *Eär* on *Ambarkanta* diagram I, *243

Eär (XII) The Great Sea. 363

Eärambar (IV) The Walls of the World. *242–5, 252, 261. (Replaced *Ilurambar*.)

Eärambar (X) The Walls of Eä. 63

Eärámë (II) 'Eaglepinion', Earendel's first ship. 253–4, 261, 265, 267. *Earum* 260–1, 276, *Earam* 276. See *Earnhama, Earrámë*.

Eärámë (IV) 'Eagle's Pinion', Tuor's ship. 37, 69, 149, 151, 155, 195, 198, 308. (Replaced *Alqarámë*; replaced by *Eärramë*.)

Eärámë (V) 'Eagle's Wing', Tuor's ship. 71, 143; *349, 382* 'Sea-wing'. *Eärámë* (XI) Tuor's ship. 352

Eärendel (I) 13, 15, 18, 24, 48, 141; the *Tale of Eärendel* 27, 221, 230–1, 233; later form *Eärendil* 135

Eärendel (II) 130, 144–5, 149, 165, 167, 169–71, 174, 177–8, 185, 187–93, 196, 199–201, 213, 215–17, 219, 221, 242, 252–70, 272, 274, 276, 278, 281, 286, 290, 302, 304, 306–10; unnamed, in Ulmo's words to Tuor, 155, 205. See especially 266–7. *Lay of Eärendel* 270. Later form *Eärendil* 212, 265–6; *Eärendl* 267

Eärendel (III) 141–2, 144–5, 149; son of Fengel 141, 145. Later form *Eärendil* 83

Eärendel (IV) 36–8, 41, 50, 68–71, 74–5, (98–9), 101, 142–5, 148–56, 160, 162, 164–5, 172, 193, 195–8, 201–5, 213–15, 238, 252–3, 306–9, 326–7; later form *Eärendil* 197–8. *The Lay of Eärendel* (referred to in the *Quenta*) 149–50, 152; alliterative fragment 66, 220. See *Evening Star, Morning Star*.

Eärendel (V) 9, 18, 20, 22–3, 25–6, 60, 64, 68–71, 73–4, 77, 100, 141–4, 152, 176, 194, 247, 275, 323–7, 329, 332–6; later form *Eärendil* 102, 219. See especially 326–7.

Eärendel (VI) 215, 254

Eärendel (VII) 91, 95–6, 99, 102, 108, 110, 266, 290; *Eärendil* 95, 103, 266, 290; *Eärendel's star* 276, *the Evening Star* 266; *the Short Lay of Eärendel: Eärendillinwë* 102–3 (development of the 'Rivendell version' of *Errantry*, 90–105).

Eärendel (VIII) 155 *(the half-elven)*, 158–9, 168, 193, 203; *Earendel's star* 224, *the evening star* 210; *Alla (Aiya) Earendel Elenion Ankalima* 223

Éarendel (IXb) In Old English. 236–7, 278, 284–5, 299–301, 308. Lowdham's second name (changed to *Arundel*) 234, 281–2. See *Aurvandill*.

Éarendel, The (IXb) Edwin Lowdham's ship. 234, 280, 284; *Earendel('s) Star* 284, 308. *Éarendel*, the ship of Eadwine father of Ælfwine the Mariner, 270

Eärendil (X) (134), 247, 340, 359

Eärendil (XI) 135, *184, 190, 224, 231, 234–5, 299, 345–6, 348, 351–2, 354; *Eärendel* (XI) 22, 302, 311–12, 348; called *the Blessed* 224, *Half-elven* 348, 351, *a new star* 76. See *Ardamir*.

Eärendil (XII) (1) 143, 145, 152, 158, 173–5, 179, 346, 348, 363–5, 367, 369–71, 373, 375–6, 381, 386–7; *Eärendel* 168, 170; *Lay of ~* 163; *Heir of ~* (King of Númenor) 154–5. See *Ardamir*.

Eärendil (XII) (2) Fifth King of Gondor. 197, 212. (3) Tenth and last King of Arnor. 32, 64, 189, 208, 247. (Replaced by *Eärendur* (2).)

Eärendil the Mariner (IXb) 237, 241, 285, 301, 305–6, 308, 333, 340, 342–3, 346, 349, 356, 359, 375, 393, 408; the wife of Eärendil 342. Earlier form *Eärendel* 257–8, 279, 284, 292, 313–15, 333–5, 342, 344–5, 356, 399–400, 402–4, 406, 412. *Eärendil* as second name of Elendil 346, 348; Lowdham so addressed by Jeremy 290. See *Azrubêl*.

Eärendil was a mariner (VI) 393, 412

Eärendilyon (II) 'Son of Eärendel', mariner. 264

Eärendur (XII) (1) Fifteenth Lord of Andúnië. 159, 164. (2) Tenth King of Arnor. 64, 189, 193, 208, 227–8, 247, 253. (Replaced Eärendil (3).)

Earliest Days (VI) 311, 329, 349; *oldest days* 179. See *Ancient Days*, *Elder Days*.

Earliest Days (XII) 8, 15. See *Elder Days*.

Earnhama (II) (Old English) 'Eagle-dress', see 276

Eärnil I (XII) Thirteenth King of Gondor. 197, 213

Eärnil II (XII) Thirty-second King of Gondor. 201, 204, 212, 216–18, 232–3, 245, 248, 252, 254, 256, 262

Eärnur (VIII) Last king of the line of Anárion. 153. See *Elessar* (1).

Eärnur (IXa) Last king of the line of Anárion. 59

Eärnur (XII) (1) Second son of Isildur. 191, 208. (Replaced by *Aratan*.) (2) Thirty-third King of Gondor. 201–2, 204, 212, 217, 225–6, 233–4, 245, 247, 256, 378

Eärrámë (II) 'Sea-wing', Tuor's ship. 265. See *Alqarámë*, *Eärámë*.

Eärrámë (IV) 'Sea-wing', Tuor's ship. 69, 155, 198. (Replaced *Eärámë*.)

Earth (IV) As used explicitly =lands east of the Great Sea, 6, 38, 99; see *World*. *Rim of Earth* 98

Earth, (The) (IXb) 168, 181, 198, 202, 204–5, 207–9, (213), 221, 227, 246–7, 249, 258, 274, 311, 335–8, 341–5, 348, 351, 353–4, 357–

8, 360–6, 369, 372–4, 377, 379, 381–2, 387–98 *passim*, 401–12 *passim*. See *(The) Talkative Planet, Thulcandra*.

Earth *(The)* (X) 7, 12–20, 23–9, 31–7, 40–4, 51–4, 58, 60, 67, 70–2, 74, 78–9, 81, 85, 99, 104–5, 112, 120, 131–2, 136, 144–6, 153–4, 160, 162, 166–7, 174, 178, 185, 188, 212, 229, 266, 275, 277, 281–2, 286, 299, 330, 334, 337, 345–9, 355, 358–9, 366, 371, 374–6, 381–5, 387, 389, 391–5, 421, 426–8, 431; *Earthly* 42. For use in sense 'Middle-earth', excluding Aman, see 282, 431.

Earth (The) (X) *Girdle of the Earth* 130, 135; *Kingdom of Earth* 144. See *Arda, Ambar, Imbar*.

Earth, *(The)* (XI) 9, 39, 106, 174–5, 203, 210, 220, 348 *('on earth')*, 402, 418–2 1. See *Ambar, Imbar; Arda*.

Earth's middle (IV) 238; *Earth-middle* *249, 254. See *Endon, Endor*.

Earth-lady (I) Kémi (Yavanna Palúrien). 71, 79, 179–80, 214; *Earth-queen* 177

Earthroots (IV) 236. See *Martalmar, Talmar Ambaren*.

Eärwen (X) Olwë's daughter, wife of Finarfin (=Finrod (1)). 93, 101, 126, 177 *(the swan-maiden of Alqualondë)*, 182

Eärwen (XI) Olwë's daughter, wife of Finarfin (=Finrod (1)). 32(-3), 43, 115

Eärwen (XII) Daughter of Olwë, wife of Finarfin. 337, 344, (346), 360, 365

East Anglia (IXb) Kingdom of the East Angles. 293

East Beleriand (IV) 133, 232, 297–8, 300–2, 313, 318, 326, 331, 335

East Broseliand (IV) 232

East Danes (II) 305; *East-Denum* (Old English, dative case) 305

East End (VII) Fangorn. 415–16

East Gate(s) of Moria (VI) 443, 454, 458–60, 466; *'the chief entrance was on the East'* 429

East March (XII) See *Buckland*.

East Road (VI) (including many references to *the Road*) 46–7, 50, 53, 65, 72, 103–4, 106, 108, 125–6, 129–30, 132, 134, 149, 152–3, 156–7, 159–62, 165–72, 174, 176, 178, 191–6, 198–205, 217, 219, 236, 274–5, 278, 283–4, 301, 329, 332–3, 336–7, 339, 341–56 *passim*, 359–61, 368; *the Old Road* 167, 169; *the west road* 417. Course of the Road 192, 199–203; distances along the Road 170–1, 356, 367–8

East Road (VII) See *(The) Road*.

East Road (IXa) 77, 88, 100, 105; see *Roads*.

East Road (XI) See *Roads*.

East Road (XII) 93, 117. See *Great Road*.

East Wall (VII) (of Rohan) 396, 401, 405–7; *west-cliff* 425; descent into the plain: *the Ladder, the Stair* 409. See *Sarn Gebir* (1).

East(ern) Beleriand (V) 128, 130, 132, 137, 143, 175, 261–5, 272 (its extent), 283, 287, 291

East(ern) Sea (IV) 239, *249, 253, (255), 257, 270, 283 *East Sea* =Sea of Ringil *250–1, 258

East, The (VI) 182, 398, 409

East, The (IXa) 91; *the East lands* 63

East, The (IXb) 274, 334–5, 337, 339, 345, 349, 351, 355, 363, 365–6, 369, 380–1, 383, 389, 409

East, The (X) 18, 33, 72, 76, 79, 95, 100, 111, 117, 130–2, 135, 154, 160, 162, 176, 187, 275, 289, 327, 370, 378, 382. See *Mountains of the East*.

East, The (XI) 9, 37, 39, 47, 60, 70, 116, 118, 146, 173, 216, 220, 226, 272, 386; *the Eastlands* 39

East, The (XII) 75, 149, 154, 194, 200, 229, 231, 233–4, 240, 242, 264, 305–6, 323; references to Men of the East 79, 197, 200, 205, 215, 232, 258, 272, 302, 305–6, 311, 321, 424, 427, and see *Easterlings*.

East-elves (XII) Avari. 73, 174; *Eastern Elves* 79

Eastemnet (VII) 318, 398, 404

Eastemnet (VIII) 236–7 *(East Emnet)*, 243–4, 313, 361

Eastemnet (IXa) Rohan east of the Entwash. 9

Easterling Men (I) 135

Easterling Men, Easterlings (II) 120, 126, 204. See *Incomers*.

Easterling(s) (XI) 74, 79, 81–2, 88, 90–1, 128, 137, 167, 205, 207–8, 252, 301, 377. See *Eastrons, Swarthy Men*.

Easterlings (IV) 5, 121, 179, 183, 320, 322. See *Incomers, Swarthy Men*.

Easterlings (V) 286 (described), 291, 307–8, 310, 312, 316; *Eastern Men* 291, 403. See *Rómenildi, Swarthy Men*.

Easterlings (VIII) 244, 415

Easterlings (IXa) 50

Easterlings (IXb) 398–400

Easterlings (XII) 197–8, 213–14, 219, 228, 230, 236, 258, 271–2, 296, 328

Eastern Land (IV) 239, 255; *Eastland or Easterness* *249; O.E. *Éastland* 281. See *Land(s) of the Sun*.

Easterness (VI) See *Eastern Land*.

Eastern Sea (V) 119, 245, 248, 266.

Eastern Sea (X) 78–9

Eastern Sea (XI) 173

Eastfarthing (VI) 124, 278, 298, 312–13, 387; *East Shire* 286

Eastfarthing (VII) 39

Eastfold (VII) 320, 407

Eastfold (VIII) 256, 259, 262, 319, 371

Eastfold (XII) Region of Rohan. 274

Eastlanders (VIII) 340

Eastrons (XI) Easterlings. 253, 256, 262, 264, 266, 298–9, 301

Eastward Lands (I) 233; *Eastern lands* 211; *Eastern shore(s)* 182, 214–15, 226

Ebor (XI) Man of Brethil, liege of Manthor. 263–5, 267, 270–1

Eccuilë (X) See *Almaren*.

Echil (XI) Sindarin name =*Hildor* 'the Followers', Men. 219. (The existence of *Echil* denied, 387; see *Aphadon*.)

Echoing Mountains (IV) See *Eredlómin*.

Echoing Mountains (V) See *Eredlómin*.

Echoing Mountains (X) 298. See *Lammoth*.

Echoing Mountains (XI) 176, 196; *Echoing Hills* 17. See *Eryd Lómin*.

Echoriad (XI) The mountains about Gondolin. 271–2, 302; earlier *Echoriath* 302. See *Encircling Mountains, Gochressiel*.

Echuinen (VII) See *Nen Echui*.

Ecthelion (I) 93

Ecthelion (II) (1) Lord of the people of the Fountain in Gondolin; called *Ecthelion of the Fountain, Lord of the Fountain(s)*. 173, 175, 180–4, 191, 200, 211–13, 215–16. (2) Name of two Stewards of Gondor. 212

Ecthelion (VIII) (1) A lord of Gondolin. 292. (2) *Ecthelion I*, Steward of Gondor. 292; *The Tower of Ecthelion* 278, 281. (3) *Ecthelion II*, Steward of Gondor, father of Denethor. 281, 292, 379

Ecthelion (XI) (1) A lord of Gondolin. 18, 318, 328; etymology 319. (2) Name borne by two Stewards of Gondor. 319

Ecthelion I (XII) Seventeenth Ruling Steward. 205, 219–20, 236, 249. *Ecthelion's Tower* 205, 236

Ecthelion II (XII) Twenty-fifth Ruling Steward. 206, 220, 240, 258

Ecthelion of the Fountain (IV) A lord of Gondolin. 101, 144, 194, 307

Ecthelion of the Fountain (V) A lord of Gondolin. 142, 249, 355, 388

Edain (I) 40

Edain (II) 266

114

Edain (IV) 337

Edain (V) 192, 338. See *Atani*.

Edain (VIII) 161. See *Atani*.

Edain (X) 7, 163, 304, 328, 378, 402, 418. See *Atani*.

Edain (XI) 112, 168, 206, 213–15, 219–20, 222–6, 229, 232–3, 236, 241, 253–4, 256–7, 262–4, 266, 268–9, 281, 283, 286, 299, 344, 377, 387, 406, 410; singular *Adan* 286, 387. Ancient tongue of 226, and see *Bëor*, *Haladin* (1), *Marach*; genealogical tables 229–38. See *Atani*, *Three Houses*.

Edain (XII) Men of the Three Houses. 31–2, 62, 64, 74–6, 143–6, 149, 159, 162, 173, 181, 203, 258, 269, 303, 306, 309, 325, 359, 364, 374, 419. See *Atani*.

Edda (II) (Old Norse) 125

Edda (V) (Old Norse) 96

Ëdë (XI) See *Estë*.

Edeb na Nestad (VIII) The Houses of Healing. See *Berin a Nestad*.

Edennil (X) 'Friend of Men', name of Finrod Felagund. 305–6, 349. See *Atandil*.

Edhel (XI), plural *Edhil* The general Sindarin word for 'Elf, Elves'. 364, 377–8. See *Mornedhel*.

Edhellond (XII) Elf-haven north of Dol Amroth. (313), 329

Edhelwen (XI) Name of Morwen. 142, 230–1, 234, 273–4, 291, 296. Earlier form *Eledhwen* 51, 56, 142, 230, translated *Elfsheen* 51, 61, 64, 79

Edhil (V) Eldar. 101, 103

Edmund, Saint (IXb) King of East Anglia. 293; O.E. *Éadmund* 270

Edoras (VII) See *Eodoras*.

Edoras (IXa) 62, 71–4

Edoras, Eodoras (VIII) (references up to 79 are almost all to the earlier form *Eodoras*) 3–6, 9, 12, 17–18, 22–3, 25, 27, 29, 40–1, 47–8, 51, 56, 58–60, 68–70, 73, 78–9, 102–3, 119–20, 140–2, 145–6, 182, 229, 232–3, 236–7, 240, 242, 245, 247, 249–50, 252, 254–7, 259, 262–4, 267, 270, 272–5, 289, 291, 296, 298–9, 301, 303, 308–9, 311, 318–22, 343–4, 346–50, 353–4, 368, 389, 406, 408, 423–4. The Mounds of Edoras 385, 389, 407–8, 423–4

Edrahil (V) Chief of the Elves of Nargothrond faithful to Felagund. 300. (Replaced *Enedrion*.)

Edrahil (XI) Elf of Nargothrond. 66

Edward the Elder (V) King of England. 80, 83

Edward the Elder (IXb) King of England. 287, 293; O.E. *Éadweard* 269, 271–2; *the king* 273, 278, 288

Edwin (V) =*Eädwine*, *Audoin*. 7, 31, 46, 53, 55; 'Bliss-friend' 7

Egalmoth (II) (1) Lord of the people of the Heavenly Arch in Gondolin. 173, 175, 183, 192, 212, 215, 258, 278–9. (2) Steward of Gondor. 211

Egalmoth (XI) (1) A lord of Gondolin. 318, 328; etymology 319. (2) Name borne by a Steward of Gondor. 319

Egalmoth (XII) (1) A lord of Gondolin. 419, 421. (2) Eighteenth Ruling Steward. 205, 219–20, 419. (3) See *Saelon*.

Eges-sirion (V) Mouths of Sirion. 407

Egla (XI) (Originally) Gnomish name =*Elda*. 189

Egladhrim (XI) 'The Forsaken' (the Sindar, but applied especially to the Elves of the Falas). 189, 365, 379; also *Eglain* (singular *Eglan*) 186, 189, 365, 379–81, 400, 418. See *Emyn Eglain*; *Eglath*.

Egladil (VII) In Lothlórien. 281, 288

Eglador (XI) (1) ('Land of the Elves'), Doriath. 16, 113, *183, 186, 189. (2) The land of the *Eglain*, western Beleriand. *182, 186, 343–4, 379 (cf. *Eglamar* (3)).

Eglahir, River (IV) =*Eglor*. 227

Eglahir, River (XI) 117, *182, 187. (Replaced *Eglor*, replaced by *Nenning*.)

Eglain (XI) See *Egladhrim*.

Eglain (XII) The people of Círdan. 392

Eglamar (II) =*Eldamar*. 262, 265, 272

Eglamar (III) =*Eldamar*. 157, 181–2

Eglamar (IV) =*Eldamar*. 70

Eglamar (V) 'Elvenhome'. 186, 356. See *Eldamar*.

Eglamar (XI) (1) 'Elf-home' in Valinor (=*Eldamar*). 189. (2) =*Arthórien* (Doriath beyond Aros). 112–13, 189. (3) The Land of the *Eglain*, the region of the Falas. *184, 189, 365, 370, 379; *Hills of Eglamar (Emyn Eglain)* *184, 189

Eglarest (I) 134

Eglarest (IV) 169, 229, 310, 313, 332–3. See *Eglorest*.

Eglarest (X) The southern Haven of the Falas. 85, 90, 179; earlier form *Eglorest* 90, 175, 179

Eglarest (XI) The southern Haven of the Falas. 8, 15, 18, 39–40, 80, 111, 189–91, 197, 365; *Firth of Eglarest* 380; earlier *Eglorest* 111, 117, *184, 189, 191, 197, 242

Eglath (X) 'The Forsaken People', name given to themselves by the Sindar. 85, 90, 164, 170–1. See *Ekelli*.

Eglath (XI) 'The Forsaken', the Sindar. 8–9, 57, 126, 189, 344; other forms *Eglim*, *Eglir* 344. See *Egladhrim*.

Eglavain (II) Elfinesse (?). 320, 325

Eglor, River (IV) 227, 229, 330, 334. (Replaced *Eldor*; replaced by *Nenning*.) See *Eglahir*.

Eglor, River (V) 128, 139, 267, 356, 407

Eglor, River (VI) In Beleriand. 434

Eglor, River (XI) 117, 187. See *Eglahir*.

Eglorest (IV) The southern Haven of the Falas. 227, 271, 290, 310, 313–14, 324, 326, 329–33, 335. (Replaced *Eldorest* and *Eglarest*, though *Eglarest* was the final form.)

Eglorest (V) The southern Haven of the Falas. 114, 128–9, 140, 146, 152, 175, 180, 186, 192, 222, 225, 261–2, 265, 267, 336, 356. 384. See *Battle of Eglorest*.

Egnor (I) Father of Beren. 240–1

Egnor (II) Father of Beren; called 'the forester', 'the huntsman of the Elves, of the Gnomes', 'Elf of the greenwood'. 11, 15, 22–3, 28, 43–5, 49, 51–2, 61, 65–6, 71–2, 116, 139–40, 242, 248. *Egnor bo-Rimion* (>*go-Rimion*) 'son of Rimion' 22, 51. See *Rog* (1).

Egnor (III) (1) Beren's father (replaced by *Barahir*). 25, 119, 125, 159, 168–71, 198, 220, 247. (2) Son of Finrod (later Aegnor son of Finarfin), slain in the Battle of Sudden Flame. 80, 85, 138, 213, 222

Egnor (IV) (1) Father of Beren in the Lost *Tales*. 54, 316. (2) Son of Finrod (1) =Finarfin. 15, 19, 55, 88, 95, 103, 106, 173–4, 176, 267, 271, 279, 295–6, 298, 310, 314, 318, 327–8; O.E. *Eangrim* 213

Egnor (V) Son of Finrod (1) =Finarfin. 116, 119, 127, 132, 145–6, 150, 223, 226, 234, 237–9, 264, 269, 276, 279, 281, 355, 374

Egnor (X) Son of Finarfin; see *Aegnor*.

Egnor (XI) Son of Finarfin (= Finrod (1)). 38, 52, *183, 195. (Later form *Aegnor*.)

Egyptian (IXb) 207, 289

Eiglir Engrin (III) The Iron Mountains. 33, 41, 49. (Replaced *Aiglir Angrin*.)

Eiglir Engrin (IV) The Iron Mountains. 220. See *Aiglir Angrin*.

Eiglir Engrin (V) The Iron Mountains. 266, 349. (*Oeges engrin*). (Replaced by *Ered-engrin*.)

Eilenach (VIII) The sixth (or fifth, see 344) beacon in Anórien. 233, 343, 349–54, 356; *Forest of Eilenach* 343–4, 354; *Dark Men of Eilenach* 343–6. Earliest form *Elenach* 232

Eilinel (III) Wife of Gorlim the Unhappy; called 'the white'. 162–4, 169- 70, 336–9, 350

Eilinel (V) Wife of Gorlim the Unhappy. 297

Eilinel (XI) Wife of Gorlim the Unhappy. 59

Eirien (IXa) Final form of Aragorn's translation of *Daisy* (Gamgee). 126, 128–9. See *Arien, Erien.*

Eithel Ivrin (II) 123; *Ivrin* 124

Eithel Ivrin (IV) 323. See *Ivrineithil.*

Eithel Nínui (V) The Fountain of Tinúviel in the plain of Gondolin. 301, *363 (eithel).*

Eithel Sirion (IV) 57, 318, 320, 330, 333; *Eithyl Sirion* 311, 320. See *Sirion's Well.*

Eithel Sirion (V) Sirion's Well. 127, 134, 260, 264, 288, *363 (eithel)*, 411; *Eithil Sirion, Eithil* 406–7. See *Sirion.*

Eithel Sirion (XI) Sirion's Well, often with reference to the fortress (see *Barad Eithel*). 17–18, 38, 52–3, 60, 114, 165, 168, 193, 233; *Eithel* *182; *Sirion's Well* *182

Eithil Ivrin (XI) Sources of the Narog. 85, 139, 256, 299; earlier *Ivrineithel* 139. See *Ivrin.*

Ekelli (XI) 'The Forsaken' (the Sindar). 175

Ekelli, Ecelli (X) 'The Forsaken', name given by the Elves of Valinor to the Sindar and Nandor; replaced by *Alamanyar*. 169–70

Ekkaia (X) The Outer Sea. 157. See *Vaiya.*

Eladar (XI) Name of Tuor, 'Starfather' (i.e. father of Eärendil). 234–5

elanor (III) Plant with golden flowers that grew in Beleriand. 333–4, 349

elanor (VII) Golden flower of Lothlórien. 234, 243, 284

elanor (IXa) Golden flower of Lórien. (114–15), 124, 132. For Sam's daughter *Elanor* see under *Gamgee.*

elanor (XII) Golden flower of Lórien. 266

Elbenil (II) Littleheart. 202. (Replaced by *Elwenil*.)

Elbereth (III) Sindarin name of Varda. 336, 350, 361

Elbereth (V) (1) Younger son of Dior. 142, 147, *351–2*, 403. (Replaced by *Eldûn*). (2) (Later signification) Varda. *351, 355*

Elbereth (VI) (1) Son of Dior Thingol's Heir. 68. (2) Varda. 59, 68,

70, 186, 189, 197, 212, 214, 280, 282, 324, 358, 364, 394 *Elberil*
68

Elbereth (VII) Varda. 65, 105; songs to Elbereth 84, 333–4, 336

Elbereth (VIII) (1) Varda. 210, 218. (2) Son of Dior Thingol's Heir.
297. (3) Son of Elrond. 297, 301–2. (Replaced by *Elrohir*.)

Elbereth (IXa) Varda. 112

Elbereth (X) 'Queen of the Stars', Varda. 20, 38, 387–8; etymology
387. See *Elentári*, *Tinwerontar*.

Elbereth (XII) (1) 'Star-queen', Varda. 358, 437. (2) Son of Dior (see
Elurín). 223, 372. (3) Son of Elrond (replaced by *Elrohir*). 224

Elbereth and *Elboron* (IV) Sons of Dior Thingol's Heir. 307, 325–6.
(Replaced by *Eldûn* and *Elrûn*.)

Elberin (VI) See *Ilverin*.

Elboron (V) Elder son of Dior. 142, 147, *351*, *353*, 403. (Replaced by
Elrûn.)

Elboron (VIII) (1) Son of Dior Thingol's Heir. 297. (2) Son of
Elrond. 297, 301–2, 307, 370. (Replaced by *Elladan*.)

Elboron (XII) (1) Son of Dior (see *Elured*). 223, 372. (2) Son of Elrond
(replaced by *Elladan*). 224. (3) Second Prince of Ithilien, son of
Faramir. 221, 223

Elboron and *Elbereth* (XI) Sons of Dior. 300. (Replaced by *Eldún and
Elrún*.)

Eldairon (II) Elvish name of Ælfwine: *Eldairon of Lúthien*, replacing
Lúthien of Luthany. 313

Eldakar (VII) 'Elfhelm' (366), father of Eldamir ('Elfstone'). 276, 360,
362, 366, 404; grandfather of Eldamir 362

Eldakar (XII) (1) Fourth King of Arnor. 192. (2) Twenty-first King of
Gondor. 199, 205, 213–14, 231, 255, 260–2. See *Vinitharya*.

Eldalië (I) 51, 97–8, 115, 117–18, 128, 140, 150, 165, 231, 235

Eldalië (II) 9, 42–3, 115, 130, 136, 165, 167, 180, 199, 215, 219, 224,
241, 265

Eldalië (III) 309

Eldalië (IV) 13, 20–1, 84 (*the people of the Elves*), 86, 89, 99–100,
105, 164, 335

Eldalië (V) The people of the Elves. 22, 171, 183, 214, 276, 304, 332,
356, (*369*)

Eldalië (VI) 71

Eldalië (IXb) 222, 303, 308, 313–14. See *Quenta Eldalien*.

Eldalië (X) The People of the Elves. 16, 36, 94, 162–3, 174, 186, 212,
219, 223, 229, 267, 274. See *Elvenfolk*.

Eldalië (XI) The Elvenfolk. 44, 70, 166, 174, 374–5; Telerin *Ellalië* 375

Eldalië (XII) The people of the Eldar. 400, 404

Eldalótë (XII) Wife of Angrod. 346; Sindarin *Eðellos* 346

Eldamar (I) 'Elfhome'. 19–20, 65, 68, 77, 98, 125–6, 129, 135, 137, 140, 143, 154, 164, 166, 171, 177 (in almost all occurrences the reference is to the *shores, coasts, strand, beach*, or *rocks* of Eldamar); *Bay of Eldamar* 134–5. See *Elfinesse*.

Eldamar (II) 'Elfhome'. 261–2, 272, 287. See *Eglamar*.

Eldamar (III) 'Elfhome'. 182, 331, 348, 356–8. See *Eglamar*.

Eldamar (IV) 257. See *Eglamar*.

Eldamar (V) 'Elvenhome'. 186, 300; name of the city of Tûn (Túna) 173, 185–6, 222, 226, 356. See *Eledûn*.

Eldamar (VII) Elvenhome. 284

Eldamar (VIII) 76. See *Elvenhome*.

Eldamar (IXa) Elvenhome, the region of Aman in which the Elves dwelt. 58

Eldamar (X) 'Elvenhome', land of the Eldar in Aman, and also a name of their city (Tirion). 84, 90, 95–7, 106, 176, 180, 185, 192, 256, 268; *Bay of Eldamar* 85, 97, *coast, shores, strands of Eldamar* 86–7, 90, 115, 193. See *Eldanor, Elendë, Elvenhome, Elvenland*, and for the relations of the names see 90, 176, 180.

Eldamar (XI) 'Elf-home' (=*Eglamar* (1)). 189

Eldamar (XII) 'Elvenhome' in Aman. 78

Eldameldor (XI) 'Elf-friends'. 412; Sindarin *Elvellyn* 412

Eldamir (VII) Elfstone (Aragorn). 276, 280, 293–4, 360, 362, 366. Transient names: *Eldavel* 366, *Eledon* 276, *Quendemir* 276

Eldandil(i) (XI) 'Elf-friend(s)'. 410, 412

Eldanor (V) 'Elfland'. 223, 226. See *Elendë*.

Eldanor (X) 'Elvenland', land of the Eldar in Aman. 90, 176, 180, 190, 277, 282–3; *Bay of Eldanor* 199, *strands of Eldanor* 194. See *Eldamar*.

Eldanyárë (V) 'History of the Elves'. 199–200, 202, 204, (374)

Eldanyárë (X) 'History of the Elves' (title). 141, 143, 200

Eldar (I) (Singular *Elda*). Selected references (including both *Eldar* and *Elves*): reference and meaning of the terms *Eldar, Elves* 50–1, 131, 235; tongues of, 47–8, 50–1, 177, 215, 232, 235–6; origin, nature, and fate 57, 59–61, 66, 76, 80, 90, 97, 142, 157, 213; stature in relation to Men 32, 233, 235; relations with Men 32, 98, 150–1,

159, 175, 235; awakening 113–16; summoning to Valinor 115–17, 132; fading 32, 179

Eldar (II) Selected references: used of all Elves including Dark Elves 9, 64, 82; in reference to Noldoli 95, 149; distinct from Noldoli 153, 165, 178, 215, 218, 289. References to the language of the Eldar (as opposed to Gnomish) 8, 70, 85, 148–9, 169, 192, 199, 215–16 (see *Eldarissa, Elfin*); *Eldar* as adjective referring to the language 148. See *Elves*.

Eldar (III) 138, 334, 347

Eldar (IV) 12–15, 21, 26, 28, 43–5, 48, 51–2, 58, 68, 72, 78, 84–6, 88, 90, 99–100, 104, 108, 118, 168, 171, 276, 289, 337; *the Eldar or Elves* 12, 78, *Eldar whom we call Elves* 84. On the name Eldar see 44, 84, 168, 276; and see *Elves*.

Eldar (V) 12, 14–15, 18, 20, 22, 24–5, 29, 63, 70, 73, 79, 112, 119, 122, 163, 165–6, 169–75, 180–3, 187–8, 191, 197–8, 201, 209, 212, 214–19, 221, 227–9, 235, 237, 240, 242, 245, 247, 266, 273–4, 276, 344, *356*, 405; *Eldain* 63, 72. On the meaning of the name see 122, 169–71, 181–3, 218–19, 344

Eldar (VII) 292

Eldar (VIII) 161

Eldar (IXb) 222, 290, 303, 308, 314–15, 332–3, 354–5, 376, 379–80, 385–6, 393–5, 397, 400–2, 404–6, 409, 411; O.E. *Eldan* 313–15. *Eldaic* 409

Eldar (X) (and singular *Elda*) 12, 15, 17, 21, 30, 36–7, 42–3, 51, 57, 69, 72–4, 77–8, 80–8, 91–6, 98–101, 103, 105–6, 109, 111–13, 119, 121, 127, 131, 133, 154–5, 157, 160, 162–3, 167–70, 173–5, 177, 182–8, 198–200, 204–40 *passim*, 243, 245, 247, 250–1, 254–78 *passim*, 281, 284, 286–8, 294, 299–300, 304–6, 311, 314–28 *passim*, 336–8, 340, 342, 349, 351–3, 355, 358, 370, 373–5, 378, 387, 389, 399, 401–2, 406, 408–9, 416–17, 423, 426–9, 431

Eldar (X) *People of the Stars* (name given by Oromë) 72, 80, (81), 160, (162), 167, 372, *Star-folk* 375; *High Eldar* 318, 370

Eldar (XI) (and singular *Elda*) 6–7, 10, 12–13, 15, 17, 20–1, 23–5, 28, 30–1, 36–8, 41, 49–50, 52–3, 58–60, 69–71, 74–5, 77, 105, 118, 121, 127–8, 132, 165–6, 173–4, 186, 189, 204–7, 212, 217–26, 233, 283, 312–13, 315, 326, 328–30, 333, 343, 362–3, 365, 368–9, 372–8, 380–2, 384, 386, 388–91, 393–5, 398, 400, 402–10, 412, 418, 420–1; for the forms *Eldo*, plural *Eldor*, see 363,

374–5. Telerin *Ello (Ella)*, plural *Elloi*, 362, 364, 373, 375–6. See *Star-folk*.

Eldar (XII) (and singular *Elda*) 29–33, 36, 55, 61, 64–5, 77–8, 82, 120, 122–3, 125–6, 129, 143, 145–9, 152, 157–8, 174, 176, 178–80, 191, 193, 202–3, 227–9, 243–4, 249, 256, 296–7, 303–8, 310–11, 321, 324–6, 329, 331–5, 337, 339–42, 347–8, 357–8, 360–4, 366, 368–72, 379–82, 384, 390, 395, 397–401, 403–4, 419, 435–7; *High Eldar* 305, 342, 363; *the Fair* 435. *Laws and Customs among the Eldar* (title of work) 356–7, 359

Eldarin (V) (of language) 75, 171, 176, 181, 183, 185, 187–9, 192–5, 197, 243, 347; (peoples) 188–9, 195, 200; as a name of Quenya 185

Eldarin (IXb) (tongue) 381; *High Eldarin* 379

Eldarin (X) 103, 136, 198, 217, 363, 371, 387–8

Eldarin (XI) (of language) 361, 389, 392, 400, 404–5, 407. 410–12, 414–15, 417, 421; *Common Eldarin* (abbreviated CE) 359–61, 368, 371, 379, 387, 390, 403, 414, 416; (with other reference) 328, 377, 380, 383, 410

Eldarin (XII) (of language; also *Primitive, Common Eldarin*) 30, 145, 152, 157, 318–19, 340–2, 346–7, 352, 357–63, 366, 368, 371–2, 374, 392, 401, 436; verb *'Eldarize'* 352; (with other reference) 124, 127, 131, 137–8, 153, 357

Eldarion (XII) Son of Aragorn and Arwen. 202, 217–18, 244–6, 410, 419–20

Eldarissa (II) The language of the Eldar, as distinct from *Noldorissa*. 148–9, 280

Eldarissa (III) The language of the Eldar (in the period of the *Lost Tales*). 89

Eldaros (II) =Ælfhâm, Elfhome. 301. *Eldos* 302

Eldaros (IV) 'Elvenhome'. *249, 257

Eldaros (X) Elvenhome (land of the Elves). 90

Elder Children (XI) See *Children of Eru*.

Elder Days (II) 324

Elder Days (III) 90, 210, 346, 349

Elder Days (IV) 75–6, 262, 294, 319, 327

Elder Days (V) 32–3, 151, 259, 404, 407; *eldest days* 245; *Elder Years* 90–1

Elder Days (VI) 187, 329, 349. See *Ancient Days, Earliest Days*.

Elder Days (VII) 101, 112, 119, 135, 141, 144–5, 150, 152, 169, 247, 262, 271, 403, 416, 429

Elder Days (VIII) 161

Elder Days (IXa) 68

Elder Days (IXb) 152, 333, 337, 348, 368. *Elder World* 240; *Elder Years* 276

Elder Days (X) 3, 30, 47, 58, 64–5, 78, 122, 160, 203, 217, 303, 327, 369–70, 373, 412, 418–20, 427; *Elder World* 154, 340

Elder Days (XI) 3–5, 23, 27, 51, 105, 110, 116–17, 142, 180, 243, 245, 297, 325, 337, 342–7, 353, 390, 396; see especially 342–3

Elder Days (XII) 8, 15, 23, 143, 147, 156, 173, 184–5, 202, 233, 243, 263, 268–70, 275, 305, 338, 349, 375; on different meanings see 173, 184–5, 263, 268–9

Elder Edda (VI) 246

Elder Edda (VII) 204; *Eddaic* 452; *Völuspa* 452

Elder Kindred (I) 42

Elder King (X) Manwë. 313, 379, 399–400, 402, 404

Elder King (XI) Manwë. 246

Elder People (VIII) Elves. 159, 169

Elder Race (VI) The Elves. 364

Elder Tongue (VII) Quenya. 84; *old tongue* 83

Elder Tree (X) Telperion. 59, 90, 155

Eldest (VII) See *Tom Bombadil*.

Eldest Dark(ness) (X) See *Dark*.

Eldest Tree, Elder Tree (XII) 123, 130, 147–8. See *Galathilion, Silpion, Telperion; Two Trees*.

Eldil(s) (IXb) [Lewis] 168, 202, 212–13, 222; *Eldila* 212, 221; *Eldilic* 221

Eldor, River (IV) 227, 229, 334. (Replaced by *Eglor, Eglahir; Nenning*.)

Eldorest (IV) The southern-Haven of the Falas. 227, 278, 296, 305, 309–10, 313, 324, 326. (Replaced by *Eglarest, Eglorest*.) See *Battle of Eldorest*.

Eldûn (V) Son of Dior. 147, (376). (Replaced *Elbereth*.)

Eldûn (VIII) Son of Dior Thingol's Heir. 297

Eldûn (XII) Son of Dior. 372. See *Elboron, Eluréd*.

Eldûn and *Elrûn* (IV) Sons of Dior. 156, 191, 325–6. (Replaced *Elbereth* and *Elboron*; replaced by *Eluréd* and *Elurín*.)

Eldún and Elrún (XI) Sons of Dior. 231–2, 257, 300, 348–51

Eledâi (IXb) Eldar. 358, 377, 397–9, 401–5, 410, 412

Eledhwen (III) Name of Morwen. 92

Eledhwen (XI) Name of Morwen. See *Edhelwen*.

Eledûn (V) A name of Tûn (Túna). 222

Eledwen (IV) Name of Morwen. 311, 319. See *Elfsheen*.

Eledwen (V) (and later *Eledhwen*). Name of Morwen. 131, 133, 140, 147, 276, 282, *356*, *398*; 'Elfsheen' 131, 135, 276, 318

Elemmírë (X) (1) Vanyarin Elf, maker of the *Aldudénië*. 106, 166, 288, 292; *Elemírë* (X) 100, 106, 292. (2) Name of a bright star (the planet Mercury?). 160. See pp. 434–5.

Elen (XI), plurals *Elin*, *Eledhrim* (Sindarin) Elf, Elves. 363, 377–8

Elenach (VIII) See *Eilenach*.

Elenarda (IV) 'Stellar Kingdom', name of Ilmen. 240–1, *2423, 253

Elenarda (VIII) (1) 'Stellar Kingdom', the region of Ilmen. 167. (2) Applied to Rohan, preceding *Kalenarda* (see *Calenard(h)on*). 155, 167

Elendë (V) 'Elfland'. 223–4, 226, *356*

Elendë (X) Land of the Eldar in Aman. 90, 114, 125, 176, 178, 180; *Bay of Elendë* 190. See *Eldamar*, *Eldanor*.

Elendë (XI) Land of the Eldar in Aman. 177

Elendil (V) 7, 9, 23, 29–31, 33–4, 48, 50, 57–73, 75–8, 153, 337, *378*

Elendil (VI) 105, 169, 174–5, 192, 197–9, 215–16, 218, 271, 320, 355, 358; 'Elf-friend' 215–16, 358. See *Orendil*, *Valandil*.

Elendil (VII) 8, 10, 50, 77, 105, 110, 119–24, 126–7, 129, 137, 141, 144–7, 152, 157, 278, 333, 361, 393, 437, 444, 450. Horn of Elendil (*Windbeam*) 344, 349; Sword of Elendil 121–2, 129, 165, 194, 201, 205, 290; see *Branding*, *Sword that was Broken*.

Elendil (VIII) 14, 19, 21, 149, 275, 359, 424; *sons of* 149, 397, 424, *heir(s)*, *house*, *race of* 80, 155, 158, 247, 249, 281, 388, 391; *sword of Elendil* 253–4, 301–2, 392, 419 (see *Narsil*); *Star of Elendil* 370, *395*, *seven stars of* 411, badges, tokens of 279, 281, 385, 389, 395, 399; the name 159–60

Elendil (IXa) 56, 58–9; *the Horn of Elendil (Windbeam)* 4

Elendil (IXb) 278–9, 284, 335, 346, 348–9, (350), 352, 356, 382, 384, 387, 401; with second name *Eärendil* 346, 348; his sons 335, 352–3, 387, 401. Lowdham so addressed by Jeremy 290. *Elendil = Elf-friend* 403; modernized *Ellendel* 284. See *Ælfwine*, *Nimruzân*, *Nimruzîr*.

Elendil (XI) Meaning of the name, 410

Elendil (XII) (1) *the Tall* 32–4, 39, 74, 156–7, 163–4, 166, 169–71, 175–7, 183, 188–9, 191–3, 196–7, 201–3, 207, 212, 217–18,

253, 257, 267; his sword 186, 195, 227, 239, 263, 266. See *Nimruzír; Narsil*.

Elendil (XII) (2) Ælfwine. 401, 403

Elendili (IXb) 'Elf-friends'. 400; *Elendilli* 403

Elendili (XII) Elf-friends of Númenor. 151, 155, 160, 185; *Elendilli* 151. See *Elf-friends, (The) Faithful, Nimruzîrim*.

Elendilions (VIII) Descendants of Elendil. 76

Elendur (XII) (1) Eldest son of Isildur. 208. (Replaced *Kiryandil* (1).) (2) Ninth King of Arnor. 193

Elenna (XII) 'Starwards', Númenor. 145

Elentári (V) 'Queen of Stars', Varda. 200, 212, 216, 344, *355*. (Replaced *Tinwerontar*.) See *Tar-Elkon*.

Elentári (VII) 'Queen of Stars', Varda. 285

Elentári (X) 'Queen of the Stars', Varda. 160, 166, 384, 388–9; *Elentárië* 71, 166. See *Tintallë*.

Elentir (XII) Brother of Amandil, lover of Zimrahil. 159–63, 165

Elenwë (II) Wife of Turgon. 209

Elenwë (XI) Wife of Turgon. 323. See *Alairë, Anairë*.

Elenwë (XII) Wife of Turgon. 345–6, 361–3

Elerína (V) 'Crowned with Stars', Taniquetil. 200, 209–10, 216, *355*. (Replaced *Tinwerína*.)

Elerrína (IV) 'Crowned with Stars', name of Taniquetil. 167. See *Tinwenairin*.

Elerrína (X) 'Crowned with stars', Taniquetil. 154; *Elerína* 154, 389. See *Tinwerína*.

Elessar (The) (VII) Elfstone. 278, 294, 362, 366, 392

Elessar (The) (IXa) Elfstone, Aragorn. 52, 58, 117, 119, 128. See *Aragorn*.

Elessar (VIII) (1) Last king of the line of Anárion. 153. See *Earnur*. (2) Aragorn. 309, 370, 390, 395, 411, 427. See *Elfstone*.

Elessar (XI) The Elfstone. 177; the Green Stone of Fëanor 176–7

Elessar (XII) (1) Rejected name of King Eärnur of Gondor. 247

Elessar (XII) (2) Aragorn II. 32, 132, 196, 202–3, 207, 211, 217, 243–4, 246, 253, 255, 258, 261, 268, 410, 419; *the Elfstone* 243; *the Great King* 414; *Annals, Chronicles of the House of Elessar* 243, 245

Elf (VII) *Elf-door*, see *Moria; Elf-friend* 123 (Elendil), 227, 277 (Aragorn), 227 (Gimli); *Elf-havens*, see *Grey Havens; Elf-king* 122 (Gil-galad); *Elf-letters* 192; *Elf-lords* (of Rivendell) 165; *Elf-rings*,

see *Three Rings*; *Elf speech* 166; *Elf towers*, see *White Towers*; other compounds 257, 272, 343, 392

Elf-, Elven- (VI) *Elf-armour* (Bilbo's) 371–2, 386 (see *Mailcoat*); *Elven-fair* 181; *Elf-folk* 71; *Elf-horse* 207; *Elven-kin* 184, 187; *Elf-king(s)* 179, 215, 227, 260, 320, 358, *Elven-king(s)* 182, 258, 269; *Elf-kingdoms* 358; *Elf-letters* 449; *Elf-lord(s)* 364, 397, 400; *Elf-mail* (Bilbo's) 443–4 (see *Mailcoat*); *Elven-maid* 184; *Elf-name* 208; *Elf-race* 182; *Elf-rings* 404 (see *Rings of the Elves*); *Elf-spell* 444; *Elf-stone* 192; *Elf-way* 448; *Elvenwise* 181, (with reference to the Gnomes) 212, 217, 364

Elf-fathers (XI) 380, 420–1

Elf-friend (II) 141 (of Úrin), 313 (of Déor Ælfwine's father).

Elf-friend (V) (=*Ælfwine, Alboin, Elendil*) 7, 29, 31, 33, 37, 48, 76–7, 103. *Elf-friends* 18–19, 28, 38, 194, 274, 281, 328, 336

Elf-friends (I) 240

Elf-friends (III) 198

Elf-friends (IV) 127 (in text of *Quenta*), 175, 200, 202, 317; cf. 297

Elf-friend(s) (VI) 60, 65, 215–16, 358. See *Elendil*.

Elf-friend(s) (VIII) 157–9, 161, 168

Elf-friend(s) (IXb) 244–5, 280 288, 339, 403, 411; *Elven-friends* 244; O.E. *Ælfwinas (Ælfwines)* (IXb) 244, 257–8, 272, 288, 313–14, 403

Elf-friends (IXa) 92; *Elf-maid* 134, *Elf-prince* 92

Elf-friends (X) 370, 373; *Elf-lords* 81; *Elf-child (ren)* 209–10, 212, 220, 228, 232, 426; *Elf-strain* 402

Elf-friends (XI) 37, 39, 48, 60, 70, 80, 118, 206, 219–21, 386, (412); as translation of *Elendil* 410. See *Eldameldor, Eldandil(i), Quendil*.

Elf-friends (XII) (of Númenor) 151–2, 155, 161, 163, 174–5, 191, 203, 234, 422, 436. See *Elendili*.

Elfhelm (VII) Father of Elfstone (Aragorn). 80, 105, 146, 165, 275–7, 360–2, 366. See *Eldakar*.

Elfhelm (VIII) Rider of Rohan. 352–3, 356–8, 371, 373; called *the Marshal* 350, 352

Elfhelm the Marshal (IXa) Rider of Rohan. 59

Elfhild of Eastfold (XII) Wife of Théoden. 274

Elfin (I) Of the language of the Eldar 48, 50–1; as adjective to *Elves* 20, 123, 165, 174, 192, 211, 213, 215, *unelfin* 99, 116

Elfin (II) References only to use as name of the language of the 'Eldar' (as distinct from Gnomish). 42, 49, 149, 202, 267; probably used in general sense 304. See *Eldar, Eldarissa*.

Elfin (III) As name of the language of the Eldar (opposed to Gnomish). 139. (Other uses of *elfin*, replaced by *elven* and *elvish*, are not given.)

Elfin (IV) As name of language (opposed to Gnomish) 12. In other applications elfln is used throughout S and Q (>*elven* 148, 155, and see *Dark-elves*, *Half-elfin*); also *elvish* in Q, 133, 136, 145

Elfinesse (I) Translation of Eldamar (see Appendix, p. 251). 22, 211, 240

Elfinesse (II) 21, 38, 43, 47, 59, 130, 240, 313, 321, 323, 325; *children of Elfinesse* 159, 326, *daughter of Elfinesse* 164, 215

Elfinesse (III) 6, 108, 155, 174,176, 180, 182, 190–3, 216, 228–9, 231, 241, 243, 255, 262, 264, 267, 286, 326, 360; later form *Elvenesse* 354, 360

Elfinesse (IV) 36, 143, 147–8, 152, 159, 162

Elfinesse (X) 271

Elf-kin (IXb) 403. *Elven-kind* 261, 296. *Elven folk* 280

Elf-kind (XI) 203, 210; -*kings* 223; -*lord(s)* 50, 234–5; -*maid* 67 (Lúthien); -*man*, -*men* 363, 421–3; -*riders* 150; -*woman* 87 (Finduilas), 363, 421

Elfland (III) 34, 134, 138, 183, 208, 234. See *Elvenland*.

Elfland (IV) 94. See *Bay of Elfland*, *Elvenhome*.

Elfland (V) 223–4, 233. See *Bay of Elfland*, *Elvenhome*.

Elf-latin (V) 41, 43, 56, 75, 172, 174, 180, 184–5, 193–4; *Elven-latin* 185

Elf-latin (VI) 60, 69, 280

Elf-Latin (XI) Quenya. 22–3

Elf-march (II) The expedition of the Elves of Kôr for the rescue of the Gnomes in the Great Lands. 144, 221, 252; *March of the Elves* 253, 257–8, 278–80, 303–4, 307–8, *March of the Inwir and Teleri* 255, 278, *March of Liberation* 279. See *Faring Forth*.

Elfriniel (II) Littleheart. 148, 201, 214–16. (Replaced by *Elfrith*.) *Elfriniol* 50, 201. (Replaced by *Ilfiniol*.) See *Ilfiniol*, *Ilfrin*.

Elfrith (II) Littleheart. 148, 201–2, 216. (Replaced *Elfriniel*.) See *Ilfrith*.

Elfsheen (IV) Name of Morwen. 105, 176, 298, 311, 319. See *Eledwen*.

Elfsheen (V) See *Eledwen*.

Elfstone (VII) (1) The elfstone on the Last Bridge. 59. (2) The Elfstone of Galadriel. 274–8, 290, 431; *Elfstone, Elfstone, bearer of my green stone* 431, 448. (3) Name of Aragorn (see 277–8). 80, 105, 146–8, 165, 176, 204, 236, 239, 244, 250–1, 260, 262, 264–5,

272–3, 275–81, 290–3, 360–2, 366, 370, 378, 381, 392–3, 431, 448; *Elfstan* 276. Transient names: *Erkenbrand* 80; *Elf-friend, Elfmere, Elfspear* 277; *Elfwold* 366. See *Eldamir, Elessar*. (4) As name of Gimli. 275–7

Elfstone (VIII) Aragorn. 390, 395. See *Elessar*.

Elfstone (XII) See *Elessar* (2).

Elfstone, (The) (IXa) Aragorn. 64, 66–7, 117, 119, 128; the green stone 56; Sindarin *Edhelharn* 128–9. See *Elessar*.

Elf-tongue (VI) 58–60, 62, 67, 194, 196, 280, 449; *Elven-tongue* 324; *Ancient Tongue* 280–1, 325; *two Elf-languages* 253; called '*secret*' 58, 67, 253, 280. See *Elvish*.

Elf-towers (VI) 93, 105, 269, 310, 312–13. See *Towers, West Towers*.

Elf-wraiths (VI) 75, 78, 87, 225, 269

Elfwine the Fair (XII) Nineteenth King of Rohan, son of Éomer. 221

Elias Tobiasson (VIII) First grower of pipeweed in the Shire. 36. See *Hornblower, Smygrave*.

Elivorn (V) 'Lake-Black', earlier form for *Helevorn*. 269, 405

Elizabeth I, Queen (XI) 312; *Elizabeth II* 312

Elladan (VIII) Son of Elrond. 307, 370, 389, 403, 406, 409, 411, 425. (Replaced *Elboron* (2)).

Elladan (IXa) Son of Elrond. 57, 66, 127

Elladan and Elrohir (XII) Sons of Elrond. 196, 224, 226, 234–6, 238–9, (243), 249, 264, 273. See *Elboron, Elbereth*.

Ello, Elloi (XI) See *Eldar*.

Ellon (II) A (Gnomish) name of Tinwelint. 69, 116. See *Tinto'ellon, Tinthellon*.

Ellon, Elleth (XI) (Sindarin) 'Elf' (m. and f.), plural *El(d)rim*. 363–4, 377

Ellonel (IXa) Transient name preceding Arwen. 66. See *Finduilas* (1).

Ellor (IXb) [Ramer] 198–200, 207, 209, 218, 221–2; *Ellor Eshûrizel* 198, 207, 218; *Eshûrizel* 198, 200

Ellu (I) Lord of the Solosimpi, chosen in place of Tinwë Linto (later Olwë; distinct from Elu Thingol). 120, 130, 132–3, 155; *Ellu Melemno* 141, 155, *Melemno* 155

Ellu (II) (1) Name of Tinwelint in Eldarissa. 49–50, 69. (2) Lord of the Solosimpi in Tinwelint's place (later Olwë). 50

Ellu (IV) See *Tinwelint*.

Elmar (XII) Mother of Hazad Longbeard. 425–6, 437

Elmavoitë (II) 'One-handed', name of Beren 'in the language of the Lonely Isle.' 34. See *Ermabwed*.

Elmir (I) One of the two first Men (with Ermon). 236–7

Elmir (II) One of the two first Men (with Ermon). 305

Elmo (XI) Younger brother of Elwë (Thingol). 350

Elmoth (XI) See *Nan Elmoth*.

Elostirion (VII) (1) See *Osgiliath*. (2) White Tower on Emyn Ber-aid. 423

Elostirion (VIII) Osgiliath. 81, 122, 128, 132–3, 138, 229

Elphir (XII) Twenty-third Prince of Dol Amroth. 221, 223

Elrohir (VIII) Son of Elrond. 297, 302, 307, 370, 403, 406, 411, 424–5. (Replaced *Elbereth* (3)).

Elrohir (IXa) Son of Elrond. 57, 66, 127

Elrohir (XII) See *Elladan and Elrohir*.

Elrond (IV) 38–9, 70, 74, 101, 150–1, 153, 155, 158, 162, 195–6, 200–1, 308–9, 326. See *Half-elfin*.

Elrond (V) Called 'Half-elfin', 'Half-elven'. 18–19, 23, 25, 30, 34, (64, 74), 143–4, 148, 152, 219, 247, 332, 336–7, *355, 360, 384*; *Elrond Beringol* 148; King of Númenor 25, 30

Elrond (VI) (many references are to Elrond's house in Rivendell) 41–2, 126, 179, 193–4, 204–10, 212–19, 225, 274, 358, 362, 365, 374, 379–82, 391, 395–409, 411–14, 416–17, 419, 421, 424, 430, 432, 436, 444, 448; *Kinsmen of Elrond* 395, 398. See *Council of Elrond*.

Elrond (VII) 6, 10, 13–15, 49, 61, 63, 82–3, 95, 110–23 *passim*, 126–30, 135–6, 138, 142–3, 145–7, 149, 152–65 *passim*, 169, 173, 224, 227, 234, 236, 241, 252–5, 257, 265, 278, 286, 326, 361, 375, 390, 402, 423, 438, 445, 451. *Sons of Elrond* 163–4. See *Council of Elrond, Half-elven*.

Elrond (VIII) 145, 156, 158, 165, 168, 207, 219, 223, 274, 301–2, (305), 307, 370, 387, 394, 401, 415, 426. See *Council of, Sons of, Elrond*.

Elrond (IXa) 25, 33, 52–3, 58–9, 63–4, 66–7, 69, 109, 111, 115, 119, 124–5, 132; *Council of Elrond* 71. *Sons of Elrond* 57, (63); see *Elladan, Elrohir*.

Elrond (IXb) 333, 339–40, 378, 403, 408

Elrond (X) 135

Elrond (XI) 71, 132, 234, 242, 348–9; meaning of the name 414

Elrond (XII) 79, 146, 163, 168, 174, 179, 192, 195–6, 202, 207, 211, 224–6, 228–9, 232, 234–5, 238–44, 247, 249, 253, 256–7, 262–7, 269, 273, 319, 347–9, 364–5, 367, 369–71, (376), 378, 382,

384–5, 388, 390; the name 371; doom of the children of Elrond 234–5, 256–7, 265

Elros (IV) 70, 155, 196, 201, 326; Elros Tar-Minyatur 70. See Half-elfin.

Elros (V) Twin brother of Elrond and with him named Peringiul 'Half-elven' (152). 23, 30, 34, 74, 152, 219, 248, 332, 337

Elros (VI) 216, 412

Elros (VIII) 158, 168

Elros (IXb) 333, 340, 345, 378, 380–2, 403, 408. See Indilzar, Gimilzôr.

Elros (XI) 234, 348–9; meaning of the name 414. The Line of Elros 349

Elros (XII) 144–6, 150–1, 153–4, 160, 164, 166, 168–71, 173, 178, 202, 256–7, 348–9, 364, 367–71, (376); Elerossë 349, 367, Elroth 369. The Line of Elros (title of work) 151, 155, 163, 165, 184. See Tar-Minyatur.

Elrûn (IV) See Eldûn.

Elrûn (V) Son of Dior. 147, 384. (Replaced Elboron.)

Elrûn (VIII) Son of Dior Thingol's Heir. 297

Elrún (XI) See Eldún and Elrún.

Elrún (XII) Son of Dior. 372. See Elbereth, Elurín.

Eltas (I) Teller of the Tale of Turambar. 229

Eltas (II) Teller of the Tale of Turambar. 69–70, 112, 116, 118–19, 135–7, 144–5, 242–3; see especially 119.

Elu (IV) Gnomish form of Elwë. 13, 44, 85–6, 168

Elu (Thingol) (III) Sindarin form of Elwe (Singollo). 347

Elu Thingol (I) 132. See Thingol.

Elu Thingol (II) 50

Elu Thingol (X) See Elwë (2), Thingol.

Elu Thingol (XI) See Elwë.

Elu Thingol (XII) See Elwë, Thingol.

Eluchil (XI) 'Thingol's Heir', name of Dior. 350

Eluchil (XII) 'Thingol's Heir', name of Dior. 369, 372

Elulin (XI) Wife of Dior. 350. See Lindis, Nimloth.

Elulindo (V) Son of Elwë of Alqualondë. 403

Eluréd (XII) 'Heir of Elu (Thingol)', son of Dior. 369, 372. Earlier names Elboron, Eldûn.

Eluréd and Elurín (IV) Sons of Dior. 191. (Replaced Eldûn and Elrûn.)

Elurín (XII) 'Remembrance of Elu (Thingol)', son of Dior. 369, 372. Earlier names Elbereth, Elrûn.

Eluwaith (XI) Subjects of King Thingol. 378

Elvellyn (XI) See *Eldameldor*.

Elven- (VII) *Elven-door*, see *Moria*; *Elven-lord* 223–4 (*Amroth*); *Elven-kings* 92, 97, 101, 112, 156, 254, *the Elven-king* (in Mirkwood) 118; *Elven-smiths* 259–60; *Elven-speech*, *Elven-tongue* 84, 224, 226–7, 239; *Elven-wise* (Noldor) 167. Other compounds 92, 97, 101, 104, 223, 225, 278, 281, 285, 382, 391, 393, 397–8 *Elven-home* 92, 97–8, 100. See *Eldamar*.

Elven- (VIII) *Elven-boat* 148, 163; *-blade* 194, 207, 209; *-cloak(s)* 92, 398; *-lords* 301; *rope* 175; *-speech*, *-tongue* 161–2; *-sword* 207. See *half-elven*, *High-elven*.

Elven- (IXa) *Elven-cloak* 14, 29, 48, 50 (and see *Lórien*); *-grace* 122; *-light* 125; *-lord* 49; *-maid* 132

Elven- (X) *lore* 374; *men, women* 199; *race* 133, 169; *tongue* 167

Elven (XI) 200 (Tirion); *-child* 242 (Gilgalad); *-craft* 200; *-fair* 291 (Morwen); *-folk* 374; *-host* 17; *-king(s)* 52, 55, 66, 131, 283; *-kirtle* 151; *-light* 273; *-lords* 39, 224; *-sight* 166; *-speech* 21; *-tongue(s)* 10, 49, 217, 219, 224

Elven folk (X) 81, 84, 163, 169, 186, 274–5; *Elf-folk* 228. See *Eldalië*.

Elven tongue (IXb) 379

Elven-, Elf- (XII) *-blood* 206, 226, 247; *-folk* 29, 206; *-kind* 257; *-king* 176; *kingdom(s)* 36, 211; *-lady* 221; *-lords* 379; *-lore* 32; *-name* 222; *-peoples* 78; *-race* 234; *-realm(s)* 196, 330; *-rings* 13; *-speech* 29; *-tongue(s)* 36, 41, 146, 164, 174; *-towers* 17; *-wise* 240; *-women* 404

Elvenesse (III) See *Elfinesse*.

Elvenfolk (I) 110

Elvenfolk (II) 286, 297. *Elvenland* 272

Elvenhome (I) 38, 42, 109–10

Elvenhome (IV) 235–6, *249, 253, 257. See *Bay of Elvenhome*, *Eldaros*, *Elfland*.

Elvenhome (V) 103, 222, 224, 231, 236. See *Bay of Elvenhome*; *Eldamar*, *Eldanor*, *Elendë*; *Elfland*.

Elvenhome (VI) 180

Elvenhome (VIII) 157–60, 164, 169–70; *Bay of Elvenhome* 169. See *Eldamar*.

Elvenhome (IXb) 280

Elvenhome (X) Land of the Eldar in Aman, and also a name of their city. 90, 125, 176, 180; *Bay of Elvenhome* 176, 178, 180, 199, *shores, strands of Elvenhome* 178, 180, 193–4. See *Eldamar*.

Elvenhome (XII) 20, 22, 63. See *Eldamar*.

Elvenland (III) 231, 233, 333, 346, 360, 362. See *Elfland*.

Elvenland (X) Land of the Eldar in Aman. 176, 180; *shores of Elvenland* 178, 180; *Elfland* 125. See *Eldamar*, *Eldanor*.

Elven-lands (IV) 155 (replacing *Fairyland*).

Elven-Latin (IXb) Quenya. 241, 286, 303, 306; *Elf-Latin* 286, 308

Elven-latin, *Elf-latin* (XII) Quenya. 30, 41, 62

Elves (I) See *Eldar*; also *Dark*, *Deep*, *Grey*, *High*, *Island*, *Light*, *Lost*, *Sea*, *Shoreland*, *Elves*

Elves (II) Selected references (see also *Eldar*, *Fairies*). Used to include Gnomes 22, 26, 35, 38, etc.; distinct from Gnomes 8, 45, 48–9, 216–17. Fate of the Elves 60, 250; stature of Elves and Men 73, 80, 142, 159, 198, 220, 281, 283, 326–7; references to 'fading' 240, 242, 250, 281, 283, 285–9, 293–4, 301, 304, 306, 312–14, 323, 326–7; union with mortals, see *Men*; feud with the Dwarves 230; tongues of 4, 148, 163; written characters 163; and Old English 301–2, 304, 309.

Elves (II) *Wild Elves* 77, 95, 113, 128, 243. See *Brown*, *Dark*, *Green*, *Grey-*, *Island-*, *Lost*, *Elves*; for *Hidden*, *Secret*, *Wood(land) Elves* see *Woodland Elves*.

Elves (III) Selected references. Distinguished from Gnomes 11, 22; estimation of Men 7, 24; stature, and diminishment in relation to Men 44, 54; ruin of the Elves to be brought about by Men 98, 103–4; fate after death 20, 28, 47, 56, 58, 65, 94, 250, 258–60, 274, 308, 357–8; crossing of the Ocean to Valinor in ships 172, 182–3. See *Dark Elves*, *Woodland Elves*.

Elves (IV) Selected references (see also *Eldar*). Elves 'proper' (the First Kindred) 13, 44, 85,distinct from Gnomes 80, 168; Elves who did not leave Cuiviénen 44–5, 168, 276; the Elvish 'ambassadors' 44, 168, 276; relations with Men, see entry *Men*; union with Men 36, 38, 143, 148, 158, 162; stature of Elves and Men 21, 51, 100, 297; return into the West 39–40, 72, 101, 159, 162, 199–200, 202, 309; and England 39, 72; fading 21, 33, 39–41, 52, 63–4, 72, 99–100, 134, 159, 162–5, 171–2, 190–1, 199–200, 267, 278–9; immortality and fate 21–2, 51, 63–4, 100, 267, 278–9; rebirth 21–2, 51, 100; ultimate destiny 41, 73, 165, 205; Elvish tongue in Valinor 78; O.E. *Elfe* (*Ælfe*, *Ielfe*) 206, etc., *Wine* 212. See *Children of Ilúvatar*, *Children of the Stars*, *Firstborn*, *Half-elfin*.

Elves (V) (and *Elf-folk*, *Elvenfolk*) 11–12, 14–18, 21–30, 44, 53, 56, 72, 103–4, 111–15, 118–19, 122, 126, 129, 131, 134, 136–8,

141–4, 153, 160–5, 168–346 *passim*, 404–6. References to 'fading' and 'waning' of the Elves (Eldar) and to their immortality, rebirth, and fate: 12, 16–18, 22–3, 29, 65, 116, 118, 163–4, 166, 178–9, 206, 239, 245–8, 332–3. In old sense =the First Kindred of the Elves 211, 218. Old English *elfe*, *ylfe* 44, 103, 203

Elves (VI) Visitors to Hobbiton from Rivendell 20, 30–1, 48, 60, 63, 66, 68, 101, 106, 149, 156, 160, 235, 315, 336; to Bingo/Frodo at Bag End 36, 234, 253; in the Shire 58, 253, 280; Elves of Rivendell 60, 71, 126, 207, 209, 212, 217, 225, 364, 393–5, 416; of Gildor's company 48, 58–62, 66–71, 73, 88, 91, 101, 103, 106, 109, 160, 194, 280–1, 295, 304, 324–5; of Hollin 418, 429, 437, 444, 448–9, 463; few in South and East of the world 260; wars of the Elves and Goblins 350; in relation to hobbits 79, 93, 294, 311–13; fading (on account of the Rings) 261, 320; other references 41, 61, 64, 70, 75, 78, 87, 117, 121–2, 178, 182–4, 187–8, 190, 198, 212, 215–16, 227, 253–4, 260, 311, 364, 379–80, 394–5, 397, 402–6, 412–13, 417, 419, 451, 458, 466. See *High Elves*, *Wood-elves*; *Rings of the Elves*, *Elf-wraiths*.

Elves (VII) Of Gildor's company 10–11, 13, 33, 61, 75, 116, 215, 333, 365; of Hollin 124, 156, 167, 178, 455; of Lindon 123–4; of Lórien (general references, and see *Wood-elves*) 167, 207, 211- 13, 222, 225, 237–9, 251, 264, 275, 288, 329, 379; of Mirkwood (and see *Wood-elves*) 148, 163, 237, 242; of Rivendell 14, 82, 84, 124, 128, 147

Elves (VII) Other references: 24, 64, 114, 121, 123, 125, 127, 133, 138, 144, 150, 152, 154, 158, 162, 166, 170–1, 181, 184–5, 212, 231, 233, 243, 248, 255–7, 259, 263, 275, 281, 283, 287, 292, 326, 331, 363, 402–3, 416, 418, 429, 454–5; and the Rings 112, 154–6, 159, 254–6, 259–60; *Western Elves* 239–40, *Elves of the West* 255, 259; *first lord of the Elves* 411

Elves (VIII) Of Gildor's company 60; of Lórien 161, 168, 256, 260, 266, 345, 361, 398, 430. Divisions of the Elves 157, 168; in relation to Men 158; described by Sam 162–3; *Elflord* 300, 305; other references 77, 98, 109, 112, 131, 153, 155, 158–60, 184, 187, 213, 217, 224, 411. *Elves of the Woods*, *Middle Elves*, see *Lembi*; *Elves of Valinor* 158; *Exiled Elves* 157; *Western Elves* 161; *Wild Elves* 157. See *High Elves*, *Wood-elves*; *Eldar*, *Elder People*, *Fair Folk*.

Elves (IXa) 7, 9, 14, 26, 52–3, 58, 89, 109, 111, 115–16, 119, 123–5, 127, 132

Elves (IXb) 216–17, 244, 272, 279–80, 290, 303, 331–6, 338–9, 354, 377, 401–3, 405–13; *Unfallen Elves* 221, 308; *History of the Elves* 303, 307; the word *Elf* 242, 306

Elves (X) (and *Elf*) 5, 12, 16, 19–22, 24–5, 28, 34, 36–7, 42–4, 51, 59, 61, 66, 70–4, 76–9, 83–4, 88–90, 93, 95, 104, 106, 108, 123, 130, 133, 138, 144–9, 154, 159–80 *passim*, 187, 190, 192–4, 199–201, 203–4, 208–10, 218–21, 223–8, 232, 236, 241, 244, 247, 251–4, 265–8, 270–1, 275, 281, 283, 294, 308–9, 311, 314, 316, 318–19, 324–44, 349, 351, 355, 357–9, 361, 363–5, 372, 374–5, 377–8, 383–4, 388, 395–7, 401–21 *passim*, 424–5, 427. See *Quendi*.

  Elves (X) (and Elf) The 'fading' or 'waning' of the Elves, the 'consuming' of the body by the spirit 31, 68, 118, 126, 130, 146, 149, 203, 209–10, 212, 219, 228, 231, 266–7, 304, 327, 342, 359, 364, 402, 405, 407, 410, 427; immortality and death of the Elves 21, 37, 87, 117, 126, 206, 209, 218–19, 221–2, 225, 227, 231, 233, 242, 244–5, 247–8, 250, 254, 258–9, 266–71, 310–12, 319, 330–2, 339–41, 359, 361, 363–5, 410, 425, 427; rebirth, reincarnation 21, 37, 80, 104, 209, 219–23, 226–7, 233–4, 248, 254, 263, 266–8, 331, 339–40, 359, 361–4

  Elves (X) (and Elf) *Elves of the Air* (Vanyar) 164; *Elves of the Darkness* 163 (see *Dark-Elves, Moriquendi*); *Elves of the Earth* (*Noldor*) 164; *Elves of the Falas* 90, 175; *Elves of the Light* 163, 173 (see *Light Elves, Kalaquendi*); *Elves of the Sea* (*Teleri*) 164; *Elves of the Seven Rivers* (the Nandor of Ossiriand) 164; *Elves of the Twilight* (Sindar) 86, 164

Elves (XI) (and *Elf*) 9–12, 14–16, 22–3, 27–8, 30, 37–9, 45–6, 50, 55–6, 60–1, 64, 71–7, 79, 81–2, 87, 95, 102–4, 107, 109–12, 121–2, 124, 126–8, 131–2, 136, 139, 141, 147–50, 164–7, 174–5, 180, 186, 189, 192, 194–5, 197, 201, 203–7, 211, 213, 219–23, 228, 244, 256, 259, 272, 289, 299, 311–13, 315, 320–2, 332, 345–6, 352, 355, 359–60, 365, 371–81, 383–4, 386–90, 392–3, 396–7, 403, 407–10, 412–14, 416, 418–23

Elves (XII) (and *Elf*) 8, 19–21, 23, 29–33, 35–6, 42, 46, 54–5, 58, 62–3, 65, 73–4, 76–7, 79, 82, 127–8, 139, 144, 152–3, 168–9, 172–4, 177–80, 220–1, 227–9, 234, 240, 244, 257, 264–5, 275, 285, 295–8, 301–2, 304, 307, 311–13, 316–17, 319, 321–3, 326–8, 330, 332, 352, 356–7, 364–5, 370–1, 377–8, 380–6, 388, 390–2, 395–7, 399, 403. *Elves of Light* 312; and see *East-elves, Middle Elves, Western Elves, Woodland Elves*.

Elves of the Air (V) Lindar. 215. *Elves of the Earth* Noldor. 215. *Elves of the Seven Rivers, of the Woods* Danas. 215

Elvish (V) (of language; also references to *Elf-tongue, Elven-tongue*) 56, 75, 108, 149, 172, 179–80, 183, 188, 190, 192–5, 202, 204–5, 207, 213, 243, 248, 294, 299, 322, 341–3, 347, 405; *Elvish* opposed to *Gnomish* 210–11; (with other reference) 135, 172, 186, 197, 214, 232, 242, 248, 309, 403, 405

Elvish (VI) (of language) 217, 324, 395, 411, 432–3, 438, 451–2, 466; (of letters) 384, 449; (with other reference) 280, 454, 463. Elvish speech cited, 194, 196, 324, 361, 394, 451–2

Elvish (VII) (of language and writing) 8, 17, 114, 125, 128, 145, 166, 173, 177, 180–1, 184–5, 191, 200–1, 233, 236, 241, 250, 277, 280, 284, 287–8, 291, 348, 387, 419–20, 454–5, 459; and see under *Elf, Elven-*. Elvish cited 169, 187, 284–5, 415; Elvish words not given separate entries 114, 173, 181, 188, 226, 233, 238–9, 241–3, 261, 287, 311, 322, 404, 419, 423–4

Elvish (VII) (with other reference) 95, 243, 258, 271, 292, 299, 331, 343, 363, 366, 391, 455; *Elvishness* 243

Elvish (VIII) (with reference to language) 35, 44, 50, 55, 158–61, 163, 202, 218, 287, 379–80; *Ancient Elvish of Elvenhome* 160; Elvish cited 218, 223, 293, 394. See *High-elven, Noldorin, Quenya*. (with other reference) 53, 134, 138, 151–2, 158, 163, 167, 169, 185, 190–1, 210, 216–17, 224, 338

Elvish (IXa) (with reference to language) 58, 72, 117–18, 121, 126, 132; Elvish cited 30, 46–7, 51, 56–7, 62, 64, 68, 70, 72–3, 112, 128–9; (with other reference) 8, 26, 34, 69, 116, 125

Elvish (IXb) (of language) 220, 222 [Ramer], 293, 310, 317, 382, 408; (with other reference) 206 [Ramer], 219–20, 406–7, 409–10. *Elvish Drama, Elf-drama* 193, 216; *Faërian Drama* 216

Elvish (X) (of language) 5, 7, 77 (origin of Elvish speech), 124, 144, 157, 160, 166–7, 229, 326, 330, 358, 385, 413, 415; (with other reference) 5, 80, 90, 127, 138, 162, 170–1, 209, 225, 231, 265, 267, 281, 285, 308, 329–33, 335–40, 342, 344, 355, 361, 363, 401, 409, 411, 413–14, 422–5, 428–9

Elvish (XI) (of language) 149, 202, 209, 215–16, 226, 234, 305, 311–12, 359–60, 374, 382, 386–7, 389–91, 393, 396, 398, 404, 407–8, 410, 416–17; (with other reference) 148, 213, 220, 229, 311–13, 323, 350, 360, 369, 372–3, 375–6, 378, 419, 421

Elvish (XII) (of language and writing) 20, 22, 24, 29–3 1, 34, 36, 39–45, 54, 58, 63–5, 67–9, 70–5, 78–9, 82, 125, 138, 151, 157, 164,

193, 297, 299, 315, 320, 324, 340, 348, 368–9, 379, 390, 395; (with other reference) 4, 29–30, 61, 73, 75, 119–20, 125, 133, 144–5, 294, 305–6, 308, 339–40, 342, 351, 359, 378, 380, 382, 389–91

Elwë (IV) Leader of the Third Kindred of the Elves (later *Olwë*). 13, 44, 85–6, 88, 264, 276, 286; brother of Thingol 264, 286; O.E. *Elwingas* 'people of Elwë' 212. See *Elu, Olwë*.

Elwë (V) (1) Lord of the Third Kindred of the Elves, brother of Thingol (see 217); called 'Lord of Ships' (403). 112, 168, 174, 186, 214–15, 217–18, 224–5 (*King of Alqualondë*), 236, 334, 360, 398, 403; *Ellu* in the *Lost Tales* 217. The People of Elwë, a name of the Teleri, 215. (Replaced by *Olwë*). (2) *Elwë Singollo* =Thingol, 217

Elwë (X) (1) Brother of Thingol (later *Olwë*). 88, 168–70, 178–9, 183, 194, 196. See *Solwë*. (2) Thingol of Doriath, called *Singollo* 'Greymantle'. 81–6, 88–91, 104, 162–4, 168–173, 217; *Elwë the Grey* 164, 169; *the People of Elwë*, a name of the Sindar, 165. *Elu Thingol (Elu-thingol)*, his name in Sindarin, 86, 91, 169, 172–3, 217; *Elu* 217. See *Greymantle, Sindo, Singollo, Thingol*.

Elwë (XI) (1) Original name of Olwë. 177. (2) Thingol of Doriath, called *Singollo* 'Greymantle'. 6–9, 107, 177, 344, 350, 369, 373, 375, 379–80, 384–5, 410, 414, 418; Sindarin *Elu Thingol* 9, 21, 350, 378. See *Greymantle, Singollo, Thingol*.

Elwë (XII) Thingol of Doriath. 333, 340–1, 357, 364–5, 369, 371, 376, 385–7, 392. See *Sindikollo, Thingol*.

Elwe Singollo (I) 132–3

Elwë Singollo (II) Thingol. 50

Elwenil (II) Littleheart. 202. (Replaced *Elbenil*.)

Elwenildo (I) Earlier name of Ilverin (Littleheart). 52

Elwenildo (II) Littleheart. 201. (Replaced *Ilverin*.)

Elwin (V) =Ælfwine, Alboin. 7, 31, 53, 55

Elwing (II) 139, 214–15, 240–2, 251–6, 258–61, 264–5, 276, 279, 303, 307–8

Elwing (IV) 33, 36–9, 41, 68–71, 74, 101, 134, 143, 145, 148–56, 158, 161–2, 164, 166, 195–8, 201, 203–4, 306–9, 326–7; called 'the White' 306

Elwing (V) Called 'the White' (141, 143). 23, (64), 71, 141–3, 152, 175–6, 178, 187, 194, 247, 323–7, 330, 332, 334–6, 355, 360; Elwing's tower 327, 335–6

Elwing (VI) 215

Elwing (VII) 100, 102, 104, 110, 136; *Bird-Elwing* 102

Elwing (VIII) 297

Elwing (IXb) 284

Elwing (X) 359

Elwing (XI) 22, 224, 231, 234, 348, 350–1; called *the White* 351

Elwing (XII) 348–9, 365, 367–71, 376

Ely (VII) 107

Emberü (IXb) [Ramer] 178, 182, 197–8, 200, 209, 214–15, 217–18, 221; *Green Emberü* 198, 218–19. (Replaced *Gyönyörü*.)

Embla (I) The first Woman, in Scandinavian mythology. 245

Emeldir (X) Mother of Beren One-hand. 3 05–6

Emeldir (XI) Mother of Beren One-hand; called *the Manhearted*. 51, 56, 124, 126, 231–4

Emil a Pheriannath (VIII) 'Prince of the Halflings', Peregrin Took. 287

Emmeril (IXa) Original name of the wife of Denethor. 54. See *Finduilas* (2).

Emnon (I) Prophecies of Emnon. 170, 172, 197. (Replaced *Morniento*; replaced by *Amnos*.)

Empty Land(s) (V) 32

Empty Lands (IXb) 336

Emrahil (IXa) Transient name preceding *Arwen*. 66. See *Finduilas* (1).

Emris, Isle of (VII) Early name of Tol Brandir. 318, 323, 367

Emyn Amen (XII) Hills in Ithilien. 207, 220, 411, 415, 421; *hills of Amen* 411

Emyn Arnen (VIII) 278, 294, 353, 363, 370, 372, 397, 422, 438; *the reach of Arnen* (stretch of Anduin below the Harlond) 370, (399), 422. See *Haramon*.

Emyn Beraid (V) The Tower Hills. 30

Emyn Beraid (VI) The Tower Hills. 105

Emyn Beraid (VII) The Tower Hills. 130, 423

Emyn Beraid (XII) 176, 186, 191, 195, 210, 231; *Emyn Gwahaedir, Emyn Hen Dúnadan* 186. See *Gwahaedir, Tower Hills*.

Emyn Eglain (XI) The Hills of Eglamar. *184, 189. See *Egladhrim, Eglamar* (3).

Emyn Muil (VII) 321, 362, 388, 404, 407, 424–5, 432–3. See *Sarn Gebir* (1).

Emyn Muil (VIII) 87, 92–5, 98–102, 111–12, 118, 129, 133, 139, 165, 266, 271, 276, 355, 361, 363, 430, 438. See *Sarn Gebir* (1).

Emyn Muil (IXa) 7

Emyn Muil (XII) 198, 205, 259, 316

Emyn Rhain (Rain) (VII) The Border Hills. 268–9, 281, 287–8, 313, 315–16, 325; *Rhain Hills* 269, 271, 315

En (IXb) [Ramer] The Solar System. 204, 220

Enadar (X) See *Denethor*.

Enchanted Isles (V) 243, 323

Enchanted Isles (I) 137, 224

Enchanted Isles (II) 324–5

Enchanted Isles (IV) 155, 198, 257 (replacing *Magic Isles*); *249, 257 ('Enchanted or Magic Isles'); 258

Enchanted Isles (X) 133–4, 137

Enchanters, The (X) A name of the Sindar. 164

Encircling Mountains (III) The mountains encircling the plain of Gondolin. 143, 148, 286

Encircling Mountains (IV) About the plain of Gondolin. 34, 66, 136–7, 139, 191, 194, 221, 259 other references 37, 143–5, 299, 307; *Mountains of Turgon* 66

Encircling Mountains (V) (about the plain of Gondolin) (133, 142), 291, 301. See *Gochressiel*; *Mountains of Valinor*.

Encircling Mountains (IXa) (about the plain of Gondolin) 44. See *Gochressiel*, *(Mountains of) Turgon*.

Encircling Mountains (XI) (about Gondolin) 35, 179, (198, 200), 272, 302. See *Echoriad*, *Gochressiel*.

Encircling Mountains, Encircling Hills (II) The mountains encircling the plain of Gondolin. 163, 166, 169–71, 175–6, 189, 193, 201, 207, 211, 213–14. See especially 207, and see *Heborodin*.

Encircling Sea (V) Vaiya. 111, 116. See *Outer Sea(s)*.

Encircling Sea(s) (X) 17, 32, 118

End, The (VII) 28, 82

End, The (X) 94, 120, 129, 187, 242, 247, 251–2, 259, 267, 274, 319–20, 332, 339, 404, 411; *the End of Arda* 259, 331, 338, 341–2, (405), 430; *the Ending of the World, the World's End* 22, 31, 37, 43, 68, 112, 319, 327, 357, 399, 428; *the End of Eä* 57, 342; *end of days* 9, 21, 35, 37, 71, 76; *Ambar-metta* 'the ending of the world' 359

End, The (XI) 204; *World's end, end of the World* 66, 70

End, The (XII) 401; *the end of the world* 265, 335, 375

Endar (X) Middle-earth. 118–20, 126, 129. See *Endor*.

Endar (XI) Middle-earth. 30, 114; *Endor* 114

Endon (IV) Midmost point of the Earth. *248–9, 254. See *Endor*.

Endor (IV) Midmost point of the Earth (varying with *Endon*, see *248).

240–1, *242–5, *248–9, 254; Middle-earth 254 (Quenya *Endórë*, Sindarin *Ennor*, 255).

Endor (X) (1) Midmost point of Middle-earth. 76–7, 80, 126, 377, 385; also *Endon* 72, 76–7, 80, 126. (2) Middle-earth. 126; Quenya *Endórë*, Sindarin *Ennor*, 126; and see *Aran Endór*.

Eneadur (II) The island of the Ythlings. 319–20, 322, 325

Eneathrim (II) The Ythlings. 331, 334. See *Shipmen of the West*.

Ened (XI) Island in the Ocean west of Drengist. 181, *182

Enedhwaith (XII) Lands between Greyflood and Isen. 313, 328–30; *Enedwaith* 294, 328–9

Enedrion (V) Chief of the Elves of Nargothrond faithful to Felagund. 300. (Replaced by *Edrahil*).

Enedwaith (VII) 'Middlemarch'. 296, 304, 403, 439; 'Middle-folk' 403

Enedwaith (VIII) 268

Eneköl (IXb) [Ramer] The planet Saturn. 205, 221. (Replaced *Shomorú*.)

Enel (XI) 'Three', the third of the Fathers of the Elves. 380, 418, 420–3; *Companions of Enel* 423. See *Nelyar*.

Enelyë (XI) Spouse of Enel. 421

Enemy, The (IV) Morgoth. 163, 202, 233

Enemy, The (V) Morgoth. 19, 24, 64, 72, 310, 329

Enemy, The (VI) 179, 182–4, 207, 253, 266, 281–2, 322–3, 358, 384, 402, 423–4

Enemy, The (VII) 50, 52, 64, 77, 83, 118–19, 121, 129, 131–2, 147–9, 153–4, 156, 169, 23 1–2, 244, 252, 255–6, 270–2, 290, 326, 328, 358–9, 426

Enemy, The (VIII) 76, 97, 122–3, 158, 254, 277, 292, 327, 329–30, 375, 378, 380–1, 385, 390, 392, 400, 402–4

Enemy, The (IXb) 411

Enemy, The (X) 43, 99, 111, 287, 309–11, 313, 320, 325, 328, 348–9, 355, 372, 399, 401, 404; *the Dark Enemy* 120, 123, 194, *the Black Enemy* 421; *the Enemies* 203; *Foe of the Valar* 114

Enemy, The (XI) 17, 29, 31, 50, 55, 59, 118, 166, 253

Enemy, The (XII) 21, 24, 267, 436; *the Great Enemy* 358

Enfeng (V) 'Longbeards', the Dwarves of Nogrod. 274, 278, *348*, *387*. See *Indrafangs*.

Enfeng (XI) 'Longbeards', Dwarves of Belegost. 10–13, 75, 108, 134, 321–2, *Ennfeng* (XI) 205, *Enfengs* 112; of Nogrod 75, 108, 134. See *Anfangrim*, *Indrafangs*, *Longbeards*.

Enfolding Ocean, *Encircling Ocean* (IV) See *Vaiya*.

Engainor (III) See *Angainor*.

England (II) 285, 291, 293–4, 301, 303–4, 308–9, 311–12, 314, 316, 319, 323, 327, 330–1, 333–4; *Englaland* (Old English) 291, 301–2. See *Luthany, Lúthien* (3), *Leithian*.

England (III) 154, 157, 181–2. See *Leithien, Luthany*.

England (IV) 39–40, 72, 75, 174, 199–200, 258. See *Leithien, Lúthien* (s).

England (V) 103, 186, 204, 412

England (IXb) 159, 211, 215, 236, 272, 280, 291

England (XII) 26, 45, 50, 52, 82; *ancient England* 22, 49, (143)

England, English (I) 22–7, 202. See *Old English*.

Engle (II) (Old English) The English people. 290–1. See *Angolcynn, English*.

English (II) (both people and language) 291–3, 301–2, 304–5, 308–9, 313, 320, 322–3, 327–8; *Englisc* 292. See *Anglo-Saxon(s), Old English*.

English (III) (language) 123, 127, 139, 160. See *Old English*.

English (IV) (language) 226–7; O.E. *Englisc* 284, 338, 340. See *Old English*.

English (V) 50, 77–8, 80–1, 83, 91–2, 94, 96, 186, 203, 322; *Englishmen* 38, 55. See *Anglo-Saxon(s), Old English*.

English (VIII) 23, 123, 127, 129, 267; see *Old English*.

English (IXb) (language) 150, 159, 192, 200–1, 222, 237, 242, 259, 267, 300, 310–11, 317, 417–19, 421, 432, 434–5, 439; *ancient English*, or with reference to Old English, 236, 243–4, 256, 268–9, 277, 301, 303, 409 *English Dialect Dictionary* 150, 286

English (XI) 312, 368–9, 372, 383, 392, 407; *(Old) English* 309, 312–15, 391–2. See *Anglo-Saxon*.

English (XII) (language) 20–1, 27, 41–7, 49–50, 52–4, 58, 60–1, 70–1, 81–2, 103, 137, 298–300, 316, 320, 361–2, 368, 405. *Old English* (also 'ancient', 'ancestral', 'archaic' English) 15, 21, 27, 41, 44, 50–3, 58, 60–1, 70–1, 76, 82 (people), 83, 125, 137, 274, 301, 405

Engwar (V) 'The Sickly', an Elvish name for Men. 245, *358*

Enkeladim (IXb) [Ramer] Elves. 199, 206–7, 218–19, 221, 283, 303; other than in Ramer's account 397–8, 400, 405, 410–11 (equated with *Eleddi, Eldar*, 397)

Ennor (IV) See *Endor*.

Ennorath (III) Middle-earth. 356

Ennyn Dûr (VIII) The Gates of Mordor (name of the pass). 105, 113, 127. See *Black Gate(s)*, *Gates of Mordor*, *Morannon*.

Enquirers (X) Term used to replace *Gnomes*. 168

Enthor (XI) Younger brother of Hunthor and Manthor. See 267, 270.

Ent-house (VII) 415, 417, 419; *Entmoot* 407, 419; *Ent-strides* 417; *Ent-voices* 419

Entish Land(s) (VII) 10, 13, 16, 58, 65, 69–70, 152, 164, 250, 299, 306, 413; *Entish Dale(s)* 10, 13, 16–17, 58, 61, 65, 250, 413. Earlier names *Hoardale(s)* 10, 16, 114, *Nen fimred* 10, *Nenvithim* 114, *Wolfdale* 10; and see *Dimrill Dale*, *Ettendales*.

Entish Lands (VI) Troll-country north of Rivendell. 201, 205; *Entish Dales* 205. (Replaced by *Ettenmoors*, *Ettendales*.) See *Dimrill-dale*, *Hoardale*.

Entmark, *Entwood* (VII) Fangorn. 429

Ents (VI) 205, 254

Ents (VII) 16, 65, 214, 250, 411–14, 416, 418–21, 428–9, 434–7, 448; *Entwives* 418–20, 448; *Entings* 420; *Song of the Ent and the Entwife* 418, 421; *Entish* 415; 419–21 (marching song). Called *Lone-walkers* 411, *Shepherds of the Trees* 429, *Tree-folk* 411, 413, *treeherds* 416; cf. *tree-giants* 216

Ent(s) (VIII) 4–6, 25–6, 30–1, 39, 41–2, 45, 47–62, (64), 66–8, 70, 79, 219, 255–6, 260, 262, 266–7, 275, 285, 343–6, 351, 360–4, (404), 430, 437; (language) 50, 55. *Entish* 50 (language), 56, *half-Entish* 50, 55. *Ent-house* 3; *Entmoot* 3, 7, 100. *Tree-giants* 266

Ents (IXa) 7, 9, 53, 63, 71, 116, 119, 123; *Entwives* 63, 116, 120, 123; *Entings* 71

Ents (X) 251

Ents (XI) 341, 353, 356; *Shepherds of the Trees* 356

Entwade (VII) 318, 320, (358), 366, 392, 402, 404

Entwash, River (VII) (including references to *the River*) 210, 214, 216, 250, 268–9, 281–3, 288, 315–16, 320, 330, 357–8, 376, 389–92, 396, 398, 409, 414, 429, 442; *mouths* 296, 321, 359; *vale of Entwash* 358. See *Ogodrûth*.

Entwash, River (VIII) 133, 343, 348; *mouths of Entwash* 270, 343

Entwash, River (XII) 53, 273, 315

Entwood Fangorn. (VIII) 30

Envinyatar (VIII) The Renewer (Aragorn). 395

Eodoras (VII) 320, 369, 402, 429–34, 437, 440–3, 446, 449–50;

earlier from *Eodor* (singular) 318, 402, later form *Edoras* 407, 449

Eodoras (VIII) See *Edoras*.

Eofor (VII) Father of Eorl the Young. 435. See *Léod*.

Eofored (VII) Second Master of the Mark. 444, 446, 450

Eofored (VIII) Second Master of the Mark (preceding Théodred). 22

Eoh (I) Father of Ottor Wǽfre (Eriol). 23–4

Eoh (II) Father of Ottor Wǽfre (Eriol). 290–1, 294. (Replaced by *Déor* (1).)

Eöl (II) Father of Meglin (Maeglin). 165, 168, 199, 220, 248

Eöl (III) Father of Meglin (Maeglin). 52, 145–8

Eöl (IV) 34–5, 65, 136, 140, 191, 193, 213, 301, 321; O.E. Éor 213

Eöl (V) 136 ('The Dark-elf'), 139

Eöl (XI) 47–8, 71, 84, 121–3, 127, 139, 316, 320–30, *331, 332–3, 335–8, 344, 348, 409, 420. See *Dark-elves*.

Eöl (XII) 'The Dark Elf', father of Maeglin. 328, 367

Éomearc, Éomeark (VIII) See *(The) Mark*.

Éomer (VII) Third Master of the Mark. 390, 392–4, 399–403, 405, 407, 410, 424, 434, 436–9, 443, 445–8, 451; *Lord of Rohan* 448

Éomer (VIII) 3, 6, 8, 10–11, 13–21, 25, 29, 41, 56, 62–5, 72, 78, 141, 226, 237–8, 240, 243–4, 246, (248), 252–6, 259–60, 262–4, 266, 272, 275, 296, 298–9, 301, 303, 309, 311–12, 315–16, 318, 321, 346, 348, 351–2, 355–6, 359–61, 363, 368, 385, 388–91, 393–4, 403–4, 415, 418; *King Éomer* 369

Éomer (XII) Eighteenth King of Rohan. 53, 65, 207, 221, 240, 244, 246, 271–3; named *Éadig* 244

Éomer, King Éomer (IXa) 7, 48, 52, 54–5, 57, 61–3, 66–8, 73, 123

Éomund (VII) Father of Éomer and Éowyn. 390, 393, 402, 448, 450–1

Éomund (VIII) Father of Éomer and Éowyn. 266, 365, 368

Éomund (XII) Father of Éomer and Éowyn. 240, 242, 244, 273

Eönwë (I) Herald of Manwe. 63, 93

Eönwë (X) Herald of Manwë. 146–7, 151, 203–4, 406. (Replaced *Fionwë*, son of Manwë.)

Eönwë (XI) Herald of Manwë. 246, 417. (Replaced *Fionwë*, son of Manwë.)

Eönwë (XII) Herald of Manwë. 143, 163. See *Fionwë*.

éored (VII) Body of cavalry in Rohan. 399, 401

éored (VIII) Body of cavalry in Rohan. 13, 352–3, 356–7

Eorl the Young (VII) 404–5, 435, 440, 443–5, 449–50; *Eorl the Old* 443; *House of Eorl* 447; *Eorlingas* 447

Eorl the Young (VIII) 21, 24, 30, 155, 243–4, 408; *House of Eorl* (the Golden Hall) 77, 130, 236, (kindred) 321

Eorl the Young (IXa) 68, 72

Eorl the Young (XII) First King of the Mark. 21, 26, 50, 205, 219, 236, 261, 271–3, 312, 328; *Oath of Eorl and Cirion* 328

Éorlingas (VIII) People of Eorl, the Rohirrim. 9, 156, 236, 242, 247, 316, 348, 365, 385, 389

Eorlings (XII) The Rohirrim. 34; *Eorlingas* 272

Éothain (VII) Éomer's esquire. 400–2

Éothain (VIII) Rider of Rohan. (1) Éomer's squire. 266, 356. (2) In other applications 247, 266; 350; 352, 356

Éothéod (VII) original name of the Riders of Rohan. 307

Éothéod (XII) 'Horse-folk' and 'Horse-land' (53). 34, 53, 81, 205, 236, 271–3; earliest name *Irenland* 271

Éowin (VII) Second Master of the Mark. 393–4, 440

Éowyn (VII) Sister of Éomer. 390, 437, 445, 447–8, 450–1; *'Elfsheen'* 390

Éowyn (VIII) (1) Sister of Helm and mother of Fréalaf, tenth King of the Mark. 408. (2) Sister of Éomer. 70, 72, 79, 236, 242–4, 246–8, 255–6, 259–60, 262, 264–7, 275, 308, 311–13, 315–20, 345, 355–6, 359–60, 363, 365–6, 368–9, 372, 380, 383–7, 389–90, 393, 406, 417–18, 421, 423, 430

Éowyn (IXa) 52, 54–5, 57, 59, 62–3, 68, 123; *Lady of Rohan* 62

Éowyn (IXb) 217

Éowyn (XII) Sister of Éomer. 39, 43, 53, 68, 181, 207, 221, 240, 242, 244, 246, 273

Ephel Brandir (II) 135

Ephel Brandir (V) Dwellings of the Woodmen on Amon Obel. 412

Ephel Brandir (XI) Dwellings of the Men of Brethil on Amon Obel. 89, 92, 96–7, 145, 148, 151–2, 157–8, 164, *182, 186, 301, 306; *the Ephel* 97. See *Bar Haleth, Obel Halad.*

Ephel Dúath (VII) 145, 310, 348; earlier *Duath* 310, 343, 345, 348. Transient names *Deldúath, Daedeloth* 169

Ephel Dúath (VIII) 122, 137, 176–7, 179–80, 195, (on *Ephel* see 137). Earlier names *Dúath* 106, 122; *Hebel Dúath* 122, 131, 133, 180. See *Mountains of Shadow.*

Ephel Dûath (IXa) 22, 32, 35

Epilogue (VIII) 256. See *Sam's book*, under *Gamgee, Sam.*

Epilogue (XII) (to *The Lord of the Rings*) 68, 112

Eradan (XII) Second Ruling Steward. 204

Erceleb (VI) The first name for *mithril* or Moria-silver. 465. See *Ithil*.

Erceleb (VII) See *Mithril*.

Erchamion (III) 'One-handed', name of Beren. 121; *Er(h)amion* 119. (Replaced *Ermabwed*.)

Erchamion (IV) 'One-handed', name of Beren. 191. (Replaced *Ermabuin*.)

Erchamion (V) 'One-handed', name of Beren. 146, 301–2, *371* (*Erchamron*), 405; *Erchamui* 146, *361*, 405. See *Ermabuin*.

Erchamion (XI) 'One-handed', name of Beren. 51, 231

Erchinion (XII) Second son of Imrahil of Dol Amroth. 221, 223

Erebor (VII) The Lonely Mountain. 142, 156, 160, 306. Earlier name *Dolereb* 306

Erebor (VIII) The Lonely Mountain. 357; *The Quest of Erebor* 357–8

Erebor (IXa) The Lonely Mountain. 119

Erebor (XII) 236–42, 244, 246, 249–50, 252, 275–8, 280–1, 284, 288, 300, 323; *The Quest of Erebor* (title) 282, 288–9. See *Lonely Mountain*.

Erech (VIII) (including many references to *the Stone* and *Hill of Erech*) 268, 287, 296–7, 300, 302, 304–9, 397, 399, 409–12, 416, 418–19, 421–2, 424, 427–9, 437; *Tower of Erech* 309, 397, 410, 418, 424. The *palantír* of Erech 300, 302, 304–6, 309, 397, 399, 410, 418, 424

Erech, *Stone of Erech* (IXa) 15–17; the *palantír* of Erech 15

Ered- (XI) (in names of mountain-ranges) See *Eryd-*.

Ered Engrin (IV) The Iron Mountains (final form). 220. See *Aiglir Angrin*.

Ered Gorgoroth (II) The Mountains of Terror. 63

Ered Gorgoroth (III) The Mountains of Terror. 171, 183, 208, 234, 314; *Gorgoroth* 272–3, 350; *Gorgorath* 345 (described), 350, 361. See *Shadowy Mountains*.

Ered Lindon (XII) 34, 301, 307, 322, 325, 349, 374. See *Ered Luin*; *Blue Mountains*, *Mountains of Lune*.

Ered Lithui (VII) The Ash Mountains. 213, 322, 344–5, 349

Ered Lithui (VIII) 128. See *Ash Mountains*.

Ered Lithui (IXa) The Ash Mountains. 11, 32, 35; *the north(ern) range* 33, 39

Ered Luin (III) The Blue Mountains160

144

Ered Luin (VII) The Blue Mountains. 301. See *Eredlindon*.

Ered Luin (XII) 78, 184, 281–2, 314–15, 330. See *Ered Lindon*.

Ered Mithrin (IV) The Grey Mountains (distinct from the Grey Mountains of *the Ambarkanta*). 257

Ered Mithrin (XII) 302–3, 305, 321–3. See *Grey Mountains*.

Ered Myrn (VII) See *Black Mountains*.

Ered Nimrais (VI) The White Mountains. 399

Ered Nimrais (VIII) The White Mountains. 103, 278, 288; earlier names *Hebel Uilos*, ~ *Orolos*, 137; *Hebel Nimrath* 156, 167, *Ered* ~ 137; *Ered Nimras* 168, *Ephel* ~ 137; *Ephel Nimrais* 137; *Eredfain* 288. See *White Mountains*.

Ered Nimrais (IXa) 16. See *White Mountains*.

Ered Orgoroth (Gorgoroth) (VII) 145. See *Mountains of Terror*.

Ered Orgoroth (V) The Mountains of Terror. 298, 302, 377; *Ered Orgorath* 298; *Ered Gorgoroth* 298–9. See *Gorgoroth*.

Ered Wethrin (I) The Mountains of Shadow. 112, 158, 242

Ered Wethrin (II) The Mountains of Shadow. 62, 132, 217

Ered Wethrin (III) The Shadowy Mountains. 29, 314

Ered-engrin (V) The Iron Mountains. 258, 266, 379. (Replaced *Eiglir Engrin*.)

Eredfain (VIII) See *Ered Nimrais*.

Eredhithui (VII) The Misty Mountains. 124. Another proposed name *Hithdilias* 124

Eredlindon (IV) The Blue Mountains. 108, 173, 259, 271, 277, 310, 328, 331–3, 335, 339, 341; O.E. *Hǽwengebeorge* 339, 341. See *Eredluin*.

Eredlindon (V) The Blue Mountains. 33, 112, 119, 122, 126–30, 154, 174–6, 179, 181, 188, 196–7, 260–1, 263, 265, 267, 269, 273–5, 277, 279, 289, 311, 330, 337, 379, 404–5. On the meaning of the name see 267, 359, 369; and see *Blue Mountains*, *Eredluin*, *Luindirien*, *Lunoronti*.

Eredlindon (VII) The Blue Mountains. 123–4, 137, 301, 377. See *Ered Luin*.

Eredlómin (V) The Echoing Mountains. 117, 130, 239, 249, 259, 270–1, 367, 405–6; *Eredlúmin* 'Gloomy Mountains' 405–7; also *Eredlemrin*, *Lóminorthin* 358, 367, 379. On the changing meaning of the name see 406.

Eredlómin, Erydlómin (IV) (Also *Eredlómen*, 210). (1) The Shadowy Mountains (replaced by *Eredwethion*, later *Eredwethrin*). 139–40, 192, 221, 229, 262, 280, 295–6, 300–1, 305, 310–13, 324. (2)

The Echoing Mountains. 192–3, 210, 229–30, 258–9, 262, 268, 280, 332, 336; O.E. *Wómanbeorgas* 210. For the different meanings and applications of *Eredlómin* see 192–3.

Eredluin (V) The Blue Mountains. 267. See *Eredlindon*.

Eredluin, Erydluin (IV) The Blue Mountains. 108, 121, 132, 135, 175, 336. See *Eredlindon*.

Eredvyrn (VII) See *Black Mountains*.

Eredwethion (V) The Shadowy Mountains. 117–18, 125, 127–8, 130, 136, 139, 145, 249–50, 259–60, 264, 270, 280, 282, 300, 311, 314–15, 379, 397, 405–6; *Erydwethion* 309–10, 314; later form *Ered Wethrin* 300. See *Shadowy Mountains*.

Eredwethion (VII) Mountains of Shadow. (1) In the Elder Days. 124. (2) Mountains fencing Mordor on the West. 325, 345, 348, 374; replaced by *(Ephel) Duath*.

Eredwethion, Erydwethion (IV) The Shadowy Mountains (replacing *Eredlómin* (1)). 140, 192, 221, 262, 268, 280, 295, 310–13, 324, 328, 330, 332–3, 336, 338, 340; O.E. *Scúgebeorg* 338, 340. (Replaced by *Eredwethrin*.)

Eredwethrin (IV) The Shadowy Mountains. 192, 258–9. (Replaced *Eredwethion*.)

Ereg, River (VII) See *Erui*.

Ereg, River (VIII) See *Erui*.

Eregion (VII) Hollin. 22, 124–5, 173, 455. Earlier name *Nan-eregdos* 166

Eregion (X) Hollin. 135

Eregion (XII) 79, 168–9, 174, 177–80, 297, 305, 317–19, 390. See *Hollin*.

Eregion Hollin. (VI) 432. See *Regornion*.

Eregon, Isle of (VII) 'Stone Pinnacle', early name of Tol Brandir. 285, 323, 345, 350, 355–6, 364, 367

Ereinion (XII) See *Gil-galad*.

Erelas (VIII) The fourth (or third, see 344) beacon in Anórien. 233, 344, 349

Erellont (IV) Companion of Eärendel. 197

Erellont (V) One of the companions of Eärendel on his voyages. 324

Eremar (X) See *Almaren*.

Erendis of Númenor (XI) 230, 232

Erenol (II) 'Iron Cliffs', 'Coast of Iron', Lionesse. 334. (Replaced by *Evadrien*.)

Ereol, Eriol (XI) 246

Eressë =*Eressëa*. (IXb) 303, 313–14, 355, 399, 402–4, 406, 411–13

Eressëa (IV) See *Tol Eressëa*.

Eressëa (V) and *Tol-eressëa* 11, 13–16, 20–1, 24–5, 27, 29–33, 56–8, 64–6, 69–71, 73, 77–8, 80, 102–4, 113, 148–9, 164, 167, 171, 178, 180, 184, 190, 193–4, 201, 203–4, 222, 224–5, 243, 333, 338, 356, 394 (also *Toll-ereb*), 412–13. The Tree of Tol-eressëa 211. See *Avallon, Lonely Isle*.

Eressëa (VII) The Lonely Isle. 123, 454

Eressëa (VIII) 169; *Tol Eressëa* 168, 170. See *Lonely Isle*.

Eressëa (IXa) See *Tol Eressëa*.

Eressëa (IXb) and *Tol Eressëa* 280, 315–16, 332, 334, 336, 354–5, 357, 379–80, 386, 391, 394, 396, 400–1, 406–10. See *Lonely Isle*.

Eressëa (X) See *Tol Eressëa*.

Eressëa (XI) See *Tol Eressëa*.

Eressëa (XII) 31, 33, 144, 146–9, 152, 157–8, 163, 173, 177–8, 185, 189, 386, 401; *Tol Eressëa* 143, 158, 388; *Lonely Isle* 158. See *Avallon, Avallónë* (1).

Eressëan (V) (language) 41–3, 45, 48, 50, 56, 62, 68, 75, 185, 203; (with other reference) 60, 75; *Eressëans* 60, 66

Eressëan (IXb) (language) 286, 303–4, 308–9. *Eressëans* 401, 403. See *Avallonian, Nimrian, Quenya*.

Eressëan (X) Quenya. 136. See *Avallonian*.

Erestor (VI) Elf of Rivendell, Elrond's kinsman and counsellor. 395, 398, 400–2, 405, 413–14

Erestor (VII) '*Half-elf*' Kinsman of Elrond. 111, 153–4, 158, 162, 172

Erhamion (VI) 'Onehanded'; see *Beren*.

Eriador (VII) 306, 455

Eriador (X) 83, 89

Eriador (XI) 13, 39, 48–9, 60–1, 64, 109–10, 123, 128–9, 206, 221, 228, 232, 381, 385, 397, 410, 416

Eriador (XII) 10–11, 33–4, 36–40, 56, 66–7, 119, 125, 153, 174, 179–80, 185, 195–6, 220, 227, 229–31, 235–6, 248, 250, 263–4, 281, 293, 302–3, 305–7, 311–14, 327, 378, 384, 391

Erien (IXa) Replaced, and replaced by, *Arien*. 120–1. See *Arien, Eirien*.

Erien (XII) Daughter of Fingon (rejected). 361; earlier name *Ernis* 361

Erin (V) Ireland. 103

Erin, Ériu (IXb) See *Ireland*.

Erinti (I) Daughter of Manwë and Varda. 58, 62, 202

Erinti (V) Daughter of Manwë and Varda in the *Lost Tales*. 165. (Replaced by *Ilmarë*).

Eriol (I) 14–18, 20, 22–7, 32, 45–51, 63–5, 78, 94–8, 107, 112–13, 129, 140, 164, 166, 169, 174–5, 189, 195–7, 202–3, 225, 230, 234–5; *Eriollo* 24. For his name and history see especially 23–4; and see *Ælfwine*.

Eriol (II) 3–9, 21, 40–2, 49, 145, 148–9, 209, 258, 264, 278–9, 283–4, 286–7, 289–95, 300–1, 303, 311, 323, 326, 329–30. 'The *Eriol* story' 293–4, 300, 303, 310–11, 323, 329–30. *Song of Eriol* (poem) 298–300. See *Melinon*.

Eriol (III) 182

Eriol (IV) 41–2, 74, 76, 78, 165, 191, 205–6, 258, 263, 274, 281, 283, 292, 337; *Ereol* 166, 283. See *Ælfwine, Leithien, Lúthien* (2).

Eriol (V) 53, 155, 201, 203, 334, 356, 412; *Eriol of Leithien* 201, 203; *Ereol* 203–4

Eriol (IXb) Ælfwine the Mariner. 279; *Eriol-saga* 281–2

Eriol (X) 5, 26. See *Ælfwine*.

Erion (VII) See *Tom Bombadil*.

Erithámrod (III) Name of Húrin (translated 'the Unbending', 37 line 864), almost always in the collocation *Thalion Erithámrod*. 6, 9, 11, 13, 21, 37, 96, 101, 111, 114

Erkenbrand (VII) See *Elfstone*.

Erkenbrand (VIII) Lord of Westfold. 10–11, 23–5, 40–1, 250. Replaced *Erkenwald* 24, 29, 40, 52, 60. See *Trumbold, Heorulf, Nothelm*.

Ermabuin (IV) See *Ermabwed*.

Ermabuin (V) 'One-handed', named of Beren. 131, 146, 371 (*Ermab(-r)in*), 405. See *Erchamion*.

Ermabwed (II) 'One-handed', (Gnomish) name of Beren. 34, 36, 71–2, 116, 137, 144–5, 242. See *Elmavoitë*

Ermabwed (III) 'One-handed', name of Beren. 9, 12, 22, 25, 56, 104, 107, 112, 119–21; *Ermabweth* 119, 123. (Replaced by *Er(h)amion, Erchamion*.)

Ermabwed (IV) 'One-handed', name of Beren. 113, 297, 310; later form *Ermabuin* 310 (replaced by *Erchamion*).

Ermon (I) One of the two first Men (with Elmir), 236–7, 239, 243, 245; *people, folk, sons, of Ermon* 237–8, 240

Ermon (II) One of the two first Men (with Elmir). 305

Errantry (VI) (poem) 412

Errantry (VII) 84–91, 95, 105–6, 108; metre and nature described 85, 90. See *Eärendel*. (VII) Names in *Errantry*: *Aerie* 88, 95; *Belmarie* 88, 95; *Derion* 89; *Derrilyn* 87, 95; *Faërie* 88; *Fantasie* 88; *Lerion* 89; *Ossory* 86; *Thellamie* 88, 95

Errol, Alboin (IXb) In *The Lost Road*. 280, 284, 286–90, 304, 308–11

Errol, Audoin (IXb) Son of Alboin Errol. 289

Errol, Oswin (IXb) Father of Alboin Errol. 284, 287, (288, 308)

Eru (I) 173

Eru (V) Ilúvatar. 338

Eru (IXb) Ilúvatar; also *Êru* (see 387–8, 432). 247, 249, 251, 290, 311–12, 341, 343–8, 351–2, 357–8, 360–1, 364, 367–8, 372, 374, 377, 381–3, 387, 392, 401–2, 410–11, 432. In different sense, 'the world', 310, 313

Eru (X) 7, 48–9, 58–9, 65–6, 74, 80, 87–8, 99, 114, 117, 129, 138, 144, 159, 186, 209, 211(-12), 220–3, 236, 241–2, 244–6, 252, 267–8, 286–7, 304, 309, 311–13, 318–19, 321–2, 326–8, 330–45, 350–2, 354, 356–7, 359–65, 380, 390–3, 397–8, 401–3, 406, 409–11, 420, 425, 427, 429–30; *Eru Allfather, Eru Ilúvatar* 48, 112, 120, 286; *the Voice (of Eru)* 345–8, 360. See *Children of Eru, God, Ilúvatar, Lord of All, (The) One.*

Eru (XI) 130, 341, 399, 402–3, 405, 421; *Eru-begotten* (the first Elves) 421; *the One* 212, 402. See *Children of Eru.*

Eru (XII) 364–5, 370, 381, 391, 413; *Eru Ilúvatar* 270. See *Children of Ilúvatar, (The) One.*

Eru Ilúvatar. (IV) 279

Eru-bênî (IXb) 'Servants of God', the Powers. 341, 353, 356–7, 387; *Êru-bênî* 387

Eruchîn (III) Children of Eru. 354

Eruhil (IXb) 'Children of God', Númenóreans. 341–5, 353–5. (Replaced by *Eruhîn*.)

Eruhildi (IXb) 'Sons of God', Númenóreans. 399, 402–4, 411. (Replaced by *Eruhil*.)

Eruhîn (IXb) 'Children of God', Númenóreans; also *Êruhîn* (see 387–8). 311, 358–63, 367, 375, 377–8, 387–90, 411; *Êruhînim* 247–8

Eruhín (X) Children of Eru. 320, 330; *Eruhíni* 356, 376; *Eruséni* 423

Eruhîn (XII) (Children of Eru), Númenóreans. 149

Eruhíni (XI) Children of Eru (singular *Eruhin*). 403

Erui, River (VII) In Gondor. 312. Earlier form *Ereg* 312

Erui, River (VIII) In Gondor. 427, 436. Earlier form *Ereg* 436, 438

Eruman (I) Name interchangeable with *Arvalin*, q.v.; (originally) the region east of the Mountains of Valinor and south of Taniquetil (see especially 82–3, 91–3). 68, 70, 79, 82–3, 87, 91–3, 145, 151–2, 155, 157–8, 209; *Erumáni* 70, 79, 91, 125, 131, 149, 179, 188, 196, 200. (Earlier names of the region: *Habbanan, Harwalin, Harvalien, Harmalin*.)

Eruman (II) 68 (the giant of Eruman). *Erumáni* 264; *Battle of Erumáni* 285–6

Eruman (III) 205

Eruman (IV) (1) Region south of Taniquetil. 50 (*Erumáni*), *250–1, 260. (2) Region where Men awoke. 99, 171, 235, 257. (Replaced by *Hildórien*.) (3) Region between the mountains and the sea north of Taniquetil. 171, 239, *249–5, 257, 260. (Replaced by *Araman*.)

Eruman (V) Region north of Taniquetil. 236, 238–9, 242, 247–8, 252, 256, *356*

Eruman (X) Earlier name of *Araman*. 123, 194, 198, 266

Eruman (XI) Earlier name of Araman. 115, 175

Eryd (Ered) Engrin (XI) 6, 104, 196. See *Iron Mountains*.

Eryd (Ered) Gorgoroth (XI) 319, ~ Gorgorath 129, 188, *the Gorgorath* 319; ~ Orgoroth 15, 129, 194, ~ Orgorath 61, 64, 129, *183, 188, 194. See *Mountains of Terror*.

Eryd (Ered) Lómin (XI) 17, 38, 117, 176, 192, 196; *Eryd Lammad* 192, 196. See *Echoing Mountains*.

Eryd (Ered) Luin (XI) 5, 7, 10, 13, 32, 38–9, 60, 104, 108, 117, 179, 193, 385, 389. See *Blue Mountains, Eryd Lindon, Luindirien*.

Eryd (Ered) Nimrais (XI) 110, 385. See *White Mountains*.

Eryd (Ered) Orgoroth (X) The Mountains of Terror. 109, 127, 297, 299; *Eryd Gorgoroth* 297, *Ered Gorgoroth* 127, 299

Eryd (Ered) Orgoroth (XI) See *Eryd Gorgoroth*.

Eryd (Ered) Wethrin (XI) 17–18, 38, 40, 46, 60, 74, 85, 113–14, 117, 196, 200, 240; earlier ~ Wethion 45, 74, 89, 91, 113, 120, 134, 166, *182, 196, 200, 219, 240; *Eryd Wethian* 142, 256, 299. See *Mountains of Shadow*.

Eryd Lammad (XI) See *Eryd Lómin*.

Eryd Wethrin (X) The Mountains of Shadow. 297, 299; earlier *Eredwethion* 299

Eryd (Ered) Lindon (XI) 49, 105, *183, 193, 201–3, 206, 215, 334, 385, 388. See *Blue Mountains, Eryd Luin, Ossiriand*.

Erydlómin, Erydluin (IV) See *Eredlómin, Eredluin*.

Eryn Galen (V) Greenwood the Great (Mirkwood). 289

Eryn Lasgalen (V) Name of Mirkwood after the War of the Ring. 211

Esgalduin (II) 63

Esgalduin (III) The enchanted river of Doriath. 76, 81–2, 93, 156, 158, 160, 177, 186, 199, 202–4, 213, 223, 262; *the Elf-river* 76; earlier form *Esgaduin* 81, 93, 158, 160

Esgalduin, River (IV) 103, 173, 210, 221–3

Esgalduin, River (V) 126, 260–1, *355, 357, 386*

Esgalduin, River (XI) 11, 94, 150, *183, 188, 194, 319, 324, 328, 332–4; the Bridge over Esgalduin 188, 319, 328, *331, 332–5, and see *Esgaliant, Iant Iaur*; (earlier) the Ford of Esgalduin 324, 332

Esgaliant (XI) The Bridge of Esgalduin. 333. See *Esgalduin, Iant Iaur*.

Esgaroth (VI) Lake-town. 213, 369, 411

Esgaroth (XII) 34, 38, 65, 239; *Lake Town* 72

Esperanto (V) 341

Essekenta Eldarinwa (XI) Title of *Quendi and Eldar*. 359

Estë (I) 88, 201

Estë (IV) Wife of Lórien. 171, 263, 270, 275, 285

Estë (V) Wife of Lórien; called 'the Pale'. 110, 165, 205, 207, *357* (also Noldorin *Idh*), *385*

Estë (X) Called 'the Pale'. 49, 59, 65–6, 69, 131–2, 136, 145, 147–8, 150–1, 198, 201, 206, 237, 258. On the status of Estë see 49, 59, 65–6, 69, 146–7, 201

Estë (XI) 'Repose'; the wife of Lórien. 403–4; Telerin *Ēdë* 403–4

Estel (XII) 'Hope', name of Aragorn II in his youth. 269–70; earlier *Amin* 269

Estolad (XI) Dwelling of the peoples of Bëor and Marach south of Nan Elmoth. 112, 189, 218–22, 227–8, 233, 334; *Estoland* *183, 189, 227; translated *the Encampment* 218

Ethelion (VI) Elvish name of Peregrin Boffin (Trotter). 392, 395. See *Du-finnion, Padathir, Rimbedir*.

Ethiopians (VII) 439

Ethir (Anduin) (XII) The Mouths of Anduin. 416

Ethir Anduin (VII) 298, 307, 311, 372. Earlier form *Ethir-andon* 298–9

Ethir Anduin (VIII) 268, 437; *the Ethir* 287, 420. See *Anduin, (The) Delta*.

Ethir Anduin (IXa) 15–16; *the Ethir* 15

Ethlon (IV) Unknown. 9

Ethraid Erui (XII) The Crossings of Erui (river of Gondor). 199

Ettendales (VII) 58, 65, 250; *Ettenmoor(s)* 58, 65, 250, 306. Earlier name *Bergrisland* 306. See *Entish Land(s)*.

Ettenmoors (VI) 192, 205; *Ettendales* 205. See *Entish Lands*.

Ettenmoors (XII) Troll-fells north of Rivendell. 437

Etyañgoldi (XI) 'Exiled Noldor'. 374

Etymologies (VI) In Vol. V. 186, 188, 432–3, 435, 437, 463, 466

Etymologies (VII) In Vol. V. 8, 66, 125, 172, 233, 238–42, 261, 287, 311, 322, 364, 404, 420, 424

Etymologies (VIII) In Vol. V, *The Lost Road*. 115, 139, 222, 292, 426

Etymologies (IXa) In Vol.V, *The Lost Road*. 73

Etymologies, The (IXb) In Vol.V, *The Lost Road*. 412

Etymologies, The (X) In Vol.V, *The Lost Road*. 39, 44, 57, 69, 89, 124, 169, 202, 229, 253, 359

Etymologies, The (XI) In Vol. V, *The Lost Road*. 104, 116, 128, 137, 186, 189, 191, 201, 235, 337

Etymologies, The (XII) In The Lost Road. 68–9, 158, 371, 404–5

Europe (II) 261

Europe (IXb) 229, 241, 306, 309, 398, 410

European (XII) 41, 61, 368

Euti (II) Jutes. 306

Evadrien (II) 'Coast of Iron', Lionesse. 313, 334. (Replaced *Erenol*.)

Evair (XI) (Sindarin) Avari. 380

Evendim, Hills of (VII) 301, 304

Evendim, Lake (IXa) 78, 127; *Evendimmer* 76, 78; *the Lake* 118. See *Nenuial*.

Evendim, Lake (XII) In Arnor. 313. See Nenuial.

Evening Star (II) 267–8

Evening Star (IV) Eärendel bearing the Silmaril. 72, 154, 196, 201

Evening Star (VII) 252; *Eärendil the Evening Star* 266

Evening Star (X) 371

Evenstar (IXa) 66–7. See *Arwen*.

Evereven (VII) 93, 98, 101, 292, *Evereve* 284; *Evermorning* 91, 94, 97, *Evermorn* 93, 98; *Evernight* 93, 97, 99–100; *Evernoon* 93, 96, 99

Evermind (VIII) Flower that grew on the Mounds of Edoras. 407, 424. See *simbelmynë*.

Evermind (IXa) Flower that grew on the Mounds of Edoras. 62

Everwhite (X) Taniquetil. 67. See *Oiolossë*.

Evranin (II) The nurse of Elwing. 241

Evromord (I) Door-ward of Mar Vanwa Tyaliéva (apparently intended to replace Rúmil). 107

Exeter Book (II) (of Old English poetry) 323

Exeter College, Oxford (II) 47, 199, 273, 277, 329

Exeter College, Oxford (IV) 214

Exile, The (VII) (of the Noldor) 453–5

Exile, The (XII) (of the Noldor) 185, 337–9, 342–4, 348, 360; Exilic 332

Exiled Elves (VIII) See *Elves*.

Exiles (V) (Exiled Noldor in Middle-earth) 24, 64, 190, 346; *Exilic Noldorin*, see *Noldorin*.

Exiles (IXb) (of Númenor) 338, 353, 375, 393–6, 407, 411, 415. *Exilic* 414–15, 419, 430, 432

Exiles, The (X) The Noldor in Middle-earth. 65, 92, 115, 373; *Exiled Noldor* 263, 305; *the Exile* 103, 340

Exiles, The (XI) The Noldor in Middle-earth. 21, 23, 25–6, 32–3, 44, 176, 328, 374, 379–81, 384, 387–8, 403; *Exiled Noldor* 364, 374, 377, 379–80, 384–5 (see *Etyañgoldi*, *Gódhel*, *Ódhel*); *the Exile* 19, 21, 372–4, 386, 398, 404, 411; *Exilic (Quenya)* 384–5, 390, 396, 400

Exiles, The (XII) (also Exiled Noldor) 20, 30–1, 36, 62, 65, 73, 78, 146, 173, 331, 336, 339, 344–6, 360, 376, 379–80, 392, 400–1. Exiles of Númenor 158, 312

Eye of Morgoth (X) 419

Eye, The (VI) The Eye of Sauron. 381–2

Eye, The (VII) (in the Dark Tower) 208, 212, 254, 260, 327, 330, 343–4, 346, 366, 373, 396

Eye, The (VIII) (in the Dark Tower) 104–5, 109, 189; *Orcs of the Eye* 105

Eye, The (IXa) (in the Dark Tower) 5–6, 8, 11, 22, 31, 38; see especially 38.

Ezellohar (III) The Green Mound of the Two Trees in Valinor. 348, 350

Ezellohar (X) The Mound of the Two Trees. 69, 106, 127. See *Green Mound*, *Corolairë*.

Ezellohar (XI) The Green Mound of the Trees (Valarin name). 341, 399, 401. See *Korollairë*.

Ezellohar (XII) The Green Mound of the Trees in Valinor. 356; the plain of Ezellohar 334, 357

Fading Ilkorin (V) 189–90. *Fading Leikvian* 189. *Fading Noldorin* 189–90

Fading of the Elves (X) See *Elves*.

Fading Years (XII) The Third Age. 227

Faelivrin (II) Name given to Finduilas, daughter of Orodreth of Nargothrond. 124. See *Failivrin*, *Finduilas*.

Faërie (IXb) 170; *Faërian Drama* 216. *Fairyland* 170; *fairy-stories*, *fairy-tales* 164, 170, 193

Faërie (X) 271

Faërie, Faëry (IV) See *Bay of Faërie*.

Faëry (I) 129; *Faery Realms* 33, 36, 39. See *Bay of Faëry*.

Faëry, Faërië (II) 321; *Bay of Faëry* 260, 313, 316, 324–5; *Lamp of Faëry* (the Silmaril) 238; *shores of Faëry* 271–2; The *Shores of Faëry* (poem) 271–3, prose preface 262, 265

Faëry, Faërie (III) 16, 20, 28–32, 50, 58, 72, 93, 116, 134; *Gulf of Faërie* 17, 118, 148; *Bay of Faëry* 95; *Faëry land* 156, 268, *Fairyland* 233. The *Shores of Faëry* (poem) 182

Fafnir (II) The dragon slain by Sigurd. 125

Faiglindra (II) See *Airin*.

Failivrin (II) Daughter of Galweg of the Rodothlim. 82–7, 102, 124–5, 138. See *Faelivrin*.

Failivrin (III) Name given to Finduilas daughter of Orodreth of Nargothrond. 76, 78, 80–1, 91–2; later form *Faelivrin* 91

Failivrin (IV) Name given to Finduilas. 60, 125, 184, 213; O.E. *Fealuléome* 213

Fair Elves (X) The Vanyar (replacing *High Elves*) 168, 180; *Fair Folk* 164

Fair Folk (VI) The Elves. 60; cf. 285

Fair Folk (VIII) The Elves. 405

Fair-elves (IV) A name of the First Kindred of the Elves. 89

Fair-elves (V) The First Kindred of the Elves. 218; *the Fair Folk*, a name of the Lindar, 215. See *Írimor*, *Vanimor*.

Fair-elves (XI) The Vanyar. 246

Fairfax (VI) ('Fair-mane'), suggested name for Gandalf's horse. 351

Fairies (I) 19, 22–3, 25–6, 32, 34–6, 51, 59, 110, 166, 175, 192, 196, 212, 228, 230, 232, 235, 237, 244; *lost fairies* 231, 235; *false-fairies*, see *Kaukareldar*; *fairy speech* 13, 51.

Fairies (II) Synonymous with *Elves*. 10, 23–4, 26, 28, 31, 35, 41, 113,

223, 240, 242, 249, 252, 257, 261, 264, 270, 274, and very frequently in Chapter VI; distinguished from Gnomes 113

Fairies (III) 54, 156; *fairy* (adjective) 108, 122. See *Faëry*.

Fairies (IV) 50, 199, 274. *Fairyland* 88–9, 95, 155

Fairyland (I) 110

Fairyland (II) 316

Faithful Men, Faithless Men (V) In Middle-earth in the Second Age. 11

Faithful Stone, The (XII) A tale of the Drúedain. 309–10.

Faithful, The (V) Númenóreans not estranged from the Valar and Eldar. 75

Faithful, The (IXb) In Númenor. 346–7, 356, 367, 370, 382, 390, 392, 401; cf. also 335, 348–9, 365, 369, 399, and see *Avaltiri. Faithful Houses of Men (Eruhildi)* 402

Faithful, The (X) (of Númenor) 402

Faithful, The (XII) (of Númenor) 160, 162, 176, 182, 257, 312, 315. See *Elendili, Elf-friends*.

Falarombar (X) The horns of Ulmo. 202. (Replaced by *Ulumari*.)

Falas (I) 134

Falas (IV) 60, 121, 182, 191, 227, 229, 257, 330, 334; *Falassë* *249, 257, 334; *Western Shore* 330; Havens of the Falas 169, 227, 278, 324, 335. See *Brithombar, Eglorest, Eldorest, Western Havens*.

Falas (V) The coasts of Beleriand. 128, 146, 170, 183, 195, 222, 253, 261, 267, 269–70, 308, 381; *Falassë* 56, 171, 174, 184, 381; translated 'Western Shore' 128, 'Coast' 261

Falas (VII) 103; =*Harfalas* 124

Falas (X) The coasts of Beleriand. 90, 175; *Falassë* 90. See *Havens*.

Falas (XI) The coasts of Beleriand. 8, 12, 15–16, 72, 80, 84, 89, 107, 117, 166, 189, 192, 197–8, 242, 418. See *Forfalas, Harfalas*.

Falas, Havens of the (XII) (329), 349

Falasquil (II) Tuor's dwelling in a cove of the sea-coast. 152, 202, 204–5, 217, 253–6, 260–1, 263–4, 276

Falasquil (IV) Tuor's dwelling in a cove of the sea-coast. 69

Falasquil (XI) Bay in the Firth of Drengist. 181, *182, 344

Falassë Númëa (I) 'Western Surf', on the shores of Tol Eressëa. 124

Falassian (V) (language) 175, 178

Falastur (XII) Name taken by Tarannon, twelfth King of Gondor. 197–8, 213

Falathar (IV) Companion of Eärendel. 197

Falathar (V) One of the companions of Eärendel on his voyages. 324, (381)

Falathren (XII) 'Shore-language': see *Common Speech*.

Falathrim (XI) Elves of the Falas. 378

Falathrim (XII) Elves of the Falas. 386, 392. See *Eglain*, *Falmani* (2).

Falborn (VIII) (1) Precursor of Faramir. 136–7, 140, 145–9, 164–5, 170; becomes Boromir's brother 147. (2) Precursor of Anborn (2). 169

Fall of Men (IXb) (called also *the First Fall*) 397–8, 401–3, 405, 408, 411; references to '*the Second Fall*' 344, 363, 388, 397, 403, 405, 408. *Fall of the Elves* 410–11

Fall of Númenor (X) (title) 5–6, 22, 179

Fall, The (X) (of Men) 270, 328, 333, 344–5, 351, 354–6, 360, 378, 423; legend of the Fall (*Tale of Adanel*) 345–9; (of the Elves) 267, 355; (of the Angels) 270, 355; (in general sense) 270, 355; *fallen world* 372

Fallohides (VI) 124, 294

Fallowhides (XII) 10, 15, 37, 40, 47, 54, 56–9, 66, 229–30, 328; *Fallowhides* 248; *Fallohidish* 57

Falls of Gelion (XI) See *Gelion*.

Falls of Rhain, Falls of Rosfein (VII) See *Rhain Hills*, *Rosfein*.

Falmani (XII) (1) The Teleri of Valinor, *Sea-elves*. 392. (2) Elves of the Falas. 386, 392

Falman-Ossë (I) See *Ossë*.

Falmari (X) A name of the Teleri of Valinor. 163. (Replaced *Soloneldi*.)

Falmarindi (V) 'Foam-riders', a name of the Teleri. *381*, 403–4. See *Foam-riders*.

Falmaríni (I) Spirits of the sea-foam. 66

Falmaríni (II) Spirits of the sea-foam. 276

Fang (VI) One of Farmer Maggot's dogs. 290, 293

Fangli (I) Earlier name of Fankil. 236–7. See *Fúkil*.

Fangluin (II) 'Bluebeard', Dwarf of Nogrod. 229–30

Fangorn (Forest) (VIII) 3–4, 30, 53, 55, 59, 166, 262, 310, 339, 345, 420. See *Entwood*.

Fangorn (VII) (1) Treebeard. 71–2, 390, 412, 428. (2) Fangorn Forest (including references to *the Forest*) 10, 16, 111, 148, 167, 210, 214, 216, 250, 268–9, 282, 288, 293, 330, 347, 369, 389, 391, 394, 396, 401–4, 406, 408–9, 414–15, 417–18, 425, 427–30, 432, 438–9. Called *the Topless Forest* 167, 210, 216; and see *East End*, *Entmark*, *Entwood*. Moving trees 418–19, 435–6

Fangorn (IXa) (1) Treebeard. 71. (2) Fangorn Forest. 63, 105, 123

Fangorn Forest (VI) (including references to *the Forest*) 189, 363, 367,

381–2, 397, 399, 401, 409–1l, 419, 434, 436. 438, 440, 464. See *Neldoreth* (2).

Fangros (III) Unidentified place. 31, 49, 55; earlier form *Fangair* 49, 55.

Fangros (IV) Unknown place. 9–10; earlier form *Fangair* 9

Faniel (X) Daughter of Finwë and Indis. 207, 238, 262, 265

Faniel (XII) Daughter of Finwë and Indis. 359

Fankil (I) Servant of Melko. 107, 237. (Replaced *Fangli/Fúkil*.)

Fantur (I) (Plural *Fánturi*.) The Valar Vefántur Mandos and Lórien Olofántur. 79, 89, 101; later form *Fëanturi* 79–80

Fanturi (IV) Mandos (*Nefantur*) and Lórien (*Olofantur*). 78–9, 207; later form *Fëanturi* 275

Fanturi (V) Mandos (*Nurufantur*) and Lórien (*Olofantur*). 120, 205, 208, 387, 389, 395 (also Noldorin *Fannor*, plural *Fennir*); later form *Fëanturi* 207

Fanturi (X) See *Fëanturi*.

Fanuidhol (VII) Cloudyhead. 174; *Fanuidol* 306. Earlier name *Fanuiras (the Grey)* 174, 306

Fanuidhol (IXa) One of the Mountains of Mona. 70. Earlier name *Fanuiras* 70, 72

Fanuin (I) 'Year', child of Aluin 'Time'. 217–19, 222, 227. (Replaced *Lathos, Lathweg*.)

Fanyamar (IV) 'Cloudhome', upper region of Vista. 236, 241, *243, 253

Far Downs (VI) 107

Far Downs (IXa) 109

Far Downs (XII) 17, 112

Far Harad (VIII) See *Harad*.

Faragon (VIII) Father of Mardil the Steward. 281, 288. (Replaced by *Orondil*.)

Faramir (VII) 440

Faramir (VIII) 45, 132, 136–7, 140–2, 144, 147–76 *passim*, 179, 182, 187, 197, 207, 209, 226, 231–4, 255, 260, 262–3, 271, 274, 281, 283, 291, 294–5, 323–4, 326–42, 354, 360, 374–7, 379–81, 385, 387, 390, 403; the name 160, 169; *the captain of the guard* 377

Faramir (IXa) 7, 22, 52, 54–9, 62–3, 123; *Prince of Ithilien* 61, 70; *Steward of Gondor* 55, 70

Faramir (IXb) 217

Faramir (XI) =Gelmir (2), companion of Arminas. 299

Faramir (XII) (1) Son of Ondohir King of Gondor. 201, 215, 232. (2)

Son of Denethor II; Prince of Ithilien. 16, 43, 63–5, 67–8, 73, 181, 206–7, 220–1, 223, 240, 244, 246, 295, 312, 411; *the Prince* 421

Farang, Faranc (XI) See *Avranc.*

Faraway (VI) Fictitious home of Bingo/Frodo Baggins. 280, 324, 334

Faraway (VII) See *Hill of Faraway.*

Farewell Party (VI) See *Party.*

Farewell! farewell, now hearth and hall! (VI) 300–1, 326

Farin (XII) Father of Fundin father of Balin. 279

Faring Forth (I) 17, 19, 25–7, 97–8

Faring Forth (II) (1) The March of the Elves of Kôr. 302–4, 307–8. (2) The expedition from Tol Eressëa. 255, 276, 283–7, 289, 293–4, 301, 303, 305, 307–8

Faring Forth (IV) 70, 74

Farmer Giles of Ham (VI) 131

Farmer Giles of Ham (IXa) 12

Farrer, Katherine (X) 5–6, 39

Farthings (VI) 278; *Four Farthings* 298, 313; *Four Quarters* 380

Farthings (XII) 17, 112; the word 45, 58; *East Farthing* 10, 56–7, 122, 129, *East-farthingers* 122; *North Farthing* 9, 115, 236

Faskalan, Faskala-númen (II) 'Bath of the Setting Sun'. 138. See *Fauri, Fôs'Almir, Tanyasalpë.*

Faskala-ntimen (I) 'Bath of the Setting Sun'. 187; *Faskalan* 187, 192, 215. See *Tanyasalpë.*

Fastred (VIII) Rider of Rohan. 371

Fastred (XII) (1) Son of King Folcwine of Rohan. 206, 238, 274; earlier name *Folcwalda* 271, 274. (2) See *Fengel.*

Father Christmas Letters (VII) 349

Father(s) of Men (IV) 298, 301, 311, 317; *the three Houses of the Fathers of Men* 163, 202

Father(s) of Men (V) 11, 13–14, 18–19, 64, 73, 125, 129–31, 136, 149, 245, 274, 280, 289, 328, 336, 403; see especially 149, 274–5

Father(s) of Men (XI) 39, 52, 75, 166, 174, 227, 229, 236, 241, 345; ~ *of (the) Men of the West* 48, 206, 232. See *Atanatári.*

Fathers of Men (VI) 182

Fathers of Men (VIII) 155, 159, 161–2; *Fathers of the Three Houses* 159, 162; *Fathers of the Númenóreans* 158

Fathers of Men (IXb) 333, 341, 354, 358, 411; cf. also 359–60, 363–5, 369

Fathers of Men (X) 7, 373. See *Atanatárion.*

Fathers of Men (XII) 23, 31–2, 34, 39, 54–5, 62, 64–5, 168, 173, 324;
    Fathers of the Three Houses 63–4; *the Fathers* 77. See *Atanatári*.
Fathers of the Dwarves (XI) 204, 207–8, 210–11, 213
Fauglith (V) See *Dor-na-Fauglith*.
Fauglith (XI) See *Dor-na-Fauglith*.
Fauri (II) Earlier name of *Fôs'Almir*. 138
Fay(s) (I) 94, 108, 120, 132, 215, 232, 234, 236–7, 239
Fay(s) (II) 10, 13, 29, 32,43, 54,64, 71, 76–7, 96, 233, 263, 274
fëa (XII) The indwelling spirit of an incarnate being. 333–5, 352, 380,
    391
Fëanonian (XII) (alphabet, script) 40–1, 76, 82, 297–8, 319. *Fëanoni-*
    ans 366, 388
Fëanor (I) 128, 138, 141, 145–6, 149–51, 155–60, 162, 165, 168–9,
    171, 173, 175, 181, 192, 198, 238, 240–3; *Sons of Fëanor* 192,
    197, 238–43; Oath of Fëanor or of his sons 171, 238, 240, 243
Fëanor (II) 13, 129, 137, 204, 216, 228, 240–1, 259, 321; *Lamp of*
    Fëanor (the Silmaril) 238. See *Sons of Fëanor*.
Fëanor (III) 87, 133, 135–9, 146–7, 192, 195, 198, 210–11, 217, 222,
    242, 267, 302–3, 329; son of Finn 133, 138; *Fëanor's fire, fire of*
    Fëanor (the Silmaril) 267, 362. See *Sons of Fëanor, Oath of the*
    Fëanorians.
Fëanor (IV) Called 'the Smith'. (*Sons of Fëanor* have a separate entry.)
    6–9, 14–16, 18–19, 22, 39, 46–9, 52, 87, 90–6, 101, 151, 158,
    161, 165, 169–70, 172, 176, 205, 212, 265–9, 271, 273–4, 277,
    280, 282–3, 287–8, 295, 327–8, 333, 338; O.E. *Finbrós*
    Gimwyrhta 212, but in the texts called *Féanor* (*se smiþ*); *House*
    of Fëanor 125, 183, 265, 267, 269, 277, 279, 298, 301, 318 (see
    Dispossessed). *Fëanorians* 48, 54, 56–7, 64, 69, 170, 174, 188,
    190, 194–5, 274, 279–80, 289, 314, 321, 325, 327, 333, 337;
    Fëanorian letter 174. See *Oath of the Fëanorians, Sons of Fëanor*.
Fëanor (V) Called 'the Smith' (113). 29, 31, 33, 113–17, 122, 125,
    173–4, 177, 193, 202, 223, 225, 227–30, 232–9, 246, 248–9,
    253, 255–6, 319, 330, 333, 336, 374, 381; *House of Fëanor* 113,
    115, 118, 132, 135, 229, 235, 237, 250, 252; *folk of Fëanor* 116,
    128, 236, 238, 264, 283, 308; *Fëanáro* 226, 381. See *Dispossessed*;
    Sons of Fëanor.
Fëanor (VI) 215–16, 466
Fëanor (VII) 125, 255–6, 260, 453. Son(s) of Fëanor 63, 102; House
    of 180; Alphabet of 453; Rings of 255–6. *Fëanorians* 102, 104
Fëanor (VIII) 76, 372; *Sons of Fëanor* 161, 169; *Fëanorians* 297

Fëanor (X) 48, 65, 87, 90–2, 94–129 *passim*, 135, 151, 177, 179, 185–95, 197, 205, 210, 217, 230, 236, 240–1, 247(-8), 253, 257–8, 260–3, 267–8, (269), 272–80, 282, 287, 290, 293–6, 310, 370; *Fëanáro* 'Spirit-of-Fire' 206–7, 217, 236–41, 243, 249, 252, 257, 263; *Faenor* (Sindarin) 217; *House of Fëanor* 114, 117–18, 189, 196. See *Curufinwë*, *Finwë* (2), *Finwion*, *Minyon*; *Sons of Fëanor*.

Fëanor (XI) (including references to his house, people, host, etc.) 14, 16–22, 24–5, 27, 31–3, 38, 41–3, 45, 47, 54, 65–6, 69–70, 77, 108, 113–15, 119, 176–7, *183, 206, 215, 218, 247, 327, 329, 359, 379, 381, 384, 396, 398, 400, 405, 417, 419; his alphabetic system 396, *Fëanorian letters* 396. See *Sons of Fëanor*.

Fëanor (XII) 30, 256, 317(-18)-19, 331–9, 342–5, 352–9, 361, 363, 368–9, 379, 388–9; *alphabet of* ~ 22. Other names and forms *Fëanáro* 333, 343, 356, *Fayanáro* 343, *Faenor* 343, 359; *Finwë* 359, 365, *Finwë minya* 343, *Finwion* 359, *Minyon* 359; *Kurufinwë* (*Curufinwë*) 343, 352, 359, 365. See *Sons of Fëanor*.

Fëanorians (I) 158, 173, 242–3

Fëanorians (II) 246, 250–1, 265

Fëanorians (III) 235, 247, 272

Fëanorian(s) (V) 239, 269. See *Oath of the Fëanorians*.

Fëanorians (X) 126, 182, 196; *Fëanorian* (of letters) 350; Oath of the Fëanorians 112, 114, 117–18, 125

Fëanorians (XI) 19, 115, 132, 134, 137, 232, 334. Oath of the Fëanorians 18–19, 29, 34, 41, 62, 65–6, 69, 176, 351–2, 354

Fëanturi (I) See *Fantur*.

Fëanturi (IV) See *Fanturi*.

Fëanturi (X) Mandos (Námo) and Lórien (Irmo). 145, 148, 203–4; earlier form *Fanturi* 145

Feast after the final victory (VII) 212, 345, 448

Feast at Edoras (VIII) 45, 48, 58, 72; *at Dunharrow* 236, 240, 242, 247–8; the Feast-hall of Dunharrow 236, 240, 242–4, 248, 250, 259

Feast at Minas Tirith (VIII) 275, 397, 405

Feast of Reunion (I) 240, 243. *Feast of Reuniting*, see *Mereth Aderthad*.

Feast of Reuniting (IV) 296, 314, 328, 333; earlier *Feast of Reunion* 53, 175, *Feast of Meeting* 104, 175, 314. See *Mereth Aderthad*.

Feast of Reuniting (V) 126, 190, 253. See *Mereth Aderthad*.

Feast of Reuniting (XI) 34, 114. See *Mereth Aderthad*.

Feiniel (XI) 'White Lady' (318), Turgon's sister, wife of Eöl. 3 18–19; *Ar-Feiniel* 3 17–18, 322. See *Isfin*, *Írith*, *Aredhel*.

Feir (XI), plurals *Fîr*, *Firiath* Sindarin, =Quenya *Firya(r)* 'Mortal(s)'. 219, 387

Felagoth (III) Earlier form for *Felagund*. 169, 171, 195, 221

Felagoth (IV) Earlier name of Felagund. 15, 19, 23–6, 46, 55–6

Felagund (II) 53–6, 123–4, 126; 'Lord of Caves' 123. See *Finrod*.

Felagund (III) 80, 85, 91, 138, 166, 169, 171, 191, 195, 198, 213–19, 221–3, 225–6, 229–31, 233–4, 240–2, 245–50, 255–8, 260, 270–1, 274, 279, 310–11, 313, 350–1, 357–8; *Inglor Felagund* 335, 350, 360; (later name) *Finrod Felagund* 93, 360. See *Finrod* (2), *Inglor*.

Felagund (IV) 15, 24, 26–7, 46, 48, 54–7, 88, 95, 102–6, 108–11, 111, 116, 120, 174–5, 179–80, 213, 226–7, 229, 267, 271, 279, 295–300, 305, 314, 316, 318–19, 328–30, 332–5, 338–9, 341; *King of Narog* 330. See *Felagoth*, *Finrod* (2), *Ingoldo*, *Inglor*.

Felagund (V) 'Lord of Caves' (116, 223), 'Lord of Caverns' (126, etc.), surname of Inglor King of Nargothrond (see 257); used alone or together with Inglor. 18, 29, 33–4, 116, 123, 126, 128, 130, 132–4, 140, 146–7, 150–1, 177, 223, 226, 239, 254, 257, 261, 266–7, 269, 274–6, 279, 281–3, 288, 290, 292–3, 296–7, 299–300, 366, 381; *Finrod* (2) *Felagund* 299; speech of his people 177. See *Inglor*.

Felagund (VI) See *Finrod* (2), *Inglor*.

Felagund (VII) See *Finrod* (2).

Felagund (X) 'Lord of Caves' 177; see *Inglor*, *Finrod* (2).

Felagund (XI) King of Nargothrond; name used alone or with *Inglor*, *Finrod* (2). 35, 38, 44, 48–9, 52, 59, 62–3, 65–7, 88, 94, 116–17, 120, 123–4, 129–31, 135, 147, 149, 178–9, *183–4, 197, 215–19, 223, 225–9, 238, 242–3, 255, 323, 355, 418, 420; said to be a Dwarvish name 179; as father of Gilgalad, see *Gilgalad*; his wife 44, 242; his ring 52, 59, 65, 242; *the Doors of Felagund* 84, 86, 143, 149. *Lord of Caves* 35, ~ *Caverns* 178

Felagund (XII) Name used alone or with Finrod: see *Finrod* (2). Origin of the name 351–2; *Felagon* 352

Felaróf (VII) Eorl's horse. 443

Felaróf (XII) The horse of Eorl the Young. 274

Felegron (IV) A name for Bruithwir; also *Felëor*. 9

Fell Captain, Fell Riders (VIII) See *Black Captain, Black Riders*.

Fell Folk of the East (XII) (in the tale of Tal-elmar) 424, 427

Fell Winter (VII) 54, 169

Fell Winter (XII) (Third Age 2911) 238

Fell Winter, The (II) 126, 205, 208

Fell Winter, The (XI) The winter of the year 495, after the fall of Nargothrond. 88, 93, 256, 261

Fell Year, The (XI) The year (455) of the Battle of Sudden Flame. 52, 125

Fellowes (VI) Assumed name of Odo and Frodo Took at Bree. 141

Fellowship of the Ring (VII) 398, 409

Fellowship of the Ring, The (II) 214, 327. See also *Lord of the Rings*.

Fellowship of the Ring, The (X) (title) 76

Fellowship, Breaking of the (VII) 214, 339

Fellowship, The (VIII) See *Company (of the Ring)*.

Fen of Rivil, Fen of Serech (XI) See *Rivil, Serech*.

Fengel (III) (1) Father of Tuor (replacing Peleg of the *Lost Tales*). 145, 148. (2) Tuor. 141, 145. (3) Fifteenth King of Rohan. 145

Fengel (IV) (1) Great-grandfather of Tuor in an early text. 4–5. (2) Father of Tuor. 5. (3) Tuor. 5. See *Fingolfin*.

Fengel (VIII) (1) Substituted for *Thengel*, father of Théoden. 355. (2) Father of Thengel; fifteenth King of the Mark. 408

Fengel (XII) Fifteenth King of Rohan. 270–1, 273–4; ephemeral names *Fastred, Felanath* (XII) 274

Fenmanch (XII) Region of Rohan. 53

Fenmarch (VIII) Region of Rohan west of the Mering Stream. 349, 356

Fenn Fornen (VIII) The Closed Door (q.v.). 338; *Fenn Forn, Fenn Uiforn* 341. (In RK *Fen Hollen*.)

Ferney, Bill (VII) 42, 45–6, 48, 52, 71, 173, 448; his pony, called *Bill*, 9, 165, 171, 173, 180, 448, called *Ferny* 173

Ferny (VI) Family name in Bree. 137; cf. 141

Ferny, Bill (VI) (139), 142, 153, 158, 162, 164–6, 175–6, 191, 350, 353–4; spelt *Ferney* 334, 342, 350, 354, 359; his pony 164, 175, 191, 354, 359, 432

Ferny, Bill (VIII) 219 (his pony).

Ferny, Bill (IXa) 80, 88–9

Field of Arbol (IXb) See *Arbol*.

Field of the Worm, Field of Burning (XI) At Cabed Naeramarth. 295

Fiery Mountain (VI) 82–3, 85, 126, 189, 214, a18, 265, 323, 380–2, 397, 402, 406–7, 409, 421; *Fiery Hill* 215 *Fire Mountain* 411; *the Fire* 402, 405; *the Mountain Red* 301; eruption of the mountain 380–1

Fiery Mountain (VII) 6, 213, (250), 328, 339, 343; *Fire Mountain* 28, 207–8, 210–11, 339; *Mountain of Fire* 212, 247, 262, 343; *the*

Mountain 216; *Hill of Fire* 373; *the Fire* 153–4, 212. See *Orodruin*.

Fiery Mountain (IXa) 3; *the Mountain* 3–7, 11, 33, 37–9; *the Secret Fire* 3. See *Mount Doom, Orodruin*.

Fifth Battle of Beleriand (XI) 71, 133. See *Battle of Unnumbered Tears* (formerly the Fourth Battle).

Filey, Yorkshire (III) 150, 181

Fili (XII) Companion of Thorin Oakenshield. 277, 285

Finarfin (I) 44, 171, 173, 223

Finarfin (II) 123

Finarfin (III) 198, 357–60. (Replaced *Finrod* (1)).

Finarfin (IV) Later name of Finrod (1) son of Finwë. 48, 170, 174, 185, 196, 213, 262, 279

Finarfin (V) Later name of Finrod (1) son of Finwë. 299–300, 334

Finarfin (VI) 72, 188

Finarfin (VII) 263

Finarfin (X) 103, 197, (207), 262, 276, 278, 282, 305, 350; *Finarphin* 103–4, 128, 177, 181–2, 197, 262, 265, 276, 282, 305, 350; *House of Finarphin* 311. (Replaced *Finrod* (1).) See *Arafinwë, Ingalaurë, Finrod* (1).

Finarfin (XI) Later name of Finrod (1), son of Finwë. 115, 130, 142, 179, 188, 197, 226, 240, 243, 319, 343, 383; *Finarphin* 179, 246

Finarfin (XII) 77, 317 (Finarphin), 336–8, 344, 346–7, 349, 351, 360, 363, 365, 389; *Nothrim, Nost* - the house of Finarfin 360. Other names *Arafinwë* 344, 360, *Arfin* 344; *Ingoldo* 360, *Ingalaurë* 360. See *Finrod* (1).

Finbor (XII) Son of Fingon (rejected). 361

Findaráto (XII) See *Finrod* (2). *Findekáno* See *Fingon*.

Findis (X) Daughter of Finwë and Indis. 207, 238, 262, 265

Findis (XII) Daughter of Finwë and Indis. 343, 359

Findobar (V) Son of Fingon. 372, *381* (*Findabar*), 403

Findor (IV) Name replacing Flinding; replaced by *Gwindor*. 312, 321

Findor (XI) See *Gilgalad*.

Findóriel (III) Earlier name for Finduilas. 81

Finduilas (II) 124–5; *Mound of Finduilas* 127, 130. See *Faelivrin, Haudh-en-Elleth*.

Finduilas (III) Daughter of Orodreth of Nargothrond. 65, 70, 75–8, 80–1, 83, 91–3. See *Failivrin*.

Finduilas (IV) Daughter of Orodreth. 29–30, 60, 125–7, 131, 184–5, 213, 304–5, 323; O.E. *Friþuswiþ* 213. See *Failivrin*.

Finduilas (V) Daughter of Orodreth. 139

Finduilas (VII) See *Galadriel*.

Finduilas (VIII) (1) Daughter of Orodreth King of Nargothrond. 372. (2) Daughter of Elrond (precursor of Arwen). 370, 386, 394, 425. (3) *Finduilas of Dol Ammoth*, wife of Denethor. 340

Finduilas (IXa) (1) Daughter of Elrond (precursor of Arwen). 52, 58–9, 61, 63, 66; called *Half-elven* 58. Other transient names before *Arwen: Amareth, Ellonel, Emrahil*.

Finduilas (IXa) (2) of Dol Amroth, wife of Denethor. 55, 59. Earlier names *Emmeril, Rothinel*.

Finduilas (XI) Daughter of Orodreth King of Nargothrond. 83–5, 87–9, 91–2, 95, 101, 138–43, 147–8, 160, 180, 256–7, 299

Finduilas (XII) (1) of Nargothrond. 350–1. (2) Earlier name of Arwen. 226, 247. (3) of Dol Amroth, wife of Denethor II. 36, 206, 220–1, 240

Finellach (XII) See *Gil-galad*.

Finglas (VII) Ent ('Leaflock'). 412

Fingolfin (I) 87, 132, 156, 173, 243

Fingolfin (III) 21, 24, 86, 96, 98, 102, 136–8, 140, 145–7, 152, 222, 275, 284–7, 290, 293–4; Fingolfin's cairn 286–7. See *Golfin*.

Fingolfin (IV) (including references to his sons, house, people) 8–9, 14–19, 23–4, 27, 34, 46, 48, 52–4, 57, 65–6, 88, 90–1, 94–7, 102–3, 105–7, 112, 119, 122, 136–7, 139–40, 170, 176, 178, 182, 213, 265–9, 271, 273–4, 279–80, 287, 294–9, 314, 316–18, 328–30, 332–4, 336–40; *King of Hithlum* 330, *Lord of the Falas* 330, 334; the cairn of Fingolfin 35, 66, 107, 136, 139, 299, 308, *Mount of Fingolfin* 107; O.E. *Fingold Fengel* 213 (but *Fingolfin* in the texts). See *Golfin*.

Fingolfin (V) (including references to his sons, house, people) 113, 115–16, 118–19, 125–8, 130–3, 145–6, 148, 177, 189, 223, 226, 228–9, 234–9, 241, 244, 250, 252–7, 259, 264, 266–7, 270, 274, 276, 279–80, 282–5, 290, 308, 312, *381, 389* (his titles *Taur Egledhriur* 'King of the Exiles', *Aran Chithium* 'King of Hithlum'), 407; *High-king of the Noldor, King of Hithlum and Nivrost, Lord of the Falas*, etc. 145–6, 266–7, 270, 279, 285. The cairn of Fingolfin (*Sarnas Fingolfin*) 133, 142, 285, 291, 406, *mount of Fingolfin* 285; speech of his people 177, 189

Fingolfin (VI) 122

Fingolfin (IXa) 44–5

Fingolfin (X) 92, 96, 100, 102, 104–6, 112–14, 116, 118–21, 125, 131, 177, 182, 188–9, 193, 196–7, (207), 253, 262, 276–9, 282,

287, 290, 326; *Fingolphin* 265, 282, 310. See *Nolofinwë*, *Ingoldo* (1), *Finwë* (2).

Fingolfin (XI) (including references to his house and people) 17, 21, 23, 25–6, 29–34, 36, 38, 40, 43, 45–6, 49–50, 52, 54–6, 72–3, 75, 77, 114–15, 117, 121, 124–6, 134, 136, 177, *182, 195, 206, 219, 223, 227–8, 235, 243, 323, 327, 329, 343, 379; his wife *Anairë* 323

Fingolfin (XII) 336, 343–5, 348, 354, 357, 360–2, 365, 388–9; other names *Nolofinwë* 344, 360; *Anakáno* 345, 360; *Ingoldo* 360

Fingolma (I) Name of Finwë Nólemë. 238–9

Fingolma (II) Name of Finwë Nólemë. 220

Fingolma (III) Name of Finwë Nólemë. 146–7

Fingolma (IV) Name of Finwë Nólemë. 8

Fingon (I) 173, 243

Fingon (II) 216

Fingon (III) Son of Fingolfin, brother of Turgon; slain in the Battle of Unnumbered Tears. 5, 80, 86, 102–3, 137–8, 146–7, 152, 212, 219, 222, 287, 292. (Replaced *Finweg* (2)).

Fingon (IV) 9, 46, 48, 52, 57, 89, 97, 103, 108. 120–1, 169, 173, 180–2, 213, 280, 295–6, 298–303, 316, 321, 328, 330, 332–3, 336–7, 339; O.E. *Finbrand* 213, 337 (but *Fingon* 339), his son *Fingár* 213. (Replaced *Finweg*.)

Fingon (V) 126–7, 130, 132–7, 223, 226, 234, 238, 251–2, 255, 259, 264, 266, 271, 278, 282, 285, 289, 307–15, 362, 381, 403, 407; *Overlord of all the Gnomes* 266

Fingon (VIII) High King of the Noldor, slain in the Battle of Unnumbered Tears. 218, 372

Fingon (X) 113–14, 116, 118–19, 121, 125–6, 177, 182, 188, 195–6

Fingon (XI) 31, 38, 46–7, 52, 56, 59–60, 70–7, 115, 117, 122, 124, 128, 133–4, 165–8, 174, 177, *182, 243, 287, 312, 315; as father of Gilgalad, see *Gilgalad*.

Fingon (XII) 344–5, 349, 351–2, 357, 361, 388; other names *Findekáno* 345, 361, *Finicáno*, *Findicáno* 361

Finland (IXb) 159

Finn (III) Gnomish form of Finwë. 133, 137–8, 212, 222

Finn (IV) Gnomish form of *Finwë*. 13–16, 18–19, 44, 46, 85–7, 89–94, 97, 102–3, 168–9, 212; O.E. *Finningas* 'people of Finn' 212

Finn (V) =*Finwë*. 192

Finno-Ugric (IXb) 151, 159

Finntan (V) See 80, 82

Finrod (II) 246; *Finrod Felagund* 123. See *Felagund*.

Finrod (III) (1) Earlier name of Finarfin. 80, 85, 138, 191, 198, 213, 216, 218, 221–2, 247, 260, 360. (2) Later name of Inglor (Felagund). 93, 357–60

Finrod (IV) (1) Third son of Finwë; later Finarfin) 15, 19, 23, 46, 48, 50, 88, 95–7, 170, 196, 213, 262, 265, 267, 279, 287, 293. Son(s) of, house of, people of Finrod 19, 23–4, 46, 48, 88, 95–7, 103, 105–6, 111, 114, 127, 138, 169, 174, 185, 267, 269, 271, 279, 295–6, 298, 310, 316, 328–30, 339; O.E. *Finred Felanóþ* 213 (but Finrod in the texts). (2) Finrod Felagund, son of Finarfin: later name of Inglor Felagund. 174, 213, 334

Finrod (V) (1) Third son of Finwë; later Finarfin. 113, 116, 123, 194, 223, 234–5, 237, 239, 299–300, 334, *381*, *383*; son(s), house, people of Finrod 33, 116, 118, 125–7, 131, 192, 194, 223, 235, 237, 250, 264, 276, 281, 284, 299–300. (2) *Finrod Felagund*, son of Finarfin (later name of *Inglor Felagund*) 299

Finrod (VI) (1) Third son of Finwë, later *Finarfin*. 60, 71–2, 188. (2) Finrod Felagund, son of Finarfin. 72, 188; *Finrod Inglor* 188

Finrod (VII) (1) Third son of Finwë, later *Finarfin*. 123, 125. (2) *Finrod Felagund*, son of Finarfin. 263; *Felagund* 123, 125; *Inglor* 124–5

Finrod (X) (1) Earlier name of Finarfin. 92–3, 101, 103–4, 106, 112–14, 118, 121, 125–6, 128, 137, 177, 181–2, 195–7

Finrod (X) (2) Later name of *Inglor*; references include also *Finrod Felagund* and *Felagund* used alone. 104, 125, 128, 177, 181, 197, 265, 303–25, 327–30, 333–6, 342, 345, 349–54, 356–8, 365, 378, 385, 390, 393, 411–13. See *Atandil, Edennil*.

Finrod (XI) (1) Earlier name of Finarfin. (Most references are to his children or his house.) 22, 31–4, 38, 40, 42–4, 49, 52, 54, 67, 83, 115, 119, 130, 142, 178–9, 188, 197, 217, 219, 226–7, 240, 243, 319, 343. *Finrodian* (language) 22

Finrod (XI) (2) Later name of Inglor (see 65, 130); references include *Finrod Felagund*. 65, 130, 179, 197–8, 225, 240, 243, 355, 383, 406, 414; *Finrod Inglor* 130. See *Felagund*.

Finrod (XII) (1) Earlier name of Finarfin. 77, 79, 389

Finrod (XII) (2) Finrod Felagund. (References include *Finrod* and *Felagund* used alone) 77, 173–4, 185, 307–8, 317–18, 325, 336–7, 344, 346, 349–52, 358, 360, 363–4, 372–3, 389, 419; *Friend of Men* 307. Other names *Findaráto* 346–7, *Artafindë* 346, 360; *Ingoldo* 346, 360, 363. His wife 317–18, 349–50. See *Felagund*.

166

Finrod Felagund (I) 44, 173. See *Inglor*.

Finrodian (V) (speech) =*Kornoldorin*. 194–5

Finvain (X) Daughter of Finwë and Indis. 262, 265. (Replaced *Írimë*.)

Finvain (XII) Daughter of Finwë and Indis. 359

Finwë (I) Lord of the Noldoli; called also *Nólemë*, *Nólemë Finwë*, *Finwë Nólemë* (all references in (I) are collected here). 115–6, 119, 123, 132, 135, 138, 141–2, 156–7, 162–3, 167, 170–1, 173, 213, 238–41, 243, 245. See *Fingolma*, *Golfinweg*.

Finwë Nólemë (II) 200, 220; *Nólemi* 208. See *Fingolma*.

Finwë (III) The first lord of the Noldoli (Noldor), father of Fëanor, Fingolfin, and Finrod(1)/Finarfin. 24, 137–8, 146–7, 221–2; *Finwë Nólemë* 21, 86, 140, 146–7. See *Fingolma*, *Finn*, *Finweg* (1), *Gelmir*.

Finwë (IV) 8–9, 13, 19, 46–7, 85, 89, 93, 97, 103, 169, 196, 212–13, 265–6, 270–1, 277–9, 287–8; *Finwë Nólemë* 8, 48, 57. A fourth child of Finwë, O.E. *Finrún Felageómor* 213. See *Fingolma*, *Finn*.

Finwë (VI) 72, 188

Finwë (X) (1) 81–93, 96–7, 99, 101–3, 105, 108, 111, 114, 122, 125, 127, 162–3, 168, 172–3, 177, 179, 185–6, 188–90, 193, 205–9, 217, 225, 230–1, 233, 236–65 *passim*, 268–9, 271, 274, 276–80, 282–3, 287, 289, 293(-4), 298, 300, 305, (310), 326, 339, 361; *House*, *Kin of Finwë* 92, 101, 113, 125, 177, 207, 239, 261–2, 264–5; *Followers of Finwë*, a name of the Noldor, 164. See *Statute of Finwë and Míriel*.

Finwë (X) (2) Original name both of Fëanor and of Fingolfin. 230

Finwë (XI) 6–8, 21, 33–4, 41, 62, 67, 246, 327, 379, 383, 387

Finwë (XII) 77, 293, 331, 333–7, 339–40, 343–50, 359, 361, 364–5, 367, 389; his title *Noldóran* 343

Finweg (III) (1) =Finwë (Nólemë). 6, 21, 24, 86, 137–8, 146. (2) Earlier name of Fingon. 5, 71, 80, 86, 92, 96, 102–3, 111, 123, 136–8, 146, 152, 219, 222, 292

Finweg (IV) Earlier name of Fingon (also *Finnweg* 14, 16). 9, 14–16, 18, 22–4, 26–7, 46, 48, 52, 57, 88–9, 95, 97, 102–3 107–8, 116–20 169, 173, 180–1, 213, 220, 316

Finwi (V) 112–14, 122, 173–5, 180, 188, 192, 214–15, 218, 223–4, 227, 229–30, 232, 234, 251, 300, 326, 381, 398; *Father of the Noldor* 180, 226, *King of Thû* 224. *The Followers of Finwë*, a name of the Noldor, 215

Finwion (X) 'Son of Finwë', original name of Fëanor. 217

Fionwë (IV) 37, 39–40, 68, 71, 73, 149, 154, 156–65, 195–6, 200–2, 205, 293, 309–10, 326; *Fionwë Úrion* 73

Fionwë (V) 13–14, 18–19, 24, 143–4, 153, 165, 176–9, 205–8, 325–33, 336, *381*, 398, 405; *Fionwë* 11 *Úrion* 162, 165, *396*

Fionwë (VII) Son of Manwe. 198

Fionwë (IXb) Son of Manwë. 331–2

Fionwë (X) Son of Manwë. 76, 145–6, 150–1, 204, 399, 406; *Fionwë Úrion* 20, 34. See *Eönwë*.

Fionwë (XI) Son of Manwë. 6, 105, 246, 345; Herald of Manwë 417. See *Eönwë*.

Fionwë (XII) Son of Manwë. 142–3, 163, 166, 172, 185, 374–5. See *Eónwë*.

Fionwë, Fionwë-Úrion (I) Son of Manwë and Varda. 58, 62–3, 93, 101, 194, 202, 215, 219

Fionwë, Fionwë-Úrion (II) Son of Manwë and Varda. 116, 281–3

Fiord of the Mermaid (II) 254, 256, 263

Fiord of the Mermaid (IV) 69

Fire, The (VIII) 134, 362. See *Orodruin*.

Fíreb (XI), plurals *Fírib, Firebrim* (XI) Sindarin, =Quenya *Fírima(r)* 'Mortal(s)'. 387

Firebeards (XII) One of the kindreds of the Dwarves. 301, 322

Firefoot (VI) Suggested name for Gandalf's horse (see *Narothal*). 351

Fire-well, Sauron's (VII) 344; *Sauron's well of fire* 209, 349

Firiath (XI) 'Mortals', see *Feir*.

Fíriel (V) Daughter of Orontor of Númenor. 62–3, 71, 73, and see *382*

Firiel (IXb) Passing name for a son of Elendil. 401

Fíriel (X) Later name of Míriel. 250, 253

Fíriel (XI) Name given to Míriel wife of Finwë. 419

Fíriel (XII) Daughter of King Ondohir, wife of King Arvedui. 195, 201–2, 215–16, 232

Firien (VIII) Forerunner of the Dwimorberg. 251, 257, 259, 266; *Halifirien* 257, 262

Firien Wood (VIII) On the border of Rohan and Gondor (in *Unfinished Tales* p.306 called *Firienholt*). 356

Firienfeld (VIII) The field of Dunharrow. 245, 251, 266, 312–13, 322

Firienholt (VIII) The pinewood before the Door of Dunharrow. 251, 257, 266, 315, 320–1. (Replaced by *Dimholt*.)

Firienlode (VIII) The Mering Stream (?). 356

Firilanda (II) See *Airin*.

Fírima(r) (XI) 'Mortal(s)'. 387, 419; *Fírimor* 419. See *Fíreb*.

Fírimor (V) 'The Mortals', an Elvish name for Men. 63, 72 (*fírimoin*), 245, *381*

First Age (II) 66, 208–9

First Age (III) 83

First Age (VII) 263, 322, 377

First Age (VIII) 161, 372

First Age (X) 51, 58, 142, 337, 374, 394, 405, 407

First Age (XI) 342, 345–6, 349

First Age (XII) 62, 65, 78, 143, 163, 168, 172–3, 185, 187, 256, 275, 301, 304, 306, 308–10, 312, 330, 340, 357, 378–9, 381, 383, 390, 395

First Age(s) of the World (IV) 269, 273, 294, 310

First Age(s) of the World (V) 23, 118

First Age, The (IXb) 217, 287, 340; O.E. *frumaældi* 242, 287

First Battle (X) See *Battles of the Gods*.

First Battle of Beleriand (IV) The Battle-under-Stars (*Dagor-os-Giliath*). 22, 101, 172, 268, 295, 328, 336; later, the battle in which Denethor was slain, before the return of the Noldor, 278, 381

First Battle of Beleriand (V) The Battle-under-Stars. 117, 239, 249. See *Dagor-os-Giliath*.

First Battle of Beleriand (XI) 15, 111–12. (Formerly the Battle-under-Stars.)

First Clan (XI) The Vanyar. 382–3; *First Kindred* 418. See *Minyar*.

First Design, The (IV) 240

First Elves, The (XI) 421, 423

First Kindred (III) 28, 139

First Kindred (of the Elves) (IV) 44, 168–9, 196, 212, 276, 289; O.E. names 212. See *Fair-elves, High-elves, Light-elves, Lindar, Quendi, Vanyar*.

First Kindred (V) (1) The Elves. 14. (2) The First Kindred of the Elves (see *Lindar, Qendi, Vanyar*) 56, 107, 122, 180, 182–3, 197

First Kindred (VI) (of the Elves). 188

First Kindred of the Elves (XII) 356

First Map (VII) See *Maps*.

First War of the Gods (VI) 122

Firstborn, The (IV) The Elves. 163

Firstborn, The (V) The Elves. 25, 29, 63–6, 68, 72–3, 327, 332; cf. *Estanessë* 'the Firstborn' 356

Firstborn, The (IXb) The Elves. 333–4, 339

Firstborn, The (X) The Elves. 12, 18–19, 31, 33, 35, 68, 159–60, 206, 225, 270, 286, 327, 361–2, 384. *Firstcomers* 309

Firstborn, The (XI) Elves. 65, 341

Firstborn, The (XII) The Elves. 147, 150, 378

First-created, The (X) 413

Firya(r) (XI) 'Mortal(s)'. 219, 387. See *Feir*.

Fladrif (VII) Ent ('Skinbark'). 412; earlier *Fladrib* 412

Flame Imperishable, The (X) 8–9, 13, 28, 345. See *(The) Secret Fire*.

Flat World (X) 4–6, 40; *Flat Earth* 6, 370–1, 373

Flend, River (IV) Earlier name of Gelion. 135, 189, 210, 232

Flight of the Noldoli (IV) (alliterative poem) 42–4, 46–7, 166, 170; *the song of the Flight of the Gnomes*, referred to in the *Quenta*, 95, 170

Flight, The (XI) (of the Noldor) 396, 398, 417

Flinding (II) Gnome of the Rodothlim, companion of Túrin (later Gwindor of Nargothrond). 62, 78–82, 84–5, 116, 118–19, 123–4, 141–2. See *Duilin* (1), *Gwindor*.

Flinding (III) Gnome of Nargothrond, companion of Turin. 36–9, 41, 43–8, 52–60, 62–5, 67, 69–72, 74, 76–8, 80, 86–92, 94, 148, 306; frequently called *Flinding go-Fuilin*, i.e. Flinding son of Fuilin. (Replaced by *Gwindor*.)

Flinding (IV) Earlier name of Gwindor of Nargothrond. 28–30, 58–60, 116–17, 121, 123–6, 131, 180, 184, 193, 220, 222, 302, 304–5, 312, 321, 325. See *Findor*.

Flinding (XI) Earlier name of Gwindor of Nargothrond. 138, 140

Flói (VI) Dwarf, companion of Balin in Moria. 467

Flói (VII) Companion of Balin in Moria. 191, 200, 204, 458

Flower of the Plain (II) Gondolin. 158, 184. See *Lothengriol*.

Fluithuin (II) An ogress, mother of Gothmog son of Melko. 216. See *Ulbandi*.

Flying ships (V) (of the Númenóreans after the Downfall) 12–13, 17, 22, 76

Flymarshes (VI) First name of the Midgewater Marshes. 165–6

Foalókë (II) The dragon Glorund. 70, 91, 94–9, 103, 105–6, 108, 129, 131, 138; *lókë* 102. See *Fuithlug*.

Foalókë (III) The Dragon in the *Tale of Turambar*. 29

Foamriders (II) 'Elves of the Sea-marge'. 314

Foamriders (III) The Third Kindred of the Elves (Solosimpi of the *Lost Tales*, later the Teleri). 133, 140, 231, 235

Foamriders (IV) 9, 13, 85, 87, 94, 169, 277. See *Sea-elves, Solosimpi, Teleri.*

Foam-riders (V) A name of the Teleri. 215, 403. See *Falmarindi.*

Foam-riders (X) A name of the Teleri. 164

Foen (XI) Mountain in Dorthonion. *183, 187; *Taur-na-Foen* 'Forest of the Foen' 187

Foes of Melkor (X) A name of the Noldor. 164

Folca (VIII) Thirteenth King of the Mark. 408

Folca (XII) Thirteenth King of Rohan. 274

Folcred (XII) Son of King Folcwine of Rohan. 206, 238, 271, 274

Folcwalda (XII) See *Fastred.*

Folcwine (VIII) Fourteenth King of the Mark. 408

Folcwine (IXa) Fourteenth King of the Mark. 68

Folcwine (XII) Fourteenth King of Rohan. 206, 238, 271, 274

Folde (VIII) Region of Rohan near Edoras. 349, 356

Followers (IXb) Men. 401. See *Hildi.*

Followers (X) 12, 309, 318, 355. See *Aftercomers, Atani, Hildi.*

Followers (XI) Men. 31, 219, 386. See *Aphadon, Echil, Hildor.*

Followers of Finwë (X) See *Finwë.*

Fonstad, Karen (VI) *The Atlas of Middle-earth.* 204–5, 305

Fonthill, Funtial (VII) See *Wellinghall.*

Forannest (VIII) The north gate in the Wall of the Pelennor. 353–4, 358–9

Ford (of Rivendell) (VI) 126, 163, 170–1, 176, 190–3, 195–204, 206–7, 211–12, 219, 355, 359–61, 364–5, 368, 416–17, 440; *Ford of Bruinen* 199, 367

Ford of Bruinen (VII) See *Bruinen.*

Ford of Isen (VII) See *Isen.*

Ford(s) of Aros (XI) See *Aros.*

Fords of Isen (VIII) (including references to *the Fords*) 4–5, 10, 12, 25, 27–8, 31, 393, 46–7, 50–1, 54, 56, 60, 68–70, 72, 79, 140, 275; *Isenford* 25, 48–9, 78–9. *Battles of the Fords of Isen* 29, 47, 52; *First Battle* 22, 51, 59; *Second Battle* 4–5, 8, 23, 51. See *Isen.*

Forest of Night (II) Taurfuin, the great pine-forest on the Mountains of Night (afterwards Dorthonion, Taur-nu-Fuin). 21, 47, 62, 78. See *Taurfuin.*

Forest of Night (III) Taur-na-Fuin. 38, 55, 233–4

Forest of Night (IV) Taur-na-Fuin. 26, 180, 299

Forest of Night (V) See *Taur-na-Fuin; Forest of Pines,* see *Taur-na-Danion.*

Forest River (VI) 218

Forest River (VII) 272–3, 296

Forfain (VII) See *Calenbel*.

Forfalas (XI) *182, 186; *North Falas* *182, 186

Forgoil (VIII) 'Strawheads', name of the Rohirrim among the Dunland-
    ers. 21

Forgotten Caves (V) See *Caves of the Forgotten*.

Forgotten Men (XII) The Dead Men of Dunharrow. 267

Forhend (XI) Man of Brethil. 274–6, 303

Forlindon (XII) Lindon north of the Gulf of Lune. 313

Forlond (VII) The North Haven in the Gulf of Lune. 301, 423; earlier
    form *Forlorn* 301, 423

Forlong (VIII) (1) Name of Gandalf in the South (see *Fornold*). 153.
    (2) *Forlong the Fat*, Lord of Lossarnach. 153, 229, 262, 276, 287,
    289, 293, 371

Formen North. (IV) *244–5, *248–9, 255. (Replaced *Tormen*.)

Formenos (I) 156–9, 161

Formenos (IV) 47–8, (91), 169, 277–8

Formenos (X) Stronghold of the Fëanorians in the north of Valinor.
    96–7, 99, 105, 107–8, 122, 189, 191, 253, 268, 279–80, 282,
    287, 289–92, 294, 296, 298

Formenos (XII) Stronghold of the Fëanorians in Valinor. 361

Forn (VII) See *Tom Bombadil*.

Fornobel (VII) See *Fornost*.

Fornobel (VIII) See *Fornost*.

Fornold (VIII) Name of Gandalf in the South. 153. (Replaced *Forlong*
    (1), replaced by *Incânus*.)

Fornost (Erain) (VII) Norbury (of the Kings). 125, 304. Earlier names
    Osforod, the Northburg 120–1, 125, 129, 147, 304; *Fornobel, the
    North Burg* or *Northbury* 147, 157, 296, 304

Fornost (VIII) City on the North Downs, Norbury of the Kings. 76–
    8, 153–4, 311. The *palantír* of Fornost 76–8. Ealier name *Fornobel*
    76, 154

Fornost (XII) 5, 9, 20, 39, 186, 193–5, 208–10, 225, 228, 230, 232,
    253; *Battle of Fornost* 232. See *Norbury*.

Fornost Erain (IXa) City on the North Downs, Norbury of the Kings.
    78

Forochel (XII) 195, 232; *Bay of* ~ 32; *Snowmen of* ~ (*Lossoth*) 210,
    258

Forochel, Icebay of (VII) 301, 322; *Cape of Forochel* 301

Forod (VIII) The North. *Lord of the (Rangers of) Forod,* Aragorn, 386, 389, 394–5

Forodwaith (II) The Men of the North (Vikings). 313–14, 317–18, 323, 330, 334. (Replaced *Forwaith.*) See *Gwasgonin, Men of the North, Men of the Sea, Winged Helms.*

Forodwaith (VII) 'Northerland'. 296, 304, 306

Forontë (X) The Northern Lamp. 7, 32, 38, 60. (Replaced *Foros*; replaced by *Illuin.*)

Foros (X) The Northern Lamp. 7, 17–18, 38. (Replaced *Helkar.*)

Forsaken (People), The (X) 85, 90, 164, 169–71, 173. See *Eglath, Ekelli.*

Forsaken Inn (VI) 170

Forsaken Inn (VII) East of Bree. 296

Forwaith (II) Earlier form for *Forodwaith.* 334

Fôs Almir (XII) The Bath of Flame (I.187, II.138). 374

Fôs'Almir (II) The Bath of Flame. 115, 138. (Replaced *Fauri.*) See *Faskalan, Tanyasalpë.*

Fôs'Almir (IV) The Bath of Flame. 205

Foster, Robert (VI) *The Complete Guide to Middle-earth.* 284

Foster, Robert (VII) *The Complete Guide to Middle-earth.* 164, 288

Foster, Robert (XII) *The Complete Guide to Middle-earth.* 117, 278

Fountain, The (II) Name of one of the kindreds of the Gondothlim (*Fountain of the South* 181). 173, 180–2, 215. See *Ecthelion.*

Fountains of the South (II) In Gondolin. 186. The king's fountain in Gondolin: see *Square of the Palace.*

Four Farthings (VI) See *Farthings.*

Fourth Age (XII) 133, 172–3, 185, 202, 211, 223, 278, 304, 339, 410

Fourth Age, The (IXa) 135

Fourth Battle of Beleriand (IV) The Battle of Sudden Flame. 333, 336; see 336, and *Third Battle of Beleriand.*

Fourth Battle of Beleriand (V) The Battle of Unnumbered Tears (afterwards the Fifth Battle, 305). 136, 293, 302, 305. See *Nirnaith Arnediad, Nirnaith Dirnoth.*

Fourth Battle of Beleriand (XI) 121. See *Battle of Sudden Flame* (formerly the Third Battle).

Frána (VIII) Wormtongue. 55. See *Gríma.*

Frána (IXa) Wormtongue. 65, 73. (Replaced by *Gríma.*)

Frána Wormtongue. (VII) 445. (Replaced by *Gríma.*)

Frankish (XII) 46–7

Frankley, Philip (IXb) Member of the Notion Club. 150–1, 159–70,

172–9, 182, 185, 187–8, 191, 194–5, 197, 202–5, 211, 214, 222–30, 232–6, 242, 244–6, 250, 252–6, 259–65, 272, 277, 283, 285, 288, 295, 304, 412; called by Lowdham *Pip*, also *Horse-friend of Macedon*, *Lover of Horses*, *Horsey* (see 285); his poems 161, 172, 205, 211, 221, and *The Death of Saint Brendan* 261–5. Earlier name *Franks* (IXb) 150, 214, 295

Franks (II) 330

Franks (V) 91

Franks (IXb) 276

Frár (VI) Dwarf (son of Balin?) accompanying Glóin at Rivendell (replaced by Burin). 397–8, 412

Frár (VII) (1) Companion of Glóin at Rivendell. 204. (2) Companion of Balin in Moria. 191, 204

Fréa (VIII) Fourth King of the Mark. 408

Fréafíras (IXb) (O.E.) 'Lordly Men' (Númenóreans). 242, 286, 317; *Héafíras* 317. See *Turkildi*.

Fréalaf (VIII) Tenth King of the Mark (see *Éowyn* (1)). 408

Fréalaf (XII) Tenth King of Rohan. 237 (~ *Hildeson*), 271

Fréawine (VIII) Fifth King of the Mark. 408

Fréawine (XII) Fifth King of Rohan. 53

Free Fair, The (XII) On the White Downs. 6

Free Folk (VII) 161

Free, The (V) A name of the Teleri (cf. 169 and *Mirimor* 373). 215

Free, The (X) A name of the Teleri. 164

French (VI) 247

French (IXb) 151, 222, 286; *Anglo-French* 265; *Old French* 150, 265; *Frenche men* 245

French (XII) 52

Frenin (XII) Brother of Thorin Oakenshield. 276, 281, 287

Freyr (V) God of fruitfulness in ancient Scandinavia. 96–7

Friend of the Noldor (X) See *Aulë*.

Friends of Aulë (X) See *Aulë*; *Friends of Ossë*, see *Ossë*; *Friends of the Gods*, see *Gods*.

Frisians (II) 306. See *Firisandi*.

Frisians (V) 91

Frisians (IXb) 276

Fróði (V) Legendary King of Denmark. 96–7

Frodo (IXb) 409

Frodo (X) 365–6, 412; and see 341.

Frodo (XII) See *Baggins*.

Frodo Baggins (VII) See under *Baggins*.

Frodo Baggins (VIII) See under *Baggins*.

Frodo Baggins (IXa) See under *Baggins*.

Frodo Baggins, Frodo Took (VI) See *Baggins, Took*.

Frogmorton (IXa) Village in the Eastfarthing. 80–1, 95, 104, 106–7; earlier name *Frogbarn* 104

Frór (XII) Brother of Thrór. 276

Fruit of Noon (I) 186–7, 191, 193, 201

Fruit of Noon (IV) 49

Frumbarn (VII) See *Tom Bombadil*.

Fui (I) Death-goddess, called also *Nienna*, *Fui Nienna* (all references are collected here). 66, 76–7, 79–80, 82, 88–90, 92, 117, 144–5, 167, 189, 202, 213; *Fui* as name of her abode 77, 90. See *Heskil*, *Núri*, *Qalmë-Tári*.

Fui (II) Death-goddess (Nienna). 115

Fui (IV) 45; *Fui Nienna* 170

Fui (XII) Death-goddess (Nienna). 374

fuilas (VIII) See *galenas*.

Fuilin (III) Father of Flinding. 72–4, 92–3; *folk of, children of, Flinding* 72, 74, 80. All other references are to Fuilin as Flinding's father: 36, 38, 44, 47, 53, 56, 65, 67, 69–72, 78, 80, 89. (Replaced *Duilin*.)

Fuilin (IV) (Only referred to as the father of Flinding) 28, 116, 124–6, 131, 180, 302, 304, 312, 321. (Replaced by *Guilin*.)

Fuin Daidelos (V) 'Night of Dread's Shadow', Taur-na-Fuin. *354–5, 382*, 406. See *Gwathfuin-Daidelos*.

Fuin, Mountains of (XI) 333. See *Taur-nu-Fuin*.

Fuithlug (II) Gnomish form for *Foalókë* 70, 118; earlier forms *Fothlug, Fothlog* 118

Fuithlug (III) Gnomish form for *Foalókë*. 29

Fúkil (I) Earlier name of Fankil. 236–7. See *Fangli*.

Fumellar (I) Poppies in the gardens of Lórien. 74

Fundin (VI) Father of Balin. 444, 460. See *Burin* (2).

Fundin (VII) Father of Balin. 186, 192, 457

Fundin (XII) Father of Balin and Dwalin. 279, 281, 287, 300, 322

Furth, Charles (VI) 11, 40, 43, 108–9

Gabilān (XI) Dwarvish name, 'Great River' (see *Gevelon*). 336

Gabilgathol (V) Dwarvish name of Belegost. 274, 278

Gabilgathol (XI) Dwarvish name translated as *Belegost*. 10, 108, 201, 206, 209, 389

Gaelic (IXb) 417

Gaerys (XI) Sindarin name of Ossë. 400. See *Yssion*.

Galadhon (XI) Son of Elmo and father of Celeborn. 350

Galadlóriel (V) Gnomish name of Laurelin. 210–11, 357 (also *Galagló-riel*), 358, 368

Galadlóriel (VI) Gnomish name of Laurelin. 187; *Galagloriel* 187–8

Galadlóriel (X) (Gnomish >) Sindarin name of Laurelin. 155

Galaðon (V) Name of Oromë. 404 (and cf. 357). See *Aldaron*.

Galador (XII) First Lord of Dol Amroth. 220–2

Galadriel (I) 44

Galadriel (IV) 48, 185, 195

Galadriel (V) 299

Galadriel (VII) 218, 233, 236, 246–7, 249–50, 254–86 *passim*, 293, 331, 343, 354, 363, 366, 380, 412–13, 430–1, 433, 440, 445, 448, 451; *The Lady* (also *The Lady of Lothlórien, of the Galadrim*) 233, 236, 246, 248–50, 253–4, 256–8, 263, 266, 270–1, 274–5, 277, 279, 290, 358, 363, 368, 393, 402 (*Lady of the Wood*). Galadriel's Ring, see *Ring of Earth*; her parting gifts 268, 274–8, 280, 282–3, 293 (and see *Elfstone* (2)); her phial, or 'glass of light' 276, 331–2, 335–6, 438, 440; her songs 279, 281, 284, 286; as wife of Elrond 236. See *(The) Mirror*.

Galadriel (VII) Earlier names *Finduilas* 249, 261; *Rhien* 249–50, 261–2; *Galdrin* 262, *Galdrien* 249–50, 262, *Galadhrien* 249, *Galadrien* 249–50, 252, 367

Galadriel (VIII) 22, 148, 160, 162–3, 168–9, 210, 219, 256, 274, 296, 301, 310, 361, 386, 420 (other references under *Phial* &c. below); *The Lady, The White Lady, The Lady of Lórien, The Lady of the Golden Wood* 150, 157, 160, 163, 203, 419

Galadriel (VIII) *The Phial (star-glass, glass) of Galadriel* 184–5, 187, 189–94, 198–200, 203, 205–11, 214, 221, 223–4, 230, 267; *the Mirror* 189, 220, (263, 267); *the green stone* 389–90; Galadriel's Ring 425

Galadriel (IXa) 52–3, 58, 64, 73–4, (90), 108–9, 112, 125, 132–3; *the Lady* 32, 115–16. *The Phial of Galadriel, the Phial* 8, 13, 23–4, 32, 39, 41, 46, 67; *the box, her gift to Sam* 39, 41, 46, 52, 90, 108

Galadriel (X) 93, 104, 106, 112, 120–1, 125, 128, 135, 177, 181–2, 195–6, 211; etymology of the name 182

Galadriel (XI), *Galaðriel* (for the spellings see 116, 119) 35, 40–2, 44, 50, 64–5, 116, 119, 123, 129–30, 178, 242, 341, 383; *Concerning Galadriel and Celeborn* 352, 355

Galadriel (XII) 36–7, 74, 77, 79, 82, 174, 185, 226, 234–5, 239, 243–4, 264–6, 293, 317–18, 320–1, 331–2, 336–8, 346–9, 351, 357, 363–5, 385; her 'Lament' 299, 320, 338, 363; as daughter of Felagund and sister of Gil-galad 174, 185, 349. Other names *Alatáriel(lë)* 346–7, *Altariel* 347; *Antanis* 346–7; *Nerwen(dë)* 337, 346, 363

Galadrim (VII) 'Tree-people'. 224–5, 233–4, 236, 239, 243, 246, 256–7, 270, 272, 274–5, 279, 290, 393. Earlier name *Ornelië* ('Tree-folk') 239

Galadwen (XII) Sindarin name of Vidumavi. 260

Galathil (XI) Brother of Galadhon. 350

Galathilion (V) Gnomish name of Silpion. 209, 211, 357 (*Galathilvion*), 392

Galathilion (VI) Gnomish name of Silpion (Telperion). 187

Galathilion (IXa) The White Tree of Valinor. 58. Afterwards the Tree of Tirion, 58

Galathilion (X) (1) (Gnomish >) Sindarin name of Telperion. 90, 155, 180. (2) The White Tree of Túna (Tirion), image of Telperion. 85, 90, 155, 157, (176), 180; called *Galathilion the Less* 155, 157, 180

Galathilion (XII) Name of the White Tree (1) of Valinor 147–8; (2) of Tirion (Túna), *Galathilion the Less* 147–8; (3) of Eressëa 147–8

Galathir, Galdaran (VII) See *Keleborn*.

Galbedirs (VIII) 'Talking Trees'. 47, 50, 59. See *Lamorni, Ornómi*.

Galdaran, King (IXa) Early name of the Lord of Lothlórien. 32

Galdor (II) Lord of the people of the Tree in Gondolin; called *Galdor of the Tree*. 173–6, 181–2, 185, 189, 191–3, 215–16, 258, 278–9. See *Nos Galdon*.

Galdor (IV) Father of Húrin and Huor. 176, 320. (Replaced *Gumlin* (2).)

Galdor (V) See 77–9; 357

Galdor (VI) (1) Father of Húrin. 413. (2) Elf of Mirkwood (precursor of Legolas). 400, 413. (3) Elf of the Grey Havens. 413

Galdor (VII) (1) A lord of Gondolin. 172. (2) Elf of Mirkwood (replaced by *Legolas*). 114–16, 118, 126, 129–30, 141, 143, 148, 157, 161, 172. (3) Elf of the Grey Havens. 130

Galdor (VIII) The seneschal of Edoras. 262, 267. (Replaced *Ealdor*.)

Galdor (XI) Son of Hador and father of Húrin and Huor; called *the Tall* (234), *Galdor Orchal* (287, 305). 123, 146, 170, 224, 229, 232, 234–5, 237, 240–1, 268, 270, 275, (280), 283, 287, 305, 344. (Replaced *Galion*.)

Galdor (XII) (1) of Goldolin. 387–8. (2) of the Havens 387–8

Galdor the Tall (III) Húrin's father in the later legend (replacing *Gumlin* (2)). 126

Galdrien (VII) See *Galadriel*.

galenas (VIII) pipeweed. 396; *green galenas* 38 (with other names *fuilas, marlas, romloth*). See *westmansweed*.

Galeroc (VII) Gandalf's horse. 68, 70, 79, 132, 139, 149. See *Narothal*.

Galhir (XI) Man of Brethil. 303

Galion (XI) Earlier name of Galdor Húrin's father. 49, 51, 53, 56–8, 60–1, 71, 81, 86, 123, 126, 128, 137, 146, 170, 202, 229, 232–3, 240, 246, 268, 344. (Replaced *Gumlin*.)

Galmir (I) 'Goldgleamer', a name of the Sun (Gnomish). 187, 196

Galvorn (XI) The metal of Eöl. 322–3. For rejected names see *Rodëol, Morlîn, Targlîn, Glindûr, Maeglin*.

Galway (IXb) 261, 264, 267, 296, 299; (town) 293; *Galway Bay* 267, 293

Galweg (II) Gnome of the Rodothlim, father of Failivrin. 82, 84–5, 114, 124

Galweg (III) Father of Failivrin in the *Tale of Turambar*. 91

Gamgee (VIII) (family name) 122–3. See *Goodchild*.

Gamgee (IXa) 79

Gamgee, Andy (VIII) Sam's uncle (first called *Obadiab Gamgee*). 95

Gamgee, Bilbo (IXa) Sam's tenth child. 134

Gamgee, Daisy (IXa) Sam's eighth child, as first spelt *Daisie*. 114, 117, 120–2, 126, 128, 134. See *Arien, Eirien, Erien*.

Gamgee, Elanor (IXa) Sam's eldest child. (71), 109, 111, 114–18, 120–9, 132–5; nicknamed *Ellie*, and called by Samwise *Elanorellë*. See *elanor*.

Gamgee, Frodo (IXá) Sam's second child and eldest son. 114–18, 120–2, 126, 128; called also *Frodo-lad*, and nicknamed *Fro*. See *Iorhael*.

Gamgee, Gaffer (VI) 26–7, 30–1, 35, 38, 71, 222–3, 241, 243–4, 249, 253–4, 275, 277, 279, 315, 329–30, 372; *Ham Gamgee* 244, 394

Gamgee, Gaffer (VII) 9, 11, 29, 32, 39, 71, 135, 249, 253

Gamgee, Gaffer (VIII) 89, 95, 122; *Ham, Hamfast* 122–3

Gamgee, Halfast (VI) 254

Gamgee, Hamfast (IXa) Sam's seventh child. 114, 117, 121, 126, 128; nicknamed *Ham*. See *Baravorn, Marthanc*.

Gamgee, Merry (IXa) Sam's fourth child. 114–17, 119–21, 123, 126, 128. See *Gelir, Riben*.

Gamgee, Sam (II) 333

Gamgee, Sam (VI) 70–1, 113, 127–8, 144, 175, 190, 193, 210, 213, 221, 243–4, 249–50, 253–6, 267, 273–84 and 287–94 *passim*, 299–300, 302–3, 321–4, 326–9, 332–4, 352, 356–7, 359–62, 366–8, 371, 373, 375, 381–2, 394–5, 397–8, 400, 406–12, 417, 420–1, 423, 427–30, 432, 436, 448–9, 452–4, 456–8, 463, 465

Gamgee, Sam (VII) 6, 8, 30–1, 42, 47, 50–2, 56–9, 61, 63–4, 69, 75–6, 78–9, 82, 114, 126, 161, 163, 165, 167, 171–3, 179, 183–4, 193–5, 198, 200–1, 208–16, 218–21, 224, 226, 228, 231, 235, 237–8, 243, 248, 253–4, 260, 264–6, 269, 273–5, 279–80, 283, 286–7, 290, 313, 321, 324–57 *passim*, 363–72 *passim*, 375–6, 378, 385–7, 389, 404, 412–13, 427, 437–8, 440, 448, 451. His songs 56, 59–61, 64, 331, 333–4, 339; his uncle Andy 235

Gamgee, Sam (VIII) 50, 60, 68, 80–1, 85–106 *passim*, 109–11, 113, 115–16, 121–9, 131, 134–41, 144–6, 148–55, 158–60, 162–6, 169, 171–2, 175–8, 182–222 *passim*, 224, 226, 230, 235, 256, 271, 275, 286, 291, 294–5, 326–7, 339, 341, 386, 398; called *Samwise* 122, 127, 139, 158, 163, 211, 309. Sam's book 219, 256, 275, 386; his *Lament for Frodo* 185, 189

Gamgee, Sam (IXb) 407

Gamgee, Sam(wise) (XII) 6, 13, 25, 42–4, 48, 51, 63, 68, 87, 108, 111–16, 120, 126, 131, (242), 268–9; *Sam Gardner* 139; his true Hobbit name 51, 60, 83; *the Great Red Book of Samwise* 19

Gamgee, Samwise or *Sam* (IXa) 4–14, 18–53 *passim*, 56, 61–2, 64, 70–1, 77, 79–81, 83–6, 88–90, 92, 95–129 *passim*, 132–5; Old English *Samwís* 47. The Praise of Frodo and Sam at Kormallen 46–7, and at Edoras 62, 70–1; his song in the Tower of Kirith Ungol 27–8, 30; his sword from the Barrow-downs 25–7, 29, 32, 48, 50; his book 52; Galadriel's gift to him, see *Galadriel*. See *Lanhail, Panthael, Perhael*.

Gamgee. Gaffer (IXa) (62), 71, 77, 81, 85, 88, 99–100, 106

Gamgee. Goldilocks (IXa) Sam's sixth child. 114, 117, 121, 126, 128. See *Glorfinniel*.

Gamgee. Pippin (IXa) Sam's fifth child. 114–18, 121, 126, 128, 134. See *Cordof*.

Gamgee. Primrose (IXa) Sam's ninth child. 122, 134

Gamgee. Rose (IXa) (1) Rose Cotton, Sam's wife. 97 *(Rosie)*, 98, 108, 114, 117–19, 121–2, 125, 127–8, (132), 133, 135. (2) Sam's third child. 114–18, 121, 123, 126, 128; called also *Rosie-lass*. See *Beril, Meril.*

Gamil Zirak (II) Dwarf smith, master of Telchar of Nogrod. 129

Gamling (VIII) Rider of Rohan. 21, 24–5, 41, 256, 259, 262; *Gamling the Westmarcher* 21

Gamling the Old (XII) Man of Rohan. 65

Gamlost (V) See *Camlost.*

Gamlost (VI) 'Empty-handed'; see *Beren.*

Gamlost (XI) See *Camlost.*

Gamwich Village of the Shire. (XII) 112, 115–16

Gandalf (III) 127

Gandalf (IV) 73

Gandalf (V) 23, 337, 345. See *Mithrandir.*

Gandalf (VI) 17–22, 26–7, 31, 38, 41–3, 47–8, 55, 63, 66, 68–71, 73–4, 76–88, 101–2, 106, 109, 120, 122–3, 126, 131, 142, 149–64 and 167–78 *passim*, 185–6, 190, 194–5, 203–14, 217, 219, 221–9, 233–75 *passim*, 279, 281–4, 301–4, 314–15, 318–23, 326–8, 332; 334, 336–87 *passim*, 392–465 *passim*. Letters from Gandalf 154, 156, 158–60, 170, 172–3, 352, 355, 368; the loss of Gandalf 381, 443, 462

Gandalf (VII) 5–16, 19–44, 47–58, 61–3, 65, 68–83, 105, 110–16, 118–19, 125–7, 129–43, 146–73 *passim*, 177–207 *passim*, 210–12, 214–15, 218–19, 227, 233, 236, 244, 247–52, 257–8, 264–6, 268, 271, 278, 289, 298, 311, 329–30, 347, 361, 365–7, 369, 375, 379, (380), 382, 385, 389–90, 394, 396–7, 400–1, 403–5, 409, 411–13, 417, 422–50, 452, 456, 458

Gandalf (VII) Names in Rohan: *Gondelf* 405, *Hasupada* 402, 405, 424, *Láthspell* 444; called *the Grey* (75), 82, 133, etc. (see especially 136), *Greyhame* 405; clad in white 211, 214, 236, 250, 252, 380, 412, 430, 433, *Gandalf the White* 425, *the White Rider* 435, 437; see *Saruman, White Wizard, Mithrandir.*

Gandalf (VII) Letters from Gandalf cited 49–50, 63, 77; his tale to the Council of Elrond 130–6, 149–52 *Gandalf* (VIII) 3–6, 9, 11–12, 17–18, 22, 25–30, 35–81 *passim*, 96–7, 119–20, 126, 129–30, 138, 140–3, 145–6, 151–4, 167, 182, 213, 219, 226, 229–36, 242, 245–7, 249, 253–7, 259–60, 262–4, 270–1, 274–8, 281–4, 287–9, 291–2, 294–6, 301, 310, 320–342 *passim*, 357–62, 364, 367, 374–82, 384–7, 389–96, 400–4, 415, 420, 423–4, 427,

430–1. References to him in white or shining 229, 263, 274, 389; *the White Rider* 30, 229, 326. His other names 153; and see *Mithrandir*.

Gandalf (IXa) 3, 5, 7–8, 11, 26, 32, 45–6, 48–50, 55–9, 61–5, 68–71, 73–80, 84, 90, 92, 95–6, 102, 104, 109–12, 117, 120, 123, 132 (*'Guardian of the Third Age'*)

Gandalf (X) 135, 152, 192, 396–7, 400. See *Olórin*.

Gandalf (XII) 4, 7, 12–14, 38, 42, 57, 66, 68, 148, 157, 206, 228, 234–5, 237–8, 240–2, 251, 276, 282–3, 287–8, 299, 321, 377–8, 381, 384–5, 388. See *Mithrandir*, *Olórin*.

Gap (of Rohan) (XI) 385

Gap of Rohan (VII) 150, 168, 177, 296, 320, 432, 434, 439–40

Gap of Rohan (VIII) 3–5, 28, 42, 386

Gap of Rohan (IXa) 52, 63–4

Gar Ainion (II) 'The Place of the Gods' in Gondolin. 164, 186, 199, 202, 218; rejected form *Gar Ainon* 202. See *Place of the Gods*.

Gar Eglos (I) Original Gnomish name of Tol Eressëa (replaced by *Dor Edloth* etc.) 21

Gar Furion (II) Earlier form for *Gar Thurion*. 202

Gar Lossion (I) 'Place of Flowers', Gnomish name of Alalminórë 16, 21. (Replaced *Losgar*.)

Gar Lossion (V) Gnomish name of Alalminórë in Tol Eressëa. 148

Gar Thurion (II) 'The Secret Place', one of the Seven Names of Gondolin. 158, 202. (Replaced *Gar Furion*.)

Garathon (VIII) See *Targon*.

Gargaroth (III) See *Carcharoth*.

Garman (XII) Father of Eorl the Young. 272–3. (Replaced by *Léod*.)

Garsecg (II) (Old English) The Great Sea. 312–13, 315–17, 326, 329; *Garsedge* 329, 332

Garsecg (IV) (Old English) See *Belegar*. *Garsecges fréa*, Ulmo, 208

Garsecg (V) (Old English) the Ocean. 80, 82

Gársecg (IXb) (O.E.) The Ocean. 243, 258, 270, 272–3, 288, 292, 316

Gársecg (X) (Old English) The Great Sea. 153

Gartharian (XI) Doriath ('hidden realm'). *183, 189

Gate of the Dead (VIII) 313, 418. See *Dark Door*, *Dead Men of Dunharrow*.

Gate of the Noldor (II) 123, 204

Gate of the Noldor (IV) 174, 230. See *Annon-in-Gelydh*.

Gate(s) of Mordor (VIII) Originally name of the pass into Mordor (see 113). 104–6, 112–13, 128, 415; *Gates of the Land of Shadow*

(chapter-title) 121. See *Black Gate(s)*, *Ennyn Dûr*, *Morannon*.

Gates of Dread (III) (probably) the Door of Night. 149

Gates of Moria (VII) See *Moria*.

Gates of Morn (I) 216, 221, 226; *Gates of East and West* (i.e. the Gates of Morn and the Door of Night) 219

Gates of Morn (IV) 49, 252, 255; *Gates of East and West* 73

Gates of Morning (V) 14, 20, 25

Gates of Morning (IXb) 334, 380

Gates of Morning (XII) 149

Gates of Summer (II) Great festival in Gondolin. 172, 201, 211. See *Tarnin Austa*.

Gates of Summer (IV) Great festival in Gondolin. 144, 194

Gate-stream (VI) See *Caradras dilthen*, *Sirannon*.

Gate-stream (VII) Sirannon. 178, 187

Gatherers of Pearl (X) A name of the Teleri. 164

Gaurhoth (III) The Werewolves of Thû. 340, 350; *Gaurhoth Isle* 337, see *Tol-in-Gaurhoth*.

Gaurin (III) Unknown; named in Beleg's 'whetting spell'. 45, 54

Gaurwaith (III) The Wolf-men, the outlaw-band which Túrin joined in the later legend. 50

Gawkroger (VI) Hobbit family name. 236, 246, 254; *Gaukrogers* 315

Gazmog (VIII) Orc of the Tower of Kirith Ungol. 212, 225. (Replaced by *Yagûl*.)

Geatas (V) People in the south of Sweden of whom Beowulf became king; Old Norse *Gautar*. 94–5

Gelduin (XI) Proposed name replacing *Gelion*. 336

Geleidhian (IV) Beleriand (Broseliand), 'the kingdom of the Gnomes'. 108, 116, 174, 179, 219, 225–6, 233; earlier spelling Geleithian 108

Geleriand (III) Rejected name for Beleriand. 160

Gelimer (II) Earlier name for Ælfheah. 332, 334. (Replaced *Helgor*.)

Gelion (II) 249

Gelion, River (IV) 135, 189, 210, 224, 230, 232–4, 259, 331–2, 335; *Greater Gelion* 233; O.E. *Glæden* 210. (Replaced *Flend*.)

Gelion, River (V) 127–9, 260–5, 267–9, 272, 274, 283, 359; described, 262–3; mouths of 261; vale of 262, 264; the arms of Gelion 268, 283: *Greater Gelion* 263, 268, 272, (412), *Little Gelion* 263, 265, 272

Gelion, River (X) 83, 89, 104, 172–3

Gelion, River (XI) 5, 7, 13, 15, 45, 53, 105, *183, *185, 190–1, 193,

195, 197, 206, 216, 218, 221, 334–6, 338, 347, 349, 385; *Greater Gelion* *183, 188; *Little Gelion* *183; *the Falls of Gelion* 335–6, 338. See *Duin Daer, Gelduin, Gevelon.*

Gelir (IXa) Aragorn's translation of *Merry* (Gamgee). 117, 126, 129. (Replaced *Riben.*)

Gelmir (II) See Arminas. 123, 125, 204

Gelmir (III) Father of Fingolfin in the *Lay of the Fall of Gondolin.* 146–7

Gelmir (IV) (1) King of the Gnomes. 6–9. (2) Brother of Gwindor of Nargothrond. 180

Gelmir (XI) (1) Brother of Gwindor of Nargothrond. 73, 134, 168

Gelmir (XI) (2) Companion of Arminas. 141–2, 256, 299. See *Faramir.*

gems, jewels, of the Noldor (X) 19, 92–3, 96, 101, 103, 108, 116, 176, 178, 181, 183, 185, 189, 191–2, 279, 285, 292, 296, 298

Geoffrey of Monmouth (IXb) 192, 216

Gepids (V) Eastern Germanic people. 37, 53–4

Geraint (IXb) Cornishman, companion of Ælfwine and Tréowine. 279

Gereth (II) Gnome who aided the flight of Elwing from Artanor. 241

German (IXb) 307, 417

Germanic (V) 43, 53–4, 91–3, 95; *Germany* ='Germania' 92; the *Germania* of Tacitus 97

Germanic (VII) 455

Germanic (IXb) 151, 159, 286; (language) 243

Germanic (XII) 47, 50, 94, 361

Gethron (V) Guardian (with Grithron) of Túrin on the journey to Doriath. 138, 151, 317–18, 322

Gevelon, Gevilon (XI) Proposed name replacing *Gelion,* derived from Dwarvish *Gabilan.* 336

Ghân(-buri-Ghân) (XII) 316

Ghân-buri-Ghân (VIII) 351–2, 356

Ghán-buri-Ghán (IXa) 56, 61–2, 67; *Ghán* 67

Ghash (IXa) See *Muzgash.*

Giants (VI) 253–4, 319, 384; and see *Treebeard.*

Giants (XII) 46, 58

Gift of Ilúvatar, The (X) (of Man's mortality) 21, 26, 36–7, 42–3, 267, 326, 354, 356; (of Light to the Valar) 380, 385

Gil (II) =*Ingil.* 281–2, 328

Gilammoth (III) Rejected name for Nan Elmoth. 349

Gilbarad (XII) Father of Ivorwen. 263, 270

Gildis (XI) Wife of Hador Goldenhead. 234

Gildor (III) One of the twelve companions of Barahir on Dorthonion. 335, 349

Gildor (Inglorion) (XII) 36

Gildor (V) Companion of Barahir. 133, 150, 282, 289

Gildor (VI) 60, 62–5, 68–71, 73, 76, 88–9, 106, 109, 122, 141, 160, 173, 194, 280–2, 300, 325; *Gildor Inglorion* 60, 71, 282

Gildor (VII) 61; see *Elves*.

Gildor (VIII) 53

Gildor (XI) Companion of Barahir. 56

Gil-Estel (XI) 'Star of high hope' (Eärendil's star); other names *Gil-Amdir*, ~ *Orestel*, ~ *Orrain*. 246

Gilfanon (I) *(Gilfanon a·Davrobel, Gilfanon of Tavrobel)* 51, 174–5, 188–9, 194–8, 203–4, 219, 222, 228–31, 235. (Replaced *Ailios*.)

Gilfanon (IV) (1) Elf of Alqualondë. 9–10. (2) Gilfanon of Tavrobel. 10, 274. For *Gilfanon's Tale* see *Lost Tales*.

Gilfanon of Tavrobel (II) (not including references to his Tale) 69, 145, 281, 283–4, 286, 288–9, 292, 294, 326. (Replaced *Ailios*.)

Gilfanon of Tavrobel (V) 412–13

Gil-galad (V) Elf-king in Beleriand after the Downfall of Númenor. 29, 31, 33–4, 77, 337, 362; descended from Fëanor 29, 31; son of Felagund 33–4

Gil-galad (VI) 105, 169, 174, 179, 192, 197, 199, 214–16, 218, 226–7, 260–2, 271, 320, 358; translated 'Starlight' 179, 215, 358; descendant of Fëanor 215–16

Gil-galad (VII) 10, 25, 56, 64, 110, 122–5, 126–7, 138, 144, 361, 444, 450. Descendant of Fëanor 125; son of Inglor Felagund 123–4. *The Fall of Gil-galad* 65

Gil-galad (VIII) 21

Gilgalad (IXb) 408

Gilgalad (XI) ('Starlight', 242). As son of Fingon 56, 126, 243; as son of Felagund 120, 242–3; named *Findor* 56, 243

Gil-galad (XII) 78, 150, 152–3, 168–9, 173–4, 176, 179, 185, 189, 192, 313, 317–18, 328–9, 347–51, 358, 364, 382, 390; other names *Ereinion* 'Scion of Kings' 347–8, 351, 364; *Finellach*, *Finhenlach*, *Finlachen* 351; *Artanáro*, *Rodnor* 350–1

Gilim (II) A Giant ('Winter'?) 19, 46, 67–8

Gilim (III) 'The giant of Eruman', named in Lúthien's 'lengthening spell'. 205

Gilmith (XII) Sister of Galador, first Lord of Dol Amroth. 221

Gilraen (VII) Mother of Aragorn. 291

Gilrain (XII) (1) River of Gondor. 294. (2) Mother of Aragorn. 196, 238, 263, 268, 270; *Gilraen* 269–70

Gilrain, River (VII) In Gondor. 312. See *Lameduin.*

Gilrain, River (VIII) In Gondor. 411–12, 422, 437; *Gilrain-mouth* 412. (Replaced *Lameduin.*)

Gilthoniel (VI) Varda. 59, 68, 186, 189, 212, 364, 394; *Gilthonieth* 68

Gilthoniel (VIII) Varda. 218

Gilthoniel (IXa) Varda. 112

Gilthoniel (X) Varda. 388

Gilthoniel Varda. (VII) 65

Gilwen (XI) Sister of Barahir. 231

Gim-Githil (I) Gnomish name of Inwë. 22, 131–2. (Replaced *Githil*, replaced by *Inwithiel*.)

Gim Githil (III) Original Gnomish name of Inwë (replaced by *Inwithiel*). 28

Gimilkhâd (XII) Father of Ar-Pharazôn. 154, 159, 161–2, 164

Gimilnitîr (IXb) 'Star-kindler', Varda. 428. See *Avradî*

Gimilzôr (IXb) Elros. 380, 382, 433. (Replaced *Indilzar.*) See *Ar-Gimilzôr.*

Gimlad (IXb) 'Starwards', Númenor. 378, 396

Gimli (II) A Gnomë, captive in the castle of Tevildo. 29, 55, 214

Gimli (III) Dwarf of the house of Durin, member of the Fellowship of the Ring. 158, 316

Gimli (VI) Dwarf, son of Glóin. 398, 400, 411, 413, 415, 435–6, 438, 444–5, 460, 466

Gimli (VII) 114–15, 162, 166, 169–71, 174, 178, 180–1, 183–5, 186–8, 194–203 *passim*, 205, 210–11, 214–25 *passim*, 231–4, 236–8, 246, 248, 257, 263, 268, 271, 275–7, 279, 288–9, 291, 329–30, 347, 350, 354, 375, 378, 381–2, 385–7, 390–2, 395, 397, 399–400, 403–4, 406, 411–13, 425–8, 431, 434, 437–8, 441–3, 449. His song in Moria 183–4; called *elf-friend* 227. See *Elf-stone* (4).

Gimli (VIII) 3–5, 13–15, 18, 20, 24–7, 37, 39, 47, 53–4, 59, 61–3, 65–7, 72, 78–9, 140–1, 146, 229, 238, 241, 243–4, 246, 249, 264, 272, 274, 276, 297–302, 304–5, 310, 313, 317, 321, 370, 386, 392, 397, 399, 403, 405–7, 409–10, 414–21, 423–9; *Glóin's son* (VIII) 392, 421

Gimli (IXa) 48–9, 51–2, 61, 63, 66, 69–70, 116, 119, 122–3, 135

Gimli (XII) 242, 244, 246, 261, 270, 285–6, 296, 391

Ginglith (III) River flowing into the Narog above Nargothrond. 66, 88, 215, 222

Ginglith, River (IV) 184, 221, 324

Ginglith, River (V) 152

Ginglith. River (XI) 139, *182

Gip (VI) Farmer Maggot's dog. 94, 96

Girdle of Melian (XI) 16, 32, 50, 61, 81, 90, 151, 178, 188, 222, 225, 228, 321, 333, 352, 355; other references, as *Girdle of Doriath, Fence of Melian* 64, 114, 333. See *List Melian; Doriath.*

Girdle of the Earth (IV) 266

Girdle of the Earth (XII) 150

Girdley Island (VI) In the Brandywine River. 284

Githil 22. (I) See *Gim-Githil.*

Gladden Fields (VI) 416, 432, 438

Gladden Fields (VII) 114, 224, 248, 307. See *Palath-ledin.*

Gladden Fields (XII) 38, 57, 177, 192, 227, 233, 238, 251. *The Disaster of the ~* (title of work) 207–8, 293, 327

Gladden Fields, Gladden River (IV) 210. See *Gelion.*

Gladden River (VI) 416, 432, 438, 440. See *Palathrin.*

Gladden River (VII) 164, 172

Gladden, River (XII) 38, 57, 66–7, 230, 280, 323

Gladuial (XI) Name of Nan Elmoth (?). *183, 188

Glad-uial, Glath-uial (III) Rejected name for Nan Elmoth (replaced by *Gilammoth*). 349

Glamdring (VI) 'Foe-hammer', Gandalf's sword. 442–4, 454, 464

Glamdring (VII) Gandalf's sword. 188, 192, 198, 205

Glamdring (VIII) Gandaif's sword. 223

Glamdring (IXa) Gandalf's sword. 78. See *Orcrist.*

Glamdring (XI) Gandalf's sword. 391

Glamhoth (II) 'Folk of dreadful hate', Gnomish name for Orcs. 160, 219

Glamhoth (III) Gnomish name for Orcs. 16, 22, 30, 34, 41–2, 46, 48, 57, 71, 92, 96, 116, 146–7

Glamhoth (IV) 'People of Hate', Orcs. 8, 12, 82

Glamhoth (V) 'Hosts of hate', Orcs. 233, *358, 364, 377*

Glamhoth (X) 'Host(s) of tumult', Orcs. 109, 128, 195

Glamhoth (XI) ('Yelling-horde'), Orcs; also *Glam*, singular *Glamog.* 391

Glanduin, River (VI) (flowing from the Misty Mountains to the Greyflood above Tharbad) 441

Glanduin, River (IXa) 72. See *Swanfleet*.

Glassmere in Dimrill-dale (VI) Earliest name of Mirrormere. 433, 437, 466. See *Helevorn*.

Glastonbury (IXb) 271

Glaurung (II) 68, 125–6, 129, 131–2, 134–5, 143, 213. See *Glorund*.

Glaurung (IV) Final name of the great Dragon. 60, 180, 185, 317, 324; *the gold-worm of Angband* 182. See *Glómund*.

Glaurung (V) 290. See *Glómund*.

Glaurung (X) 306

Glaurung (XI) (including references to *the Dragon, the (Great) Worm* 46, 49, 52, 74–5, 85–8, 90, 93, 96–102, 121, 139–43, 148–50, 152–64, 167, 180, 224, 238, 240, 254–8, 266–7, 273, 285, 290–1, 299–300, 310, 329, 347, 350; *Father of Dragons* 52, 74, *the Serpent of Angband* 264, and see *Urulókë* his speed and power of sight 149. (Replaced *Glómund*.)

Glend (II) The sword of the giant Nan. 67

Glend (III) The sword of the giant Nan. 205

Gléowine (IXa) Minstrel of Théoden. 73 (and earlier form *Gleowin*).

Glewellin (V) 'Song of gold', a Gnomish name of Laurelin. 210, *368*

Glewellin (X) 'Song of gold', (Noldorin >) Sindarin name of Laurelin. 155

Glindûr (XI) Earlier name of Maeglin. 48, 58, 76, 91, 122–3, 127, 135, 146, 322–3, 344; as name also of the metal of Eöl 48, 122, 322. See *Maeglin, Galvorn*.

Glingal (III) The Golden Tree of Valinor (Laurelin). 5, 80–2, 192, 195, 210; earlier form *ngol* 5, 73, 80–2, 195, 219

Glingal (V) Gnomish name of Laurelin; the Golden Tree of Gondolin. 210–11, 359, *369*; earlier form *Glingol* 211

Glingal (X) Image of Laurelin in Gondolin. 155

Glingal (XI) Image of Laurelin in Gondolin. 200

Glingna Nauglir (IV) The Necklace of the Dwarves. 33

Glingol (I) Gnomish name of the Golden Tree of Valinor. 22

Glingol (II) 'Singing-gold', the Tree of Gondolin with golden blossom. 160, 184–6, 207, 216. Later form *Glingal* (Tree of Gondolin made of gold by Turgon) 207

Glingol (IV) Gnomish name of the Golden Tree of Valinor. 81–2, 167, 210, 283; O.E. *Glengold* 210, 283; later form *Glingal* 167

Glinnel (XI), plural *Glinnil* Sindarin, =*Lindar* (Teleri). 378, 385

Glirhuin (XI) Seer and harper of Brethil. 296

Glithui, River (XI) *182, 186; *Gilthui* 186

Glittering Caves (VIII) See *Aglarond*.

Glittering Caves (IXa) 63, 116, 119,122

Gloaming-fields (VII) 94, 97, 108; *Gloaming-bree* 108

Glóin (VI) Dwarf, companion of Thorin Oakenshield. 209–10, 213, 217, 220–1, 225–6, 362, 366, 369, 391–2, 395, 397–400, 403–4, 411–14, 429, 437, 444

Glóin (VII) 81–2, 112–18, 126, 129, 141, 143, 154–5, 158–9, 162, 188, 204, 246, (248), 263–4, 392

Glóin (VIII) See *Gimli*.

Glóin (XII) (1) Son of Thorin I. 275–7. (2) Companion of Thorin Oakenshield. 242, 244, 276–7, 279, 287

Glómund (III) Later name of Glórund (itself replaced by *Glaurung*). 205, 208–9

Glómund (IV) Name of the great Dragon in the *Quenta* and the *Annals of Beleriand*; called 'the Golden', 'Father of Dragons', 'First of Dragons'. 32–3, 60, 108, 118–19, 126–32, 176, 181–2, 185–6, 298, 302, 305–6, 317, 322, 324, 332–3, 336–7; image on the Helm of Gumlin 118, 182; other references 184, 187, 322. See *Glórund, Glórung, Glaurung*.

Glómund (V) 130, 132, 137, 139–40, 152, 255, 257–8, 274–5, 280, 283, 290, 310, 319

Glómund (XI) Earlier name of Glaurung. 121, 154, 180, 206, 240. (Replaced *Glórund*.)

Gloomweaver (I) Translation of *Wirilóme, Gwerlum*, the great Spider. 152–3

Gloomweaver (II) The Great Spider. 160. See *Wirilómë, Ungweliant(ë)*.

Gloomweaver (III) The great Spider. 132. See *Ungoliant*.

Gloomweaver (IV) 16, 69, 91. See *Ungoliant, Wirilómë*.

Gloomweaver (V) 230. See *Ungoliantë*.

Glóredhel (V) Daughter of Hador. 314. (Replaced *Glorwendel*.)

Glóredhel (XI) Daughter of Hador, wife of Haldir of Brethil. 234–5, 237, 268, 270, 309. (Replaced *Glorwendil*.)

Glorfalc (II) 'Golden Cleft', by which Tuor came to the Sea. 150, 202. See *Cris Ilbranteloth, Golden Cleft, Teld Quing Ilon*.

Glorfalc (IV) 'Golden Cleft', early name of Cirith Ninniach. 193

Glorfindel (II) Lord of the peoplë of the Golden Flower in Gondolin; called *Glorfindel of the golden hair, golden Glorfindel, Gold-tress* (216). 173, 175, 182–3, 186, 192–4, 196, 211–12, 216, 243, 260

Glorfindel (III) Lord of the people of the Golden Flower in Gondolin. *Glorfindel the golden* 142

Glorfindel (IV) Lord of the House of the Golden Flower of Gondolin. 37, 145, 194, 308

Glorfindel (V) Lord of the house of the Golden Flower of Gondolin. 142, *358* (also *Glaurfindel*), *368*, *387*

Glorfindel (VI) Elf of Rivendell. 193–6, 198, 207, 209, 212–15, 361–2, 364–5, 367–8, 384, 392, 395, 397–8, 400, 405–6, 409–10, 414; on the identity of Glorfindel of Rivendell and Glorfindel of Gondolin see 214–15.

Glorfindel (VII) 14, 61, 75, 112–13, 116, 153–4, 158, 172

Glorfindel (XI) A lord of Gondolin. 318, 328

Glorfindel (XII) (of Gondolin and Rivendell) 67, 377–82, 384–5, 387–91

Glorfindel of Gondolin (X) 364

Glorfinniel (IXa) Aragorn's translation of *Goldilocks* (Gamgee). 117, 126, 129

Glorindol (XI) Name of Hador, 'Goldenhead'. 223, 225, 228, 232–3, 235; *Glórindol* 225; *Glorindal* 226, 235. See *Lorindol*.

Glorious Battle (IV) See *Dagor Aglareb*.

Glorious Battle (V) 127, 254. See *Dagor Aglareb*, *Second Battle*.

Glorious Battle (XI) The Third Battle of Beleriand (formerly the second). 28, 36, 116. See *Dagor Aglareb*.

Glorund (II) The Dragon, precursor of Glaurung. References include passages where he is called the *drake*, etc; see also *Foalókë*. 19, 41, 46, 68, 84–8, 94–8, 103–16, 118, 123, 125–6, 128–37, 140–4, 221–3, 229–31, 235–6, 238–9, 241, 246; *Glorunt* 84. See *Laurundo*, *Undolaurë*

Glórund (III) The Dragon. 5–6 (in title of first version of *The Children of Húrin*), 103, 208; *the Worm of Greed* 8, 100. (Replaced by *Glómund*.)

Glórund (IV) Name of the great Dragon in the *Lost Tales*. 33, 60, 186

Glórund (XI) Original name of Glaurung, replaced by *Glómund*. 154(-5)

Glórung (IV) Name of the great Dragon in the 'Sketch'. 30–3, 60–1

Glorvent (I) 'Ship of Gold', a name of the Sun (Gnomish). 187

Glorwendel (V) Daughter of Hador. 147, 314; *Glorwendil* 310. (Replaced by *Glóredhel*.)

Glorwendil (XI) Daughter of Hador, wife of Hundor of Brethil. 51, 79, 126, 128, 136, 233, 268. (Replaced by Glóredhel wife of Haldir.)

Glossamnach (VIII) See *Lossarnach*.

Glund (IXb) [Lewis] The planet Jupiter. 203, 220; *Glundandra* 220

Gnomes (I) (including *Gnome-folk, Gnome-kin*) 13, 16–7, 21–2, 24, 27, 43–4, 49–51, 62, 94, 129, 140–2, 144, 146, 150–1, 153, 156–7 160, 163, 165–9, 171, 174–6, 178, 187, 192, 196, 198, 207–10, 213, 220, 234, 237–43. See especially 43–4, 50–1, and see *Noldoli*.

Gnomes (II) Selected references (including *Noldoli*). Slaves of Melko 9–11, 31, 42–3, 65, 77–8, 154, 156–7, 159, 161, 163, 166, 170, 205–6, 219, 279; free Noldoli 44, 65, 77, 82, 248; in Artanor 9, 43, 65, 122, 254, 276; in Dor Lómin 15, 43, 52, 65, 149, 204; among the Dwarves 224, 245; confusion with Orcs 159; tongue of 148–9, 158, 198, 216–17; art of 224; lanterns of 78, 80–1, 123, 153; steel, chainmail of 83, 85, 164; miners 168; release of, and return into the West 161–2, 278, 280, 285

Gnomes, Gnomish (III) 7, 11, 18, 21–2, 25, 28–9, 31, 35–8, 40, 45, 58–9, 61, 63–6, 69–70, 74 (*the Gnome-river*), 83–6, 90, 92, 94, 99, 104, 107, 111, 133, 136–9, 145–6, 148, 150, 152–3, 173, 187, 191–2, 195–6, 210, 212, 214, 217, 219–22, 226, 231–3, 235–7, 244, 247, 263, 270, 275, 283, 285; *Doom of the Gnomes* 16, 116; lamps of 35, 148. See *Noldoli, Noldor*.

Gnomes (IV) Selected references (see also *Noldoli*). The name *Gnome* 85, 87, 105, 108, 175; described 87; their horses on Bladorion 330, 334; relations with the Dwarves 104, 108, 174–5, 331, 335–6; some remained in Valinor 95, 149, 154, 195; return into the West 159, 162, 202, 309, and to Valinor 159, 162; thrall-Gnomes 107, 117, 121; those who remained free at the end 309, 326; *Kingdom of the Gnomes* 108 (*Geleidhian*), 174 (*Ingolondë*).

Gnomes (IV) References (in the texts) to Gnomish speech: 4, 12, 78–82, 84–5, 87, 101, 104, 108, 127, 226–7, 329, 339; O.E. *noldelfisc* (*gereord*) 206, 285, 291, *noldisc* 338. See *Noldorin*.

Gnomes (V) 'The Wise' (275; cf. *Ainimor, Istimor*). 13–15, 18, 28–30, 60, 71, 113–15, 117–18, 125–46 *passim*, 153, 174–7, 179–80, 190–2, 201–88 *passim*, 298, 305, 307–8, 312, 323, 328, 331–3, 405. *Thrall-Gnomes* 177, 286, 309; *Song of the Flight of the Gnomes* 236; *Kingdom of the Gnomes (Ingolondë)* 253

Gnomes (VI) 71, 212, 217, 364. See *Noldor, Wise-elves*. Gnomish (tongue) 131, 187. See *Noldorin*.

Gnomes (VII) 124–5, 158, 256. Gnomish 390; *Gnome-elvish* 277, 291

Gnomes (VIII) 158, 160, 169, 224. Gnomish 159, 161–2

Gnomes (IXa) 58

Gnomes (X) 103, 124–5, 137, 146, 154–5, 163, 168, 177–8, 188–9,

194; language of 144, 177; *Song of the Flight of the Gnomes* 125

Gnome(s) (XI) 108, 113, 125, 131, 137, 175, 177–8, 189, 193, 195, 202–4, 206, 209, 239, 244

Gnome(s) (XII) Noldor. (23), 24, 63, 76–7, 81–2, 351, 379

Gnomish (I), *Gnome-speech, tongue of the Gnomes* 21–2, 24, 43, 48, 50–2, 89, 91, 108, 130, 132, 138, 160, 200, 235, 245

Gnomish (III) (language) 28–9, 61, 87, 93, 138–9, 160, 182; early Gnomish dictionary 22, 87, 89, 93, 124, 139, 160, 170, 198

Gnomish (V) (of language) 29, 33, 126, 148, 190, 192, 211, 226, 256, 262, 280, 298, 342, 405–6; (with other reference) 150, 231, 263

Gnomish (X) (language) 90, 103, 195

Gnomish (XI) (of language) 194, 206, 209, 215, 240, 315

Gnomish (XII) 20, 23–4, 71, 74–7

Goatleaf, Harry (VI) Keeper of the west-gate of Bree. (333–4), 336, 342, 344–5, 347–9, 354; his brother (Ned?) 344, 349

Goatleaf, Harry (VII) Gatekeeper at Bree. 40–2, 44–5, 62, 71, 73–4, 80; Ned his brother (?) 41

Goblin Feet (I) (poem) 32, 136; on the meaning of *Goblin* here see the Appendix, entry *Noldoli*, p. 262.

Goblin Gate (VI) In the Misty Mountains. 416, 432. See *Annerchin*.

Goblins (I) 47, 237, 245

Goblins (II) Frequently used as alternative term to Orcs (cf. *Melko's goblins, the Orcs of the hills* 157, but sometimes apparently distinguished, 31, 230). 14, 31, 35, 67, 76–80, 154, 156–7, 159, 176–7, 179–82, 219, 230, 247, 279. See *Orcs*.

Goblin(s) (III) 34, 46, 48, 64, 148, 225–6, 282

Goblins (IV) Orcs (see 82). 12, 82

Goblins (V) A translation of *Orcs*. 233, 406

Goblins (VI) 55, 75, 78–81, 84, 86, 110, 128, 176, 178, 187–8, 211, 227, 253, 261, 263–4, 271–2, 282, 320, 364, 381–2, 391, 429, 437, 442–3, 451, 453–4, 462; goblinish 165, 176, 354; *Wars of the Elves and Goblins* 350; *Dwarf and Goblin War* 391, *Goblin invasions* 391; language 451; Goblins as Ring-wraiths 75, 78. On the relation of *Orcs* and *Goblins* see 437, 443.

Goblins (VII) 24–5, 114, 142–3, 155–7, 181, 184, 193, 199, 201, 205, 336–7, 340, 353, 382, 423; *goblin-spirit* 411. On Goblins and Orcs see 199–200, 205. *Goblin Gate* 114 (see *Annerchion*), *Goblins' door* 114. See *Dwarves, Orcs*.

Goblin(s) (VIII) 18, 96, 213, 215; *Goblin-men* 52; *Goblin-wars* 224

goblin(s) (IXa) 14, 119; *goblin-king* 119

goblins (IXb) 397

Goblins (XII) 4, 21, 23, 249–50, 323

Gochnessiel (IXa) 44. See *Encircling Mountains*.

Gochressiel (V) The Encircling Mountains about Gondolin. 285, 290–1, 301, *363*

Gochressiel (XI) The Encircling Mountains about Gondolin. 239. See *Echoriad*.

God (IXb) 249, 310–11, 314, 391, 400–3, 408–9, 432; O.E. 313. See also *Children of God, Servants of God*.

God (X) 329–30, 355, 357, 397; *Children of God* 330, 356, 377, 379, 398. See *Eru, Children of Eru, (The) One*.

God (XI) 212

Gods (I) *Passim*; on the nature and character of the Gods (*Valar*, see 63) and their relation to Manwë see especially 103–4, 111, 149, 182, 189–90, 199, 209, 213, 219–20, 222–3, 225–6, 228; language of the Gods 47–8, 51–2, 235. See *Children of the Gods*.

Gods (II) See *Valar*.

God(s) (III) Selected references. Passages concerning the relation of the Gods to Elves and Men 11–12, 26, 43, 54, 111–12; 'a dream from the Gods' 203, 210; the Gods 'gaze on the world' 17; 'wrath of the Gods' 73; *Wrack of the Realm of the Gods* 31; *God of Hell* 6, *of Darkness* 102, *of Sleep* 180. See *Valar*.

Gods (IV) 3, 12, 14–21, 27, 39–45, 47, 49, 65, 68, 71–4, 78–82, 84–91, 93–9, 110, 119, 147, 149, 151, 153–9, 161, 163–6, 168–70, 196–7, 199–200, 202–3, 205, 215, 217, 236–8, 252, 255, 263–7, 269–71, 275, 277–9, 288, 295, 299, 328; O.E. *Fréan* 208, *Ése* 208, 211, *Godu* 206, 281–2, 285–8, 291, 338. *Land(s) of the Gods* 13, 78–9, 85–6, 98, 134, 142, 190, 240, 261. See *Battle of the Gods; Powers, Valar*.

Gods (V) 11–12, 14–22, 24–9, 32, 44, 56, 162–3, 74–6, 79, 111–16, 118, 171–4, 184–5, 193, 195, 204–46 *passim*, 252, 275) 283, 290, 303, 305, 313, 325–8, 330, 332–5, 338; Old English *Ése* 44, 103, 203, cf. also *Oswin* 53. *Land of the Gods* 16, 19, 21, 25, 170, 172, 181, 205, 215, 221, 224; *Mountains of the Gods* 222, 300; *Plain of the Gods*, see 12, 17; *God of Dreams* 220; *the Black God* 206; *Friends of the Gods*, a name of the Lindar, 215. See *Battle of the Gods; Lords of the West, Powers, Valar; Children of Sons of the Valar*.

Gods (VI) 184, 187; *land of the Gods* 182, 187 *hound of the Gods* 183

Gods (VII) 432. See *Rulers of the World.*

God(s) (VIII) 136, 168, 292, 401

Gods (IXb) 241, 244, 305, 332–9, 344, 354–5, 357, 362, 376–7, 387, 395, 400–4, 408–9, 412–13; *Goddess* 428 (see *Avalië*); (*a, the*) God 341, 345, 358, 363, 371, 398, 401, 404, 407; *Land of the Gods* 333, 336, 407, 409; *First Battle of the Gods* 383; *Haven of the Gods,* see *Avallondë, Avallôni; Lord of the Gods* (Manwë) 316–17, O.E. *Ôsfruma* 316–17; *Children of the Gods* 332, *sons of Gods* 334

Gods (IXb) *Norse Gods: Æsir* 214, *Regin* 286, *Tívar* 286; Old English *Ése* 244 (singular *Ós* 317), *Tíwas* 242, 286 (=Valar)

God(s) (X) 18, 20, 26, 32, 54–5, 67–9, 95–9, 106, 111, 116–18, 129–30, 133, 136, 144, 147, 150, 153–5, 160–2, 167, 172–3, 175–9, 181, 185, 187–91, 196, 198, 271, 273, 282, 321, 372, 387, 407; of Melkor as 'God' 344, 351, 354, 397. *City of the Gods* 146, 154; *Land of the Gods* 90, 145, 148, 174, 178, 180; *Mountains of the Gods* 22, 176, 180; *language of the Gods* 77, 166; *Sickle of the Gods,* see *Valakirka; Friends of the Gods,* a name of the Vanyar, 164; *the Black God* 146; *the Nine Gods* 144; and see *Battles of the Gods, Valar.*

Gods (XI) 42, 55, 65, 175, 177, 217, 220, 227, 240, 246–7, 420; *Battle of the Gods* 207, *People ~* 239, *Sons ~* 246

God(s) (XII) 148, 306 (of Morgoth), 312, 374–5; *God* (Eru Ilúvatar) 157, 420

Gódhel (XI), plurals *Gódhil, Gódhellim* (Sindarin) The Exiled Noldor. 364, 379. See *Ódhel.*

go-Dhuilin, go-Dhrauthoḍauros, go-Rimion (II) 'son of' Duilin, etc.; see the names. (*go-* replaced by *bo-*).

go-Fëanor, go-Maidros (I) 'son of Fëanor, of Maidros'. 155; 146, 155, 158

Go-hilleg (XII) Númenóreans (in the tale of Tal-elmar). 427–8, 430, 433

Golasgil (VIII) Lord of Anfalas. 287, 289. (Replaced *Asgil-Golamir.*)

Golda (III) Original Gnomish equivalent of *Noldo.* 160. See *Golodh.*

Goldberry (VI) 115, 117, 122, 125–6, 128, 130

Golden Book (IV) 76, 78, 274. See *Parma Kuluina.*

Golden Book (V) 201, 203–4, 278

Golden Book, The (II) 283, 285, 287, 291, 293, 310. See *Panna Kuluinen.*

Golden Cleft (II) 150, 153, 219. See *Glorfalc.*

Golden-elves (V) A name of the Noldor. 215, 403. See *Kuluqendi*.

Golden Elves (X) A name of the Noldor. 164

Golden Flower of Gondolin (IV) See *Glorfindel*.

Golden Flower, The (II) Name of one of the kindreds of the Gondothlim, ruled by Glorfindel. 173, 182, 186, 195, 211, 216. See *Los'lóriol*.

Golden Hall (VII) 440–1, 449; described 444. See *Winseld*.

Golden Hall (XII) 71, 236. See *Meduseld*.

Golden Hall, The (VIII) 3–4, 21, 29, 244, 321, 347, 407, 424; other references 56, 70, 231, 249, 270, and see *Eorl*, *Meduseld*.

Golden Hall, The (IXa) 62–3, 68

Golden Perch (VI) The inn at Stock. 286–7, 291, 295, 325

Golden Tree (XII) The *mallorn* planted by Sam Gamgee. 139

Golden Tree 167. (IV) See *Laurelin*.

Golden Wood (VII) 222, 236, 238, 243, 286, 367, 415

Golden Wood, The (VIII) Lothlórien. 148, 158; *Lady of the Golden Wood* 150, 157

Goldo (XI) (Telerin) =*Noldo*. 383. *Goldorin*, *Goldolambë*, Telerin names of Quenya. 375

Goldriel (I) Earlier name of Golthadriel. 22

Goldwine (VIII) Sixth King of the Mark. 408

Golfimbul (IXa) Leader of the Orcs of Mount Gram (in *The Hobbit*). 119

Golfimbul (XII) Orc-chief slain by Bandobras Took. 236

Golfin (III) Son of Gelmir (=Fingolfin). 147

Golfin (IV) Earliest name of Fingolfin. 6–8

Golfinweg (I) Gnomish name of Nólemë Finwe. 115, 132

Gollum (III) 49

Gollum (VI) 75, 79–81, 84–7, 224, 226–9, 233, 241–2, 261–5, 268, 271–2, 314, 320–2, 370, 380–2, 401, 410, 413, 438, 442, 444; his relation to hobbits 75, 78–9; his grandmother 320; his (second) ring 370, 381. See *Dígol*.

Gollum (VII) 7, 9–10, 15, 23–9, 38–9, 83, 111, 116, 118–19, 126, 129–30, 134, 137, 147–8, 157, 208–18 *passim*, 225, (229), 240, 250, (252), 260, 265, 328–32, 339, 343–4, 346–7, 355, 357, 361, 367, 370–1, 410, 437–8. See *Deagol* (1), *Smeagol*.

Gollum (VIII) 78, 85–6, 89, 92, 95–129 *passim*, 132–8, 140–1, 151–5, 164, 169–203 *passim*, 206–9, 211–14, (217), 220–4, 291, 361. See *Smeagol*.

Gollum (IXa) 3–6, 8–9, 11–12, 14, 33, 36–7, 40–1, 71, 120

Gollum (XII) 3–5, 7, 11–14, 38, 54, 57, 66, 112, 167–9, 225, 227, 233, 239, 241, 248, 251. See *Sméagol*.

Golodh (III) Sindarin equivalent of Quenya *Noldo*. 160. *Golodhinand*, rejected name for Beleriand. 160

Golodh (IV) Sindarin equivalent of Quenya *Noldo*. 174. *Golodhinand*, rejected name for Beleriand. 174

Golodh (XI), plurals *Goelydh*, *Golodhrim* Sindarin form of *Noldo*. 323, 364, 379 383

Golosbrindi (II) Earlier name of Hirilorn. 51

Golthadriel (I) Gnomish name of Salmar (Noldorin). 22. (Replaced *Goldriel*.)

Gon Indor (II) Name of Eärendel as great-grandson of Indor. 217. See *Indor*, *Indorildo*.

Gondelf (VII) See *Gandalf*.

Gondobar (II) 'City of Stone', one of the Seven Names of Gondolin. 158, 172; in another application 275–6. See *City of Stone*.

Gondobar (III) 'City of Stone', one of the Seven Names of Gondolin.145–6

Gondobar (V) 100, 102–4, *359* (also *Gonnobar*), 372

Gondolin (I) 25, 27, 47, 52, 93, 158, 167–8, 172, 239, 242, 245; the tale of *Tuor and the Exiles of Gondolin* ('The Fall of Gondolin') 45, 52, 88–9, 112, 172, 203, 231, 233, 242, 245

Gondolin (II) 'Stone of Song'. 43–4, 65, 70, 77, 119–20, 130, 158–64, 166, 168–72, 175, 178, 184–6, 188–91, 193, 195–9, 201, 203–16, 218, 220, 240–2, 248, 251, 253, 255, 257–8, 260, 266, 276, 289; the Trees of Gondolin 160, 171, 184–5, 207–8, 215–16 (see *Bansil*, *Glingol*); the birds that flew from Gondolin to Kôr 253, 255, 257, 260, 263, 278; ruins of Gondolin 215–16, 253, 255, 258, 264; time of the founding of Gondolin 120, 208

Gondolin (III) 23, 51, 81, 83, 90, 141–3, 145–9, 160, 286–7, 292, 309–10

Gondolin (IV) 5, 15, 34–8, 49, 56, 58, 65–9, 74, 88, 101, 107, 115, 120, 132, 136–40, 142–8, 150–2, 162, 167, 173, 178, 181, 190–4, 210, 214, 219, 221–2, 226, 259, 263, 274, 280, 282–4, 290–2, 296, 299, 301–3, 305–8, 316, 318, 321, 324–7, 329–31, 333–4, 339; O.E. *Stángaldorburg* &c. 210, 283, but *Gondolin(d)*, *Gondoelin* in the texts. Discovery of Gondolin 34, 58, 136; later story of its foundation 120, 138, 181, 192, 296, 316, 329–31, 334, 339; *city of seven names* 142, 147, 194; the great square of Gondolin 36, 142, 144

Gondolin (V) 22, 104, 123, 126–9, 132–3, 136, 138–42, 145, 148, 150, 152, 167, 176–7, 179–80, 187, 189–92, 194, 201, 203, 210–11, 223, 249, 254, 257–8, 264, 269, 272, 274, 278, 285, 287–8, 291, 301, 307–8, 311, 313–15, 324, 332, *355*, *359* (also *Gondost*; and *Ardholen 358, Garthoren 360*); *the forbidden city* 288; language of Gondolin 177, 187, 189–90, 194; the Trees of Gondolin 211

Gondolin (VI) 214–15; *King of Gondolin* 444

Gondolin (VII) 110, 172, 454; *Gondolinic Runes* 452

Gondolin (VIII) 161, 169, 207, 224; *the Fall of Gondolin* 292

Gondolin (IXa) 44

Gondolin (IXb) 280, 290, 316

Gondolin (X) 155, 177, 359, 364, 373

Gondolin (XI) 5, 18, 22–3, 25–8, 35, 40, 44–5, 47–8, 53, 55, 57(-8), 68, 70, 72–6, 84, 91, 110, 116, 118–23, 125–7, 133, 135–6, 139, 146, 166, 169, 177, 179, *182, 193, 198–201, 203, 206, 234, 239, 241, 243–5, 254–6, 258, 260–1, 272, 298, 300–2, 313–14, 316–17, 319, 324, 326, 328, 330, 333, 344–8, 351, 353, 356, 396–7, 409; translated *the Hidden Rock* 199–201; *the Guarded City, ~ Realm* 53, 57, *the Hidden City, ~ Kingdom, ~ Realm* 56–7, 91, 195, 260. *Lay of the Fall of Gondolin* 121, 320; the tongue of Gondolin 22–3, 25–8, and its population 25–8, 40, 44–5, 55–6, 119, 126; etymology 201. See *Ondolindë*.

Gondolin (XII) 317, 348, 358, 370, 374, 377–81, 387–91, 395, 419, 421; *The Fall of Gondolin* (title of work) 379, 387–8; *Ondolindë* 374

Gondolindeb, Gondolindren, Gondolic (V) Names of the language of Gondolin. 177

Gondolindrim (II) The people of Gondolin. 209

Gondolindrim (IV) The people of Gondolin. 191

Gondor (V) 7, 34. See *Ondor*.

Gondor (VI) 379–80, 409, 411, 438; '*Stone-land*' 379. See *Ond*.

Gondor (VII) 146, 215, 312–13, 318, 321–2, 362, 395–6, 400–1, 420, 423, 445, 448, 450; *Gondorian* 437; *South Gondor (Harondor)* 310. See *Ond, Ondor*.

Gondor (VIII) 21, 24, 49, 71–3, 76–8, 80, 95, 106, 122, 127, 135–6, 142–8, 151–4, 156, 158, 160–2, 165, 168, 170–1, 174, 180, 182, 219, 231–3, 235–6, 238, 241, 243–4, 246, 253, 256–7, 259–60, 262–3, 268, 271–2, 274, 278–9, 281–4, 286, 291, 293–4, 299–301, 304, 306, 309, 311–12, 315–19, 321–2, 331, 338, 343, 349–

53, 356, 360, 362, 367, 369, 371, 375, 377, 379, 385, 387, 389, 392–3, 398, 401, 410–11, 413–14, 416, 424–5, 431, 436; *South(ern) Gondor* 253, 255, 413, 422; *the Realm* 401

Gondor (VIII) Languages of Gondor 136, 144, 159–62, 356; Kings of Gondor 238, 246, 263, 276, 278–9, 281–2, 292, 294, 337, 380, 383, 385, 425; customs 283–4, 293, 385; relations with the Rohirrim 155–6

Gondor (IXa) 8, 10, 20, 30, 46, 48–50, 52, 55–6, 59, 61, 69, 71, 83, 86, 91, 117, 122, 126, 128–9, 135

Gondor (IXb) 331

Gondor (X) 370, 373

Gondor (XI) 189, 314, 319, 391

Gondor (XII) 6, 20–2, 25, 32, 34, 38, 42–3, 45, 53, 63, 68, 74, 120–2, 124, 128, 132–3, 136, 163, 167, 169–71, 176, 188, 190–2, 194–207, 210–20, 225–33, 235–6, 238–45, 247–50, 252–5, 258–60, 265–7, 269, 271–4, 283, 293–4, 296, 311–12, 315–16, 328, 330, 332, 339, 360, 371, 410–11, 414, 419; *Gondorian* 138, 410; *Council of Gondor* (XII) 203, 256; early name *Ondor* 71

Gondor, Stewards of (II) 211–12

Gondorian(s) (VIII) 113, 135–7, 397, 422; *a dark Gondorian* 58

Gondothlim (II) 'Dwellers in Stone', the people of Gondolin. 155–66, 168, 170–4, 176, 179–81, 184–5, 187, 190, 193, 196, 198–200, 206, 208, 211, 213–16, 267; speech of, secret tongue of 158, 164–5, 198–9, 267; stature of 159, 198

Gondothlim (III) The people of Gondolin. 103

Gondothlim (IV) The people of Gondolin. 67

Gondothlim (XII) Old name of the people of Gondolin. 388

Gondothlimbar (II) 'City of the Dwellers in Stone', one of the Seven Names of Gondolin. 158

Gondothlimbar (III) 'City of the Dwellers in Stone', one of the Seven Names of Gondolin. 145

Gong of Littleheart (II) 6–7, 41, 254, 256, 263; the *Gong-warden* 144–5, 149, 201

Gong of the Children (I) In Mar Vanwa Tyaliéva. 15, 17, 27, 230. See *Tombo, Littleheart.*

Gongs (I) See 245

Gongs (II) Evil beings, obscurely related to Orcs. 136–7, 283, 288, 328

Gonlath (I) A great rock on Taniquetil. 219

Gonnhirrim (XI) 'Masters of stone', the Dwarves. 205, 209

Goodbody (VI) Hobbit family name. 236

Goodchild (VIII) Name proposed to replace *Gamgee*. 122–3

Gorbag (VIII) Orc of Minas Morghul. 226, 361. (Replaced *Yagûl*.)

Gorbag (IXa) Orc of Minas Morgul (but also of the Tower of Kirith Ungol, see 9). 8–10, 13–14, 18, 23–4, 26, 28

Gorbelgod, Swans of (XII) In the tale of Tal-elmar. 426, 437; earlier *Dur nor-Belgoth* 437

Gordon, E.V. (VI) 144–5

Gore, The (VII) (of Lothlórien) 231, 236, 242, 244, 261, 288, 368. See *Angle; Bennas, Naith, Narthas, Nelen, Nelennas*.

Gore, The (VIII) Below Helm's Deep. 310

Gorfalon, Gorfalong (I) Site of the Battle of Unnumbered Tears. 238, 240, 244. See *Vale of Weeping Waters, Valley of the Fountains*.

Gorgol (III) An Orc, called *the Butcher*, slain by Beren. 344, 350

Gorgor (VIII) =*Gorgoroth*. 137, 256

Gorgor (IXa) 8 (*fields of Gorgor, the Gorgor plain*), 22 (*valley of Gorgor*); replaced by *Gorgoroth*. See *Kirith Gorgor*.

Gorgorath, Gorgoroth (III) See *Ered Gorgoroth*.

Gorgoroth (V) The Mountains of Terror. 298, 377 (*Fuin Gorgoroth* = Taur-na-Fuin); *Gorgorath* 298. See *Ered Orgoroth*.

Gorgoroth (VII) 208–9, 211, 213–14, 330, 339, 343–5, 347–9, 373, 412, 450; *Gap of Gorgoroth* 208, 213, 313, 339, 347; *mouth of* 438; *valley (vale, plain) of* 144–6, 213, 313, 333; Orc guard-towers 208, 213, (310), 344, 349, 412–13, 437, 440 (see *Gorgos, Nargos*). See *Battles*.

Gorgoroth (VIII) 104, 116, 184, 190, 230, 438; *Pass of Gorgoroth* 431; *Battle of the Field of Gorgoroth* 21, 155

Gorgoroth (IXa) 20, 23, 34, 51. See *Gorgor, Kirith Gorgor*.

Gorgoroth (XII) 176

Gorgos (VII) 'Dire-castle', eastern guard tower in Kirith Ungol. 344–5, 349. See *Nargos*.

Gorgos (VIII) Eastern guard-tower of the pass into Mordor. 116

Gorgos (IXa) Eastern guard-tower of Kirith Ungol as the main pass into Mordor. 28

Gorgumoth (II) The hound of Mandos. 278

Gorgûn (VIII) Ghân-buri-Ghân's name for Orcs. 351

Gorgûn (XI) Name of the Orcs in the language of the Druedain. 391

Gorlim (III) The companion of Barahir who betrayed his hiding-place on Dorthonion; called 'the Unhappy'. 162–5, 169–70, 318, 330, 333, 335–41, 348–51

Gorlim (IV) Companion and betrayer of Barahir. 300, 311, 319

Gorlim the Unhappy (II) 52

Gorlim the Unhappy (V) Companion and betrayer of Barahir. 133–4, 282, 289, 292, 296–8

Gorlim the Unhappy (XI) Companion and betrayer of Barahir. 56, 59, *183

Gormok (IXb) [Ramer] The planet Mars 205, 220. See *Karan*.

Gorothress(?) (XI) See *183, 188

Gorsodh (XI) Name of Sauron 'in Beleriand'. 54

Gorthaur (XI) Sindarin name of Sauron. 240, 246; replacing *Gorthú* (Noldorin name) 239–40, 246

Gorthol (III) 'Dread Helm', the name that Túrin took in Dor-Cúarthol. 51

Gorthû (III) Later name of Thû. 153, 232–3

Gorthû (V) Gnomish name of Sauron. 33, 333, 338

Goth (V) Morgoth. See 406.

Gothic (IV) 210, 283

Gothic (VI) 145

Gothmog (I) Lord of Balrogs. 93. See *Kosomot*.

Gothmog (II) (1) 'Strife-and-hatred', lord of Balrogs, son of Melko and captain of his hosts. 67, 176, 179, 183–4, 212–13, 215–16. See *Kosmoko*. (2) Lieutenant of Minas Morgul. 216

Gothmog (III) Lord of Balrogs. 103

Gothmog (IV) Lord or captain of Balrogs. 22, 52, 101, 144, 181, 268, 282–3, 295, 307, 321, 328, 338

Gothmog (V) Lord of Balrogs. 117, 125, 142, 249, *359*, 372, 406

Gothmog (VIII) (1) In the First Age: Lord of Balrogs. 372. (2) Lieutenant of Morghul. 369.

Gothmog (XI) 18 ('Lord of the Balrogs'), 168 ('High-captain of Angband'), 169

Goths (V) 91; *East Gothfolk* 86

Goths (IXb) 276, 295; *Gothic* (language) 286–7

Gow, Professor Jonathan (IXb) 200

Graidon Hills, Grailaws (VII) See *Sarn Gebir* (1).

Gram (VIII) Eighth King of the Mark. 408

Gram, Mount (IXa) 119. See *Golfimbul*.

Great Battle (IV) At the end of the First Age. 160, 166, 252–3, 309, 327. See *Last Battle* (1).

Great Battle (V) At the end of the Elder Days. 13, 22, 24, 31, 33, 125, 144, 153–4, 190, 328, 333, 335–7; *Terrible Battle* 144, 328, 405. See *Dagor Delothrin, Last Battle, Long Battle, War of Wrath*.

Great Battle (VII) See *Battles*.

Great Battle (VIII) The battle between Sauron and the Last Alliance of Elves and Men. 105; *the Battle, a great battle* 109, 112, 116

Great Battle (IXb) At the end of the Elder Days. 331, 354

Great Battle (X) See *Battles of the Gods*.

Great Battle (XI) (at the end of the Elder Days) 345. See *Last Battle*.

Great Battle (XII) At the end of the First Age. 142–3, 163, 166–8, 172, 177, 187

Great Bear (I) 133; *Silver Bear* 33, 35; *Silver Wain* 39, 43. See *Seven Stars, Valacirca*.

Great Bear (III) 170, 259. See *Burning Briar, Seven Stars, Sickle of the Gods, Timbridhil*.

Great Bear (IV) 168, 289. See *Burning Briar, Seven Stars, Sickle of the Gods*.

Great Bear (X) (constellation) 166. See *(The) Plough, Burning Briar, Valakirka*.

Great Dark(ness) (VII) 416–17; *the Darkness* 416–17; *the Dark Days* 415–16

Great Darkness (VIII) See *Darkness out of Mordor*.

Great Door (IXb) [Ramer] 206; *the Door* 206, 221

Great Dwarf Road (XII) 323. See *Old Forest Road*.

Great End (I) 53, 59, 63, 77, 90–2, 97, 157, 182, 219

Great End (II) 60, 170, 281–3, 285. See *Great Wrack*.

Great End (IV) 51, 73; *the End* 73, 75, 150, 164; *Great Wrack* 73

Great End (V) 164; *the End* 304, 332; *the end of all* 227

(Great) Explosion (IXb) 157, 167, 186, 212, 215; *the Black Hole* 186

Great Folk of the West (I) Name of the Gods among the Ilkorins. 231

Great Folk of the West (II) Name of the Gods among the Ilkorins. 142

Great Fortress (XI) 108, 201, 209. See *Belegost, Mickleburg*.

Great Gulf (IV) *250–1, 258, (259)

Great Gulf (V) (260), 267

Great Gulf (XI) 6, 104–5, 109

Great Haywood (I) Village in Staffordshire (Tavrobel). 25, 196

Great Haywood (II) Village in Staffordshire (Tavrobel). 146, 290, 292–3, 328; (Old English) *Hagwudu* 290, 292, 328

Great Haywood (V) In Staffordshire. 412–13

Great Hole of Bucklebury (VI) 234, 245, 386. See *Brandy Hall*.

Great Isles (V) 23, 153, (247), 248, 33;, 337

Great Journey (II) (of the Elves from the Waters of Awakening) 64, 307

Great Journey (III) 182

Great Journey (V) See *Great March*.

Great Journey (VII) (of the Eldar) 292

Great Journey (X) 103, 106, 169, 171, 281. See *Great March*.

Great Journey (XII) (of the Eldar to the Sea) 340, 366, 387, 391–2, 403; *the (Great) March* 76, 366, 403

Great Lake (X) 7, 18, 23, 25, 27, 32, 38, 52, 153, 179. See *Almaren*.

Great Lands (I) The lands east of the Great Sea. 15, 18–21, 24–7, 32, 48–9, 51, 68, 81–2, 85 *(i Nori Landar)*, 94, 106, 111, 114, 118, 125, 129, 134–5, 157–60, 166–8, 170, 177, 197–8, 212, 220, 224, 226, 230, 234, 244

Great Lands (II) The lands east of the Great Sea. 4–6, 60, 64–5, 68, 140–1, 206, 208, 249–50, 255, 257–8, 264, 279–81, 283, 285, 289, 292–4, 299–300, 302–3, 306–8, 317, 326–7. See *Lands Without, Outer Land(s)*.

Great Lands (III) 26, 149, 212, 224. See *Outer Lands*.

Great Lands (IV) 5–6, 8, 15, 43–4, 68, 72, 75, 87, 89, 110, 115, 170–1, 197, 233, 274; *the great land* 238; *Great Lands of the East* 224, 230, 233

Great Lands (V) 23, 190, 242, 247–8

Great Lands (VI) 215; *Great Land* 319

Great Lands (VII) 119

Great Lands (VIII) 154, 158–9, 167–8, 401

Great Lands (IXb) Middle-earth. 314, 341–2, 344, 359, 362, 398–9, 402; *Great Central Land* 410. See *Kemen*. *A Great Land beyond the sun*, see *Blessed Realm*.

Great Lands (XII) Middle-earth. 72, 149, 175

Great March (IV) The great journey of the Elves from Kuiviénen. 13, 44–5, 84. See *March of the Elves*.

Great March (V) The great journey of the Elves from Kuiviénen. 112, 115, 169, 171, 175, 181–3, 188–9, 194, 197, 214–15, 217, 221, 225, 344, 405

Great March (IXb) (of the Elves) 406

Great March (X) (of the Eldar from Kuiviénen; including references to *the March, the Westward March*) 82–3, 88–9, 162–3, 169–70, 277, 378, 417, 423. See *Great Journey*.

Great March (XI) (of the Eldar) 122; *the March* 13, 20–1, 23, 106, 195, 373, 375, 381–4, 390; *the Westward March* 371; *Marchers* 374; *Great Journey* 174

Great March, Great Journey (I) 44, 50, 132–3, 144, 244; described 118–20

Great Market, The (II) In Gondolin. 182

Great Men (VI) Númenóreans (cf. V.376, stem NDŪ). 215

Great Music, Great Song (X) See *Music of the Ainur*.

Great One, The (VIII) Orc name for Sauron. 185

Great Ones, The (X) 15, 73; *the Great* (115), 147, 156, 161, 308; *the Seven Great Ones* (X) 15, 44, 147, 151. See *Aratar*.

Great Plains (I) 240

Great Plains (II) 61

Great River (VI) (also *the River*) 214, 397, 399, 410–11, 417, 419, 429, 432, 434, 437–8, 440, 461. See *Anduin, Beleghir*.

Great River (VII) (including many references to *the River*) 67, 119, 122–6, 128, 138, 144–5, 213, 231, 234, 244, 261, 267–73, 280–3, 285, 289, 291–2, 3 15–16, 324–5, 327, 333, 345–6, 350–3, 355–60, 367, 370, 372–3, 379–81, 384, 386, 397–8, 401, 411, 426–7. See *Anduin*.

Great River (VIII) (including many references to *the River*) 50, 69, 116, 128, 133, 145–7, 150, 154, 177, 187, 214, 226, 233, 256, 260, 262–3, 278, 283, 288–9, 291, 294, 313, 326–7, 330–1, 333, 339–40, 345, 356, 363, 366, 370–1, 378, 388, 392, 400, 404, 412, 414, 420, 422, 427–8. See *Anduin*.

Great River (IXa) 49; *the River* 116. See *Anduin*.

Great River (XI) 13, 109, 173–4; *Vale of the* ~ 13. See *Anduin*.

Great River (XII) 56, 238, 311, 437; *the River* 66, 177, 183, 218, 239, 248, 259. See *Anduin*.

Great River of Wilderland (X) 89

Great Road (XII) 193. See *East Road*.

Great Sea (II) (not including many references to the *Sea, the Ocean*) 151, 155, 162, 196, 312, 315, 324. See *Garsecg, Western Sea (s)*.

Great Sea (VI) 122, 320, 399; *Great Seas* 183–4, 331. See *(the) Sea, Western Seas*.

Great Sea (VIII) See *(The) Sea*.

Great Sea (IXa) See *(The) Sea*.

Great Sea (X) 57, 75, 78, 83, 108, 115, 118, 134–5, 271, 295, 423; *Great Sea of the West* 54, 58, 78, 154. See *(The) Sea, Western Sea, Gársecg*.

Great Sea (XI) 6, 8, 91, 104–7, 111. See *(The) Sea, Western Sea*.

Great Sea (XII) See *(The) Sea*.

Great Sea(s) (I) 21, 36, 46, 53, 64, 68–9, 71, 81–3, 85 (*Haloisi Velikë*),

106, 118, 120, 125, 135, 137, 146, 166, 194; also called *the Sea, the mighty Sea*, etc.; *Western Water* 125

Great Sea(s) (IV) 45, 198–9, 208, 210, 214, 239, *249–51, 258–60, 263, 265–7, 271, 296, 328. See *Belegar, West(ern) Sea(s)*.

Great Sea(s) (V) 14, 21–2, 24, 31–2, 64–5, 95, 111, 113–16, 171, 186, 209, 225, 260. See *Belegar, Garsecg, Western Sea*.

Great Sea(s) (VII) 33, 355, 382, 400; *the Sea(s)* 5, 15, 34–6, 82, 92–3, 95, 98–100, 104, 112, 122–4, 137, 153, 156, 158, 177, 210, 212, 216, 232–3, 244, 248, 252, 255, 257, 265, 272, 284, 295, 311–12, 331–3, 384, 395, 411, 416, 418; *Western Sea* 119, 123, 144

Great Sea(s) (IXb) 270, 272, 290, 308, 336, 342, 354, 359, 386, 398–400, 402; *Shoreless Sea* 229, *Western Sea* 398, ~ *Ocean* 289; also many references to *the Sea(s)*, not indexed. See *Gársecg*. *Great Seas* (of Space) 204

Great Stars (X) 34, 39, 384, 387–8

(Great) Storm (IXb) 157–8, 211, 252, 254, 267, 290; *the Black Night* 267

Great Tale, The (X) 377–8, 380, 389, ~ *of Eä* 375, 388; *the Great History* 382; *the Tale* 377, 382, 405; *the Tale of Arda* 68, 223, 232, 240, 246–7, 25 1–2, 389, 392, 405; *the Tale of the Eldar* 246. See also 332, 338

Great Tales (X) 373

Great Tales (XI) 314

Great Theme (X) The Great Music. 240, 242, 244, 246–7

Great War (VII) The War of the Ring. 455; *Great Wars* (of the Elder Days) 110

Great War of the Gods (X) See *Battles of the Gods*.

Great Water (IXb) The Great Sea. 332; *great waters* 351, 373, 391–3

Great Wave (IXb) 217; *Green Wave* 194; *Fluted Wave* 206, 221

Great Wrack (II) 116, 282; *Wrack of Things* 283; *Wrack of the Gods* 285. See *Great End*.

Great, The (XI) 212. See *Aratar*.

Greater Folk (XII) See *Hador*.

Greek (V) 39, 41, 43, 279

Greek (IXb) 206, 221, 240, 249, 285, 409, 419; *Greeks* 289

Greek (XII) 46, 69, 103, 320, 368

Green Dragon (VI) The inn at Bywater. 249, 253–4, 318, 323

Green Dragon (VII) The inn at Bywater. 29

Green Dragon (IXa) The inn at Bywater. 82

Green Elves (II) 234, 248–9; the *brown Elves and the green* 237, 240, 242, 248; (Elves) 'clad in green and brown' 234, 248. See *Laiquendi*.

Green Hill (X) The hill of Túna. 178

Green Hill Country (VI) 50, 72, 107, 278, 284; *Green Hills* 46, 50

Green Hills (VII) (about the middle course of Anduin) 269–71, 273, 285, 313, 315–16, 325; *Green Ravines* (?) 268–9

Green Hills (IXa) In the Shire. 99–100, 107

Green Hills (X) In the north of Valinor. 294

Green Isle (VII) See *Tol Galen*.

Green Mound (X) The Mound of the Two Trees. 55, 61–2, 69, 100, 106–7, 288, 293. See *Ezellohar, Korolairië*.

Green Mound (XI) (of the Two Trees) 401. See *Ezellohar, Korollairë*.

Green Spit (VII) See *(The) Tongue*.

green stone (VII) of Galadriel, see *Elfstone* (2); of Theoden, 431, 444, 448

Green Stone (XI) See *Elessar*.

Green, Howard (IXb) Editor of The Notion Club Papers. 148, 155–7, 211–12, 215, 217, (283)

Green, Mr. (VI) Assumed name of Odo Took at Bree. 135–6, 140–1, 150, 152

Green, Mr. (VII) Frodo's assumed name at Bree. 37, 41–3, 48–9, 71–2, 76, 80. See *Hill of Faraway, Underhill*.

Green-elves (IV) 108, 133–4, 190, (223), 270–1, 277, 311, 313, 320, 331, 336. See *Laiqi*.

Green-elves (V) 114, 119, 126, 128, 141, 148, 175–6, 179, 182–3, 186–8, 194, 196–7, 215, 253, 264–5, 268–9, 274, 283, 307–8, 313–14; described, 176, 263–4. See *Danas, Laiqendi*; other names 215

Green-elves (VI) 412

Green-elves (VII) 377. See *Danians*.

Green-elves (X) 93, 164, 169, 171. See *Laiquendi, Nandor*.

Green-elves (XI) 13, 16, 21, 28, 39, 111–12, 118, *185, 216, 218, 349, 355–6, 385. See *Danas, Laegel, Nandor*.

Green-elves (XII) 349, 365, 367; *Green-elvish* 368. See *Danians, Nandor*.

Greenfields, Battle of (IXa) 101, 107; *of the Green Fields* 119

Greenfields (XII) See *Battle of (the) Greenfields*.

Greenholm (XII) On the Far Downs. 112

Greenland (II) 261

Greenland (VII) 216; *a green land* 212, 216

Greenleaf (VIII) Legolas. 22, 420

Green-tine (VII) See *(The) Tongue.*

Greenway (VI) 142, 332–4, 342, 346–8

Greenway (VII) 45, 69–7 1, 74, 79, 131; *Greenway-crossing, Cross Roads* 74, 80; *the old North Road* 164

Greenway (IXa) 83

Greenwood (the Great) (XII) 79, 174, 193, 229, 244, 258–9, 303, 324; *the Wood, the (Great) Forest* 303, 305–6, 323. See *Mirkwood.*

Greenwood the Great (V) 289. See *Eryn Galen, Eryn Lasgalen.*

Greenwood the Great (IXa) Later name of Mirkwood. 123

Gregory the Great (V) 55

Grendel (V) In *Beowulf* 94

Grendel (VII) (in Beowulf) 65

Grey Annals (IV) The last version of the *Annals of Beleriand.* 294

Grey Annals (V) The last version of *the Annals of Beleriand.* 124, 154, 290, 296, 298–301, 305, 324

Grey Annals (X) The final version of the *Annals of Beleriand.* 3, 49, 123, 142, 307, 326, 357, 423

Grey Annals (XII) 62, 79, 142, 146, 185, 190, 318, 349–50, 362, 387, 388–9

Grey Company (XII) 267

Grey Company, The (VIII) (including references to *the Company*) 254, 308, 310, 313, 320, 397, 399, 409–10, 414, 419–21, 423, 428, 437

Grey flood, River (IXa) 72, 76, 103

Grey Havens (VI) 254, 319, 412–13; *the Havens* 397, 402

Grey Havens (VII) 130, 158, 301, 423; *Havens in the Gulf of Lhûn* 123; *Havens of the High-elves* 244, *Elf havens* 144; *Havens of Escape* 124, 232, 244; *(the) Havens* 154, 167, 232, 235, 244, 286. See *Mithlond.*

Grey Havens (VIII) 78, 219; *the Havens* 405. See *Mithlond.*

Grey Havens (IXa) 53, 80, 109, 112, 132; *the Havens* 52–3, 112, 115, 125. See *Mithlond.*

Grey Havens (XII) 36, 168, 173–4, 178–80, 236, 243, 257, 264; *the Havens* 228, 384, 387–8, 435

Grey Mountains (IV) (1) In the *Ambarkanta.* 239, *249, 255–6, 258. (2) *Ered Mithrin.* 257

Grey Mountains (VII) 306

Grey Mountains (XII) 233, 322–3. See *Ered Mithrin.*

Grey Wanderer (VIII) Gandalf. 153. *Grey Pilgrim* 153; *Grey Fool* 378. See *Mithrandir*.

Grey Wood (IXa) (also *Greywood*, *Grey Woods*). Under *Amon Dîn*. 61, 67, 70

Grey Woods (VIII) South-east of Amon Dîn. 353

Grey-elves (I) 51, 132, 243

Grey-elves (II) of Doriath 64; of Beleriand 64, 128; of Hithlum 204; of Mithrim 205

Grey-elves (IV) 51

Grey-elves (V) 181, 190; *Grey-elven tongue* 299. See *Sindar*, *Sindarin*.

Grey-elves (X) 86, 91, 164, 170, 173, 349. See *Sindar*.

Grey-elves (XI) 5, 9, 18–19, 26, 28, 33–5, 39, 72, 79, 101, 104, 114, 117, 136, 192–3, 214, 315, 344, 375, 384, 410 (origin of the name). *Grey-elven* (tongue) 223, 313. See *Sindar*.

Grey-elves (XII) 78–9, 221, 385; see *Sindar*. *Grey-elven* (language) 78–9, 145; see *Sindarin*.

Greyfax (VII) See *Shadowfax*.

Greyflood River 437. (VIII) See *Gwathlo*, *Odothui*.

Greyflood, River (VI) 192, 201, 441

Greyflood, River (XII) 198, 229, 271, 273, 313, 315, 329–30; see *Gwathló*.

Greyflood. River (VII) 59, 164, 282, 289, 304, 311–12, 402, 439. Called *the Seventh River* 149, 177, 282, 292, 304, 311. See *Gwathlo*, *Odothui*, *Seven Rivers*.

Greylin. River (VII) A source-stream of Anduin. 307

Greymantle (X) Translation of *Singollo*, Thingol (Elwë). 84, 88, 93, 163, 169, 173; *King Greymantle* 86; *Greycloak* 217

Greymantle (XI) Translation of *Sindikollo*, *Singollo*, Thingol (Elwë). 7, 9; *Greycloak* 410

Gríma (VIII) Wormtongue. 355

Gríma Wormtongue. (VII) 445. See *Frána*.

Gríma Wormtongue. (IXa) 65, 73. (Replaced *Frána*.)

Grimbeorn the Old (VII) Son of Beorn. 248, 263

Grimbold of Grimslade (VIII) Rider of Rohan. 370–1

Grímhelm (VIII) See *Dernhelm*.

Grinding Ice (I) See *Helcaraxë*.

Grinding Ice (IV) (Also *the Ice*). 10, 11, 16, 18, 22, 25, 47–9, 55, 86, 92, 95–7, 102, 170, 295, 314, 328. See *Bridge(s) of Ice*, *Straits of Ice*, *Helkaraksë*.

Grinding Ice (V) 125, 221, 232, 236, 238–9, 250, 255, 303; *the Ice* 274. See *Helkaraksë*.

Grinding Ice (X) 108, 174, 281, 295; *the Ice* 283, 295, 310. See *Helkaraxë*.

Grinding Ice (XI) 29, 43; *the Ice* 6, 31, 206, 323; *the Straits of Ice* 343. See *Helkaraxë*.

Grip (VI) One of Farmer Maggot's dogs. 290, 293

Grishnákh (VII) Orc of Mordor. 408, 410; earlier form *Gríshnak* 409

Grishnákh (VIII) Orc of Mordor. 49, 59; *Grishnákh* 59

Grishnákh (XII) 83

Grithnir (II) The elder of Túrin's guardians on the journey to Doriath. 127. See *Gumlin*.

Grithnir (V) Later name for *Grithron*. 151

Grithron (V) Guardian (with Gethron) of Túrin on the journey to Doriath. 138, 151, 317–18, 322. (Replaced by *Grithnir*.)

Grodnof (XI) Variant of *Novrod* (Nogrod). 414

Gróin (XII) Father of Óin and Glóin. 279

Grond (III) The great mace of Morgoth, 'Hammer of the Underworld'. 285, 293

Grond (IV) The great mace of Morgoth. 107

Grond (V) The great mace of Morgoth, 'Hammer of the Underworld'. 284–5, *384*

Grond (XI) 'The hammer of Angband'. 55

Grór (XII) Brother of Thrór. 277

Grubb (VI), *Gorboduc* A friend of Bilbo's. 15, 17–18, 26, 32, 36. (Replaced by *Orlando Grubb*.)

   Grubb (VI), ~ *Iago* (VI) Lawyer. 33, 36

   Grubb (VI), ~ *Inigo* (VI) A great glutton. 38, 247; earlier called *Inigo Grubb-Took*, 15, 17–18, 26–7, 32, 36, 38, 315. (Replaced by *Primo Grubb*.)

   Grubb (VI), ~ *Orlando* (VI) 17, 26, 32, 36. (Replaced *Gorboduc Grubb*; replaced by *Orlando Burrowes*.)

   Grubb (VI), ~ *Primo* (VI) 247, 315. (Replaced *Inigo Grubb*.)

Grubb family, Grubbs (VI) 13–14, 18, 22–3, 25, 31, 33

Gruir (II) River in Tol Eressëa, joining the Afros at the bridge of Tavrobel (see 288). 284, 287

Gruir, River (V) In Tol-eressëa, joining the Afros at Tavrobel. 413

Guarded City (XI) See *Gondolin*; ~ *Kingdom*, see *Doriath*; ~ *Realm*, see both *Doriath* and *Gondolin*.

Guarded Plain (IV) (1) Of Gondolin (*Tumladen*). 34, 36, 66. (2) North of Nargothrond. 126, 128, 184, 225

Guarded Plain (XI) North of Nargothrond. 85, 139–40, 149, 228. See *Talath Dirnen.*

Guarded Plain of Nargothrond (I) See *Talath Dirnen.*

Guarded Plain of Nargothrond (II) See *Talath Dirnen.*

Guarded Plain of Nargothrond (III) 66, 88, 214, 222

Guarded Realm (III) Doriath. 352

Guarded Realm (IV) Valinor. 158, 161

Guarded Realm, The (X) Valinor. 54, 98, 117

Guardians (IXb) [Ramer] 196–7, 217

Guardians, The (XII) The Valar 181 (~ *of the World*), 182

Guest-elves (XI) Nandorin Elves in Doriath. 112

Guests, The (V) An Elvish name for Men. 66

Guests, The (X) An Elvish name for Men. 21, 37, 315–16

Guiðlin (II) Invaders of Tol Eressëa. 294

Guildford, Nicholas (IXb) Member of the Notion Club and its reporter; often called *Nick.* 149–51, 156, 159–74, 176–8, 180, 183, 191, 195, 198, 200, 202, 205, 211–15, 217, 219, 221, 223–4, 227–33, 235, 245, 252–5, 260, 266, 272, 276–7, 281–4, 291, 293, 302. *Maister Nichole of Guldeforde* 150. (Replaced *Latimer.*)

Guilin (IV) (Only referred to as the father of Gwindor) 120–1, 125, 131, 180, 312, 321. (Replaced *Fuilin.*)

Guilin (V) Father of Gwindor of Nargothrond. 136, 138, 308–9

Guilin (XI) Father of Gelmir (1) and Gwindor. 73, 82

Guilwarthon (II) See *I·Guilwarthon.*

Guingelot (XII) The ship of Wade. 371

Guingelot Wade's boat. (III) 144

Gully of the Rainbow Roof (II) See *Cris Ilbranteloth, Teld Quing Ilon.*

Gulma (III) Original Gnomish name of Ulmo. 93. See *Ylmir.*

Gumlin (II) The elder of Túrin's guardians on the journey to Artanor. 74, 76, 92–3, 127. See *Grithnir.*

Gumlin (III) (1) The elder of Túrin's guardians on the journey to Doriath. 9, 12, 14, 22, 25, 126. (Replaced by *Mailgond, Mailrond.*) (2) Húrin's father. 115, 126. (Replaced by *Galdor the Tall.*)

Gumlin (IV) (1) The elder of Túrin's guardians on the journey to Doriath. 58. (Replaced by *Mailgond.*) (2) Son of Hador and father of Húrin and Huor. 23–5, 54, 104–5, 108, 118, 124, 127, 175–6, 297–300, 310, 312, 315, 320; *Helm of Gumlin* 124. (Replaced by *Galdor.*)

Gumlin (V) Called 'the Tall' (146); son of Hador and father of Húrin and Huor. 64, 130–2, 134–5, 146, 179, 275–6, 282, 287–8, 317, 319–20, 328; *the helm of Gumlin* 319–20 (see *Dragon-helm*).

Gumlin (VI) Father of Húrin. 413. See *Galdor*.

Gumlin (XI) Original name of Húrin's father (see *Galion*, *Galdor*). 123, 202, 229, 232, 240–1, 246

Gumniow (II) Apparently an alternative name for Tevildo's doorkeeper (see *Umuiyan*). 24

Gundabad, Mount (XII) 301, 305, 322–3

Gundor (IV) Son of Hador and brother of Gumlin (2). 108, 175–6, 200, 297–8, 315, 317–18

Gundor (V) Son of Hador and brother of Gumlin. 130, 132, 146, 275, 282, 289, 328

Gundor (XI) Son of Hador. 49, 53, 123, 224, 232–4, 241

Gungliont (I) Earlier name of Ungoliont. 156, 160

Gunthorpe Park in Matfield (IXb) 181, 215

Gurthang (XI) 'Iron of Death', Túrin's sword. 83, 86, 92, 98–9, 101–3, 138, (160), 304. Earlier names *Gurtholfin, Gurtholf* 138, 160. See *Anglachel*.

Gurtholfin (II) 'Wand of Death', Túrin's sword (later *Gurthang*). 83, 85, 90, 99, 107–8, 112, 115 earlier form Gortholfin 119

Gurtholfin (III) Túrin's sword. 28

Gurtholfin (IV) 'Wand of Death', Túrin's sword. 31–2, 130–1, 186, 304, 306; *olfir* 32

Gurtholfin (V) 'Wand of Death', Túrin's sword. 139–41, 147, 406; *Gurtholvin* 405; *Gurtholf* 147, *359*, 377 (also *Gurtholv*, *Gurutholf*), 406

Gurthrond (III) 'The valley of the Dead Awaiting' (?) 20, 28; earlier form *Guthrond* 23, 28

Guthláf (VIII) Rider of Rohan, banner-bearer of Théoden. 368, 373. Earlier name *Guthwin* 368, 371, 373

Guthrond (VIII) See 427.

Guthwin (VIII) See *Guthláf*.

Gwaehir (X) 410; *Gwaihir the Windlord* 412

Gwaeron (III) (Sindarin) the month of March. 87

Gwaewar (the Windlord) (VII) 134–5, 139, 151, 426–7, 430; *Gwaiwar* 151. Later name *Gwaihir* 139, 151, 369, 397, 427, 430; *Gwaehir* 430–1

Gwaewar (V) Vassal of Thorondor. 301

Gwaewar (IXa) See *Gwaihir*.

Gwahaedir The (XII) *Palantíri.* 186; *Emyn Gwahaedir*, the Tower Hills, 186. See *Emyn Beraid*.

Gwaihir (V) Later form for *Gwaewar*; see 301

Gwaihir (VI) Lord of Eagles. 120

Gwaihir (VIII) 362. See *Eagle(s)*.

Gwaihir (IXa) 'The Windlord', Eagle of the North; earlier name *Gwaewar* (45). (1) In the Elder Days, vassal of Thorondor. 45. (2) In the Third Age, descendant of Thorondor. 7, 44–5

Gwaihir (XI) The eagle, vassal of Thorondor. 68, 131

Gwanwen (XI), plural *Gwenwin* 'The departed', Sindarin name of the Elves who went to Aman; also *Gwanwel*, plural *Gwenwil*. 378

Gwar, Gwâr (II) =*Mindon Gwar* (Kortirion). 291, 313; *hill of Gwar* 313; *Prince of Gwar* 313, 323. *Gwarthyryn* 307. See *Caergwâr*.

Gwarestrin (II) 'Tower of Guard', one of the Seven Names of Gondolin. 158

Gwareth, mount of (III) The hill of Gondolin (*Amon Gwareth*). 142

Gwasgonin (II) 'Winged Helms', earlier name for the Forodwaith. 334

Gwath-Fuin-daidelos (IV) 'Deadly Nightshade', Taur-na-Fuin. 311. (Replaced *Math-Fuin-delos*.)

Gwathfuin-Daidelos (V) 'Deadly Nightshade', Taur-na-Fuin. 133, 147, 354–5, 382, 397. See *Deldúwath, Fuin Daidelos*.

Gwathlo, River (VII) The Greyflood. 304, 312

Gwathlo, River (VIII) 436–7. See *Greyflood, Odothui*.

Gwathló, River (XII) 198, 294. See *Greyflood*.

Gwathuirim (XII) Dunlendings. 330

Gwedheling (II) Queen of Artanor; name replacing *Gwendeling* in the *Tale of Turambar*. 73, 76, 94–6, 119, 244; *Gwedhiling* (replacing *Gwendeling* in the Gnomish dictionary) 50, 119, 244. See *Artanor*.

Gwedheling (IV) Name of Melian in the *Tale of Turambar*. 59

Gwendelin (II) Queen of Artanor; name replaced by *Gwenniel* in the *Tale of the Nauglafring*. 228, 231–5, 237, 239–40, 243–4, 246, 249–50. See *Artanor*.

Gwendelin (IV) Name of Melian in the *Tale of the Nauglafring*. 63

Gwendelin (XI) Old name of Melian. 347

Gwendeling (II) Queen of Artanor; name replacing *Wendelin* in the *Tale of Tinúviel*. 8–10, 12, 14–15, 17–19, 22–3, 30, 33, 35–7, 49–51, 63–4, 66, 119, 243–4. See *Artanor*.

Gwendeling (III) Name of the Queen of Artanor in the *Tale of Tinúviel*. 125

Gwenethlin (II) Queen of Artanor; name replaced by *Melian* in the typescript text of the *Tale of Tinúviel*. 51, 244, 259

Gwenethlin (III) Name of the Queen of Artanor in the second version of the *Tale of Tinúviel*. 4

Gwenniel (II) Queen of Artanor; name replacing *Gwendelin* in the *Tale of the Nauglafring*. 223, 225, 227, 230, 243–4, 249. See *Artanor*.

Gwerin (XI) Another name for Brandir's kinsman Hunthor (Torbarth). 97, 156, 163–5; his wife 163

Gwerlum (I) 'Gloomweaver', Gnomish name of the great Spider. 152 (*Gwerlum the Black*), 153, 160. See *Wirilómë*.

Gwerth-i-cuina (IV) (Also *Gwairth-*, *Gweirth-* 233.) The Dead that Live Again, and their land. 116, 135, 179, 224, 233

Gwerth-i-Cuina (V) The Land of the Dead that Live. 305–7; *Gwerth-i-Guinar* 313; *Gyrth-i-Guinar* 305, 313; cf. 366, 381–2 (*Dor Firn i guinar*).

Gwerth-i-guinar (XI) The Land of the Dead that Live. 71; earlier forms *Gwerth-i-cuina*, *Gyrth-i-Guinar* 132

Gwindor (II) Elf of Nargothrond, companion of Túrin (earlier *Flinding*). 62, 123–4. See *Flinding*.

Gwindor (III) Elf of Nargothrond, companion of Túrin (earlier Flinding). 83, 89–92

Gwindor (XI) Elf of Nargothrond. 73, 82–6, 134, 138–42, 168, 180, 256, 299, 311, 352. See *Flinding*.

Gwindor of Nargothrond (IV) 59, 120–1, 125, 131, 180–1, 184, 193, 312, 321, 324–5. (Replaced *Flinding*.)

Gwindor of Nargothrond (V) 136, 138–9, 308–10

Gwingloth (XII) See *Vingilot*.

Gwinhir (VIII) Boy of Minas Tirith, precursor of Bergil. 285–6, 293. Earlier name *Ramloth* 293

Gwirith (IXa) April. 129

Gylfaginning (I) A part of the 'Prose Edda' by Snorri Sturluson. 245

Gyönyörü (IXb) [Ramer] 214–15, 218. (Replaced by *Emberü*.)

Gyürüchill (IXb) [Ramer] The planet Saturn. 221. (Replaced by *Shomorú*.)

Habbanan (I) Earlier name of the region Eruman/Arvalin. 79, 82, 91–2, 130–1, 155, 170; poem *Habbanan beneath the Stars* 91–2

Hadhod, Hadhodrim (XI) Sindarin name of the Dwarves (derived from *Khazâd*). 388, 414

Hadhodrond (XI) 'Dwarrowvault', city of the Dwarves in the Misty

Mountains (replaced *Nornhabar*). 389, 414 (etymology), 419; rejected form *Hadhodrad* 419. See *Khazad-dûm*; *Casarrondo*; *Nornhabar*; *Dwarrowdelf*.

Hador (III) 92, 126, 343, 350; *Helm of Hador* 27 (see *Dragon-helm*).

Hador (IV) Called 'the Tall', and 'the Golden-haired'. (Also *Hádor*: see 317.) References include those to the house, son(s), people, etc. of Hador. 104–5, 108, 118, 127, 138, 158, 175–6, 182, 185, 200, 202, 297–8, 300–3, 311–12, 315, 317–18, 332–3; the people described 297, 317

Hador (the Golden-haired) (VIII) Father of Men. 157, 159, 168; *people, folk of Hador* 168–9

Hador (V) Called 'the Golden-haired'. (Also *Hádor*, see 146). 130, 132, 146, 149, 274–5, 282, 289, *363*; the sons, daughter, house, people of Hador 18, 25, 64, 130–2, 134, 136–8, 147, 149, 151, 179, 189, 191, 276, 281, 287, 289, 291, 310–12, 314, 316, 326; the people described, 111, 276; their language 131, 149, 179, 191–2 (see *Taliska*).

Hador (VII) (house of) 455

Hador (IXb) 333

Hador (X) 306, 373, *Hador Lorindol* 305–6; *House of Hador* 306, 344–5

Hador (XI) Lord of Dor-Lómin; called 'the Goldenhaired', and later 'Goldenhead' (see *Glorindol, Lorindol*). 48–9, 51–2, 56, 79, 123–4, 126, 128, 142, 202, 206, 223–6, 228, 230, 232–7, 241, 268; *House of Hador* 48–9, 53, 57, 60–1, 64, 77–8, 135, 165, 224, 228, 232, 234–6, 259, 263–9, 277, 289, 297, 302, 308–9, 311, 313; *People, Folk, Men of Hador* 49–51, 75–7, 79, 90, 123, 128, *182. For the changed genealogy of the House of Hador see 232–5.

Hador (XII) (1) 'Father of Men'. 63, 144, 146, 308, 325, 370; *House, Folk, People of Hador* 294, 303, 307–8, 311–13, 325–6, 330, 348, 368, 373–4; *Hadorians* (XII) 326, 372–3; *Greater Folk* 370

Hador (XII) (2) Seventh Ruling Steward. 204, 219; former name *Cirion* 219

Hador, House of (II) 120, 126

Hægwudu (II) See *Great Haywood, Heorrenda*.

Half-elven (X) 340; *Half-eldar*, see *Pereldar*.

Halabor (XI) See *Angbor*.

Halad (XI) 'Warden', title of the Chieftain of Brethil (see 263, 270,

and *Haladin* (2)). 263, 270–1, 275–80, 283–91, 304, 309. See *Brethil*; *Obel Halad*; *Halbar*.

Haladin (IV) Later name for the People of Haleth. 175, 337

Haladin (XI) (1) The People of (the Lady) Haleth. 217–18, 221–2, 226–8, 233–4, 236–7, 240–1, 265, 268–70, 279, 299, 303–4, 309; ancient tongue of 217, 226, 238, 270, 283, 296, 304; genealogical table 237. See next entry.

Haladin (XI) (2) (Later sense) The kindred of the Lady Haleth, descendants of Haldad; 'wardens' (see 263, 270, 278, and *Halad*). 262–3, 267, 270, 293, 296–7, 302, 304, 306, 309

Haladin (XII) The people of (the Lady) Haleth. 325, 372

Halbar (XI) Proposed replacement of the term *Halad*, and of the name *Haldar*. 238, 309

Halbarad (VII) (1) See *Shadowfax*. (2) Ranger, bearer of Aragorn's standard. 157

Halbarad (VIII) (1) Shadowfax. 265. (2) Messenger from Minas Tirith to Théoden (sister-son of Denethor). 236, 242, 244. See *Hirgon*. (3) Ranger of the North. 297–300, 302, 304–7, 309, 370–1, 389, 3 95–6, 424

Haldad (XI) Father of the Lady Haleth, slain by Orcs in Thargelion. 221–3, 236–7, 265, 270, 278, 303 (name translated 'watchdog' 270).

Haldan (XI) Proposed replacement of *Hardan*. 228, 238

Haldar (XI) Son of Haldad, slain with him in Thargelion; brother of the Lady Haleth. 221–3, 228, 237–8, 278, 303, 308–9. See *Halbar*.

Haldir (V) Son of Orodreth; see *Halmir*.

Haldir (VII) Elf of Lórien, guide of the Company. 235–6, 240–1, 246–7, 256, 262, 279–80, 285–6, 288–9; *Halldir* 246, 262. Earlier name *Hathaldir* 227–36, 240–2, 244, 250–1, 262, 288; originally *Haldir* 240, 262

Haldir (XI) (1), *of Nargothrond* Son of Orodreth. 82, 137. See *Halmir* (1).

Haldir (XI) (2), *of Brethil* Son of Halmir and husband of Glóredhel; fourth chieftain of the Haladin, slain in the Nírnaeth. 133, 234–7, 266, 268–70, 281, 303. See *Hundor*.

Haleth (IV) (1) Originally the son of Hador, later one of the Fathers of Men (see 175, 317); called 'the Hunter' (108, 175). References include those to the people of Haleth. 104, 108, 120, 127, 129, 175–6, 180–1, 185, 297–9, 301–3, 305, 311, 315, 317–18, 320–

1, 324, 332–3, 337; the people described 297, 317. See *Woodmen*. (2) The Lady Haleth. 175

Haleth (V) Called 'the Hunter'. 130, 132–3, 136 ('last of the Fathers of Men'), 147, 149–50, 274–6, 287–9, 291; son, house, people of Haleth 64, 130–3, 135–6, 147, 151, 179, 191, 276, 287, 291, 308, 310, 313–14; the people described, 131, 276; their language 179, 191 (see *Taliska*).

Haleth (VII) (house of) 455

Haleth (VIII) Father of Men. 157, 159

Haleth (XI) (1), *the Hunter* 48–9, 51, 53, 56–7, 60, 70, 74, 97, 123, 125–6, 128, 133, 136, 157, 168, 206, 227–8, 235–6, 240–1, 268; *House, Kin, People, Folk of Haleth* 50–1, 53, 56, 77, 89, 92, 98, 124, 127–8, 132, 147, 157, *182, 186, 228, 267; and see *Halethrim*.

Haleth (XI) (2), *the Lady* 221–3, 227–8, 236–8, 263, 270, 278, 303, 308–9; *People, Folk of Haleth* 133, 222–4, 235–7, 240, 269, 303, 307; *House of Haleth* 289, 295, 297, 308; *Nothlir Haletha* 237, (309); and see *Haladin* (1).

Haleth (XII) (1) Haleth the Hunter. 63, 325. (2) The Lady Haleth. 307, 309, 325; *Folk, People of Haleth* 307–8, 310, 314, 325–6, 329–30, 368, 372, 374; *Halethian* (language) 372. See *Haladin*. Haleth (2) Son of Helm of Rohan. 274; earlier *Haeleth* 271, 274

Haleth, People of (III) 91

Halethrim (XI) The People of Haleth. 164, 255

Half-elfin, Half-elven (IV) 38–9, 70, 75, 151, 155, 158, 162–3, 195, 200, 308–9 (*Half-elfin >Half-elven* 155, 163). See especially 38, 70, 158, and see *Elrond, Elros*.

Half-elven (II) 130, 215, 265–6, 293

Half-elven (V) 23, 34, 148, 152, 219, 332, 337; *Half-elfin* 143–4, 148. See *Peredhil, Pereldar, Peringol*.

Half-elven (VII) 120, 128 (Elrond); *Half-elf* 162, 172 (Erestor); *Half-elves* 326

Half-elven (VIII) 155, 158

Half-elven (IXa) See *Finduilas* (1).

Half-elven (IXb) 333, 340

Half-elven (XI) 71, 242, 257, 348, 351; *Half-elfin* 242

Half-elven (XII) 256, 319, 347–8, 369. See *Peredhil, Pereldar*.

Half-elvish (VI) 395, 400, 413; *Half-elven* 412; *Half-eldar* 412

Half-high (VII) Hobbits. 122, 125, 128, 146, 232, 244, 400; Old English *Halfheah* etc. 465

Half-high (VIII) 36, 139, 145, 164, 166

Halfling(s) (XII) 10, 133, 196, 229, 231, 242–3, 265, 285, 310

Halfling(s) (VIII) 139, 149, 166, 284–5, 311, 382, 390

Halflings (VII) Hobbits. 241, 244, 400, 409

Halflings (IXa) 46–7. See *Periain, Periannath*.

Halifirien (VIII) (1) See *Firien*. (2) The first beacon in Anórien. 233, 257, 343–4, 346–7, 349, 356. See *Mindor Uilas*.

Halifirien (XII) Beacon-hill of Gondor. 53

Hall of Fire (VI) In Elrond's house. 392. *Hall of Feasting* in Elrond's house, also called the *Great Hall*. 392

Hall of Fire (VII) In Elrond's house. 173

Hall of Play Regained (I) In Mar Vanwa Tyaliéva. 15

Hall of Play Regained (II) In Mar Vanwa Tyaliéva. 4

Hall(s) of Iron Angamandi. (II) 166, 264; *halls of darkness* 169

Hallas (XII) Thirteenth Ruling Steward. 205

Halls of Awaiting (IV) 22, 115

Halls of Iron (VI) See *Angband*.

Halls of Iron Angband. (IV) 69

Halls of Waiting (Awaiting) (X) 94, 219, 223, 227, 248, 260–1, 264, 325, 364; other references to the 'waiting' of the Dead 219, 221–2, 233, 235, 266, 268; *the place of waiting of Men* 365

Halls of Waiting (VI) 184, 187

Halls of Waiting (XII) 333, 378, 380–1

Halmadhurwion (I) Another name for Turuhalmë. 244

Halmir (III) (1) Son of Orodreth, slain by Orcs; called 'the hunter'. 75, 82, 91. (2) A ruler of the People of Haleth. 91

Halmir (IV) (1) Son of Orodreth, hanged by Orcs. 312, 323. (2) (later) Lord of the People of Haleth at the time of the Union of Maidros. 181, 323

Halmir (V) Son of Orodreth. 138, 147, 403; subsequently *Haldir*, 147, 354, 386

Halmir (XI) (1), *of Nargothrond* Earlier name of Haldir son of Orodreth. 137

Halmir (XI) (2), *of Brethil* Third chieftain of the Haladin, father of Haldir and grandfather of Húrin. 168, 234–7, 240–1, 268–70, 289

Halog (III) The younger of Túrin's guardians on the journey to Doriath. 9, 11–12, 22, 25, 105–8, 110–11, 113–14, 121–5

Halog (IV) The younger of Túrin's guardians on the journey to Doriath. 28, 58, 183

Halog (V) Earlier name of the younger of Túrin's guardians on the journey to Doriath. 151

Halog (VI) Turin's guardian. 180

Háma (VII) Rider of Rohan. 437, 447

Háma (VIII) (1) Eleventh King of the Mark. 408. (Replaced by *Brytta*.) (2) Rider of Rohan. 5–6, 9, 22, 41, 236, 264, 352. See *Hamelow*.

Háma (IXa) Eleventh King of the Mark. 68. (Replaced by *Brytta*, also named *Léofa*.)

Háma (XII) Son of Helm of Rohan. 271

Hamelow (VIII) The Mound of Háma. 41; *Hamanlow* 41

Hamfast Gamgee (XI) 268

Hammer of Wrath (II) Name of one of the kindreds of the Gondothlim. 174, 176, 179, 183, 218. See Rog (2), *Stricken Anvil*.

Handir (IV) Father of Brandir the Lame; in the *Quenta* son of Haleth (129), but in *the Annals of Bekriand* son of Hundor son of Haleth. 129, 185, 298, 303, 305, 310, 315, 317, 324

Handir (V) Grandson of Haleth and father of Brandir the Lame. 131, 139–40, 289, 363

Handir (XI) (Old genealogy) Son of Hundor, son of Haleth the Hunter. 51, 53, 84–5, 89, 92, 125–6, 139, 141, 145, 147, 152, 157, 199–200, 241. (Later genealogy) Son of Haldir son of Halmir; fifth chieftain of the Haladin. 231, 234, 237–8, 256, 268, 270, 299

Hannar (VI) One of the Dwarves who accompanied Bilbo from Bag End. 238, 240, 315

Hanstovánen (I) The beaching-place of the ship Mornië. 167, 170; also *Vanë Hansto* 170

Happy Mariners, The (I) (poem) 221

Happy Mariners, The (II) (poem) 273–6

Happy Mariners, The (V) (poem) 104

Harad (VII) The South. 313, 333

Harad (VIII) The South. 135–6, 142, 243, 366, 413, 426; =the people of Harad 274, 321; *ships of Harad* 226, 231, 256

Harad (VIII) *Far Harad* 369, 372, 439; *Near Harad* 372, 439; *Harad Road* 439

Harad (IXa) The South. *Men of Harad* 15

Harad (XII) Lands of the South. 79, 175, 197–9, 201, 206, 213–14, 216, 232, 271; *Near Harad* 198

Haradhoth, Haradoth (VIII) People of Harad. 365

Haradrim (VIII) People of Harad. 254, 321, 397–8, 412–13, 420, 427, 437

Haradrim (XII) People of the Harad. 201, 206, 229, 238, 420

Haradwaith (VII) 'Sutherland'. 304, 313, 389; people of the Harad 389, 403, 434, 437, 439–40, 442. See *Harrowland*.

Haradwaith (VIII) People of Harad. 58, 155, 229, 254, 311, 398, 422, 426, 437

Haradwaith (IXa) People of the South. 15–17; *Haradrians* 17

Haramon, Hill(s) of (VIII) Earlier name of Emyn Amen. 359, 363, 372, 397–8, 421, 438

Harathor (XI) (1) Proposed replacement of *Hardan*. 238. (2) Chieftain of the Haladin when Húrin came to Brethil (replaced by *Hardang*). 237–8, 265–71, 278, 303–5, 307–8, 310

Harathrad (XI) The 'South Ford', Sarn Athrad. 335–6. See *Athrad Daer*, *Sarn Athrad*; *Northern Ford*.

Harbour of the Lights of Many Hues (II) In Tol Eressëa. 321; *Haven of Many Hues* 322, 333

Harbourless Isle(s) (II) 317–18, 324–5, 331–2; *Isle of the Old Man* 322; other references to the Isles 5, 7, 311, 315–16, 333

Harbourless Isles (IV) 257

Hardan (XI) Son of Haldar and father of Halmir; second chieftain of the Haladin. (XI) 222, 228, 237–8. See *Haldan*, *Harathor* (1).

Hardang (XI) Chieftain *(Halad)* of the Haladin when Húrin came to Brethil (replaced *Harathor* (2)). 256, 258, 263–6, 269–71, 274–8 1, 283–4, 287–95, 297, 299, 302–4, 307–9

Harding (VIII) Rider of Rohan. 371

Hareth (XI) Daughter of Halmir, wife of Galdor, and mother of Húrin. 234–5, 237–8, 268–70, 280, 289, 309. See *Hiriel*.

Harfalas (VII) Southern coastal regions. 124, 137; *Falas* 124

Harfalas (XI) *184, 187, 190; *South Falas* *184, 187

Harfoots (VI) 124, 294

Harfoots (XII) 10–11, 15, 37, 54, 56–7, 59, 66, 229–30, 247, 328

Harlindon (XII) Lindon south of the Gulf of Lune. 313, 328

Harlond (VII) The South Haven in the Gulf of Lune. 301, 423; earlier form *Harlorn* 301, 423

Harlond (VIII) Quays on the west bank of Anduin at Minas Tirith. 278, 294, 370, (415), 419, 422. Earlier name *Lonnath-Emnin* 294, 370

Harlond (XII) The harbour of Minas Tirith. 421

Harmalin (I) Earlier name of the region Eruman/Arvalin. 22, 79, 82, 85, 130, 155

Harmen (IV) South. *244–5, *248–9, 254–5. (Replaced by *Hyarmen*.)

Harmen (V) South. 200, 345, 372; later form *hyarmen* 200, 345, 365

Harnen, River (VII) 306

Harnen, River (VIII) 237, 265

Harnen, River (XII) 197–8

Harns (VIII) =*Haradwaith, Haradrim* (?). 253–4

Harondor (VII) South Gondor. 310

Harp, The (II) Name of one of the kindreds of the Gondothlim. 173, 182. See *Salgant.*

Harrowdale (VIII) 77, 80, 141, 219, 231, 235–8, 240, 244–5, 249–51, 257, 259, 262, 267–8, 272–4, 289, 296–7, 301, 308, 311–13, 315–20, 322, 346, 355

Harrowdate (IXa) 123

Harrowland, Men of (VII) Haradwaith. 435, 439. Other names *Harwan, Silharrows, Men of Sunharrowland* 435, 439

Harvalien (I) Earlier form for Arvalin. 155

Harwalin (I) Earlier form for Arvalin. 22, 79, 82, 91, 131

Harwan (VII) See *Harrowland.*

Hasen of Isenóra (II) Uncle of Ottor Wǽfre (Eriol); alternative to Beorn. 291

Hasofel (VII) 'Greycoat', Aragorn's horse of Rohan. 402, 424, 439; *Hasufel* 424. Earlier name *Windmane* 402

Hasufel (VIII) Aragorn's horse of Rohan. 301, 305–6, 423

Hasufel (IXa) Aragorn's horse of Rohan. 61 (error for *Arod*), 70, 72

Hasufel (XII) Horse of Rohan. 53

Hasupada (VII) 'Greycoat', see *Gandalf.*

Hathaldir (III) One of the twelve companions of Barahir on Dorthonion. 335, 349

Hathaldir (V) Called 'the Young'; companion of Barahir. 282

Hathaldir (VII) (1) Hathaldir the Young, companion of Barahir. 240. (2) See *Haldir.*

Hathaldir (XI) Companion of Barahir. 56

Hathol (XI) Father of Hador in the revised genealogy. 223, 225, 232, 234 ('the Axe'), 235; later, son of Hador 226, (235)

Haudh-en-Arwen (XI) The burial-mound of the Lady Haleth. 223. See *Tûr Haretha.*

Haudh-en-Elleth (II) The Mound of Finduilas. 130. See *Finduilas.*

Haudh-en-Elleth (XI) The burial-mound of Finduilas. 95, 148, 256, 267, 269, 271, 274, 288, 297. 299, 307; earlier *Haudh-en-Ellas* 92–3, 95, 99, 101, 148; *Mound of the Elf-maid* 148

Haudh-en-Ndengin (I) The Hill of Slain in the desert of Anfauglith. 243

Haudh-en-Ndengin (XI) The Mound of the Slain in Anfauglith. 169; *Haudh-na-Dengin* 72, 79, 133; other variants 79; *Haudh-en-Nírnaeth* 169. See *Hill of Slain*.

Hauð-na-Dengin (V) (136), 312, 314, 316, 322, 363, 375 (*Hauð i Ndengin*). See *Amon Dengin, Cûm-na-Dengin, Mound of Slain*.

Haunted Mountain (VIII) The Dwimorberg. 421

Havard, Dr. Robert (IXb) 150, 152

Haven of the Gods (IXb) See *Avallondë, Avallôni*.

Haven of the Moon (I) 215–16

Haven of the Moon (II) 269

Haven of the Sun (I) 213, 215, 221, 225, 236

Haven of the Sun (II) 266, 268–9

Haven of the Swans (II) See *Swanhaven*.

Haven of the Swans (IV) See *Swanhaven; Havens of Sirion*, see *Sirion; Havens of the Falas*, see *Falas*.

Haven of the Swans (X) 116, 178; *Swanhaven* 86; *the Haven* 116, 125; *Battle of the Haven* 119

Haven of the Swanships (I) 164; *Haven of the Swans* 208; *Swanhaven* 164; *the Haven* 160, 171, 176. See *Ielfethýp, Kópas Alqaluntë*.

Havens (V) *Western Havens* and other references to the Havens of the Falas (Brithombar and Eglorest) 114, 126, 128, 146, 186, 195, 253, 261, 265–7, 269, 404. *Haven of the Swans* 224, 236, 242, *Swan-haven* 113, 326, *the Haven* 237 (see *Alqualondë*). *Havens in the Gulf of Lhûn* (the Grey Havens) 33–4. See *Sirion*.

Havens (VII) (1) Havens of Sirion. 102 (and see *Sirion*). (2) North and South Havens in the Gulf of Lune, see *Forlond, Harlond*. (3) See *Grey Havens*. (4) Haven(s) in the South 372

Havens (XI) (1) Of the Falas (see *Brithombar, Eglarest*). 5, 8, 16, 34, 56, 77, 80, 89, 104, 107, 111, 117, 135, 197, 242–3. (2) The *Ship-havens* at Cape Balar. *184, 190. (3) Of Sirion: see *Sirion*.

Havens (XII) See *Grey Havens, Falas*.

Havens of Sirion (II) See *Sirion*.

Havens of the Falas (X) 90; *Lord of the Havens* 90. See *Brithombar, Eglarest*.

Havens of the Sun and Moon (IV) 255

Havens of Umbar (VIII) See *Umbar*.

Havens, The (IXa) See *Grey Havens*.

Haysend (VI) The southern end of the High Hay. 100, 112, 298–9

Hayward, Hob (IXa) Hobbit; a guard at the Brandywine Bridge. 79–80

Hazad Longbeard (XII) Father of Tal-elmar. 423–3 1, 435, 437; earlier *Tal-argan* 437

Hazowland (VII) See *Sarn Gebir* (1).

Healfdene (V) Father of Hrothgar King of the Danes. 94

Heath of the Sky-roof (V) Near Tavrobel. 413

Heath of the Sky-roof, Battle of the (II) 284–5, 287, 293; *Battle of the High Heath, of the Heaven Roof* (II) 287. See *Dor-na-Dhaideloth, Ladwen-na-Dhaideloth, Withered Heath*.

Heathen Kings (VIII) 376

Heathen, The (IXb) Vikings. 270, 272; *the heathen earls* 269

Heathertoes (VI) Family name in Bree. 137

Heaven (I) 92

Heaven (IXb) 200, 261, 292, 296, 364, 381, 392, 395, 401; *High Heaven* 262, 295, 297, 400. See *Deep Heaven*; *Menel, Pillar of Heaven*.

Heaven Roof, Battle of the (II) See *Heath of the Sky-roof*.

Heaven(s) (X) 40, 71, 84, 86, 130, 132, 134, 146, 160, 202, 284, 346, 355, 371–2, 387; *the far heaven* 17, 27, 38, 41. See *Ilúvë*.

Heavenfield (VII) 94–5

Heavenly Arch, The (II) Name of one of the kindreds of the Gondothlim; also the *Arch of Heaven, the Arch, the Rainbow*. 173, 176, 179–83, 215. See *Egalmoth*.

Heavens, Sky (XII) (in name of a day of the week) 123, 130

Heavyhanded, The (V) An Elvish name for Men. 245

Hebel Dúath (VIII) See *Ephel Dúath*; *Hebel Nimmath*, ~ *Orolos*, ~ *Uilos*, see *Ered Nimrais*.

Heborodin (II) The Encircling Hills about the plain of Gondolin. 166. See *Encircling Mountains*.

Hebraic (XII) 51, 70

Hebrew (IXb) 238, 300

Hecelloi; Heculbar (XI) See *Hekeldi; Hekelmar*.

Heden (I) Father of Eoh, father of Ottor Wǽfre (Eriol). 23

Hedge, The (VI) Fencing Buckland from the Old Forest. 100, 105, 107, 110–12, 327. See *High Hay*.

Hekeldi (XI) Quenya name of the Eldar who remained in Beleriand. 365, 371, 374, 379; singular *Hekel* 365. Telerin *Hecello*, plural *Hecelloi*, 365, 376, 379

Hekelmar (XI) Quenya name of Beleriand. 365; also *Hekeldamar* 365, 374. Telerin *Heculbar* and *Hecellubar* 365, 376

Helcar (I) The Inland Sea. 87. See *Helkar*.

Helcaraxë (I) The Grinding Ice. See *Helkaraksë*.

Helcaraxë (II) 209

Helcaraxë (III) 136

Helevorn (V) Lake in Thargelion beside which Cranthir dwelt. 265, 269, 283, 365, 405. See *Elivorn*.

Helevorn (VI) (1) Lake in Thargelion. 466. (2) Early name for Mirrormere. 459, 466. See *Glassmere*.

Helevorn (XI) Lake in Thargelion. 34, 45, 121, *183

Helgor (II) Earlier name for Ælfheah. 334. (Replaced by *Gelimer*.)

Heligoland (I) 23–4

Heligoland (II) 290–2

Helkar (I) The pillar of the Southern Lamp. 69–71, 87, 106, 118. See *Helcar*.

Helkar (IV) Originally the pillar of the Southern Lamp, 256; in the *Ambarkanta* the Northern Lamp, which became the Inland Sea, (238), 239, *249, 256, 258; later spelling Helcar, the Inland Sea, 256, 259. See *Illuin*.

Helkar (V) The Inland Sea. 261, 267, (364)

Helkar (X) (1) The Northern Lamp. 7, 22, 77. See *Foros*, *Forontë*, *Illuin*. (2) The Inland Sea of Helkar. 72, 77, 82, 87

Helkar (XI) The Inland Sea. 174

Helkaraksë (I) 'Icefang', promontory of the Outer Land in the far North. 167–9, 172, 177, 210, 220, 224, 237, 241. See *Helcaraxë*, *Icefang*.

Helkaraksë (IV) Originally the Icefang (170), subsequently the Strait of the Grinding Ice. 95, 170, 227, *249–51, 260, 267, 269, 279, 338, 340; later spelling *Helcaraxë* 254, 258; O.E. *Isgegrind* 338, 340. See *Bridge(s) of Ice*, *Grinding Ice*, *Straits of Ice*.

Helkaraksë (V) 116, 118, 125, 236, 259, 270–2, 362 (also Noldorin *Helcharaes*), (364). See *Grinding Ice*.

Helkaraxë (X) 108, 118–20, 126, 128, 194, 295; *Helkaraksë* 194. See *Grinding Ice*.

Helkaraxë (XI) 6, 29, 191, 323; *Helkaraksë* 191. See *Grinding Ice*.

Helkaraxë (XII) 362–3; *the Ice* 345, 362–3

Hell (I) 92

Hell (II) Angamandi. 239

Hell (IXb) 262, 297

Hells of Iron (I) 77, 92, 158, 198, 242. See *Angamandi*.

Hells of Iron (II) Angamandi. 45, 61, 77, 157, 159, 161, 196, 206; *Hells of Melko* 187. See *Angamandi, Angband*.

Hells of Iron (III) Angband. 6, 49

Helluin (I) Sirius. 200. See *Nielluin*.

Helluin (X) The star Sirius. 160, 185

Helm (VIII) Ninth King of the Mark. 10–11, 408

Helm (IXa) Ninth King of the Mark. 72

Helm Hammerhand (XII) Ninth King of Rohan. 236–7, 271–2, 274

Helm of Húrin (III) 114–15. See *Dragon-helm*.

Helm's Deep (VII) 320

Helm's Deep (VIII) (including references to *the Deep*) 4–6, 10–12, 15– 19, 21, 23, 25, 27, 29, 39, 41–2, 49, 52, 57–8, 68–72, 76, 78, 100, 120, 140, 238, 241, 248, 250–1, 262, 266, 272–3, 305–6, 310, 396. See *Dimgræf, Heorulf's Clough, Nerwet; Aglarond*.

Helm's Deep (IXa) 63

Helm's Deep (IXb) 292

Helm's Deep (XII) 53, 236, 271, 274

Helm's Dike (VIII) (including references to *the Dike*) 13, 16–19, 22– 3, 40–1, 298, 305–6. *'Inlets'* in the Dike 13, 15–19. See *Stanshelf*.

Helm's Gate, Helmsgate (VIII) (1) The fortress of Helm's Deep (replaced by *the Hornburg*). 10–11, 13, 17, 19. (2) Later sense, the entrance to Helm's Deep. 11. See *Heorulf's Hold*.

Helmshaugh (VIII) Helm's Deep. 11, 23

Helsings (III) Germanic tribe ruled by Wada (Wade). 142–4; Old English *Hælsingas* 143–4

Hendor (II) Servant of Idril who carried Eärendel from Gondolin. 190, 216

Hengest (I) Invader of Britain 23; son of Ottor Wǽfre (Eriol) 24

Hengest (II) Son of Ottor Wǽfre (Eriol), with his brother Horsa conqueror of Tol Eressëa. 290–4, 304, 323

Henion (XII) Third Ruling Steward. 204

Henneth Annûn (VIII) 119, 140–3, 154, 163–4, 166, 175, 178–9, 182, 271, 291, 294–5, 322, 327, 332–3, 338–42, 431; rejected Elvish names 164. *Pool of Annûn* 182. See *Window of the Sunset*.

Henneth Annûn (IXa) 50, 55

Henneth Annûn (XII) 206

Heofonsýl (X) (Old English) 'Pillar of Heaven'; with reference both to Taniquetil and the Meneltarma. 154, 157

Heorot (V) The hall of the Danish kings in *Beowulf* 97; *Hart* 95

Heorrenda (II) (1) Son of Eriol, born in Tol Eressëa. 145, 197, 290–4, 323, 328, 334; *Heorrenda of Hægwudu* 290, 292, 328; *the Golden Book of Heorrenda* 290. (2) In the Old English poem *Déor* 323

Heorrenda (IV) Son of Eriol. 76

Heorulf (VIII) Precursor of Erkenbrand. 8–11, 16–17, 19, 23–4; *Herulf* 8, 10–11, 17, 23; called *the Marcher* 10. See *Trumbold*, *Nothelm*.

Heorulf's Clough (VIII) Original name of Helm's Deep. 9–12, 23; *Herulf's Clough* 11; *Herelaf's Clough* 23; *the Clough* 11, 23, *the Long Clough* 23; *Theostercloh* 23

Heorulf's Hold (VIII) Original name of the Hornburg. 9–12, 17; *Herulf's Hold* 10, 23; *Herulf's Burg* 23. *Heorulf's Hoe* (properly the rock on which the fortress stood) 10–11, 23. See *Helm's Gate*.

Heorulf's Wall (VIII) The Deeping Wall. 19

Herefordshire (V) 80

Herefordshire (IXb) 293–4

Herelaf's Clough (VIII) See *Herorulf's Clough*.

Herendil (V) Son of Elendil. 9, 49, 51–2, 56–63, 65, 68–70, 72–3, 75–8, 364, 378

Herubrand (VIII) Rider of Rohan. 371

Herufare (VIII) Rider of Rohan. 371, 373; later form *Herefara* 373

Herugrim (VII) Théoden's sword. 450

Herugrim (VIII) Théoden's sword. 15

Herulf (VIII) See *Heorulf*, *Heorulf's Clough*, *Heorulf's Hold*.

Herumor (XII) (1) 'Black Númenórean', a lord of the Haradrim. 420. (2) In *The New Shadow*. 414

Herunúmen (IXb) 'Lord of the West'. 310–11; *Númekundo* 311. *Númeheruvi* 'Lords of the West' 246, 311

Herunúmen (XII) Quenya name of Ar-Adûnakhôr. 164

Hesiod (IXb) 289

Heskil (I) 'Winter One', name of Fui Nienna. 66

Hesperia (IXb) Western land. 303, 309. See *Westfolde*.

Hesperides (IXb) 289

Hibernia Ireland. (IXb) 267, 293–4

Hidden City, *Hidden Realm* (XI) See *Gondolin*; *Hidden Kingdom*, see *Gondolin* and *Doriath*; *Hidden Way* (into Gondolin) 48

Hidden Elves (V) A name of the Danas. 215

Hidden Half (IV) (of the Earth) *242–3

Hidden King (V) (1) Turgon. 135. (2) Thingol. 266

Hidden Kingdom (III) Doriath. 10, 106

Hidden Kingdom (V) Doriath. 318, 326

Hidden Kingdom (VI) Doriath. 182

Hidden People (III) The Elves of Doriath. 11, 16, 111, 114, 116–17. See *Woodland Elves*.

Hidden People, The (X) A name of the Nandor. 164

Hiding of Valinor (I) See *Valinor*.

Hiding of Valinor (II) 317, 324–5, 332

Hiding of Valinor (X) See *Nurtalë Valinóreva*, *Valinor*.

High Eldar (X) 318, 370

High Elves (I) 43; *High-elven* 44

High Elves (VI) Elves of Valinor. 188, 280, 285, 324; *High Elves of the West* 71, 187, 225, 260. The High Elves 'live in both worlds', 212, 225, 260, 324

High Elves (VIII) 157–8, 219; *High Men*, see *Men*.

High Elves (IXa) 124

High Elves (XI) 341

High Elves (XII) 31, 73, 78, 174, 221, 246, 256–7, 312, 339, 364; *High Eldar*, see *Eldar*.

High Elves (IXb) 409

High Faroth (II) Highlands above Nargothrond. 124

High Faroth (III) See *Hills of the Hunters*.

High Faroth (XI) 35, 116, 189. See *Taur-en-Faroth*, *Hills of the Hunters*

High Faroth (XII) The highlands above Nargorthrond. 350

High Hay (II) 328

High Hay (VI) The Hedge of Buckland. 298, 304

High Hay (VII) The Hedge of Buckland. 10, 173

High Heath (IV) 259

High Heath (V) Near Tavrobel. 413

High Heath, Battle of the (II) See *Heath of the Sky-roof*.

High Heaven (I) 187

High Men (XII) Númenóreans. 312; *High Men of the Sea* 427

High Moor (VI) South of Rivendell. 201; *high moors* 417

High Pass (VI) Pass over the Misty Mountains east of Rivendell. 416

High Pass (VII) Over the Misty Mountains. 114

High Speech of the West (V) 190

High Speech (of the West) (XI) 21, 26–7, 44; *High Tongue (of Valinor)* 25

High tongue (VIII) 390, 395; *noble tongue* 394. See *Quenya*.

High-elven (VIII) 160–1, 169; *High Ancient Elven* 160; *High Elvish, high-elvish* 159–60

High-elven (XII) (language) 20, 22–3, 30, 36, 77–8, 193, 219, 228, 234, 253, 379; *High-elvish* 63

High-elves (IV) The First Kindred of the Elves. 89; O.E. *héahelfe* 212

High-elves (V) A name of the Lindar. 214, 218, 223, 334, 403 (see *Tarqendi*); in later sense, the Elves of the West, 7

High-elves (VII) 128, 144, 180, 244; *high elven-tongue* 84; *High-elvish* 95

High-elves (X) (1) Name of the (Lindar>) Vanyar (see *Fair Elves*). 163, 168, 176, 180. (2) The Elves of the West. 127, 267–8, 308, 349, 360, 370, 384–5; *High-elvish* (X) (speech) 182. See *Tareldar*.

Hild (XII) Sister of Helm of Rohan. 271

Hildi (V) The Followers, Men. 72, 245, 248, 364; *Hildor* 248

Hildi (VII) 'The Followers', Men. 8

Hildi (IXb) 'sons, or followers', Men. 401. See *Eruhildi*.

Hildi Men. (X) 130. See *Aftercomers, Followers*.

Hildor (I) The Aftercomers, Men. 223

Hildor (IV) The Aftercomers, Men. 257

Hildor (XI) 'The Followers', Men. 219, 386–7; earlier form *Hildi* 31, 174, 219. See *Aphadon, Echil*.

Hildórien (IV) The land where the first Men awoke. 171, 235, 239, *249, 257. See *Eruman* (2).

Hildórien (V) The land where the first Men awoke. 245, 248, 275, 364 (another name *Firyanor*, 381)

Hildórien (X) Land of the awakening of Men. 423

Hildórien (XI) The region where Men awoke. 30, 114, (site of) 173–4

Hill of Death (I) The cairn raised over Finwë Nólemë. 241, 243

Hill of Death (III) The mound raised by the Sons of Fëanor after the Battle of Unnumbered Tears. 87. See *Mound of Slain*.

Hill of Faraway, Mr. (VII) Frodo's assumed name at Bree. 37, 80. See *Green, Underhill*.

Hill of Guard (VIII) The hill of Minas Tirith. 260, 279. See *Tower of Guard*.

Hill of Hearing (VII) Amon Lhaw. 387

Hill of Sight (VII) Amon Hen. 387; *Hill of the Eye* 374

Hill of Slain (I) See *Haudh-en-Ndengin*.

Hill of Slain (IV) 146, 193; *Mound of Slain* 220, 303; other references 27, 56, 58, 119, 302. See *Amon Dengin, Cûm-na-Dengin*.

Hill of Slain (XI) 133, 135; *Mound of the Slain* 169. See *Haudh-en-Ndengin*.

Hill of Spies (II) 128–9. See *Amon Ethir*.

Hill of Spies (IV) Near Nargothrond. 128, 185, 225

Hill of Spies (V) East of Nargothrond. 412

Hill of Spies (XI) 149–50; *the Spyhill* 149; origin of 149. See *Amon Ethir*.

Hills of the Hunters (XI) 116, 190; *Hunters' Wold* 116. See *High Faroth*, *Taur-en-Faroth*.

Hill of Watch (II) 158; *hill of vigilance* 161, 208. See *Amon Gwareth*.

Hill, Mr. (VI) Assumed name of Bingo/Frodo at Bree. 135–6, 138, 140–1, 149–50, 152, 155–6, 223, 280, 324, 334, 338, 340–1

Hill, The (VI) 20, 30, 34, 222, 234–6, 238, 240–1, 244, 247, 315, 385; *Hobbiton Hill* 284

Hills of Iron (I) See *Iron Mountains*.

Hills of Iron (II) See *Iron Mountains*.

Hills of Iron (III) See *Iron Hills*.

Hills of the Hunters (III) The highlands west of the river Narog. 61, 88–9, 214, 222–3; *Hunters' Hills* 66, 88; *Wold of Hunters* 72, 89, *Hunters' Wold* 67, 88, 92; later names *High Faroth* 88–9, *Taur-en-Faroth* 88. The Land of the Dead that Live in the Hills of the Hunters, 61, 89

Hills of the Hunters (IV) The highlands west of Narog. 55, 223–5, 227, 229. See *Duil Rewinion*, *Hunters' Wold*.

Hills of the Hunters (V) 268. See *Taur-na-Faroth*.

Hills of the Hunters (VII) See *Duil Rewinion*.

Himlad (IV) Land between the rivers Aros and Celon. 335

Himlad (XI) 'Cool-plain', land between the upper waters of Celon and Aros. *183, 188, 320, 326, 332–3, 336, 338; for the name see 338.

Himling (Hill of) (VII) Remaining as an island. 124, 138, 301; *Himring* 137–8

Himling (III) Great height east of the Gorge of Aglon. 263, 274; later form *Himring* 274, 313, 361

Himling, Hill of (IV) 103, 106, 108, 111, 115–16, 119–20, 173, 224, 233, 297–8, 300, 316, 318, 330; the passes to the east 298, 318; island of Himling 199; later form *Himring* 57, 108, 115, 120, 199

Himring, Hill of (V) 'Ever-cold' (265). 145, 177, 189, 263, 265 (described), 268–9, 283, 289, 307, 311, (364, 383–4); earlier form

Himling 127, 132, 134, 145, 189, 268–9; the speech of Himring 177

Himring, Hill of (XI) 34, 53, 59, 67, 70, 77, *183, 219, 319, 321, 324, 326, 332, 334–5, 337–8; earlier form *Himling* 127

Himring, Hill of (XII) 330

Hiradorn (III) =*Hirilorn*. 208

Hirgon (VIII) Messenger from Minas Tirith to Théoden. 316–17, 319, 321, 352. For earlier names see *Barahir* (2), *Dirgon*, *Halbarad* (2); and see *Messenger(s) from Minas Tirith*.

Híri (I) Stream in Valinor. 142, 156

Hiriel (XI) Earlier name of Hareth. 235, 269

Hiril (XI) (1) Daughter of Barahir. 232. (2) Daughter of Halmir of Brethil, sister of Hareth. 264, 266, 269–70, 280, 289, 308–9

Hirilorn (II) 'Queen of Trees' in Artanor. 18–19, 46, 51, 54. (Replaced *Golosbrindi*.)

Hirilorn (III) 'Queen of Beeches' in Doriath. 186, 202–3, 206–9, 312

Hirluin the Fair (VIII) Lord of Pinnath Gelin. 287, 371

Hirwen (XI) Sister of Barahir. 231

Hisildi (I) The twilight people: Dark Elves. 232, 244

Hisilómë (I) 101, 106–7, 111–12, 115, 118–19, 132, 135, 138, 158–9, 175, 196, 237–9, 241–4; see especially 111–12, 135, and see *Aryador, Dor Lómin, Land of Shadow*.

Hisilómë (II) 10–11, 13, 17, 21, 23, 31, 38, 43, 45, 47, 51, 61–6, 70, 88, 92, 102–3, 115, 117, 119–20, 126, 138, 140, 204, 215, 222, 234, 240, 243, 248–51, 280. See *Aryador, Dor Lómin, Hithlum, Land of Shadow(s), Mathusdor*.

Hisilómë (III) 28, 89. See *Hithlum*.

Hisilómë (IV) 4, 22, 53, 101, 220–1; translated 'Twilit Mist' 4, 'Land of Mist' 101, 107, 296, 316. See *Aryador, Dor-lómin, Hithlum*.

Hísilómë (V) Hithlum. 266, (364), 370, 406; *Hísilumbë* 370, 406

Hísilómë (XI) Exilic Noldorin name =North Sindarin *Hithlum*. 192, 400

Histories, The (IV) 240

Hithaeglir (IV) The Misty Mountains. 256–7

Hithaeglir (V) The Misty Mountains. 336

Hithaeglir (X) 'Towers of Mist'. (82), 83, 89. See *Misty Mountains*.

Hithaeglir (XI) The Misty Mountains. 322, 384–6, 389

Hithdilias (VII) See *Eredhithui*.

Hither Lands (IV) Middle-earth. (In the *Quenta* replacing *Outer Lands* and *Great Lands*). 85, 89, 99, 101, 115, 148, 155, 163, 171, 233,

*250–1, 258, 266–7, 269–70, 295, 309, 328; *hither world* 103; O.E. *Hiderland* 281, 338

Hither Lands (V) Middle-earth. 118–19, 125, 170–2, 176–8, 184, 220–1, 326, 328, 332, 334, 405. See *Cinderion*.

Hither Lands (VI) Middle-earth. 71

Hither Lands (X) Middle-earth. 77, 172, 174

Hither Lands (XI) Middle-earth. 22

Hitherland (VII) 94, 97. *Hither Shore(s)* 94, 98, 102, 225, 284

Hithliniath (V) 'Pools of Mist'. 262, 268, 364. See *Aelin-uial, Umboth Muilin*.

Hithliniath (XI) 'Pools of Mist'. 194. See *Aelin-uial, Umboth Muilin*.

Hithlum (I) 107, 112, 135

Hithlum (II) 61, 71–2, 74–7, 87, 120–2, 126–7, 131, 142, 204–5, 218, 238, 240–2, 248–52. See *Hisilómë*.

Hithlum (III) 6, 8, 10–11, 14, 16, 19–20, 24–5, 27, 29, 34, 37, 44, 54, 59–60, 62, 73, 87, 96–7, 101, 105–7, 111–17, 119, 125–6, 148, 170, 274, 284, 287, 314. See *Aryador, Dorlómin, Hisilómë, Land of Shadows, Lands of Mist*.

Hithlum (IV) 22–5, 27–8, 30, 35–6, 39, 53–4, 57, 59–67, 101–5, 107–8, 116–23, 126–7, 131, 138–9, 141–2, 146, 151, 157, 160, 163, 176, 180–2, 185, 192–4, 202, 210, 220–2, 229, *250–1, 258–9, 268, 280, 296–7, 299–300, 302–3, 305, 313, 316–17, 319–22, 324, 330, 332, 334; O.E. *Hasuglóm, Hasuland* 210; *Hithlum* equated with Dor-lómin 22, 101, 221. See *Aryador, Dor-lómin, Hisilómë*.

Hithlum (V) 19, 117, 127, 130–1, 133–40, 145, 147, 151–2, 239, 249–52, 255, 259–60, 263–4, 266, 269–71, 276, 280–2, 284–5, 287, 289, 291, 307–8, 310–14, 316, 318–23, 328, 364, 370, 404, 406; *Men of Hithlum* 19, 311, 319–21; *King of Hithlum* (Fingolfin) 128, 146, *Aran Chithlum* 322; northern edge of Hithlum 270–1; origin of the name 'Land of Mist' 259, 266

Hithlum (X) 297

Hithlum (XI) 5–6, 17, 29, 31–2, 38, 46, 49–52, 54, 56, 59–60, 70–2, 76–81, 85, 104, 120, 123, 125–8, 134–7, 139, 162, 166, 168, 176, 192, 202, 219, 227, 234–5, 239, 251–4, 256–7, 260, 262, 264–5, 275, 277, 294, 313, 400; *the North-realm* 287. See *Hísilómë*.

Hlýda, Hlýdingaburg (III) (Old English) Narog, Nargothrond. 87

hnau (VII) See 411, 419.

Hnau (IXb) [Lewis] 175, 202, 204–5, 207, 210, 214, 220

Ho! ho! ho! To my bottle I go (VI) 91, 287

Ho! Tom Bombadil/Whither are you going (VI) 115–16

Hoardale (VI) Briefly replaced *Dimrill-dale* in the earlier sense. 205, 432

Hoardale(s) (VII) See *Entish Land(s)*.

Hoards of the Dwarves (VI) 78, 87, 226–7, 260, 399

Hoarwell, River (VI) 192, 200–5, 360, 368; *Hoarwell Bridge* 200–1. See *Mitheithel, Last Bridge*.

Hoarwell, River (VII) 10, 14, 16–17, 5 8–9, 69, 152, 164; *Hoarwell springs* 61. See *Mitheithel*.

Hoarwell, River (XII) 67, 229, 250, 315

Hobbit families (XII) References include all occurrences of members of families (women by maiden name, not married name) except for *Bilbo, Frodo, Meriadoc, Peregrin, Samwise*, which are separately entered. For the true names (not referenced here) of families and individuals see 45–51, 58–60, 68–9, 81, 83.

Baggins (XII) 5, 85–98, 100–1, 103–7, 109–11

Banks (XII) 108

Boffin (XII) 5, 15, 88–92, 94, 96–101, 106, 108–11, 117–18

Bolger (XII) 40, 51, 61, 70, 87–111, 117–18

Bracegirdle (XII) 89–92, 99–101, 103, 105

Brandybuck (XII) 40, 47, 57, 59, 69, 80, 89–92, 95–7, 99–106, 108–11, 117

Brockhouse (XII) 100–1

Brown (XII) 114–16

Brownlock (XII) 88

Bunce (XII) 88, 91–2

Burrows (XII) 86, 88–90, 92, 94, 99–103, 105–6

Chubb (XII) 86, 88, 90–2, 109–11; *Chubb-Baggins* 88, 92, 94, 97

Cotton (XII) 44, 68, 108, 112–16, 118

Diggle (XII) 94, 97

Drinkwater (XII) 102

Fairbairn (XII) 25, 112–13, 116

Gamgee (XII) (including *Gardner, Greenhand, Roper*) 45, 83, 108, 111–16

Gaukroger (XII) 87–8, 91–2, 94, 96

Goldworthy (XII) 103

Goodbody (XII) 88, 97

Goodchild (XII) 114–15

Goodenough (XII) 100–1

Goold (XII) 102–3, 105

Grubb (XII) 88–92, 100–1

Headstrong (XII) 103

Hogpen (XII) 102–3, 105

Hornblower (XII) 6, 17, 51, 69–70, 88–92, 94, 97

Lightfoot (XII) 94, 97

Noakes (XII) 86

Oldbuck (XII) 40, 80, 83, 102–3, 105–6, 232, 235

Proudfoot (XII) 86, 88–92

Sackville (XII) 89–92

Sackville-Baggins (XII) 69, 86–92, 94, 99–101, 118

Sandyman (XII) 86

Smallburrow (XII) 6

Smygrave (XII) 69

Took (XII) 5–7, 10–11, 15–18, 40, 47, 85–6, 89–92, 97–102, 104–11, 115–18, 121, 226, 235–8, 243, 249–50, 283, 288;

Took-Bolger (XII) 106; *Took-Brandybuck* 105–6; *North-tooks of Long Cleeve* 108

Whitfoot (XII) 112, 115

Hobbit, The (I) 23, 43

Hobbit, The (VI) 11, 17–18, 25–8, 31, 33, 35, 38, 43–4, 85–6, 108–9, 131, 173, 186, 193, 203–5, 218, 222, 224, 226, 245–6, 261, 268, 271, 283, 310, 314, 329–30, 374, 381–2, 384, 387, 399, 411, 414, 432, 437–8, 440, 444, 460, 465; '*sequel to The Hobbit*' 40, 43–5, 108–9, 173, 370, 384

Hobbit, The (VII) 27, 29, 38–9, 137–8, 142–3, 155–6, 159–60, 172, 187–8, 298, 452

Hobbit, The (VIII) 223; referring to *The Lord of the Rings* 77

Hobbit, The (IXa) 12, 119, 132

Hobbit, The (X) 89, 414. *Hobbit world, Hobbit-lore* 5–6

Hobbit, The (XI) 207–8

Hobbit, The (XII) (title) 3, 7, 10, 12, 15, 18, 25, 29, 53, 71–2, 76, 81–2, 249, 283, 286, 288, 319, 322–3

Hobbiton (VI) 13, 15, 19–21, 25–6, 29, 32, 37, 40–1, 43, 46, 50, 54–5, 62, 64, 69, 71–2, 76, 83, 92, 95–6, 106–7, 122, 133, 160, 210, 217, 221–2, 228, 233–4, 237, 244, 247, 249–50, 253–4, 265, 268, 272–4, 276, 278–80, 284, 288, 294–5, 299–300, 304, 312,

318, 323, 326, 336, 338, 366–7, 372–6, 379, 385, 391, 401, 407, 459; *Hobbitonians* 41

Hobbiton (VII) 6–8, 10–13, 43, 68, 70, 73, 78, 80, 83, 116, 130; the mill 249, 253; the Hill 264, 266

Hobbiton (IXa) 80, 82–3, 85, 87–8, 99–101, 103, 105–7, 118, 127; *the Hill of Hobbiton* 103; *the Old Mill* 88, 106, *the Old Grange* (88), 106, the bridge 89

Hobbiton (XII) 85, 89–92, 112–13, 116, 118, 241; ~ *Hill* 98; *the Hill* 98, 288

Hobbits (V) 98, 199, 293–4

Hobbits (VI) (Selected references). Stature 311; beardlessness 52, 294, 312; shoelessness 312; silence of movement 46, 50, 61, 312; short memories 20; weddings 15 and their children 14, 24; and dragons 19, 29, 41; presents 21, 312; money (ducats, double-dragons, silver pennies) 16, 34, 164, 174, 252, 268; houses, holes (architecture) 92, 289, 294, 310, 312–13; families and their lands 313; maps 252; language 311; 'Hobbit translation' of Elvish names =English 432. A general account of hobbits 3 10–14. *Wild Hobbits*, see *Rangers*.

Hobbits (VII) (general references) 24–6, 31, 84, 114–15, 228–9, 232, 241, 244, 326, 379, 386, 397. See *Half-high*, *Halflings*.

Hobbits (VIII) (general references) 36, 38–9, 66, 75–6, 123, 127, 150, 156, 160, 163, 241, 282, 284–5, 306, 388; the name 36, 44; *Hobbit-ells* 89, 99. See *Half-high*, *Halfling(s)*, *Holbytla*.

Hobbits (IXb) 409

Hobbit(s) (XII) (Often used attributively, as *Hobbit legend*, ~ *year*) 3, 5–8, 10, 13–20, 24–5, 27–9, 37–61, 66–7, 69–74, 86, 94, 102, 119, 121–5, 127–33, 136–7, 168, 209, 211, 225, 229, 236, 245, 247, 253, 262, 268, 283, 288, 302, 309–11, 314, 326–7; true Westron words for 'Hobbit' 83; *wild Hobbits* 10, 121, 127; *western Hobbits* 37–8, 311; *Shire-Hobbits* 126. See *Halflings*, *Periannath*.

Hobbit(s) (XII) Language of Hobbits 8, 10, 15, 17, 20, 27, 37–9, 43, 45, 48–55, 57–8, 67, 72–3, 311; the word *Hobbit* (etymology and 'translation') 10, 49–50, 53, 59–60, 69, 83

Hocker-men, *Hoker-men* (VIII) Earlier name of the Púkel-men. 245–6, 248, 260

Holbytla (VIII) Hobbit. 44, 348; *Holbytlan* (plural) 36; *Holbylta(n)* 36, 44

Holbytlan (IXa) (Old English) Hobbits. 47

Hold of Dunharrow (VIII) See *Dunharrow*.

Holdwine (IXa) Merry Brandybuck's name in Rohan. 68

Holdwine (XII) Meriadoc's name in Rohan. 261, 273

Hollin (V) 345, (*Regornion 356*)

Hollin (VI) 418–21, 4z9, 432, 435, 438, 440–1, 444, 448–9, 463. See *Eregion, Regornion*.

Hollin (VII) 124–5, 156, 165–6, 167, 169, 178–9, 204, 365, 367–8. See *Eregion*.

Hollin (XII) 76, 79, 168, 174, 248. See *Eregion*.

Hollowbold (XI) Nogrod. 206, 209, 389; translation of the original form *Novrod*, see 389, 414.

Holy Elves (V) A name of the Lindar. 215

Holy Elves (X) A name of the Vanyar. 164

Holy Mount (V) Taniquetil. 234

Holy Mountain (X) Taniquetil. 100, 112, 154, 289; *Holy Hill* 159

Holy Ones (X) See *Ainur*.

Homecoming of Beorhtnoth, The (VII) Early version in rhyme. 106–7

Homer (IXb) 289, 413; *Homeric* 408; *the Iliad* 186

Hope (X) 245, 311, 320, 322–3, 327, 332, 338; *the Hope 351, the Great Hope 351–2, 356; the Old Hope 321, 356. See *amdir, estel* in the Index of Elvish terms, X.470

Hopton Heath (V) In Staffordshire. 413

Horn (VIII) Rider of Rohan. 371

Horn of Cloud (VII) See *Cloudyhead*.

Horn of Oromë (X) 7, 39, 70, 76, 202, and see *Rombaras, Valaróma*.

Hornblower family. Hornblowers (VI) 31, 33, 78, 284; *Hornblower country* 278, 284, 295

Hornblower, Adam (VI) The Hobbiton blacksmith. 82, 265

   Hornblower, Adam (VI) ~ *Carambo, Colombo* (VI) 247, 315. (Replaced *Cosimo Hornblower*.)

   Hornblower, Adam (VI) ~ *Cosimo* (VI) 38, 247. (Replaced *Cosimo Chubb*.)

   Hornblower, Adam (VI) ~ *Tobold* (VI) First grower of pipeweed in the Shire. 284

Hornblower, Tobias (VIII) First grower of pipeweed in the Shire. 37–40, 45; *Old Toby* 38, and as name of a pipeweed 45; replaced by *Tobold Hornblower*, 37, 39, 45. Family name 59. See *Elias Tobiasson, Smygrave*.

Hornburg (XII) 296

Hornburg, The (VIII) (including references to *the Battle of the Hornburg* and to *the Gates, the Burg, the Tower*) 5–7, 10, 18–19, 21–22, 25, (30), 40–2, 47, 52–3, 60, 70–3, 92, 95, 100–2, 120, 250, 257, 274, 276, 291, 296–9, 301–2, 305–11, 405, 410–11, 424. The *palantír* of the Hornburg 71–2. See *Helm's Gate, Heorulf's Hold*.

Hornpipe Shag (VIII) Name of a pipeweed. 45

Hornpipe Twist (XII) A variety of pipeweed. 6, 18; ~ *Cake* 18

Hornrock, The (VIII) 310. See *Stanrock*.

Horns of Ylmir (IV) (poem) 213–18

Horsa (I) Invader of Britain 23; son of Ottor Wæfre (Eriol) 24

Horsa (II) See *Hengest*. 290–4, 304, 323

Horse-kings (VI) 422, 435, 440; *Horse-lords* 435, 440; *Horsemen* 434; *Horseland* 434. See *Rohan, Rohiroth*.

Horsemasters (VII) 135, 351, 357, 392, 395–6, 398, 412, 430, 433. *Horse-kings* 140; *Horse-lords* 168; *Horsemen (of Rohan)* 148, 208, 210–11, 214, 330, 372, 374, 408–9, 437, 442

Horsemasters (VIII) 154; *Horse-marshals* 155; *Horsemen* (of Rohan) 56, 156, 229, 254, 351; *Horseboys* (Orc-name for Rohirrim) 213, also used of Orcs of Minas Morghul, 217

Horserland (VII) Rohan, 71; *Horsermark* 151

Host of Dân (X) See *Dân*.

Host of the West (VII) 142, 263

Houghton Mifflin Company (VI) 200, 305

House of a (the) Hundred Chimneys (II) The house of Gilfanon at Tavrobel. 283–4, 310

House of a Hundred Chimneys (IV) The house of Gilfanon at Tavrobel. 274

House of Lost Play (I) 189; poem *The Little House of Lost Play* 28, 30–1

House of the Hundred Chimneys (I) The house of Gilfanon at Tavrobel. 175, 196

House of the Hundred Chimneys (V) The house of Gilfanon at Tavrobel. 413

House, The (X) (1) As image of the body. 362–3; *the House and the Indweller* 316–17, 352–3; *houseless* (of the Dead) 218–19, 221–5, 232, 248, 330–1, 339, 353, 361–5, 403 (of Melkor); *housed, unhoused, rehoused*, etc. 218, 221, 236, 243, 248–9, 269, 337, 339–40, 342, 349, 353, 361–5

House, The (X) (2) Of Melkor in the *Tale of Adanel.* 347–8

Houses of Healing (VIII) (374–5, 377, 379–80, 385); 379–80, 386, 389–93, 403, 406, 416–17, 419, 421; *Warden of* 394. See *Berin a Nestad.*

Houses of Healing (IXa) 54

Houses of Healing (XII) 68

Houses of the Dead (X) 145, 148

Hravani (XI) Men other than the Edain, 'the Wild'. 219; Sindarin *Rhevain* 219

Hressa-hlab (IXb) [Lewis] 213, 220. See *Old Solar.*

Hrívion (I) The third part of the poem *The Trees of Kortirion.* 42

hröa (XII) The body of an incarnate being. 391

Hroald (V) Viking leader. 80

Hrossa (IXb) [Lewis] 203, 220

Hrothgar (V) King of the Danes in *Beowulf* 93–4

Huan (II) Called 'lord of the Hounds of Hisilómë (47), 'Captain of Dogs' (21, 231), 'Huan of the Dogs'. 21–3, 26–7, 30–1, 34–6, 38–9, 41, 47–8, 53–9, 62, 68, 231, 233–4, 239, 243

Huan (III) 87, 107, 236, 238–9, 241–8, 251–8, 260, 263–7, 269–73, 278–9, 283–4, 287–8, 290, 294, 306, 311–12, 314, 358; *the hound of Hithlum, Huan wolf-bane* 107

Huan (IV) 25–6, 56, 62, 110–16, 123, 138, 169, 177–8, 219, 221, 225, 300–1; *lord of dogs* 25; his speaking 112, 115

Huan (V) The Hound of Valinor. 135, 151, 300, 364–5

Húan (VI) 183 (*hound of the Gods*), *Huan* (see III) 197

Huan (X) The Hound of Valinor. 251, 408, 410–12

Húan (XI) The Hound of Valinor. 62–3, 66–8, 129, 131

Humarni (I) A name of the Dark Elves. 244

Hundad (XI) Son of Hundar and father of Hardang. 237, 263, 269–70, 284, 289, 308

Hundar (XI) (1) Name intermediate between *Hundor* and *Haldir* (of Brethil). 166, 168, 235–6. (2) Brother of Haldir of Brethil, slain with him in the Nírnaeth; grandfather of Hardang. 133, 236–8, 269–70, 281, 303, 308–9

Hundor (IV) Son of Haleth and father of Handir. 297–8, 301–3, 310–1l, 315, 317, 321; see especially 317

Hundor (V) Son of Haleth. 130–1, 136, 146–7, 275, 310, 314, 364

Hundor (XI) (Old genealogy) Son of Haleth the Hunter. 49, 51, 70, 72, 74, 126, 128, 133, 136, 157, 168, 233, 236, 268. (Later genealogy)

Name retained as son of Halmir, 235–6; replaced by *Hundar* (1), and finally by *Haldir*, q.v.

Hundor (XII) Son of Haleth the Hunter. 325

Hundredweight Party (VI) 251

Hungary (IXb) 159, 201; *Magyarország* 201; *Magyar* 201

Hungry Sands (II) On the coast of the Isle of the Ancient Mariner. 318

Hunleth (XI) Daughter of Hundar (2). 237–8

Hunters' Wold (III) See *Hills of the Hunters*.

Hunters' Wold (IV) 25, 55, 189. See *Hills of the Hunters*.

Hunters' Wold (V) 268. See *Hills of the Hunters*.

Hunthor (II) Companion of Turambar in the attack on Glaurung. 133

Hunthor (XI) Companion of Túrin in the attack on Glaurung. 152, 156, 164, 237–8, 256–7, 264–7, 269–70, 297, 299, 303, 309. See *Albarth*, *Gwerin*, *Torbarth*, and for the development of his story and genealogy see 155–6, 267, 269–70.

Huor (II) 214

Huor (IV) 24, 35, 39, 54, 67, 104, 108, 116, 118, 120, 122, 141, 146, 176, 181, 183, 192, 298, 301–3, 312, 315, 318, 321

Huor (V) 64, 131, 136–8, 140, 179, 191, 275, 289, 307, 311, 316, 328, 359, *364*

Huor (VI) 413

Huor (VIII) Brother of Húrin Thalion. 155

Huor (IXb) 340

Huor (XI) 51, 57(-8), 71, 75–6, 79, 81–2, 89–91, 126–7, 133, 135, 166, 169–70, 200, 224, 23 1–2, 234, 237, 241, 302, 314

Huor (XII) Father of Tuor. 348

Huorns (VIII) 6, 30–1, 40, 43, 46, 56–8, 69–70, 345; *Huorn-forest*, *Huorn wood* 39, 70, 297; other references 4, 16, 18, 22, 25–7, 47, 49, 51, 59, 404. See *Galbedirs*, *Lamorni*, *Ornómi*.

Húrin (I) 239, 242; *folk of*, 244. See *Úrin*.

Húrin (II) 52, 118, 120, 126, 128, 131, 135, 137, 210, 216, 245. See *Úrin*.

Húrin (III) 4,7, 11–14, 21–7, 37, 55–6, 71, 92, 96–8, 100, 102–5, 111–15, 117, 119, 125–6 (references to Túrin as *son of Húrin* etc. are included under *Túrin*). Called *the Steadfast* 11–12; *Prince of Mithrim* 96, 103; *Lord of the Lands of Mist* 96; and see *Erithámrod*, *Thalion*. Earlier form *Úrin* 21–2, 25 (*Urinthalion* 21).

Húrin (IV) (including references to the Children of Húrin) 23–8, 32, 34–5, 38–40, 54–6, 58–9, 61, 104–5, 108, 116–22, 132, 136,

141, 146, 165, 175–6, 181–3, 185, 88–9, 192, 194, 199, 222, 298–303, 306, 311, 315, 3 17–18, 320–2, 325; original form *Úrin* 56, 188

Húrin (V) Called 'the Steadfast' (131, 312, 318, sc. *Thalion*, 388). 30, 131–2, 134–8, 141, 147, 150, 275–6, 287–9, 291, 307, 309, 311–20, 322, 328, 333, 361, 364, 403

Húrin (VI) 413

Húrin (VIII) (1) Húrin Thalion. 155, 293. (2) Húrin the Tall, *Warden of the Keys* of Minas Tirith. 369, 401–2, 423; *Warden of the City* 369

Húrin (X) 76, 373; *Children of Húrin* 76; *Narn i Chîn Húrin* 373

Húrin (XI) (including *Húrin Thalion*, 'the Steadfast') 51, 53, 57–8, 60–1, 63–4, 71–2, 74–80, 83–90, 92–3, 96, 99–101, 125–9, 134–5, 137–8, 143, 145–6, 148, 152, 162–3, 165–70, 181, 199–200, 224, 231–2, 234–5, 237, 241, 244–5, 251–5, 257–308, 310–11, 314, 346–7, 349–50, 352–5, 409; *Húrin Hadorion* 294. See *Thalion*.

   Húrin (XI) *The children of Húrin* (XI) (not as title) 102–3, 164–5, 252, 254, (258, 274), 290, 301, 403; *Hîn Húrin* 403. See *Lay of the Children of Húrin, Narn i Chîn Húrin*.

Húrin (XII) (1) Húrin of Dor-lómin. 144, 309, 327, 372, 374–5; *The Children of Húrin* 357–8; old form *Úrin* 374. *The Wanderings of Húrin* (title) 372

Húrin (XII) (2) Steward to King Minardil. 202–3. (3) *Húrin I.* Fifth Ruling Steward. 204. (4) *Húrin II.* Fourteenth Ruling Steward. 205. (5) *Húrin of the Keys* (of Minas Tirith). 271

Húrin the Steadfast (IXb) 332–3, 340

Húrinien, iChúrinien (XI) 'The Children of Húrin' (title). 311, 313. See *Narn i Chîn Húrin*.

Hurinionath (XII) Descendants of Húrin (2). 202–3, 218

Husbands, Winifred (VI) 144–5

Huxley, Thomas (IXb) 208, 222

Hwiccian 291. (IXb) [*Hwicce*, a West Midland people whose name survives in the Forest of Wychwood.]

Hy Bresail (V) See 81

Hyarantar (X) Earlier name of Mount Hyarmentir. 98, 105, (190), 291, 386

Hyarantë (X) The Southern Lamp. 7, 32, 38, 60. (Replaced *Hyaras*, replaced by *Ormal*.)

Hyaras (X) The Southern Lamp. 7, 17, 38. (Replaced *Ringil*, replaced by *Hyarantë*.)

Hyarmen (IV) South. *244–5, *248–9, 255. (Replaced *Harmen*.)

Hyarmendakil I (XII) Name taken by Kiryahir, fifteenth King of Gondor. 197–8, 210, 212–13, 260, 315; translated *South-slayer* 198, 213

Hyarmendakil II (XII) Name taken by Vinyarion, twenty-fourth King of Gondor. 199, 214

Hyarmentir (IV) The highest mountain south of Taniquetil. 47; unnamed 16, 91

Hyarmentir (X) Highest peak of the southern Pelóri. 105, 285, 291. (Replaced *Hyarantar*.)

Hyarmentir, Mount (I) 160

I sit beside the fire and think (VII) 165, 173

i·Chúrinien (V) The Lay of the Children of Húrin (q.v.). 317, 322. See *Narn i Hîn Húrin*.

i·Cuilwarthon, i·Guilwarthon (IV) See *Cuilwarthien*.

I·Cuilwarthon (II) The dead that live again. 41, 51, 245, 249. (Replaced *i·Guilwarthon*.)

I·Guilwarthon (II) The dead that live again. 51, 233, 243, 245; *the Guilwarthon* 240. (Replaced by *i·Cuilwarthon*.)

I·Guilwarthon (III) The dead that live again. 314

Ialassë (IV) 'Everlasting Whiteness', Taniquetil. 81, 167; later form *Oiolossë* 167. See *Amon Uilas*.

Ialassë, Iolossë (V) Earlier forms for Oiolossë. 210, 357–9.

Iant Iaur (XI) 'The Old Bridge'. 188, 333, 338. See *Esgalduin*, *Esgaliant*.

Iarwaeth (XI) Name taken by Túrin in Nargothrond. 83–4, 138, 142, 256, 299. (Replaced by *Agarwaen*.)

Iathrim (XI) Elves of Doriath *(Dôr Îath)*. 378

Iaur (VII) See *Tom Bombadil*.

Ice, The (X) See *Grinding Ice*, *Helkaraxë*

Ice, The (XI) See *Grinding Ice*.

Ice, The (XII) See *Helkaraxë*.

Icebay of Forochel (VII) See *Forochel*.

Icefang (I) 167, 169, 172, 224. See *Helkaraksë*.

Iceland (II) 261

Iceland (IXb) 234; *Land of Ice* 272. Icelandic 151, 159, 282; Icelander 214

Iceland, Icelander (V) (80), 81, 96

Icelandic (VI) 144–5

Icelandic (XI) 303

Icy Realms (I) 166

Icy Seas (II) 254

Idis (VII) Théoden's daughter. 445, 447, 450. Suggested name *Ælflæd* 450

Idril (Celebrindal) (XI) Daughter of Turgon, mother of Eärendil. 200, 234 *(Iðril)*, 235, 258, 301–2, (323), 325, 345–6, 348, 351–2, 354; *Irildë* 235

Idril (II) Wife of Tuor, mother of Eärendel. 130, 162, 164–5, 167–70, 174, 177, 185–93, 199–201, 209–16, 219–20, 253–6, 260, 262–7, 276; *Idril Talceleb, Idril of the Silver Feet* 165, 199, 210, 216. See *Irildë*.

Idril (IV) Wife of Tuor, mother of Eärendel; called 'the far-sighted' and *Celebrindal* 'Silverfoot' (see 36, 143, 148). 36–7, 67–70, 143–4, 147–9, 151–2, 162, 195, 213, 274, 306–8, 325, 327; O.E. *Ideshild Silfrenfót* 213

Idril (V) Wife of Tuor, mother of Eärendel. 25, 71, 141–3, 326, 361, 366–7 *(Idhril,* also *Irildë)*; *Idril Celebrindal* 'Silverfoot' 141, 332, 337, 366–7 (also *Gelebrendal; Taltelepsa, Taltelemna)*.

Idril (IXb) Wife of Tuor, mother of Eärendil. 333

Idril (XII) Also ~ *Celebrindal.* 82, 346, 348, 363, 380, 387; *Itaril* 346, 363, *Itarillë* 346, 364, *Itarildë* 348, 364

Idril Celebrindal (III) Daughter of Turgon, wife of Tuor. 83

Idril Celebrindal (X) Daughter of Turgon. (128), 359

Ielfethýp (I) 'Swanhaven' *(Old English).* 164

Ifan Belaurin (IV) See *Belaurin.*

Ilmarë (X) (1) Daughter of Manwë and Varda. 20, 34, 145, 150–1. (2) 'The handmaid of Varda'. 147, 152, 204

Ilwë (III) The middle air that flows among the stars. 139

Ilbranteloth (II) See *Cris Ilbranteloth.*

Ildramir (IXa) Transient name replacing *Imrahil.* 66

Ilfiniol (II) Littleheart. 5, 50, 144–5, 201, 221, 244. (Replaced *Elfriniol,* replaced by *Ilfrin.)*

Ilfiniol (IV) Littleheart, son of Bronweg. 3

Ilfrin (II) Littleheart. 7, 50, 201. (Replaced *Ilfiniol.)*

Ilfrith (II) Littleheart. 276

Ilien (V) See *Tar-Ilien.*

Ilien (IXb) See *Tar-Ilien.*

Ilinsor (I) Spirit of the Súruli, steersman of the Moon. 192–5, 207, 215, 218–19, 222, 227; called *the huntsman of the firmament* 195, 227

Ilinsor (II) Spirit of the Súruli, steersman of the Moon. 259

Ilinsor (IV) Steersman of the Moon. 49, 73, 171. See *Tilion*.

Ilinsor (V) Steersman of the Moon. 244

Ilkorin (V) (of languages) 148, 175, 181, 183, 187–9, 192, 194, 196, 260, 267–8, 346–7, 405 *Fading Ilkorin* 189–90

Ilkorin(s) (I) Elves 'not of Kôr'. 175, 196, 231, 235–41, 243; Ilkorin tongue 236 *Illuin* (I) The Northern Lamp. 87

Ilkorin(s), Ilkorindi (IV) Elves 'not of Kôr'. 13, 20–1, 23–7, 35, 39–40, 44–5, 51, 53–4, 58, 72, 85, 99–100, 105, 116, 123, 175, 202, 232–3. See *Dark-elves*.

Ilkorindi (II) Elves 'not of Kôr' (see especially 64). 9, 64–5, 70; *Ilkorin(s)* 74, 122, 285

Ilkorindi (V) or *Ilkorins* Elves 'not of Kôr': originally 'Dark-elves' in general (122, 181), but narrowed in sense to the Telerian Elves of Beleriand and the Danas (see 181–2, 219). 112, 122, 170–2, 175–7, 181–4, 186–90, 194, 197–8, 215, 219, 246, 323, 344, *349, 367* (also *Alchoron*, plural *Elcheryn*), 405; adj. *Ilkorin* 200, 344. See *Alkorin*, and next entry.

Ilkorindi (X) Elves 'not of Kôr', used in the sense of the 'lost Eldar'. 169–70

Ilkorins (III) Elves 'not of Kôr'. 84

Ilkorins (VII) 124, 453–5; *Ilkorin* (adjective) 453

Ilkorins (XI) Old name of the Sindar and Nandor. 22, 107, 175; *Ilkorindi* 22. *Ilkorin* (language) 23, 193

Illuin (IV) Final name of the Northern Lamp. 256. See *Helkar*.

Ilma (IV) Earlier form for *Ilmen*, itself replacing *Silma*. 240, *242, *244, *249

Ilma (V) (1) In the *Ambarkanta*, earlier form for *Ilmen*. 9, 13, 207. (2) 'Starlight'. 205, 207, *358*

Ilmandur (VII) Eldest (?) son of Elendil. 119, 122

Ilmarë (I) Handmaid of Varda. 62

Ilmarë (V) Daughter of Manwë and Varda. 165, 205, 207, *358*; earlier form *Ilmar* 162, 165

Ilmarë (XII) Daughter of King Ondohir (rejected name; see *Fíriel*). 210, 216

Ilmarin, Hill of (VII) Taniquetil. 92, 95, 97, 100, 109, 292

Ilmen (IV) 'Place of light' (240–1), the middle air (replacing *Ilma*).

236–7, 240–1, *242–5, *247, 253–4; *Chasm of Ilmen* (*Ilma* 236–9, *248–9, 254, 258–60. See *Elenarda, Tinwië-mallë; Ilwë.*

Ilmen (V) The region of the stars. 9, 11–13, 17, 78, 165, 207–8, *358*; *Chasm of Ilmen* 207, 241–2, 244, 270–1 (=*Ilmen-assa 357*)

Ilmen (VII) Region of the stars. 122

Ilmen (VIII) The region of the stars. 167. See *Elenarda.*

Ilmen (IXb) The region above the air, region of the stars. 338, 394, 396

Ilmen (X) Region of the firmament in which the Sun, Moon, and Stars have their courses. 29, 130–1, 133, 135, 137; *Chasm (of Ilmen)* 26, 132, 136–7

Ilmen-assa (IV) The Chasm of Ilmen. 240

Ilsaluntë (I) 'Silver Boat', a name of the Moon. 192, 194–5

Ilterendi (I) The fetters set on Melko. 101, 104

Ilu (I) =Ilúvatar. 52, 60–1

Ilu (IV) The World. 241, *242–3, *245, 252

Ilu (V) The World. 57, 56, 63, *361*

Ilu (IXb) The World, the Universe. 310, 313, 401, 412; *Ilúve* 401, 412

Ilu (X) The World, as described in the *Ambarkanta*. 28–9, 39, 63, 373

Iluin (X) The Northern Lamp. 7, 22, 32, 38, 52–3, 58, 60, 67, 72, 84, 98, 153, 179. See *Helkar, Foros, Forontë.*

Ilurambar (I) The Walls of the World. 227

Ilurambar (IV) The Walls of the World. 235, 241, *242–5, 252. (Replaced by *Eärambar.*)

Ilurambar (V) 303, *361, 382*. See *Walls of the World.*

Ilurambar (X) The Walls of the World. 28, 63. See *Eärambar.*

Ilúvatar (I) 49, 52–7, 59–63, 67, 74, 86, 90, 92–3, 97, 99, 113–14, 116, 118, 141, 144, 150–1, 162, 180, 182–3, 185, 187, 199, 214, 218–20, 225–7, 230, 232–3, 236, 244; *Lord for Always* 49, *Lord of All* 233. See *Children of Ilúvatar.*

Ilúvatar (II) 8, 42, 163, 209, 219, 223, 247, 283–4, 287; *the Lord for Always* 163, 209

Ilúvatar (IV) 9, 78–9, 90, 100, 160, 205–6, 263, 275, 281, 285, 290–3. See *Allfather, Eru, Children of Ilúvatar.*

Ilúvatar (V) 15–16, 24–5, 28–9, 31–2, 47, 63, 65, 72–4, 110, 120, 129, 146, 149, 155–61, 163–6, 178, 180, 204–6, 208, 212–14, 217, 228, 247, 273, 294, 302–5, 330, 333, 349, 361; *Lord of All* 15; *the One* 63. See *All-father, Children of Ilúvatar, Mountain of Ilúvatar.*

Ilúvatar (IXb) 246, 249, 290, 310, 312, 332–3, 335–6, 338, 346, 386,

391, 395, 399–401, 404, 408; *Allfather* 317, 401. *The Mountain of Ilúvatar* 317, 335, 339, 356, *the Mountain* 251, 289–90, 301, 373; O.E. *Ealfæderbeorg* 317; see *(The) Pillar of Heaven*.

Ilúvatar (X) 7–16, 19, 21, 24–9, 31, 33–4, 36–40, 42–4, 48, 71, 77, 80, 92, 95, 144–7, 149, 151, 160–2, 187–8, 202, 204, 206, 241–5, 253, 259, 268, 271, 275, 282, 358–9, 362, 364–5, 375–6, 378–80, 383, 385, 405, 408; *Eru Ilúvatar* 48, 120, 286; *Servants of Ilúvatar*, the Valar, 67, 69. See *Children of Eru, Eru, Gift of Ilúvatar; All-father*.

Ilúvatar (XI) 203–4, 210–13, 340–1, 402. See *Children of Eru*.

Ilúvatar (XII) 150, 157, 322, 396, 420; *Eru* ~ 270. See *Children of Ilúvatar*.

Ilúvë (X) 'Heaven'. 355

Ilverin (I) Littleheart son of Bronweg. 46, 52. (Replaced *Elwenildo*.)

Ilverin (II) Littleheart. 201–2. (Replaced *Elwenildo*.)

Ilverin (VI) (1) Minstrel of Doriath (in the place of Dairon). 180, 187. Other names *Neldorín, Elberin, Diarin* 187. See *Iverin*. (2) A name of Littleheart of Mar Vanwa Tyaliéva. 187

Ilwë (I) The middle air that flows among the stars. 65, 69, 73, 83, 85, 113, 127, 138, 181, 193–4

Ilwë (II) The middle air that flows among the stars. 281, 328

Ilwë (IV) In the original cosmology, the middle air that flows among the stars. 253. See *Ilmen*.

Ilweran (I) 'Bridge of Heaven', the Rainbow. 212–13. See *Rainbow*.

Imbar (X) 'The Habitation'; the Earth as 'the principal part of Arda' (see 337). 337–9, 342, 358–9, 383, 385. See *Ambar*.

Imbar (XI) The Earth. 419. See *Ambar*.

Imin (XI) 'One', the eldest of the Fathers of the Elves. 380, 418, 420–3; *Companions of Imin* 423. See *Minyar*.

Iminyë (XI) Spouse of Imin. 421, 423

Imlach (XI) Son of Marach. 220, 233–4; earlier form *Imrach* 233

Imlad Morghul (VIII) The vale of Morghul. 176, 223. See *Minas Morghul*.

Imlad Morghul (IXa) The vale of Morghul. 43

Imlad Morthond (VIII) The vale of Morthond. 287. See *Blackroot, Morthond*.

Imlad Ringlo (VIII) The vale of Ringlo. 287. See *Ringlo*.

Imladris (VII) Rivendell. 122, 125, 146. Earlier forms *Imladril* 120, 125; *Imladrist* 120, 123–5, 128, 146

Imladris (XII) Rivendell. 36, 44, 58, 79, 83, 168–9, 174, 176, 179–

80, 184, 186, 192–3, 195–6, 207–8, 225, 228, 232, 235, 239, 241, 263–5, 267, 330; earlier *Imladrist* 36, 44, 168, 184, 209; Westron *Karningul* 68, 83 (earlier forms 44, 58, 68, 76, 83)

Imladris(t) (V) Rivendell. 33–4, 345, *384*

Imladrist (VIII) Rivendell. 139, 165, 401, 423

Imloth Melui (VIII) In Gondor (nowhere identified). 396

Imrahil (VIII) Prince of Dol Amroth. 278, 294, 333, 338, 340, 369, 374, 381, 388–91, 394, 400–4, 409, 415–16, 418, 423; and see *Dol Amroth*.

Immortal Elves (X) A name of the Vanyar. 164

Immortals, The (V) A name of the Lindar. 215

Imrahil (IXa) 55, 66; and see *Dol Amroth*, *Ildramir*.

Imrahil (XII) Twenty-second Prince of Dol Amroth. 32, 36, 221, 223, 244, 271

Imram (V) (poem) 82, 100; *imrama* 81

Imrám (IXb) (Irish) tale of seavoyaging, plural *Imráma*. 222, 283; (the poem) 296–9

Imrazór the Númenórean (XII) Father of Galador first Lord of Dol Amroth. 220–3

Incânus (VIII) Name of Gandalf in the South. 153. See *Forlong* (1), *Fornold*.

Incarnate(s) (XI) 212, 359–60, 372, 375–6, 388, 393–4, 397, 402, 405–6, 408; *Self-incarnate* (the Valar) 406

Incomers (II) Easterlings. 126

Incomers (XI) Easterlings in Hithlum. 253 (and see *Brodda*). Used of Asgorn and his companions in Brethil 262, 274; of Húrin 279

Incomers, Incoming Men (IV) 122, 183

Indilzar (IXb) Elros. 363, 365, 380–2. (Replaced by *Gimilzôr*.)

Indilzar (XII) Elros. 164

Indis (I) Mother of Fingolfin and Finarfin. 44

Indis (X) (1) Wife of Finwë, mother of Fëanor. 87, 91, 102, 230. (2) Second wife of Finwë, mother of Fingolfin and Finarfin; called 'the Fair'. 101, 103, 127, 193, 205, 207–8, 230–1, 233, 237–9, 247–9, 252–3, 261–2, 264–5, 273, 276, 279–80, 300

Indis (XI) Second wife of Finwë. 327, 383

Indis (XII) Second wife of Finwë. 77, 334–7, 343, 347, 359, 365

Indo-European (V) 279

Indo-European (VII) 455

Indo-European (IXb) 415, 418

Indor (II) Father of Peleg father of Tuor. 160, 217. See *Gon Indor*, *Indorildo*.

Indor (III) Father of Peleg father of Tuor (in the tale of *The Fall of Gondolin*). 145

Indor (IV) Father of Peleg father of Tuor. 4–5

Indorildo, Indorion (II) Name of Eärendel, great-grandson of Indor. 217. See *Gon Indor*.

Indowns (VI) In the Shire. 294–5

Indrafangs (II) The Longbeard Dwarves of Belegost. 46, 68, 223, 230, 232–5, 243, 247–8; *Indrafangin* 234, *Indravangs* 19, 68. See especially 247.

Indrafangs (IV) The Longbeard Dwarves of Nogrod. 104, 175

Indrafangs (V) The Longbeard Dwarves of Nogrod. 278. See *Enfeng*.

Indrafangs (XI) Old name of the Longbeard Dwarves. 108, 208. See *Anfangrim, Enfeng*.

Ing (I) Earlier name of Inwë. 22, 132

Ing (II) (1) *Ing, Ingwë* King of Luthany; many references are to his kin, sons, or descendants. 301–10, 312; on the relationship between Ing and *Ingwë* see 305. (2) Earlier name of Inwë. 305. (3) *Ing* in Old English legend. 305

Ing (III) (1) Gnomish form of *Ingwë*. 28, 133, 138–9; *sons of Ing* 17, 28, 127; *tower of Ing* 73, 82, 93. (2) King of Luthany. 28

Ing (IV) (1) King of Luthany. 75. (2) Gnomish form of *Ingwë*. 13, 17, 44, 84, 86, 89–90, 93–4, 96, 168–9, 212; the tower of Ing 18, 87, 91; O.E. *Ingwine*, the First Kindred, 212

Ing (V) In Old English legend. 95

Ingalaurë (X) Mother-name of Finarfin (Arafinwë). 230, 265

Ingar (X) The people of Ingwë. 230, 265

Ingársecg (IV) See *Belegar*.

Ingil (I) Son of Inwe. 16, 22, 25–6, 95–6, 129, 132, 200. (Replaced *Ingilmo*.)

Ingil (II) Son of Inwë. 5–6, 258, 280–2, 289, 292, 305, 328. See *Gil*.

Ingil (IV) Son of Inwe in the *Lost Tales*. 72, 75, 197; Ingil's tower 197. See *Ingwiel*.

Ingildon (XI) Tower on the cape west of Eglarest. 40, 80, 118, 190, 196–7. (Replaced *Tindobel*; replaced by *Barad Nimras*.)

Ingilmo (I) Earlier name of Ingil. 22, 132

Inglor (I) Earlier name of Finrod (Felagund). 44

Inglor (III) Eldest son of Finrod (1) (later Finarfin), called *Felagund*. 335, 350–1, 360. (Replaced by *Finrod* (2)).

Inglor (IV) Later 'true' name of Felagund (replaced by *Finrod* (2)). 213, 339, 341; O.E. *Ingláf Felahrór* 213, 341. See *Ingoldo*.

Inglor (V) Son of Finrod (1) =Finarfin; King of Nargothrond; called 'the Faithful' (223). Used alone or with *Felagund*. 116, 118–19, 123, 125–6, 145, 223, 226, 234–5, 237–9, 250, 253–4, 257, 262, 264–6, 269, 281, 284, 290, 292, 300, *361*, 368. See *Felagund*.

Inglor (VII) Felagund. See *Finrod* (2), *Gil-galad*.

Inglor (X) Earlier name of Finrod (2); references include also *Felagund*. 93, 104, 106, 112, 114, 120–1, 125, 128, 177, 181–2, 195–7

Inglor (XI) Earlier name of Finrod (2); references include *Inglor Felagund*. 31–2, 34–5, 38, 42–4, 48–50, 52, 54, 62, 65, 67, 116–18, 130, 178–9, 197–8, 228, 238–40, 242–3, 343. See *Felagund*.

Inglor Felagund (VI) 72, 188. See *Finrod* (2).

Inglorel (VII) See *Nimrodel*.

Inglorion (VI) See *Gildor*.

Inglormindon (V) The tower on Tol Sirion. 146, 269, *373*, *395*. (Replaced by *Minnastirith*.)

Ingold (VII) Name for a time replacing Aragorn, Elfstone (see 277–8). 80, 236, 244, 246–7, 256–8, 260, 262, 265, 268, 270–8, 281, 289–90, 292–3, 360, 381

Ingold (VIII) Man of Minas Tirith. 233, 277, 340. (Replaced *Cranthir*.)

Ingold (XII) Man of Minas Tirith. 360

Ingoldo (IV) Mother-name of Finrod Felagund. 174

Ingoldo (X) (1) Mother-name of Fingolfin (Nolofinwë). 230, 249, 253, 265, *Ingoldo-Finwë* (X) 230. (2) Mother-name of Finrod Felagund. 265

Ingoldo (XII) See *Finarfin*, *Fingolfin*, *Finrod* (2).

Ingolondë (IV) Beleriand, 'the kingdom of the Gnomes'. 108, 174

Ingolondë (V) Beleriand, 'the Kingdom of the Gnomes'. 253, 256, *377* (also Noldorin *Angolonn*, *Geleidhien*).

Ingrim (VII) Father of Ingold. 246, 256, 262, 277

Inguaeones (II) See 304–5.

Ingwaiwar (II) People deriving their origin from Ing(wë) as their founder-ruler, Anglo-Saxons. 304–7, 309, 312, 323

Ingwaiwar (IV) See 75.

Ingwë (I) Lord of the Vanyar. 26, 132, 135, 223. See *Inwë*.

Ingwë (II) (1) See Ing (1). (2) Lord of the Vanyar. 305. See *Inwë*.

Ingwë (III) Lord of the First Kindred of the Elves (Gnomish Ing). 28, 93, 138–9

Ingwë (IV) (1) King of Luthany. 75. (2) Lord of the First Kindred of

the Elves (*Inwë of the Lost Tales*). 13, 44, 85, 89, 93, 96, 149, 154, 156, 168–9, 196–7, 212, 309; the tower of Ingwe 89, 169

Ingwë (V) King of the First Kindred of the Elves and High-king of the Eldalie (of the *Lost Tales*, (165, 183). 144, 165, 173, 183, 185, 188, 193, 195, 214, 217, 225, 326, 334, *361, 398*; house of, people of Ingwë 171–2, 228, 233 (see *Ingwëlindar, Ingwë*); *the Children of Ingwë*, a name of the Lindar, 215; the tower and lamp of Ingwë 112, 173, 185, 222, 234–5 (see *Ingwëmindon*).

Ingwë (X) King of the Vanyar, and *High-king of all the Elves* (179), 81–2, 84–5, 87, 90, 133, 162, 168, 176, 179, 186, 206–7, 230, 23 7–8, 249, 258, 261–2, 265. See *Children of Ingwë, Ingwëmindon*.

Ingwë (XI) King of the Vanyar. 6, 246

Ingwë (XII) King of the Vanyar. 334, 340, 343, 356–7, 364–5; *Ingwë Ingweron* 340

Ingwëa (V) The 'noble dialect' of the speech of the Lindar (=*Ingwelindarn, Ingwiqen(d)ya*). 183, 195

Ingwelindar (V) The house and people of Ingwë. 171, 183 (see *Ingwë*); *Ingwelindarin* =*Ingwëa*, 185, 195

Ingwemindon (V) The tower of Ingwë. 222, 225, 373, 395. See *Ingwë*.

Ingwëmindon (X) 90, 180; *Tower of Ingwë* 84–5, 90, 176. See *Mindon Eldaliéva*.

Ingwer, Ingwi (XII) Vanyar. 332, 340, 356. *Ingwi, Ingwëlindar*, house and people of Ingwë, 356; *Ingar* 360

Ingwi (V) =*Ingwelindar*. 171, 183

Ingwiel (IV) Son of Ingwë, leader of the First Kindred at the Battle of Eldorest (> Eglorest). 156, 196–7, 313, 326. See *Ingil, Ingwil* (2).

Ingwiel (V) Son of Ingwë. 144, 326, 334, 336

Ingwil (III) Stream falling from the Hills of the Hunters into the Narog at Nargothrond. 68, 72, 80, 88, 214, 222. (Replaced by *Ringwil*.)

Ingwil (IV) (1) River flowing into Narog at Nargothrond. 225. (2) Earlier form for *Ingwiel*. 309, 313, 326

Ingwil (V) River flowing into the Narog at Nargothrond. 262

Ingwil (XI) Tributary stream of Narog. *184, 190, 197. (Replaced by *Ringwil*.)

Ingwinë (II) See 305.

Ingwion (XI) Son of Ingwë. 246; *Ingwiel* 246

Ingwiqen(d)ya (V) A tongue whose relations are differently described (see 195). 172, 184–5, 193–5

Inias Beleriand (X) The Annals of Beleriand. 200; *Inias Valannor (Balannor), Ínias Dor-Rodyn* (X) 200

Inias Valannor or *Inias Balannor* (V) The Annals of Valinor. 202; *Inias Velenand* or *Inias Beleriand*, the Annals of Beleriand, 202; *400*

Inklings, The (IXb) 148–51, 211, (216, 219), 220; *Inklings' Saga,* ~ *Saga-book* 148–9

Inklings, The (XII) 19–20, 25, 140

Inklings. The (VII) 85

Inland Sea (I) See *Helcar*.

Inland Sea (II) The Mediterranean. 294.

Inland Sea (VIII) The Sea of Nurnen (?) 243–4. See *Nurnen*.

Inland Sea (XI) See *Helkar, Rhûn*.

Inland Sea (XII) 258, 294, 326, 373. See *Rhûn*.

Inland Sea(s) (IV) 238, *250–1, 256, 258

Inlands (VI) The Mittalmar, central region of Númenor. 295

Inner Lands (V) Middle-earth. 245

Inner Lands (XII) (of Middle-earth) 185. *Inner Seas* 149

Inner Sea (V) The Great Sea of the West. 209. *Inner Seas* (of Middle-earth) 25, 161

Inner Sea (XI) See 173–4.

Inner Seas (IV) The Great Seas of East and West. 236–7, 254

Inner Seas (IXb) (of Middle-earth). 334, 380

Inner Seas (X) 20, 35, (145)

Inram the Tall (VIII) Man of Gondor, from the vale of Morthond (?). 252, 254

Inscrutable, The (V) An Elvish name for Men. 245

Insula Deliciarum (V) 80–1

Inwë (I) King of the Eldar of Kôr (later Ingwë). 16, 18, 22, 25–6, 49–50, 59, 82, 116–18, 122–3, 129, 132, 135, 141, 144, 162, 196, 200, 213; called also *Isil* 115, *Isil Inwë* 115–16, 132. (Replaced *Ing*.) See *Ingwë, Inwithiel*.

Inwë (II) King of the Eldar of Kôr (later Ingwë Lord of the Vanyar). 208, 253, 258, 280, 282, 289, 292, 305 *the Arch of Inwë* in Gondolin 182

Inwë (III) Earlier form for *Ingwë*. 28

Inwë (IV) King of the Eldar of Kôr in the *Lost Tales*. 44, 72, 197. See *Ingwë* (2).

Inwë (V) See *Ingwë*

Inwir (I) The royal clan of the Teleri (=the later Vanyar), kindred of Inwë. 26, 48–50, 52, 115, 126, 132, 143, 163, 235

Inwir (II) The royal clan of the Teleri (the later Vanyar), kindred of Inwë. 4, 253, 255, 278, 281, 283

Inwir (V) The house of Inwë in the *Lost Tales*. 183

Inwithiel (I) Gnomish name of Inwë. 16, 22, 115, 131–2. (Replaced *Githil, Gim-Githil*.)

Inwithiel (II) Gnomish name of Inwë. 258

Inwithiel (III) Early Gnomish name of Inwë. 28. (Replaced *Gim Githil*.)

Inziladûn (XII) 154, 159–60, 162. See *Tar-Palantir*.

Inzilbêth (XII) Queen of Ar-Gimilzór. 159–60, 162

Iôn (XI) Eöl's first name for Maeglin ('Son'). 337

Ior (IV) (1) Ilúvatar? 6, 9. (2) Gnomish name of Ivárë. 9

Ioreth (IXa) Woman of Gondor. 55; earlier spelling *Yoreth* 55

Iorhael (IXa) Aragorn's translation of *Frodo* (Gamgee). 126, 129; earlier spelling *Iorhail* 117, 135

Ipswich (VII) 106

Iranian (IXb) 418

Íras (II) (Old English) The Irish. 290

Ireland (II) 285, 293, 312, 323. See *Íverin*.

Ireland (V) 39, 80–1, 84, 103; see Erin. *Irish, Irishmen* 39, 78, 81–2

Ireland (IV) 199

Ireland (IXb) 234, 261, 264, 267, 278–80, 293, 296, 299; O.E. *Íraland* 270, 272, 294; *Ériu* 270, 294, *Erin* 280, 294. See *Hibernia*.

Ireland (X) 5

Iren, River (VII) See *Isen*.

Irenland (XII) See *Éothéod*.

Irensaga (VIII) 'Ironsaw', mountain at the head of Harrowdale. 312–13. See *Iscamba*.

Íreth, Ínith (XII) See *Írissë*.

Irildë (II) name of Idril in Eldarissa. 199, 210, 216, 254, 276; *Irildë Taltelepta, Irildë of the Silver Feet* (II) 216. See *Idril*.

Irildë (XI) See *Idril*.

Írimë (X) Daughter of Finwë and Indis. 207, 238, 265. (Replaced by *Finvain*.)

Írimë (XII) Daughter of Finwë and Indis. 343, 359; other names *Írien* 343, 359; *Lalwen(dë)* 343, (*Glaðwen* 359)

Írimor (V) 'The Fair', a name of the Lindar. 361, 403–4. See *Fair-elves*.

Irish (IXb) 211, 294, 296; the Irish 273, O.E. *Íras* 294

Írissë (XII) Daughter of Fingolfin. 345, 362–3; Sindarin *Íreth, Írith* 345, 362–3. See *Ar-Feiniel*.

Írith (XI) Turgon's sister. 318, 409, 420. See *Isfin, Aredhel, Feiniel*.

Írith Daughter of Fingolfin, called 'the White'. 177, 182. See *Isfin, White Lady of the Noldor*.

Irmo (X) True name of the Vala Lórien. 145, 147–8, 150–2, 236, 257; rendered 'Desire' 150. See *Olofantur, Lís.*

Irmo (XI) 'Desirer', true name of the Vala Lórien. 403

Iron Crown (II) See *Melko.*

Iron Crown (III) The crown of Morgoth. 52, 192–3, 221, 272, 296, 302, 352; *iron-crowned* 285, 293, 301

Iron Crown (V) 125, (135 144), 154, 233, (284), 303, 329

Iron Crown (XI) 38, 63, 68; other references to Morgoth's crown 62, 65, 69, 347

Iron Crown of Morgoth (IV) 17, 24, 39, 71, 74, 93, 109, 113, 157, 160, 197, 201, 295, 310, 328; O.E. *irenhelm, isern helm*, 282, 338

Iron Crown of Morgoth (X) 110, (371)

Iron Doom, The (VIII) Underground entry into the Tower of Kirith Ungol. 226

Iron Halls (VI) See *Angband.*

Iron Hills (III) The Iron Mountains. 33, 49; *Hills of Iron* 30, 50

Iron Hills (XII) 233, 237, 239, 250, 276, 282, 286, 302, 305–6, 323–4

Iron Mountains (I) 112, 118, 149, 158–9, 176, 198, 238, 240, 242; called also Mountains of Iron 101, 112, 166, 243, Hills of Iron 209, 243, mountains of the North 77, Bitter Hills 238, 240, 242. See especially 112, 158–9.

Iron Mountains (II) 10–11, 14, 43, 61, 70, 77, 140, 153, 215, 217, 279; *Mountains of Iron* 13, 156, 217; *Hills of Iron* 87, 154, 161, 169, 219, 279; *Bitter Hills* 12, 22, 29, 61. See *Angorodin.*

Iron Mountains (III) 29, 49, 148; *Mountains of Iron* 39, 96. See *Angorodin, Aiglir Angrin, Eiglir Engrin, Bitter Hills, Iron Hills, Mountains of the North.*

Iron Hills (VII) 143, 298, 306–7

Iron Mountains (IV) 22, 26, 47, 52–3, 67, (101, 139), 220, 239, *249, 259–60; *Mountains of Iron* (IV) 102–3, 105, 222; *Mountains of Morgoth* 296, 330. See *Aiglir Angrin; Bitter Hills, Black Mountains, Northern Towers.*

Iron Mountains (V) 251, 254–5, 257, 259, 266, 270–2; *Mountains of Iron* 125, 280; *Mountains of Morgoth* 127, *of Melko* 259, 270. See *Eiglir Engrin, Ered-engrin.*

Iron Mountains (XI) 6, 15, 31, 36, 60, 104, 112, 128. See *Eryd Engrin.*

Iron Prison (XI) See *Angband.*

Ironfists (XII) One of the kindreds of the Dwarves. 301, 322

Iron-forest (V) 12, 23

Irongarth (VII) See *Isengard*.

Irtinsa, Lake (I) 193, 215

Irtinsa, Lake (IV) 49

Iscamba (VIII) A name of the mountain Irensaga. 312, 320

Isen, River (VII) 177, 187, 241, 298, 304, 306, 311–12, 434, 436–8, 446, 450; *Ford of Isen* 320; *Battle of Isen* 438, 450. Earlier form *Iren* 187, 298, 306

Isen, River (VIII) (including references to *the river*) 4, 8, 24, 28–31, 39–41, 43, 47–8, 51–2, 56–8, 68–9, 79, 230, 362, 436; and see *Fords of Isen*.

Isen, River (IXa) 64, 69, 76

Isen, River (XII) 271, 273, 313, 436. *The Battles of the Fords of Isen* (title) 293

Isenford (VIII) See *Fords of Isen*.

Isengard (VI) 189, 225

Isengard (VII) 36, 72, 132, 139, 149–51, 161, 177, 211–12, 214–16, 296, 320, 333, 347, 372, 379, 382, 386, 390, 400–1, 408, 410, 412, 418–20, 422, 434–7; its original site 132, 139, 149; *Great Gate* 436. Earlier name *Irongarth* (Angrobel) 71–2, 130–1, 139. See *Angrenost*.

Isengard (VIII) (including references to the *Ring, Circle*, and *Gates* of Isengard) 4–8, 17, 21, 25–7, 31, 37, 39, 41–3, 45, 47–54, 56–9, 64, 68–75, 78–81, 92, 109–10, 119–20, 126, 129, 142, 235–7, 243, 247–9, 266, 272, 285, 297, 301, 362, 430. North gate of Isengard 39, 44–5, 47, 57–8

Isengard (IXa) 53, 63–4, 68, 71, 74, 82–3, 91, 95, 103, 106, 120, 123; *the Circle of Isengard* 136

Isengard (XII) 7, 69, 191, 229, 233, 238, 241–2, 248, 251, 262, 267; *Angrenost* 191

Isengarders (VII) 408, 435–6

Isengarders (VIII) 12, 51

Isenmouthe (VII) 213

Isenmouthe (IXa) 33–6, 38, 41, 43. See *Carach Angren*.

Isfin (II) Sister of Turgon, mother of Meglin. 165, 168, 199, 210, 220, 248. See *Aredhel*.

Isfin (III) Sister of Turgon, mother of Meglin. 145–7, 222. (Afterwards named *Aredhel*.)

Isfin (IV) Sister of Turgon, mother of Meglin; called 'the White' (88) and 'the white-handed' (136). 8, 15, 34–5, 65, 88, 136, 140, 191, 193, 213, 301, (305), 321; O.E. *Finhwít* 213. See *Aredhel*.

Isfin (V) Sister of Turgon, mother of Meglin; called 'the White' (223). 136, 139, 152, 223, *361, 381*

Isfin (X) Earlier name of Írith. 102, 106, 177, 182

Isfin (XI) Called *the White*; original name of Turgon's sister. 47–8, 71, 84, 121–3, 127, 139, 316–20, 322, 324–5, 332, 336, 420. On the name see 317–18; and see *Írith, Aredhel, Feiniel, Rodwen.*

Isfin (XII) Original name of Fingolfin's daughter Irissë, Íreth. 367

Ishmalog, valley of (XII) In the tale of Tal-elmar. 424; earlier *Rishmalog* 437

Isil (V) 'The Sheen', name of the Moon. 41, 56, 72, 240, 243, *361, 385, 392.* See *Ithil, Rana.*

Isil (IXb) The Moon. 241, 302, 306; *Ithil* 303, 306

Isil (X) 'The Sheen', name of the Moon. 130–1, 135–6, 198. See *Ithil.*

Isil, Isil Inwë (I) See *Inwë.*

Isildur (V) 71, 376

Isildur (VI) 85, 227, 320; *Isildor* 261–2, 271, 320; *Ithildor* 251; *son of Elendil* 358. Earliest germ of the story of his death 78

Isildur (VII) 25, 50, 105, 119–21, 123, 126–9, 144–5, 147, 359, 361–2, 364, 366, 393, 395, 444, 450

Isildur (VIII) 21, 123, 149, 152–4, 304, 307, 310, 397, 410, 412, 418, 424; *heir of* 301, 304, 310, 370, 411, 419, *sons of* 374; *sword of Isildur* 301, 309; the name 159–60

Isildur (IXa) 15; the standard of Isildur 15

Isildur (IXb) 335, 384, 387, 401

Isildur (XII) 32, 157, 163, 166–70, 172, 176–7, 186, 189, 191–2, 194–6, 198, 202, 208–9, 225–8, 230–3, 237–8, 247, 253, 257, 263–4, 266–7; *Isildur's Bane* 241

Isildur's Bane (VII) 129–30, 146–8

Isildur's Bane (VIII) 145, 149, 151, 164, 166

Isildurioni (XII) Heirs of Isildur. 192, 208

Island Elves (I) Elves of Tol Eressëa. 48–9, 129

Island-elves (II) Elves of Tol Eressëa. 283, 285

Isle of (the) Werewolves (IV) 221–2, 311, 319. See *Tol-na-Gaurhoth.*

Isle of Balar (IV) See *Balar.*

Isle of Balar (V) See *Balar; Isle of Werewolves,* see *Tol-na-Gaurhoth.*

Isle of Seabirds (II) 253, 255–6, 259–60, 262, 264; tower on 264

Isle of Seabirds (IV) 70; the tower on the isle 38, 70, 150, 154, 156, 195, 197, 203–4

Isle of Werewolves (II) 53. See *Tol-in-Gaurhoth.*

Isle of Werewolves (III) Tol-in-Gaurhoth. 87, 350. See *Wizard's Isle.*

Istar (V) Queen of Númenor. 15–16, 27. (Replaced by *Tar-Ilien*.)

Istari (VII) Wizards. 422

Istari (X) The Wizards. 397

Istari (XII) 228–9, 247, 360, 384–5, 392. See *Ithryn Luin*, *Wizards*.

Istarnië (X) See *Nerdanel*.

Istimor (V) 'The Wise', a name of the Noldor. 361, 403–4; cf. 215

Italian (XII) 368

Italy (V) 54–5, 91; Old English *on Eatule* 55

Italy (IXb) 236, 276

Itaril (XII) See *Idril*.

Ithil (III) (Sindarin) the Moon. 354

Ithil (V) Name of the Moon in Noldorin. 41, 56, 243, *361*, *385*, *392* (another name *Elfaron* 'Star-hunter' 387, cf. 241). See *Isil*, *Rana*.

Ithil (VI) Moria-silver, *mithril*. 458, 465. See *Erceleb*.

Ithil (VII) See *Mithril*.

Ithil (VIII) The Moon. 172

Ithil (X) The Moon. 42, 377, 382

Ithil (XI) The Moon. 401

Ithildin (VI) Element from which the design on the West Gate of Moria was made. 463

Ithildin (VII) 'Starmoon'. 180, 185, 187–8. Earlier name *Thilevril* 187

Ithildor (VI) See *Isildur*.

Ithilduin (VII) See *Duin Morghul*.

Ithilduin (VIII) Former name of Duin Morghul. 436

Ithilien (VII) 318

Ithilien (VIII) 133–6, 140–2, 145–7, 165, 170, 182, 190, 226, 252–4, 256, 259–60, 262–3, 271, 276–7, 286, 291, 294–5, 329, 331, 431; *lower Ithilien* 370, 422; *South Ithilien* (VIII) 398

Ithilien (IXa) 7–8, 20, 49–50, 116; *Prince of Ithilien* (Faramir) 61, 70

Ithilien (XII) 45, 200–1, 204–7, 215–16, 219, 233, 235, 238, 244, 250, 262, 315; *North* ~ 206, 218; *South* ~ 201, 206, 216–17, 238, 315; *Prince of* ~ 207, 223, 244

Ithil-stone (VIII) The *palantír* of Minas Ithil. 80. See *Minas Morghul*.

Ithryn Luin (XII) Blue Wizards. 385

Ivárë (II) Minstrel of the Elves, 'who plays beside the sea'. 10, *59*

Ivárë (III) Minstrel of the Elves 'who plays beside the sea'. 181–2

Ivárë (IV) Minstrel of the Elves. 9. See *Ior* (2).

Iverin (VI) Minstrel of Doniath. 188. See *Ilverin*.

Íverin, Isle of (II) Ireland. 283, 285–6, 293, 323. See *Ireland*.

Ivorwen (XII) Mother of Gilrain. 263, 270; earlier *Evorwen* 263

Ivorwin (XII) See *Yavannildi.*

Ivrin (II) See *Eithel Ivrin.*

Ivrin (III) The lake and falls beneath the Shadowy Mountains where the river Narog rose. 60, 62–3, 76, 87–91, 94, 170, 224, 234, 244

Ivrin (V) 260, 272, 412; *Falls of Ivrin* 261

Ivrin (XI) 91, 139–40, 145–6; *the Pools of Ivrin* 34, 83, 88–9. See *Eithil Ivrin.*

Ivrin, Lake (IV) 29, 124, (125), 184, 221, 324; *Pools of Ivrin* 175; *Ivrin's Well,* see *Ivrineithil.*

Ivrineithel (V) Ivrin's Well. 139

Ivrineithel (XI) See *Eithil Ivrin.*

Ivrineithil (IV) 313, 323; *Ivrin's Well* 304, 313. See *Eithel Ivrin.*

Ivriniel (XII) Daughter of Adrahil of Dol Amroth. 221, 223

Ivy Bush (VI) Inn on the Bywater road. 222, 243–4, 249, 314, 323, 329

Ivy Bush (VII) Inn on the Bywater road. 29

Japan (IXb) 241, 306

Japheth (IXb) Son of Noah. 411

Jeremy, Wilfrid Trewin (IXb) Member of the Notion Club. 151, 159, 164–5, 169–71, 173, 175, 177, 179–81, 188–9, 191–4, 196–7, 199–203, 205, 207, 211, 216, 218–20, 223–4, 227–33, 245, 249–55, 260, 265–9, 277–9, 281, 283, 286, 289–90, 293, 300–1, 303, 306–9, 316, 356, 389, 413, 432–3, 440; called Jerry 231, 250; the name *Trewin* 290, 293, spelt *Trewyn* 266, 268–9, 293; his books 159, 164, 200. For Jeremy's *'alter ego'* in Anglo-Saxon England see *Tréowine,* in Númenor see *Abrazân, Voronwë.*

Jewels, The (X) The Silmarils. 107, 268, 377; *War of the Jewels* 395. See *gems, jewels, of the Noldor*

Jewel(s), The (XI) The Silmaril(s). 63, 65, 68–9, 254, 351, 354

Jewels, War of the (XII) 163, 302–3, 306, 312; *the (Great) Jewels,* the Silmarils, 30, 78, 363

Jewel-wrights (X) A name of the Noldor. 164

John the Baptist (IXb) 285

Jones, James (IXb) Member of the Notion Club. 159, 173, 186, 198, 211, 215, 223, 233, 245

Jötunheim (IXb) Land of the Giants in Norse mythology. 308

Jupiter (IXb) (the planet) 220. See *Glund.*

Jutes (II) 306. See *Euti.*

Jutland (IXb) 223

Kalakilya (V) The Pass of Light. 168, 173, 185, 223–4, 242, 362, 365 (also *Cilgalad*). See *Kôr*.

Kalakilya (VII) See *Calacirian*.

Kalakiryan (X) The Pass of Light. 84, 86–7, 89, 97, 102, 133–4, 176, 178, 180, 183, 194, 197, 262, 283, 288(-9), 291, *Calaciryan* 183. Earlier forms *Kalakirya* 87, 89, 102, 180, 190, 192, *Kalakilya* 22, 89, 102, 197

Kalakiryan (XI) 'The Cleft of Light'. 119, 403

Kalamor (V) Light-elves. 197, 362

Kalaqendi (V) Light-elves. 197, 362; *Calaquendi* 197

Kalaquendi (X) Elves of the Light. 163, 169. See *Light Elves*.

Kalaquendi (XI) 'Light-elves', Elves of Aman. 19, 175, 361, 373, 375–6; Telerin *Calapendi* 362, 375. See *Calben*.

Kalaventë, *Kalavénë* (I) 'Ship of Light', a name of the Sun. 188, 198, 221–2

Kalenarda, *Kalinarda* (VIII) See *Calenard(h)on*

Kalimehtar (XII) (1) Younger brother of Rómendakil II. 199, 213. (2) Thirtieth King of Gondor. 200, 212, 215–16, 232

Kalimmakil (XII) Son of Narmakil II, father of Siriondil (2). 201, 216

Kaliondi (I) A name of the Dark Elves. 244

Kalmakil (XII) Eighteenth King of Gondor. 198–9, 212–13, 259–60; *Calmacil* 259

Kalormë (I) Great mountain in the furthest East. (83), 212, 225

Kalormë (IV) Great mountain in the furthest East. 255

Kama (X) 28. See *(The) Void*.

Kapalen (II) name preceding Tifanto (Dairon). 49–50

Kapalinda (I) Source of the stream Kelusindi in Valinor. 157

Karan (IXb) [Ramer] The planet Mars. 220. (Replaced by *Gormok*.)

Karkaras (II) 'Knife-fang', 'father of wolves'. 19, 21, 31, 33–4, 36, 38–9, 56, 58–9, 68, 227, 231, 239; *Carcaras* 46, 68; *Hell-wolf* 38. See *Knife-fang*; *Carcharoth*.

Karkaras (III) See *Carcharoth*.

Karma-kundo (XII) Title of Minalkar as Regent of Gondor. 260

Karnil (X) The planet Mars. 160, 166; *Carnil* 166. See pp. 434–5.

Kasari (XI) Quenya name of the Dwarves (derived from *Khazâd*); singular *Kasar*. 388, 402; *Kasallië* 388. Cf. *Casarrondo*.

Kastamir (XII) 'The Usurper', twenty-second King of Gondor. 199, 213–14, 231, 248

Kaukareldar (I) 'False-fairies'. 239, 245

Kay, Guy G. (V) 302

Kay, Guy G. (XI) 356

Keladian (IXb) [Ramer; cf. *Enkeladim*] 206, 222

Keleborn (VII) 246–9, 256–7, 262–3, 267–85 *passim*, 289–91, 293, 315–1 6, 320, 402, 415, 451; *Celeborn* 218, 261; *The Lord* (also *The Lord of Lothlórien, of the Galadrim*) 233–4, 236, 246–9, 256–7, 263, 270–1, 274, 279, 290. Other names: *Tar* 249, 261; *Aran* 249, 261–2; *(King) Galdaran* 249–50, 262 (*King Galdaran's Mirror* 249–50); *Galathir* 249, *Arafain* 256

Keleborn (IXa) See *Celeborn* (1) and (2).

Kelebrant (VII) See *Celebrant*.

Kelebras (VII) See *Celebdil*.

Kelegorn (VII) Father of Aragorn. 50–1, 63, 77, 80, 82, 105, 113, 120, 146, 165, 277, 361, 404, 451. See *Arathorn*.

Kelos, River (VII) In Gondor. 312; *Celos* 322

Kelos, River (VIII) In Gondor. 436; *Celos* 427

Kelufain (VII) See *Calenbel*.

Kelusindi (I) Stream in Valinor. 157

kelvar (XI) Animals, living things that move. 340–1. See *olvar*.

Kemen (IXb) The Great Lands, Middle-earth. 402–4, 412

Kemendur (XII) Fourth King of Gondor. 197, 212

Kementári (I) Name of Yavanna. 79

Kementári (X) Name of Yavanna. 157, 202. (Replaced *Palrúrien*.)

Kementári (XI) Name of Yavanna. 246. (Replaced *Palúrien*.)

Kémi (I) Name of Yavanna Palúrien. 71–2, 79, 100, 179, 209. See Earth-lady.

Kerin Amroth (VII) See *Cerin Amroth*.

Kerin Amroth (XII) See *Cerin Amroth*.

Kerin Muil (VII) See *Nen-uinel*.

Kerry (IXb) 293

Khand (VIII) Land south-east of Mordor. 369, 372, 439. See *Variags*.

Khand (XII) Land south-east of Mordor. 79

Khazâd (VIII) The name of the Dwarves in their own language. 20

Khazad (IXb) The Dwarves. 414. *Khazadian* (language) 414–15, 433

Khazâd (XI) The Dwarves. 205, 209–10, 214, 387–8, 414; earlier form *Khuzûd* 205, 209–10, 214. See *Hadhod, Kasari*.

Khazâd (XII) The Dwarves. 24, 296, 302

Khazaddûm (V) Dwarvish name of Nogrod. 274, 278. (Replaced in this sense by *Tumunzahar*.) In later application, Moria, 278, 336

Khazad-dûm (VI) (1) Dwarf-city in Eredlindon; Elvish *Nogrod*. 466.

(2) Moria. 462 (*the Bridge of Khazad-dûm*), 465–6; *Kazaddûm* 467

Khazad-dûm (VII) 117, 125, 143, 166, 185–6, 199, 264, 266, 304, 333, 430, 457; *Kazaddûm* 457–8; the Bridge in Khazad-dûm 186, 190, 197–200, 203, 206, 215, 236, 247, 257, 266, 422, 430, 446 (*Durin's Bridge* 431). See *Dwarrowdelf, Moria.*

Khazad-dûm (XI) 201–2, 204–9, 389, 397, 419; originally name of Nogrod 108, 201, 209. See *Casarrondo, Hadhodrond, Nornhabar; Dwarrowdelf.*

Khazad-dûm (XII) 24, 44, 278, 286, 304, 321. See *Dwarrowdelf, Moria.*

Kheled-zâram (VI) Mirrormere. 466

Kheled-zâram (VII) Mirrormere. 166–7, 174, 219–20, 237, 275, 290

Kheled-zâram (IXa) Mirrormere. 135

Kheled-záram (XII) Mirrormere. 275, 281, 286

Kheru (IXb) See *Arûn.*

Khuzdul (VI) Language of the Dwarves. 466

Khuzdul (VII) 174

Khuzdul (VIII) The language of the Dwarves. 20

Khuzdul, Khuzdûl (XII) The language of the Dwarves. 297, 300–1, 317, 319, 321–3, 358

Khuzûd (V) The Dwarves. 274, 278; *Khazad* 278

Kibil-nâla (VII) Silverlode. 174–5, 241, 290

Kibil-nâla (XII) Silverlode. 279, 286; (Mirrormere, see 275, 286). See *Zigil-nâd.*

Kilby, Clyde S. (XI) 310

Kili (XII) Companion of Thorin Oakenshield. 277, 285

Kindred of Lúthien (X) A name of the Sindar. 165

Kindreds Three Kindreds of the Eldar (X) 162, 168, 184, 256; *Two Kindreds* (Elves and Men) 209, (247, 338), and see 308. See *Second Kindred.*

King of the Dead (VIII) See *Dead Men of Dunharrow.*

King of the World (X) Name taken by Morgoth. 110, 121, 124 (and see *Lord of the World* in entry *World*); *King of Middle-earth* 121, 126 (see *Aran Endór, Tarumbar*).

King Stones (VIII) 98, 132, 137

King under the Mountain (XII) 236, 239, 275–7, 286

King, The (IXa) See *Aragorn.*

King's hall, palace, tower, fountain, square (II) In Gondolin. See *Square of the Palace.*

King's House, Royal House (II) Of the Gondothlim. 172, 183–5, 187, 213

King's Men (XII) (in Númenor) 151–3; *King's Folk* 151, 174–5

King's Reckoning (XII) 128, 131–3, 138; *Kings' Reckoning* 132

Kingless, The (X) A name of the Nandor of Ossiriand. 164

Kings from over the Sea (VII) 82; *Kings of Men* 185, 400

Kings of Men (VI) Númenóreans. 331, 458

Kings of Men (VIII) Dúnedain. 310, 335

Kings of Men (IXb) The Númenóreans. 337, 346, 348, 366, 368, 385, 392–3, 395, 410

Kings of Men (XII) Númenóreans. 31, 55, 261, 263, 270

Kings' Norbury (IXa) 76. See *Fornost Erain.*

Kingsfoil (VIII) The healing herb *athelas.* 394

Kinslaughter, Kinslaying (I) *(at Swanhaven)* 164, 169, 171, 176, 199, 239

Kinslaying (V) The First Kinslaying, see *Alqualondë.* The Second Kin- slaying (the attack on Dior), 142. The Third Kinslaying (the attack on the Havens of Sirion), 143

Kinslaying at Alqualondë (III) 17, 70, 90, 104, 118, 136, 231

Kinslaying at Swanhaven (II) 258

Kinslaying, The (IV) 68, 170, 266–7, 279, and see *Swanhaven.*

Kinslaying, The (IXb) 411

Kinslaying, The (X) At Alqualondë. 115, 117–18, 120, 196

Kinslayings, The (XI) The first (at Alqualondë) 19, 26, 37, 41; the second (the attack on Dior) 232, 345–6, 348–9; the third (the attack on the Havens of Sirion) 345, 348

Kin-strife (of Gondor) (XII) 190, 198–9, 213–14, 230, 254–5, 258– 60, 262

Kirdan (VIII) See *Cirdan.*

Kiril, River (VII) In Gondor. 312

Kiril, River (VIII) In Gondor. 411, 427, 436–7; *Ciril* 419; *crossings of Kiril* 425 (see *Caerost, Calembel* (2)).

Kirith Gorgor (VIII) The great pass into Mordor, 'the Dreadful Pass', 'the Haunted Pass' (122). 121–2, 127, 270, 360–2, 431; *Cirith Gorgor* 122, 431

Kirith Gorgor (IXa) The great pass into Mordor. 8, 11, 20, 34. [Kirith Gorgor originally not separated from Gorgor(oth): see 32–3.]

Kirith Helvin (IV) 'Rainbow-cleft'. 146, 193. (Replaced *Cris-Ilfing,* replaced by *Cirith Ninniach.*)

Kirith Naglath (VIII) 'Cleft of the Teeth', proposed name for the Morannon. 137. See *Naglath Morn*.

Kirith Ninniach (XI) See *Cirith Ninniach*.

Kirith Ungol (VII) The great pass into Mordor (see 333, 344). (214), 283, 285, 310, 313, 321–2, 329–30, 333–4, 344, 346–9, 437–8, 450; *Kirith* 344; *gates* of 438; translated *'Spider Glen'* 330. See *Cirith Ungol*.

Kirith Ungol (VIII) (1) Original sense, the main pass into Mordor. 104–6, 111, 116, 121, 184, 220, 229; guard-towers of 106; translated *Spider Glen* 104, 184. (2) Cleft near the main pass. 106. (3) Pass below Minas Morghul. 113, 124. (4) Final sense, the high pass above the Morghul Vale (including references to the Stairs, the cleft, the pass, &c.). 101, 121, 124–6, 129, 136–7, 171, 173, 181–4, 186–7, 190–6, 198–200, 202, 208–9, 211–16, 218, 220–1, 223, 225–6, 252, 254, 256, 327, 329, 360, 431; *Ungol top* (Orc name) 216. For the tunnel (the Spider's lair) see *Shelob*.

Kirith Ungol (VIII) *The Tower of Kirith Ungol* 113, 125–6, 183–4, 187, 190–1, 195, 199–200, 202, (207), 211–16, 218–20, 225–6, 398; *Ungol* (Orc name) 216

Kirith Ungol (IXa) The high pass or cleft above the Morgul Vale. 8–10, (14, 18), 20, 22, 25.

Kirith Ungol (IXa) *The Tower of Kirith Ungol* guarding the pass (including references to *the Tower* and to *Kirith Ungol* in this sense) 7–10, 12–14, 18, 20–7, 29–30, 51 (some references are imprecise, whether to the pass or the fortress, 11, 25, 31, 35–6). *The turret* (or *horn-turret*) of the Tower (visible from the western side of the pass) 18, 20, 22, 24, 26–7; *the under-gate, brazen door, brazen gate* 18, 21–2, 24, 26, 28; the fortress described 18–20, 22, 26.

Kirith Ungol (IXa) Original sense, the main pass into Mordor, 28

Kirith Ungol (XII) 201

Kirith Ungol, Tower of (IXb) 407

Kirith-thoronath (IV) 'Eagles' Cleft'. 146, 194. (Replaced *Cristhorn*.)

Kiryahir (XII) Fifteenth King of Gondor (see *Hyarmendakil I*). 198, 210, 212; *Ciryahir, Ciryaher* 210. See also *Kiryandil* (2).

Kiryandil (XII) (1) Eldest son of Isildur. 191, 208. (Replaced by *Elendur* (1).) (2) Fourteenth King of Gondor. 197, 212–13; former name *Kiryahir* 212. (3) Father of Eärnil II King of Gondor (rejected). 216

Kiryatan (XII) See *Tar-Kiryatan*.

Knife-fang (II) 21, 31, 33, 68, 227. See *Karkaras*.

Knife-fang (III) See *Carcharoth*.

Koivië-néni (I) 'Waters of Awakening'. 85, 115, 117, 232; *Waters of Koivië* 115. See *Cuiviénen, Waters of Awakening*.

Koivië-Néni (III) See *Cuiviénen*.

Koivië-néni (IV) See *Cuiviénen*.

Koivië-néni (XI) Original form of *Kuiviénen*. 424

Kópas (II) Haven (of the Swanships). 255. See *Cópas Alqalunten*.

Kópas Alqaluntë (I) (*Alqalunten*) 'Haven of the Swanships'. 163–4, 171; *Kópas* 164, 166, 171, 178, 209, 223; *Cópas, Cópas Alqaluntë* 163, 169; *Alqaluntë* 176, 239. See *Haven of the Swanships*.

Kópas Alqaluntë (IV) 'Haven of the Swanships'. 277, 283. See *Alqualondë*.

Kópas Alqaluntë (VII) 322

Kôr (I) City of the Elves in Eldamar and the hill on which it was built. 15–16, 18–20, 25–7, 31, 48–50, 58, 65, 83, 98, 115, 122–3, 126–9, 135, 137, 141–4, 146–7, 149–54, 156, 159, 162–4, 169, 171, 175, 177, 196, 207, 209–11, 213, 220, 222, 225, 230–1, 235, 242; see especially 122–3. The Trees of Kôr 123, 135, 213, 221. Poem *Kôr* (renamed *The City of the Gods*) 136. See *Tûn*.

Kôr (II) City of the Elves in Eldamar and the hill on which it was built. 8–9, 42, 64, 71, 77, 115, 119, 123, 141, 145, 148–9, 161, 197, 202, 208, 215, 219, 253–65, 271–2, 278, 280, 285–6, 289, 291–2, 303–5, 307–8, 329; see especially 291–2, and see *Tûn, Túna, Tirion*.

Kôr (III) See *Côr*.

Kôr (IV) See *Côr*.

Kôr (V) 27, 112, 114, 167, 170–1, 173–4, 176, 180–1, 185, 192, 195, 198, 215, 218–19, 222, 224, 230, 234, 242, 246, 325, 365, 405; *in Kôr* 180, 192, 215, 218; *Pass of Kôr* 233, 244 (see *Kalakilya*).

Kôr (VII) 95

Kôr (X) 90, 180, 194, 197; *the Pass of Kôr* 194

Kôr (XI) Original name of the city of the Elves in Valinor. 23, 175, 189, 246. See *Tûn, Túna, Tirion*.

Koreldar (I) Elves of Kôr. 50, 143

Koreldar (II) Elves of Kôr. 276

Koreldar (IV) Elves of Kôr. 21, 51

Koreldar (XI) The Elves of Kôr. 107

Koreldarin (V) The tongue of the Lindar and Noldor before the departure of the Lindar from Kôr. 193, 195

Korin (I) Enclosure formed by elm-trees in which Meril-i-Turinqi dwelt. 16, 95

Korin (II) Enclosure formed by elm-trees in which Meril-i-Turinqi dwelt. 144, 197

Kormallen, Field of (IXa) 45–6, 49–50, 55, 83, 92; *Cormallen* 105

Kornoldorin, Korolambë (XI) The ancient Noldorin tongue of Kôr. 22–3

Kornoldorin. (V) 'Noldorin of Kôr', *Korolambë.* 174, 194–5, 347; *Ancient* or *Old Noldorin* 174, 193, 347 (in different sense 177).

Korolairë (X) The Mound of the Two Trees. 127, *Corolairë* 288; *Korlairë* 107, 122, 127. See *Ezellohar, Green Mound.*

Korolambë (V) 'Tongue of Kôr', =*Kornoldorin.* 174, 347

Korollairë (XII) The Green Mound of the Two Trees. 356

Korollairë, Koron Oiolairë (XI) The Green Mound of the Trees. 401. See *Ezellohar.*

Koromas (I) The town of Kortirion. 16, 22, 24–6; earlier form *Kormas* 22

Koromas (II) The town of Kortirion. 280, 292

Kortirion (I) Chief town of Alalminórë in Tol Eressea. 16, 24–6, 32–3, 35–43, 49, 132, 175, 222. Poem *Kortirion among the Trees* 25, 32–9, 50, late version *The Trees of Kortirion* (I) 32, 39–43. See *Koromas.*

Kortirion (II) Chief town of Alalminórë in Tol Eressëa. 4, 7, 280, 282–3, 288–9, 291–3, 298, 300, 302, 307–8, 310, 313, 323–4. Poem *Kortirion among the Trees* 276, 328, prose preface 289, 308

Kortirion (IV) See *Cortirion.*

Kortirion (V) 155, 201; *Cortirion* 334

Kosmoko, Kosomok(o) (II) Name of Gothmog in Eldarissa. 216; *Kosomot* 216

Kosomot (I) Son of Melko (=Gothmog Lord of Balrogs). 93

Kronos (IXb) Greek god (identified with Saturn). 221

Kuiviénen (IV) See *Cuiviénen.*

Kuiviénen (V) The Waters of Awakening. 168, 181–3, 212, 216, 263, 366, 406. See *Nen-Echui.*

Kuiviénen (X) The Water(s) of Awakening. 51, 71–4, 76–7, 81–2, 88, 91, 111, (130), 160, 166–7, 170, 281, *Cuiviénen* 277, 417. On the site of Kuiviénen see 72, 76–7

Kuiviénen (XI) See *Cuiviénen.*

Kulullin (I) The cauldron of golden light in Valinor. 71, 73, 76, 88, 99, 127, 154, 177–8, 180–1, 183, 186, 190, 208, 212

Kulullin (V) The cauldron of golden light in Valinor. 244

Kuluqendi (V) 'Golden-elves', a name of the Noldor. 403; cf. 215.

Kulúrien (V) Name of Laurelin. 210–11

Kulúrien (X) A name of Laurelin. 155

Kúma (IV) The Void, the Outer Dark. 237, 241, *243, *245, 252. See *Avakúma*.

Kurufinwë (X) See *Curufinwë*.

Kurufinwë (XII) See *Curufin, Fëanor*.

Kurúki (II) An evil magician in a preliminary sketch of the *Tale of Turambar*. 138–9

Lachend (XI), plural *Lechind* 'Flame-eyed', a Sindarin name of the Noldor. 384

Ladros (III) Lands to the northeast of Dorthonion. 344, 350

Ladros (XI) Land in the east of Dorthonion. *183, 187, 224, 229

Ladwen-na-Dhaideloth (II) 287; *Ladwen Daideloth* 287. See *Dor-na-Dhaideloth, Heath of the Sky-roof*.

Ladwen-na-Dhaideloth (IV) 259

Lady of the Stars (VI) Varda. 364

Laegel (XI), plurals *Laegil, Laegrim, Laegel(d)rim* (Sindarin) The Green-elves; whence Quenya *Laiquendi*. 385

Laer Cú Beleg (III) The Song of the Great Bow. 89. See *Beleg*.

Lagduf (IXa) Orc of the Tower of Kirith Ungol; earlier name *Lughorn*. 26

Laiqalassë (II) Name of Legolas Greenleaf of Gondolin in Eldarissa. 217

Laiqendi (V) The Green-elves. 176, 188, 198, 368 (also Noldorin *Lhoebenidh, Lhoebelidh*); *Laiqi* 188; *Laiqeldar* 188

Laiqi, Laiqeldar (IV) The Green-elves. 270, 277; later form *Laiquendi* 277

Laiquendi (II) The Green-elves of Ossiriand. 249

Laiquendi (X) Green-elves. 169. See *Nandor*.

Laiquendi (XI) See *Laegel*.

Lake Town (XII) See *Esgaroth*.

Lake-men (VI) Men of the Long Lake. 186

Lake-town (VI) 237. See *Esgaroth*.

Lake-town (VII) 187

Lalaeth (X) Sister of Túrin. 374

Lalaeth (XI) See *Urwen*.

Lambë Valarinwa (XI) Valarin. 397

Lamben (VII) See *(The) Tongue*.

Lambengolmor (XI) 'Loremasters of Tongues'. 396–8

Lamedon (VII) Region of Gondor. 312, 388

Lamedon (VIII) 287, 398, 411–12, 414, 419, 436–7, 439. For changing application of the name see 436–7.

Lamedon (IXa) 15–16

Lameduin, River (VII) In Gondor. (Afterwards *Gilrain*.) 312

Lameduin, River (VIII) In Gondor (later *Gilrain*). 398, 422, 427, 436–7; *Fords of Lameduin* (VIII) 397, 422, 437; *Lamedui* 436

Lameduin, River (IXa) 16–17; *Lamedui* 15–16; *Fords of Lameduin* 16; *Mouths of Lamedui(n)* 15–16

Lammas (I) (Harvest festival, 1st of August) 41

Lammas The (XI) 'Account of Tongues' by Pengolodh. 205–6, 208, 393, 397, 416; older form *Lhammas* (the work as published in *The Lost Road*) 3, 22–3, 108–9, 118, 208–9, 419; *Lammasethen* 22

Lammoth (X) Region north of the Firth of Drengist. 295–9; *the Great Echo* 296; *Echoing Mountains of Lammoth* 298

Lammoth (XI) Region north of the Firth of Drengist. 176, *182

Lammoth (XII) Region north of Drengist. 362; *Battle of the Lammoth* 345, 362

Lamorni (VIII) 'Talking Trees'. 50, 60. See *Galbedirs*, *Ornómi*.

Lamp of Vána (I) The Sun. 187

Lamps, The (I) 69–71, 87, 100, 110–11, 118, 134, 152, 182

Lamps, The (III) 148

Lamps, The (IV) 12, 42–3, 45, 80, 82, 238, *249, 256, 263–4, 270, 276, 314; O.E. *Blácern, Léohtfatu*, 281, 283, 285–6. See *Helkar, Illuin, Ringil*.

Lamps, The (V) 110–11, 121, 208, 211

Lamps, The (VI) 122

Lamps, The (IXb) The original lights of Middle-earth. 412

Lamps, The (X) 7, 17–18, 25–7, 32–3, 38, 41, 43, 52–3, 60–1, 66, 78, 105, 153, 156, 158, 165, 375, 384. See *Forontë, Illuin; Hyarantë, Ormal*.

Lamps, The (XI) 106

Lampwrights, Street of the (VIII) In Minas Tirith. 287, 396. See *Rath a Chelerdain*.

Land of Bow and Helm (XI) 144, 314. See *Dor-Cúarthol*.

Land of Dread (III) The land of Morgoth. 155, 158, 168, 350

Land of Dread (IV) 221, 269. See *Dor Daideloth*.

Land of Dread (V) See *Dor-Daideloth, Dor-deloth*.

Land of Echoes (IV) See *Dor-lómin*.

Land of Elms (I) 16, 25, 33, 36, 39–40, 95. See *Alalminórë*.

Land of Five Streams (VII) 310–11. See *Lebennin*.

Land of Gift (IXb) (Also *Land of his Gift*, i.e. the gift of Amân) 241, 247, 259, 312, 332, 343, 353, 361, 373, 375, 378, 385, 388, 391–2, 394, 397; *the Gift* 396; O.E. *léanes lond* 258. See *Andórë*; *Athânâte, Amatthânê, Zen'nabâr, Abarzâyan, Yôzâyan*.

Land of Ice (IXb) See *Iceland*.

Land of Light (III) The Blessed Realm. 236

Land of Mist (IV) See *Hisilómë*.

Land of Seven Rivers (V) See *Ossiriand*.

Land of Seven Rivers (VIII) 254, 278. See *Lebennin*.

Land of Seven Rivers (XI) 13, 385. See *Ossir, Ossiriand*.

Land of Seven Streams (IV) Ossiriand. 116, (135, 230), 233; *Land of Seven Rivers* 301

Land of Seven Streams (VII) See *Lebennin, Seven Rivers*.

Land of Shadow (VII) Mordor. 178

Land of Shadow(s) (I) 112, 138, 239–40; *land of shade* 118. See *Aryador, Dor Lómin, Hisilómë*.

Land of Shadow(s) (II) 61, 88, 149, 161, 166, 215, 218. See *Aryador, Dor Lómin, Hisilómë, Hithlum, Mathusdor*.

Land of Shadow(s) (III) Hithlum. 8, 104, 108

Land of Shadows (IV) See *Dor-lómin*.

Land of the Blessed (X) See *(The) Blessed Realm*.

Land of the Dead that Live (II) 249. See *I·Cuilwarthon, I·Guilwarthon*.

Land of the Dead that Live (III) 89. See *I·Guilwarthon*.

Land of the Dead that Live (IV) 55, 133–4, 179, 189–90, 224, 230, 233. See *Cuilwarthien, Gwerth-i-cuina*.

Land of the Dead that Live (V) 268, 305, 307. See *Gwerth-i-Cuina*.

Land of the Dead that Live (XI) 71, 132, 347. See *Gwerth-i-guinar*.

Land of the Lost (III) See *Valley of the Dead Awaiting*.

Land of the Star (IXb) 368, 390. See *(The) Star of Eärendil*.

Land of Thirst (III) Dor-na-Fauglith. 275

Land of Thirst (IV) See *Dor-na-Fauglith*.

Land of Waiting (III) See *Valley of the Dead Awaiting*.

Land of Willows (II) 140, 153–4, 195–6, 205, 214, 217, 278–80. See *Nan-tathren, Tasarinan*.

Land of Willows (III) Nan-Tathrin. 141–2

Land of Willows (IV) 36, 67, 104, 141, 175, 193, 195, 214–17, 225, 296, 314, 329; *Valley of Willows* 35. See *Nan Tathrin*.

Land of Willows (V) 253, 261; *Vale of Willows* 126. See *Nan-tathren*.

Land(s) Beyond Artanor. (II) 9, 11, 21, 62, 72, 77, 91–2, 117, 126, 140. See *Artanor, Doriath*.

Land(s) of the Sun (IV) The Eastern Land. 239, *249; *Burnt Land of the Sun* *250–1

Land's End (IXb) In Cornwall. 266

Landroval (IXa) See *Lhandroval*.

Landroval (X) Brother of Gwaihir the Windlord. 410, 412

Landroval, Lhandroval (V) 'Wide-wing', vassal of Thorondor. 301, 382.

Lands of Ease (III) The Blessed Realm. 172, 187, 308; *a land of ease* 148

Lands of Mist (III) Hithlum. 96

Lands Without (II) The lands 'without Valinor', i.e. the Great Lands. 233. See *Outer Land(s)*.

Langobards (IXb) Lombards. 236–7, 284, 301; *Longobards* 273, 276; O.E. *Longbeardan* (IXb) 273; *Langobardic* 237, 301

Langon (I) Servant of Melko. 102

Langstrand (VIII) 287, 293, See *Anfalas*.

Langstrand (XII) Coastal fief of Minas Tirith. 422

Langwell, River (VII) A source-stream of Anduin. 307

Lanhail (IXa) 'Plain-wise', Aragorn's name for Samwise. 118. See *Núrnen*.

Lanthir Lamath (XII) Waterfall in Ossiriand. 349, 372; cf. 369

Larmindon (VII) See *Amon Lhaw*.

Lasgalen (X) 'Green of leaf', (Noldorin >) Sindarin name of Laurelin. 155

Lassiriand (III) Rejected name for Beleriand. 160

Last Alliance (V) 12, 18, 23, 29, 31, 33, 35, 153, 337

Last Alliance (VI) 174, 216–18, 260, 320

Last Alliance (VII) 122, (123), 126–7, 138, 144–5, 361. See *Battles*.

Last Alliance (VIII) 129

Last Alliance (IXb) 331

Last Alliance (XII) (also the *Alliance*) 166, 169–70, 176, 192, 420

Last Alliance, The (IXa) 20

Last Battle (II) 138

Last Battle (IV) (1) At the end of the Elder Days. 39–40, 71, 73, 75, 157, 168, 198, 200, 203–5, 309; see *Battle of the Gods, Battle of Wrath and Thunder, Great Battle, Terrible Battle*. (2) The ultimate

battle of the world, declared in prophecy. 40–1, 71, 73–4, 165, 205; see *Dagor Dagorath*.

Last Battle (V) (1) The Great Battle (q.v.). 11, 405. (2) The ultimate battle of the world, declared in prophecy. 16, 333

Last Battle (IXb) 336, 386

Last Battle (XI) At the end of the Elder Days. 27, 117; *last war of the Elder Days* 345–6; *the Great Battle* 345. The final battle of Arda 204, 207

Last Battle (XII) (at the end of the First Age) 371, 375; ('at the end of Days') 374–5

Last Battle, The (X) See *Battles of the Gods*.

Last Bridge (VI) 192, 194, 199, 202–4, 219, 360, 367–8; *Hoarwell Bridge* 200–1; *Mitheithel Bridge* 201

Last Bridge (VII) See *Mitheithel*.

Last Homely House (VI) Elrond's house at Rivendell. 208, 417

Later Ages (X) 31, 68, 327

Later Tales (X) 5. *Last Tales* 22

Lathos, Lathweg (I) Earlier names of Fanuin. 222

Láthspell (VII) 'Ill-news'. See *Gandalf*.

Latimer (IXb) Member of the Notion Club (precursor of Guildford). 150, 212, 214

Latin (V) 38–9, 41–3, 53–4, 92, 186, 279

Latin (VI) 145

Latin (IXb) 150, 217, 220, 222, 225, 238, 241, 283, 285–6, 294, 300, 306–7, 418. See *Elven-Latin*.

Latin (XI) 372, 391. See *Elf-Latin*.

Latin (XII) 46–7, 52, 69, 88, 102–3, 368

Laurelin (I) 72–3, 75–6, 88–9, 99, 116–17, 119, 122, 126–8, 135, 153, 162, 178–9, 181–2, 184–6, 190–1 193, 200–1. See *Glingol, Lindelos, Lindeloksë*.

Laurelin (II) 216, 285

Laurelin (III) 353

Laurelin (IV) 20, 49–50, 74, 80–3, 92, 97, 171, 210, 237, 255, 269, 281, 283; O.E. *Goldléoþ* 281, 283. See *Glingol*.

Laurelin (V) 111, 118, 209–11, 231, 240–2, 244, 358–9, 368–9

Laurelin (VI) 187–8. See *Galadlóriel*.

Laurelin (X) 55–6, 62, 98, 130–2, 157–8, 177, 197, 238, 261–2, 371–2, 386; 'founded on the laburnum' ('Golden-rain') 157

Laurelin (XI) 20, 401

Laurelin (XII) 130, 334, 337

Laurelindórenan (IXa) The old Elvish name of Lórien used by Tree-beard, earlier *Laurelindórinan*. 73

Laurundo, Laurunto (II) Forms of the name of Glorund in Eldarissa. 84. See *Undolaurë*.

Lavaralda (V) A tree of Tol-eressëa. 57–8, 70; earlier *lavarin* 70

Lay of Eärendel (IV) See *Eärendel*.

Lay of Leithian (II) 52, 54, 57, 67, 330

Lay of Leithian (IV) 5, 24, 43, 46, 52, 54–5, 60, 66, 71, 167–8, 173, 176–9, 181, 189, 219–22, 224–6, 233, 289, 316; references in the *Quenta* 109–10, 112 (*Lay of Lúthien*), 115 (*Lay of Leithian*).

Lay of Leithian (V) 22, 107, 151, 186, 290–2, 295–7, 299–303, 338, 368

Lay of Leithian (VI) 187, 197

Lay of Leithian (VII) 108

Lay of Leithian (IXb) 149

Lay of Leithian (X) 3, 89, 142, 182, 423

Lay of Leithian (XI) 59, 62, 65, 69, 108, 125, 129–31, 187

Lay of the Children of Húrin (II) 62

Lay of the Children of Húrin (IV) 9, 11, 43–4, 46, 52–5, 57–9, 64, 167, 172–3, 175, 180–4, 189, 215, 219–26, 229, 232, 259, 310, 312, 320, 323; referred to in the 'Sketch' 28, in the *Quenta* 122, 183; *Túrin and the Dragon* 11

Lay of the Children of Húrin (V) 149, 151, 256, 266, 314–17, 322–3, 338. See *i·Chúrinien, Narn i Hîn Húrin*.

Lay of the Children of Húrin (VI) 180

Lay of the Children of Húrin (XI) (in *The Lays of Beleriand*: alliterative verse) 109, 137–8, 314

Lay of the Fall of Gondolin (IV) 5, 8, 46, 65, 193, 222

Lay of the Fall of Gondolin (XI) 121, 320

Lëa the Young (X) Wife of Tulkas. 66–7; *Lëa-vinya* 67

Leaflock (VII) Ent. 412. See *Finglas*.

Lebennin (VII) 'Land of Five/Seven Streams'. 310–12, 318, 322

Lebennin (VIII) 229, 236, 243, 252, 254–5, 263, 276, 278, 283, 287, 289, 293–4, 330, 372, 398, 411–15, 420, 425, 427–8, 436–7; *five streams of Lebennin* 252, 254, 294, 436. See *Land of Seven Rivers*.

Lebennin (IXa) 15–16

Lebennin (XII) 45, 199, 238

lebethron (VIII) Tree of Gondor. 180. Earlier names *melinon, lebendron, lebethras* 176

lebethron (IXa) Tree of Gondor. 55

Leeds (I) 108, 136, 204

Leeds (V) 98

Leeds, University of (III) 3, 81, 94, 120–2, 131, 142, 145

Leeds, University of (IV) 42, 219

Leeds, University of (VI) 142, 144–5, 180

Leeds, University of (VII) 59

Lefnui, River (VII) In Gondor. 298, 307, 311–12; earlier *Lhefneg* 'fifth'
    312

Legolas (VI) Elf of Mirkwood. 398, 413, 415, 436. See *Galdor* (2).

Legolas (VII) (1) Legolas Greenleaf of Gondolin. 172. (2) Elf of
    Mirkwood. 129, 141, 148, 157, 161–2, 167, 169–72, 180, 193–
    4, 197–8, 200, 203, 210–33 *passim*, 237–40, 242, 246, 248, 251,
    256–8, 263, 268, 271–4, 279, 289, 29 1–2, 329–30, 347, 353–
    5, 360, 363, 365, 378, 381–2, 385–90, 392, 395–7, 399, 402–3,
    406, 411–13, 425–9, 431–2, 434, 437–9, 441–3, 446, 449; called
    Greenleaf 392, 431 *Lembas* 'waybread'. 271, 279, 398

Legolas (VIII) 3–5, 13–15, 20, 22, 24–5, 27, 37, 40, 59, 66–7, 72,
    78, 140–1, 146, 229, 238, 241, 243–4, 246, 249, 264, 272, 274,
    276, 297–301, 304–5, 308, 310–11, 313, 321, 361, 370, 386,
    392, 397, 399, 403, 405–7, 409–11, 414–21, 423–4, 426–9;
    Green-leaf 22, 420

Legolas (IXa) 48–9, 57, 61, 63,70–1, 116, 120, 123

Legolas (XII) 36, 64, 79, 82, 220, 242, 244, 246, 286, 391

Legolas Greenleaf (II) (1) Elf of Gondolin. 189, 191–2, 214, 217. See
    (I).267 and *Laiqalassë*. (2) Elf of Mirkwood, member of the Fellow-
    ship of the Ring. 327

Legolin, River (IV) 135, 233. (Replaced *Loeglin*.)

Legolin, River (V) 128, 263, 368

Legolin, River (XI) In Ossiriand. 13, *185

Leikvian (V) Tongue of the Leikvir. 188, 196; *Fading Leikvian* 189

Leikvir (V) Danian Elves who remained east of the Blue Mountains.
    188, 197

Leire (V) On the island of Zealand. 97

Leithian (II) =*Lúthien* (3) (England). 330; *Leithien* 300

Leithian, Lay of (III) Date of 3–4, 150–1, 159; named in *The Children
    of Húrin* 107, 121, and in the introductory verses to *Light as Leaf
    on Lindentree* 120; meaning of the name 154

Leithien (IV) 'Britain or England' (40). 40–1, 72, 75, 162, 165–6, 199,

258; *Eriol of Leithien* 76, 78, 191, 206, 263; *Leithian* 72. See *Lúthien* (3).

Leithien (V) *Land of Leithien* 332; *Eriol of Leithien* 201, 203

Leithien (IXb) Britain. 280

Leithien, Leithian (III) England. 154. See *Lúthien* (2).

lembas (VIII) 86, 105, 139; *waybread, elvish bread* 130, 134, 138–9

lembas (IXa) 11, 25

Lembas (XII) The 'waybread' of the Eldar; Quenya *coimas*. 395, 403–4

Lembeni (XII) Early name for the Sindar. 62; *Lembenin* (language) 30, 36, 41, 62, 65, 73

Lemberi (X) 'The Lingerers'. (1) Name of the Eldar 'lost upon the long road'. 169. (2) A name of the Sindar. 164, 171

Lembi (V) Dark-elves. 169–70, 175–6, 179, 181–3, 187–8, 197–8, 200, 215, 218–19, 256, 344, 368. Translated 'those that were left' 181,'the Forsaken' 198, 'those that lingered', 'the Lingerers', 169, 215, 218. On change of the application of the name see 219.

Lembi (VIII) Elves of the Great Journey who never went to Valinor. 158. *The Lingerers* 157–8. Called also *Middle Elves, Elves of the Woods,* 157

Lembi (X) =*Lemberi* (1). 169 *letters* (devised by Rúmil, Fëanor) 92, 103, 184–5, 191, 256, 350. See *tengwar*.

Lembi (XII) Earlier term for Lemberi. 30, 61–2, 76

Lembi Dark-elves. (XI) 118

Lembian (V) and *Lemberin* Languages of the Lembi. 171, 176, 185, 183, 188–90, 194–5, 197

Lenwë (IV) Leader of those Teleri who abandoned the Great March. 277. (Replaced *Dan*.)

Lenwë (XI) First leader of the Nandor (replaced *Dân*). 384–5, 412, 418. See *Denweg*.

Léod (VII) Father of Eorl the Young. 440. See *Eofor*.

Léod (XII) Father of Eorl the Young. 273–4. (Replaced *Garman*.)

Léof (XII) See *Brytta*.

Léofa (IXa) Name given to Brytta, eleventh King of the Mark, earlier *Léof*. 68, 72

Lesser Folk (XII) See *Bëor*.

Lesser Market, Square of the (II) In Gondolin. 182

Letters of J. R. R. Tolkien (I) 22, 25, 44–5, 192

Letters of J. R. R. Tolkien (II) 265–7, 271, 329

Letters of J. R. R. Tolkien, The (VII) 66, 90, 106, 173, 299, 315, 406–7, 410, 413, 422, 432; other letters 85, 89, 107, 452

Letters of J. R. R. Tolkien, The (VIII) 45, 65, 77–8, 80, 85–6, 92, 100, 104, 115, 121–3, 127, 129, 131, 134, 136–7, 144, 147, 162, 170–1, 180, 183–4, 218–20, 233–4, 255, 274

Letters of J. R. R. Tolkien, The (IXa) 12, 18, 53, 68, 109, 129, 132; other letters 12

Letters of J. R. R. Tolkien, The (IXb) 145, 147, 150–3, 212, 217, 220, 285, 291–2, 381, 407–10

Letters of J. R. R. Tolkien, The (X) 3, 6, 26, 43, 124, 126, 141, 181, 267, 270, 290, 300, 328, 354, 356–8, 365–6, 372, 408, 411–13; other letters 5, 300

Letters of J. R. R. Tolkien, The (XI) 118, 212, 341, 353, 356

Letters of J. R. R. Tolkien, The (XII) 7, 15, 18, 26, 69, 80, 158, 190, 321, 410; other letters 71–3, 88, 246

Levain tad-dail (XI) 'Two-legged animals' (see 416), original Sindarin name of the Petty-dwarves. 388; *Tad-dail* 388

Levin-tree (VII) 94–5; *Tree of Lightning* 99

Lewis, C. S. (III) 150–1, 153, 157–8, 169, 181, 194–6, 208, 315–29

Lewis, C. S. (V) 7, 9; *Out of the Silent Planet* 8

Lewis, C. S. (VI) 44, 108

Lewis, C. S. (VII) 85; 419 (*Out of the Silent Planet*).

Lewis, C. S. (VIII) 104, 107, 137, 144, 171–2, 183–4

Lewis, C. S. (IXb) 145, 148–50, 152–3, 164, 168, 175, 199–200, 202–3, 213, 216, 219–22, 303, 307–9; with reference to his nickname *Jack* 200, 219. *Out of the Silent Planet* 152, 164, 174, 199, 212, 220; *Perelandra* 152, 199, 202, 212–13; *That Hideous Strength* 152–3, 309; other works 153, 219

Lewis, W H. (XII) 140

Lhammas (XI) See *Lammas*.

Lhammas (XII) The 'Account of Tongues'. 62, 356

Lhammas, The (VI) 69

Lhammas, The (VII) 138, 453

Lhammas, The (VIII) 169

Lhammas, The (IXb) 280, 286

Lhammas, The (X) 77, 89–90, 102, 104, 169–70; *Lammas* 415 Light (of various reference, not including those expressly to the Light of the Trees) 43, 73, 83, 85–6, 98, 100, 108–9, 111–12, 122, 132, 153–4, 158, 163, 178, 195, 198–9, 247, 250, 284, 288–9, 294–5, 308–9, 313, 321–2, 326, 346, 351, 354, 372, 379–80, 382,

389–90, 401; *the Primeval Light*, the Light of Varda, 377, 380–1, 385–6

Lhandroval (V) See *Landroval*.

Lhandroval (IXa) 'Wide-wing', Eagle of the North. (1) In the Elder Days, vassal of Thorondor. 45. (2) In the Third Age, descendant of Thorondor and brother of Gwaihir. 44–5, 50. Later form *Landroval* 50

Lhandroval (XI) The eagle, vassal of Thorondor. 68, 131

Lhasgalen (V) 'Green of Leaf', Gnomish name of Laurelin. 210–11, 367–8

Lhefneg, River (VII) See *Lefnui*.

Lhefneg, River (VIII) In Gondor. 436–7. (Later *Lefnui*.)

Lhothland, Lhothlann (XII) Plain east of Dorthonion. 68

Lhûn (VII) 'Blue River' (124). 123–4, 144; written *Lune* 301, 415–16. *Gulf of Lhûn* 123–4; written *Lune* 301. *Mountains of Lune* 416. See *Lindon*.

Lhûn, River (V) 33–4; *Gulf of Lhûn* 33–4

Light as Leaf on Linden tree (VI) 179–80, 187. See *Tinúviel*.

Light as Leaf on Lindentree (III) (poem) 108–10, 120–6, 159, 181–2

Light Elves (X) 169; *Elves of the Light* 163, 173. See *Kalaquendi*.

Light, (The) (XI) (and ~ *of Aman, of the Trees, in the West*, etc.) 6–9, 17, 39, 41, 217, 220, 225, 227, 373, 403

Light-elves (I) 43

Light-elves (IV) The First Kindred of the Elves. 13, 44, 85, 87, 89, 149, 151, 154, 159–60, 162, 196, 289, 309; O.E. *Léohtelfe* 286, 289

Light-elves (V) (1) The First Kindred of the Elves (Lindar). 143, 197, 218, 326, 328, 331, 334. (2) The Elves who went to Valinor. 197, 215, 218–19; see *Kalamor, Kalaqendi*.

Light-elves (IXb) 410; Old Norse *Ljós-alfar* 398

Light-elves (XI) (1) The Lindar (Vanyar). 246. (2) Elves of Aman. 320, 361. See *Kalaquendi*.

Limhir, River (XI) Late replacement of *Celon*. 320, 326, 337.

Limlight, River (VII) 318, 320, 356–7, 365

Limlight, River (VIII) 313

Limlight, River (XI) 337

Limlight, River (XII) 259

Limpë (I) The drink of the Eldar. 17, 95–8, 107, 166, 174–5, 230

Limpë (II) The drink of the Eldar. 279, 283–4, 290, 292, 306, 308, 310; given the Old English equivalent *líþ* 290

Linaewen, Lake (XI) In Nivrost (Nevrast). *182, 186, 192

Lindai (XI) See *Lindar*.

Lindalambë (XI) The language of the Lindar (Teleri). 375. See *Lindarin*.

Lindar (IV) The First Kindred of the Elves. 86, 89, 93, 96, 168–9, 270, 272, 276, 289. (Replaced *Quendi* (2), replaced by *Vanyar*.)

Lindar (V) The First Kindred of the Elves. 56, 107, 112, 122, 162, 165, 168 ('the fair'), 171–4, 180, 182, 184–5, 192–5, 197–8, 211, 214–15, 218, 221–4, 226, 228, 231, 233, 235, 242, 326, 331, 334, *369* (also *Melimar 372*), *386*, 403; language of the Lindar 171–4, 180, 184–5, 192–3, 222. See *Fair-elves*, *High-elves*, *Light-elves*; other names 215, 403

Lindar (VI) The First Kindred of the Elves. 188

Lindar (VII) The First Kindred of the Elves. 453

Lindar (X) (1) Earlier name of the Vanyar. 20, 24–5, 34, 88, 90, 162, 168, 171, 174–6, 178–9, 181, 184. (2) A name of the Teleri. 349, 360

Lindar (XI) The 'Third Clan' (formerly the name of the 'First Clan', the Vanyar, 246, 418). 378, 380–3, 410–11, 418, 423; meaning of the name 382. Original and Telerin form *Lindai* 378, 382, 385; Nandorin *Lindi* 385; Sindarin *Lindil*, *Lindedhil* 385. See *Glinnel*, *Nendili*; *Teleri*.

Lindar (XII) (1) The Vanyar. 30, 62, 356; *Lindarin* (language) 30. (2) The Teleri. 332, 356

Lindarin (V) (of speech and race) 172, 174, 184, 186, 188, 192–6, 347

Lindon The undrowned land west of the Blue Mountains. 32–4, 154, 267 ('region of music'), 269, 337, *369* (also *Lhinnon*).

Lindarin (XI) (1) The language of the Lindar =Vanyar. 22. (2) The language of the Lindar =Teleri. 375–6, 382; as adjective to *Lindar* 376–7, 381–2, 385

Lindelaurë, *Lindeloktë* (II) Names of Laurelin. 216

Lindeloksë (I) Name of Laurelin. 22, 72, 79, 88, 119, 131. (Replaced *Lindelótë*, *Lindelóktë*.)

Lindeloktë (I) Name of Laurelin. 22. (Replaced by *Lindeloksë*.)

Lindelos (I) Name of Laurelin. 18, 22. (Replaced *Lindelokë* in one passage.)

Lindeótë (I) Name of Laurelin. 79, 131. (Replaced by *Lindeloksë*.)

Lindir (VII) Elf *of* Rivendell. 84

Lindis of Ossiriand (XI) Wife of Dior. 257, 300, 350–1, 353. See *Elulin*, *Nimloth*.

Lindo (I) Elf of Tol Eressëa, master of Mar Vanwa Tyaliéva. 14–18,

20, 24, 26–7, 45, 63, 65, 78, 129, 140, 162, 166, 169–70, 174–5, 182, 189, 194–7, 200, 203, 219–20, 229–31

Lindo (II) Elf of Tol Eressëa, master of Mar Vanwa Tyaliéva. 3, 70, 144–5, 219, 221, 258, 279, 284, 302

Lindon (IV) 199

Lindon (VII) 123; *North and South Lindon* 124 (*Forlindon* and *Harlindon on* the First Map, 302). *Gulf of Lindon* 144

Lindon (X) See *Mountains of Lindon.*

Lindon (XI) Ossiriand. 193, 195, 385; *Dor Lindon* 385; *Lindónë* 385

Lindon (XII) Lands west of the Blue Mountains. 36, 78, 168–9, 173–4, 179, 183, 193–5, 209, 230, 246, 328, 351, 382, 390

Lindórië (XII) Sister of Eärendur (1), Lord of Andúnië. 159

Lindsay, David (IXb) 164, 212. *A Voyage to Arcturus* 164, 212

Lingerers (X) (1) See *Lemberi.* (2) 'Faded' Elves in Middle-earth. 224

Lingerers, The (VIII) 157–8. See *Lembi.*

Linglor, Linglorel (VII) See *Nimrodel.*

Linhir (VIII) Town in Gondor on the river Lameduin (Gilrain). 361, 364, 397–8, 411–12, 422, 424, 427–9, 436–7

Linhir (IXa) Town in Gondor, on the river Morthond. 16–17

Linqil (I) A name of Ulmo. 61

Linwë (IV) See *Tinwelint.*

Linwë (Tinto) (II) Earlier name of Tinwë (Linto), Tinwelint. 49–50, 76, 92, 116–17, 135–8

Linwë Tinto, Linwë (I) Earlier name of Tinwë Linto. 106–7, 130, 132

Lionesse (II) Legendary land now drowned between Cornwall and the Scilly Isles. 313–14. See *Evadrien, Erenol.*

Lionesse (III) Legendary land now drowned between Cornwall and the Scilly Isles. 140

Lionesse (V) 85

Lirillo (I) A name of Salmar (Noldorin). 144, 155

Lís (X) True name of the Vala Lórien. 150. (Replaced by *Irmo.*)

Lisgardh (II) Land of reeds at the Mouths of Sirion. 217. See *Arlisgion.*

List Melian (XI) *183, 188, 223, 225, 228, 333; *Lest Melian* 225, 228. Cf. *Aran Lestanórëo* 'King of Doriath' 369; and see *Girdle of Melian.*

Lithe, The; Lithedays (XII) The three Summerdays in the Shire Calendar. 6, 15, 121–2, 124, 128–9, 131–2, 136. See *Overlithe.*

Lithir, River (XI) Tributary of Sirion north of Brethil. 181, *182, 261, 301

Lithlad (VII) 'Plain of Ash'. 208, 213, 313

Lithlad (VIII) 'Plain of Ash', in the north of Mordor. 127, 438

Lithlad (IXa) 'Plain of Ash', in the north of Mordor. 20

Little Folk (VII) Hobbits. 171, 247, 249

Little Folk (XII) Hobbits. 311; *Little People* 9

Little Folk, Little People (VI) Hobbits. 121, 134, 427, 431

Little Ford (XI) (over Gelion) See *Northern Ford.*

Little Lune (XII) Tributary of the River Lune. 313, 328

Little People (VIII) Hobbits. 167, 306

Little World, Little Kingdom (X) See *(The) World.*

Littleheart (I) Son of Bronweg, called 'the Gong-warden' (of Mar Vanwa Tyaliéva). 15, 46, 48, 52, 64, 94–6, 230. See *Ilverin.*

Littleheart (II) Son of Bronweg (Voronwë), called 'the Gong-warden' (of Mar Vanwa Tyaliéva). 197, 201, 221, 228, 244, 252, 254, 256, 263, 276. For his Elvish names see 201–2, 276.

Littleheart (IV) Son of Bronweg. 69–70. See *Ilfiniol.*

Littleheart (VI) The Gong-warden of Mar Vanwa Tyaliéva. 187

Living Land (IXb) In *The Death of St. Brendan.* 261, 296

Living, The (X) (Elves) 206, 223–7, 232, 234–5, 248, 250, 255, 259–60, 264, 362

Lockholes (IXa) In Michel Delving. 80, 85, 87, 89, 98–100, 108, 110

Loeglin, River (IV) 135, 189, 233. (Replaced by *Legolin.*)

Lofar (VI) Dwarf who stayed at Bag End after the Party. 238–9, 241–3, 248, 315

Lofar (VII) Dwarf who remained at Bag End. 21

Lókë (II) Name in Eldarissa for the dragons of Melko. 85. See *Foalókë, Fuithlug.*

Lombards (V) 7, 37, 46, 53–5, 77–8, 91, 93; *Long-beards* 53; Old English *Longbearden* (V) 53, 93; *Langobards, Longobards* 87, 91; *Langobardi* 53

Lómëarni (I) A name of the Dark Elves. 244

Lomendánar (I) 'The Days of Gloaming' before the making of the Lamps. 69, 79; *Lome Danar* 79

Lóminórë (XI) 145. See *Dor-lómin.*

Lómion (XI) 'Child (Son) of Twilight', name given to Maeglin by his mother. 323, 337

Lond Daer (XII) Great Númenórean haven at mouth of the Greyflood. 329

Lonely Companies (I) 34, 37; *Faithful Companies* 41

Lonely Island (III) 48

Lonely Island, Lonely Isle (I) 13, 15–16, 22–3, 25, 37, 85, 121, 125,

134, 136–7, 224; *the Isle, our isle* 97, 174–5; *the fairies' isle* 175; poem *The Lonely Isle* 25. See *Tol Eressëa*.

Lonely Isle (IV) 14, 20, 38, 40–1, 72, 78, 87, 98, 150, 153, 159, 162, 165, 198, 200. See *Tol Eressëa*.

Lonely Isle (V) 14, 16, 20–1, 26, 29–30, 64, 104, 113, 171, 203, 221–2, 243, 323–4, 327, 331, *333*; *Lonely Island* 24, 338. See *Eressëa*.

Lonely Isle (VIII) 168–9. See *Eressëa*.

Lonely Isle (X) 5, 86, 134, 174–6, 271. See *Tol Eressëa*.

Lonely Isle (XI) 246, 312, 315. See *Tol Eressëa*.

Lonely Isle (XII) See *Eressëa*.

Lonely Isle, Lonely Island (II) 4–5, 7, 34, 148, 253, 289, 298, 301, 307, 311, 313, 316–17, 322–4, 326–7, 329; *the Isle* 42, 144, 283–4; *the holy isle* 291; *Island of the Elves* 320, 327; Old English *se uncúpa holm* 290, *seo unwemmede Íeg* 291, 301; speech of 34, 148; poem *The Lonely Isle* 291. See *Tol Eressëa*.

Lonely Isle, Lonely Island (VII) 95, 97, 100. See *Eressëa*.

Lonely Isle, The (IXb) (1) (Tol) Eressëa. 280, 316, 332, 334, 354, 394, 396, 412; O.E. *Anetíg* 316. (2) The summit of the Pillar of Heaven after the Downfall. 391–4, 407; *a lonely isle, ~ island* 351, 373, 391–3

Lonely Mountain (IV) 283

Lonely Mountain (VI) (in many references *the Mountain*) 53, 210, 221, 310, 366, 381, 391–2, 411, 429, 437, 442, 444

Lonely Mountain (VII) (also *the Mountain*) 82, 117, 142, 159–60, 306, 329; *King under the Mountain* 160. See *Erebor*.

Lonely Mountain (VIII) 415; *the Mountain* 409. See *Erebor*.

Lonely Mountain (XII) (also *the Mountain*) 35, 39, 73, 124, 131, 236, 275–6, 281–2; *the Great Hall* (within the Mountain) 281. See *Erebor*.

Long Battle (V) The Great Battle. 405

Long Cleeve (XII) Home of the North-tooks. 108

Long Lake (VI) 177, 218

Long Lake (XII) 34

Long Lists (VIII) 66, 76; *Long Rolls* 76

Long Peace, The (X) (305), 306–7, 327

Long Peace, The (XI) 46, 58, 206, 215, 329

Long Winter (XII) (Third Age 2758–9) 17, 205, 220, 236, 271

Longbeard Dwarves (III) 205

Longbeards (II) See *Indrafangs*.

Longbeards (IV) See *Indrafangs*.

Longbeards (V) See *Enfeng, Indrafangs*; *Lombards*.

Longbeards (X) The Dwarves of Belegost. 93

Longbeards (XI) The Dwarves of Belegost. 10, 108, 205, 207–8, 322; of Nogrod 108, 208. See *Anfangrim, Enfeng, Indrafangs*.

Longbeards (XII) Durin's Folk. 295, 297, 301–5, 319, 321–4, 383. See *Andafangar, Anfangrim*; *Sigin-tarag*.

Longbottom (VI) In the Southfarthing. 284

Longbottom (VIII) Village in the Southfarthing. 36–8; *Longbottom Leaf* (pipeweed) 37, 39, 45, 59

Longbottom (XII) Village in the South Farthing. 6, 18

Longholes (VI) Hobbit family name. 137, 236

Lóni (VII) Companion of Balin in Moria. 191, 204

Lonnath-Ernin (VIII) See *Harlond*.

Lord of All (IXb) (Meleko, Arûn) 347, 367, 383, 390

Lord of All (X) Eru. 241, 245; *Lord everlasting* 245

Lord of Gloaming (I) The wizard Tû 232

Lord of Gods (III) See *Manwë*.

Lord of Hell (III) Morgoth. 97–8. Also called *Lord of Lies* 348; *Lord of the World* 99; *Lord of Woe* 8, 101, 287; *Prince of the People of Hell* 16

Lord of Night, of the Darkness, of the World (X) See *Night*, etc.

Lord of Ocean (III) See *Ulmo*.

Lord of Sleep (III) See *Lórien*.

Lord of the Ring (VI) 74, 84, 209, 363, 402, 414; *The Lord of the Ring* as title of the book 84, 109, 112

Lord of the Ring(s) (VIII) Applied to Aragorn. 412, 425–6

Lord of the Rings (VI) (not as title of the book) 75, 80–1, 84, 262, 414; *the Ring-lord* 75, 87, 228, 225

Lord of the Rings, The (I) 41–4, 200

Lord of the Rings, The (II) 211, 247, 266, 328; *The Fellowship of the Ring* 333; *The Two Towers* (II) 140; *The Return of the King* 67, 216

Lord of the Rings, The (V) 21, 30, 34, 98, 100, 107, 109, 119–20, 124, 145, 149, 153–4, 164, 185, 199–200, 211, 216–17, 219, 245, 267, 271–2, 278, 292, 294–5, 298–9, 301–2, 306, 323–4, 338, 345, 412

Lord of the Rings, The (IXb) 145, 147, 152, 280, 309, 331, 339–40, 378, 405–6, 439

Lord of the Rings, The (X) (title) 3–4, 6, 8, 26, 39, 44, 47, 49, 59–60, 63, 65, 75–6, 79, 88–91, 103–4, 126, 141–2, 152, 158, 174,

181, 193, 203, 266, 271, 282, 290, 298, 303, 306, 341, 350, 356, 365, 369, 387, 406, 409–14, 424, 431

Lord of the Rings, The (XI) (title) 3, 107, 110–11, 129–30, 142, 144, 173–5, 177, 201, 207–8, 242, 245, 247, 254, 297, 314, 337, 342, 344–5, 352, 354, 419–20; The Fellowship of the Ring 417, 419; The Return of the King 420

Lord of the Rings, The (XII) (References specifically to the First and Second Editions) 11–12, 17, 24–6, 66, 98, 112, 117, 190, 210, 215, 247, 249, 255–6, 258–9, 261, 274, 317–18, 323, 420

Lords of the West (XI) 287, 402

Lord of Waters (IV) Ulmo. 3, 13, 78, 147, 208, 217, 229, 299; O.E. Ágendfréa ealra watera 207–8, Ealwæter-fréa 208

Lord of Wolves (II) Thû (the Necromancer). 54

Lord of Wolves (III) Thû (Sauron). 199, 210, 220, 233, 240, 256; Master of Wolves 228; Werewolf Lord 358

Lord of Wolves (IV) See Thû.

Lord, The (VI) Sauron. 75, 78, 81, 226, 270–1, 303, 374, 379, 381, 396, 399, 402, 404; the evil Lord 208; the Lord of the Dark Tower 209. See Dark Lord.

Lord, The (VII) Sauron. 112, 134, 151, 155, 262, 271, 338, 341, 347; Lord of the Ring(s) 136; Lord of Mordor 117, 351, 434; Great One 332, 334, Mighty One 332. See Dark Lord.

Lords of the Sea (X) Ulmo and Ossë. 116

Lords of the West (II) The Valar. 205

Lords of the West (V) The Valar; also the Lords. 14, 16, 20, 24, 26, 60–1, 63–6, 68–9, 72–4, 79; Lords of the World 64. Lord of the West 38, 47 (herunūmen), 56, 60, 62, 64–5, 75, 77–8; see especially 75–6, and see Nuaran Númen(ór)en. Eagles of the Lord of the West 38, 47, 62, 75–8, and cf. 87.

Lords of the West (VII) 422

Lords of the West (IXb) 231, 238, 246–7, 251–2, 258, 277, 281, 290, 331–2, 334, 350, 371, 400, 410; the Lords 251, 290, 332; O.E. Westfrégan 'West-lords' 258 (Westfréa 'West-lord' 317). See Bârim an-adûn, Herunúmen; Eagles.

Lords of the West (X) 81, 407; the Lords 285

Lords of the West (XII) 144, 152, 175–6, 181, 244, 396

Lórellin (X) Lake in Lórien in Valinor. 148

Loremaster(s) (X) 17, 31, 38, 50–1, 59, 62, 106, 184, 191, 251, 256, 258, 271, 290, 350, 363, 370–1, 380, 417; masters of lore 57, 72–3, 124, ~ of the lore of speech 92, 103

Loremaster(s) (XI) 10, 25, 343, 346–7, 359, 365, 374, 378, 380, 383–6, 391, 393–6, 405, 408–10, 416–17; with reference to Dairon 13, 20, 110

Loremasters (VII) 26

Loremasters (XII) 55, 158, 203, 297, 305, 308, 314, 321, 332–3, 335, 337–40, 342, 349, 356, 358, 363, 365, 367, 397

Lorgan (XI) Chief of the Easterlings of Hithlum. 82, 91, 137, 146, 253(-4), 256, 260–1, 299

Lórien (I) 27, 66, 71–4, 79–80, 88–9, 99–101, 105–6, 111, 113–15, 117, 132, 147, 177–9, 183, 189–91, 193–5, 199, 201–2, 209–11, 213, 221, 224. See *Fantur, Olofantur*.

Lórien (II) 8–9, 33, 42–3, 240, 324

Lórien (III) 137, 346–7; *God of Sleep* 180, *Lord of Sleep* 172

Lórien (IV) 13, 49, 78, 85, 95, 170–1, 207–8, 263, 275, 285–6, 289, 291–2; O.E. *Swefnfréa* 208, but *Lórien* (gen. *Lóriendes*) in the texts; *God of Dreams* 85. See *Olofantur*.

Lórien (V) 110–11, 120, 165, 205, 220, 240–1, 370 (also Noldorin *Lhuien*); *God of Dreams* 220. See *Olofantur*.

Lórien (VII) See *Lothlórien*. Nelen-Lórien 234, 236, 244; (?) Naith-Lórien 267, 287; (the ancient) *Forest of Lórien* 281–2, 292

Lórien (VIII) 89, 98, 148–9, 160–1, 163, 169, 214, 256, 260, 267, 274, 325, 345, 361, 372, 398, 425, 430. Time in Lórien 325; relation of Elves of Lórien to Galadriel 157, 168. See *Lothlórien*.

Lórien (IXa) 9, 14, 58, 64, 73, 115–16, 124, 129, 132. *Lórien-cloak, cloak of Lórien* (IXa) 9, 14; other references to the cloaks 25, 29, 39, 48, 50

Lórien (XI) (also *Lorien*) The abode of the Vala Irmo, but used also as his name. 11, 108, 403–4. See *Irmo*.

Lórien (XII) 36, 65–6, 70, 73–4, 79, 82, 174, 206, 221–3, 226, 234–5, 239–40, 264–6, 273, 283, 320, 323, 329. See *Lothlórien*.

Lórien, Lorien (X) The abode of the Vala Irmo, but used also as his name. 48–9, 56, 65–6, 84, 131–2, 136, 144–5, 148, 150–1, 172–3, 198, 201, 206, 236–8, 248–9, 252, 257–8, 261, 263–4, 407. Variant forms *Lorion* 65, 141–5, 148, 150, *Lorinen* 148; on *Lórien, Lorien* see 56, 148, 263. See *Irmo, Lís, Olofantur*.

Lórinand (VII) Lórien. 292

Lorindol (X) See *Hador*.

Lorindol (XI) Name of Hador, 'Goldenhead'. 228, 230, 233–5. See *Glorindol*.

Loruin (III) Alternative name to *Nargil*. 49

Lôs (II) Earlier form of the name *Loth* of Gondolin. 202

Los'lóriol (II) Name in Noldorissa of the Golden Flower (kindred of the Gondothlim); earlier *Los Glóriol*. 216

Losengriol (I) Earlier form for Lothengriol. 172

Lósengriol (II) Earlier form of the name *Lothengriol* of Gondolin. 202

Losgar (I) (1) Earlier name for Gar Lossion. 21. (2) The place of the burning of the ships of the Teleri. 198

Losgar (V) (1) Gnomish name of Alalminórë in Tol-eressëa. 148. (2) The place of the burning of the Telerian ships by Fëanor. 125, 148

Losgar (X) The place where Fëanor burned the ships of the Teleri. 120, 127, 196

Losgar (XI) The place of the burning of the ships of the Teleri. 16, 31, 38, 43, 115, 117, 119, 176, 329

Losgar (XII) Place of the burning of the ships by Fëanor. 355

Lossarnach (VIII) Region of Gondor south-west of Minas Tirith (see 436). 153, 278, 283, 287, 289, 294, 419, 436; *Arnach* 371; *Glossarnach* 289, 294

Lossarnach (XII) 238

Lossoth (XII) 210, 258. See *Forochel*.

Lost Elves (I) 68, 119, 138, 237, 244; *lost bands* 48–50; *lost fairies* 231, 235; *lost kindreds* 237; *lost families of the kindred* 17, 26

Lost Elves (II) Elves of the Great Lands. 9 (of Artanor), 40, 42, 283, 285, 293, 302; tongue of 22, 47. *Lost Elves of Hisilómë* 63–4, 249

Lost Folk (X) A name of the Nandor of Ossiriand. 164. *Lost Elves of the people of Dân* 93

Lost Land (VII) Númenor. 400

Lost Road, The (VI) 175

Lost Road, The (IXb) 145, 153, 280, 282, 284, 286–90, 292–5, 304, 308–10, 315, 317, 331, 340, 356

Lost Road, The (X) 44, 136

Lost Road, The (XII) 140, 156

Lost Tales (IV) 9, 42–6, 50–2, 60, 63, 68, 71, 73, 76, 166–8, 170–1, 179, 187, 197–8, 220, 223–4, 233, 235, 241, 252–7, 259, 274–5, 277–8, 293. See *Book of Lost Tales*.

Lost Tales (IV) *The Cottage of Lost Play* 167; *Music of the Ainur* 51, 253, 292; *Coming of the Valar* 42, 51, 256, 293; *Chaining of Melko* 43, 215, 283; *Coming of the Elves* 44–5, 220; *Theft of Melko* 44, 47, 52, 66; *Flight of the Noldoli* 9, 48, 283; *Tale of the Sun and Moon* 49, 170, 279; *Hiding of Valinor* 5, 50, 73, 205,

252; *Gilfanon's Tale* 5–6, 8, 44, 52–3, 56–8, 65, 171, 175, 233

Lost Tales (IV) *Tale of Tinúviel* 44, 51, 55, 57, 190, 224, 276, 289; *Tale of Turambar* 57–9, 61, 73, 180, 183–8, 205, 220–3, 225–6, 316, 322–3, 325; *The Fall of Gondolin* 3, 5, 43, 65–7, 167, 191–4, 209, 215, 225–6, 229, 283 (referred to in the *Quenta* 141, 144); *The Nauglafring* 61–4, 68, 175, 188–90, 223, 225–6, 327; *Epilogue* 259

Lost Tales (V) 20, 78, 104, 121, 123, 155, 164–5, 182–3, 185–6, 190, 201, 207, 216–17, 226, 232, 243–4, 268, 277, 342; see especially 78. *The Cottage of Lost Play* 148; *The Music of the Ainur* 107, 155–6, 164–6; *The Chaining of Melko* 121; *The Coming of the Elves* 225; *Tale of the Sun and Moon* 187, 189; *Gilfanon's Tale* 148, 180, 182; *Tale of Tinúviel* 187, 292, 304; *Tale of Turambar* 315, 323; *The Fall of Gondolin* 211; *The Nauglafring* 306

Lost Tales (VI) See *Book of Lost Tales*.

Lost Tales (IXb) See *(The) Book of Lost Tales*.

Lost Tales (X) See *Book of Lost Tales*.

Lost Tales (XI) See *(The) Book of Lost Tales*.

Lostladen, Desert of (VIII) South of Mordor. 426, 439. See *Lothland*.

Loth (II) 'The Flower', one of the Seven Names of Gondolin. 158, 202. (Replaced *Lôs*.)

Loth (III) 'The Flower', one of the Seven Names of Gondolin. 149

Loth Barodrin (III) Rejected name for *Loth-a-ladwen*. 149

Loth-a-ladwen (III) 'Lily of the Plain', one of the Seven Names of Gondolin. 149 (cf. 309–10). (Replaced *Lothengriol*.)

Lothengriol (I) 'Lily of the Valley', one of the Seven Names of Gondolin. 172. (Replaced *Losengriol*.)

Lothengriol (II) 'Flower of the Plain', one of the Seven Names of Gondolin. 158, 202. See I.172 and *Flower of the Plain*.

Lothengriol (III) Name of Gondolin as 'Lily of the Valley', replaced by *Loth-a-ladwen*. 149

Lothíriel (XII) Daughter of Imrahil; wedded King Éomer. 221, 244, 271

Lothland (V) The great plain north of the Marches of Maidros. 264, 269, 283, 367 (*Lhothland, -lann*), 370 (*Lothlann*).

Lothland desert (VIII) South of Mordor. 426; *Lothlann* 426. See *Lostladen*.

Lothlann (VII) (1) Great plain north of the Marches of Maidros in the Elder Days. 313. (2) Region south of Mordor. 313

Lothlann (XI) Great plain east of Dorthonion. 60, 128; *Lhothlann* 128; *Lothland* 128, *183, 187

Lothlim (II) 'People of the Flower', name taken by the survivors of Gondolin at the mouth of Sirion. 196, 201, 252, 259–60

Lothlórien (V) 345

Lothlórien (VI) 189, 411, 461

Lothlórien (VII) (including references to *Lórien*) 67, 167, 186, 207, 211–12, 214–15, 218, 220–5, 229, 233–7, 239–43, 246–53, 256, 259, 261, 263, 270–1, 273, 281–92 *passim*, 313, 315, 333, 343, 351, 353–5, 358, 363–9, 372, 379, 382, 385–6, 393, 397–8, 401, 405, 415–17, 424, 427, 430, 433, 443, 448, 451. References to Time in Lothlórien 249, 284–6, 354–5, 358, 363, 366–9, 431. Cloaks of Lothlórien 269, 271–2, 278–9, 285, 343, 348, 386, 391, 393–4, 397–8, (401), 408; leaf-brooches 272, 279, 283, 285, 397–8, 401, 408; making of rope 249, 251, 280

Lothlórien (VIII) 98, 159, 166, 168

Lothlórien (IXa) 32, 57, 106. See *Mirror of Lothlórien*.

Lothlórien (XI) 110

Lothlórien (XII) 82, 244, 266. See *Lórien*.

Loudwater, River (VI) 192, 199, 201-5. See *Bruinen, River of Rivendell*.

Loudwater, River (VII) 57, 59, 65, 296. See *Bruinen*.

Loudwater, River (XII) 38, 56, 67, 250. See *Bruinen*.

Lough Derg (IXb) In the Shannon. 261, 292, 296

Loughrea (IXb) In Galway. 267, 293

Lovers of jewels (V) A name of the Noldor. 215

Lovers of Lúthien (VI) The Danas, Green-elves. 412

Low Worlds (IXb) [Lewis] Planets of the Solar System. 213

Lowdham, Alwin Arundel (IXb) Member of the Notion Club. References include his earlier name *Harry Loudham*, and the later *Arry* for *Arundel* (on the changes of his name see 153, 213, 233–4, 282–3). 146, 148, 150–3, 159, 162–3, 165–8, 171–4, 179–80, 182, 184–8, 190–2, 194, 196, 199–202, 206, 211, 213–17, 219, 221–7, 230–56, 259–61, 264–6, 268–77, 279–90, 292–4, 299–312; 317, 375, 378–9, 388–9, 396, 412–13, 440; his *Report on Adunaic* 413 ff. *Alboin* preceding *Alwin* 284. See *Ælfwine, Éarendel, Elendil, Nimruzîr*.

Lowdham, Arundel (XII) Member of the Notion Club. 158

Lowdham, Edwin (IXb) Father of A. A. Lowdham. 233–6, 245, 260, 280, 284, 287, 293, 301 (all other references are to his manuscript). Called *Éadwine* 244; original name *Oswin Ellendel* 284

Lowdham, Edwin (IXb) His manuscript and the single preserved page 148, 235, 248, 253, 255–9, 279–81, 291–2, 301, 306–7, 311, 313–27, 355–6, 381, 384, 411–13

Lowdham's invented languages 235, 238–40, 256, 302, 304–5

Lowdham, Oswin (IXb) Father of Edwin Lowdham. 293

Lug (II) Orc slain by Tuor in Gondolin. 181

Lugbûrz (VII) The Dark Tower. 409

Lugburz (VIII) The Dark Tower. 49, 213–14, 216–18.

Lugburz (IXa) The Dark Tower. 8, 13, 24–5

Lugdush (VII) Orc of Isengard. 409

Lughorn (IXa) See *Lagduf*.

Luindirien (V) 'Blue Towers', the Blue Mountains. 257, 370 (*Lhúndirien*, also *Lhúnorodrim*).

Luindirien (XI) 'The Blue Towers'. 193. See *Blue Mountains*.

Luinil (X) Name of a bright star. 160. See pp. 431–5.

Lumbar (X) Name of a bright star (the planet Saturn?). 160. See pp. 434–5.

Lumbi (II) A place where Melko dwelt after his defeat. 278–9

Lúmin (I) Earlier name of Aluin. 222

Lumpkin (VI) Tom Bombadil's pony. (128), 130, 164

Lundy (V) Island off the coast of Devon. 80, 82

Lune (VII) See *Lhûn*.

Lune (XII) (River and Gulf) 312–15, 328; see *Little Lune. Círdan of Lune* 195, 232. *Mountains of Lune* 78; see *Ered Lindon*.

Lune, Firth of (IXa) 109; *Gulf of Lune* 110

Lune, Gulf of (VIII) 76–7, 213

Lungorthin (III) 'Lord of Balrogs'. 98, 102

Lunoronti (V) The Blue Mountains. 32, 370

Lúsion (II) =*Lúthien* (2). 302

Luthany (II) England. 301–10, 323, 326–30, 334. See *Lúthien* (1) and (3), *Leithian*.

Luthany (III) England. 154

Luthany (IV) 72, 75, 172

Lúthien (II) (1) 'Man of Luthany', name given to Ælfwine by the Elves of Tol Eressëa. 301, 304, 309; explained as meaning 'Wanderer', 302. (2) Son of Telumektar 302. (3) =*Luthany* (England). 312–15, 323–4, 326–7, 329–30, 334. (4) Tinúviel. 52–8, 66, 302, 330

Lúthien (III) (1) Ælfwine. 154. (2) England. 154. See *Leithien*.

Lúthien (III) (3) Daughter of Thingol and Melian. 54, 104, 107, 119–

20, 124–5; *passim* in *Lay of Leithian* and commentaries. See *Melilot, Tinúviel*.

Lúthien (IV) (1) Son of Gelmir (replacing *Oleg*). 6–8. (2) Eriol. 7. (3) 'Britain or England' (39). 39, 41, 72, 75, 199–200. See *Leithien*. (4) Daughter of Thingol. 24–6, 28, 33, 55–62-4, 69, 72, 74, 109–16, 120, 133–5, 150, 152, 162, 177–9, 190–1, 221, 225, 230, 233, 300–1, 306–7, 325; *the geste of Beren and Lúthien* 300; the destiny of Lúthien 63–4, 190–1, 325. See *Lay of Leithian, Tinúviel*.

Lúthien (V) Daughter of Thingol. 25, 32–3, 134–5, 141, 154, 176, 268, 292–6, 298–308, 313, 315, 322, 326–7, 332, 370 (also *Lhúthien, Luithien*; another name *Firiel* 382); the Choices of Lúthien 303–5; *Lovers of Lúthien*, a name of the Danas, 215. See *Tinúviel*.

Lúthien (VI) 179, 182–4, 187, 197, 199, 216, 358; *the Choices of Lúthien* 187. See *Children of Lúthien, Lovers of Lúthien*.

Lúthien (VII) 58, 110, 123, 136, 173, 271

Lúthien (IXa) 13, 45; the choice of Lúthien 66, 125

Lúthien (IXb) 333

Lúthien (X) 3, (86), 106, 141, 267, 281, 336, 340, 359, 364, 404, 408; see *Kindred of Lúthien, Tinúviel*.

Lúthien (XI) 9, 14, 61–71, 129–33, *185, 195, 224, 228, 231, 242–3, 346–51, 353. See *Tinúviel*.

Lúthien (XII) Also ~ *Tinúviel*. 211, 226, 234, 243, 265, 318, 348–9, 357, 363–4, 369; *Children of Lúthien* 364

Lúthien, Lúthien Tinúviel (I) 82, 90, 107, 132, 203. See *Tinúviel*.

Lydbrook (III) Stream-name in England. 88

Lyme Regis, Dorset (III) 223, 234

Mablon the Ilkorin (I) 239, 241

Mablon the Ilkorin (IV) 58

Mablosgen (IV) 'Empty-handed', name of Beren. 311, 317. (Replaced by *Camlost*.)

Mablosgen (V) 'Empty-handed', name of Beren. 131, 146, 371, 405. See *Camlost*.

Mablost (V) =*Mablosgen*. 361, 405. *Mablothren* =*Mablosgen*. 370, 405

Mablui (III) Name of Melian. 34, 55–6, 108

Mablung (II) 'The Heavy-hand(ed)', chief of the thanes of Tinwelint. 38–41, 49–50, 56, 59, 121, 128–30, 134, 231, 233, 243

Mablung (III) 'Heavyhand', Thingol's chief warrior (311). 25–6, 56, 310–14

Mablung (IV) Called 'Heavyhand' (113). 113–14, 117, 179, 185, 187 ('with weighted hand').

Mablung (V) 308, *370–1*

Mablung (VI) Elf of Doriath; called 'the heavy-handed'. 183

Mablung (VIII) Ranger of Ithilien. 136, 139, 145–6, 148, 151, 431; the name 159–60

Mablung (XI) Elf of Doriath, chief captain of Thingol. 34, 63, 72, 93–5, 101–2, 116, 133, 148, 150, 161–2, 164, 257, 281, 303, 311

Macedon (IXb) See *Frankley.*

Maedhros (I) Eldest son of Fëanor. 243; *Union of Maedhros* 243. See *Maidros.*

Maedhros (IV) See *Maidros.*

Maedhros (XII) 357; *Maidros* 224, 373; *Maedron* 372. Other names *Nelyafinwë* 352, (365)-6, *Nelyo* 352; *Maitimo* 353, 366; *Russandol* 353, 355, 366

Maedros (XII) Son of Fëanor. 318, 344, 352, 355, 357, 366–7, 372;

Maedros, Maedhros (V) See *Maidros.*

Maedros, Maedhros (X) See *Maidros.*

Maedros, Maedhros (XI) See *Maidros.*

Maeglin (II) Later form for Meglin. 210–12, 248

Maeglin (III) See *Meglin.*

Maeglin (IV) See *Meglin.*

Maeglin (XI) 48, 58, 76, 122–3, 127, 139, 146, 169, 302, 317, 321–7, 330, 332–3, 336–7, 344, 348, 351, 353, 409; as name also of the metal of Eöl 48, 122, 322–3; later translated 'Sharp-glance' 323 (etymology 337). See *Iôn, Lómion.* For names of the metal of Eöl see *Galvorn;* for rejected names of Maeglin see *Meglin, Morleg, Morlîn, Targlin, Glindûr.*

Maeglin (XII) 377, 389

Maelduin (V) Irish voyager. 80–1

Maelduin (IXb) Irish voyager. 270, 294

Maelor (III) Variant of *Maglor.* 353

Magbar (II) Elvish name of Rome. 315, 330. See *Rûm.*

Maggot, Farmer (VI) 92, 94–7, 103, 105, 109, 116–17, 122, 124, 223, 268–9, 286–97, 300, 303, 305, 330; see especially 117, 122. Mrs. Maggot 95–7, 291–3

Maggot, Farmer (VII) 10

Maggot, Farmer (IXa) 107 (see *Bamfurlong*).

Maggot, Farmer (XII) 326

Maggots (VI) Hobbit family of the Marish. 289

Magic Isles (I) 36, 39, 64, 68, 83, 85 (*I Tolli Kuruvar*), 121, 125, 134, 211, 220, 224 (see especially 211); *Magic Archipelago* 134

Magic Isles (II) 5, 7, 254, 260, 311, 316, 320, 324–5, 332, 334; *Magic Archipelago* 316

Magic Isles (IV) 20, 38, 69, 98, 150, 153, 155, 198, *249, 257. See *Enchanted Isles.*

Magic Sun (I) 17, 25, 35, 65, 179, 199

Magic Sun (II) 264, 281–2, 285–6, 289, 303; see especially 285–6

Maglor (II) Son of Fëanor. 241, 250

Maglor (III) (1) Transiently used =Beren. 159, 168–71, 182. (2) Son of Fëanor. 65, 84, 86, 135–6, 159, 174, 181–2, 211, 353; called 'the swift' 65, 'the mighty' 135, 211.

Maglor (IV) (1) =Beren. 5. (2) Son of Fëanor. 15, 22, 26–7, 33, 35, 38–40, 64, 69–71, 74, 88, 113, 115, 150, 152, 154–6, 158–9, 161–2, 170, 196, 201–2, 212, 308–10, 313, 321, 326, 331, 335; O.E. *Dægmund Swinsere* 212; *Maglor's Gap* 259, 335

Maglor (V) Son of Fëanor. 125, 127, 132, 134, 143–4, 147, 151, 153, 223, 250, 254, 263, 265, 283, 287, 314, 328, 330–2, 336, *371* (also Quenya *Makalaurë*). *Maglor's Gap* (128, 132), 148, (254), 257, 265, 283; *passes of Maglor* 147

Maglor (X) Son of Fëanor. 112, 117, 125, 177, 182; *Maelor* 182

Maglor (XI) Son of Fëanor. 34, 47, 49, 53, 64, 74, 116, 131, 134, *183, 215, 247, 345, 352

Maglor (XII) Son of Fëanor. 318, 352, 358; *Maelor* 318. Other names *Kanafinwë*, *Káno*, 352; *Makalaurë* 353

Magor (XI) Son of Malach Aradan, son of Marach; 'the Sword' (234–5). 219, 223, 225–6, 232–5; called *Dagorlind* 'Singer in battle' 226, 235. For the changed place of Magor in the genealogy see 225–6, 235.

Magyar (IXb) See *Hungary.*

Mahal (XI) Dwarvish name of Aulë. 10, 108

Máhanaxar (XI) The Doom-ring of the Valar. 399, 401. See *Rithil-Anamo.*

Máhani (XI) The chiefs of the Valar, the Aratar; singular *Máhan*. 399, 402

Mahtan (X) Father of Fëanor's wife Nerdanel. 272, 277

Mahtan (XII) Father of Nerdanel, Fëanor's wife. 366. See *Urundil.*

Maia (II) 246

Maiar (I) 63, 80, 88

Maiar (V) 120

Maiar (X) (and singular *Maia*) 'The Beautiful' (49). 49, 52, 55–6, 59, 61, 65–6, 69, 72, 76, 79, 84, 86, 91, 99, 110, 112, 130, 133, 137–8, 147–50, 152, 165, 172, 198, 200, 203–4, 286–7, 340, 410–12, 416, 418, 424–6; original form *Mairi* 56, 150. See *Vanimor*.

Maiar (XI) (and singular *Maia*) 5–7, 9–10, 16, 71, 113, 341, 372–3, 399, 401, 405–6; *Maia* as adjective 415; *language of the Valar and Maiar* 397, 416

Maiar (XII) 378, 381, 384, (388); *Máyar* 363–4

Maid of Tears (III) See *Nienor*.

Maidros (I) (1) Father of Fëanor's father Bruithwir. 146, 155, 158, 238. (2) Eldest son of Fëanor (later Maedhros). 158, 238–40, 242–3

Maidros (II) Son of Fëanor. 241–2, 250

Maidros (III) Eldest son of Fëanor. 65, 84, 86, 135–7, 211–12, 222; *Union of Maidros* 274 (see *Marching Forth*).

Maidros (IV) Eldest son of Fëanor; called 'the Tall' and 'the Left-handed' (298). 15, 22–3, 26–7, 38–41, 52–3, 57, 69–71, 88, 101–2, 116–18, 120–1, 135, 150, 152–4, 156, 158, 161–2, 172–3, 179, 181–2, 195–6, 201–2, 204–5, 212, 268–9, 274, 280, 282–3, 295, 298, 300–2, 307–10, 313, 318, 320–1, 325–31, 333, 335, 338–9; O.E. *Dægred Winsterhand* 212, in the texts *Maegdros* etc.; *Marches of Maidros* 331, 335. Later *form Maedhros* 180, 182, 212, 280. See *Russandol, Union of Maidros*.

Maidros (V) Eldest son of Fëanor, called 'the Tall'. 117, 125–8, 130, 132, 134–7, 142–4, 151, 153, 177 (speech of his people), 189, 223, 249–52, 254, 256–7, 260, 263, 265–6, 283, 287, 289, 293, 300, 307–1l, 314, 328, 330–1, 336, 371, *385*; other spellings *Maedros, Maedhros, Maidhros* 301, 305–6, *371, 385. Marches of Maidros* 127, 264; *hills of Maidros* 254, 260. See *Union of Maidros*.

Maidros (VIII) Son of Feanor. 297

Maidros (X) Eldest son of Fëanor, called 'the Tall'. 112, 119–21, 126, 177; later forms *Maedros* 292–5, 298, *Maedhros* 177, 292

Maidros (XI) Son of Fëanor. 18, 29–30, 32–4, 36, 38, 46, 49, 53, 59–61, 64, 69–72, 74, 114–17, 121, 128, 131–2, 134, 167–8, 176–7, 247, 345, 348–9, 351–4; later forms *Maiðros* 32, 115, 188, *Maedhros, Maeðros* 115, *183, 188, 255, Maedros* 115, 165–8, 177, *183, 188, 215, 219, 221. See *March of Maidros, Union of Maidros*.

Mailcoat (Bilbo's) (VI) Referred to also as his *ring-mail, elf-armour*,

elf-mail, etc. 18, 126, 223, (315), 371–2, 378, 386, 397–8, 443–4, 466

Mailgond (IV) The elder of Túrin's guardians on the journey to Doriath. 28, 58, 183; later form *Mailrond* 58. (Replaced *Gumlin* (1).)

Mailgond (V) Earlier name for the elder of Túrin's guardians on the journey to Doriath. 151

Mailrond (III) The elder of Túrin's guardians on the journey to Doriath. 105–6, 113, 119, 123, 126; earlier form *Mailgond* 119, 126. (Replaced *Gumlin* (1)).

Mailwin (III) See *Morwen*.

Mainlos (I) Earlier form for Minethlos. 198

Makar (I) Warrior Vala. 67, 75, 77–8, 80, 82, 89, 98, 101, 103, 105, 117, 144, 154–5, 177

Makar (IV) Warrior Vala. 7–8

Malacandra (VII) In C. S. Lewis, *Out of the Silent Planet*. 419

Malacandra (IXb) [Lewis] The planet Mars. 181, 212–13, 220; *Malacandrian* 220. See *Mars*.

Malach (XI) (also with Elvish name *Aradan* conjoined, or *Aradan* alone, see 219, 234) Son of Marach. 219, 223, 225–6, 230–5; *the people of Aradan* 233

Malaroko (V) Balrog. *384* (*Malarauko*), 404

Malbeth the Seer (VIII) 306–7, 311. Forms of the verse of Malbeth 300, 302, 305–7, 311

Malbeth the Seer (XII) Foreteller of the fate of Arvedui. 256

Maldon, Battle of (V) 38, 55

Maldon, Battle of (VII) 106

Maldon, Battle of (IXb) 236

Malduin, River (XI) *182, 186

Malevarn (VII) See *Baranduin*.

Malevarn (XII) Rejected Elvish name of the Brandywine, changed by Hobbits to *Malvern*. 39, 67

Malinalda (V) Name of Laurelin. 210–1l, (386)

Malinalda (X) Name of Laurelin. 155

Malkarauki (II) Name of the Balrogs in Eldarissa. 169

Mallor (XII) Third King of Arthedain. 193, 208

mallorn (IXa) 116; the *mallorn-seed*, gift of Galadriel, 108

mallorn, mallorn-trees (VII) 217, (218), 226–7, 230, 233–4, 239, 245, 249, 251, 280, 291; plural *mellyrn* 233; *mallorn bark* 249, 251

Malory, Sir Thomas (III) 143

Malvegil (XII) Sixth King of Arthedain. 193, 208–9

Man in the Moon (I) See *Moon, Uolë Kúvion*; poem 202, 204–6

Man of the Sea (II) The 'ancient mariner' (Ulmo) dwelling in the Harbourless Isles. 316–20, 322, 325, 331–4; other references to him 5, 7, 301, 311–12, 332

Manawe (IXb) See *Manwë*.

Mandar (X) See *Mandos*.

Mandos (I) (Vala) 66–7, 72, 76, 79–80, 82, 89–90, 101, 105, 111, 113, 117, 145, 147–8, 154, 158, 167–8, 171–2, 189, 213, 224, 234; *children of Mandos* 116, 154, 173. See *Vefántur*.

  Mandos (I) (Region of his abode) 47, 76–8, 82, 90, 99–100, 105–6, 111, 131, 142–3, 145, 156–7, 167, 170, 172, 176. See *Vê*.

Mandos (II) (both the Vala and his abode) 39–40, 53, 56, 60, 87, 92, 111, 113, 115, 125, 240, 250, 253–6, 260, 263–4, 278, 286. See *Vefántur*.

Mandos (III) 28, 103, 125, 137–8, 196, 274, 309, 312, 314

Mandos (IV) (both the Vala and his abode) 13–16, 18, 21–2, 25–6, 33, 43, 45, 48, 51–2, 54–5, 63–4, 70, 78–9, 84, 87, 89, 91, 96, 100, 115, 134, 166, 170, 172, 179, 190, 205, 207–8, 263–4, 267, 273, 275–6, 279, 285–6, 289, 291–2, 307; O.E. Néfréa 166, 208, but *Mandos* (gen. *Mandosses*) in the texts, also called *neoærna hláford* and *wælcyriga* 207. See *Nefantur, Vefántur; Prophecy, Doom, of Mandos*.

Mandos (V) (both the Vala and his abode) 20, 110, 112, 115, 120, 135, 141, 163, 166, 205–7, 213, 223, 227, 229, 237, 247–9, 255, 302–6, 326, 333, 359, 371–2, 374 (also *Mando, Mandosse; Morimando; Bannos*). See especially 205, 207, and see *Doom of Mandos, Nefantur, Nurufantur*.

Mandos (VI) The abode of the Vala Mandos. 215

Mandos (X) The abode of the Vala Námo, but used also as his name. 21, 37, 48–9, 65, 71, 76, 80, 86, 88, 93, 96–7, 103–4, 107, 117–18, 122, 126–7, 129, 134–5, 144–6, 148, 150–1, 159, 161–2, 166, 168, 176, 180, 185–7, 189–90, 202–8, 216, 219, 222–6, 228, 232–8, 241–3, 246–9, 252–5, 258–61, 263–9, 275, 278–81, 291, 293, 325, 339–41, 350, 359, 363–5, 392–3, 403, 411; *Mandar* 101, 205

  Mandos (X) Called *Námo Mandos* 225, 246, 254, 259, 403; *Doomsman of the Valar* 145, *the Mouth of Manwë* 255, *the Unmoved*, 340, *the Wise* 176, 'the strongest of all in Arda' 242. Prophecies of Mandos 76, 204, 246–7, 359; Doom of Mandos in

Araman, see *Noldor*; etymology of the name 350. See *Námo, Núr, Nurufantur, Vê, Vefántur; Summons of Mandos.*

Mandos (XI) The abode of the Vala Námo, but used also as his name. 18, 33, 43, 67, 69, 119, 130, 177, 204, 207, 247, 283, 295, 387, 402; *the Curse, Doom of Mandos* 19, (31), 37, 43, 45, 343, *the shadow of ~* 43; called *the Just* 295. See *Námo.*

Mandos (XII) 356, 359, 370, 374–5, 378, 380–1; *Doom of Mandos* 338, 389–90

Mandos, Doom of (IXb) 411

Manface, Sir Gerald (IXb) Member of the Notion Club. 160

Mani Aroman (VI) See 434.

Mánir (I) Spirits of the air, attendant on Manwë and Varda. 68, 91, 144, 181, 188, 200

Mánir (III) Spirits of the air, attendant on Manwë and Varda. 137, 306

Mannish (IXb) (tradition) 406–7

Mannish (X) (of the beliefs and traditions of Men) 370, 373, and see 5, 22.

Mannish (XI) 311

Mannish (XII) 29, 32, 34, 37–9, 41–2, 54, 61, 63–5, 67, 71, 73, 75, 141, 296, 300–1, 304, 321, 324, 330, 357, 368, 370, 384, 390

Manorhall (VIII) In the Southfarthing. 36–7

Manthor (XI) A lord of the Haladin, brother of Hunthor; 'Master of the Northmarch' of Brethil (263). 258, 263–5, 267, 269–70, 275–82, 284, 286–97, 302–9

Manwë (I) 26–7, 48, 52, 56, 58–60, 62–3, 65–7, 69–70, 73–4, 79, 88–93, 99–105, 111, 113–17, 122, 124, 126–9, 131–2, 138, 141, 143–51, 153–4, 156–9, 162, 172, 176–84, 186–8, 190, 192, 194–6, 199, 208–9, 211–21, 223, 230, 233, 244; called *Lord of the Air* 176, *of the Heavens* 190, *of Gods and Elves and Men, of the Gods, of Gods and Elves, of Elves and Men* 52, 58–9, 62, 100, 104, 115, 142, 218. See *Súlimo, Valahíru, Valatúru; Valwë.*

Manwë (III) 133, 137, 139, 211, 230, 286, 306; *Lord of Gods* 211

Manwë (IV) 5, 10, 12–14, 17, 19–20, 23, 44, 47, 50, 52, 68, 72–3, 78–81, 85, 87–90, 92, 94, 97–8, 102, 151, 153–4, 159, 162, 166, 173, 196, 198, 202, 206, 208, 236, 263, 265, 270, 275, 278, 285, 287, 289, 291–2, 294, 309; O.E. *Wolcenfréa* 208, but *Manwë* in the texts.

Manwë (V) 12–15, 20, 24, 56, 64–5, 69, 74–5, 110, 112–13, 115, 120, 143, 159–65, 187, 205–9, 213–14, 217, 223, 225, 227–8, 231–2, 234, 240, 242, 245–7, 251–2, 285, 303, 305, 325–6, 330,

332, 334, *371–2*, *398*, (called *Kalamando 362, 372*). *Mountain of Manwë* (Taniquetil) 224, 231; his hall *Taen-Nimdil 389*. See *Súlimo*.

Manwë (VII) 198

Manwë (IXb) 317, 331–2, 336, 376, 381. *Manawë* 341–3, 348–9, 351, 354, 376. See *Amân, Gods, Valar*.

Manwë (X) 7, 13–15, 19–21, 24–6, 28–9, 32, 34, 36, 40–4, 48–9, 51–4, 59–60, 65–9, 71, 74–5, 79–81, 83, 85, 87, 89, 93–4, 97, 99–101, 104–5, 107–8, 112–14, 117, 125, 128–30, 135, 137–8, 144–7, 149–52, 154, 159, 161, 163, 167, 176, 179–80, 185–6, 188, 197, 201–2, 204–6, 211, 219, 223, 225–6, 230, 235–7, 239, 241, 244, 246–7, 249, 253–5, 257–60, 264, 270, 273, 275–90 *passim*, 293–4, 300, 313, 321, 326–7, 337, 339, 349, 357–8, 361–5, 372, 374, 376–82, 390–3, 397, 399–404, 406, 410, 429

Manwë (X) Called *King of the World* 20, *of the Valar* 65, (147); *Lord of the Gods* 144; *(High-) King, Lord, of Arda* 114, 145, 279, 287, 313, *the King* 242, 244, *Lord of Aman* 247. *The Great Wind of Manwë* 377; *the Mouth of Manwë* (Mandos) 255. See *Elder King, Súlimo*.

Manwë (XI) 41, 70, 246, 272, 280, 287, 340–1, 345, 399–400, 403–4, 406, 417; *son of, herald of, Manwë* 246; *Mánwë, Mánwen*, and origin of the name 399. See *Elder King*.

Manwë (XII) 142–4, 152, 157, 334–5, 343, 357–8, 361, 370, 374, 378–81, 390, 396; *Aran Einior, the Elder King* 357–8

Manwë, Manwë Súlimo (II) 77, 115, 141, 163, 165, 193, 199, 223, 257–8, 265, 280, 282, 287; *Súlimo* 200; *Lord of Gods and Elves* 163; *Manweg* =*Wóden, Óðinn* 290

Map, Walter (III) 144

Maps (VI) See *Shire, Wilderland*. Maps of *The Lord of the Rings* 163, 200–2, 205, 438–41

Maps (VII) In *The Hobbit*: Thrór's Map 159–60, 452; Wilderland 172, 298. Maps of LR: Shire maps 39, 299, 424; the First Map 65–6, 137, 145, 157, 172, 187, 213, 238, 287, 295–323, 348–9, 364, 389, 404, 423, 440, 450, described 295–6, 299–300; 1943 map 299–301, 304, 306–7, 310, 313, 318, 320–2, 348–9; later maps 301, 307, 312, 321–2; published maps 213, 301, 307, 321–2, 424. First *Silmarillion* map 287, second 301

Maps (VIII) First Map 12, 22, 41–2, 76, 78–80, 111–12, 115, 122–3, 127–8, 136, 240, 244, 257, 265–6, 268, 270, 287, 289, 291, 293, 308, 339, 426, 433; 1943 map 12, 42, 76, 78, 80, 111, 244,

265–6, 291, 293; Second Map 268, 270, 293, 308, 354, 363, 372, 422, 424, 426–7, 433–9; map of Rohan, Gondor and Mordor in RK (and its original) 112, 118, 267, 270, 289, 291, 308, 339, 353–4, 356, 433, 436, 438 (portion redrawn, Frodo's journey to the Morannon, 117–18).

Maps (VIII) Minor maps: Minas Morghul and the Cross-roads 180–1, 438; Harrowdale 257–9, 268; White Mountains and South Gondor 264, 268–70, 291, 308, 439; mountains between Edoras and Erech 296; map accompanying 'The Ride of the Rohirrim' 353, 438

Maps (IXa) First Map 72; Second Map 14, 16–17, 34–5; Third Map 34–5; map of Rohan, Gondor and Mordor 35; general map published in LR 72; maps of the Shire 105–7; sketch-map of N.W. Mordor 34; map accompanying 'The Ride of the Rohirrim' 70; plan of the Citadel of Minas Tirith 67

Maps (XI) (1) The first *Silmarillion* map. 149, 190, 202, 334. (2) The second map. 111–13, 117, 139–40, 145, 149, 157, 159, 180–94, 198, 201, 227–9, 238, 299, 301, 330–8, 344, 353, 418; scale of this map 111, 332; photocopy used in connection with *Maeglin* 330–8. (3) Map accompanying the published *Silmarillion*. 112, 159, 187–8, 191, 333, 336, 338

Mar Vanwa Tyaliéva (I) The Cottage of Lost Play in Kortirion. 14, 21 (also *Taliéva*), 27–8, 30, 48, 97, 129, 174, 202, 229; in title of poem 28, 30

Mar Vanwa Tyaliéva (II) The Cottage of Lost Play. 4, 41, 144–5, 149, 201, 209, 279, 286; *Vanwa Tyaliéva* 145

Mar Vanwa Tyaliéva (V) The Cottage of Lost Play. 55

Mar Vanwa Tyaliéva (VI) The Cottage of Lost Play. 187

Marach (IV) Leader of the third host of Men to enter Beleriand. 175

Marach (X) Leader of the third host of Men to enter Beleriand. *The people of Marach* 305–6, 309, 344, 353, 359–60

Marach (XI) 218–20, 226–8, 230, 232–4, 241, 334. *The People, Folk, of Marach* 218, 226–7, 234; *the Children of Marach* 402; *Nothlir Maracha* 234; ancient tongue of 49, 123, 218–19, 224, 226–7, 234, 402; genealogical table 234

Marach (XII) Leader of the third host of the Edain. 325; *People of Marach* 372–4

Máraher (VIII) See *Mardil*.

March of Liberation (I) The great expedition from Kôr. 166; *march into the world* 26, 129, 196

March of Maidros (XI) 34, 38–9, 53, 77, 128; *Marches* ~ *183, 188; the March 34, 61

March of the Elves (II), *March of Liberation* See *Elf-march, Faring Forth*.

March of the Elves (IV) (1) The Great Journey from Kuiviénen. *249, 256, 264, 271–2; see *Great March*. (2) The expedition from Valinor. 68, 70, 72, 74, 168

March, The (XI) (1) Of the Eldar. See *Great March*. (2) Of the Edain. 218, 296

Marchers (IXb) 269, 272–3, 294; *Men of the Marches* 273; *West Marches* 269

Marches of Maidros (IV) See *Maidros*.

Marches of Maidros (V) See *Maidros*.

Marching Forth (III) The Union of Maidros. 265, 274

Marching Forth (IV) See *Union of Maidros*.

Marcho (XII) Hobbit, brother of Blanco. 6, 17, 87; earlier *Marco* (brother of Cavallo) 6, 9–10, 17, 86–7, 209, 225

Marculf (VIII) Rider of Rohan. 371

Mardil (VIII) The Good Steward. 153, 281, 288, 292; *Mardil's son* 156. Earlier name *Máraher* 153

Mardil (XII) 'The Good Steward', first Ruling Steward of Gondor. 132, 201–4, 217–19, 225, 233; ~ *Voronwë* 204, 219

Margoliantë, Queen (VI) See 464.

Marhath (Marhad) (VII) Second Master of the Mark. 390, 440; Fourth Master 400, 440. Other unused names in *Mar-* 390

Mârim (IXb) [Ramer] 221. (Replaced by *Albarim*.)

Marish, The (VI) 107, 116, 286–7, 289, 294, 296–7, 312, 387

Marish, The (VII) 249

Marish, The (IXa) 106

Marish, The (XII) 10, 15, 56, 103, 232, 248

Mark (of Rohan), The (XII) See *Rohan*.

Mark, The (VII) Rohan. 399–400, 402, 419, 433, 441; *Lord of the Mark* 433, 441; *King of the Mark* 440. See *Riddermark*.

Mark, The (VIII) Rohan. 21, 24, 27–8, 49, 246, 322, 350, 366, 389, 401, 407, 418; tongue of the Mark 35, 44, 389; *King, Lord, of the Mark* 41, 245, 247, 317 (Théoden), 368 (Éomer); *Kings of the Mark* 243–4, 407–8 (enumerated, 408). *Éomearc, Éomeark* 22; *Riddermark* 52

Mark, The (IXa) Rohan. 61–2, 67–8, 71, 73, 86, 98; *King(s) of the Mark* 62, 68, 72. See *(The) Riddermark*.

Markison, Dom Jonathan (IXb) Member of the Notion Club. 151, 160, 223, 227, 230, 232–3, 236–7, 241, 245, 253, 265, 277, 300–3, 306

marlas (VIII) See *galenas*.

Mar-nu-Falmar (XII) 'Land under the waves', Númenor. 157

Marquette University (VI) 309, 318

Marquette University (VII) 18, 40, 53, 94, 103, 136, 187, 206

Marquette University (VIII) 44, 235, 252

Marquette University (IXa) 121

Marrer, The (X) Melkor. 240–2, 245, 248–9, 252, 402

Marrer, The (XII) Morgoth. 359

Marring of Arda, The (X) 203–4, 209, 211, 219, 223, 239–41, 244–5, 252, 259–60, 270–1, 293, 304, 318, 321, 331, 351, 428–9

   Marring of Arda, The (X) *Arda Healed* 245, 251, 318, 327, 351, 405; *Arda Vincarna* 408, *Arda Envinyanta* 405, 408; *Arda Remade* 319–20, 333, 351–2; *Arda Complete* 251, (3 18–19), 327; *New Arda* 251–2

   Marring of Arda, The (X) *Arda Marred* 203–4, 219, 225, 239–41, 244–7, 254–5, 258, 269–70, 309, 312, 318, 327, 396, 399, 405, 408, 424, 428; *Arda Hasteina* 254, 408, *Arda Sahta* 405

   Marring of Arda, The (X) *Arda Unmarred* 239–40, 245–6, 251, 258, 260, 287, 318, 327, 351, 366, 405, 424; *Arda Alahasta* 254

   Marring of Arda, The (X) Other references to 'marring': 53, 217–18, 225, 232, 241, 243, 245, 247, 259, 269, 315, 333–4, 342–3, 351, 381, 390, 396; *the Marring of Men* 328 (see *(The) Fall*).

Mars (IXb) (the planet) 163, 167, 169, 204, 212–13, 220; *Martian(s)* 212; (the god) 286. See *Gormok, Malacandra; Tíw*.

Marshal of the Mark, Chief (VIII) Éomund. 266 *Master of the Mark, Second* 22 *Meduseld* (VIII) 316, 319, 321. (Replaced *Wínseld*.)

Marshals of the Mark (VII) 399

Martalmar (IV) The roots of the Earth. 241, *242–5, 255. See *Earth roots, Talmar Ambaren*.

Marthanc (IXa) Aragorn's translation of *Hamfast* (Gamgee). 117, 121. (Replaced by *Baravorn*.)

Master, The (VI) See *Dark Lord*.

Masters of the Mark (VII) 399. *First Master* (Théoden) 400; *Second Master*: Marhath 390, Éowin 393, unnamed 435, 437, 450, Eofored 444, 446, 450; *Third Master* (Éomer) 393, 410; *Fourth Master* (Marhath) 400, 440. *Master of Rohan* (Théoden) 433. See *Mark, Riddenmark*.

Math-Fuin-delos (IV) 'Deadly Nightshade', Taur-na-Fuin. 299, 310. (Replaced by *Gwath-Fuin-daidelos*.)

mathom (XII) 8, 39, 53, 81

Mathusdor (II) Name replacing *Aryador* in manuscript A of *The Fall of Gondolin*. 202

Matterhorn (VII) 175

Mauhur (VII) Orc of Isengard. 410

Mavoinë (II) Name of Mavwin in Eldarissa. 70

Mavwin (II) Wife of Úrin, mother of Túrin and Nienóri; afterwards Morwen. 70–6, 78, 87–9, 91–9, 109, 112–17, 120–1, 126–9, 136–7, 139, 141–2, 144. (Replaced *Tirannë*.)

Mavwin (III) See *Morwen*.

Mavwin (IV) 57, 60–1, 219, 221, 229, 316. (Replaced by *Morwen*.)

Mayor, The (IXa) See *(The) Shire*.

Mazarbul (VII) *Book of Mazarbul* 125, 190–2, 200–1, 205, (247, 257), 457–9. *Chamber of Mazarbul* 67, 188, 190, 192, 195–6, 199–202, 209, 215, 237, 247, 257, 458; *Chamber of Records* 200

Mazarbul Book of (VI) (443–4, 460), 467; *Chamber of* (443–4, 460), 467

Mazarbul, Book of (XII) 22, 26, 293, 295, 298, 320; *Chamber of ~* 299

Mearas (VII) Noblest horses of Rohan. 400–1, 405

Meássë (I) Warrior goddess. 67, 77–8, 80, 82, 89, 98, 105, 117, 154, 177

Meássë (III) Warrior goddess. 127

Mediterranean (II) 261, 294. See *Wendelsæ*.

Mediterranean Sea (IV) 258

Mediterranean Sea (V) 39

Mediterranean, The (IXb) 289

Meduarn, Meodarn (VII) See *Wínseld*.

Meduseld (XII) 236, 271. See *Golden Hall*.

Megalithic (IXb) 221

Meglin (II) Son of Eöl and Isfin, betrayer of Gondolin; afterwards Maeglin. 164–5, 167–73, 175, 177–8, 189–90, 206, 210, 213, 220; *lord of the house of the Mole* 175

Meglin (III) Son of Eöl and Isfin, betrayer of Gondolin. 146–7; later form *Maeglin* 52, 83

Meglin (IV) 34–7, 65–7, 136, 140, 142–4, 147–8, 193–4, 213, 305–7, 327; O.E. *Mánfrið* (IV) 213; later form Maeglin 67, 181, 193, 318

Meglin (V) 139–42, 152, 274, 278

Meglin (XI) Original name of Maeglin. 84, 91, 121–2, 139, 146, 206, 302, 316, 323. See *Maeglin*.

Meldis (XI) Elvish name of Zimrahin wife of Malach Aradan. 234

Melegor (III) Name of Morgoth, replacing *Belegor*, replaced by *Bauglir*. 21–2

Mēlekō (IXb) Melkor-Morgoth. 341–2, 344–5, 347–8, 354, 398–9, 401–5, 407, 411–13; translated *Tyrant* 411. *Offspring of Mēlekō* 344

Mēlekō (X) See *Melko*.

Melemno, Ellu Melemno (I) See *Ellu*.

Meleth (II) Eärendel's nurse. 174

Meleth (XI) Daughter of Hiril (2) and mother of Manthor. 270, (289)

Melian (I) 107, 132–3. See *Tindriel, Wendelin*.

Melian (II) Queen of Doriath. 42–4, 46, 48, 51, 66, 244, 249; the *Girdle of Melian* 63, 249. For earlier names of Melian see 244 and *Gwedheling* and following entries; see also *Artanor*.

Melian (III) Queen of Doriath. 4, 12–13, 16, 22, 28, 33–4, 53, 55, 107, 112–14, 116–17, 125, 127, 148, 172–3, 188–94, 197, 199–200, 203–4, 207, 210, 215, 240, 242, 246, 261, 272, 287, 298, 311–13, 332, 346–7, 350, 360; *the immortal Queen* 352. See *Ar-, Tar-Melian; Gwendeling, Gwenethlin; Mablui*.

Melian (IV) 13, 23, 25–6, 28, 33, 55, 57, 59, 62–3, 85, 100, 109–10, 115–16, 123, 133–4, 162, 182, 189–90, 264, 271, 286, 288–9, 296, 307, 328, 339; her protective power over Doriath 23, 62, 105, 114, 123, 127, 278, 288 (O.E.), 300, 307, 329–30, 334. See *Gwedheling, Gwendelin, Wendelin*.

Melian (V) 111–12, 114, 126, 128, 139, 141, 168, 174–5, 186–7, 220, 246, 253, 261–2, 281, 299, 302–5, 308, 317–19, 322, 326, 332, (another name *Tóril* 389); *fences, girdle, mazes of Melian* 128, (253), 262, 299, 317

Melian (VI) Queen of Doriath. 182, 184

Melian (VII) 265–6

Melian (IXb) 333

Melian (X) 72, 77, 84–6, 89, 93, 147, 152, 172–3, 203, 281, 340, 410. See *Wards of Melian*, and on Melian's relation to Yavanna see 147, 152, 172.

Melian (XI) 5–7, 9–11, 14–16, 21, 25, 35, 40–3, 50, 59, 61, 64–5, 70–1, 82, 90, 93, 95, 105–8, 110–11, 113–14, 119, 123, 129–

30, 132, 175, 178, 194, 252, 259, 310, 312, 321, 333, 345–7, 350–3, 355. See *Girdle of Melian*; *Gwendelin*.

Melian (XII) 185, 364–5, 371, 404 (see especially 364–5).

Melilot (III) Transiently used =Lúthien. 157, 159, 182

Melilot Brandybuck (III) 159

Melineth (VII) 93, 95, 99

Melinir (II) Name given to Vëannë by Eriol. 5–6

Melinon (II) Name given to Eriol by Vëannë. 5–6, 41

melinon (VIII) See *lebethron*.

Melko (I) 25–7, 47, 49, 52–60, 62–3, 66–70, 77–9, 87, 89–90, 92–3, 98–107, 111, 113–18, 120, 128, 131, 133, 135, 140–54, 156–60, 165–9, 171, 174, 176–7, 180, 182–3, 196, 198, 200, 203, 207–11, 213, 217, 219–20, 222–3, 230, 234, 236–44; *son(s) of Melko* 93, 210, *child of Melko* 237; *Melko's Chains* 98, 107, 168; *Mines of Melko* (I) 239, 241. See *Melkor, Morgoth*.

Melko (II) Selected references: his curse on Urin and his kin 71–2, 83, 86, 102; in relation to the origin of Orcs 14, 159, 219; hawks and snakes as creatures of Melko 166, 210; no power of flight 193; in relation to Men 160, 218, 282; *Mines of Melko* 65, 78, 174; *Spell of Bottomless Dread* 65, 77, 159, 169, 206; the Iron Crown 13, 33, 53, 56, 58, 239, 246; his throne 32, 169; myth of his defeat 281–2; attack on the Sun 281, 286. Called *Ainu Melko, the Evil Prince, the Prince of Evil Heart, Vala of Iron, Lord of Iron, the Evil One, the Foe*.

Melko (III) 21, 27, 137, 139, 142, 145, 148, 219, 221, 305

Melko (IV) 3, 5–9, 42–4, 47, 50, 52–3, 56–7, 59, 61, 65, 67–9, 71, 73, 75, 79, 164–7, 180, 205, 207, 209, 238–41, *249, 252–3, 256–61, 263, 270, 275, 281, 283, 285, 290, 292; O.E. *Mánfréa* etc; 209, *Orgel* 281, 283. Later form *Melkor* 73, 166–7, 253, 260, 275, 282, 291, 336; O.E. *Melkor* (*Melcor*) 283, 290–1

Melko (V) 60, 63, 72–5, 108, 110, 120–2, 144, 148, 157–61, 163–4, 187, 205–8, 210, 221, 225–8, 234, 238, 240–1, 258–9, 263, 335, 338, 373 (also *Maeleg, Moeleg*); see especially 164. *Mountains of Melko* 259, 270; *Foes of Melko*, a name of the *Noldor*, 215. See *Alkar, Melkor, Morgoth*.

Melko (X) Earlier, or alternative, form for *Melkor* (see 350). 22–4, 26–7, 63, 76, 104, 156, 194, 198, 291, 350, 360, 407; *Melekô* 355

Melkor (I) 26, 79–80, 110, 112, 131, 133, 156–61, 198–9, 222–3, 225

Melkor (II) 216, 219

Melkor (V) Later form for *Melko*. 120, 332, and see especially 338.

Melkor (VI) 122

Melkor (IXb) 383. See *Mēlekō*.

Melkor (X) 7, 9–27, 29, 32–8, 40–3, 48–9, 51–4, 58–67, 69–75, 78–80, 82–3, 87–90, 93–101, 104–8, 110–11, 114, 121, 123–4, 129–31, 133, 138, 144–7, 149–53, 156, 158–62, 165, 167–8, 174, 179, 184–94, 197, 201–4, 209, 240–1, 243, 247–8, 253–4, 256, 258–9, 269, 271, 273–95 *passim*, 304–5, 309–10, 312, 318, 321–2, 326–7, 330–1, 333–8, 340, 342, 344–5, 349–52, 354, 356–8, 360, 362–4, 374–400, 403–24 *passim*, 428–30; unnamed, in the *Tale of Adanel*, 346–8, 360; spelt *Melcor* (X) 362; *Melkórë* 350.

Melkor (X) Etymology of the name 350; called *the Calumniator* 401, *the Diabolus* 412; *Melkorism* 334. See *(The) Marrer, Morgoth*.

Melkor (X) The power of Melkor 9–10, 12, 48, 59, 65, 97, 121, 144–6, 150, 190, 254–5, 258, 269, 273, 280, 304, 312, 322, 330, 334, 352, 357, 375, 390, 392–4; his power 'dispersed' 110, 133, 137, 259, 296, 334, 390–5, 400, 403–4, 411, 422; his inability to make living things 74, 78, 110, 123–4, 165, 409, 413–14, 417; his bodily form 187, 275, 284, 292, 346, 377, 395–6, 399, 403

Melkor (XI) 5, 9–10, 12, 14, 17, 36, 44, 78, 104–5, 109, 117, 134, 150, 177, 191–2, 196, 200, 203–4, 207, 210–12, 346, 351, 373, 384, 386, 402, 418; *'He who arises in Might'* 402; *the Chaining of Melkor* 9–10. Earlier form *Melko* 111, 121, 191–2, 195. *War of the Valar and Melkor* 373

Melkor (XII) 358, 377, 385, 388, 390, 396, 413–14, 420; old form *Melko* 374–5. See *Belegar*.

Melkorohíni (X) 'Children of Melkor'. 416, and see 406; *Melkorséni* 423

Mellyn, Meldir, Melin (VI) Forms of the Elvish word for 'friends' spoken by Gandalf before the Gate of Moria. 452, 463

Melthinorn (V) 'Tree of Gold', a Gnomish name of Laurelin. 210, 386 (also *Mellinorn*).

Melthinorn (X) 'Tree of gold', (Noldorin >) Sindarin name of Laurelin. 155

Men (II) Selected references: confinement of Men in Hisilómë 10, 70–1, 74, 120, 161, 215, 218; Tuor the first Man to reach the Sea 151, 204; Ulmo's choice of a Man 160, 218; tongues of Men 70; tales told by 70; fate of 59–60; stature of, see *Elves*; knowledge of Ilúvatar 163, 209; union of Men and Elves 101, 130, 164, 199,

215, 219, 265; in relation to Melko 160, 218, 282; in Tol Eressëa 283–4

Men (IV) Selected references. Awakening 99, 269; Men corrupted by Morgoth 26, 179–80, 202, 233, by Thû/Sauron 40, 164, 166; dispersion in Middle-earth 23, 53, 99, 104, 175; faithless Men in Hithlum 35, 58, 67, 119, 122, 141–2, 193–4, repentance of 151, 160, 163, 202; relations with Elves 17, 20–1, 26, 33, 40, 64, 90, 99–100, 105, 118, 134, 147, 163–4, 171–2, 298, 331–2, 337; union with Elves, see entry *Elves*; stature 21, 51, 100; Ulmo's prophecies concerning 36, 50, 66, 98, 142, 146–7, 151, 160, 202, 299, 318; Elf-friends allowed to depart into the West 158, 200, 202; fate of Men 21–2, 41, 51–2, 100, 135, 165, 191; O.E. *Fíras* 206, 208, 21 1–12, *Elde (Ælde)* 208, 211. See *Easterlings, Swarthy Men, Hildor.*

Men (V) Selected references. Awakening 118, 245; nature, mortality, and fate 14, 18, 25, 28, 163, 166, 247, 273, 303, 305, 333; language 30, 68, 75, 129, 131, 148–9, 176–7, 179–80, 191–2, 194, 246, 273, 275, 279; in relation to Elves 12, 17–18, 22–3, 29, 129, 131–2, 178, 228–9, 246–7, 275–6, 304, 310, 326–7, 332; to the Gods 18, 25, 160–1, 163, 229, 245–6, and to Morgoth 13, 19, 24–5, 163, 329; names of Men among the Elves 245. See *Elf-friends, Fathers of Men; Easterlings, Rómenildi; Wild Men; Brethil, Hithlum.*

Men (VI) Visitors to Hobbiton 20, 30, 54–5, 150, 221, 235; in Bree 132–3, 140–1, 223, 331, 334; *Men (out) of the West, Western Men* 128, 169, 190, 192, 218, 329, 393; *Eastern Men* 398; other references 175, 178, 182, 184, 192, 215–16, 225, 253, 260, 272, 278, 311, 357, 379, 391, 397, 403–4, 417. See *Rings of Men, Men-wraiths; Big Folk, Wild Men.*

Men (VII) Men of the North 6, 120, 128, 158, 390, 395; of the East 286, 372, 455; of the South 372, 434; of the West, see *Númenórean(s), Westernesse.* Other references 84, 113–14, 125, 127, 133, 144, 152, 158, 162, 181, 184, 186, 286, 291, 326, 331, 363, 386 (*Men of the cities*), 395, 416, 418–19, 455

Men (VIII) The divisions of Men 157 (*the High, Men of Light; Middle Men, Middle People; Men of (the) Shadow(s), Men of the Darkness*); speech of Men 21, 155, 157, 159–61 (*Man-speech* 160, *Mannish* 161); Men and Elves 158–9; and Sauron 45, 158; *Dominion of Men* 219 (Great Lands committed to Men 401); other references 45, 76–7, 109, 112, 134, 162, 184, 213, 219, 400, 402–

3. See *Fathers of Men, Three Houses, Swart Men, Wild Men*.

Men (IXa) 57; *Men of the West* 20; *Dominion of Men* 57, 68

Men (X) (also *Man, Mankind*) 5, 12, 20–6, 28, 36–7, 39, 42–4, 66, 71, 76, 95, 108, 111–12, 130, 133, 135–8, 144–5, 147–8, 154, 157–8, 160–1, 163, 173, 176, 187–8, 199, 204, 208–10, 212, 215, 218–19, 224–5, 232, 241, 245, 250–1, 266–7, 270, 275–6, 282, 294, 304–5, 307–44 *passim*, 349–58, 364–5, 370, 373–5, 378, 385, 389, 395–7, 401–31 *passim*

   Men (X) The awakening or coming of Men 95, 130, 135, 138, 187, 275, 327, 378 ('in an Isle amid the floods'), 385, 409, 417, 420, 423, 431; the mortality and death of Men 21, 37, 43, 219, 250, 267, 304, 307–17, 326, 330–3, 339–41, 354–6, 365–6, 424–6, 429–30. See *Dominion of Men*.

Men (XI) Selected references. Awakening, coming of Men 30, 37, 49–50, 217; their fate, doom 52, 225, 247, 387; languages 39, 60, 118, 128, 205, 208–9, 402 (and see *Bëor, Haladin*) (1), *Marach*); in relation to Elves 39, 49–50, 77, 124, 128, 219–21, 224, 386–7; Elvish names for Men 219, 386–7; corruption by Morgoth and rebellion 37, 39, 118, 217; Men of Eriador 61, 64

Men Falros (VIII) See *Cair Andros*.

Men of Middle-earth (IXb) (in the age of Númenor) 332, 334, 339, 344–5, 348, 356, 359, 362, 368, 380, 403 (and see *Wild Men*); their tongues 344, 362, 380

Men of the Mountains (VIII) The Dead Men of Dunharrow. 307, 410; *Dark Men of the Mountains* 397, 410, 424; their King 397, 410, 424

Men of the North (II) (1) Tuor's people. 160. (2) *Forodwaith*, Vikings. 313, 318. See *Forodwaith, Gwasgonin*.

Men of the Sea (II) *Forodwaith*, Vikings. 304, 312

Men of the South (II) Romans. 315, 330. See *Romans, Rúmhoth*.

Men of the West, Western Men. (V) 26, 191, 194, 196

Men of the Wood(s) (IV) See *Woodmen*.

Men of the Woods (V) The people of Haleth. 136. See *Brethil, Woodmen*.

Men, Mankind (I) 16, 18–20, 25–7, 31–2, 45, 47, 49, 52–3, 56–7, 59–61, 63–4, 68, 77, 80, 82, 90–3, 97–9, 105, 118–19, 125, 134–5, 138–9, 146, 150, 156, 159, 174–5, 177, 180, 187, 189, 198, 207–8, 211–13, 215–16, 219–21, 223–5, 230, 233–42, 244. On the nature and fate of Men see especially 59–61, 77, 90–3, 150–1

Menegroth (II) The Thousand Caves in Doriath. 63, 129, 245. See *Thousand Caves.*

Menegroth (III) The Thousand Caves in Doriath. 28, 50–1, 332, 349

Menegroth (IV) 188–9, 271, 278, 288, 311, 329, 333, 336, 339. See *Thousand Caves.*

Menegroth (V) 114, 125–6, 138, 178, 220, 254, 261, 272, 319, 321, 384. See *Thousand Caves.*

Menegroth (X) 'The Thousand Caves' in Doriath. 93, 104, 173

Menegroth (XI) 10–12, 14–16, 18, 20–1, 23, 32, 35, 43, 63–5, 67, 69–70, 81–2, 95, 108, 110–12, 132, 135, 138, 140, 149, 178, *183, 244, 334–5, 347–8, 350, 352–3, 355, 414–15, 418; Menegroth described 11, 415; etymology 414. See *Thousand Caves.*

Menegroth (XII) 'The Thousand Caves' in Doriath. 371

Menel (IXb) The heavens. 241, 305, 401, 412, 414–5

Menel (XI) The heavens. 411, 422

Meneldil (VIII) Son of Anárion. 154

Meneldil (XII) Son of Anárion; third King of Gondor. 170, 177, 191–2, 197, 208, 212

Meneldor Eagle of the North. (IXa) 45

Meneldur (XII) See *Tar-Meneldur.*

Menelkemen (IXb) [Ramer] 218

Menelmakar (X) 'Swordsman of the Sky'. 71, 76, 160, 166; *Menelmacar* 76. See *Menelvagor, Orion.*

Menelmakar (XII) Orion. 375

Menelmakil (XI) Orion. 411. See *Telumehtar.*

Menelmin (IXb) The Pillar of Heaven. 335. Other abandoned names (in order of succession) *Menelminda* 302, 353, 356, 412, *Menelmindo* 315; *Meneltyúla* 302, 314–15, 346–7, 351–3, 355–6, 375, 384, 395; *Menel-tûbel* 302, 353, 375, *Menel-tûbil* 302, 305, 353, 375, *Menel-Tûbal* 363, 365, 367, 372–3, 375, 383, 388, *Menil-Tûbal* 371, 383, 388, 391. See *Minul-Tárik.*

Menelmindon (XII) See *Meneltarma.*

Menelrond (XII) 'Heaven-dome', Hall of the Throne in Menegroth. 37, 376

Meneltarma (V) The mountain in the midst of Númenor. 30. See *Mountain of Ilúvatar.*

Meneltarma (IXb) The Pillar of Heaven. 378, 393–4; *Isle of Meneltarma* 393–4

Meneltarma (X) 154, 157; *the mountain of Númenor* 154. See *Heofonsýl.*

Meneltarma (XII) The Pillar of Heaven in Númenor. 145–6, 153, 158; earlier *Menelmin, Menelmindon*, etc. 146

Menelvagor (VI) Orion. 325

Menelvagor (X) Sindarin form for *Menelmakar*. 76

Mengas Dûr (XI) See *Cabed-en-Aras*.

Men-orcs (X) 419

Men-wraiths (VI) 75, 78

Meoita (II) See *Tevildo*.

Mercia (IV) 290

Mercia (IXb) Kingdom of the Mercians. 291. *Mercian* 291, 294; (dialect of Old English) 257, 292, 313. See *West Midlands*.

Meres of Twilight (II) See *Aelin-uial*.

Meres of Twilight (V) 253, 260–1; *Twilight Meres* 262. See *Aelin-uial, Hithliniath, Umboth Muilin*.

Mereth Aderthad (I) The Feast of Reuniting. 243

Mereth Aderthad (IV) 329, 333, 337, 339; O.E. *Sibbegemótes fréols* 339. See *Feast of Reuniting*.

Mereth Aderthad (V) 126, 148, 253, 372. See *Feast of Reuniting*.

Mereth Aderthad (XI) 34, 114, 116. See *Feast of Reuniting*.

Merethrond (IXa) The Great Hall of Feasts in Minas Tirith. 67

Meriadoc (Merry) (XII) See *Brandybuck*.

Meriadoc Brandybuck, Merry (VI) See *Brandybuck*.

Meriadoc Brandybuck, Merry (VII) See under *Brandybuck*.

Meriadoc Brandybuck, Merry (VIII) See under *Brandybuck*.

Meriadoc Brandybuck, Merry (IXa) See under *Brandybuck*.

Meril (IXa) Aragorn's translation of *Rose* (Gamgee). 121, 126, 129. (Replaced *Beril*.)

Meril (XI) Wife of Felagund. 242. See *Felagund*.

Meril-i-Turinqi (I) The Lady of Tol Eressëa; also *Meril, Turinqi*. 16–17, 20, 22, 26, 48, 50, 52, 95–8, 107, 111–13, 129–30, 134, 175, 230, 235; *Lady of the Isle* 175

Meril-i-Turinqi (II) The Lady of Tol Eressëa; also *Meril, Turinqi*. 144–5, 197, 258, 280, 283–4, 290, 294; *Lady of the Isle* 144, 283–4

Meril-i-Túrinqi (IV) The Lady of Tol Eressëa. 72

Meril-i-Turinqi (VII) The Lady of Tol Eressëa. 242

Mering Stream (VIII) The 'Boundary-stream' between Rohan and Gondor. 354, 356. (VIII) See *Firienlode*.

Merlin (IXb) [Lewis] 309

Mermaids (II) 259–60, 263; *seamaids* 260. See *Fiord of the Mermaid, Oarni*.

Merrill (VI) The stream of Rivendell. 205

Merryburn (VII) 91, 93, 96, 98

Merton College (X) 5, 350, 352, 385, 390, 409

Mesopotamia (IXb) 410

Messenger(s) from Minas Tirith (VIII) Sent to ask Théoden for aid; also *errand-rider(s)*. 141, 231–4, 236, 244, 255–6, 259, 262–4, 270, 272, 274–5, 312, 315–17, 319, 321, 343, 349; and see *Hirgon*.

Methedras (VII) 320, 404, 426–7. Earlier names *Methen Amon* 391, 404; *Methendol* 404

Methedras (VIII) Last great peak of the Misty Mountains. 8

Methiriad (XI) Mid-Beleriand. *184, 187, 190

Mettanyë (I) The last part of the poem *The Trees of Kortirion*. 43

Miaugion (II) See *Tiberth, Tifil*.

Miaulë (II) Tevildo's cook. 28, 54

Micelgeard, Mickleyard (II) (Old English, 'the great town') Rome, 'the Heartless Town'. 330. See *Rûm*.

Michel Delving (VI) 107, 244–5, 278, 284, 295, 312, 334. (Replaced *Much Hemlock*.)

Michel Delving (VII) 41, 185; *the Town Burrow* 41; *the Museum, Mathom-house* 185

Michel Delving (IXa) 80–2, 85, 87–8, 91–2, 98–100, 105, 108

Michel Delving (XII) 15, 89–91

Mickleburg (XI) Belegost. 206, 209, 389. See *Great Fortress*.

Middle Age (VIII) Equivalent to the Second and Third Ages (cf. *the Middle Days* VII. 150). 219

Middle Age (IXa) Equivalent to the Second and Third Ages. 68. *Middle Days* 68

Middle Days (VII) 150

Middle Elves (VIII) See *Lembi. Middle Men, Middle People*, see *Men*.

Middle Elves (XII) 312, 329. *Middle Men* 312–14

Middle English (VI) 145

Middle English (IXb) 291

Middle lands (I) 234

Middle Stone, The (VIII) The single pillar of stone before the Door of Dunharrow. 248, 250; see also 246, 312–13, 315, 406

Middle-earth (I) 21, 23, 26, 51, 81, 89, 110–11, 132–5, 199, 222–3

Middle-earth (II) 64, 266, 327, 333

Middle-earth (III) 90, 224, 269, 313, 331, 334, 349, 356; *midworld* 28. See *Ennorath, Great Lands*.

Middle-earth (IV) 6, 46, 52–3, 64, 171–2, 180, 187, 233, 235–9, 241,

*249, 253–9, 262, 264, 272–3, 278, 280, 283, 292, 314, 326–7; O.E. *middangeard* 282–3, 285–6, 289, 338. See especially 283, and see *Ambar-endya, Endor, Pelmar, Great Lands, Hither Lands, Outer Lands* (1).

Middle-earth (V) (in QS to 61 and occasionally later, and elsewhere, *the Middle-earth*). 9–35 *passim*, 64–6, 71, 73–4, 76, 89, 97–8, 103, 111, 114, 116, 118–19, 121, 125, 144, 148, 152–3, 164, 168, 170, 173–4, 178–9, 184, 189, 193–4, 206–61 *passim*, 268, 273–4, 281, 290, 298, 300–1, 303, 305, 324, 330, 332, 336–7, 344, 407; (Elvish names *Entar, Entarda* 356, *Endamar* 356, 372, *Ambarenya, Emmerein, Emerin* 372, *Endor* 376). See *Hither Lands, Inner Lands, Outer Lands*.

Middle-earth (VI), *the Middle-earth* 75, 105, 122, 176, 179, 182, 184, 187–90, 215, 218, 260, 263, 270, 320, 431, 438, 440; *the Middle-world* 182, 260, 270

Middle-earth (VII) 26, 82, 101, 104, 112, 117, 123–4, 127, 129, 144–5, 154, 158, 161, 180, 241, 248, 250–1, 255, 257, 259, 263, 266, 295, 429, 452; *the Middle-earth* 121, 123–4, 233

Middle-earth (VIII) 45, 167–8, 172, 217, 405, 409

Middle-earth (IXa) 44, 56, 58,110,119,128

Middle-earth (IXb) 152, 241, 258, 275, 280, 287, 305–6, 316, 331–2, 334–9, 343–6, 352–3, 358, 361–3, 365–6, 368, 374–5, 379–80, 382–3, 386, 389, 394–6, 399, 403, 405–11, 439; *the Middle-earth* 236, 348, 387, *the Great Middle-earth* 398; O.E. *Middangeard* 236, 257, 285, 313, 316. See *Great Lands, Kemen*.

Middle-earth (X) (also *the Middle-earth*) 12, 17–20, 25–7, 32–3, 35, 38, 50, 53–4, 65, 70–86 *passim*, 90–1, 95, 102–3, 108, 111–13, 115, 118–21, 123, 126, 129–30, 132–3, 138, 146–7, 149, 153, 156, 158–65, 168, 173, 175, 177, 179, 182–3, 185, 188, 196, 201–3, 208, 210, 214, 219, 221, 223, 232, 241, 248, 250, 254, 257–8, 265, 269, 271, 276, 281–3, 290–1, 295, 307–10, 321, 339–41, 349, 359, 361–5, 370, 372–3, 377, 382, 384–5, 390, 397, 400, 402, 404, 406–7, 416–17, 419–20, 423–6, 430–1

Middle-earth (X) Middle-earth as *Morgoth's Ring* 372, 377. See *Ambar; Endar, Endor; Hither Lands, Outer Lands*.

Middle-earth (XI) 5–6, 8–10, 13–14, 16, 18, 20–4, 26, 30, 33, 37, 39, 42, 45, 50, 62, 67, 69, 85, 104–7, 109, 114, 116, 118, 130, 161–3, 173–6, 178, 180, 186, 193, 196, 203, 205, 207, 210–11, 217, 220, 224, 253, 320–1, 341, 343, 345, 350, 355, 360, 365, 373, 378, 381, 384, 386, 393, 397, 409, 412, 416. See *Endar*.

Middle-earth (XII) 12, 20–2, 25–33, 55, 61, 64–5, 71, 73–5, 78–9, 82, 119–20, 124, 144–6, 149, 151–4, 156–7, 159, 164, 168–73, 175–6, 178, 180–3, 187–8, 191–2, 227–8, 234, 236, 243–4, 254, 257, 263–5, 296, 304–6, 312–15, 321, 323–4, 327–9, 338–9, 341–2, 344, 346–8, 354, 356–7, 359, 361, 364, 366, 370, 377–9, 381–3, 386–8, 390–2, 398, 401, 403–4, 422; Maps 187, 328, 373

Middle English (VII) 65

Middlemarch (VII) 296, 304, 320, 403, 439; *men of the Middlemarch* 434. See *Enedwaith*.

Midgewater Marshes (VI) 166, 354; the marshes 174–5, 178, 355–6. (Replaced *Flymarshes*.)

Midgewater Marshes (VII) 11, 44, 56, 296

Mid-land (IV) *249; *middle land* 238–9

Midyear('s) Day (XII) 121, 128–9, 131–5, 288; *Midyear Days* 128, 131; *Midyear* 135–6

Mighty, The (X) The Valar. 273, 277

Mikligarðr (II) (Old Norse) Constantinople. 330

Mîm (XI) 180, 187, 255, 257–8, 300, 310–12, 314, 354–5, 389

Mîm (XII) The Petty-dwarf. 352

Mîm the Dwarf (II) Called 'the fatherless'. 103, 113–14, 118, 122, 134, 137, 222–3, 230, 246; curse of, spell of, Mîm 223, 228, 231, 233, 235, 238–41, 246, 264

Mîm the Dwarf (III) 52

Mîm the Dwarf (IV) 32, 61, 63, 132–3, 187–9, 306

Mîm the Dwarf (V) 141

Min Rimmon, Minrimmon (VIII) The third (or sixth, see 344) beacon in Anórien. 233, 319, 343–4, 349–52, 354, 356; *Rimmon* 351–2. See *Rimmon (Forest)*.

Minalkar (XII) Regent, and later the nineteenth King of Gondor (Rómen-dakil II). 259–60; *Minalcar* 259

Minal-zidar (IXb) [Ramer] 199–200, 218; translated *Poise in Heaven* 200

Minardil (XII) Twenty-fifth King of Gondor. 199–200, 202–3, 214–15, 231

Minas Anor (VII) 119–21, 123, 125–7, 129, 144–6, 298–9, 333 (error for *Ithil*), 347, 366; *Tower of the Sun* 119, *of the Setting Sun* 119, 144; *City of the Sun* 333

Minas Anor (VIII) 76, 154

Minas Anor (X) 44

Minas Anor (XII) 163, 170, 176–7, 191–2, 199–201, 213, 215–18, 228, 231–3

Minas Ithil (VII) 119–20, 123, 125–7, 144–5, 212, 298–9, 333, 347, 366 (error for *Anor*); *Tower of the Moon* 119, 384, *of the Rising Moon* 119, 144; *City of the Moon* 333; *Lord of Minas Ithil* (Aragorn) 212

Minas Ithil (VIII) 76, 106, 125, 136, 152; see *Ithil-stone.*

Minas Ithil (IXa) 20

Minas Ithil (XII) 176, 191, 195, 201, 215–17, 233, 240; *Stone of Ithil, -stone* 206, 217, 240–1

Minas Morghul, Minas Morgul (VIII) 71–2, 106, 113, 115–16, 123–6, 129, 132, 134, 136, 171, 173, 177, 180, 182–6, 192, 215, 217–18, 222, 225–6, 229–30, 256, 275, 291, 327, 330, 360, 364, 400, 430, 438; *Minas Morgol* 229. For changes in the site of Minas Morghul see 106, 113, 115–16, 124.

Minas Morghul, Minas Morgul (VIII) *Morghul, Morgul* 106, 213–14, 226, 260, 275, 386, 403, 431. (In the following references spelt here *Morghul* only.) *Morghul-host, Host(s) of Morghul* 182, 187, 192, 260, 262–3, 274–5, 359. *Lieutenant of Morghul* (Gothmog) 369, 431. *Vale, valley of Morghul, Morghul Vale* 176–7, 186–7, 327, 431, and see *Imlad Morghul*; *Morghul dale* 195; *Vale of Dread* 327; *Valley of the Wraiths* 180. *The Morghul Pass* 195, 431; *the main pass* 124, 192, 222. *Meads of Morghul* 202, (360, 364). *Morghul-road*, see *Roads.* The *palantír* of Minas Morghul (taken to Barad-dûr) 71–2, 76, 80 (*Ithil-stone*), 362, 404.

Minas Morgol (VII) 116, 120–1, 125, 127–8, 138, 145–7, 151, 209, 212, 214–15, 298–9, 310, 339; *Minas Morghul* 146–7, 372, 389; *Minas Morgul* (also *Morgul*) 215, 310, 322, 332–3, 335, 338–40, 344–5, 347–9, 366, 412–13, 440; the City described 333, 337.

Minas Morgol (VII) *City of Sorcery* 343, *Tower of Sorcery* 127; *the Tall Tower* 333, *the Loathly Tower* 336, 338, 343, and cf. 372; *Captain of Morgul* 338; *Morgul-spells* 128; *the Gate* 337–8, 340–1, 343, 372, *the Sentinels* 337–8, 340–1, 343, 348

Minas Morgul (II) 216

Minas Morgul (IXa) 18, 22, 29; earlier form *Minas Morghul* 7, 9–10, 13; *Morghul* 7; original form *Minas Morgol* 4. *Pass of Morgul* 22

Minas Morgul (X) 350

Minas Morgul (XII) 195, 201, 203, 207, 215–18, 233–4; *Morgul* 204–5, 217–19, 241, *Lord of* ~ 233

Minastan (XII) Son of Minardil. 200

Minastir (XII) See *Tar-Minastir.*

Minas Tirith (II) Fortress on Tol Sirion 55, 123

Minas Tirith (VII) 115–16, 120–2, 125–9, 147, 151, 154, 157, 161–2, 165, 177, 207, 210–14, 216, 248, 258, 268, 270–1, 278, 281–2, 287, 289, 298–9, 307, 310–11, 320, 322, 326, 328–30, 333, 336, 345, 347, 358–9, 366, 370–2, 375–6, 378, 385, 389, 392, 400, 412–13, 418, 429, 434–5, 437–40, 442, 449. Early names *Minas-berel* 115–16, *Minas-ond* 115, *Minas Giliath* 116, *Minas rhain* 116, 287, *Othrain* 116

Minas Tirith (VII) *Tower of Guard* (VII) 127, 381; *the white tower* 384; *Lord of Minas Tirith* 128, 210–11, 214, 378, *Lords of* 395; earliest history of 116, 119–21, 127; prophecies in, prophetic verse 116, 120, 122, 125, 127–9, 146, 400. See *Mundbeorg.*

Minas Tirith (IXa) 10, 18, 22, 44, 48–51, 55–7, 59–61, 67, 73, 83, 119, 122, 128–9; *the City* 54, 58, 67, 73, 116, 119, 122–3; *the City of the South* 62; *the Stone City* 115; *the Lord (of Minas Tirith)* 22, 83. See *Mundburg, Stonehouses.*

Minas Tirith (IXa) *The Citadel* 56–7, 67 (plan of, 67); *the White Tower* 22, 67; *Hall of the Kings, Court of the Fountain, the King's house,* 67; *Hall of Feasts,* see *Merethrond. The Hallows* 61, 67; *the Gates, Gateway* 22, 55

Minas Tirith (IXb) 217

Minas Tirth (VIII) (including many references to *the City*) 58, 70–3, 76, 79–80, 126, 129–30, 135, 138, 140–3, 145–7, 150–2, 155, 161, 164–8, 182, 219, 226, 229, 231–2, 234–5, 242, 244, 247, 249, 252–6, 259–60, 262–4, 266, 270–95 *passim*, 301, 304, 306, 318, 322, 324–5, 332–60 *passim*, 364, 366, 368–9, 372–405 *passim*, 410–19 *passim*, 422, 425, 428, 431–3, 438; *Tirith* 145, *Tirith*-man 135; Minas Tirith described 278–9. See *Mundbeorg; Hill, Tower, of Guard.*

Minas Tirth (VIII) Prophetic verse of Minas Tirith 145, 149, 164–6, 328, 339. The *palantír* of Minas Tirith 71–2, 76, 231, 257, 263, 374–81, 391

Minas Tirth (VIII) *The Circles of the City* 279, 284, 377, 405, 417; *first circle* 353, also *lowest* 284, 336, *outer(most)* 288, 336; *sixth circle* 284, 338; *upper circle* 396. The Citadel 276, 279, 281, 294, 324, 326, 329, 335–8, 374, 382, 384, 387, 389, 415, 426. *The Fountain* 276, *Court of the Fountain* 281.

Minas Tirth (VIII) *The Gates: the outer and lowest gate* 278, called *the Great Gate* 278–9, 286, 288, 359, *City Gates* 293, *East Gate*

284, 286, *First Gate* 278, and *the Gate(s)* 300, 306, 326, 332, 335–6, 340, 353, 359–60, 363, 368–70, 374, 380, 384–5, 388, 415, 422; other gates 278–9, 291; *the Seventh Gate* 279, 291.

Minas Tirth (VIII) *The Hall of the Kings* 281, *great hall* 281, 288, *Tower Hall, Hall of the Tower* 323, 385, 389. *The Tombs* 276, 279, 336–7, 360, 375. *The Tower*, see *White Tower*. See also *Othram, Taurost.*

Minas Tirith (XII) 74, 157, 181, 201–2, 204–5, 207, 215–17, 233, 236, 238, 240–3, 265, 267, 271, 274, 282, 332, 371, 421; *the City* 43, 411–12, 415. See *Mundburg.*

Mindeb (III) Tributary of Sirion. 261, 274, 360

Mindeb, *River* (IV) 222, 224, 330, 334

Mindeb, *River* (V) 128, 260–1, 267, 412

Mindeb, *River* (VI) 432

Mindeb, *River* (XI) 81, *183, 188, 193–4, 333

Mindolluin, *Mount* (VII) 310, 322

Mindolluin, *Mount* (VIII) 80, 130, 133, 138, 142, 172, 260, 271, (276), 278–9, 287, 336–7, 353. See *Tor-dilluin.*

Mindolluin, *Mount* (IXa) 49, 57; *the mountain* 58

Mindolluin, *Mount* (XII) 148, 414

Mindon Eldaliéva (I) 135

Mindon Eldaliéva (III) The tower of Ingwë in Tirion. 93. See *Ing.*

Mindon Eldaliéva (X) (including references to *the Mindon*) 85, 90, 110, 115, 118, 176, 180, 196, 278. See *Ingwëmindon.*

Mindon Gwar (II) Gnomish name of Kortirion. 291–2, 313–14, 321, 324. See *Gwar.*

Mindon, *The* (IXa) The tower of Ingwe in Tirion. 58

Mindor Uilas (VIII) Original name of the first beacon in Anórien (Halifirien). 233

Mines of Moria (VI) See *Moria.*

Minethlos (I) A name of the Moon (Gnomish). 192, 198. (Replaced *Mainlos.*)

Minhiriath (XII) Lands between Brandywine and Greyflood. 294, 313–14, 329–30

Miniel (XI), plural *Mínil* Sindarin name of the Vanyar. 383

Minnastirith (V) The tower on Tol Sirion. (128), 146–7, 264, 269, 283–4, 287, 290, 373, 394; later form *Minastirith* 146, 269. (Replaced *Inglormindon*).

Minnas-tirith (XI) The fortress on Tol Sirion. 38, 54, 125

Minnónar (XI) 'The First-born', Elves. 403

Min-Rimmon (IXa) The third beacon in Anórien. 59

Minul-Târik (IXb) The Pillar of Heaven. 238, 241, 249, 302, 375, 388, 391–2, 394, 413, 428. See *Menelmin*.

Minyar (XI) Elves of the First Clan (Vanyar). 380–2, 420. See *Imin*.

Minyon (X) 'First-begotten', Fëanor. 87

Mircwudu (IXb) 'Mirkwood', the Eastern Alps (see V.91). 276

Míriel (IV) Mother of Fëanor. 47

Míriel (X) First wife of Finwë, mother of Fëanor. 92, 101, 103, 127, 185, 191–3, 205–9, 217, 221, 231, 233, 236, 238–44, 246–50, 253–71 *passim*, 276, 293, 300, 339, 361–3. Called *Byrde* (Old English) 92, 103, 185, 192, 205, 257; *Serendë* 185, 192, 205, *Serindë* 236, 254, 257. See *Fíriel*; *Statute of Finwë and Míriel*.

Míriel (XI) First wife of Finwë, mother of Fëanor. 327, 387, 419

Míriel (XII) (1) First wife of Finwë, mother of Fëanor. 332–6, 342, 356–7; named *Þerindë* 333, 336, 342, *Serindë* 356. (2) See *Tar-Míriel*.

Mirkwood (IV) 257

Mirkwood (V) 23, 211, 289; with reference to Taur-na-Fuin 282, 289; Old English *Myrcwudu* 91 (with reference to the Eastern Alps).

Mirkwood (VI) 53, 128, 131, 216, 218, 253, 261, 264, 268, 320, 387, 412–14, 416; *Eastern Mirkwood* 395, 400. Mirkwood in Mordor 216, 218

Mirkwood (VII) 106, 114–16, 118–19, 126, 131, 138, 143, 147–8, 163, 211, 230, 237–8, 264, 272, 295–6, 298, 306, 331, 333, 372, 395, 402, 431, 442–3, 451; called *the Great* 296, 402; *Southern Mirkwood* 111, 177–8, 234, 296, 298, 351. See *Mountains of Mirkwood*.

Mirkwood (VIII) 22, 122, 157; with reference to the spiders 184, 187, 217; *the* Wood 415; *Woodmen of Mirkwood* 242, 247, 249, 253

Mirkwood (X) (82), 89

Mirkwood (XI) 110; translation of *Taur-na-Fuin* 239

Mirkwood (XII) (including *the* Forest) 10, 34, 36, 65, 73–4, 82, 166, 193, 198, 208, 214, 219, 225, 229, 234, 239, 242, 244, 248, 272, 275, 280, 311, 316, 329. See *Greenwood*.

Mirröanwi (X) Incarnate beings, Children of Eru. 315–16, 326, 329, 349–50. Earlier forms *Mirruyaina(r)* 326, 352, *Mirroyainar* 326

Mirror of Galadriel (VIII) See *Galadriel*.

Mirror of Lothlórien (IXa) 32, 77, 90, 106

Mirror, The (VII) Of King Galdaran 249–50; of Galadriel (Galadrien)

251, 253–4, 256, 259–60, 264–6, 272, 289, 367, 379–80, 4 12–13

Mirrormere (VI) 437–8, 466. See *Glassmere, Helevorn, Nen Cenedril.*

Mirrormere (VII) 166–7, 184, 191, 203–4, 218–20, 237, 306. See *Nen Cenedril, Nen Echui*

Mirrormere (IXa) 135. See *Kheled-zâram.*

Mirrormere (XII) 275, 286. See *Kheled-zâram.*

Miruvor (I) 153, 160; *miruvórë* 161

miruvor (VII) Cordial of Elrond. 169

miruvórë (XI) The cordial of the Valar. 399, 419

Misty Mountains (IV) See *Hithaeglir.*

Misty Mountains (VI) (including many references to *the Mountains*) 79, 71, 178, 189, 191, 193, 200, 203, 205, 207–8, 214, 216, 263, 314, 331, 342, 360, 374, 381–2, 397, 401, 409, 416–19, 422–4, 429, 432–4, 438, 440–1, 445–6, 448, 462; demons of the mountains 424. Passes south of the Red Pass 422, 428, 434, 438; configuration of the Mountains 440–1

Misty Mountains (VII) (including references to *the Mountains*) 10, 16, 111, 117, 122, 124, 134, 139, 142, 149, 151, 166, 168, 172, 177, 203, 218–20, 222, 225–6, 228, 230, 232–3, 235, 238–9, 247, 257, 262–4, 289, 298, 306, 320, 333, 347, 351, 356, 372, 378, 391, 402, 404, 419, 426–7. See *Eredhithui.*

Misty Mountains (VIII) (including references to *the mountains*) 8, 16, 21–2, 31, 43, 52, 68, 133, 230, 362, 386

Misty Mountains (IXa) 69, 72; *the mountains* 64–5, 71, 136

Misty Mountains (X) 89, 103; *Towers of Mist*, reared by Melkor, 83, (87), 89. See *Hithaeglir.*

Misty Mountains (XI) 202; *Mountains of Mist* 13, 201, 206. See *Hithaeglir.*

Misty Mountains (XII) (including *the Mountains*) 4, 9, 34–6, 38, 56, 65–6, 72, 174, 176, 193, 196, 205, 219–20, 225–6, 229–30, 233, 235, 237, 239, 241, 248, 264, 272, 275–6, 278, 302, 305–6, 311, 323, 327, 329

Mitheithel (VI) The River Hoarwell. 192, 201, 360; *Mitheithel Bridge* 201. See *Hoarwell, Last Bridge.*

Mitheithel, River (VII) 14, 17, 58, 299; *Bridge of Mitheithel, Last Bridge* 14, 17, 58–9, 61. See *Hoarwell.*

Mithlond (VII) The Grey Havens (see 423). 301, 423 *Mithrandir* Gandalf. 251, 264, 432

Mithlond (VIII) 76–7, 80–1; *Mithond* 77, 80, *Mithrond* 80–1. The *palantír* of Mithlond 76–8. See *Grey Havens*.

Mithlond (IXa) 109, 133. See *Grey Havens*.

Mithrandir (V) 'The Grey Pilgrim', Gandalf. 345, (*373, 383*)

Mithrandir (VIII) Gandalf. 153, 158, 163, 284–5, 328, 330, 332, 335, 338, 387, 390. See *Grey Wanderer*.

Mithrandir (XII) 206, 228, 240, 243, 251, 265, 281–2, 287, 392. See *Gandalf*.

Mithrellas (XII) Companion of Nimrodel, mother of Galador. 220–2

mithril 184, 233, 244, 275, 318; *true-silver* 233, *Moria-silver* 318

Mithril (VI) 223, 465–6. See *Erceleb, Ithil, Moria-silver*.

Mithril (VII) 98, 101, 104, 137, 184–5, 188, 191, 200–1; *mithril-coat, -corslet, -mail, -rings* 185, 211, 218, 221, 331, 336; called *Moria-silver* 185, 188, *true-silver* 185, 191, 200, 459. Early names *Erceleb* 184, *Ithil* 184, *Thilevril* 184, 188

mithril (VIII) (with reference to Frodo's mithril-coat) 92, 185, 190, 210, 219, 230, (257), 361–2, 430; (helms of the guards of the Citadel of Minas Tirith) 279

mithril (IXa) (of Frodo's mithril-coat) 9, 14, 24, 48, 52, 72, 92 (other references to the coat 8, 52, 64); (of the rings given to Frodo at Kormallen) 48, 51; (of the ring Nenya) 112

Mithrim (I) (lake and region) 160, 238–9, 241, 243. See *Asgon*.

Mithrim (II) Lake and (149, 153) the river flowing from it. 149, 151–3, 202, 204; *Grey-elves of Mithrim* 205. (Replaced *Asgon*.)

Mithrim (III) (Lake and perhaps also region, see 103). 103, 105, 115, 118–19, 126; *Prince of Mithrim* (Húrin) 96, 103; *Men of Mithrim* 97, 103

Mithrim (IV) Lake Mithrim 3–4, 7–8, 22–3, 35, 52–3, 101–2, 141, 210, 221–2, 229–30, 268, 270, 272, 280, 295–6, 304, 316, 328, 333, 337–8; the land of Mithrim 172, 268–9, 274, 280, 295, 310, 328, 333, 338; O.E. *Mistrand* 210, *Mistóra* 210, 337, but *Miþrim* 338; *Mountains of Mithrim* 221, 268, 280, *hills of Mithrim* 230

Mithrim (V) Lake Mithrim 117–18, 125–6, 138, 151, 249–50, 259, *373, 384*; the land of Mithrim 117–18, 125–6, 151, 189, 239, 249–50, 252, 255, 259, 289; *Mountains of Mithrim* 117, 249, 259, 412; speech of Mithrim 177

Mithrim (VI) 122

Mithrim (XI) The Elves of Mithrim (primary meaning of the name). 378, 410–11, 420; name of their dialect of Sindarin 400. Lake Mithrim (originally ='Lake of the Mithrim', 410) 17–18, 31, 81,

176, *182, 378, 410; the land of Mithrim 17–18, 31, 33–4, 79–82, 89, 91, 113–14, 128, 136–7, 146, 176, *182, 238, 261–2, 411 (language); *the Mountains of Mithrim* 17, 181, *182

Mittalmar (VI) The 'Inlands' of Númenor. 295

Modred (IXb) Nephew of King Arthur. 283

Moeleg (IV) Gnomish form *of Melko*. 79, 164, 167. (Replaced *Belcha*.)

Mogru (XII) Master of Agar (tale of Tal-elmar). (428), 429–34

Mole, The (II) Name of one of the kindreds of the Gondothlim (*House of the Mole, Mole-kin, Mole-folk, warriors of the Mole*). 175, 177–8, 220; sign of the Mole 165, 171, 220; Meglin's folk bore no emblem 172. See *Meglin*.

Monoliths, Road of (VIII) The line of standing stones across the Firienfeld. 320–1; *the Stony Road* 315, 321

Months (XII) Hobbit names 9, 16, 122, 125, 129, 136–8; Quenya names 134–6, 138; Noldorin (Sindarin) names 135–6, 138

Moon, The (I) 60, 64, 83, 85, 88, 119, 151, 174–5, 182, 187, 192–3, 195, 197, 199–203, 206–8, 214–20, 227–8, 242; *Ship of the Moon* 192, 194, 216; *Man in the Moon* 193, 202; *King of the Moon* 202; *Harvest Moon* 41. See *Haven of the Moon*; and for other names of the Moon see 192.

Moon, The (II) Selected references: the Moon mariner or shipman chases Eärendel 255, 259, 262, 264, 269, 271; ship of 268–9; haven of 269; gateway of 272–3; recall of 285–6; imprisonment of 286; Melko seeks to hurt the Moon 281; beyond the Moon 162, behind the Moon 274–5, East of the Moon 271–2; an emblem of the King's House in Gondolin 172

Moon, The (III) Selected references. *Halls of the Moon* 47, 56, 65, 259; the Moon as a ship (see *Silver Wherry*) 74, 93, 128–9; Fëanor's foreknowledge of the Sun and Moon 138

Moon, The (IV) Selected references. Making of 20, 49, 97; ship of 20, 49, 253, island of 97, 171; course of 20, 49, 97–8, 165, 170–1, 236–7, 241, 253–4; first Moonrise 22, 269, 272; prophecies concerning 50, 73–4, 98, 165, 205; 'magic Moon' 20, 49, 98; the Moon and Eärendel 38, 41, 70–1, 150, 164, 195, 197, 203–4; *Song of the Sun and Moon* 97, 170. See *Rána*.

Moon, The (V) 13, 20, 31–2, 41, 56, 64, 72, 109–10, 118, 123, 125, 168, 171–2, 177, 184, 189, 215, 240–1, 243–5, 248, 250, 252, 299, 325, 331, 333, 335; the Moon and the Elves 64, 72, 118, 240; *Elder Moon* (the White Tree) 242, 244; *Song of the Sun and Moon* 240. See *Isil, Ithil, Rana*.

Moon, The (VI) 57, 121–2, 329; on the West Gate of Moria 449. References to the Moon's phases 58, 61, 168, 184, 191, 281, 325, 330, 409, 421, 434, 462; *Hunter's Moon* 409

Moon, The (VII) 37, 92–4, 98, 101, 212, 284; in design on the West Gate of Moria 180–1, 187; phases of the Moon 167–8, 179–80, 187, 219, 228, 253, 343–4, 353–4, 357–8, 363, 365–9, 391; phases those of 1941–2, 369, 387; runic Moon-letters 452 *Morannon* 213; *the Black Gate* 321

Moon, The (VIII) 167, 172, 174, 359, 363, 399, 422. See *Ithil*. Phases of the Moon 16, 27, 40–1, 51, 81, 109, 131–5, 137, 140–3, 147, 152, 172, 174, 176, 180, 232, 237, 240, 245, 249, 251–2, 255, 259, 262–4, 270–3, 276, 295, 299, 303, 309, 316, 319–22, 432

Moon, The (IXa) (phases) 49, 51

Moon, The (IXb) 165–7, 169, 182, 241, 302, 306, 426; *moons* 199. See *Isil, Nîlû*.

Moon, The (X) (41), 42–4, 50–1, 57–8, 60, 94, 120, 130–2, 134–8, 163–4, 169, 196, 198, 271, 346, 370–7, 382–5, 390; *island of the Moon* 130–1, *Flower of Silver* 131; *the Elder Moon* (the White Tree) 198, 372. See *Isil, Ithil, Râna*.

Moon, The (XI) 17, 20, 30, 114, 176. See *Ithil*.

Moon, The (XII) 119, 121, 123, 125, 127, 130, 137, 398. For 'Moon's day' see 123, 130, 137

Moors of the Neweglu (XI) (Petty-dwarves) *182, 187. See *Neweg*.

Moot (of Brethil) (XI) See *Brethil*.

Morannon (VIII) The Black Gate; originally name of the pass into Mordor (see 122). 112, 118, 120, 122, 125, 127, 129–42 *passim*, 173, 260, 263, 271, 275, 359–61, 363, 399, 416, 418–19, 430, 432, 438. *Morennyn* 113, *Mornennyn* 112–13, 127, (names of the pass). See *Black Gate(s)*, *Gates of Mordor*, *Ennyn Dûr*, *Kirith Naglath*.

Morannon (IXa) 7–8, 32–5, 44. See *Black Gate*.

Morannon (XII) 200, 215, 265. See *Black Gate*.

Morben (XI), plural *Moerbin (Morbin)* Sindarin name derived from *Moriquendi* (XI) (for the meaning see 376–7, 409). 362, 376–7, 380, 408–9, 420

Mordor (V) 29, 31, *33–4*. See *Black Country*.

Mordor (VI) 131, 197, 199, 209, 214, 216–18, 226–7, 253, 258, 261, 264, 268–9, 272, 321–3, 370–1, 373, 380–1, 397–9, 401, 403, 410–14, 466; *Lord of Mordor* 364. See *Black Country*.

Mordor (VII) 10, 68, 72–3, 111, 117–18, 121, 123, 127, 129–30,

135–6, 139, 144–5, 148, 165, 169, 186, 205, 210, 212–15, 247, 262–3, 289, 298, 310, 322, 325, 333, 339, 343, 345, 347–9, 351, 360, 366, 371, 374, 381–2, 385, 389, 408–10, 413, 418, 423, 427, 430, 434–5, 450; *the Black Country* 123, 144; *passes of Mordor* 281, 283, 285, 313, 320–1, 352, *gates of Mordor* 285, 321, 324; the host of Mordor riding out 208, 212–13, 345. See *(The) Lord, Mountains of Mordor.*

Mordor (VIII) 48–50, 66, 68, 70–5, 77, 81, 85, 104–5, 107, 110–11, 115, 119–20, 122, 124, 136–7, 143, 148, 151–2, 154, 163, 165, 177, 179, 182–4, 215, 219–20, 226, 233, 247, 249, 254, 256, 260, 265, 268, 270, 275, 289, 295, 303, 317, 319, 322, 329, 333, 346, 359–60, 362, 369, 375, 378, 381, 391, 398, 401–3, 410, 412–14, 419–20, 425–9, 437–8. *Lord of Mordor* 401; *the pass into Mordor* 85, 104, 111, 270; *the mountains of Mordor* 265, 268. See *Gates of Mordor; Teeth of Mordor; Black Land, Nameless Land.*

Mordor (IXa) 3, 5, 7–9, 11–12, 14, 20, 22, 29, 32–4, 40, 46, 56, 90, 106; *Plain of Mordor* 10; map(s) of Mordor in Elrond's house 25. 32–3. See *Black Land.*

Mordor (X) 350

Mordor (XI) 370, 390

Mordor (XII) 83, 153, 168–9, 174, 176, 178–9, 182, 191, 196, 200–2, 204, 206, 215, 217, 226, 231–3, 240–3, 251–2, 256, 265–7, 283, 305, 315, 324, 384, 390

Mordu (?) (VIII) Sauron's messenger. 256, 267

Moreldar (V) Dark-elves. 405

Morennyn (VIII) See *Morannon.*

Morgai (VIII) 438

Morgai (IXa) The inner ridge beyond the Ephel Dúath. 14, 22, 26, 31, 34–6; unnamed 9–11, 25. *The Trough* below the Morgai 10–11; the bridge over 33, 35

Morghul, Morgul (VIII) See *Minas Morghul.*

Morgoth (I) 26, 135, 222, 242–3

Morgoth (II) 44, 58, 62, 67–8, 120, 124, 134, 138, 143, 204, 206, 210–11, 213, 328; see especially 67, and see *Belcha, Melko(r).*

Morgoth (III) *Passim.* Other names: see *Bauglir, Belcha, Belegor, Melegor, Melko, Delu-Morgoth, Lord of Hell,* and under *Gods.*

Morgoth (IV) *Passim.* See *Melko(r); Belcha, Bauglir, Moeleg; Demon of Dark, the Enemy.*

Morgoth (V) 9–33 *passim,* 64–6, 68–9, 73–4, 110–44 *passim,* 150–

3, 174- 9, 187, 190, 194, 206, 208, 211–13, 216, 228–97 and 307–38 *passim*, 405–6; the name *Morgoth* 206, *365*, *373*, 406; *Mountains of Morgoth* 127. Called *the Strong, the Eldest Power, the Master* 67–8, *the Black God* 206, *King of the World* 233; and see *Alkar, Bauglir, the Enemy, Melko(r), the Shadow*.

Morgoth (VI) 122, 187–8, 218, 270

Morgoth (VII) 122, 142, 175, 256, 260, 454

Morgoth (VIII) 168; *the Dark Power of the North* 161

Morgoth (IXa) 44–5

Morgoth (IXb) 317, 331–2, 334–6, 339, 354, 406, 412; O.E. *Malscor* 317

Morgoth (X) 48, 76, 78, 108–12, 114–15, 119–25, 130–1, 133–5, 137, 146, 156, 186, 192–5, 198–9, 223–4, 240, 268, 294–8, 341, 350, 371–3, 385, 394–7, 399–409, 411, 416–23; *the Morgoth* 310, 312–13, 322, 390–1, 393; *Moringotto* 194, 294, *Moriñgotho* 294; Melkor so first named by Fëanor 108, 186, 194, 294. See *(The) Black Foe, (The) Enemy, King of the World*.

Morgoth (XI) 14–19, 22, 29–33, 35–42, 45–6, 50, 52–6, 58–9, 61–6, 68–80, 82–5, 89, 91, 99, 105, 109–11, 113–21, 127–8, 134–7, 141–2, 146, 149–50, 159, 166–70, 176–7, 195, 200, 203–4, 220–1, 223, 239–40, 242, 247, 251–9, 261, 264, 266, 272, 275, 281, 296, 298–302, 306–7, 310, 320–1, 328, 333–4, 343–8, 353, 355, 376, 381, 383–6, 391, 397, 408–9, 411, 415, 418–19; the Eye of Morgoth 259. See *Bauglir, Dark Foe*.

Morgoth (XII) 65, 142–4, 163, 166, 168, 173, 181–2, 185, 256, 275, 302–7, 312, 314, 323, 325, 327, 329, 336, 338, 342, 344, 357–9, 361–2, 366, 370–5, 404; *the Black Enemy* 358. See *Melkor*.

Morgul (XII) See *Minas Morgul*.

Morgulduin (VIII) Stream flowing through Imlad Morghul. 180. See *Duin Morghul, Ithilduin*.

Morgul-knife (VI) 211, 363

Moria (II) 329

Moria (III) 158, 316

Moria (V) 336, 345, 400. See *Khazaddûm*.

Moria (VI) (including references to *the Mines of Moria, the Mines*) 173, 213, 226, 381–2, 391, 398, 403, 410–1l, 429–31, 435, 437–8, 440, 442–6, 448–9, 451, 454–5, 457–8, 460–6; *Lord of Moria* 449 (Durin), 443, 460, 467 (Balin). See *East Gate(s), West Gate(s), of Moria*

Moria (VII) (including references to *the Mines of Moria, the Mines*) 5,

10, 16, 67, 115, 117, 125, 129, 141–3, 155–6, 158, 160–1, 166–8, 173, 175, 178–9, 181, 183–6, 188, 190, 192, 199–202, 204, 206, 215, 218–21, 224, 227–8, 235, 240, 247, 250, 257, 263–4, 266, 278, 280, 333, 354, 367–9, 378–9, 381, 401, 422, 430, 432, 446, 452, 455–8. *Black Gulf, Black Pit* 166, 173. *Lords of Moria* 178; *Runes of Moria* 200, 455. See *Balin; Khazad-dûm; Mithril; Mountains of Moria.*

Moria (VII) Gates (Doors) of Moria: 184–5, 204, 206, 219, 372. In the West: 178, 181, 215; two entrances, the Elven-door and the Dwarven-door 178, 190–1, 201, 204–5. In the East: 143, 178, 191, 199, 201, 204, 219–22, 238, 372; *Dimrill Gate* 183; *Great Gate(s)* 191, 199. Design on the West Gate 180–1, 187–8. For the Bridge in Moria see *Khazad-dûm. Deep(s) of Moria* 191–2, 194, 211, 432; *Third Deep* 191, 201, 459

Moria (VIII) 17, 20, 214; *the Bridge of Moria* 285 Mornennyn See *Morannon.*

Moria (IXa) 74, 122, 135, *Mines of Moria* 122; *Gates of Moria* 70; *Mountains of Moria* 70, 74

Moria (XI) 201–2, 206, 209

Moria (XII) 24, 45, 58, 76, 78–9, 173–4, 179, 184–5, 221, 223, 227, 233, 235, 237, 240, 246, 249–50, 261, 275–9, 281, 286, 293, 297, 300, 302, 304–5, 318–21; *Gates of Moria* (XII) 79, 179, 237, 278, 319; *Lord(s) of* ~ 300, 319. See *Dwarrowdelf, Khazad-dûm; mithril.*

Moria-silver (VI) (391), 458, 465–6; *true-silver* 458. See *Erceleb, Ithil, Mithril.*

Morimor (V) Dark-elves. 197, 374 (cf. also *Dúrion, Dureðel, Duveledh* 'Dark-elf', *354, 374*)

Morinehtar (XII) One of the Blue Wizards. 384

Moriondë (V) Haven in the east of Númenor. 67, 74

Moriqendi (V) Dark-elves. 197, 374

Moriquendi (II) 'Elves of the Darkness'. 64

Moriquendi (X) 163, 169–70, 173. See *Dark-elves.*

Moriquendi (XI) 'Dark-elves', 'Elves of the Dark' (8). 8–9, 19, 361, 373, 376–7, 380–1, 384, 417; Telerin *Moripendi* 362, 375. See *Morben.*

Moritarnon (I) 'The Door of Night'. 215, 222; *Móritar* 222. See *Door of Night, Tarn Fui.*

Morleg (XI) Rejected name of Maeglin. 323–5, 332. See *Maeglin.*

Morlîn (XI) Rejected name of (1) Maeglin, 323; (2) the metal of Eöl, 322 (see *Galvorn*).

Mormacil (X) 'Blacksword', name of Túrin in Nargothrond. 216. (On the different forms of the name see the Index to Vol.IV, *Mormakil*.)

Mormael (V) 'Black-sword', name of Túrin in Nargothrond. 139–40 (see *371*)

Mormagli (II) 'Black Sword', Túrin (Gnomish). 84, 125. See *Mormakil, Mormegil*.

Mormakil (II) 'Black Sword', Túrin, said (84) to be one of the forms of the name among the Gnomes, though *makil* is an 'Eldar' form (I.259). 84, 86, 94, 112, 116, 118, 125, 128. See *Mormagli, Mormegil*.

Mormakil (IV) 'Black Sword', Túrin in Nargothrond. 29, 73, 184, 304–5, 313. *Mormakil* became the Quenya form (313); in addition successive Gnomish forms were *Mormagli* 184; *Mormaglir* 125, 128, 131, 184, 323 *Mormegil* 184, 304, 313, 323 *Mormael* 313, 323. See *Black Sword*.

Mormakil (XII) Túrin Turambar. 374

Mormegil (II) 'Black Sword', Túrin (later form of the name). 125, 128

Mormegil (XI) Name of Túrin in Nargothrond. 83–5, 89, 92–3, 138, 147–8, 256; *Mormael, Mormaglir* 138. See *(The) Black Sword*.

Mornedhel (XI) 'Dark-elf'. 377, 380, 409, 420

Mornië (I) The black ship that ferries the dead from Mandos. 77, 90, 92, 167, 170, 172

Morniento (I) Earlier name of the beaching-place of the ship Mornië. 170. (Replaced by *Emnon, Amnos*.) See *Hanstovánen*.

Morning Star (II) 266

Morning Star (IV) Eärendel bearing the Silmaril. 154, 196

Mornvenniath (VII) See *Black Mountains*.

Morris, William (IXb) 213; *News from Nowhere* 172, 213

Morthond, River (VII) Blackroot. (1) Earlier name of Silverlode. 166–7, 218, 222, 230–1, 235, 237. (2) River of Gondor. 310–12, 316. See *Blackroot*.

Morthond, River (VIII) 268, 296, 397, 409, 436–7, 439; *Morthond Vale, Vale of Morthond* (VIII) 254, 266, 287, (370), 397, 409; *meres of Morthond* 371. See *Blackroot, Imlad Morthond*.

Morthond, River (IXa) 16; *Morthond Vale, the Dale* 15–16; *source of Morthond* 16, *outflow of Morthond* 15–16

Morthond, River (XII) 313, 436

Morthu (VI) 'Black Thû', Sauron. 186, 188

Móru (I) The 'Primeval Night' personified in the great Spider. 151, 156, 160; *Muru* 160

Móru (II) The 'Primeval Night' personified in the Great Spider. 286

Morwë (X) Leader of a kindred of the Avari. 81, 88, 168

Morwë (XI) Leader of a kindred of the Avari. 418

Morwen (II) 120–1, 126–8, 135, 139. (Replaced *Mavwin*.)

Morwen (III) Wife of Húrin. 5, 22–7, 92–4, 104–6, 111–16, 126–7; *Morwen Eledhwen* 92. Earlier forms *Mavwin* 5, 22–5, *Mailwin* 22, *Morwin* 5, 8–14, 16–18, 22–3, 27

Morwen (IV) 23–4, 28, 30, 32, (58), 60, 105, 122–3, 125–8, 131–2, 176, 182–3, 185, 188, 199, 221–2, 229, 298–9, 301, 303–6, 311, 315–16, 319, 322–3, 325. (Replaced *Mavwin*.) See *Eledwen*, *Elfsheen*.

Morwen (V) Mother of Túrin and Nienor. 131, 133, 135, 137–41, 151, 276, 282, 289, 316–20, 322, 398. See *Eledwen*.

Morwen (XI) 51, 56, 61, 64, 78–9, 81, 85, 87–8, 90, 93–5, 102, 124, 126, 129, 137, (142)-3, 145, 148–50, 161–4, 181, *182, 224, 230–1, 234, 251–2, 254, 256–9, 268, 273–4, 291, 294–6, 298–300, 302, 306, 409, 420; *the Grey Lady* 296. See *Edhelwen*; *Tol Morwen*.

Morwen (XII) (1) Wife of Húrin of Dor-lómin. 374; old name *Mavwin* 374. (2) Sister of Orodreth Steward of Gondor. 205, 219–20. (3) Daughter of Húrin of the Keys. 271

Morwinyon (I) Arcturus. 114, 133, 182, 200

Mound of Avarice (II) See *Cûm an-Idrisaith*.

Mound of Avarice (IV) See *Cûm an-Idrisaith* and *Cûm-nan-Arasaith*; *Mound of Slain* see *Hill of Slain*.

Mound of Slain (III) (58–9), 87. See *Hill of Death*.

Mound of Slain (V) 137, 147. See *Amon Dengin*, *Cûm-na-Dengin*, *Hauð-na-Dengin*.

Mound of the First Sorrow (I) See *Cûm a Gumlaith*.

Mound of the Slain (XI) See *Hill of Slain*.

Mount Doom (VII) 209, 343–5, 348–9, 373; spelt *Mount Dûm* 373. See *Amon Amarth*.

Mount Doom (VIII) 118, 190, 219, 268, 433; spelt *Mount Dûm* 118. See *Orodruin*.

Mount Doom (IXa) 3–4, 8, 10–11, 21, 33–9, 41; spelt *Mount Dûm* 8, 14; described 39–41. See *Fiery Mountain*, *Orodruin*.

Mount Doom (IXb) In *The Death of St. Brendan*. 292, 295

Mount Doom (XII) 176, 206, 240, 242, 267. See *Amon Amarth*.

Mount Fang (VII) Orthanc. 419

Mount Fang (VIII) Translation of Elvish *Orthanc*. 35

Mountain of Fire (VII) See *Fiery Mountain*.

Mountain of Fire (XII) 174, 178. See *Orodruin*.

Mountain of Ilúvatar (V) The mountain in the midst of Númenor. 27, 30; *the Mountain* 67–8; *Mountain of Númenor* 77. See *Meneltarma*.

Mountain of Ilúvatar (IXb) See *Ilúvatar*.

Mountain of Manwë (V) See *Manwë*.

Mountain of Manwë (X) Taniquetil. 178

Mountain of the World (I) See *Taniquetil*.

Mountain of the World (II) See *Taniquetil*.

Mountains of Aman (V) See *Aman*; *Mountains of Iron, of Melko, of Morgoth*, see *Iron Mountains*; *Mountains of Mithrim*, see *Mithrim*; *Mountains of Ossiriand*, see *Ossiriand*; *Mountains of Shadow*, see *Shadowy Mountains*.

Mountains of Aman (X) The Pelóri. 54, 70, 154, 174, 190; *Mountains of Defence* 132; *Mountains of the Gods*, see *Gods*; *Mountains of Valinor* 7, 18, 33, 174. For references to *the Mountains* see *Pelóri*.

Mountains of Aman, ~ of Valinor (XI) See *Aman, Valinor, Pelóri*; ~ *of Mist*, see *Misty Mountains*; ~ *of Mithrim*, see *Mithrim*; ~ *of Ossiriand*, see *Ossiriand*.

Mountains of Darkness (II) =*Mountains of Iron*. 162

Mountains of Iron (I) See *Iron Mountains*.

Mountains of Iron (II) See *Iron Mountains*.

Mountains of Iron (III) See *Iron Mountains*.

Mountains of Iron (IV) See *Iron Mountains*; *Mountains of Mithrim*, see *Mithrim*; *Mountains of Morgoth*, see *Iron Mountains*; *Mountains of Shadow*, see *Shadowy Mountains*.

Mountains of Lindon (X) 93. See *Blue Mountains*.

Mountains of Lune (VII) See *Lhûn*.

Mountains of Lune (XII) See *Lune*.

Mountains of Mirkwood (VII) 119

Mountains of Mondor (VII) 299, 327, 374; *mountain-fences of Mordor* 450

Mountains of Moria (VI) 441

Mountains of Moria (VII) 166–7, 174, (203, 219), 237, 288, 306

Mountains of Night (II) The mountains on which grew Taurfuin, the Forest of Night. 20, 46, 62

Mountains of Shadow (I) Ered Wethrin. 112, 158–9, 242

Mountains of Shadow (II) 61–2, 122, 205, 217. See *Ered Wethrin*.

Mountains of Shadow (III) See *Shadowy Mountains*.

Mountains of Shadow (VII) West-fences of Mordor. (Including references to *the Mountains*) 144–5, 169, 310, 312, 322, 333, 337, 343, 348–9, 374. See *Eredwethion* (2).

Mountains of Shadow (VIII) 106, 113, 115–16, 122, 182, 317; *the mountains* 112, 118, 124–5, 128–9, 131, 137, 173, 176, 180, 184, 187, 194, 207, 215, 292, 294. See *Ephel Dúath*.

Mountains of Shadow (X) 297. See *Eryd Wethrin*.

Mountains of Shadow (XI) 272; *Shadowy Mountains* 128, 146; *the mountains* 18, 31, 34, 52, 73, 77, 79, 91, 257, 260–1. See *Eryd Wethrin*.

Mountains of Terror (II) See *Ered Gorgoroth*.

Mountains of Terror (III) Ered Gorgoroth. 170–1, 183, 208, 234, 314, 350–1

Mountains of Terror (IV) 55, 115 (referred to as *the Shadowy Mountains* 24, *the Mountains of Shadow* 109).

Mountains of Terror (V) Ered Orgoroth. 298

Mountains of Terror (VII) North of Doriath. 145, 331. See *Ered Orgoroth*.

Mountains of Terror (VIII) North of Doriath. 184, 187

Mountains of Terror (XI) 15, 111, 194, 222, 332(-3). See *Eryd Gorgoroth*.

Mountains of the East (II) 6, 295, 300, 311

Mountains of the East (IV) *242 (Walls of the Sun); 256 (Red Mountains).

Mountains of the East (X) 72, 77. See *Orokarni*.

Mountains of the Gods, Mountains of the West (V) See *Mountains of Valinor*.

Mountains of the North (III) The Iron Mountains. 59, (101)

Mountains of the South (VII) See *Black Mountains*.

Mountains of the Sun (IV) See *Walls of the Sun*.

Mountains of the West (III) The Mountains of Valinor. 74

Mountains of the West (VII) The Mountains of Valinor. 263

Mountains of the Wind (IV) 239, *249, 257

Mountains of the Wind (V) 248

Mountains of Turgon (IV) See *Turgon*.

Mountains of Valinor (I) 68, 70, 74–7, 82–3, 85, 87, 93, 100, 118, 122, 125–6, 135, 137, 141, 144–7, 149, 154–5, 157–8, 162, 167, 169, 172, 177, 190, 194, 199, 209–10, 220, 223, 226

Mountains of Valinor (II) 161, 171, 285, 320, 325

Mountains of Valinor (IV) 12–14, 16, 20, 41, 45, 50, 73–4, 80, 82, 86–7, 98, 165, 198, 236–9, *249, 253, 255, 257, 260, 263, (O.E. *miclebeorgas* 285); *Mountains of the Gods* 87, 91; *Mountains of the West* 20, *242; *hills of Valinor* 3

Mountains of Valinor (V) 207, 209, 211, 221–2, 230, 303, 333; (unnamed) 111–12, 114, 121, 206, 223, 242, 245; *Mountains of the Gods* 222, 300; *Mountains of the West* 64; *encircling mountains* 222; *mountains of defence* 241

Mountains of Valinor (VII) See *Valinor.*

Mouth of Manwë The (X) Mandos. 255, and see 339.

Much Hemlock (VI) 278, 284, 295. (Replaced by *Michel Delving.*)

Much Wenlock, Shropshire (VI) 278

Mugwort (VI) Family name in Bree. 137. *Mr. Mugwort* 141

Mugwort (VIII) Family name in Bree. 44

Mugworth (VIII) Village in the Southfarthing. 36, 44

Múlanoldorin (V) Language of the slave-Noldor. 177, 189, *373*

Mulkhêr (IXb) 'Lord of Darkness' (358), Morgoth. 358–61, 363–4, 367–8, 384, 390, 411; *Arûn-Mulkhêr* 367, 384; *offspring of Mulkêr* 362

Mull (Island of) (IXb) Argyll, Scotland. 267

Mûmak (VIII) Elephant of the Southrons. 136; plural *Mûmakil* 370. Earlier forms *Múmar, Múmund, Mâmuk* 136. See *Andabund, Oliphaunt.*

múmak (XII) Great elephant of the Harad. 79

Mundbeong (VII) Name in Rohan of Minas Tirith (in LR *Mundburg*). 449. Other suggested names *Heatorras, G(i)emenburg* 449

Mundbeorg (VIII) Name in Rohan of Minas Tirith. 348, 355; *Mundberg* 356, 371; later name *Mundburg* 355–6; alliterative song *The Mounds of Mundburg* 352, 371, 373

Mundburg (IXa) Name in Rohan of Minas Tirith, earlier name *Mundberg.* 73

Mundburg, Mundberg (XII) Minas Tirith. 274

Murmenalda (I) The vale in which Men first awoke. 233, 235–7; *Vale of Sleep* 233, *Slumbrous Dale* 235

Murmenalda (IV) The vale in which Men first awoke. 171

Murmuran (I) The dwelling of Lórien in Valinor. 74, 100

Muru (I) See *Móru.*

Music of the Ainur (I) (not including references to the Tale itself) 49, 56, 59–63, 65, 74, 92, 107, 144, 150, 159, 180, 209, 219, 226;

the Music of Ilúvatar 220, the Great Music 227. See Ainulindalë.

Music of the Ainur (II) (not including references to the Tale) 146, 163, 209. See Ainulindalë.

Music of the Ainur (IV) 42. (For references to the Tale see Lost Tales.)

Music of the Ainur (V) 155–60, 163–4, 204, 207, 212, 217, 232, 247; Second Music of the Ainur 157, 163, 166

Music of the Ainur (X) (not as title; including references to the Music) 9–12, 15, 21–4, 27, 31, 36, (40), 68, 77, 144, (160), 166, 275, 282, 318–19, 327, 336, 338, 351–2, 358, 363, 388–9, 395, 399, 401–2, 405, 408–9, 425; Music of Eru (99), 327, (351); Great Music 8–9, 14, 144, 336; Song of the Ainur 144, 149, the Song 379, the Great Song 378–9; Second Music of the Ainur 21, 37, 43. See Ainulindalë, Great Theme, Themes.

Music (of the Ainur), The (XI) 341

Music of the Ainur (XII) 365, (413, 415), 420

Musicians of the Shore (V) A name of the Teleri. 215, 403. See Soloneldi.

Muzgash (IXa) Orc of the Tower of Kirith Ungol; earlier name Ghash. 26

Naglath Morn (VIII) The Teeth of Mordor. 122, 137. Cf. Kirith Naglath, and see Nelig Myrn, Teeth of Mordor.

Naglath Morn, Nelig Myrn (IXa) The Teeth of Mordor. 28

Naglur-Danlo (VIII) Orc of the Tower of Kirith Ungol. 212, 225

Nahar (III) Oromë's horse. (186, 198), 356

Nahar (X) Oromë's horse. (35), 70, 72–3, 76, 79, 82, 87, 101, 162, 203, 281, 289

Nahar (XI) Oromë's horse. 14, 401 (etymology).

Naimi (II) Ælfwine's wife, Elf of Tol Eressëa. 290–1, 323, 330. See Eädgifu (1).

Náin (VII) (1) Náin I, son of Durin. 143. (2) Father of Dáin. 143

Náin (XII) (1) Náin I. Slain by the Balrog of Moria. 252, 275, 277, 288. (2) Náin II. Grandfather of Thrór. 276, 284, 288. (3) Náin father of Dáin Ironfoot. 277

Naira (X) The Sun. 198

Naith (of Lórien) (VII) Of varying application (see 287–8). 244, 267–8, 280, 287–8

Naith of Lothlórien (V) 345, 387

Náli (VII) Companion of Balin in Moria. 191, 204

Namárië (I) (poem) 161

Namárië (VII) 284–5

Namárië (XI) 419

Nameless Land (VIII) Mordor. 196, 400

Nameless Land, The (V) (poem) 82, 98–100

Nameless, The (X) Andreth's reference to Melkor. 312, 320–1

Naming of the Eldar (X) 214–17, 229–30, 263

Námo (X) 'The Judge', true name of Mandos; often *Námo Mandos*. 145, 148–51, 202–3, 207, 219, 225–6, 246, 254–5, 259, 403. See *Nurufantur, Núr.*

Námo (XI) 'Judge', true name of the Vala Mandos. 402

Nan (II) A Giant. 19, 46, 67–8

Nan (III) A Giant. 205, 208; *Nann* 208

Nan Dumgorthin (II) 'The Land of the Dark Idols'. 35, 62, 68; *Nan Dungorthin* 62

Nan Dungortheb (I) 161

Nan Dungortheb (II) 'The Valley of Dreadful Death'. 62–3

Nan Dungortheb (X) 'Valley of Dreadful Death' (297). 127, 297, 299; earlier *Nan Dungorthin* 109, 123, 127, 299, original form *Nan Dumgorthin* 299

Nan Dungortheb (XI) 110, 180, *183, 197, 319, 333, *Dungortheb* 329; earlier *Nan Dungorthin* 47, 61, 64, 110, 122, 180, 194, 197, *Dungorthin* 319, 328–9

Nan Dungorthin (III) 59, 87, 89, 148, 312, 314 *Dungorthin* 148, 332, 348, 350; earlier form *Nan Dumgorthin* 87, 314; later form *Dungortheb* 348. See *Nan Orwen.*

Nan Dungorthin (IV) 222, 334; *Dungorthin* 222; later form *Nan Dungortheb* 222

Nan Elmoth (II) 248

Nan Elmoth (III) 346–7, 349–50. See *Glad-uial, Gilammoth.*

Nan Elmoth (X) 83–4, 89, 91, 172–3

Nan Elmoth (XI) 6–7, 9, 21, 47–8, 106, 122, *183, 218, 321–3, 326–30, 333–6; *Elmoth* 327, 332, 335. See *Gladuial.*

Nan Elmoth (XII) Forest in Beleriand. 328, 330

Nan Gurunír (VII) Valley of Saruman. 420

Nan Gurunir (VIII) The Wizard's Vale. 4–8, 26, 29, 31, 38, 43, 50–1, 59, 70, 72; later form *Nan Curunír* 41. See *(The) Wizard's Vale.*

Nan Gurunir (IXa) The Wizard's Vale; later form *Nan Curunír*. 136

Nan Orwen (III) Transient substitution for *Dungorthin*. 148.

Nan Tathren (VII) Land of Willows. 95. Cf. *Weepingwillow Pool(s)* 91, 94–5, 97. See *Tasarinan.*

Nan Tathren (XI) The Land of Willows. 80, 116, 180, *184; earlier *Nan Tathrin* 90, 180

Nan Tathrin (IV) 35, 65, 141, 145, 195, 225–6, 296, 305, 329, 339, 341; *Dor Tathrin* 214–15; O.E. *Wiligwangas* (*Wiligléagas*) 339–41. See *Land of Willows*.

Nandini (I) Fays of the valleys. 66

Nandor (X) The people of Dân (Nano), who abandoned the Great March; the Green-elves of Ossiriand. 83, 89, 102, 164, 169–71; *Nandar* 169. See *Danas, Green-elves*.

Nandor (XI) The people of Lenwë (Dân) who abandoned the Great March; the Green-elves of Ossiriand. 13, 34, 109–10, 112, 126, 195, 218, 377, 381, 384–6, 409, 412, 418–19; origin of the name 109, 412. See *Danwaith*.

Nandor (XII) 76, 364; *Nandorin* (language) 368. See *Danians, Green-elves*.

Nandorin (II) 122

Nandorin (VII) Green-elven. 292

Nandorin (XI) (of language) 390, 407, 411–12; (with other reference) 412

Nanduhiriath (VI) Dimrill-dale. 433. *Nanduhirion* 433

Nanduhirion (VII) Dimrill Dale. 166, 174; earlier form *Nanduhiniath* 174

Nanduhirion, Battle of (XII) 237, 281. See *Azanulbizar, Dimrill Dale*.

Nan-dungorthin (V) 261, 267, *355*, 374, 377 (also *Nan Dongoroth, Nann Orothvor*); *Dungorthin* 299; later form *Dungortheb* 299

Nan-eregdos (VII) See *Eregion*.

Nano (X) Leader of the Nandor (Dân). 83, 89, 169

Nan-tathren (II) 140, 214. See *Land of Willows, Tasarinan*.

Nan-tathren (V) 145, 261, 267, *374*, *391*; earlier form *Nan-tathrin* 126, 140, 145, 267. See *Land of Willows*.

Nan-Tathrin (III) The Land of Willows. 61, 89; *Nantathrin* 89. See *Dor-tathrin, Tasarinan*.

Nar (VI) One of the Dwarves who accompanied Bilbo from Bag End. 238, 240, 315

Nár (XII) (1) Brother of Dáin I. 276–7, 279. (Replaced by *Borin*.) (2) Companion of Thrór to Moria. 276, (278)

Narag-zâram (VI) Dwarvish name, probable origin of *Helevorn*. 466

Narch Udûn (VIII) Region behind the Morannon (later *Udûn*). 438

Narch, The (IXa) Original name of the vale of Udûn. 33–4, 41, 51; the *Narch-line* 34

Narchost (IXa) The westward(?) of the Towers of the Teeth. 23. (Replaced *Nargos*.)

Nardol (VIII) The fifth (or fourth, see 344) beacon in Anórien. 233, 344, 349

Nardol (XI) (1) Beacon-hill in Anórien. 187. (2) *Nardol* and *Amon Narðol*, see *Amon Rûdh*.

Narfi (VI) Dwarf, maker of the West Doors of Moria. 449, 463

Narghil (Nargil) (VII) *Pass* In the southern mountains of Mordor. 310

Nargil (III) Unknown; named in Beleg's 'whetting spell'. 45, 49, 54. See *Loruin*.

Nargil Pass (VIII) In the southern mountains of Mordor. 237, 265; *Narghil Pass* 265; *Nargul Pass* (VIII) 243–4, 265

Nargos (VII) Western guard-tower in Kirith Ungol. 344, 349. See *Gongos*.

Nargos (IXa) Western guard-tower of Kirith Ungol as the main pass into Mordor, 28; one of the Towers of the Teeth, 20, 28 (replaced by *Narchost*).

Nargothrond (I) 270

Nargothrond (II) 53–4, 56, 61, 123–6, 128–9, 131, 135, 137, 140-I, 205, 208, 245–6, 251; see especially 123–4

Nargothrond (III) 36, 38, 51, 53, 55, 58, 61–2, 64–6, 69, 74, 80, 83– 8, 90–3, 151, 171, 191, 195, 213–15, 217–18, 220–1, 223–4, 229, 231, 233–4, 237, 240–7, 257, 260–1, 268, 270–4, 287, 310– 13, 321–2, 335, 351, 358–9. *Winter comes to Nargothrond* (poem) 128–9. See *Hlýdingaburg*.

Nargothrond (IV) 23–7, 29–32, 35, 54–6, 59–61, 106, 109–12, 114, 116–17, 119, 121, 125–9, 131–2, 137–8, 140, 173, 176, 179– 81, 184, 187–9, 192, 210, 219, 224–7, 229, 279, 299–306, 310– 1l, 315–16, 318–20, 322–4, 327, 329–31, 334–5, 339 O.E. *Hlýd-ingaburg, Stángaldorburg,* 210; *the hidden city* 128; (written) characters of Nargothrond 31. Later story of its foundation 296, 316, 319, 329, 331, 339

Nargothrond (V) 18, 29, 126, 128–9, 133, 135–6, 138–41, 146–7, 150–2, 177, 189, 254, 257, 261–2, 264–6, 268, 272, 281, 283, 287–8, 290, 292, 301, 308–9, 312, *374, 379, 384,* 407; speech of Nargothrond 177

Nargothrond (VII) 454

Nargothrond (VIII) 372

Nargothrond (X) 104, 328, 336, 357–8

Nargothrond (XI) 5, 35, 38–9, 44, 52, 54, 62–3, 65–7, 70, 72–3, 77,

82–6, 89, 92–4, 97, 99, 101, 116–17, 120, 125, 129–31, 133–4, 137–47, 149–50, 152, 157, 162, 166, 168, 177–80, *184, 186, 189–90, 197–8, 203, 223, 242, 245, 251, 254–8, 260, 298–301, 306–7, 310–11, 313–14, 347, 350, 352, 354–5, 414 (etymology), 418; *Realm of Nargothrond* 85, *182, *184, 193. See *Nulukkhizdîn.*

Nargothrond (XII) 185, 317, 349–52, 358, 421

Nargûn (VI) Dwarvish name of Mordor. 466

Narmakil I (XII) Seventeenth King of Gondor. 198, 212–13, 259–60

Narmakil II (XII) Twenty-ninth King of Gondor. 200–1, 215–16

Narn i Chîn Húrin (XI) 103, 160. 251, 255, 311, 313–14; *Glaer nia ~* 160, 251; *(the Tale of) the Children of Húrin* 144, 160, 165, 313–14; the *Narn* (excluding detailed references to the last section 'NE', see 144–5) 112, 139–45, 148, 156, 164–5, 167–9, 174, 180, 186–7, 236, 241, 251, 267, 269, 303–4, 307, 309, 312–16, 354; the name and the verse-form 311, 313–15. See *Harinien* and 'Túrins Saga' in entry *Túrin.*

Narn i Hîn Húrin (II) 119–22, 124, 126–35, 142

Narn i Hîn Húrin (III) 5, 21, 24–8, 50–2, 88, 91–2, 126

Narn i Hîn Húrin (IV) 182–7, 324

Narn i Hîn Húrin (V) 316, 322, 374; see especially 322, and *i·Chúrinien, Lay of the Children of Húrin.*

Narodûm (VI) The Red Vale; early name of Dimrill-dale. 433

Narog (II) 123, 132, 135, 141, 244. See *Aros.*

Narog (III) 61–2, 65–9, 74–5, 79, 84–5, 87–9, 151, 213–15, 224, 234, 237; *the Gnome-river* 74; =‘torrent’ 61. Used of the realm of the Gnomes of Nargothrond (*Lord of Narog, folk of Narog,* etc.) 67, 69, 75, 213, 215, 217, 224, 228, 237, 260, 311; *Wards of Narog* 66, 88. *Storm over Narog* (poem) 128. See *Hlýda.*

Narog, River (IV) 23–4, 29–32, 59–60, 106, 124–5, 128–9, 141, 184–5, 211, 223, 225–6, 229, 259, 296, 305, 316, 319, 324, 329–30, 334; O.E. *Hýlda* 211, but *be Naroge stréame* 339; Narog as realm 29–30, 111, 116, 120, 125–6, 128, 226, 229, 306, *King of Narog* (Felagund) 330; the bridge over Narog at Nargothrond 32, 59, 128, 184–5, 305

Narog, River (V) 128, 139, 152, 254, 260–2, 268, 272, 320, 374; *caves of Narog* 126, 254; *realm of Narog* 139, (*Narogardh* 374); *King of Narog* (Felagund) 528

Narog, River (VI) In Beleriand. 433

Narog, River (VII) 287

Narog, River (XI) 15, 34–5, 38, 84–6, 88, 93, 116, 139–40, 150, 178, *182, *184, 193–4, 197, 228, 379, 414; *Caverns of Narog* 35, 116

Narog, River (XII) 350

Narosîr (VI) River Redway (later Silverlode). 433

Narothal (VI) 'Firefoot', earliest name of Gandalf's horse. 345, 347, 351

Narothal (VII) Gandalf's horse. 70. See *Galeroc*.

Narquelion (I) Autumn. 32; the second part of the poem *The Trees of Kortirion* 41

Narrow Crossing (III) From the Western Lands to the Great Lands. 31

Narrow Ice (VII) 100

Narrow Land (XI) The Pass of Sirion. 256–7, 261, 299, 301. See *Sirion*.

Narrows, The (IXa) The gap between the mountain-spurs enclosing the Narch. 33

Narsil (VIII) The sword of Elendil. 370, 372. See *Elendil*.

Narsil (XII) The sword of Elendil. 195, 227, 239. See *Elendil*.

Narsilion (IV) The Song of the Sun and Moon. 170

Narsilion (X) The Song of the Sun and Moon. 130, 372

Narthas (VII) The Gore of Lórien. 236, 244, 288

Narthseg (II) The Elf who betrayed Artanor to the Dwarves. 231, 243

Narvi (VII) Dwarf of Maria. 188; *Narfi* 188

Narya (IXa) One of the Three Rings of the Elves, borne by Gandalf. 111; *the Red Ring* 132, *the Third Ring* 109

Narya (XII) The Ring of Fire. 392

Naugladur (II) Lord of the Dwarves of Nogrod. 225, 230–8, 243, 246–7 (called *king* 225).

Naugladur (IV) Lord of the Dwarves of Nogrod. 62, 189

Nauglafring (II) The Necklace of the Dwarves (references include both names). 41, 59, 72, 136–7, 144, 221, 227–8, 231–2, 234–5, 237–41, 243, 245–7, 252–6, 259, 264; see especially 228

Nauglafring (IV) The Necklace of the Dwarves. 33, 38–9, 62–4, 68–9, 71, 74, 134–5, 149–50, 152–3, 155, 190, 197, 306–7, 313, 325; O.E. *Dweorgmene* 33, *sigelmǽrels* 211. See *Glingna Nauglir*, *Nauglamír*.

Nauglamír (IV) Later form for Nauglafring. 135, 155, 190, 313, 325

Nauglamír (V) 141–2, *373, 375* (also *Mír na Nauglin*, *Nauglavir*).

Nauglamír (XI) 244, 298, 345–7, 350–1, 353, 355. See *Necklace of the Dwarves*.

Nauglar (IV) The Dwarves. 311. Earlier forms *Nauglath* 175, *Nauglir* 104, 175, 311; final form *Naugrim* 175, 336

Nauglar, *Nauglath*, *Nauglir* (V) Earlier forms of the Elvish name of the Dwarves. 277, 405. See *Naugrim*.

Nauglath (I) Dwarves. 236

Nauglath (II) The Dwarves of Nogrod. 68, 136–7, 223–6, 229, 233–4, 243, 247, 328; see especially 247

Nauglath, *Nauglar*, *Nauglir* (XI) See *Naugrim*.

Nauglian (V) Languages of the Dwarves. 197, 277. See *Aulian*.

Naugrim (X) The Dwarves. 93, 102–3, 106; earlier *Nauglath* 102–3, 106. See *Nornwaith*. (X) [The entry *Naugrim* was omitted from the Index to Vol.V: see X.103.]

Naugrim (V) 273, 277, 405.

Naugrim (XI) 'The Stunted Folk', the Dwarves. 9–14, 16, 20, 45, 60, 70, 75, 107–9, 126, 134, 167, 201, 203–7, 209–10, 214, 322, 324, 388, 395, 408; earlier *Nauglath* 28, 107–8, 209, *Nauglar*, *Nauglir* 209; *Naug* 205, 209–10, 214, 388, 413–14; *Naug-neben* (Petty-dwarf), see *Nibin-noeg*.

Naugrim (XII) The Dwarves. 27, 174, 295. Earlier name *Nauglir* 23, 26

Nauko (XI) (Quenya) Dwarf; *Naukalië*, the people of the Dwarves. 388. See *Naugrim*.

Nautar (II) Apparently =*Nauglath*. 136, 247, 283, 285, 328

Návarot (XI) (Quenya) Nogrod. 389

Návatar (XII) A name of Aulë. 391

Nazgûl (II) 327

Nazgûl (VI) 434 (Winged Nazgûl).

Nazgûl (VII) 149, 213, 365, 389, 409, 451. See *Black Riders, the Nine, Ringwraiths, Vultures*.

Nazgûl (VIII) (All references are to the Winged Nazgûl) 48, 59, 71–3, 77, 109–10, 112, 118–20, 127, 141–2, 217, 219, 229, 231, (232, 249), 253, 255, 257, 260, 262–3, 267, 274–6, 283, 289, 320, 322, 324, 326, (329), 331, 335, 359–69, 372, 375, 380, 387, 430–1. *Nazgûl* used as if specifically =Ringwraith borne on wings 359, 362–4. See *Black Rider(s), Ringwraith(s)*.

Nazgûl (VIII) *King* or *Lord of the Nazgûl* 256, (260, 263), 267, 334, 336, 363, (365), 366–8, 372, (375), 377, (380), 390, 395. Prophecy concerning him 326, 334–5, 368, 390, 395. See *Angmar, Black Captain, Wizard King*.

Nazgûl (IXa) 4–8, 10, 13–14, 25, 38

Nazgûl (XII) 178, 217. See *Úlairi*.

Near Harad (VIII) See *Harad*.

Near Harad (XII) See *Harad*.

Neave, Jane (X) 360

Neben-naug, Nebin-nog (XI) See *Nibin noeg*.

Necklace of the Dwarves (I), *Tale of the* 231, 233; *Tale of the Naugla-fring* 204

Necklace of the Dwarves (II) See *Nauglafring*.

Necklace of the Dwarves (IV) (32), 33, 61, 63, 134, 211, 306–7, 326. See *Glingna Nauglir, Nauglafring, Nauglamír*.

Necklace of the Dwarves (V) 306; *Dwarf-necklace* 141. See *Nauglamír*.

Necklace of the Dwarves (XI) 244, 258, 297, 347; *the Necklace, Thingol's necklace* 350–1, 353; *Sigil Elu-naeth* 'Necklace of the Woe of Thingol' 258, 297. See *Nauglamír*.

Necromancer, The (II) 53–5

Necromancer, The (V) 23

Necromancer, The (VI) 42, 81, 85, 117, 131, 208, 211–12, 215, 218, 226, 253, 255, 258, 261, 264–5, 268, 270, 272, 311, 321, 363–4, 380, 399; *land of the Necromancer* 77, 85, 255, 269, 319; *Necromancer-rings* 225

Necromancer, The (VII) 48, 83, 147, 154–5, 159, 234, 244, 255

Necromancer, The (IXa) 3

Necromancers (X) 224

Nefantur (IV) Mandos. 78–9, 100, 166, 207–8. See *Vefántur*.

Nefantur Mandos. (V) 207. (Replaced by *Nurufantur*.)

Neldoreth (III) The forest forming the northern part of Doriath. 355, 360

Neldoreth (IV) The forest forming the northern part of Doriath. 278

Neldoreth (V) The forest forming the northern part of Doriath. 126, 148, 261, 376

Neldoreth (VII) (1) The northern forest of Doriath. 322. (2) Forest bordering the Sea of Rhûnaer. 307

Neldoreth (XI) The northern forest of Doriath. 7, 9, 11, 15–16, 61, 64, 106, 111, *183, 333, 355

Neldoreth, Forest of (VI) (1) The northern part of Doriath. 384. (2) Passing name for Fangorn. 384, 399

Neldorín (VI) See *Ilverin*.

Neleglos (VIII) 'The White Tooth', Minas Ithil. 106, 113; replaced *Neleg Thilim*, 106

Nelen, Nelen-Lórien (VII) The Gore of Lórien (and other applications). 231, 234, 236, 242–4, 261, 268, 288

Nelennas (VII) The Gore of Lórien. 236, 241–2, 245, 261, 288; name of Caras Galadon (?) 233, 242, 261

Nelig Myrn (VIII) The Teeth of Mordor. 113, 122, 128; *Nelig Morn* 113, 122, 128. See *Naglath Morn*.

Nellas (II) Elf of Doriath who bore witness at the trial of Túrin. 121

Nellas (III) Elf of Doriath who bore witness against Saeros in the trial of Túrin before Thingol. 50

Nellas (V) Elf of Doriath, friend of Túrin in his boyhood. 316

Nelyar (XI) Elves of the Third Clan (Lindar). 380–2, 420. See *Enel*.

Nemorie (III) Unknown. 122

Nen Cenednil (VII) Mirrormere. 184

Nen Cenedril (VI) Mirrormere. 466

Nen Echui (VII) (1) Cuiviénen. 184. (2) Mirrormere. 184; also *Echu-inen* 184

Nen fimred (VII) See *Entish Land(s)*.

Nen Girith (II) 'Shuddering Water', name given to the falls of Celebros in the Forest of Brethil. 130, 133–4, 140

Nen Girith (IV) 'Shuddering Water', name given to the falls of Silver Bowl Dimrost). 130, 186–7, 313

Nen Girith (XI) 'Shuddering Water', name given to the falls in the stream Celebros. 96–100, 151, 156–9, 163, 295–6, 306–7. See *Dimrost*.

Nen Hithoel (XII) Lake in Anduin. 259

Nen Lalaith (II) Stream rising under Amon Darthir in Ered Wethrin. 126

Nen Lalaith (XI) The stream that flowed past Húrin's house in Dorló-min. 181

Nen(e), River (I) 205–6

Nénar (X) Name of a bright star. 160. See pp. 434–6.

Nendili (XI) 'Water-lovers', the Lindar. 411

Nen-Echui (V) Waters of Awakening, *Kuiviénen*. 366, 376, 406

Nen-girith (V) 'Shuddering Water'. 140, *358*

Nenning (VI) (1) River in Beleriand (replacing Eglor). 433. (2) Passing name for the River Redway. 433

Nenning, River (IV) Later name for the Eldor (Eglor, Eglahir). 60, 227, 229

Nenning, River (XI) 39, 80, 84, 117–18, *182, 187. See *Eglor, Eglahir*.

Nenuial (VII) Lake beneath the Hills of Evendim. 301

Nenuial (IXa) The lake in Arnor beside which Annúminas was built. 76, 78. See *Evendim*.

Nenuial (XII) Lake in Arnor. 192. See *Evendim*.

Nen-uinel (VII) The great lake in Anduin north of Tol Brandir (in LR *Nen Hithoel*). 364; unnamed 361; another name *Kerin-muil* 364

Nenvithim (VII) See *Entish Land(s)*.

Nenya (IXa) One of the Three Rings of the Elves, borne by Galadriel. 112; *the White Ring* 132

Neorth (II) 'Lord of Waters', Ulmo. 331–2. (Cf. the Scandinavian god *Njörð*, especially associated with ships and the sea.)

Neorth (V) Early name of Ulmo. 97

Neowollond, -land (IXb) (O.E.) 'The Land that is fallen low' (315), *Atalante*. 258, 292, 313; *Niwelland* 292, 313–14.

Neptunians (IXb) Inhabitants of Neptune. 175

Nerdanel (IV) Wife of Fëanor. 212

Nerdanel (X) Wife of Fëanor, called 'the Wise' (274). 253, 272–4, 277, 279; rejected name *Istarnië* 273

Nerdanel (XII) Wife of Fëanor. 353–5, 365–6, 368

Nereb (III) Riddling reversal of *Beren* (replaced by *Wrath*, 233). 229, 233

Nermir (I) Fays of the meads. 66

Nerthus (V) 'Mother Earth', goddess worshipped in antiquity in the islands of the Baltic. 97

Nerwen(dë) (XII) See *Galadriel*.

Nerwet (VIII) Helm's Deep. 9, 23; *Nerwet Gate* 10. *Neolnerwet*, *Neolnearu* 23

Nessa (I) 75, 79, 89, 99, 117, 126, 154, 177, 209

Nessa (II) 10, 218, 240

Nessa (III) 127

Nessa (IV) 97, 263, 275, 285, 291

Nessa (V) Wife of Tulkas. 110, 206, 376–8 (also *Neth*, *Dineth*; Nessa was also named *Indis* ('bride'), 361, 375)

Nessa (X) Sister of Oromë and wife of Tulkas, called 'the Young' (65). 49, 53, 60–1, 65–6, 69, 146, 149, 150–1, 201; said to be a Maia 65. When replaced by Lëa as wife of Tulkas (see *Lila the Young*) called the *Ever-maid*, 66

Nessa (XI) Wife of the Vala Tulkas. 404, 416 (etymology).

Nether Darkness (XII) 149

Nevrast (II) 204, 208, 217

Nevrast (IV) 229, 259, 324

Nevrast (V) Later form for *Nivrost*. 256, 266

Nevrast (IXb) 316

Nevrast (XI) The region south of Drengist. 107, 179, 181, *182, 197, 200, 318, 396; *Nevrost* 318; translated 'Hither Shore' 197. Earlier form *Nivrost* 28, 35, 38, 40, 44–5, 80, 91, 104, 107, 120, 146, 178–9, 181, 192 (described), 195, 197–200, 256, 318; translated 'West Vale' 197. *The Marches of Nevrast (Nivrost)* 181, *182, 186

New Age, The (IXa) The Fourth Age. 68

New Arda (X) See *(The) Marring of Arda.*

New Era (XII) (of Calendar) 132–6, 202, 243

New Hebrides (IXb) 300

New Lands (IV) (after the Cataclysm) *246–7

New Lands (V) In the World Made Round. 16; *New World* 17, 28

New Lands (IXb) 387, 393, 395; *a New Land* (west of Eressëa) 403; *the New Land (Númenor)*, see *Vinya.* See *(The) World.*

New Year (IXa) (in Gondor) 45–6, 49, 59

New Year (XII) 121, 128–9, 133, 139; *New Year's Day* 121, 127, 129, *Yearsday* 121, 129

Neweg (V) 'Stunted', Gnomish name for the Dwarves. 274, 375

Neweg (XI) The Dwarves. 187, 209; *Neweglin*, Petty-dwarves, 187, *Neweglu* *182, 187

Nibin-noeg (XI) Petty-dwarves. 187, 420; *Nibennog, Nibinnogrim, Nebinnog, Neben-naug, Naug-neben, Niwennog* 187. See *Nogoth.*

Nibinnogs (XII) Petty-dwarves. 352

Nielíqui (I) Daughter of Oromë and Vána. 75, 89, 93

Nielluin (I) Sirius. 182, 192, 200; *Bee of Azure, Blue Bee*, 182, 200. See *Helluin.*

Nielluin (II) Sirius. 282. See *Bee of Azure.*

Nielthi (II) Handmaid of Gwendelin Queen of Artanor. 231–2

Nienna (I) See *Fui.*

Nienna (IV) 79, 81, 97, 167, 170, 207, 263, 265, 270, 275, 277, 285, 287, 289. See *Fui.*

Nienna (V) 110, 113, 206–9, 227, 241, 376; *Fui Nienna* 207, 382

Niënna (X) (also *Nienna*) 15, 49, 55, 62, 65–6, 68–9, 93, 104, 107, 129, 135–6, 146–7, 149, 151, 154, 186, 197–8, 201–4, 241–3, 245, 247–9, 253, 264, 273, 293, 295, 326–7, 389; called *queen of Shadow* 65

Nienor (II) Later form for *Nienóri* (see 118–19). 118–20, 128–30, 134–5

Nienor (III) Turin's sister. 9, 13–14, 22, 25, 93, 104, 113, 115; *Maid of Tears* 20; *Nienóri* 22

Nienor (IV) 28, 30, 32, 59, 60–1, 73, 123, 126, 128–32, 185–7, 205, 303, 305–6, 312, 322, 327. See *Níniel*.

Nienor (V) 138 ('the Sorrowful'), 139–40, 317 ('Mourning'), 358, 320 (cf. *Nuinoer, Nuinor* as the name of Túrin's sister, 375).

Nienor (X) Sister of Túrin. 374

Niënor (XI) 79, 81, 85, 87–8, 90, 93–5, 100–3, 137, 143, 148–50, 162–4, 234, 256–7, 290, 295, 298–300. See *Níniel*.

Nienóri (II) Daughter of Úrin and Mavwin. 71, 73–4, 87, 89, 91–9, 103, 109–1l, 113, 115–21, 127–31, 134, 137–9, 142, 144. (Replaced *Vainóni*.) See *Níniel*.

Nienóri (XII) Old form of Niënor, sister of Túrin Turambar. 374

Nieriltasinwa (II) The Battle of Unnumbered Tears. 84. See *Nínin-Udathriol*.

nifredil (VII) Pale green flower of Lothlórien. 233–4; flowers on the burial mounds at Eodoras 443

nifredil (VIII) Flower on the burial mounds at Edoras. 423

nifredil (XII) White flower of Lórien. 266

Night (X) (with reference to Melkor) 312, 376–7, 382; *Night of the Void* (28), 53, 58, *Outer Night* 383; *Lord, Realm, of Night* 219. See *Door (of Night), Walls of (the) Night*.

Nightfearers, The (V) An Elvish name for Men. 245

Nîlû (IXb) The Moon. 241, 306, 426; *Nil, Njâl* 306

Nimbrethil (VII) Birchwoods in Arvernien. 99, 103

Nimbrethil (XI) Birchwoods in Arvernien. *184, 190

Nimîr (XI) The Elves (Adunaic). 386; singular *Nimir* 419

Nimladel, Nimlorel, Nimlothel (VII) See *Nimrodel*.

Nimloth (V) 'Pale blossom', a Gnomish name of the White Tree of Valinor; afterwards the Tree of Númenor. 210–1l, *370*, (*378*). See *Ninquelótë*.

Nimloth (IXa) The White Tree of Valinor. 57–8. Afterwards the Tree of Númenor, 58

Nimloth (IXb) The White Tree of Númenor. 384–5

Nimloth (X) 'Pale blossom', a name of Telperion, and also of the White Tree of Númenor. 155, (176), 180

Nimloth (XI) Wife of Dior. 349–50. See *Elulin, Lindis*. (*Nimloth* was a name of Telperion, and the name of the White Tree of Númenor.)

Nimloth (XII) Name of the White Tree (1) of Eressëa 14 7–8; (2) of Númenor 147–8

Nimphelos (XI) A great pearl given by Thingol to the Lord of Belegost. 10, 108

Nimras (XI) See *Barad Nimras*.

Nimrî (IXb) 'The Shining Ones' (Eldar). 358–62, 364, 372, 376, 378–9, 385–6, 388, 405–7, 410; later form *Nimîr* 377–8, 388, 391, 394, 405, 407, 410, 413–14, 436

Nimrian (IXb) (tongue) 361, 375, 378–9, 396, 414–15, 419; *Nimrië* 'Nimrian tongue' 414. See *Avallonian, Eressëan, Quenya*.

Nimrodel (VII) (references both to the Elf of Lóriel and to the stream) 223, 228–31, 233, 235, 239–40, 258, 265, 292, 296, 354. Earlier names *Inglonel* 223, *Linglor* 222, 239; *Linglorel* 223–6, 237, 239; *Nimladel* 223, 239; *Nimlorel* 223, 239; *Nimlothel* 223; and see *Taiglin*. First mention of the stream, unnamed, 221; the bridge 221–2

Nimrodel (VIII) Elf of Lórien. 338

Nimrodel (XII) Elf of Lórien, beloved of Amroth. 36, 65, 82, 221–3, 294

Nimrûn, Towers of (IXb) Unknown. 381; earlier *Nimroth* 364, 381

Nimruzân (IXb) Elendil. 365, 369–70, 374–5, 382, 387, 389; his sons 374–5, 387. (Replaced by *Nimruzîr*.)

Nimruzîr (IXb) Elendil. 247, 290, 312, 389–90, 396; Lowdham so addressed by Jeremy 250, 252

Nimruzîr (XII) Elendil the Tall. 164

Nimruzîrim (XII) Elf-friends. 151, 164

Nindalf (VII) The Wetwang. 281, 283, 307, 3 15–16. Earlier name *Palath Nenui* 268, 287, 299, 313

Nindalf (VIII) The Wetwang. 112, 118.

Nine Rings (of Men) (VII) 149, 259

Nine Rings (of Men) (VIII) 335 (repossessed by the Nazgûl).

Nine Rings (VI) See *Rings of Men*. Nine Rings of the Elves, and of the Dwarves, 269

Nine Rings (XII) See *Rings of Power*.

Nine Walkers (VI) 409

Nine Walkers (XII) 242. See *Company of the Ring*.

Nine, The (VI) 270, 364; *the Nine Servants of the Lord of the Ring* 363; *the Nine Riders, Nine Ring-wraiths* 416

Nine, The (VII) (Riders, Ringwraiths) 50, 73, 116, 131–2, 135, 149, 151–2, 161–2, 177, 311. *Chief of the Nine*, see *Black Riders*.

Nineveh (II) See *Ninwë*

Niniach, Vale of (IV) Site of the Battle of Unnumbered Tears. 4–5

Níniel (II) 'Child of Tears', Turambar's name for Nienóri. 100–8, 110–12, 117, 129–35, 141–2

Níniel (III) Turambar's name for Nienor. 6, 96

Níniel (IV) 31, 61, 129–30, 186, 306; 'the Tearful' 31, 306, 'Tear-maiden' 129

Níniel (V) Name of Nienor. 140 ('the Tearful'), 376

Níniel (X) Name given to Nienor. 374

Níniel (XI) 'Tear-maiden', name of Niënor. 96–101, 103, 151–2, 156–61, 163–4, 234, 257, 300

Nínin Udathriol (III) 'Unnumbered Tears'. 21–2, 79. (Replaced by *Nínin Unothradin*.)

Nínin Unothradin (III) 'Unnumbered Tears'. 5–6, 11, 21, 79; *Nirnaithos Unothradin* 21, 79. (Replaced by *Nirnaith Únoth*.)

Nínin-Udathriol (II) The Battle of Unnumbered Tears. 84. See *Nieriltasinwa*.

Ninqendi (V) 'White-elves', a name of the Lindar. 403; cf. 215

Ninquelótë (V) A Quenya name of the White Tree of Valinor (Noldorin *Nimloth*). 209, 211, (*370, 378*)

Ninquelótë (IXa) The White Tree of Valinor (Sindarin *Nimloth*). 58

Ninquelótë (X) A name of Telperion. 155

Ninwë, Ninwi (II) Nineveh. 196, 203; *Nineveh* 203

niphredil (III) A white flower that bloomed in Doriath. 333, 349

Niphredil (V) A white flower. 102, *376, 378* (*nifredil* 'snowdrop').

niphredil (IXa) White flower of Lórien. (115), 124

niphredil (XI) A white flower in Doriath. 9, 107

Nirnaeth Arnoediad (I) 135. See *Battle of Unnumbered Tears*

Nirnaeth Arnoediad (II) The Battle of Unnumbered Tears. 208, 211

Nírnaeth Arnoediad (XI) (including references to *the Nírnaeth* used alone, and spellings *Nírnaith* and *Arnediad*; the element *Nír-* often without accent) 28, 71, 73, 77, 128, 133, 136, 165, 167, 236, 255, 262, 264, 266, 269, 281, 287, 303, 307, 312, 315, 377; *Dagor Arnediad* 22, 28; and cf. *Haudh-en-Nírnaeth* 169. See *Battle of Unnumbered Tears*.

Nirnaith Arnediad (III) 'Unnumbered Tears'. 5, 102–3; later form *the Nirnaeth*. 91. (Replaced *Nirnaith Ornoth*.)

Nirnaith Arnediad (IV) The Battle of Unnumbered Tears. 121, 312. Earlier names: *(Nirnaith) Únoth* 232–3, 312; *Ornoth* 232, 312; *Irnoth* 312; *Dirnoth* 312

Nirnaith Arnediad (V) The Battle of Unnumbered Tears. 147, 293, 310, 349, 375–6, 378, 399. See *Fourth Battle*.

Nirnaith Dirnoth (V) The Battle of Unnumbered Tears, 136, 147. (Replaced by *Nirnaith Arnediad*.)

Nirnaith Ornoth (III) 'Unnumbered Tears'. 5, 59, 61, 79, 84, 96, 102, 111. (Replaced by *Nirnaith Arnediad*.)

Nirnaith Únoth (III) 'Unnumbered Tears'. 5, 79–80, 84–5, 102, 123. (Replaced by *Nirnaith Ornoth*.)

Nivrim (II) Doriath beyond Sirion. 249

Nivrim (V) 'West-march', Doriath-beyond-Sirion. 261, 267, *378, 383* (cf. *Radhrim* 'East-march' of Doriath, *382*). See *Doriath*.

Nivrim (XI) 151, *182, 187; *the West-march of Doriath* 56, 150–1; *Doriath beyond Sirion* *182. Cf. *Radhrim*.

Nivrost (V) 'West Vale' (259), the land west of Dor-lómen and south of Drengist. 145–6, 239, 253–4, 256–61, 264, 266, 269, 271, *378* ('West-dales'), *384*; earlier form *Nivros* 145, 256, 266. See *Nevrast*.

Nivrost (XI) See *Nevrast*.

Nivrost (XII) Earlier form of Nevrast, region of Beleriand. 389

Niwennog (XI) Petty-dwarves. See *Nibin-noeg*.

Njörth (*Njörðr*) (V) Norse god, father of Freyr. 97

No Man's Land (VIII) 111–12; *Noman-lands* 112, 120, 139; *Field of Nomen's Land* 229; *Nomenlands* 270; *the desert* 430

Noad, Charles (XI) 157, 159

Noakes (VI) Hobbit family name. *Old Noakes (of Bywater)* 243–4, 249

Nob (VI) Servant at *The Prancing Pony*. 135–6, 141, 148, 150–1, 159, 164, 338–9; originally called *Lob* 141

Nob (VII) Servant at *The Prancing Pony*. 46, 48

Nob (IXa) Servant at *The Prancing Pony*. 76

Nobottle (VII) Village in the Westfarthing. 424

Nobottle (VIII) Village in the Westfarthing. 44

Nognith (XI) Petty-dwarves. 187

Nogoth (XI), plurals *Noegyth*, *Nogothrim* 'Stunted'; Dwarf, Dwarves. 388, 412, 419. *Nogoth niben*, Petty-dwarf, 388, plural *Noegyth niben* 408, 419–20; *Nogotheg* 388. See *Athrad i-Nogoth*.

Nogrod (II) City of the Nauglath. 224–6, 229–30, 232, 235–6, 238, 245, 247–9

Nogrod (III) City of the Dwarves. 32, 45, 52, 56, 111, 127, 264, 274, 303, 306, 343

Nogrod (IV) 32, 61–2, 103–4, 116, 132–3, 174–5, 178, 182, 188–9, 220, 232, 300, 331, 335

Nogrod (V) 'Dwarfmine'. 129, 134, 141, 274, 277–8, 303, 307, 322, 375. See *Khazaddûm*.

Nogrod (VI) Dwarf-city in Eredlindon. 466. See *Khazad-dûm*.

Nogrod (VII) Dwarf-city in Eredlindon. 301

Nogrod (XI) 'Hollowbold', city of the Dwarves in the Blue Mountains (for the different applications and relations of the name see 201–2, 209). 10, 12, 45, 75, 108–9, 134, *185, 201–2, 206, 208–9, 215, 322, 324, 326–7, 329, 335–6, 347, 350, 352–3, 389, 408, 414 (etymology). See *Tumunzahar; Návarot; Novrod, Grodnof, Bar-goll; Hollowbold*.

Nogrod (XII) Dwarf-city in Ered Lindon. 185, 275, 322

Noldolantë (IV) 'The Fall of the Noldor', lament made by Maglor. 170

Noldolanti (X) 'The Fall of the Noldor', Maglor's lament. 117, 121, 125

Noldoli (I) The Gnomes, the second kindred of the Elves. 21, 25–6, 43, 47–52, 58, 62, 94, 110, 115, 117, 119, 121–4, 126–8, 132, 134–5, 137–8, 140–52, 154, 156–65, 167–9, 171–3, 175–8, 181, 189, 192, 196, 198–9, 207–10, 215, 220, 223–4, 230–1, 238, 241–3. See *Gnomes, Noldor*.

Noldoli (II) See *Gnomes; Noldor*.

Noldoli (III) 21, 24, 55, 82, 84, 90, 138, 140, 146–7, 149, 282; singular *Noldo* 53, 160. See *Noldor, Gnomes*.

Noldoli (IV) 10, 13–15, 17–20, 37, 42, 44–5, 48, 50, 52–3, 57, 66–8, 77, 85–7, 89–92, 95, 98, 105–6, 155, 169, 176, 202, 211–12, 229, 264–8, 270–4, 278–9, 292, 314, 327, 336; O.E. *Noldelfe* (*Noldielfe*) 207, 282–3, 286–8, 338–9 (also *Noldena* gen. pl. 282–3), *Noldelfaracu* 'History of the Noldoli' 284, 288, 290; *Noldelfisc* (see *Gnomes*). See *Deep-elves, Gnomes, Noldor*.

Noldoli (V) 71, 107–8, 119, 121, 181, 182. (Replaced by *Noldor*; see 108, 121.)

Noldoli (XI) See *Noldor*.

Noldolindarin (V) See 192

Noldor (I) 21, 24, 43–4, 49–51, 132, 134–5, 138, 156, 158–60, 171, 173, 198, 223, 242–3, 245; form occurs in the original text 162, 169. Adjective *Noldorin* 43, 49–50, 62, 156, 171, 242

Noldor (II) 120, 123, 204, 206, 246; adjective *Noldorin* 204. (Replaced *Noldoli*.) See *Gate of the Noldor*.

Noldor (III) 104, 139, 284; *Doom of the Noldor* 248; adjective *Noldorin* 83, 137, 147, 350. See *Noldoli, Gnomes*.

Noldor (IV) 6, 44, 46, 49–50, 57, 66, 167, 170, 173–4, 180, 196, 277,

279–80, 292, 335; sing. *Noldo* 174; *curse of the Noldor* 66

Noldor (V) 55, 60, 107–8, 113–26 *passim*, 134, 146, 162, 169–78, 180, 182–4, 187, 190–5, 197, 214–58 *passim*, 266, 271, 275, 279, 285, 287–8, 296, 298, 305, 309, 313, 320, 323, 326, 330, 334, 346, 403; *Thrall-Noldor* 189. Etymology 377; other names 215, 403.

Noldor (VI) 71–2. See *Gnomes*, *Wise-elves*.

Noldor (VII) 167 (the Elven-wise), 263, 453–5

Noldor (VIII) 76, 159–61, 168–9

Noldor (IXb) 406, 411

Noldor (X) (and singular *Noldo*) 17, 19–20, 22, 24–5, 31, 34, 38, 41, 65, 82–97 *passim*, 99, 101–20, 122, 125–6, 128–30, 134, 137–8, 146, 155, 157, 159, 163–5, 168–9, 172, 174–89 *passim*, 192–6, 207–8, 211, 214–17, 225, 229–31, 236–8, 240–1, 249–50, 254, 256–7, 261–5, 268, 272–82, 287, 289, 305, 312, 340, 350, 375, 402, 407, 419–20; Old English *Noldelfe*, *Noldielfe* 168 (and see *Witan*).

Noldor (X) *The Doom of the Noldor (Doom of Mandos)* 108, 115, 117, 120, 122, 125, 266–7, 295; *The Prophecy of the North* 117, 125. On the spelling *Noldor* see 101, 350; etymology 350. See *Gnomes*, *White Lady of the Noldor*.

Noldor (XI) (and singular *Noldo*) 5–9, 12, 15–29, 31–48, 50, 52, 54–6, 59–60, 62, 70, 72–7, 79, 83, 90, 106–7, 113–16, 119, 121–2, 124–6, 136, 165–6, 168, 175–7, 181, 189, 192–5, 197, 200, 203–7, 210, 214–15, 219, 224, 239–40, 243, 246, 317–18, 321, 323, 327–8, 333–4, 338, 343, 364, 372–89, 393, 396–7, 399, 403–5, 409–12, 417, 420, 422–3; meaning of the name 383; earliest form *Noldoli* 244. See *Gódhel*, *Golodh*, *Goldo*; *Nómin*, *Samûri*; *Exiles*; *Second Clan*.

Noldor (XII) (and singular *Noldo*) 23, 30–1, 33, 36, 62–3, 65, 73–9, 143, 145–7, 163, 173–4, 185, 203, 293, 305, 312, 318, 324–5, 331–4, 336–45, 348, 350, 356, 358–62, 366, 370, 374, 378–80, 383, 386–90, 392, 401–2; *Flight of the Noldor* 361. See *Exiles*, *Gnomes*.

Noldórien (IV) Beleriand. 108, 174

Noldorin (I) Name of Salmar. 16, 22, 27, 66, 75, 80, 89, 93, 155

Noldorin (II) Name of Salmar. 154, 201, 219, 278–80

Noldorin (IV) (1) Name of Salmar. 68, 71. (2) Adjective to *Noldor*. 8, 46–7, 53, 58, 169, 284, 323; language of the Noldor 206

Noldorin (V) (of language) 172, 174, 177–8, 180, 186–96, 226, 279,

323, 338, 343, 345–7,404, 406, 412; *Ancient Noldorin*, see *Kor-noldorin*, *Korolambë*; *Exilic Noldorin* 243, 298, 322, 346–7; *Fading Noldorin* 189–90. (With other reference) 148, 175, 182, 188, 226, 256, 300

Noldorin (VI) (tongue) 186, 432, 435, 463. See *Gnomish*.

Noldorin (VII) (of language and writing) 173, 184, 238, 242, 287, 311, 322, 404, 453–7; with other reference 454

Noldorin (VIII) (language) 139, 169, 226

Noldorin (X) (of language) 7, 125, 136, 198 (see *Gnomish* with other reference 121, 125, 182, 195–6

Noldorin (XI) (of language) 20–8, 116, 120, 191, 201, 240, 315, 323, 337, 359, 361, 363, 373–4, 384, 391, 399–400, 407, 413, 417; (with other reference) 4, 26–8, 119, 136, 141, 188, 373, 379, 381–2, 385, 391, 394–7, 404, 406, 408, 412, 416–17

Noldorin (XII) (of language; in almost all cases =later Sindarin) 20, 22, 26, 30–4, 36, 39–41, 45, 52–5, 61–3, 65, 68–9, 74–5, 125, 130, 133, 135–6, 138, 146, 189, 193, 203, 217, 219, 228, 234, 371, 400, 404–5; Noldorin Quenya 331, 368, 400; (with other reference) 36, 40, 76–7, 79, 310, 317, 328, 331, 333, 339, 368, 379, 389, 401. See *Gnomish*.

Noldórinan (III) Rejected name for Beleriand. 160

Noldórinan (IV) Beleriand. 174. See *Noldórien*.

Noldorissa (II) Language of the Noldoli. 149, 216, 280

Nólemë (I) See *Finwë*.

Nólemë (II) See *Finwë Nólemë*.

Nolofinwë (X) Fingolfin. 230, 238–9, 252, 265

Nolofinwë (XII) See *Fingolfin*.

Nóm (IV) 'Wisdom', name given to Felagund in the language of Bëor's people. 175

Nóm (V) 'Wisdom', name given to Felagund in the language of Bëor's people. 279. See *Widris*.

Nóm (XI) 'Wisdom', name given to Felagund in the language of Bëor's people. 217. See *Sômar*, *Vidri*.

Nomenlands (VII) Also *Nomen's Land*, *Noman-land(s)*, *No Man's Land*. 281, 283, 310, 320–1, 325, 345, 352. See *Úvanwaith*.

Nómin (XI) 'The Wise', name given to the Noldor in the language of Bëor's people (rejected form *Nómil*). 217. See *Samûri*.

Noon, Fruit of (II) 271

Norbury (XII) 5, 7, 39, 47, 103; *Northburg*, *Northbury* 5; *Northworthy* 5, 7, 15, 225, 247. See *Fornost*.

Norbury of the Kings; *North Burg, Northbury* (VII) See *Fornost*.

Nordic (IXb) 174, 236; *Nordics* 222, 283

Norfolk (I) 206; *Norwich* 206

Nori (VI) Dwarf, companion of Thorin Oakenshield. 210

Nori (XII) Companion of Thorin Oakenshield. 279

Norman Keeps (IXb) An uninstructed barber. 230–1, 283

Normans (II) 301, 312, 323, 328

Norn-folk (XI) The Dwarves. 9, 107, 209. See *Norno, Nornwaith*.

Nornhabar (XI) 'Dwarrowdelf', city of the Dwarves in the Misty Mountains (replaced by *Hadhodrond*). 206, 209, 215, 419. See *Khazad-dûm; Casarrondo; Hadhodrond; Dwarrowdelf*.

Norno (XI) (Quenya) Dwarf; *Nornalië*, the people of the Dwarves. 388, 413. See *Norn-folk, Nornwaith, Nyrn*.

Nornorë (I) Herald of the Gods. 77, 93, 101–3, 115–18, 131, 144, 231

Nornorë (II) Herald of the Gods. 60

Nornwaith (X) The Dwarves. 93, 106. See *Naugrim*.

Nornwaith (XI) The Dwarves. 107, 209, 324. See *Norno, Norn-folk*.

Norse (V) 39, 77, 97; *Norsemen* 80–1; *Northmen* 91

Norse (XI) 303

Norse (XII) 27, 41, 54, 60, 70–1, 81, 278, 300, 322, 324

Norse, Old Norse (II) 125, 323, 330

Norse, Old Norse (IXb) 174, 214, 286, 295, 307, 410

North Downs (VII) 296, 301, 304

North Downs (IXa) In Arnor. 76

North Downs (XII) 313

North Gate (VIII) The Black Gate (Orc name). 213

North Haven (VII) 301, 423. See *Forlond*.

North Kingdom (VII) Arnor. 59; *Northland* 120

North Kingdom (VIII) The northern realm of the Dúnedain. 369, 395. See *Arnor*.

North Kingdom (XII) (Arnor and Arthedain) 38, 40, 121, 125, 127– 9, 171–2, 176, 186, 193, 195, 201, 208, 210, 227–8, 230–2, 254, 258, 268–9, 327, 330

North March (VIII) (of Gondor) 167

North Moor(s) (VI) 54, 66, (71), 72, 84, 254, 278, 319, 324, 386; *moors of the Northfarthing* 385, 423

North Road (VII) 164. See *Greenway*.

North Sea (I) 23–4; *Ocean of Almain* 205–6

North Sea (II) 290–1, 303, 307, 309

North Sea (V) 7, 91

North Sea (VII) (of Middle-earth) 301

North Stair (VII) Portage-way beside Rauros. 359, 370

North Wind (II) 261

North, The (IXa) 55–6, 58, 64–5, 68, 91, 122

North, The (IXb) 308, 334, 341, 344, 358, 362, 366, 383, 399, 402; *Isles of the North* 273; *North-seas* 273, *North-countries* 275, *Northern lands* 276

North, The (X) 7, 17–18, 25–7, 32–3, 38, 53, 67, 71, 74–5, 82, 88, 98, 108–10, 115, 118, 120, 153, 156, 159–61, 174, 177, 191, 197, 283–4, 291, 293, 295, 297, 307, 323, 376–8, 381–2, 388, 412; *the Northlands* 109, ~ *of Endar* 120, *the Northern Lands* 131, 163–4, *the Northern World* 296; *the North-west* (of Middle-earth) 400. *The Prophecy of the North*, see *Noldor*.

North, The (XI) 6, 12–15, 30–2, 34, 36, 46, 50, 57, 60, 79, 88, 90, 92, 109, 111–12, 117, 121, 124, 128, 176, 178, 200, 216, 220, 227, 263, 272, 297, 377, 410–11; *the northlands* 31, 33, 56; *the North-realm* (Hithlum) 287

North, The (XII) (References to Men of the North) 21, 30, 39, 64, 71, 303–5, 323–4, 328

Northburg, Northbury (XII) See *Norbury*

Northerland (VII) 296, 304. See *Forodwaith*.

Northern (XII) (of language) 21–2, 34–5, 49, 53–4, 60, 260, 296

Northern Ford (XI) (over Gelion) 335–6; *Little Ford* 335

Northern Line (XII) The Heirs of Isildur. 32, 64, 188–90, 192, 207–8, 216, 254–5, 257, 279

Northern Towers (IV) The Iron Mountains. 239

Northern Venture, A (II) (Anthology containing poems by J. R. R. Tolkien) 273

Northfarthing (VI) 298, 313, 385, 423

Northfarthing (IXa) 101

Northland (IV) 239, *249; *northern land* 238

Northlands (VIII) 371

Northmen (VII) Vikings. 106

Northmen (IXb) 276

Northmen (XII) 198–9, 205, 214, 230, 258–60

Northope (VI) Village north of Hobbiton Hill. 319, 385–7. (Replaced by *Overhill*.)

Northope (XII) Village north of Hobbiton. 98. (Replaced by *Overhill*.)

Northworthy (XII) See *Norbury*.

Norway (II) 323

Norway (IXb) 185, 234

Nos Galdon (II) People of Galdor of Gondolin living in Tol Eressëa. 215. (Replaced by *Nos nan Alwen*.)

Nos nan Alwen (II) 215. (Replaced *Nos Galdon*.)

Nosdiligand (VIII) Lord of the people of the Delta. 252, 255, 266; *Northiligand* 266

Nost-na-Lothion (II) The spring festival of 'The Birth of Flowers' in Gondolin. 172, 202; rejected form *Nost-na-Lossion* 202

Nothelm (VIII) Name briefly replacing *Heorulf* (precursor of Erkenbrand). 11, 23

Notion Club Papers (IXb) Division into two parts 146–7, 153; original extent 156; suggested course of development 281–2

Notion Club Papers (XII) 140, 146, 158, 372

Notion Club Papers, The (X) 4, 7, 44, 135–6, 157

Notion Club, the Club (IXb) 146, 148, 150–2, 155, 157–61, 164, 170, 173, 196–7, 200, 211, 213, 218–19, 228, 253–4, 260–1, 277, 281–2, 284, 293, 308

Novrod (XI) 'Hollowbold', the original name later transformed to *Nogrod*: see 389, 414. See *Bar-goll, Grodnof*.

Nówë (XII) See *Círdan*.

Nówendaland (IXb) (O.E.) 'Land of Seafarers', Númenor. 242, 286, 317

Nuaran Númen(ór)en (V) 'Lord of the West', 'Lord of Westernesse (Númenor)'. 60, 71

Núath, The Woods of (XI) Forest to the west of Ivrin. *182, 186

Nuin (I) Dark Elf, finder of the first Men, 232–3, 235–7, 244; called *Father of Speech* 236–7

Nuin (V) Dark-elf, called 'Father of Speech'. 148

Nulukkhizdîn (XI) Dwarvish name of Nargothrond; also *Nulukhizidûn*. 180

Númar (V) (1) Númenor. 11. (2) The chief city of Númenor. 14, 19. See *Númenos*.

Númen (IV) West. *243, *249

Númendil (XII) Seventeenth Lord of Andúnië. 159, 161–2, 165

Númenor (IV) 200, 261

Númenor (V) 7–78 *passim*; 149, 152, 337, 404; *Númenorë* 14, 47, 58, 376. *Downfall of Númenor* 13, 21–3, 29–32, 56, 75, 77, 98, 153–4, 337; White Tree of Númenor 211. See *Andor, Andúnië, Atalantë, Vinya, Westernesse*.

Númenor (VI) 105, 122, 215–16, 295, 320; *the Island* 260, 320, *the*

Far West Island 215; 'The Fall of Númenor' 155, 131, 174–5, 216, 218. See *Avallon, Westernesse.*

Númenor (VII) 82–3, 106, 119, 122–3, 144; *Númenórë* 124; Men of Númenor in Middle-earth 127, 158, 374; tongue of Númenor 390; *The Fall of Númenor* (title) 111, 122–3, 137, 301. See *Lost Land, Westernesse.*

Númenor (VIII) 72, 157–61, 164, 169–70, 309, 326, 363, 397, 410, 424; *the Fall of Númenor* (VIII) 161, (title) 169; *old speech of Númenor* 426. See *Westernesse.*

Númenor (IXa) 15; *White Tree of Númenor* 58 (*Nimloth*). See *Westernesse.*

Númenor (IXb) 146–7, 217, 221, 231–2, 238, 240, 247, 249, 277, 279, 281, 284, 286, 290, 300–3, 305–7, 309–10, 315–16, 331–40, 343–7, 349–57, 379–80, 382, 384, 386, 395, 400–1, 403–10, 412 (other references under *(The) Downfall*). *A Description of Númenor* 406

Númenor (IXb) *Númenóre* 240, 242, 247, 310, 303, 305, 310, 343, 351–2, 354, 361, 378. *Numinor* [Lewis] 153, 303, 307, 309

Númenor (IXb) Speech of Númenor 333, 343, 354, 361, 379; the number of Kings before Ar-Pharazôn 335, 339–40, 363, 381–2, 404, 412, 433; *the White Tree of Númenor*, see *Nimloth*. See *Anadûnê, Westernesse, Land of Gift.*

Númenor (X) 65, 154–5, 176, 180, 370, 373–4; the destruction of Númenor 339, 341, 344, 356, 397. See *Meneltarma, Nimloth.*

Númenor (XI) 224, 230, 232, 243; *Númenórë* 386; *Drowning of Númenor* 105; *Númenóreans* 386; *Númenórean* (tongue, tales) 226, 314

Númenor (XII) (including references to the Downfall or Drowning of Númenor, not as title of work) 31–3, 55, 63–5, 71, 74–5, 123, 128, 130, 140–1, 144–55, 157–8, 160–1, 163, 166–78, 180–3, 185, 187–8, 191, 193, 202–3, 208, 234, 239, 244, 246, 249, 256–7, 263, 306, 312–15, 317, 329–30, 348, 357, 359–60, 364, 368–71, 381–2, 422, 436. *A Description of Númenor* (title) 141, 144, 351. See *Westernesse.*

Númenórean (V) 7–8, 23, 28, 31, 34, 57, 71, 75–7, 153, 207, 337; (language) 8, 56. *Númenóreans* 12–30 *passim*; 56, 71, 74, 76, 79, 149; *Lie-númen* 12, *Númenórië* 12, 19; language 30, 149; stature 25; aging 71

Númenórean (VI) 215–16, 227, 332, 414; Númenórean kingdoms in Middle-earth 189

Númenórean (IXa) 30

Númenórean (IXb) (of language) 148, 240, 256, 279, 291, 302, 305, 309, 379, 381, 397; (of script) 256, 279, 291, 313, 318; (with other reference) 152, 281, 290, 315–16, 381, 385, 387, 397, 404–5, 407

Númenórean (XII) (language; see *Adûnaic*) 31–2, 64–5, 75, 145, 151–2, 158, 163, 174, 327, 371, 436; (with other reference) 34, 36, 65, 74, 124, 131–2, 141, 151, 153, 156, 169, 172, 179–80, 186, 188, 191, 199, 203–4, 206, 211, 214, 218, 234, 293–4, 296–7, 310, 312–17, 329, 332, 379, 382, 435

Númenórean(s) (X) 342, 344, 360, 373–4, 387, 389, 398, 401–2, 404, 427. Númenórean tradition in *The Silmarillion* 65, 342, 344, 360, 370, 373–4, 389, 401

Númenórean(s) (XII) 31, 33, 55, 63–4, 74–5, 138, 146–7, 149–50, 152–6, 160, 164, 167–70, 173–5, 178–82, 184, 186, 194, 196, 198, 206, 209, 220–3, 225, 227, 230, 267, 304, 312–14, 323–4, 327–30, 382, 420, 422, 436

Númenóreans (II) 325; *Black Númenórean* 67

Númenóreans (III) 269

Númenóreans (IV) 240, *246–7, 261

Númenóreans (VII) 84, 95, 121, 124, 145; *Men of the West* 83, 120–1, 157, *Men that came out of the Sea* 416. Númenórean kingdoms in Middle-earth 117, 121, 144

Númenóreans (VIII) 129, 153–5, 157–9, 161–2, 168–9, 424; *Black Númenóreans* 431. *Númenórean* (language) 159, 394

Númenóreans (IXb) 251, 258, 290, 292, 315, 317, 333–40, 343–4, 346–7, 350–2, 354–7, 378–82, 386, 400–1, 403–4, 408–13; O.E. *Númenoriscan* 257, 314. Called *Men out of the Sea* 344, 356, *Sea-kings* 362, 388; and see *Kings of Men*, *Adûnai*, *Adûnâim*.

Númenóreans (IXb) Life-span of the Númenóreans 332–3, 337, 340, 343, 361, 378, 400, 403, 408, 433; religion 400; the Ban on their westward sailing 313–14, 333–4, 343–5, 351, 354, 356–7, 361–2, 364–5, 372, 379, 404, 408, 412

Númenos (V) (1) Númenor. 11. (2) The chief city of Númenor. 14, 19, 30. (3) The high place of the king. 25, 30, 337. See *Númar*.

Númenos (IXb) City of the Númenóreans. 292, 333, 335, 339. See *Armenelos*, *Arminalêth*; *Antirion*, *Tar Kalimos*.

Númenos (XII) Early name of Armenelos. 145, 147

Numessir (I) Earlier name of Sirnúmen. 155

Núnatani (XI) (Quenya) The Dúnedain. 386

Núr (X) True name of Mandos. 150. (Replaced by *Námo*.)

Núri (I) Name of Fui Nienna. 66

Nur-menel (X) The 'lesser firmament' of the Dome of Varda. 388

Nurn (VIII) Region of Mordor. 438

Núrnen, Lake (IXa) 56

Nurnen, Sea of (VIII) 265, 438; called *the Inland Sea of Nurnen* 127, 236, and cf. 243–4.

Nurqendi (V) 'Deep-elves', a name of the Noldor. *378*, 403–4. See *Deep-elves*.

Nurtalë Valinoréva (I) The Hiding of Valinor. 224

Nurtalë Valinóreva (X) The Hiding of Valinor. 133, 137

Nurufantur (V) Mandos. 205, 207, 377, 387 (also Noldorin *Gurfannor*). (Replaced *Nefantur*.)

Nurufantur (X) Mandos. 145, 150.

Nurwë (X) Leader of a kindred of the Avari. 81, 88, 168

Nurwë (XI) Leader of a kindred of the Avari. 418

Nûzu (VIII) Orc of the Tower of Kirith Ungol. 212, 218

Nyarna Valinóren (V) The Annals of Valinor. 202 (see *Yénië Valinóren*); *Nyarna Valarianden*, the Annals of Beleriand, 202; *374*

Nyrn (XI) 'The hard', the Dwarves. 205, 209, 214. See *Norno, Norn-folk*.

O! Wanderers in the shadowed land (VI) 112, 114

O! Water warm and water hot! (VI) 98

Oäreldi, Oäzeldi (XI) Elves who left Middle-earth for Aman (=*Aureldi, Auzeldi*); singular *Oärel, Oäzel*. 363–6, 374

Oaritsi (I) Mermaids (?). 227

Oarni (I) Spirits of the sea. 66, 70, 74, 121, 123–4

Oarni (II) Spirits of the Sea (identified with 'mermaids' 259, identity denied 263). 253–4, 259–60, 263, 276. See *Mermaids*.

Oarni (III) Spirits of the sea. 148

Oath of the Fëanorians (III) 31, 50, 135–6 (in alliterative verse), 193, 210, 211–12 (in rhyming couplets), 216, 217 (as spoken by Celegorm), 219, 221–2, 245

Oath of the Fëanorians (IV) 19, 21, 23, 25, 39, 47, 51, 69, 74, 94, 100, 102, 109, 116, 134, 145, 150–3, 158, 161–2, 170, 201, 266–8, 308, 326

Oath of the Fëanorians (V) 115–17, 142–4, 234, 237, 239, 246, 252, 308, 330–1, 336

Obel Halad (XI) The fortified place in which stood the Hall of the

Chieftains of Brethil. 148, 258, 263–7, 271, 276, 292, 301–2, 306; *the Obel* 296–7, 306, 308. See *Brethil*, *Halad*.

Ocean, The (IXb) 273, 317, 398. See *Gársecg*.

Odda of Portloca (IXb) King's thegn under Edward the Elder. 271–2

Ódhel (XI), plurals *Ódhil*, *Ódhellim* The Exiled Noldor (= *Gódhel*). 364, 366, 378–9

Óðinn (II) 290. See *Wóden*.

Odo (VI) (including *Odo Took* and *Odo Bolger*) See *Bolger*.

Odothui (VII) Seventh River (Greyflood); changed from *Odotheg*. 312. See *Greyflood*.

Odothui, River (VIII) Seventh River (Greyflood); changed from *Odotheg*. 437

Odysseus (IXb) 289

Ogbar (III) Unknown; named in Beleg's 'whetting spell'. 45, 54

Ogden (VI) Hobbit family name. 17

Ogodrûth, River (VII) Entwash. 250, 268–9, 288

Ohtar (XII) Esquire of Isildur. 227

Ohtor (V) Viking leader. 80

Oikeroi (II) A cat, thane of Tevildo, slain by Huan. 27–8, 30–2, 55–8

Oikeroi (III) A cat, thane of Tevildo, slain by Huan. 258, 270–1, 282

Óin (IV) Gnomish form of *Uinen*. 13–14, 46, 169

Óin (VI) Dwarf, companion of Thorin Oakenshield. 217, 226, 369, 381, 391

Óin (VII) Companion of Balin in Moria. 82, 117, 141–2, 191, 201, 459

Óin (XII) (1) Father of Náin II. 276, 284. (2) Companion of Thorin Oakenshield. 240, 276–7, 279

Óinen (I) See *Uinen*.

Óinen (II) See *Uinen*.

Oiolossë (I) 88

Oiolossë (IV) See *Ialassë*.

Oiolossë (Oron Oiolossë) (XI) '(Mount) Everwhite', 'Eversnow'. 403. See *Amon Uilos*.

Oiolossë (V) 'Everlasting Whiteness', Taniquetil. 209–10, 359, 379. See *Amon Uilos*, *Ialassë*.

Oiolossë (VII) Taniquetil. 285

Oiolossë (X) 'Everlasting Whiteness' (154), Taniquetil. 67, 154, 238, 262, 313. See *Everwhite*.

Oiolossë (XII) Mount Everwhite. 334, 396

Oiomúrë (X) Region of mists near the Helkaraxë. 295

Oivárin (I) Earlier name of Ainairos. 222

Old English (I) 23–4, 28, 32, 91, 108, 138, 164, 204, 217, 245

Old English (II) (including citations, words, titles of poems) 197, 200, 266–7, 271, 276, 290–2, 294–5, 298, 301, 304–5, 309, 323, 325, 328–31. Old English spoken by the Elves of Tol Eressëa 301–2, 304, 309

Old English (III) 23, 87, 95, 127, 140–1 (metre), 143–5, 151, 271

Old English (IV) (including all O.E. names and connected passages) 12, 33, 80–1, 166, 205–14, 230, *250–1, 261, 263, 277, 280–93, 310–11, 316, 323, 325, 333, 337–41

Old English (V) 38–9, 53–5, 80, 84–5, 91–6, 103, 120–1, 123, 202–3, 209, 243, 279, 300, 412; see also *Anglo-Saxon(s)*.

Old English (VI) 35, 86, 131, 141, 145, 173, 205, 304; Runes 467

Old English (VII) 16, 56, 61, 65, 78, 106, 150, 158, 244, 250, 274, 288, 290, 298, 349, 387, 402, 405, 409, 420, 423–5, 439, 442–3, 446, 449–50, 455–6; *Anglo-Saxon* 405, 413, 452

Old English (VIII) 23, 36, 41, 44–5, 69, 122–3, 127, 138, 245, 257, 265–7, 292, 320–1, 355–6, 369, 372, 389, 408

Old English (IXa) 46–7, 107

Old English (IXb) 148, 239, 243, 255, 257, 284–7, 29 1–5, 304, 309, 313, 315–18, 355–7, 381, 384, 412–13; other references under *Anglo-Saxon, English*.

   Old English (IXb) Words or passages cited 236, 239, 242–4, 257–8, 268, 271–3, 277–8, 285–7, 292–5, 304, 313–14, 316–17, 384

Old English (X) (including names) 124, 130, 136, 143, 154, 157, 163, 168, 185, 192, 198, 205, 257, 422. See *Anglo-Saxon*.

Old English (XI) See *English; Anglo-Saxon*.

Old English (XII) See *English*.

Old Forest (II) 328

Old Forest (IV) 211

Old Forest (VI) (also often *the Forest*) 29–30, 35, 37, 40, 42–3, 100, 103–5, 109–12, 121, 124–5, 160, 206, 221, 273, 286, 299, 301–3, 326–7, 334, 349–52, 365–6, 401. See *Buckwood*.

Old Forest (VII) 6, 10, 36, 69, 72–3, 111, 152, 402, 415, 417

Old Forest (IXa) 77

Old Forest (XII) 235; *the Forest* 194.

Old Forest Road (XII) (in Mirkwood) 323. See *Great Dwarf Road*.

Old Home (XII) See *Bree*.

Old Human (IXb) (language) 203, 220; *Old Humane* 220; *Primitive Adamic* 203, 220, *Adamic* 220

Old Lands (IV) (after the Cataclysm) *246–7

Old Lands (IXb) 393, 395. See *(The) World*.

Old Man Willow (VI) See *Willow-man*.

Old Man Willow (VII) 36

Old Norse (I) 23, 245

Old Norse (IV) 207–10

Old Norse (VI) 246, 444

Old Norse (VII) 138, 204, 306, 405, 424, 455

Old Norse (VIII) 353, 372

Old Norse (X) 406

Old Road, The (IXb) See *(The) Straight Road*.

Old Solar (IXb) [Lewis] 151, 168, 199–202, 204, 213, 219–20; *Hlab-Eribol-ef-Cordi* 213. See *Hressa-hlab*.

Old Took (VI) See *Took, Frodo* (1) and *Took, Gerontius*.

Old Universal (IXb) (language) 204, 219–20

Old Winyards (VI) Wine of the Southfarthing. 241

Old World (V) (after the Cataclysm) 12, 16–18, 21, 28

Old World (VI) (after the Cataclysm) 215, 311

Old World (XII) 30; *ancient world* 55, 257

Old Year (XII) 121, 128–9; *Old Year's Day* 121, 127, 129, *Yearsend* 121, 129, 133–4, 136

Oldbuck, Gorhendad (VI) Founder of the Brandybuck clan. 298, 326

Oleg (IV) See *Lúthien* (1).

Oliphaunt (VIII) 127, 129, 136–7, *Oliphant* 129. See *Andabund, Mûmak*.

Oliphaunt (IXa) 50

Olney, Austin (VI) 200, 305

Olofantur (I) 'Fantur of Dreams', the Vala Lórien. 66. See *Fantur, Lórien*.

Olofantur (IV) Lórien. 78–9, 207

Olofantur (V) Lórien. 205, 379, 387 (also Noldorin *Olfannor*).

Olofantur (X) Lórien. 145, 150, 172–3

Olog-hai (X) The great Trolls of the Third Age. 414

Olog-hai (XII) Race of Trolls. 79; earlier forms *Horg-hai* 79, *Olg-hai* 79–80

Olórë Mallë (I) 'Path of Dreams'. 18, 27, 212, 220–1, 224–5; *the magic way of Lórien* 213

Olórë Mallë (II) 'The Path of Dreams'. 48, 70, 119, 258. See *Way of Dreams*.

Olórin (VIII) Gandalf's name in the West, changed from *Olórion*. 153

Olórin (X) Gandalf. 147, 152, 203

Olórin (XII) Gandalf's name in Valinor. 377–8, 381

olvar (XI) Living things that grow in the earth. 340–1. See *kelvar*.

Olwë (I) 132–3. See *Ellu*.

Olwë (II) Lord of the Solosimpi in Thingol's place. 50. See *Ellu* (2).

Olwë (IV) Lord of the Teleri. 44. See *Elwë*.

Olwë (V) Later name of Elwë (1), brother of Thingol. 217

Olwë (X) 81–6, 88–9, 93, 101, 104, 115–16, 118, 125–6, 163–4, 169–70, 173, 177–9, 182–3, 194, 196, 206, 258; *People of Olwë* a name of the Teleri, 164. See *Elwë* (1), *Solwë*.

Olwë (XI) Brother of Elwë (Thingol), lord of Alqualondë. 7–8, 13, 19, (32), 41, 115, 177, 344, 369, 379–80. See *Elwë* (1).

Olwë (XII) Brother of Elwë Lord of Alqualondë. 76, 337, 340–1, 357–8, 364–5, 385–7, 392; *Ciriáran* (mariner king) 341

Olympians (I) 160

Ómar (I) Youngest of the great Valar, called also Amillo. 47, 52, 67, 75, 80, 89, 93, 101, 122, 177, 184, 228

Ómar (II) Youngest of the great Valar, called also *Amillo*. 279

Ond (VI) Earliest name of Gondor. *(Land of) Ond* 381–2, 398, 400, 409–10, 427; *Men of Ond* 403, 409; *King of Ond* (father of Boromir) 411, 462. See *Stone-land*, *City of Stone*.

Ond (VII) Original name of Gondor. 110, 115–16, 122, 126–8, 146–7, 157, 177, 187, 216, 241, 299, 310–11; *King of Ond* 216, 376

Ondohir (XII) Thirty-first King of Gondor. 195, 200–4, 210, 212, 215–16, 218, 232, 245, 254, 256; *Ondonir* 195, 200–2, 210, 216; final form *Ondoher* 210

Ondolindë (XII) See *Gondolin*.

Ondolindë (XI) 'Rock of the Music of Water', Quenya name of Gondolin. 201

Ondor (V) Earlier name of Gondor. 33–4

Ondor (VII) Replaced *Ond*. 123, 144, 146–7, 157, 187, 270, 272–3, 278, 289, 293, 310, 318, 333, 358–60, 362, 376, 381–2, 390, 393, 395, 401, 418, 420, 423; *Ondor! Ondor! Between the Mountains and the Sea* 395; tongue of Ondor 390; throne of Ondor 395–6, 404; name changed to *Gondor* 423. See *Staniland*.

Ondor (VIII) Earlier name of Gondor. 155

Ondor (IXb) Earlier name of Gondor. 331

Ondor (XII) See *Gondor*.

One, The (X) Eru. 144, 224, 311, 313–14, 320–1, 329–30, 335, 351, 353, 358, 360, 379–80; *the One God* 356, *the One Great* (of Melkor) 347

One, The (XI) See *Eru*.

One, The (XII) 182, 370, 380, 389, 413. See *Eru*.

Ónen (I) Earlier name of Uinen. 58, 61, 63, 66, 68, 74, 79, 83, 120, 130, 220. (Replaced *Ówen*.)

Onen (II) Earlier name of Uinen. 51

Onótimo (X) See *Quennar (i) Onótimo*.

Opening Hour. Hour of Opening (IV) (when Silpion shone alone) 80, 82–3, 167

Orald, Oreald, Orold (VII) See *Tom Bombadil*.

Orchal (XI) Name of Galdor. 287, 305

Orc-men (X) 419. See *Men-orcs*.

Orc-mountains (IV) 229

Orcobal (II) Champion of the Orcs, slain by Ecthelion in Gondolin. 181

Orcrist (VIII) The sword of Thorin Oakenshield. 223

Orcrist (IXa) The sword of Thorin Oakenshield, attributed to Gandalf. 78

Orcs (I) 236, 238, 240–3, 245

Orcs (II) Selected references: origin of 14, 159, 219; *children of Melko* 193; described 99, 159–60; sight and hearing of 78–9, 165–6; wolfriders 44, 67, 84, 190, 195; Orcs' blood in Meglin 165; *sons of the Orcs* 165; mercenaries of the Dwarves 230, 247. Singular *Ork* 202, plural *Orqui* 136, 202, 219. See *Goblins*.

Orcs (III) *Passim*. See *Glamhoth, Goblins, Wolfriders. Orc-road*, see *Taur-na-Fuin*.

Orcs (IV) Selected references. Origin of the Orcs 82, 93, 295, 314, 328, 338; 'Goblins' 82; tongue of 104, 107; numbers of 302; laughter at Morgoth 113, 178; Orcs' road of haste, see *Taur-na-Fuin*; O.E. *Orcas* 282, 288, etc. See *Glamhoth, Goblins*.

Orcs (V) 24, 29, (65, 74), 114, 117–51 *passim*, 161, 177–9, 190–1, 212, 216, 233, 238–9, 249–94 *passim*, 307, 309–12, 315, 320–1, 323, 328, 332, 404, 406. Origin of the Orcs 24, 29, 114, 122, 125, 148, 212, 216, 233, 238–9; numbers 137; language 177–9, 190–1, 404, 406; etymology 379, 406. See *Glamhoth, Goblins*.

Orcs (VI) 187–8, 211, 320, 364, 429, 437, 443, 462, 467. See especially 437, 443; and see *Goblins*.

Orcs (VII) (in many instances used attributively, as *orc-arrow, -chieftain, -draught, -prints, -trail, -work*, etc.) 71, 119, 134–5, 142–3, 156, 181, 184–5, 191, 193–4, 197–203, 205, 207–9, 213–14, 218–19, 221, 224, 227, 229, 231, 233, 241, 248, 264, 273, 281, 331–41, 343–4, 347, 349, 351, 353, 357–8, 365, 368–9, 371–2, 376–402 *passim*, 405–10, 418, 424, 427, 434, 437–8, 440, 458–9; *orch*, plural *yrch*, 229

Orcs (VII) With reference to place of origin (Isengard, Mordor, Moria) 378–9, 381–2, 401, 408–9, 434; and see *Isengarders*. *Black Orcs* 193, 347; *great Orcs* 408; language 181, 202, 336, 424. See *Dwarves, Goblins*.

Orcs (VIII) (including many compounds as *orc-drums, -laughter, -make, -path, -raid, -tower, -voices*) 3, 5, 9–10, 13–20, 22, 24, 26, 28, 40–1, 47, 49, 51, 54–5, 58–60, 105–6, 109, 119, 122, 124, 132, 134–5, 148, 150–1, 154, 165, 172, 184–6, 189–91, 195, 199- 200, 207, 211–16, 218, 222–6, 237, 249, 253–6, 259, 266, 275, 281, 285–6, 300, 310, 313, 332, 343–6, 348, 350–1, 355, 367, 404, 411, 413–15, 420; *orch* 135. *Orc-men* 345. See *Goblins, Gorgûn*.

Orc(s) (IXa) (including compounds, as *orc-blade, orc-rags, orc-voices*) 8–11, 13, 18, 21, 23–32, 34–6, 38–9, 43, 46, 63, 68, 71, 103, 107, 116, 122; *orc-man, orc-men* 91–3. 103, 105–6, *half-orcs* 84; *orcish, orc-like* 31, 91, 94; orc-speech 31 (see *Orkish*).

Orcs (IXb) 332

Orcs (X) 78, 80, 106, 109, 123–4, 127–8, 159, 165, 194–5, 251, 391, 396, 406, 408–23; *Great Orcs* 418; *Orks* 165, 414, 421–2; *Orkor* 73–4, 78, 109, 120, 194–5, 409; *Orkish* (X) 418, 424; *orch, yrch* 195. Origin of the name 124, 422, and its spelling 414, 422–3; etymology 413. See *Glamhoth*.

Orc(s) (XI) (including many compounds as *Orc-camp, -host, -legion*, etc.) 15–18, 33, 36–7, 46, 49, 52–3, 56–60, 66, 70, 72–7, 79–82, 84–9, 92–7, 105, 109, 111–13, 118, 121, 125, 127–8, 132, 138–44, 147, 150, 162, 169, 176, 195, 203–4, 206, 212, 216, 220–3, 236–8, 241, 244, 255–6, 262, 275, 277, 279, 285, 307, 329, 359, 372, 377, 386, 389–91, 408–9, 418; *Ork(s)* 321, 330; *orkish* 267. Origin of the Orcs 12, 109, 195

Orc(s) (XI) Sindarin *Orch*, plurals *Yrch, Orchoth* 390–1. Quenya *Orko*, plural *Orqui* 390, also *Orkor* 12, 36–7, 390; and see *Urko*. Etymology 389–91

Orc(s) (XII) (including many compounds, as *Orc-chief, -holds*) 9, 21,

24, 35–6, 42, 65, 70, 75, 80, 83, 177, 192–3, 196, 204–6, 211, 219–20, 223, 225–7, 230, 235–9, 242–3, 249–50, 264, 271–3, 276–8, 280, 323, 326, 410, 412–15, 420; *Orks* 301–5, 309, 319, 326, 345, 347, 358, 362; *ork-plants* (fungi) 327; *Orkish* 35, 414

Orendil (VI) Name varying with *Elendil*. 175, 197, 260–1, 270–1. See *Valandil*.

Orfalas (VII) 108

Orfalch Echor (II) The great rift in the Encircling Mountains by which Gondolin was approached. 207, 211

Orfalch Echor (III) The ravine through the Encircling Mountains about Gondolin. 83

Orfalch Echor (IV) The great rift in the Encircling Mountains. 66

Orfin (VII) See *Orofin*.

Orgof (II) Elf of Artanor, slain by Túrin. 74–6, 122, 142

Orgof (III) Elf of Doriath, slain by Túrin. 18–20, 23–5, 28, 30, 51, 127

Orgof (IV) Elf of Doriath, slain by Túrin. 28, 58, 123, 183, 304, 323

Orgof (V) Elf of Doriath, slain by Túrin. 138, 316, 321. (Replaced by *Saeros*.)

Orgof (XI) Earlier name of Saeros. 81, 135, 138, 244; *Orgoph*, *Orgol* 112

Ori (VI) Dwarf, companion of Thorin Oakenshield. 217, 226, 369, 381, 391

Ori (VII) Companion of Balin in Moria. 82, 117, 141–2, 201, 459

Ori (XII) Companion of Thorin Oakenshield. 240, 279

Orion (I) 224. See *Telumehtar*.

Orion (II) 281–2, 302. See *Telimektar*.

Orion (IV) 68, 75. See *Telimektar*.

Orion (IXb) 236, 285, 308

Orion (X) 76, 166, 388. See *Menelmakar*, *Menelvagor*.

Orion (XI) 411. See *Menelmakil*, *Telumehtar*.

Orion (XII) 375. See *Menelmakar*.

Orkish (IXa) (language) 30, 106

Orkor, *Orks* (X) See *Orcs*.

Orlin (II) Man of Hisilómë, slain in Brodda's hall by Turambar. 90

Orm (II) Sea-captain of the Forodwaith, slayer of Déor Ælfwine's father. 318–19, 323, 331

Ormaid (III) Rejected name for Tavros (Oromë), changed from *Ormain*. 195

Ormal (I) The Southern Lamp. 87

Ormal (X) The Southern Lamp. 7, 22, 32, 38, 52–3, 60, 67, 98, 153. See *Ringil*, *Hyaras*, *Hyarantë*.

Ornelië (VII) See *Galadrim*.

Ornendil (XII) Son of Eldakar King of Condor. 199, 214

Ornil (XI) Elf of Nargothrond. 86

Ornómi (VIII) 'Talking Trees'. 52, 54–6, 59; *Ornómar* 50, 60. See *Galbedirs*, *Lamorni*.

Orocarni (IV) The Red Mountains. 256

Orodlin (V) Son of Orodreth. 403

Orod-na-Thôn (VII) Dorthonion. 420. Earlier *Orod Thon*, *Orod Thuin* 420

Orodras (VIII) Original name of the second beacon in Anórien. 233

Orodreth (II) Lord of the Rodothlim. 82–4, 98, 117, 123–4

Orodreth (III) King of Nargothrond. 65, 69–71, 75, 80, 82–6, 90–1, 138, 213, 218–19, 221–2, 229, 237, 242, 246–7, 260, 272–3, 358–9; see especially 91, 246

Orodreth (IV) Second king of Nargothrond, son of Finrod (1) =Finarfin. 15, 19, 25, 27, 29, 46, 48, 57, 59, 88, 95, 103, 106, 110–11, 116, 120, 125–6, 128, 174, 176, 180, 184, 213, 267, 271, 279, 295–6, 298–300, 304, 310, 312, 314, 318–19, 321, 323, 327–8, 330, 334; O.E. *Ordred* 213, his sons *Ordhelm* and *Ordláf* 213, 323

Orodreth (V) Son of Finrod (1) =Finarfin. 116, 119, 127, 132–3, 135–6, 138–9, 145–7, 150, 223, 226, 234, 237, 239, 264, 269, 283, 290, 292, 308, 379, 403; see especially 239

Orodreth (VIII) King of Nargothrond. 372

Orodreth (X) Son of Finarfin. 112, 121, 125, 128, 177, 182, 195

Orodreth (XI) Son of Finarfin (Finrod (1)); second king of Nargothrond. 38, 54, 63, 66–7, 73, 82–5, 92, 125, 131, 133–4, 137–9, 141–2, 149, *183, 187–8, 239–40, 242, 256

Orodreth (XII) (1) Originally brother of Felagund and second King of Nargothrond. Later names and genealogical history 349–51; finally son of Angrod and father of Gil-galad, see *Arothir*. (2) Sixteenth Ruling Steward. 205, 219

Orodruin (VII) 28, 39, 209, 247, 262–3, 313, 438; *Orodnaur* 39. See *Fiery Mountain*.

Orodruin (VIII) 275, 361–2, 364, 404, 438–9; *the Fire* 134, 362; *the Mountain* 362. See *Mount Doom*.

Orodruin (IXa) 3, 6–8, 10–11, 22, 38. See *Fiery Mountain*, *Mount Doom*.

Orodruin (XII) 168, 174, 176, 179, 240, 242, 390. See *Mountain of Fire*.

Orofin (VII) Elf of Lórien, companion of Hathaldir (Haldir). 235, 279, 285; earlier form *Orfin* 227, 229, 235–6; in LR *Orophin*, 236. Earlier names of this Elf *Rhimdir*, *Rhimlath* 240

Orokarni (X) The Red Mountains, the Mountains of the East. 72, 77

Oromë (I) Son of Aulë and Palúrien (67). 27, 66–7, 75–6, 78–80, 89, 93, 99, 101–2, 104, 106, 110–11, 114–15, 117–20, 124, 126–8, 131, 145, 154, 157, 194, 209–12, 214, 220, 224–5, 231. See *Aldaron*.

Oromë (II) 8, 42, 240, 279

Oromë (III) 127, 137, 198, 235–6, 248. See *Ormaid*, *Tauros*, *Tavros*.

Oromë (IV) 3, 12–13, 16, 43–4, 79, 82, 84, 88, 91–2, 97, 110, 168–9, 171, 207–8, 239, 255–6, 263–4, 272, 275–6, 278, 285–6, 291–3; O.E. *Wáðfréa*, *Huntena fréa* 208 (*Oromë* in the texts); Oromë's horse 13, 84. See especially 293, and see *Aldaron*, *Tauros*.

Oromë (V) 110–13, 120, 122, 168–9, 175, 180–3, 186, 192–3, 205–8, 212–14, 216–19, 221, 223, 225, 230–1, 240, 379, 384 (also Noldorin *Araw*); *Lord of Forests* 168. See especially 110, 120, and see *Aldaron*, *Galaðon*, *Tauros*.

Oromë (VIII) 292, 353. See *Araw*.

Oromë (X) 7, 19, 25, 33, 35, 39, 48–9, 53, 59, 65, 69–83 *passim*, 87–9, 97–8, 101, 105, 110, 123–4, 131, 136, 144, 146, (149), 151, 159–60, 162, 166–7, 170, 174, 177, 179, 190, 192, 201–4, 276, 281, 283–5, 289, 377–8, 382, 384, 416–17, 425. Called *the Hunter* 73, *the (Great) Rider* 73, 78. See *Aldaron*, *Araw*, *Tauron*; *Horn of Oromë*.

Oromë (XI) 5–6, 11, 14, 55, 105–6, 109–10, 295, 343, 360–1, 368, 373, 383, 400–1, 419. See *Araw*.

Oromë (XII) 341, 357–8, 366, 403; his horn 358. See *Araw*, *Tauron*.

Oromet (XII) The hill of Tar Minastir's tower, near Andúnië. 164

Oromian (V) Languages derived from Oromë's instruction of the Elves (=*Quendian*). 168, 178, 193–5

Oromian (X) (languages) 77

Orondil (VIII) Father of Mardil the Steward. 288. See *Faragon*, *Vorondil*.

Orontor (V) Númenórean. 62, 71

Orossi (I) Fays of the mountains. 66

Orothanador (VI) See *Rohan*.

Orqui (II) Earlier plural of *Orc* (*Ork*). See *Orcs*.

Orquin, Orquian (V) Language of the Orcs. 178

Orthanc (VI) 120

Orthanc (VII) 36, 105, 130, 132–4, 139, 150–1, 372, 400, 404, 419, 426, 436; on the name see 419.

Orthanc (VIII) 26, 31–3, 35, 39, 44, 47–8, 52–3, 55–6, 58, 61–79 *passim*, 119–20, 127, 129–30, 289, 301, 304, 307, 381. On the name see 35, and on the structure of Orthanc see 31–5, 61–2. The *palantír* of Orthanc (all references, including *Orthanc-stone, the Stone, the Glass, the Dark Crystal, the palantír*, &c.) 60, 64–7, 69–76, 78–81, 119–20, 126, 142, 274, 289, 296, 300–1, 304, 307, 339, 342, 362, 381

Orthanc (IXa) 53, 63–4, 71, 136

Orthanc (XII) 176, 191, 205–6, 229, 233, 240–1, 248, 384

Osforod (VII) See *Fornost*.

Osgiliath (VII) 119, 122, 125–8, 138, 144–5, 147, 211, 267, 271–2, 290, 298, 307, 310, 322, 358, 360, 382, 389, 423–4, 440; 'Fort(-ress) of Stars' 119, 126, 144. *Bridges of Osgiliath* 267, 271–2, 290. Name changed to *Elostirion* 389, 423, 435, 440; and to *Ostechain* 424

Osgiliath (VIII) 69–72, 76, 79, 81, 115, 122, 128, 133, 135, 138, 147, 165, 175, 178, 182, 187, 213, 243, 247, 253, 255–6, 262–3, 268, 270, 278, 283, 291–2, 294–5, 324, 326, 329–30, 333–4, 338–40, 342, 353–4, 356, 360, 364, 369, 379, 389, 391, 432, 438. *East Osgiliath* 330–1, 334, *West Osgiliath* 324; *the Fords of Osgiliath* (213), 253, 278, 291, 327, *the Crossings* 283, 292, 294, 324. The *palantír* of Osgiliath 71–2, 76. *The Battle of Osgiliath* 365–7. See *Elostirion*.

Osgiliath (IXa) 10, 51

Osgiliath (XII) 169, 179, 191–2, 197, 199–200, 203–4, 207, 215, 217–19, 231, 235, 238

Öshül-küllösh (IXb) [Ramer] The waterfall in Ellor. 199–200; translated *Falling Water* 200. Earlier names 218

Ossë (I) 58, 63, 66, 68, 70–1, 74–5, 79–80, 83, 85–6, 89, 100, 104, 106, 117–21, 123–6, 129, 134–7, 144, 152, 154, 177, 194, 210–11, 214, 220, 224; *Falman-Ossë* (I) 66, 101, 118, 121, *Falman* 119

Ossë (II) 150, 197, 254, 256, 263, 283, 285, 293, 304, 306–9, 323–4, 331

Ossë (III) 137, 148

Ossë (IV) 13–14, 42, 45–6, 75, 78, 86–8, 94, 168, 207, 209, 215–17, 227, 263, 275, 285, 289–92; O.E. *Sæfréa* 209

Ossë (V) 11, 14, 24, 110, 113, 120, 161, 171, 186, 205, 208, 221–2, 224–5, 233, 236, 239, *359* (also Noldorin *Oeros*).

Ossë (IXb) 332, 412

Ossë (X) 20, 35, 48–9, 69, 84–6, 88, 90–1, 116, 144–5, 151, 175, 178, 183, 199, 201–2, 204, 286. *Friends of Ossë*, a name of the Sindar, 164, 171

Ossë (XI) 5, 7–8, 80, 104, 107, 112, 192, 400, 404. See *Balar*; *Gaerys*, *Yssion*.

Ossë (XII) 387

Ossir (XI) Ossiriand. 351, 353; *the Seven Rivers of Ossir* 353

Ossiriand (II) 249

Ossiriand (IV) 108, 116, 135, 173, 179, 189–90, 224, 227, 233, 259, 270–1, 277, 301, 306–7, 320, 325, 331; *Ossiriand(e)* rejected name for Beleriand 233; earlier form *Ossiriath* 233. See *Assariad*, *Land of Seven Streams*.

Ossiriand (V) 32, 34, 112, 114, 119, 126, 128, 135, 141, 146, 153–4, 175- 80, 182, 186, 189, 193–4, 196, 253, 260–1, 263, 265, 267–8, 274, 281, 283, 305, 307–8, 314, 331, 404; *Land of Seven Rivers* or *Streams* 128, 135, 175, 253, 263, 305, 307; *Elves of the Seven Rivers* and *Lost Folk of Ossiriand*, the Danas, 215; *Mountains of Ossiriand*, Eredlindon, 267

Ossiriand (VII) 124, 271, 311, 377, 454

Ossiriand (X) 93, 104, 164

Ossiriand (XI) 13, 15–16, 22, 24, 28, 34, 39, 48, 71, 80, 110–12, 193, 195, 216, 218, 257, 300, 347, 350–1, 353, 385, 406; *the Mountains of Ossiriand* 193. See *Land of Seven Rivers*, *Lindon*.

Ossiriand (XII) 76, 307, 349, 365, 367–8, 373

Ossiriand(e) (III) Rejected name for Beleriand. 158–60

Ossiriandeb (V) Language of Ossiriand. 189, 347; *Ossiriandic* 180, 194, 347

Ost Belegost (II) See *Belegost*.

Ostechain (VII) See *Osgiliath*.

Ostohir (XII) (1) Seventh King of Gondor. 197, 210, 213, 228; *Ostonir* 197, 210, 213; final form *Ostoher* 210. (2) *Ostohir II* (rejected), see 212, 215

Oswin Errol (V) 36–7, 39–44, 53–5, 104

Óswine (II) Prince of Gwar (Kortirion). 313, 323

Óswine (IXb) Father of Éadwine father of Ælfwine the Mariner. 270

Othrain (VII) See *Minas Tirith*.

Othram (VIII) The City Wall of Minas Tirith. 288

Othrod (II) A lord of the Orcs, slain by Tuor in Gondolin. 181

Othrondir (XII) Man of Condor. 417, 421; earlier *Othrondor* 421

Ottor Wǽfre (I) Original name of Eriol. 23–4

Ottor Wǽfre (II) Eriol. 290, 292; Wǽfre 291

Out of the Silent Planet (IXb) See *Lewis, C. S.*

Outer Dark (I) 216, 221, 226

Outer Dark (II) 273, 276

Outer Dark (IV) 40–1, 49, 73–4, 91, 164, 166, 204, 238, 252–3, 255; *Eldest Dark* 80, *Everlasting Dark* 97. See *Ava-kúma*, *Kúma*.

Outer Dark (VI) 122. *Outside* 121–2

Outer Dark (XI) 346

Outer Darkness (V) 14, 230; *Outer Dark* 20, 157, 335; *the Dark* 225, 335; *the Darkness* 206; *Everlasting Dark, Darkness* 234, 330; *Eldest Dark* 209. See *Ava-kúma*, *Void*.

Outer Darkness (X) See *Dark. Outer Night*, see *Night*.

Outer Land(s) (II) (1) The Great Lands (Middle-earth). 254, 265. See *Lands Without*. (2) The lands West of the Great Sea. 316–17, 324–5, 334

Outer Lands (I) (1) Originally used of the Great Lands. 21, 81. (2) Valinor, Eruman/Arvalin (I), and the Twilit Isles (68). 21, 64, 67–8, 77, 81–2, 125, 158, 160, 220; *Outer Land* 134

Outer Lands (III) The Great Lands (Middle-earth). 211, 224

Outer Lands (IV) (1) Middle-earth (in the *Quenta* replaced by *Hither Lands*) 12, 14, 21, 43, 72, 82, 85–6, 89, 100–1, 137, 139, 142, 147–8, 151, 153, 155–6, 160, 162–4, 168, 196–7, 200, 204, 233; *Outer Earth* 3, 89, *Outer World* 3, 13, 20, 93, 98, 154, 197. (2) The Western Land, Valinor. 233, *250–1, 258

Outer Lands (V) (1) Middle-earth. 22, 326; also *Outer World* 327. (2) *Outer Land*, the western land, beyond the Great Sea, 221

Outer Lands (X) (1) Middle-earth. 19, 35, 54, 71, 79, 85; *Outer World* 295. (2) *Outer Land of Aman* 174

Outer Night (IXb) 264, 292, 298

Outer Oceans, Outer Sea(s) (II) 154, 160, 276. See *Vai*.

Outer Sea (X) 28, 33, 54, 58, 62–3, 132, 135–7, 154, 156–7, 161, 179, *Outer Seas* 145, 204, *Outer Ocean* 20, 24–5, 29, 34. See *Ekkaia*, *Vaiya*.

Outer Sea (XI) 175

Outer Sea(s) (I) 68, 70, 74, 82, 90, 114, 126, 142, 162, 188, 196, 215–

16, 226; *Outermost Seas* (I) 67; *Outermost Waters (Neni Erú-mëar)* 85; *Outer Ocean* 58, 62, 83, 85; *the Sea* 179, 196. See *Vai.*

Outer Seas (III) 356; *outmost sea* 172

Outer Sea(s) (IV) Vaiya. 12–13, 20, 41, 74, 78, 80, 98, 208, 210, 241, *250–1, 254, 258, 263, 267

Outer Sea(s) (V) Vaiya. 205, 209, 225, 241–2, 248; *Outer Ocean* 161. See *Encircling Sea.*

Outer World (III) The lands east of the Blue Mountains. 156, 160, 332

Outlands (VIII) The fiefs of Gondor. 286–7, 289, 370

Outsiders (VI) Hobbits not of the Shire. 132–3, 175, 343; Hobbits not of the Bree-land 136, 345

Ovenhill (VII) Village in the Westfarthing. 30

Over Old Hills and Far Away (I) (poem) 115–16

Overhill (VI) Village north of Hobbiton Hill. 254, 284, 319, 386–7. (Replaced *Northope.*)

Overhill (XII) Village north of Hobbiton. 98, 113–15. (Replaced *Northope.*)

Overlithe (XII) 121, 124, 129, 130–1; *Leapday* 124, 130

Ówen (I) Earliest name of Uinen. 61, 79, 220. (Replaced by *Ónen.*)

Owl and the Nightingale, The (IXb) 150

Owlamoo (IXb) 231, 284

Oxford (I) 23, 25, 27, 45, 107–8, 203; *Oxford English Dictionary* 44–5, 203

Oxford (II) 146, 269, 292–3, 295, 300, 323; (Old English) *Oxenaford* 292; poem *The City of Present Sorrow* (II) 295–8. See *Taruithom, Taruktama.*

Oxford (III) 3, 81, 94, 120, 127, 330

Oxford (V) 41, 53, 93, 155

Oxford (VI) 35, 382; *Oxford Magazine* 115–16, 412

Oxford (VII) *Oxford English Dictionary* 64; *Oxford Magazine* 86, 89–90, 106, 108; *Oxford University* 67, 107, 362, 377

Oxford (VIII) 44, 193; *Oxford Dictionary* 116

Oxford (IXb) 146, 149–50, 153, 155–7, 159–60, 200, 211, 213, 215, 219, 222, 230, 233, 260, 269, 307, 389

Oxford (IXb) Colleges: *All Souls'* 160, 231; *Brasenose (B.N.C.)* 159, 223, 283; *Corpus Christi* 159; *Exeter* 160, 213; *Jesus* 159, 213, 245; *Lincoln* 159, 213; *Magdalen* 160; *New College* 160; *Pembroke* 132, 256, 291; *Queen's* 159, 224; *St. John's* 159; *Trinity* 159; *University College* 160; *Wadham* 159

Oxford (IXb) *Oxford University* (IXb) 152, 211; *University Press*

149. *The Schools:* faculties 149, 156; =examinations 255. 291; *Examination Schools* (building) 155, 254, *Clerk of the Schools* 155. *English Board* (Board of the Faculty) 219

Oxford (IXb) Streets, etc.: *High Street, the High* 213, 222, 283; *Turl Street, the Turl* 173, 213, 223, 283; *Broad Street* 213; *Brasenose Lane* 283; *Radcliffe Square* 211, 222, 281, 283; *Radcliffe Camera, the Camera* 211, 222–3, 238, 281–3; *Bodleian Library* 222, 284; *St. Mary's Church* 211, 222; *Banbury Road* 157, 179, 215

Oxford English Dictionary (II) 69, 147

Oxford English Dictionary (IXb) 150, 222, 283, 286; *New English Dictionary* 225, 283

Oyarsa (IXb) [Lewis] The Eldil of Malacandra. 212

Padathir (VI) Elvish name of Trotter. 194–5, 198, 217, 361. See *Dufinnion, Ethelion, Rimbedir.*

palantír (VII) 423

palantír (VIII) 65, 76, 79; of Orthanc 60, 67, 69, 75, 78, 80–1, 120, 126, 274, 289, 301, 307; of Barad-dûr 80; of Minas Tirith 231, 257, 263, 374–9, 381, 391; of Erech 309, 397, 399, 410, 418, 424. Plural *palantírs* 76–7, 81; *palantíri* 65, 78, 81, 309, 397, 399. See *Seeing Stones*; and for complete references to the *palantíri* however named see *Aglarond, Barad-dar, Erech, Fornost, Hornburg, Minas Morghul, Minas Tirith, Mithlond, Orthanc, Osgiliath.*

palantír (IXa) 15, 63; *palantíri* 15

Palantir, Palantíri (XII) 176, 186, 191, 193–5, 199–201, 206, 208–10, 217, 230, 232–3, 240, 245. See *Gwahaedir, Seven Stones.*

Palantíri (V) 30–1, 344, 380, 394

Palantíri (X) (185), 192, 396

Palath Nenui (VII) See *Nindalf.*

Palath-ledin (VII) The Gladden Fields. 114

Palathrin (VI) The Gladden River. 432

Palisor (I) The 'midmost region' (114) of the Great Lands, where the Elves awoke. 85, 106, 114–19, 131, 141, 231–2, 234–8; *Battle, War, of Palisor* 236–8, 243

Palisor (II) Region of the Great Lands where the Elves awoke. 8–9, 21, 42, 47, 49, 64–5, 115, 136, 141, 206, 307

Palisor (IV) Region of the Great Lands where the first Men awoke. 171, 256

Palisor (V) Land where the first Men awoke (afterwards called *Hildórien*). 181–2

Pallando (XII) One of the Blue Wizards. 385

Palúrien (I) Yavanna. 66–8, 71–5, 79–80, 88–9, 98–100, 105–6, 114, 117, 123–4, 126, 131, 133, 154, 179–80, 184, 237; *children of Palúrien* 94. See *Earth-lady*, *Kémi*, *Yavanna*.

Palúrien (II) Yavanna. 281, 328. See *Belaurin*.

Palúrien (IV) 3, 12, 41, 78–9, 81, 165, 167, 207, 275; 'Bosom of the Earth' 78; O.E. *eorþan scéat* 207. See *Belaurin*, *Yavanna*.

Palúrien (V) Name of Yavanna. 205–6, 209, 333, *380*; *Bosom of the Earth* 207, *Lady of the Wide Earth* 205, 207

Palúrien (X) 'Lady of the Wide Earth' (145). 32, 34, 145–6, 149, 151, 154, 157, 202, 393. (Replaced by *Kementári*.)

Palúrien (XI) Name of Yavanna. 246. (Replaced by *Kementári*.)

Palúrien Yavanna. (III) 160; Aule's wife 139

Panthael (IXa) 'Fullwise', Aragorn's name for Sanwise. 126, 128–9; earlier spelling *Panthail* 120, 135; *Panthail-adar* 135 (*adar* 'father'). See *Lanhail*.

Papar (V) Irish hermits in Iceland. 81; *Papey*, *Papafjörðr* 81

Paracelsus (I) 43–4

Paracelsus (XII) Physician and visionary theorist of the sixteenth century. 23, 76

Paradise (IXb) 263, 265–6, 292, 297, 409; *earthly paradise* 344, 398, 402, 410

Parley at the Black Gate (VIII) See *Black Gate(s)*.

Parma Kuluina (IV) The Golden Book. 78, 274; *Patina Kuluinen* 78

Parma Kuluinen (II) 310. See *Golden Book*.

Parmalambë (V) 'Book-tongue', Quenya. 56, 172, 184, *380*

Parth Celebrant (XII) See *Celebrant*.

Parth Galen (VII) Lawn beneath Amon Hen. 377, 382. See *Calenbel*.

Parth Galen (VIII) 20, 79, 307. See *Calembel* (1).

Parting of the Ways, The (IXb) In *The Death of St. Brendan*. 264–5, 298

Party Field, The (IXa) At Bag End. 90, 106, 108

Party, The (VI) (including references to *Birthday Party*, *Farewell Party*). Given by Bilbo: 13–15, 19–26, 40; (later story) 160, 225, 227–9, 233, 236–7, 245, 247, 252, 268, 276–7, 305, 315–16, 370, 372, 376–8, 386. Given by Bingo: 30–2, 36, 40, 42, 63, 74, 76, 85, 87, 106, 123, 138, 150, 160, 221–2, 224, 228, 233, 255, 284, 336, 371–2, 375. Given by Frodo (or 'Folco'): 370–1, 373

Party, The (VII) 5, 8, 15, 21, 38, 62

Pass of Light (V) See *Kalakilya*.

Pass of Light (X) See *Kalakiryan*.

Path of Dreams (I) See *Olórë Mallë*.

Path of Dreams (II) 119. See *Olórë Mallë, Way of Dreams*.

Paths of the Dead (VIII) 262, 274, 297, 300, 302–5, 307–8, 312, 320, 392, 397–8, 405, 407, 416–17, 419, 421–3, 427–8; described 406–7, 409. See *Dead men of Dunharrow*.

Paths of the Dead (IXa) 15–16, 50; *the Dead* 15

Paths of the Dead (XII) 265, 267, 270

Paul the Deacon (V) Historian of the Lombards. 53–4.

Pearl (V) Mediaeval English poem. 98

Pearl-gatherers (V) A name of the Teleri. 215

Pelargir (VIII) Town on Anduin. 268, 379, 386, 398, 411–15, 419–20, 422, 424, 426–9

Pelargir (IXa) Town on Anduin. 15–16

Pelargir (XII) City and port on Anduin. 32, 65, 74–5, 79, 152–3, 175, 183, 197, 199–200, 206, 215, 231, 312–13, 315, 416, 421

Peleg (II) Father of Tuor. 88, 160, 181, 204

Peleg (III) Father of Tuor in the *Lost Tales*. 145. See *Fengel* (1).

Peleg (IV) Father of Tuor in the early legends. 4–5

Pelendur (XII) Steward to King Ondohir. 203–4, 215–18, 232, 248, 256

Pelennor (VIII) (1) The wall surrounding the 'townlands' of Minas Tirith. 277 (other early references, 260, 263, are ambiguous: see 277). (2) The 'townlands' (many references are to 'the wall of (the) Pelennor', 'the Pelennor wall'). 143, 233, 260, 263–4, 270, 275, 277, 283, 288–9, 291, 324–6, 330–3, 339–40, 342–3, 349, 353–4, 359–60, 363–4, 370, 372, 388, 392, 399–400, 415–16, 422, 438. *Townlands* 277–8, 287, 330, 332, 354; *Cityland* 260, 277. *Pelennor Gate* (at the Causeway?) 326; see also *Forannest*.

   Pelennor (VIII) *Battle of the Pelennor Fields* 153, 326, 352, 367, 371, 373, 399, 419, 428–30, 432, (438); and see *Osgiliath*.

Pelennor Fields (XII) 360; *Battle of the* ~ 242, 265, 267

Pelennor Fields, Battle of the (VII) 157

Pelennor Fields, Pelennor (IXa) 7, 14, 36, 49

Pelmar (IV) 'The Enclosed Dwelling', Middle-earth. 241, *243, *245, *249, 255. See *Ambar-endya*.

Pelmar (V) 'The Enclosed Dwelling' (IV. 241), Middle-earth. 32, (380)

Pelóri (VII) The Mountains of Valinor. 95

Pelóri (X) 7, 18, 23, 33, 54–5, 67, 84, 97–8, 105, 133, 154, 175, 284–5, 291, 295, 312, 394, 401, 405; *Pelóri (Pelóre) Valion* 18, 23, 33; *the Mountains* 33, 54, 98–100, 108, 111, 117, 122, 137, 146, 149, 154, 158, 190, 284–5, 287, 289, 295. See *Mountains of Aman*.

Pelóri (XI) The Mountains of Aman. 30, 403–4

Pembrokeshire (IXb) 234, 279, 284, 309, *Pembroke* 246

Penannon (VIII) Original name of the third beacon in Anórien. 233

Pen-Arduin (XII) The dwelling of Borlas in the Emyn Amen. 411

Pendi (XI) (Telerin) = *Quendi*. 362, 375, 408

Pendrethdulur (VI) The Dimrill-stair. 433

Pengoloð (the Wise) (XII) 143, 152–3, 392, 395–6, 403, 405; *Quendingoldo* 401, *Quengoldo* 404–5

Pengoloð (X) (also *Pengoloth, Pengolodh*) 'The Sage' (of Gondolin). 7–8, 17, 22, 25–7, 30–1, 35, 38, 41, 48, 51, 65, 68, 93, 102, 110, 123, 143, 160, 165, 188, 192, 202, 281, 326–7, 415; *Pengolod* 8, 17, 22, 31, 41, 104, 143, 155, 160, 166, 281

Pengolod of Gondolin (IV) Called 'the Wise'. 263, 274, 292; O.E. *Pengolod, Pengoloð*, called *se Úþwita*, 28 1–2, 284, 290–1

Pengolod of Gondolin (V) Called 'the Wise'. 113–14, 116, 122–3, 167, 178, 192, 201–4, 228, 231, 273, 275, 278–9, 412–13; *Pengoloð* 167. See especially 277–8

Pengolod of Gondolin (VII) 454–5

Pengolod the Wise of Gondolin (IXb) 280

Pengolodh (XI) 107, 109, 210, 343, 393, 396–404, 406, 416, 419; called the *Loremaster of Eressëa* 393; his origin and history 396–7. Earlier form *Pengolod* 110 ('the Wise, of Gondolin'), 192, 201–3, 206, 210, 343. See *Thingódhel*.

Penian In Pembrokeshire. (IXb) 234, 284

Penian In Pembrokeshire. (IXb) 234, 284

Penlod (II) Called 'the Tall'; lord of the peoples of the Pillar and of the Tower of Snow in Gondolin. 173, 175, 179

Pennas (IV) 205–6, 270, 280, 284, 290, 292; *Pennas-na-Ngoelaidh* 77, 205, 280, *Pennas nan Goelið*. 284, *Pennas na Ngoeloeð* 290. See especially 206, 284, and see *Quenta Noldorinwa*, *Noldoli*.

Pennas (V) (1) *Pennas in Geleidh, Pennas na-Ngoelaidh* =*Qenta Noldorinwa*. 201, 366, 377. (2) *Pennas Hilevril, Pennas Silevril* = *Qenta Silmarillion*. 202, 385

Pennas (XI) The *Quenta Silmarillion*. 192, 206

Pennas Silevril (X) =*Quenta Silmarillion*. 200

Pensarn (VII) The rapids in Anduin. 353, 357–8, 360, 364, 366, 370. Replaced by *Ruinel* 366. See *Sarn Ruin, Sarn Gebir* (2).

People of Elwë (X) See *Elwë* (2). *People of Olwë*, see *Olwë*.

People of the Stars (X) See *Eldar*.

Peredhil (V) The Half-elven (Elros and Elrond). 219. See *Pereldar, Peringol*.

Peredhil (VI) The Half-elven (Elrond and Elros). 412

Peredhil, Pereðil (XII) 348, 364, 369; *i·Pheredhil* 256. See *Pereldar, Half-elven*.

Peregrin (Pippin) (XII) See *Took*.

Peregrin Took, Pippin (VI) See *Took*.

Peregrin Took, Pippin (VII) See under *Took*.

Peregrin Took, Pippin (VIII) See under *Took*.

Peregrin Took, Pippin (IXa) See under *Took*.

Perelandra (IXb) [Lewis] The planet Venus. 168, 203; as title, see *Lewis, C. S.*

Pereldar (II) 'Half-elven'. 266. See *Half-elven*.

Pereldar (V) 'Half-eldar', Danas. 200, 215, 218–19

Pereldar (VI) Half-elven, 'Elrond's kinsfolk'. 412. See *Children of Lúthien*.

Pereldar (X) 'Half-eldar'. 169

Pereldar (XII) 348, 364. The Half-elven (see *Peredhil*); old sense, the Nandor, 364

Perhael (IXa) Aragorn's translation of *Samwise* ('Half-wise'). 126, 128–9, *(a) Pherhael* (IXa) 129; *Perhael-adar* 127 (*adar* 'father'); earlier spelling *Perhail* 118, 120, 135. See *Lanhail, Panthael*.

Periain (IXa) Halflings. 55. (Replaced *Periannath* in Second Edition of LR.)

Periannath (IXa) Halflings. 55; *(i) Pheriannath* 46–7, 55

Periannath (XII) 193–4, 196, 229–32, 236, 247–8. See *Halflings, Hobbits*.

Peringol, Peringiul (V) The Half-elven (Elros and Elrond). 152, 219, 380; *Elrond Beringol* 148, 152

Peringol, Peringiul (VI) The Half-elven (Elrond and Elros). 412

Petty-Dwarves (IV) 188

Petty-dwarves (XI) 187, 299, 313, 388–9, 408, 415, 419; *Petty-dwarf* (referring to Mîm) 180, 258, 389. For Elvish names see *Neweg, Nibin-noeg, Nogoth; Attalyar, Levain tad-dail, Pikinaukor*.

Petty-dwarves (XII) 352. See *Nibinnogs; Mîm*.

Pharazîr (IXb) See *Azrubêl*.

Pharazôn (XII) See *Ar-Pharazôn.*

Phial of Galadriel (VIII) See *Galadriel.*

Phial of Galadriel (IXa) See *Galadriel.*

Pictures by J. R. R. Tolkien (I) 85

Pictures by J. R. R. Tolkien (II) 123, 214

Pictures by J. R. R. Tolkien (VII) 457

Pictures by J. R. R. Tolkien (VIII) 17, 44, 193, 250, 310

Pictures by J. R. R. Tolkien (IXa) 40, 136

Pictures by J. R. R. Tolkien (XII) 26, 320

Pikinaukor, Pitya-naukor (XI) (Quenya) Petty-dwarves. 389

Pillar of Heaven (IXb) 315, 317, 335, 353, 356, 373, 375, 384, 388, 391–4, 400–1, 407, 412, 429; O.E. *Heofonsýl* 287, 314–15, 317, archaic *Hebaensuil* 242; a Volcano 410, 412, and cf. 265, 289–90. *The Mountain (of Ilúvatar)*, see *Ilúvatar*; and see *(The) Lonely Isle* (2), *Menelmin, Meneltarma, Minul-Târik.*

Pillar, The (II) Name of one of the kindreds of the Gondothlim. 173, 179. See *Penlod.*

Pillars of the Kings (VII) See *Argonath.*

Pillars of the Kings (VIII) 132. See *Argonath, King Stones.*

Pine of Belaurin, Pine of Tavrobel (II) 281–2, 310, 328

Pinnath Gelin (VII) Hills in the west of Gondor. 312

Pinnath Gelin (VIII) Hills north of Anfalas. 287, 419, 429, 436–7; un-named 371

Pinnath Gelin (IXa) Hills in the west of Gondor. 59

Pipeweed (VIII) (including references to *tobacco*) 36–9, 44–5, 47, 49, 58–9, 72–3, 162, 169, 396. Used by wizards 36–8, but not by orcs 49. See *galenas, westmansweed.*

pipeweed (IXa) (including references to *tobacco, leaf*) 65, 76, 80, 95

Pipeweed (XII) 6–7, 16–17, 69; *tobacco* 6, 16; *sweet galenas* 6

Pitt, Dr. Abel (IXb) Member of the Notion Club. 159

Place of the Fountain (II) In Gondolin. 207

Place of the Gods (II) In Gondolin. 164, 186–7, 199–200, 218. See *Gar Ainion, Place of the Wedding.*

Place of the King (II) In Gondolin. See *Square of the Palace.*

Place of the Well (II) In Gondolin. See *Square of the Folkwell.*

Place of Wedding (II) The same as the Place of the Gods (see 164). 186, 200

Plague, The (Great) (XII) 17, 194, 200, 203, 209, 231, 254–5, 327

Plain of Thirst (IV) See *Dor-na-Fauglith, Thirsty Plain.*

Plains of Drouth (III) Dor-na-Fauglith. 36, 55, 232; *fields of drouth* 227, 232

Planet(s) (IXb) 204–5, 210, 212–13; of another Solar System 207

Plato (IXb) 249, 289; Dialogues: *Critias*, 289; *Timaeus* 249, 289

Pleiades (I) 35. See *Seven Stars*.

Pleiades (IXb) Daughters of Atlas. 289

Plough, The (X) The constellation of the Great Bear. 388

Poldor (V) Númenórean. 70

Poldórëa (I) Name of Tulkas. 66, 75, 79, 103, 148, 154

Poldórëa (IV) 'The Strong One' > 'the Valiant' (79) name of Tulkas. 79, 207

Poldórëa (V) 'The Valiant', name of Tulkas. 206, 382

Poldórëa (X) 'The Valiant', Tulkas. 146, 149. (Replaced by *Astaldo*.)

Pool of Annûn (VIII) 182

Pools of Twilight (II) Region on the lower course of Sirion, afterwards *Aelin-uial, the* Meres of Twilight. 195, 217, 220, 225, 248, 279–80. See *Silent Pools, Umboth-muilin*.

Pools of Twilight (III) 56, 142. See *Twilight Meres, Umboth-Muilin*.

Pools of Twilight (V) 268. See *Aelin-uial*.

Porlock (V) In Somerset. 80–1; Old English *Portloca* 80

Porlock (IXb) In Somerset. 266, 268–9, 271, 277, 293; *Porlock Weir* 268; O.E. *Portloca* 272

Poros, River (VII) 'Boundary'. 312

Poros, River (VIII) 'Boundary'. 426, 436

Poros, River (XII) 198

Poseidon (IXb) 289

Powers, The (IV) The Valar. 74, 78, 86, 151, 158, 161, 165, 211, 263, 288, 292, 331; *Battle of the Powers* 258; O.E. *Þá Mægen* 206–7, 211, *Þá Mihta* 281, *Þá Mihtigan* 285, 291

Powers, The (V) The Valar. 63–4, 66, 73–4, 110, 129, 161, 191, 204, 214, 245, 273, 277, 330, 333; *offspring of the Powers* 66

Powers, The (VI) 187–8; *the Power of darkness* 215

Powers, The (VIII) The Valar. 157

Powers, The (IXb) (Valar) 241, 246–7, 310–11, 314–15, 341, 355, 357–8, 377, 399–404, 407, 410, 412; *Powers of the World* 251, *of the West* 290; wars of the Powers 402; O.E. *Waldend* 313, 355, *Héamægnu* 317. See *Avalôi, Avalôim, Gods, Valar*.

Powers, The (X) 21, 37, 144, 162, 273, 326, 350, 394, 421; *the Powers of Arda* 152, 270, *of Eä* 48, 62, *of the World* 14, 16, 28, 36

Powers, The (XI) 6, 39, 403; *Powers of Light,* 39; *War of the Powers* 6, 106; *the (Dark) Power* 39, 43

Powers, The (XII) The Valar. 29–30, 130, 149, 183; *the Great* 149, *the Rulers* 30, 123; *the evil Power* 36, 83, *the Dark Power* 78

Prancing Pony, The (VI) (including references to *The Pony* and to *the inn*) 126, 129, 131–4, 142, 144–5, 149, 156–7, 159–62, 172, 174–5, 206, 214, 217, 223, 236, 333–4, 338–9, 342–54 *passim,* 359, 414, 430. See *White Horse.*

Prancing Pony, The (VII) (including references to *The Pony* and *the inn*) 11, 13, 16, 33, 36, 40–5, 48–9, 52–3, 55–6, 59, 62–3, 69–71, 74, 83, 106, 116, 196

Prancing Pony, The (IXa) 75–6

Prancing Pony, The (XII) 70; *the Pony* 52, 60

Precious, The (VII) The Ring. 332

Precious, The (VIII) The Ring. 97–9, 107, 109, 112, 186, 211; *precious* used by Gollum of himself 97, 109–10, 115, 193, 196, 198

Prologue (VI) (to *The Lord of the Rings*) 31, 105, 124, 284, 294, 310, 316

Prophecies of Amnos, Prophecy of Amnon (I) See *Amnos, Amnon.*

Prophecy of Mandos (IV) 18, 49, 96–7; 170, 278; *Prophecy of the North* 97, 170, 172, 262; *(Second) Prophecy of Mandos* (40–1, 73), 165, 205, 253. See *Doom of Mandos*

Prophecy of the North (I) 171–3

Prophecy of the North (III) 103–4, 136

Prophecy of the North (V) 109, 192, 237, 239. See *Doom of Mandos.*

Prophecy of the North (X) See *Noldor; Prophecies of Mandos,* see *Mandos.*

Prophecy of the North (XII) 388

Prose Edda, Snorra Edda (IXb) See *Snorri Sturluson.*

Proudfoot (VI) Hobbit family name. 14, 23, 25, 31; *Proudfeet* 13–14, 17, 223; *Proudfoots* 14, 17–18, 23, 31, 78; *Mr. and Mrs. Proudfoot* 15, 23–5; *Old Proudfoot* 248; *old Odo Proudfoot* 248

Proudfoot, Sancho (VI) 33, 36, 39, 241–2, 276

Public-house School, The (IXb) Jeremy's name for writers of the Inklings. 200, 219–20

Puck (VIII) 265

Pudda (VII) Precursor of Torhthelm (Totta) in *The Homecoming of Beorhtnoth.* 106–7

Puddifoot, Farmer (VI) 105, 295–6

Puddifoots of Stock (VI) Hobbit family of the Marish. 105, 289

Púkel-men (VIII) 245, 251, 259–60, 262–3, 265, 316, 319, 350, 356; spelt *Pookel-men* 245–6, 248, 260. See *Hocker-men*.

Púkel-men (IXa) 137; earlier name *Hoker-men* 137

Pûkel-men (XII) 309

Purgatory (I) 92

Pygmies (II) 254

Qalmë-Tári (I) 'Mistress of Death', name of Fui Nienna. 66

Qalvanda (I) 'Road of Death'. 213

Qendemir (VII) See *Eldamir*.

Qendi (I) Elves, but used of the Ilkorins as opposed to the Eldar of Valinor. 231–2, 234–5. See *Quendi*.

Qendi (VII) 453

Qendi, Quendi (V) (1) The First Kindred of the Elves (replaced by *Lindar*). 107, 122, 180–1. (2) All Elves. 119, 122, 168, 171, 174, 178, 180, 182–3, 197, 212–14, 218–19, 225, 246, 247, 366 (also *Qendië*, Noldorin *Penedhrim*), 403

Qenta (III) *Quenta Noldorinwa*, the 'Silmarillion' version of 1930. 219

Qenta, Quenta (V) (References in the texts themselves) 119, 171, 180, 185, 191, 201–2, 226, 366. See *Pennas*.

Qenya (I) (with reference to the entries in the early Qenya dictionary) 86, 92, 160, 200, 227. See *Quenya*.

Qenya (II) With reference to the entries in the early 'dictionary' of Qenya. 216, 264, 285, 292, 310

Qenya (IV) 9, 78

Qenya, Quenya (V) 'The Elvish Tongue'. 8, 56, 75, 172–5, 180, 184–6, 188, 192–5, 200, 217, 343–5, 404, 406, 412; *Qendya* 185. See *Elf-latin, Parmalambë, Tarquesta*.

Qenya, Quenya (VI) 69, 435, 463

Qerkaringa (I) The Chill Gulf, between the Icefang (*Helkaraksë*) and the Great Lands. 166–9, 172, 177, 224

Qerkaringa (IV) The Chill Gulf, between the Icefang and the Great Lands. 170

Qorinómi, Tale of (I) 202, 215, 221, 227

Queen, The (IXa) See *Arwen*.

Quenderin (XI) 'Of the Quendi'. 407

Quendi (I) 44, 132, 223, 236

Quendi (II) 219

Quendi (IV) (In the 'Sketch' spelt also *Qendi*) (1) In the *Lost Tales*, the original name of all Elves, becoming distinct from *Eldar*. 44.

(2) The First Kindred (replaced by *Lindar*). 13–15, 17, 37, 40, 44, 72, 85–7, 89–90, 93–6, 149, 151, 153–4, 159, 168, 196, 202, 264, 270, 272, 276, 289; O.E. *Cwendi* 286, 289. (3) (Final sense) The original name of all Elves. 86, 168. See *First Kindred*.

Quendi (X) 71–5, 77–8, 81, 86–7, 91, 109–10, 123–4, 130, 160–3, 166–8, 179, 187, 195, 206, 209, 259–60, 268, 275–7, 281, 309–12, 314–15, 322–3, 326, 364, 387, 390, 408, 416–18, 424, 426–7; *Qendi* 77 *Quendian* (languages) 77

Quendi (XI) Elves (see 372). 5–6, 28, 37, 105, 117, 204–5, 217, 361, 372–5, 382, 386, 391, 393, 401, 403, 405–6, 409–10, 421–3; singular *Quende* 361, 372, 374. See *Awakening of the Elves*; *Pendi*.

Quendi (XII) Elves. 29, 31, 77, 295, 395–6, 399–401. *Quendi and Eldar* (title) 325, 328, 356, 367, 392

Quendi and Eldar (X) (title of work also called *Essekenta Eldarinwa*) 415

Quendian (V) Languages derived from Oromë (*Oromian*). 168, 181, 188, 192–7, 205, 207, 342, 347; *Quendian race* 178

Quendian (VIII) 159 (*High Elvish Quendian*).

Quendian (IXb) 439

Quendian (XI) 'Of the Quendi'. 407; with reference to language 20, 319, 373, 411; *Primitive Quendian* (abbreviated PQ) 359–61, 363–5, 368, 375–6, 380, 382–4, 390, 409, 411, 413

Quendil, *Quendendil* (XI) 'Elf-friend'. 410; plural *Quendili* 412

Quendingoldo, *Quengoldo* (XII) See *Pengoloð*.

Quennar (i) Onotimo (X) Eldarin loremaster. 48–50, 56–7; *Quennar* 51, 57, *Onotimo* 57

Quennar (i) Onótimo (XI) Eldarin loremaster. 343

Quenta Eldalien (IXb) 'The History of the Elves'. 303, 307–8; *Quenta Eldaron* 308

Quenta (VII) *Quenta Noldorinwa* 96. *Quenta Silmarillion* 63, 95, 115–16, 138, 256, 453–4. See *(The) Silmanillion*.

Quenta Noldorinwa (IV) (Also *Qenta*) 77, 205–6, 270, 280, 284, 290–2. See especially 206, 284, and see *Pennas*, *Noldoli*.

Quenta (Noldorinwa) (VI) 437; *Quenta Silmarillion*, See *Silmarillion*.

Quenta Noldorinwa (IXb) 279, 412; *the Quenta* 279, 317, 356 *Quenta Silmarillion* 280, 284, 292, 354, 356, 377, 383, 411–12. See *(The) Silmarillion*.

Quenta (Noldorinwa) (XI) The *Quenta Silmarillion* (references in the texts only). 27–8, 32, 38, 48, 59, 117, 120

Quenta Silmarillion (VIII) 157, 174, 426

Quenta Silmarillion (IXa) 44–5, 58

Quenta Silmarillion (XII) 27, 61–2, 76, 142–3, 147–8, 190, 285, 295, 325–6, 349, 351, 355–6, 361, 372–3, 375, 389; *Quenta Noldorion* 30, 62

Quenta, The (Quenta Noldorinwa) (IXa) 44

Quenta, The (XII) *(Quenta Noldorinwa)* 27, 374–5

Quentalë Ardanómion (XI) Unknown work of learning referred to by Ælfwine. 206

Quenya (I) 41, 51, 112, 132

Quenya (II) 50, 140

Quenya (III) 87, 160

Quenya (IV) 174, 255, 313

Quenya (VII) 174, 242, 291, 311, 322; *Qenya* 453. See *Elder Tongue.*

Quenya (VIII) 20, 139, 161. See *High tongue.*

Quenya (IXa) 30, 47, 64, 73

Quenya (IXb) 218, 290, 304, 309–11, 313, 317, 379; Quenya words and passages cited 240–1, 246–9, 289–90, 302–3, 305–6, 308, 310, 317, 415, 419. See *Avallonian, Eressëan, Nimrian.*

Quenya (X) 39, 76, 80, 89, 126, 136, 217, 231, 284, 349–50, 359, 387–9, 415, 431 See *Avallonian, Eressëan.*

Quenya (XI) (=*Quenya lambë* 407) 22–3, 145, 201, 318–20, 337, 359, 361–78, 380–5, 387–400, 402–3, 405–7, 410–17; original and Vanyarin form *Quendya* 361, 373, 375, 393

Quenya (XII) 30–2, 36–7, 41, 52, 55, 62, 69, 78, 126, 129–30, 133, 135, 138, 154, 164, 193, 210, 217, 219, 234, 299, 315, 318–21, 324, 331–2, 335, 339–49, 352–4, 356–61, 363, 365–8, 370–1, 374, 376, 392, 404; *Quenyarin* 379; verb '*Quenyarize*' 347, 370

Quest, The (VII) 115, 248–9, 269–70, 289, 329, 371, 422, 445

Quickbeam (VIII) Ent. 26, 30, 49, 54. See *Bregalad.*

Quickbeam (IXa) Ent. 71

Radagast (VI) 379, 387, 397

Radagast (VII) 73, 76, 78, 80, 131–4, 136, 138–9, 149, 164, 173, 177, 212, 311; *the Grey* 132, 136, *the Brown* 132–3, 136, 173

Radagast (X) 397

Radagast (XII) 384

Radbug (IXa) Orc of the Tower of Kirith Ungol. 26

Radhrim (XI) 'East-march', Doriath beyond Aros. *183, 188–9. Cf. *Nivrim.*

Radhrost (V) 'East Vales, Dark-elvish name of Thargelion. 262, 265, 268–9, *382, 384*

Radhrost (XI) 'East Vale', Thargelion. 194, 197, 218, 221, 225, 227. Cf. *Nivrost* 'West Vale' (entry *Nevrast*), and see *Talath Rhúnen*.

Radhruin (III) One of the twelve companions of Barahir on Dorthonion. 335, 349

Radhruin (IV) Companion of Barahir on Taur-na-Danion. 319. (Replaced *Radros*.)

Radhruin (V) Companion of Barahir. 147, 282; *Radruin* 147, 289. (Replaced *Radros*.)

Radhruin (XI) Companion of Barahir. 56, 126. Earlier name *Radros* 126

Radros (IV) Earlier name of Radhruin. 311, 319

Radros (V) Companion of Barahir. 133, 147, 289. (Replaced by *Rad(h)ruin*.)

Ragnarök (IV) 207

Ragnarök (IXb) 286

Ragnarök (X) 399, 406

Ragnir (XI) (1) Servant of Morwen. 302. (2) Companion of Asgon. 262, 265, 302

Ragnor (III) One of the twelve companions of Barahir on Dorthonion. 335, 349

Ragnor (V) Companion of Barahir. 282

Ragnor (XI) Companion of Barahir. 56

Rainbow (I) 212, 220–1, 224–5. See *Ilweran*.

Rainbow Cleft (IV) 5, 141, 193. See *Glorfalc, Cris Ilbranteloth, Cris-Ilfing, Kirith Helvin, Cirith Ninniach*.

Rainbow, The (II) 179. See *Heavenly Arch*.

Ramandur (I) Earlier name of Sorontur. 89

Ramandur (II) Earlier name of Sorontur. 203

Ramas Coren (VIII) Earlier name of *Rammas Echor*. 288, 324, 339–40, 359, 399. Other names *Corramas* 340; *Rammas Ephel* 288; and see *Pelennor* (1).

Ramathor, Ramathir (VII) See *Belfalas*.

Ramdal (V) 'Wall's End' in East Beleriand. 262–3, 268; *Rhamdal* 283, *390*

Ramdal (XI) See *Rhamdal*.

Ramer, Michael (IXb) Member of the Notion Club. 146, 148–53, 159, 161–4, 166, 169–224, 226, 228–9, 231–3, 235–8, 245–6, 249–57, 259–60, 264, 266, 277, 281, 283–4, 291–2, 302–3, 305, 308–9, 311, 317, 353, 410; his book *The Stone-eaters* 177, 214

Ramer, Michael (X) Member of the Notion Club. 135

Ramloth (VIII) See *Gwinhir*.

Rammas Echor (VIII) The wall about the Pelennor. 277, 291, 294, 354, 371; *the Rammas* (VIII) 340, 344, 352–4

Rammas Ephel (VIII) See *Ramas Coren*

Rána (I) Name of the Moon given by the Gods. 192–3, 218

Rána (IV) Name of the Moon given by the Gods. 97, 170

Rana (V) 'The Wayward', the Moon. 56, 240, 243, *383* (also Noldorin *Rhân*). See *Isil, Ithil*.

Rana (VI) The Moon. 122

Rána (X) (also *Rana*) 'The Wayward', the Moon. 130, 136, 198, 376–7

Rangers (VI) 137–8, 154, 158, 165–7, 171, 173, 175–6, 178, 186, 204, 223–4, 331–2, 352, 354, 356, 374, 376, 393, 420; identified as *wild folk* 137, *wild hobbits* 154, 158, 173 (other references to *wild hobbits* 162, 166, 174). See especially 223–4, 331–2.

Ranger(s) (VII) 6–7, 10, 48–9, 56–8, 63–4, 75–6, 79, 82, 157, 379, 393, 399

Ranger(s) (VIII) (1) Of the North. 38, 49, 242, 244, 247, 249, 253–4, 260, 262–3, 274, 296–7, 299, 301–2, 304–5, 307–9, 360, 371, 378, 389, 391, 394–5, 406, 411, 413–14, 423–5, 438. (2) Of Ithilien. 136, 145–6

Rangers (XII) 195, 225

Ranuin (I) 'Month', child of Aluin 'Time'. 217–19, 222, 227. (Earlier forms *Ranos, Ranoth, Rôn* 222.)

Ransom, Dr. Elwin (IXb) [Lewis] 168, 212–13, 309

Rashbold, John Jethro (IXb) Member of the Notion Club. 151, 160, 211, 223, 245, 277

Rashbold, Professor (IXb) 151, 256–7, 259, 291–2. On the name *Rash-bold* see *Tolkien, J. R. R.*

Ras Mewrim (XI) Cape south-west of Eglarest. *184, 190, 418. See *Bar-in-Mŷl*.

Ras-Arphain (XI) Sindarin name of Taniquetil. 403. See *Arfanyarassë*; *Amon Uilos*.

Rateliff, John (VII) 159

Rateliff, John (XII) 140

Rath a Chelerdain (VIII) 'The Street of the Lampwrights' (q.v.) in Minas Tirith. 388; *Rath a Chalardain* 287; *Rath Celerdain* 287

Rath Dínen (VIII) 'The Silent Street' in Minas Tirith. 288, 338, 341, 375, 380, 391

Rath Dinen (IXa) 'The Silent Street' in Minas Tirith. 61, 67

Rathcarn, Rathgarn (VI) The River Redway (later Silverlode). 433 *Redhorn Gate* The pass beneath Caradhras. 381, 433; *Redhorn Pass* 381, 441

Rathloriel, River (V) 'Bed of Gold'. 141, 263, *368, 383*, 407; earlier form *Rathlorion* 407

Rathlóriel, River (XI) (also *Rathloriel*) Name given to the Ascar: 'Bed of Gold'. 180, *185, 190, 345–8, 351, 353; earlier name *Rathlorion* 180, 190, 353; late names *Rathmalad, Rathmallen* *185, 191, 353

Rathlorion, River (IV) 'Golden-Bed', name given to Ascar after the drowning in it of the treasure of Doriath. 134–5, 189–90, 234, 307, 313, 325; later form *Rathloriel* 135, 189, 234, 313

Rauros (VII) 'Rush-rain' or 'Roar-rain' (285). 285, 296, 316, 318, 346, 350, 355–6, 358–9, 361, 364, 370, 373, 378, 413. For earlier names see *Rhain Hills, Rhosfein, Dant-ruin.*

Rauros (VIII) 118, 145, 147–8, 268, 270, 361, 437

Rauros (XII) 206, 242

Realm, The (VIII) Gondor. 401

Realms in Exile (XII) 188–91, 225, 245, 254, 256, 263, 268, 279, 315

Rebirth of the Elves, the Reborn (X) See *Elves.*

Red Book (of Westmarch) (VII) 95

Red Book of Westmarch (IXa) 111; *the* (or *a*) *Red Book, the Book* (109), 112, 114, 120–3, 125–6, 132, 134

Red Book of Westmarch (XII) 12, 25; *the Red Book* 12, 25, 29, 35, 41, 47–8, 52, 61, 123–4, 126, 130–1, 217, 243–4, 253, 255, 262, 282, 327; *Great ~ of Samwise* 19

Red Eye, The (VIII) Orc-emblem. 49, 132, 138

Red Fire (VII) The fire of the Balrog. 203; *the red flame* 198

Red Maw (III) See *Carcharoth.*

Red Mountains (IV) 239, *249, 255–6. See *Orocarni.*

Red Mountains (X) 77. See *Orokarni.*

Red Pass (VI) Earlier name of the pass beneath Caradhras. 381, 397, 419–20, 422, 434, 440, 444, 461. See *Cris-caron, Dimrill-stair.*

Red Valley (VI) Earlier name of Dimrill-dale. 419, 433; *Red Vale* 433; *vale of Redway* 464. For Elvish names see 433, and *Dunruin.*

Redhorn (VII) Caradras. 166. *Redhorn Gate* 164, 240; *Redhorn Pass* 164, 174, 240; *Red Pass* 161

Redhorn Mountain (XII) 275; *Redhorn Pass* 229, 248, 250. See *Caradras.*

Redhorn, The (VI) Caradhras. 440. See *Ruddyhorn*.

Redwater, River (XII) 316. See *Carnen*.

Redway, River (VI) Earlier name of the Silverlode. 381, 397, 415, 419, 432–3, 438, 462, 464. For Elvish names see 433–4. *Little Redway*, see *Caradras dilthen*.

Redway, River (VII) Original name of the river flowing out of Dimrill Dale. 114, 164, 166, 173, 190, 213, 296, 306; see *Blackroot*, *Silverlode*. Elvish name *Ruinnel* 114

Refusers, The (VIII) See *Avari*.

Regeneard (IXb) (O.E.) Valinor. 242, 286, 317; *Regenrice* 317

Region (IV) The forest forming the southern part of Doriath. 278

Region (V) The forest forming the southern part of Doriath. 126, 148, 261, *356* (also *Eregion, Taur-nan-Erig*)

Region (XI) The southern forest of Doriath 7, 11, 15–16, 106, 112, *183, 321, 334, 355; *Region over Aros* 112

Regornion (VI) Hollin. 432. See *Eregion*.

Renewer, The (VIII) Aragorn. 390, 395. See *Envinyatar*.

Rerir, Mount (V) Outlier of Eredlindon, on which was a fortress of the Noldor. 263, 265, 268, 283, 290

Rerir, Mount (XI) Source of Greater Gelion. 34, *183, 188

Return of the King, The (IXb) 217

Return of the King, The (X) (title) 4, 6, 135, 359, 412

Reynolds, R. W. (IV) 11, 41

Reynolds. R. W. (III) 3

Rhain Hills (VII) See *Emyn Rhain. Falls of Rhain* 273, 315; see *Rhosfein*.

Rhamdal (XI) 'Wall's End' in East Beleriand. *185, 191; *Ramdal* 191. See *Andram*.

Rhascaron (VI) Early name for Caradhras. 433; *Rhascarn* 438

Rhevain (XI) See *Hravani*.

Rhibdath, Rhimdath (V) [River Rushdown. 384. This name only appears in the *Etymologies*, but it should have been mentioned there that the Rushdown is the river that flowed from the Misty Mountains to join Anduin north of the Carrock.]

Rhibdath, River (VII) See *Rushdown*.

Rhien (VII) See *Galadriel*.

Rhimbron (VII) Elf of Lórien, companion of Hathaldir (Haldir). 227, 230–1, 236, 240. Replaced by *Rhomrin, Romrin* 236, and finally *Rúmil* 240

Rhimdad, Rhimdath, River (VII) See *Rushdown*.

Rhimdath (VI) The River Rushdown. 205

Rhimdir, Rhimlath (VII) See *Orofin.*

Rhomrin (VII) See *Rhimbron.*

Rhosfein, Rosfein, Falls of (VII) In Anduin. *(Rosfein)* 273, (281), 282, 285, 315; *cataracts of Rhosfein* 283, 285. See *Dant-ruin, Rhain Hills, Rauros.*

Rhosgobel (VII) Home of Radagast in Mirkwood. 149, 164, 172–3, 296, 306. See *Brownhay.*

Rhovan(n)ion (XII) 198, 213–14, 259, 262, 280, 302, 312–13, 437; *Róvannion* 214. See *Wilderland.*

Rhovanion (VII) Wilderland. 296; *Rhovannion* 318

Rhovanion (VIII) Wilderland. 253

Rhudaur (XII) One of the divisions of earlier Arnor. 193–4, 208–9, 228, 230

Rhûn (VII) The East. 296, 307, 333; *Rhûn the Great* 434. *Sea of Rhûn* 307, 333, 347

Rhûn (VIII) The East. 281

Rhûn, Sea of (III) 26

Rhûn, Sea of (IXa) 71

Rhûn, Sea of (XI) 174

Rhûn, Sea of (XII) 204, 294, 306, 316, 373, 387, 391–2, 437; *fields of Rhûn* 219; *Sea of Rhúnaer* 198, 229 (*Rúnaer* 198)

Rhûnaer, Sea of (VII) 296, 298, 306–7, 347. On *Rhûn* and *Rhûnaer* see 307

Rhymes of Lore (VIII) 65, 75–7, 306

Rían (IV) Mother of Tuor. 35, 67, 122, 141, 146, 183, 193, 298–9, 301, 303, 311–12, 315–16, 319, 321–2

Rian (V) Mother of Tuor. 131, 133, 136–7, 151, 282, 289, *383* (*Rhian*); *Rían* 316

Rían (VII) Mother of Tuor. 261

Rían (XI) Mother of Tuor. 52, 56, 71, 79, 126, 133, 135, 224, 231, 234

Rían (XII) Sister of Dior Steward of Gondor. 204, 219, 249.

Riben (IXa) Aragorn's translation of *Merry* (Gamgee). 117. (Replaced by *Gelir.*)

Riddermark, The (VII) 135, 139, 148, 151, 351, 393. See *Horserland, (The) Mark, Rohan.*

Riddermark, The (VIII) 52. See *(The) Mark, Rohan.*

Riddermark, The (IXa) 61, 72. See *(The) Mark.*

Riddle-game (VI) 80, 86, 262–3, 314

Riddle-game (VII) 24–5, 38, 147

Rider Haggard (XII) 320

Rider Haggard, Henry (II) 329

Rider(s) of Rohan (VIII) 4–5, 13, 16, 18, 22, 26, 28, 36, 40–2, 48, 50–1, 68, 92, 95, 102, 219, 226, 231, 238, 240, 242, 245, 250, 252, 256–7, 265, 273, 298–9, 303–4, 306–7, 309–10, 316–19, 322, 337, 345–9, 352–3, 356, 360, 369, 371, 373, 385, 413; Old English *Ridend* 389

Riders (of Rohan) (IXa) 46, 57, 61, 72, 120, 123; *Riders of the King's House* 62; *Knights of Rohan* 67; *Lady of Rohan* (Eowyn) 62. See *Gap, Wold, of Rohan.*

Riders (VII) (1) See *Black Riders.* (2) Riders of Rohan. 390, 392–5, 399–400, 402, 404–6, 409–10, 449

Riders of Rohan (XII) 34, 52, 71, 272–3. See *Rohirrim.*

Rigel (IXb) Star in Orion. 236, 285, 308

Rim of Earth (II) (Also *World's Rim, Rim of Things, Lip of the World, (bar at the) Margin of the World*) 151, 255, 260–2, 268–9, 274, 314, 316, 322, 325

Rimbedir (VI) Elvish name of Trotter. 198, 207, 217. See *Du-finnion, Ethelion, Padathir.*

Rimion (II) Father of Egnor; *Egnor bo-Rimion* 22, 51

Rimmon (Forest) (VIII) Forest about Min Rimmon Beacon. 351–2; *Taur-rimmon* 350–1. *Rimmon* used of the beacon-hill 351–2

Ring of Doom (II) Earlier reading for *Necklace of the Dwarves.* 136

Ring of Doom (IV) The council-place of the Valar. 81, 167

Ring of Doom (V) The council-place of the Valar. 209, 229

Ring of Doom (X) The council-place of the Valar. 55, 61, 80, 88, 96, 106, 110, 114, 129, 154, 189, 278, 288, 291–2, 294, 386

Ring of Earth (VII) Galadriel's Ring. 252, 255, 260–1, 265, 279; other references 254, 266, 358, 363, 366. *Ring of Sea* 255. *Ring of Sky* 255.

Ring, The (VI) 15–16, 25–6, 32, 34, 38, 41–3, 47, 49, 54, 58, 64, 70–1, 73–87, 94, 123, 126, 138–9, 154, 173, 185–6, 188–9, 197, 199, 206, 208, 211, 217–18, 224–9, 233, 237, 239–43, 245, 248–9, 255–6, 258, 261–6, 271–2, 282, 285, 287–8, 290, 293–4, 297, 300–1, 314–15, 319–22, 325, 334, 336, 352–3, 358–60, 362, 364–5, 371, 373–4, 376–81, 392, 394, 396–406, 409–10, 414, 436, 442, 455, 459, 461. See especially 42–3, 64, 73–5, 78–82, 87, 226–7, 396–7.

Ring, The (VII) 5–6, 8, 13, 19–28, 38, 49–51, 54–5, 63, 69, 71, 77,

81–3, 105, 110–12, 114, 117–18, 121, 126–7, 129–30, 143–4, 146–8, 153–4, 157–8, 161–2, 207–18 *passim*, 254–5, 269, 271, 325–48 *passim*, 366, 370, 372–4, 378–80, 385, 426–7, 437–8, 444. The Ring confers understanding of Orc-speech 332, 337, 340; the Ring worn on Amon Hen 373–4, 381; *the Ring* as title of the work 407

Ring, The (VIII) 50–1, 56, 67, 85–6, 98–9, 104–5, 109, 112, 115, 145, 151–2, (154), 160, 163–4, (167), 169, 173, 177, 185–7, 189–92, 195, 199, 211–15, 219, 224, 230, 256, 262, (304, 310), 329, (332), 333, 361–2, 386, 400–3, 432. *The One Ring* 98, 401; *the Ruling Ring* 151. *The War of the Ring* 71, 162; *The Ring* as title of the work 130, 136, 184; powers conferred by the Ring 186, 190–2, 212–14. See *(The) Precious*.

Ring, The (IXa) 3, 5–7, 9, 12, 14, 21–3, 25, 30, 37–9, 59, 133; *the Great Ring* 111; *the Ring of Doom* 44, 55; *Frodo of the Ring* 125; *Companions of the Ring* 57; *War of the Ring* 111

Ring, The (IXb) 217, 382

Ring, The (XII) (including references to the *Great Ring, One Ring, Ruling Ring*) 3–5, 7, 11, 13, 15, 19, 25, 29, 33, 124, 131, 153, 166–70, 172–4, 177–80, 186, 225, 233, 237–43, 247–8, 251, 264–7, 282–3, 310, 320, 338, 382. See *Company, War of the Ring*.

Ring, The One (VI) 226, 258, 260–2, 264, 266, 269–71, 319, 399, 404; *the Master-ring* 258, 397; *the Great Ring* 403. See *Ruling Ring*.

Ring, The One (VII) 26, 148–9, 154, 237, 255, 259–60, 265, 286; *the One Treasure* 337, *the Great Ring* 154. See *Ruling Ring*.

Ringbearer (VII) 114, 168, 208, 265–6, 327, 329, 332, 334, 337, 345–7, 389, 397; *the Bearer* 338

Ringbearer(s) (XII) 242–3, 246, 265, 267, 378

Ringbearer, The (VI) 189, 199, 224, 406

Ringbearer, The (VIII) 50, 105, 185, 229, 334; *the bearer* 329.

Ringbearer, The (IXa) (9), 14, 45, 66, 83,112; *Ringbearers* 47, 112

Ringhay (VI) Original name of the house at Crickhollow. 299

Ringhay (VII) Crickhollow. 173

Ringil (I) (1) The pillar of the Northern Lamp. 69–70, 82, 87, 101, 106, 118. (2) Fingolfin's sword. 87

Ringil (III) Fingolfin's sword. 285–6, 293

Ringil (IV) (1) Originally the pillar of the Northern Lamp, 256; in the *Ambarkanta* the Southern Lamp, which became the Sea of Ringil,

(238), 239, *249, 256, 258. See *East(ern) Sea*. (2) Fingolfin's sword. 106–7

Ringil (V) (1) The Sea of Ringil, formed from the fall of the Lamp Ringil. 32, *383*. (2) Fingolfin's sword. 284–5, *383*

Ringil (X) The Southern Lamp. 7, 22. See *Hyaras, Hyarantë, Ormal*.

Ringil (XI) Fingolfin's sword. 55

Ringlo, River (VII) In Gondor. 311–12

Ringlo, River (VIII) In Gondor. 268, 287, 411, 436–7; *crossing of Ringlo* 437, 439; *Ringlo Vale* (VIII) 287. See *Imlad Ringlo*.

Ringlo, River (IXa) 17; *Ringlo Vale* 15–17

Ringló, River (XII) 313

Ring-lord (VI) See *Lord of the Rings*.

Ringlord, The (VIII) 401, 404; *Ring-master* 105

Ringmaker, The (VII) 25

Rings (VI) 75, 78, 80–2, 85, 87, 173, 225–7, 255, 258, 260–2, 265, 269–71, 319, 364, 396–7, 404. See *Lord of the Rings*.

Rings (VII) 22–3, 26, 38, 112, 117, 130, 132, 138, 149, 155, 255, 259; *Rings of Fëanor* 255–6; *Saruman's Ring* 133, 138; *'ring from Mazarbul'* 209, 215

Rings (VIII) 48, 71, 73, 98, 156. Ring of Galadriel 425; Ring of Aragorn 425–6. See *Three Rings, Seven Rings, Nine Rings*.

Rings of Men (VI) 75, 78, 87, 258, 260, 269–70, 404

Rings of Power (VI) 265, 270, 272

Rings of Power (VII) 22, 28, 117, 149, 255, 259–60; *the Great Rings* 22. *Of the Rings of Power* in *The Silmarillion* 138, 144–6, 260. See *Three Rings, Seven Rings, Nine Rings*.

Rings of Power (XII) 79, 168, 172, 174, 177–9, 235, 237, 251–2; *Elven-rings* 13. The Three Rings of the Elves 33, 179–80, 227, 243, 265. The Seven Rings of the Dwarves 237, 250, 252, 276, 280, 283; *the Ring-wearer* 286; the Ring of Thrór and Thráin 250, 252, 276, 280–1, 283–4. The Nine Rings of Men 175–230.

Rings of Power, The (X) (title) 5–6

Rings of the Dwarves (VI) 75, 78–9, 87, 210, 226, 258, 260, 269, 320, 397–9, 403–4, 414

Rings of the Elves (VI) 75, 78, 87, 225, 258, 260, 269–70, 319, 397, 399, 403–5. See especially 225, 404.

Rings of the Goblins (VI) 75, 78

Rings, The (IXa) 52 (of the Elves); *The Lord of the Rings* 111. See *Three Rings*.

Rings, The (X) 395, 400; *the Ring* 400; *Morgoth's Ring*, Middle-earth, 400, 406

Ring-verse, The (VI) 258–9, 269–70

Ringwil (III) Later name of the stream Ingwil. 89

Ringwil, River (XI) Tributary stream of Narog. 190, 197–8. (Replaced Ingwil.)

Ringwraith(s) (VIII) 115, 120, 186, 363–4. See *Wraiths.*

Ringwraith(s) (IXa) 5, 20, 38, 40, 109

Ringwraiths (IXb) 382

Ringwraiths (III) 124

Ring-wraiths (VI) 74–6, 173, 176, 186, 189–90, 198–9, 211–12, 223–5, 260, 270, 363–5, 367, 373, 375, 396, 408, 416; *Wraiths* 78, 81, 87, 168, 206, 208, 256, 261, 270, 362, 364; *wraith-world* 208, 217. See *Elf-wraiths, Men-wraiths; Black Riders, (the) Nine Rivendell* 41–3, 45–6, 60, 63–4, 68–9, 74, 84, 88, 106, 109, 125–6, 131, 133, 155, 159, 162, 164, 168, 170, 176, 178–9, 191–217 *passim*, 220, 223, 225–6, 229, 233, 270, 274, 283, 305, 309, 353, 355–6, 359–76 *passim*, 379–82, 391–2, 395–6, 398, 400, 402–3, 406–7, 413, 415–19, 428, 430–2, 435, 437, 440, 444, 455, 461. See *Elves.*

Ringwraiths (VII) (also *Wraiths*) 14, 49, 72–3, 78, 130–1, 149, 158, 162, 208, 210, 254, 332, 335, 343, 422–3. Borne upon vultures, see *Vultures; the Winged Messenger* 428. See *Black Riders, Nazgûl, (The) Nine.*

Ringwraiths (XII) 153, 175, 177, 193, 200–2, 207, 215–16, 230, 233–4, 240–1, 245, 252, 265; *Chief, Lord of the Ringwraiths* 195, 201, 217, 230, 233, 242, 245. See *Nazgûl, Úlairi; Black Captain, Witch-king.*

Rithil-Anamo (XI) The Doom-ring of the Valar. 401. See *Máhanaxar.*

Riven River (VI) The river of Rivendell. 360

Riven River, Rivendell River (VII) 59

Rivendell (VII) 5–10, 13–14, 18, 31, 49, 57, 59, 61–3, 65–6, 68–70, 72–3, 75–6, 80–4, 95, 116, 120, 124–5, 127–8, 130, 134, 136, 140, 146, 152–3, 156–8, 161, 164–5, 169, 173, 183, 212, 221, 223, 238, 247–50, 255, 258, 263–4, 280, 286, 290, 292, 311, 361, 367–9, 390, 401, 405, 409, 417, 423, 438–9, 445, 451. See *Imladris.*

Rivendell (VIII) 76, 98, 139, 145, 218, 256, 267, 275, 296, 301–2, 305, 307, 310, 386. See *Imladrist.*

Rivendell (IXa) 32, 52, 57–8, 63–4, 69–70, 73–4, 111, 115, 127, 132

Rivendell (X) 90

Rivendell (XI) 190

Rivendell (XII) 36, 44, 76, 79, 168, 174, 177, 225, 239–42, 246, 253, 255, 269–70, 273, 283, 339, 377–80. See *Imladris*.

River of Rivendell (VI) 204; *Rivendell River* 360; unnamed 126, 162, 191–2, 196–8, 200, 204, 207, 212, 360–1, 400, 409, 417. See especially 204–5; and see *Bruinen, Loudwater*.

Rivers, Mr. (VI) Assumed name of Merry Brandybuck at Bree. 135, 141, 152, 159, 164

Rivil (XI) Tributary stream of Sirion. 72, 113, 181, *183; *Rivil's Well* 59, 113, *183; *Fen of Rivil* 113, 181, 238 (see *Serech*).

Rivil, Rivil's Well (III) Stream rising in Dorthonion and flowing into Sirion in the Fen of Serech. 171, 342, 350

Rivil's Well (V) 298

Road goes ever on and on, The (VI) 47, 53, 65, 70, 236, 240, 246–7, 278, 284, 324

Road goes ever on and on, The (IXa) 64

Road Goes Ever On, The (I) 160

Road Goes Ever On, The (VII) 85

Road Goes Ever On, The (XI) 419

Road Goes Ever On, The (XII) 299

Road of Arches (II) In Gondolin. 182

Road of Pomps (II) In Gondolin; 186

Road, The (VI) See *East Road*.

Road, The (VII) 7, 14, 29–30, 42, 52, 57, 59, 61, 69, 71–4, 79, 83, 296; *East Road* 9, 13, 17

Roads (VIII) From Helm's Deep 27, 42, 72. From Isengard 31, 41, 43, 56, 68–9, 78. From Edoras to Minas Tirith 253, 318, 340, 347, 351 ('horsemen road'), 353–4, 373, 404; old wain-road in Anórien 351–2.

Roads (VIII) From Minas Tirith into South Gondor 283; across the Pelennor to the Causeway 353, 389, 391, 416 (and see *Causeway*). From Osgiliath to Minas Morghul (*Morghul-road, Osgiliath road*) 135, 175–8, 182, 192, 291, 294–5, 327; *Wraith-road* over the pass above Minas Morghul 195, 222

Roads (VIII) Roads to the Black Gate 123, 128; south road through Ithilien 121, 123, 125, 128–9, 131–2, 135, 139, 151, 177, 360, 432, *Harad Road* 439

Roads (IXa) Coast road in South Gondor 15–17. Main road from

Minas Morgul to Barad-dûr 10, 20–2; from Durthang to the Isenmouthe 35–6; from the Isenmouthe to Barad-dûr 39, 43.

Roads (IXa) 'North Roads' from Minas Tirith 61; the East Road 77–8, 88, 100, 105; the Bywater Road, leaving the East Road at the 'waymeet' (105), 87–8, 92, 96, 98, 100, 105, 107. The old South Road 103

Roads (XI) In Brethil 157, 186; to Nargothrond 157, 186, 398. *The East Road (East-West Road)* 319, 324–5, 332–5. See *Dwarf-road(s)*.

Rochallor (XI) Fingolfin's horse. 55–6, 125

Rodëol (XI) The metal of Eöl. 322–3. See *Galvorn*.

Rodnor (XII) See *Gil-galad*.

Rodothlim (II) Noldoli of the Caves with whom Túrin sojourned (precursors of the Noldor of Nargothrond). 81–4, 91–2, 94–8, 107, 112–13, 117–19, 123–4, 128, 135–6, 140–2, 222–3, 226, 228, 236, 246, 248. (Replaced *Rothwarin*.)

Rodothlim (III) Precursors of the Gnomes of Nargothrond. 53, 83, 85, 90, 247

Rodothlim (IV) Precursors of the Gnomes of Nargothrond. 60, 180, 223

Rodrim (III) Unknown; named in Beleg's 'whetting spell'. 45, 54

Rodwen (XI) Proposed name to replace *Isfin*. 3 17–18

Rog (II) (1) Orcs' name for Egnor father of Beren (*Rog the Fleet*) 45. (2) Lord of the people of the Hammer of Wrath in Gondolin. 174–6, 178–80, 203, 211

Rog (IV) Lord of the people of the Hammer of Wrath in Gondolin. 144, 194

Rohan (II) 329

Rohan (VI) 189, 351, 411, 422, 434–5, 438, 440; *Rochan(dor)* 'Horseland' 434; *Gap of Rohan* 434. Other names *Borthendor, Orothanador, Thanador, Ulthanador* 434

Rohan (VII) 68, 71–2, 79, 130, 135–6, 139, 144, 148, 151–2, 177, 210, 212, 214–15, 232, 282–3, 293, 311, 322, 330, 351, 357–8, 372, 385–8, 390, 393–412 *passim*, 419, 424, 426, 429–30, 433–5, 437, 441, 443–6, 448–50. *Master of Rohan* 386; tongue of Rohan 419, 424, 442–3. See *Horseland, (The) Mark, (The) Riddermark; Gap of Rohan, Wold of Rohan*.

Rohan (VIII) 4, 16, 35, 39, 42, 45, 50–2, 54, 68, 71, 80, 92, 95, 100, 102, 110, 126, 129–30, 141, 150, 152, 155–6, 158–9, 162, 166–7, 182, 219, 226, 229, 233, 235, 238, 243–5, 247, 249–51, 253–

7, 259–60, 263, 274–6, 298–9, 301, 303–4, 306, 310–11, 317–21, 324, 329, 337, 339, 346–7, 355, 359–60, 362, 369, 371, 373, 385–6, 389, 408, 411, 423. Tongue of Rohan 35, 44, 155, 159, 243–4, 267, 389. *Rohan* (VIII) =Men of Rohan 16, 18, 22, cf. *Rochann, Rohann* 22. See *(The) Mark*; *Riders of Rohan*; *Gap of Rohan, Wold of Rohan.*

Rohan (IXa) 48, 57, 70, 73, 120, 123; see *(The) Mark, (The) Riddermark.*

Rohan (XII) 10, 21, 34, 38–9, 41, 49–50, 52–4, 58–60, 65, 68–71, 81, 83, 122, 157, 205–7, 219–21, 236–40, 242, 244, 255, 261, 267, 271–4, 296, 301, 314–16, 319, 329; *Rochann* 53, 236, *Rohann* 60; *Gap of* ~ 271, 273, *Wold of* ~ 205, 271; and see *Riders of Rohan.*

Rohan (XII) *Mark of Rohan, the Mark* 49, 52–3, 76, 81, 261, 270, 272, 274, 316

Rohan, Rochan(d) (XI) 104; and see *Gap (of Rohan).*

Roheryn (VIII) Aragorn's horse. 301, 423

Rohir (VIII) Rohirrim. 24, 40, 56, 155, 157, 167–8, 236, 249

Rohiroth (VII) Earlier form for *Rohirrim.* 135, 139, 151, 347, 389–90, 392, 395, 398–9, 412, 418, 433–5, 442, 449; *Rochiroth* 139; *Rohir* 433. See *Horsemasters, Riders* (2).

Rohiroth (VIII) Rohirrim. 22 (*Rochirhoth, Rohirhoth*), 24, 156–7, 168

Rohiroth, Rochiroth (VI) The Horse-lords. 440. See *Horse-kings.*

Rohirrim (VII) 214, 357, 395, 407, 450

Rohirrim (VIII) 4–5, 22, 24, 40, 254–5, 266–7, 273–4, 318, 320, 342, 344–6, 349, 351–4, 359, 381, 385–6, 389, 392–3, 404–6, 415, 420, 422–3, 428. See *Eorlingas.*

Rohirrim (XII) 34, 38, 41, 49, 52–3, 60, 65, 71, 75, 82, 236, 238–9, 242, 245, 271–2, 296, 312, 328; earlier name *Rohiroth* 71; Horse-lords 272. See *Riders of Rohan, Eorlings.*

Rohirwaith (VIII) Rohirrim. 22

Romance (IXb) (languages and literatures) 151, 418

Romans (II) 294, 304, 309, 330. See *Rúmhoth, Men of the South.*

Romans (IXb) 221

Rombaras (X) The horn of Oromë. 7, 35, 39, 151, 202. (Replaced by *Valaróma.*)

Rome (II) See *Rúm.*

Rome (V) 55; *Roman(s)* 39, 91–2; Old English *Walas, Rúm-walas* 92

Rómelonde (IXb) 'East-haven' in Númenor. 314–15; earlier (in O.E. text) *on Rómelónan* 315. (Replaced by *Rómenna.*)

Rómen (IV) East *243, *249, 255

Rómendakil I (XII) Name taken by Tarostar, eighth King of Gondor. 197, 213, 228; translated *East-slayer* 197, 213, 228, *East-victor* 213

Rómendakil II (XII) Name taken by Minalkar, Regent and later the nineteenth King of Gondor. 198, 213–14, 258–60, 315

Rómenildi (V) Easterlings. 286, 291, (364)

Rómenna (V) Haven in the east of Númenor. 74

Rómenna (IXb) 'Eastward', haven in Númenor. 315, 384–5; cf. 310

Rómenna (XII) Great haven in the east of Númenor. 151–2, 160, 162

Rómestámo (XII) One of the Blue Wizards. 385; *Róme(n)star* 391

romloth (VIII) See *galenas*.

Romrin (VII) See *Rhimbron*.

Room of Logs (II) In Mar Vanwa Tyaliéva. 197, 221; *Room of the Tale-fire* 298. See *Tale-fire*.

Room of the Log Fire (I) See *Tale-fire*.

Roos (IV) 215

Root of the Boot, The (VI) The original 'Troll Song'. 142–4

Root of the Boot, The (VII) The original 'Troll Song'. 59, 66

Rope of Years (I) 219

Rôs (II) (1) Promontory of the Great Lands; Battle of Rôs. 283–6, 293, 302. (2) Capital of Tol Eressëa. 302. (3) Name of Tol Eressëa? 302. (4) See the Appendix on Names, II 347.

Rosamund (IXb) Wife of Alboin the Lombard. 236, 285

Rosamunda (V) Wife of Alboin the Lombard. 37, 54

Rose of Silpion (I) The Moonflower. 191–3, 195, 218; *Rose of Silver* 192. See *Sil*.

Rosfein (VII) See *Rhosfein*.

Rothinel of Amroth (IXa) Wife of Denethor. 54, 58. (Replaced *Emmeril*, replaced by *Finduilas* (2).)

Rôthinzil (IXb) 'Flower of the Foam', the ship of Azrubêl. 360, 377–8. See *Vingalótë*.

Rothinzil (XII) Adûnaic name of Vingilot. 143, 163, 365, 369–71

Rothwarin (II) Earlier name for the Rodothlim. 117, 119, 135–6

Round World (X) 4–6, 22, 39; *Round Earth* 383

Ruddyhorn (VI) Caradhras. 419, 421, 433; *Ruddihorn* 433. See *Redhorn*, and for early Elvish names see 433.

Ruddyhorn (VII) Caradras. 167

Ruffian(s) (IXa) (in the Shire) 80, 83–8, 91–7, 99–105, 108, 117, 119, 126, 128

Rufus (IXb) See *Dolbear, Rupert*.

Ruinel (VII) See *Pensarn*.

Ruinnel (VII) See *Redway*.

Rúkhs, plural *Rakhās* (XI) Dwarvish name for Orcs. 391

Rulers of Arda, The (X) 49, 99, 224, 232, 248, 271; *the Rulers* 147

Rulers of the World (VII) The Valar. 255. *The Gods* 432.

Ruling Ring, The (VI) 87, 189, 227, 250, 258, 260, 265, 270, 322, 364, 396, 403–4. See *Ring, The One*.

Ruling Ring, The (VII) 23, 28, 112, 148, 155, 159, 254, 259–60, 266

Rûm (II) Rome. 196, 203, 315, 330; *Rome* 203. (The form of the name with *u* is found in Old English; see 315.) See *Magbar, Micelgeard*.

Rúmhoth (II) Romans. 294, 304, 306, 309. See *Romans, Men of the South*.

Rúmil (I) Door-ward of Mar Vanwa Tyaliéva, called *the Sage* (65). 46–52, 59, 64–5, 78–9, 94, 107, 129, 134, 167, 169, 171, 230, 235. See *Evromord*.

Rúmil (II) 149, 209 *Alphabet of Rúmil* 69; *book of Rúmil* 217

Rúmil (IV) 235, 271, 274, 292–3; called *the Elfsage of Valinor* 292

Rúmil (V) 113–14, 116, 122–3, 155–6, 164, 167, 178, 191–2, 203–4, 278; called *the sage of Kôr, of Tûn* 167, *the Elf-sage of Valinor* 123, 203–4

Rúmil (VII) (1) See *Rhimbron*. (2) The alphabet of Rúmil of Túna. 453

Rúmil of Tûn (IXb) 280

Rúmil (X) 8, 17, 22, 25, 30–1, 48, 64–5, 92, 103, 145, 150, 174, 184–5, 191, 256, 373

Rúmil (XI) 'The ancient sage of Tirion' (398). 343, 398–9, 401, 407; *I Equessi Rúmilo* 'the Sayings of Rúmil' 397–8, 401; *Rúmilian letters* 396

Rúmil (XII) The sage of Tirion. 360; *alphabet of Rúmil* 22

Rúnaeluin (IXa) See 65, 71

Runes (VI) 82, 145, 154, 156, 158, 170, 173, 194, 235, 343, 352, 355, 448, 460, 467

Runes (VII) 47, 49–50, 56, 61, 78, 92, 97, 101, 104, 186, 189, 200, 220, 274, 276, 382, 387, 452–9

Runes (VIII) 138, 218; *north-runes* 407

Runes (IXb) (Old English) 285

Runes (X) (of Daeron) 106

Runes (XI) (all references are to the Runes of Dairon or 'of Doriath') 14, 20, 26, 28, 103, 110. See *Cirth*.

Runes (XII) 22, 72, 75–6, 81, 297–300, 319–20, 324; *moon-runes*

319; *dwarf-letters* 297. *Runic* 297–8, 319. See *Angerthas, Cirth*.

Running River (VI) 218

Running, River (VII) 298, 307

Running, River (XII) 259, 316, 330. See *Celduin*.

Rushdown, River (VI) Rhimdath, a tributary of the Anduin. 205

Rushdown, River (VII) Tributary of Anduin. 296. Elvish names *Rhibdath, Rhimdad, Rhimdath* 296

Rushey (VI) Village in the Marish. 298, 304; *Rushy* (erroneous) 304

Rushlight (VI) Family name in Bree. 137

Rúsitaurion (II) 'Son of the weary forest' (Eldarissa), name given to himself by Turambar. 89. See *Dhrauthodavros*.

Russandol (IV) Name of Maedhros. 212

Sackville (VI) Hobbit family name. 31

Sackville-Baggins, Ainalda (VI) Earliest name of Lobelia. 16–18, 35–6

Sackville-Baggins, Cosimo (IXa) 32, 34, 52, 65–6, 77–9, 82–5, 88, 90–1, 94–5, 99, 103–4, 106, 110; called *Pimple* 84, 96; *the Boss* 82, 88–91, 94, 97–8, 104; *the Chief* 98, 101, 104, 107. (Replaced by *Lotho*.)

Sackville-Baggins, Lobelia (IXa) 32, 52, (85, 91), 96, 98–100, 108, 110

Sackville-Baggins, Lotho (IXa) 34, 78, 99, 103. (Replaced *Cosimo*).

Sackville-Baggins, Otho (XI) 104

Sackville-Bagginses (VI) 13–16, 19, 22–3, 29, 31, 33, 36–7, 39, 221–2, 228, 241–3, 248, 273, 275, 283, 315, 371, 377

Sackville-Baggins,~ *Cosimo* (VI) Son of Lobelia and Otho. 276, 283, 324, 380. (Replaced by *Lotho*.)

Sackville-Baggins,~ *Cosmo* (VI) Early name of Otho. 18, 36. (Replaced *Sago*.)

Sackville-Baggins,~ *Grimalda, Griselda* (VI) Early names of Lobelia. 18, 33, 36

Sackville-Baggins,~ *Lobelia* (VI) 32–3, 36, 39, 239, 241, 243, 247–8, 276, 283, 324

Sackville-Baggins,~ *Lonicera* (VI) Early name of Lobelia. 17, 36

Sackville-Baggins,~ *Lotho* (VI) Son of Lobelia and Otho. 283. (Replaced *Cosimo*.)

Sackville-Baggins,~ *Miranda* (VI) Wife of Cosimo. 283, 324

Sackville-Baggins,~ *Otho* (VI) 33, 36, 39, 239, 241, 243, 248

Sackville-Baggins,~ *Sago* (VI) Earliest name of Otho. 16, 18, 36

Sackville-Bagginses (VII) 6, 8, 21, 135, 286; *Lobelia* 32; *Cosimo* 32, 216, 249

Sador (I) Servant of Húrin. 244

Sador (XII) Old servant of Húrin of Dor-lómin. 327; *Sadog* 309, 327

Sador Labadal (XI) Servant of Húrin. (90), 145–6, 257, 300, 314

Saelin (XI) Name of Andreth. 230, 232–3; *Saelind* 233; *Saelon* 233–4

Saelind (X) 'Wise-heart', Andreth. 305, 360; earlier form *Saelon* 351–2, 360

Saelon (XII) (1) Young man of Gondor. 409–18, 421; earlier names *Almoth*, *Egalmoth* 409, 419, *Arthael* 409–10, 418, 420. (2) See *Andreth*.

Saeros (II) 121–2, 142

Saeros (III) Elf of Doriath, enemy of Turin. 51.

Saeros (V) Elf of Doriath, slain by Túrin. 187, 316. (Replaced *Orgof*.)

Saeros (X) Elf of Doriath, enemy of Túrin. 374

Saeros (XI) Nandorin Elf of Doriath, enemy of Túrin. 112, 409, 420. See *Orgof*.

Sagroth (XI) Man of Brethil. 274, 278, 303

Sailors, The (V) A name of the Teleri. 215

Saithnar (III) Unknown; named in Beleg's 'whetting spell'. 45, 54

Saksani (II) Saxons. 306

Salgant (II) Lord of the people of the Harp in Gondolin. 173, 175, 177, 182, 190–1

Salmar (I) Companion of Ulmo, called also Noldorin, Lirillo, and (Gnomish) Golthadriel. 58, 63, 66, 75, 79–80, 89, 93, 101, 126, 155, 177, 184

Salmar (II) Companion of Ulmo, called also Noldorin. 219, 279

Salmar (IV) Companion of Ulmo, called also Noldorin. 68

Salmar (V) Companion of Ulmo. 161, 165

Salmar (X) Companion of Ulmo. 20, 35

Sam Gamgee (VI) See *Gamgee*.

Sam Gamgee (VII) See under *Gamgee*.

Sam Gamgee (VIII) See under *Gamgee*.

Sam Gamgee (X) 412

Samírien (I) Feast of Double Mirth in Valinor. 143–4, 222; *Samírien's road* 222 (see *Vansamírin*).

Sammath Naur (VII) The Chambers of Fire in Orodruin. 349

Sammath Naur (IXa) The Chambers of Fire in Orodruin. 40–1, 50. *The Chamber of Fire, (fire-) chamber* 4–7, 37

Samûri (XI) 'The Wise' (the Noldor), name replaced by *Nómin*. 226

Sam(wise) (XII) See *Gamgee*.

Samwise Gamgee, Sam (IXa) See under *Gamgee*.

Sanavaldo (IXb) The Almighty. 401

Sandheaver (VI) Hobbit family name. 137

Sandyman (VI) The Hobbiton miller. 243–4

Sandyman, Ted (II) 333

Sandyman, Ted (VI) Son of the Hobbiton miller. 249, 254, 269; earlier
    Tom Sandyman 249, 269 (replaced *Tom Tunnelly*).

Sandyman, Ted (IXa) 89, 100. *Sandymans* 106

Sandymans (of Hobbiton) (VII) 216, 264; *Ted Sandyman* 253

Sangahyanda (XII) Corsair of Umbar. 199, 215, 231, 248; later *San-
    gahyando* 215

Santoski, T. J. R. (VII) 94, 157, 159, 181, 457

Santoski, T. J. R. (VIII) 308, 323, 354, 356, 396

Santoski, T.J. R. (VI) 328

Sári (I) Name of the Sun given by the Gods. 186, 193, 195, 198, 215–
    16, 218, 221–2

Sári (IV) Name of the Sun given by the Gods. 170

Sári (V) Name of the Sun in the *Lost Tales*. 243

Sarmo (XII) Father of Nerdanel. 366. See *Urundil*.

Sarn Aran, Sern Erain (VIII) The Pillars of the Kings. 98. See *Sern
    Aranath*.

Sarn Athra(d) (IV) The Stony Ford, Ford of Stones. Original form

Sarn Athrad (V) The Stony Ford over Gelion. 129, 141, 274, 349, 383,
    385, 406 ('Stone of Crossing')

Sarn Athrad (XI) The Stony Ford over Gelion. *185, 190, 206, 216,
    334–6, 338, 346–7, 349, 355. See *Athrad Daer, Harathrad*.

Sarn Ford (VII) 9, 16, 71, 78, 131, 299, 356, 365

Sarn Ford (IXa) 103

Sarn Gebir (VII) (1) The highlands afterwards called *Emyn Muil*. 283,
    285, 316, 318, 320–1, 325, 345, 351–2, 355, 357–8, 360, 362,
    385, 389, 394, 396, 403, 423, 429, 432–3; hills of *Gebir* 358;
    Sern Gebir 283, 395; and see *East Wall*. Gates of *(Sarn) Gebir*
    357 (of obscure meaning), 359–60, 362 (=*Gates of Argonath*, q.v.),
    the Gates 370. Proposed names *Graidon Hills, Grailaws* 423–4;
    Hazowland 424; *Sern Lamnach, Tarn Felin, Trandóran* 424. (2)
    The rapids in Anduin. 318, 360. See *Pensarn, Sarn Ruin*.

Sarn Gebir (VIII) (1) Old name of Emyn Muil. 85–6, 98–100, 111,

136, 139, 165. *Gates of Sarn Gebir*, the Pillars of the Kings, 98–
9. (2) The rapids in Anduin. 343, 348, 354, 361, 404

Sarn Ruin (VII) The rapids in Anduin. 318, 320, 361, 366, 380, 387,
428. See *Pensarn, Sarn Gebir* (2).

Sarn Ruin (VIII) The rapids in Anduin. 270. See *Sarn Gebir* (2).
Saruman 6–8, 11, 21–2, 26, 29–30, 35, 37–9, 41, 43, 47–53, 55–
6, 59, 61–7, 71–7, 79–80, 119–20, 126, 130, 240, 243, 249, 317,
339, 342, 362, 380. *Valley of Saruman*, see *Wizard's Vale*.

Sarnas Fingolfin (V) The cairn of Fingolfin. 406

Sarnathrod (II) 'Stony Ford'. 236. Later form *Sarn Athrad* 249. See
Stony Ford.

Sarnathrod (IV) 190, 223, replaced by *Athrasarn* 223–4 and *Sarn
Athra* 133, 135, 32–3, 307, 313, 333; final form *Sarn Athrad* 135,
233, 313, 332–3. For the site see 232.

Sarqindi (II) 'Cannibal-ogres'. 254

Saruman (VII) 23, 70, 72–3, 75, 116, 130–41, *passim*, 149–52, 154,
157, 168, 177, 210–12, 214–16, 236, 250, 252, 287, 311, 330,
333, 379, 382, 385, 389, 394–5, 400–1, 403, 405, 408, 411–
12, 414, 417–20, 422, 426–8, 432, 434–6, 440; earlier forms
Saramond, Saramund 70–2, 75, 105, 140; called *the Grey* 70, 132,
136, 138–9, *the White* 70, 132–3, 136, 138–9, 149; proposed
identification with the Balrog of Moria 236, 422; his ring 133,
138; confusion with Gandalf 389, 401, 403, 405, 425, 428

Saruman (X) 396–7, 418

Saruman (XII) 83, 205–6, 227–8, 233, 235, 237–42, 248–9, 251, 262,
267, 274, 283–4, 384–5. See *Curunír*.

Saruman (IXa) 52–3, 64–6, 68–9, 71–2, 74, 76, 83–4, 90–1, 93–5,
100, 102–4, 106–7, 115

Saruman's staff (VIII) 64–5, 67

Satan (IXb) 265

Satan (X) 270

Saturn (IXb) (the planet) 205, 221; *Saturnian* 205; (the god) 221. See
Eneköl, Gyürüchill, Shomorú.

Sauron (I) 52

Sauron (II) 53–5, 57; *Wolf-Sauron* 55; *Mouth of Sauron* 67

Sauron (III) 153, 170, 232–3, 284, 304, 306, 313, 337–40, 342, 344,
348, 350

Sauron (IV) 73, 108, 120, 166, 173, 205. See *Thû.*

Sauron (V) 7, 9, 26–31, 33, 47–8, 56–7, 61, 65–71, 74, 76–7, 283,
289–90, 296–7, 299–300, 307, 333, 338, 393 (also *Sauro, Súro*);

called *the wizard* 296. See especially 290, and see *Sûr, Thû, Gorthû.*

Sauron (VI) 11, 85, 131, 215–16, 218, 258, 260–1, 270–1, 318, 397, 399, 402–5, 414, 416–17, 422, 435; called *the Magician* 215. See *Dark Lord, (the) Lord, Lord of the Ring(s), Necromancer, Thû.*

Sauron (VII) 54–5, 65, 71–2, 112, 116, 119–21, 123, 126–7, 129–30, 134–5, 137, 140, 144–6, 148, 150, 153–6, 158, 177, 184, 188, 207, 209–11, 247, 254–5, 259–60, 262, 265, 286, 289, 298, 321, 330, 335, 344, 347, 349, 360, 382, 393, 395, 404, 409, 431, 437–8, 444–5, 450; *Sauronites* 71, 74; Sauron's well of fire 209, 344, 349. See *Dark Lord, (The) Lord.*

Sauron (VIII) 21, 45, 48–50, 68, 72–4, 76–7, 79–80, (86), 95, 98, 105–6, (107), 110, 112, 122–3, (124), 127, 129, 135, 155, 179, 212, 214, (216, 218), 219, 229–30, 236, 238, 241, 243, 256–7, (300–1, 304, 306, 309–10, 326, 329, 339), 342, 358, 360–2, 364(-5), 372, 381, 386, 401–2, 404, 410, 412, 420, 430. *Mouth of Sauron* 431. See *Dark Lord.*

Sauron (IXa) 6–11, 13–14, 20, 38, 45–6, 51, 55, 59, 133; *ambassador of Sauron* 14; *Sauron's Fire-well* 3–4 (see *Sammath Naur*).

Sauron (IXb) 246, 250, 284, 289–90, 310, 313–15, 317, 334–7, 339, 345–8, 350–3, 355–6, 380, 382–4, 393, 395, 400–1, 404, 407–9, 412; O.E. *se Malsca, Saweron* 317. See *Zigûr.*

Sauron (X) 52, 60, 66, 124, 147, 152, 156, 223–4, 232, 341, 344, 391, 394–8, 400, 404, 406–14, 419–21, 423; see especially 394–8

Sauron (XI) 37, 54, 56, 59, 62, 66–7, 82, 125, 131, 135, 196, 239–40, 247, 351, 390, 397; *Sauron's Isle* (Tol-in-Gaurhoth) 62, 67, 131. See *Gorsodh, Gorthaur.*

Sauron (XII) 31–3, 65, 74, 79, 129, 133, 150–4, 158, 163, 166–84, 191–3, 196, 200–2, 206, 208, 211, 215, 219, 225–9, 234–5, 237–40, 242–3, 249–52, 257, 264–7, 280, 283–4, 287, 301, 304–5, 310–11, 317–18, 324, 328, 330, 378, 382, 385, 390, 410, 418, 436, 438; *Eye of ~* 266, *Messenger of ~* 68; called *the King* in the tale of Tal-elmar 434, 436, 438. See *(The) Sorcerer.*

Saxo Grammaticus (IXb) Danish historian. 301, 307

Saxon (VIII) 123

Saxons (II) 306. See *Saksani.*

Saxons (V) 54, 91

Saxons (IXb) 276

Sayer, George (VII) 59, 66

Scada Pass (VIII) In the White Mountains. 243–4, 25 1–3

Scandinavia(n) (V) 53, 96; Old English *Scedeland* 93, 95

Scandinavian (XII) 53–4, 61

Scarlet Heart, The (I) Emblem of the King's Folk in Gondolin. 245

Scarlet Heart, The (II) Emblem of the King's House in Gondolin. 172, 200

Scarlet Heart, The (III) Emblem of Turgon. 146

Scarlet Heart, The (IV) Emblem of Turgon. 57

Scary (VII) Village in the Eastfarthing. 39

Scary (XII) Village in the East Farthing. 117

Scatha the Worm (IXa) Dragon of Ered Mithrin (the Grey Mountains). 68

scop (IXb) (O.E.) minstrel. 272

Scotland (IXb) 234, 267

Scyldingas (V) (Old English) Danish royal house ('Shieldings'). 93–5; *House of the Shield* 95. See *Shield*.

Sea Chant of an Elder Day (IV) (poem) 214

Sea-danes (IXb) See *Danes*.

Seafarer, The (IXb) Old English poem. 243–4, 272, 287–8, 304

Sea of Rhûn, Sea of Rhûnaer (VII) See *Rhûn, Rhûnaer*.

Sea(s), The (VII) See *Great Sea(s)*.

Seas of sunlight, Seas of shadow (IXb) 360

Sea, The (VI) 59–60, 71, 93, 216, 260, 313, 320, 402; *the Seas* 331–2, 364, 393; *the bending of the seas* 121–2. See *Great Sea, Western Seas*.

Sea, The (VIII) 36, 38, 150, 153, 155, 157–9, 168, 184, 187, 219, 278, 283, 293, 310, 369, 401, 409, 413–14, 419–20; *the Great Sea* 41

Sea, The (IXa) 6, 15, 49, 53, 57, 59, 65, 109–10, 116, 119, 123, 128, 132; *the Great Sea* 56

Sea, The (X) (5), 19, 54, 84–6, 89, 98–9, 101, 111, 113, 115–16, 119, 125, 128, 133–4, 156, 163–4, 170, 174–6, 178–9, (191), 272, 277, 282, 284, 286–7, 289, 291, 293, 296, 309–10, (349), 366. See *Great Sea, Shadowy Seas, Sundering Seas, Western Sea*.

Sea, The (XII) 21, 30–3, 62, 64, 73–4, 78–9, 153, 156–8, 163, 173–4, 176, 178–9, 183, 191, 235–6, 238, 244, 251, 265–7, 313, 329, 363, 379, 387, 423–4, 426–7, 430, 433–4; *the Great Sea* 61, 145, 306, 363, 370, 373, 379, 385–6; Elvish names 363. For 'Sea's day' see 123, 125, 130, 138

Sea, The 6–8, 11–13, 16–17, 20, 22, 24, 38–41, 44–6, 80, 91, 106, 109–10, 112, 118, 164, 176, 192–3, 196–7, 200, 212, 216, 218, 220, 227, 296, 343–5, 348, 354, 365, 382, 400, 404. See *Great Sea, Western Sea*.

Sea-elves (I) 43, 50

Sea-elves (IV) 13, 44, 85; O.E. *sǽelfe* 212. See *Foamriders, Solosimpi, Teleri.*

Sea-elves (V) The Teleri. 214, 403; *Elves of the Sea* 215. See *Veaneldar.*

Sea-elves (X) The Teleri. 163; *Elves of the Sea* 164

Seafarer, The (V) Old English poem. 85

Sea-kings (XII) Kings of Númenor. 153, 155; *King of the Sea* 156

Seasons (XII) (of the Calendars) *Spring* 121, 127, 133–5; *Spring-days* 133–5. *Summer* 133–7; *Summer-day(s)* 121–2, 124, 128, 131–2, 136, and see *Lithe. Harvest* 121, 123–4, 127, 131–3, 137; *Autumn* 133–5. *Winter* 123, 129, 133–7. *Stirring* 133–5; *Stirring-days* 133–4. For Elvish names see 134–5.

Seat of Sight (VII) On Amon Hen. 374. *Seat of Seeing* 374, 380–1

Sea-wing (II) See *Eärrámë.*

Second Age (IV) 327

Second Age (V) 8, 12, 23

Second Age (VI) 215

Second Age (VII) 455

Second Age, The (IXb) 217, 407–8

Second Age (X) 341, 394, 419, 423

Second Age (XI) 61, 64, 128, 349, 390, 397

Second Age (XII) 74, 78, 140, 150, 166–73, 177–8, 184–6, 188, 192, 208, 225–6, 246, 256, 262, 293–4, 297, 301, 303–5, 312–15, 317–18, 323, 328, 378, 381–5, 391

Second Battle of Beleriand (IV) The Battle of Sudden Flame. 106, 108–9, 115, 121, 173, 179, 182, 301. Later *Dagor Aglareb*, the Glorious Battle, became the Second Battle, 182, 329, 336

Second Battle of Beleriand (V) The Glorious Battle. 127, 254–5, 257–8, 264–5. See *Dagor Aglareb.*

Second Battle of Beleriand (XI) 17, 111. See *Battle-under-Stars* (formerly the First Battle).

Second Battle of the Gods (IV) See *Battle of the Gods.*

Second Children (X) See *Children of Eru.*

Second Clan (XI) The Noldor (and Avari of this clan, see 381). 383, 409, 420. See *Tatyar.*

Second Kindred (I) The Gnomes or Noldoli. 21

Second Kindred (of the Elves) (IV) O.E. names 212. See *Deep-elves, Gnomes, Noldoli, Noldor.*

Second Kindred (V) Men. 15.

Second Kindred (IXb) Men. 401

Second Kindred (X) Men. 355

Second Prophecy of Mandos (V) 324, 333

Second Theme (X) See *Themes*.

Secondborn, The (XI) Men. 341. See *After-born, Apanónar, Atani*.

Secret Fire (I) 53, 55, 60

Secret Fire (VI) In the Fiery Mountain. 82

Secret Fire, The (X) 9, 144, 148; *the Fire* 9. See *(The) Flame Imperishable*.

Seeing Stones (VIII) The *palantíri*. 72–3, 75–6; also *Stones of Sight* 381, *Stones of Seeing* 403, *Stones* 72, 282, 300–1, 304 (in *Rhyme of Lore* 65, 281.) *The Seeing Stone, the Stone*: of Orthanc 70–5, 81, 119–20, 300, 304, 339, 342 (also *Orthanc-stone*); of Minas Tirith: 257, 375, 378, 380–2; of Barad-dûr 362, 404 (also *Ithilstone*); of Erech 300, 302, 304–6, 309, 399. See *palantír*.

Seekers, The (X) Western Men. 320

Self-cursed, The (V) An Elvish name for Men. 245

Semitic (IXb) 241, 415

Sentinels of Minas Morgul (IXa) 29. See *(The) Watchers*.

Sentinels, The (VIII) See *(The) Silent Watchers*.

Separation, The (XI) Between the Eldar and the Avari. 360, 373, 375–6, 380, 382, 391, 393, 407, 410, 421

Serech, Fen of (III) North of the Pass of Sirion, where Rivil flowed in from Dorthonion. 171, 335, 342, 350–1

Serech, Fen of (V) 298

Serech, Fen of (XI) 17, 52, 59, 76, 113, 168, 181, *182–3, 187, 238, 272. See *Rivil*.

Serendë, Serindë (X) 'Broideress'. See *Míriel*.

Sern (Sairn, Sarnel) Ubed (VIII) See 132, 137–8

Sern Aranath (VII) See *Angonath*.

Sern Aranath (VIII) The Pillars of the Kings. 99, 132, 137. *Sern Erain* 98; *Annon Torath* 132

Sern Lamnach (VII) See *Sarn Gebir* (1).

Serni, River (VII) In Gondor. 312

Serni, River (VIII) In Gondor. 43 6–7

Servants of God (IXb) 341, 353, 357, 359. See *Eru-bêni*.

Seven Fathers (of the Dwarves), the Fathers (XII) 322–3, 382–3, *Seven Ancestors* 301, 322; *Seven Kindreds* 302 (for names of the kindreds see 301).

Seven Great Ones, The (X) See *(The) Great Ones*.

Seven Rings (of the Dwarves) (VII) 112, 149, 259; other references to the Rings of the Dwarves 117, 154–5, 158–9

Seven Rings (VI) See *Rings of the Dwarves.*

Seven Rings (XII) See *Rings of Power.*

Seven Rings of the Dwarves (VIII) 357–8

Seven Rivers (IV) See *Land of Seven Streams.*

Seven Rivers (of Ossiriand) (X) 93, 104; *Elves of the Seven Rivers,* see *Elves.*

Seven Rivers (VII) 132, 138, 177, 311. *Country, Land, of Seven Streams,* region between the Black Mountains and the Sea, 177, 272, 310–11. *Land of Seven Rivers,* Ossiriand, 311

Seven Rivers (XI) See *Land of Seven Rivers, Ossir.*

Seven Stars (I) 38, 42 (perhaps referring to the Pleiades); 114 (referring to the Great Bear); *Seven Butterflies* 133. See *Great Bear, Valacirca.*

Seven Stars (III) The constellation of the Great Bear. 170, 251, 259

Seven Stars (IV) The Great Bear. 84 (*the crown of Seven mighty Stars*).

Seven stars and seven stones and one white tree (VIII) 65, 76, 281

Seven Stones (IXb) The Palantíri. 385

Seven Stones (XII) The *Palantíri.* 176, 191; *Seeing Stones* 400–1; other references to *the Stone(s)* 176, 195, 206, 209–10, 217, 232, 240–1, 245

Seventh River (VII) See *Greyflood.*

Severn, River (V) 80–1; *Severn sea* 83

Severn, River (IXb) 293; *Severn Sea, Severn-mouth* 268–9, 293

Shadow Folk (I) (1) Name among Men of the Lost Elves of Hisilómë. 119, 138–9, 237. (2) Fays of unknown origin encountered by the Noldoli in Hisilómë. 237, 239

Shadow Host (IXa) The Dead Men of Dunharrow. 16; *Shadowy men, Shadow-men* 15

Shadow Host, Host of Shadow (VIII) The Dead Men of Dunharrow. 275, 311, 398, 412, 414, 420, 422, 426; *the grey host* 414, 420; *Shadow-men* (VIII) 397, 410–11, 416, 418, *Shadows of Men* 423, *Shadows* 406, 413

Shadow, The (V) (of Morgoth) 15, 18, 21, 25–9, 47, 56, 58, 68; *the shadow of the East* (in *King Sheave*) 86

Shadow, The (VI) 270, 300, 398, 400

Shadow, The (VII) 48, 118, 122, 129, 203, 225, 232, 237, 264, 374, 397, 416–17, 426; *Song of the Banished Shadow* 212

Shadow, The (VIII) 306–7, 311; (the Lord of the Nazgûl) 365–6, 374,

385; *the Black Shadow*, malady caused by the Nazgûl, 387; *Men of (the) Shadow(s)*, see *Men*.

Shadow, The (IXb) 258, 334–5, 339, 362–3; *the Ancient Shadow* 363; *the Deathshadow* 247, 315, *-shade* 258–9, 312, O.E. *Déaþscúa* 257–8, 314, 317

Shadow, The (X) (of Melkor, but used in different senses) 21, 37, 53, 65, 97, 99–100, 110, 167, 210–11, 217, (218), 219, 222–4, 228, 232, 240–1, 247, 254, 269, 283, 289, 305, 307–8, 310, 312, 315, 322–3, 326, 348, 374, 379, 401–2, 404, 412, 422, 428, and see 399; the Shadow upon Men 305, 316, 331

Shadow, The (XI) Of Morgoth. 34, 200, 220, 275, 280–1, 296–7, 354; of Húrin, or of the House of Hador 255, 264, 266, 281, 294, 297–8, 308, 310; of Túrin 90; of Sauron 397; of Mandos 43; a shadow over Aman 40; *the shadows* 281

Shadow, The (XII) (in various applications) 68, 143, 145, 150, 152, 154, 174, 177, 180, 193, 228–9, 234–5, 240, 248, 262, 264–5, 267, 269–70, 303, 306, 311, 314, 323, 333, 338, 382, 413; *Men of the Shadow* 330; *unshadowed Men* 314

Shadowfax (VII) 152, 390, 400–1, 405, 412, 433–5, 438–9, 441, 443, 445–6, 450; Old English *Sceadufax* 425; his return from the North 438–9. Earlier names: *Arfaxed* 412; *Greyfax* 135–6, 152, 390; *Halbarad* 152, 390

Shadowfax (VIII) 4, 9, 12, 28–9, (54), 126, 143, 232–3, 235, 265, 282, 284, 320, 336, 374, 380, 382, 387, 391

Shadowfax (IXa) 61, 120, 123

Shadowfax (XII) 53, 157

Shadow-folk of Hisilómë (II) 64, 215, 249

Shadowland (VII) 87, 89, 92–3, 97–8, 101. *Shadowmere* 92–3, 95, 97–8, 100–1, 292; *Shadow-meres* 284, 292

Shadowy Isles (IV) *249, 257

Shadowy Mountains (III) (1) =Ered Wethrin. 16, 29, 59, 62, 87, 116, 148, 170, 224, 233–4, 312, 314. (2) =Ered Gorgoroth. 168, 170, 183, 201, 208, 234, 314; *Mountains of Shadow* 170; described 175–6, 345

Shadowy Mountains (V) 118, 125, 259–60, 282, 285, 317, 406; *Shadow Mountains* 250; *Mountains of Shadow* 266. See *Eredwethion*.

Shadowy Mountains (XI) See *Mountains of Shadow*. *Siege of Angband* See *Angband*.

Shadowy Mountains, Mountains of Shadow (IV) (1) =Mountains of

Terror. 24, 55, 109, 115. (2) 'The northward bending mountains on the borders of Hithlum' (103). 28, 60, 105, 107, 117–18, 122, 127, 137, 139, 172, 192–3, 221–2, 229, 262, 268, 272, 280, 295–6, 303, 316, 320, 322, 324, 328. See *Eredlómin* (1), *Eredwethion*, *Eredwethrin*.

Shadowy Sea(s) (V) 82, 99, 101, 103, 222, 243, 323

Shadowy Seas (I) Region of the Great Sea west of Tol Eressëa (see especially 68, 125). 15, 27, 68, 70, 74, 76, 83, 118–21, 125, 134, 137, 152, 154, 164, 188, 209, 211, 224; *Shadowy Sea* 101, 163, *the Shadows* 134

Shadowy Seas (II) Region of the Great Sea west of Tol Eressëa. 256, 275, 286, 324–5; the *great (sea-) shadows* 260, 272; the *Shadows* 316

Shadowy Seas (III) 73, 93, 95, 148, 187, 192; *Shadowy Sea* 346

Shadowy Seas (IV) 14, 20, 87, 98, 150, 153, 198, 256

Shadowy Seas (X) 110, 134, 176

Shadowy Spring (IV) Source of Aros and Esgalduin. 222

Shannon, River (IXb) 261, 292, 296

Shagram (VIII) Orc of the Tower of Kirith Ungol. 218

Shagrat (VIII) (1) Orc of Minas Morghul. 225 (replaced by *Yagûl*). (2) Orc of the Tower of Kirith Ungol. 216–18, 225 (replaced *Yagûl*).

Shagrat (IXa) Orc, commander of the Tower of Kirith Ungol (but also from Minas Morgul, see 9). 8–9, 13, 18, 23–6, 28

Sharkey (IXa) One of the Hobbiton ruffians. 82–3, 85–6, 94; Orc-man ('the Boss') at Bag End 91–2, 94, 103, 106; (with the same reference?) *Big Sharkey* 82, 94, 104; name of Saruman 93–5, 97, 102, 107–8, 110, *Sharkû* 106

Sharkûn (VIII) See *Tharkûn*.

Shathûr (VII) See *Bundu-Shathûr*.

Shaw, G. B. (IXb) *Shavian* 167

Sheaf, Sheave (V) (and Old English *Sceaf*, *Scef*, *Sceafa*) 7, 78, 80, 82, 85–7, 89–97; *Sheafing, Scefing* 7, 92–5; *the mill of Sheaf* 86, 96; *Sheaf-lords* 86, 96; *King Sheave* (poem) 87–92

Sheaf, The (IXb) 227; *King Sheaf* 236, 278, 284, 294, *King Sheave* 273–6, 294, 380

Shelob (VIII) (115), 183 (the name *She-lob*), 199, 202, 207, 212–18, 222, 224–6. Earlier name *Ungoliant(ë)* 196–200, 205–6, 209–11, 221–2. *The Great Spider* 191, 199, 222, *the Spider* 184, (196), 205–6, 208–9, 214, 218, 224. *Shelob's Lair* (including all references to the tunnel beneath Kirith Ungol) 124–5, 180, 184, 187,

190–2, 194–5, 197–200, 202–3, 205–17, 222–6. See *Spiders*; *Torech Ungol*.

Shelob (IXa) 23, 112; *the Spider* 115

Shelob (XII) 251

Shepherds of the Trees (VII) See *Ents*.

Sheppey, Isle of (V) 83–4; Old English *Sceapig* 84

Shield (V) (and Old English *Scyld*, Latinized *Sceldius*, Norse *Skjöldr*) Legendary ancestor of the Danish royal house (Old English *Scyldingas*). 7, 78, 92–6. See *Scyldingas*.

Shem (IXb) Son of Noah. 411

Shining Isles (I) Dwelling of the Gods and the Eldar of Valinor, as imagined by the Ilkorins. 231

Shining Isles (II) Dwelling of the Gods and the Eldar of Valinor as imagined by the Ilkorins. 142

Ship-burial (IXb) 338, 400, 411

Ship of the Heavens, Ship of (the) Morn(ing) (I) See *Sun*.

Ship of the Moon (I) See Moon

Ship of the World (I) 83–7, 134, 225

Ship-burial (V) 7, 12, 17, 22, 28, 77, 86, 93–6

Ship-friends (V) A name of the Teleri. 215

Ship-kings (XII) (of Gondor) 198

Shipmen, Ship-folk, of the West (II) The Ythlings. 319, 322, 325, 331, 334. See *Eneathrim, Ythlings*.

Shippey, T. A. (II) *The Road to Middle-earth*, 57

Shippey, T. A. (VI) *The Road to Middle-earth*. 145

Shippey, T. A. (IXa) *The Road to Middle-earth*. 60

Ship-wrights, The (X) A name of the Teleri. 164

Shire Reckoning (VIII) (37–8), 45, 59, 309, 408, 424

Shire, The (VI) 13–14, 18, 22, 29–31, 35, 37, 46, 50–2, 54–5, 58, 63–4, 69, 71–2, 74, 76–8, 83–4, 92–3, 95, 99–101, 103, 110, 119, 122, 124, 129, 132–4, 136–9, 149–51, 153, 155, 157, 168, 171, 175; 179, 194, 210, 212–13, 221, 223–5, 228, 233–6, 239–40, 243–5, 250–4, 256, 264, 266, 268, 272, 277–8, 280–1, 285, 288–9, 294–5, 298, 312–14, 318, 322, 324, 331, 337–8, 340, 342, 344–7, 349, 358, 362–4, 366–7, 370–1, 374–5, 379–80, 385–7, 392–4, 397–8, 403, 407–8, 412, 415, 423; see especially 31.

Shire, The (VI) *Shire-folk* 135, 138, 333–4, 349; *South Shire* 241, 278; *East Shire* 286. Maps of the Shire 43, 66, 105–8, 114, 200, 202, 284, 296, 299, 304–5, 313, 387

392

Shire, The (VII) 6–7, 9–11, 13, 16, 25, 31–2, 34, 38, 41, 43, 46–7,
49, 51, 55, 63, 68, 70–4, 78, 80, 82, 130–1, 134–5, 139, 162,
185, 193, 212, 216, 221, 232, 246, 248–50, 253, 265, 286, 356,
424. *Shire Reckoning* 9; *Shire-folk* 125, 152; language 424; maps
of, see *Maps*.

Shire, The (VIII) 37–8, 44, 59, 123, 219, 241, 256, 283–4, 292, 308,
323, 338, 394; *Shire-folk* (VIII) 38, 304–5

Shire, The (IXa) 32, 52–3, 62–6, 68–9, 74, 76, 78, 80–1, 84, 87–91,
93–5, 98–103, 105–12, 116–18, 121, 126–9, 132, 134; Sindarin
Drann 129

Shire, The (XII) (Often used attributively, as *Shire word*) 5–6, 8–10,
12, 15–17, 20, 36–7, 40, 42–3, 45–56, 58–60, 69–70, 83, 87,
112, 118–19, 121–31, 136, 138, 168, 209, 220, 225–6, 231–2,
235–6, 238–9, 241, 243, 248, 251, 255, 268, 281–3, 287, 289,
311, 327; true name of the Shire *Suza* 45, 58; Maps 11, 18, 93,
98, 117

Shirebourn (VI) River in the Shire. 296

Shire-folk (IXa) 123, *Shire-rats* 90; *Shire-house(s)* 81, 85, 99, 104, *Shir-
riff-house* 104; *Shirriffs* 80–2, 95; *Chief Shirriff* 79–80, (91), 104;
Mayor 79–81, 91, 104, 108, 117, 128, 132, Sindarin *Condir* 129;
Deputy Mayor 108; *Thain* 99, 101, 103; *Scouring of the Shire* (not
as chapter-title) 94, 103, 129

Shire-reckoning (IXa) 18, 22, 46, 104, 117, 119, 128 (and see *Chronology*); Sindarin *genediad Drannail* 129

Shire-reckoning (XII) 6, 9, 85–6, 106, 119, 121, 125, 128–9, 131,
133–4, 138, 225, 231, 247–8, 270. *Shire-reform* (of the Calendar)
121–2, 129, 133

Shire-records, Note on the (XII) 14, 261

Shirking (XII) Original name of the Thain of the Shire. 5–7, 11, 87,
107–8, 111, 248–9; *Shire-king* 6, 107, 248–9

Shirriffs (XII) 6, 9, 14; *Shirriff* < *Shire-reeve* 6

Shirriffs, Chief Shirriff (IXa) See *(The) Shire*.

Shomorú (IXb) [Ramer] The planet Saturn. 221. (Replaced *Gyúrúchill*,
replaced by *Eneköl*.)

Shorab or *Shorob* (VIII) Gandalf's name in the East. 153

Shoreland Elves (I) See *Shoreland Pipers*.

Shoreland Pipers (I) The Solosimpi (afterwards called Teleri). 16, 50,
94, 123, 160, 223; *Pipers of the Shore* 230; *the Pipers* 106; *shoreland dancers* 129; *Shoreland Elves, shoreland folk* 125, 165, 210,
shore-elves 165

Shoreland Pipers (II) 42; *pipers of the shore* 8; *shoreland Elves* 304.
  See *Solosimpi.*

Shoreland Pipers (IV) See *Solosimpi.*

Shoreless Sea (IXb) See *Great Sea(s).*

Shores of Faërie (IV) See *Bay of Faërie.*

Shores of Faëry (II) See *Faëry.*

Shores of Faëry, The (V) (poem) 186

Short Lay of Eärendel (VII) See *Eärendel.*

Shrouded Island(s), The (VII) 92, 95

Shugborough Hall (V) In Staffordshire. 413

Sickle of the Gods (III) The constellation of the Great Bear. 170, 266;
  Sickle of the Valar (III) 259; *sickle of the heavenly field* 169–70

Sickle of the Gods (IV) The constellation of the Great Bear. 84, 168,
  264, 270, 272, 276; O.E. *Godasicol* 286

Sickle of the Gods (V) The constellation of the Great Bear. 111, 212
  (see *365 Valakirka*, and also *379 Otselen, Edegil* 'Seven Stars')

Sickle of the Gods (X) 71, 76, 160, 388. See *Valakirka.*

Sickle of the Valar (I) See *Valacirca; the Silver Sickle* 133

Sidmouth, Devon (VI) 214

Siege of Angband (V) 127, 129, 131–2, 145, 148–9, 151, 252, 254–
  9, 272, 279, 281, 208, 301; dates of the Siege 257–8

Siege of Angband (X) See *Angband.*

Siege of Angband, Leaguer of Angband (IV) 23–4, 53–5, 57–8, 103–
  5, 173, 176, 191, 296–7, 314, 319, 329, 331, 333–4, 336–7; O.E.
  Angbandes Ymbsetl 340

Sigelwara land (VII) (J. R. R. Tolkien, article in *Medium Ævum*) 439

Sigin-tarâg (XII) 321. See *Longbeards.*

Sigurd Fafnisbane (II) 125

Sil (I) Name of the Moon. 85, 192

Sil (V) Name of the Moon in the *Lost Tales.* 243

Silent Pools, Battle of the (II) 278–9. See *Pools of Twilight, Umboth-
  muilin.*

Silent Watchers, The (VIII) In Minas Morgul. 123–6, 129; *the
  Watchers* 125, 216; *the Sentinels* 126; *the Night Watcher* 217

Silent Water, The (VII) 92

Silharrows (VII) See *Harrowland.*

Silindrin (I) The cauldron of silver light in Valinor; name varying with
  Telimpë. 71–4, 79, 88, 130, 196

Silivros (V) 'Glimmering Rain', A Gnomish name of the White Tree of
  Valinor. 210–11, *384–5.* See *Silmerossë.*

Silivros (IXa) The White Tree of Valinor. 58

Silivros (X) 'Sparkling rain', a name of Telperion. 155

Silma (IV) Earlier name for *Ilma, Ilmen*. 240, *242, *244, *248–9

Silma (V) Earlier name for *Ilma, Ilmen*. 9, 13

Silmarien (XII) Ancestress of the Lords of Andúnië. 154–5, 257

Silmaril(s) (II) 13, 30, 33–4, 36–40, 53, 56–8, 95, 136–7, 223–4, 227–8, 238–41, 245–6, 259, 265; *Lamp of Faërv, Lamp of Fëanor* 238

Silmaril(s) (III) 52, 125, 134–6, 138–9, 151, 192–3, 196–7, 211–12, 216–7, 220–1, 237, 262, 265, 270, 272, 296, 301, 303–5, 307–9, 311–12, 329, 353, 361–2; *the Gnome-crystal* 107, *Fëanor's fire* 267, *fire of Fëanor, Light of Morn* 362; *the Three* 133–4

Silmaril(s) (IV) 9, 14–17, 19, 21, 23–6, 32–3, 37, 39–41, 47–8, 57, 63–4, 68–9, 71–4, 88, 90, 92–4, 98, 100–2, 109–10, 113–14, 116, 122, 133–5, 145, 149–54, 156–66, 169, 173, 182, 187, 189–90, 195–7, 201–2, 204–5, 211, 265–6, 269, 283–4, 295, 300–1, 306–10, 313, 321, 325–9, 340; O.E. *Sigel, Sigelmǽrels* 211, *Eorclanstánas* 282–4, 338, *Silmarillas* 282–3, 287–8, 340, *Silmarillan* 340

Silmaril(s) (V) 113–15, 118, 125, 127, 135, 141–4, 162, 176, 180, 202, 204, 227, 229, 231–5, 242, 246–7, 249, 252, 254, 292–3, 303, 306, 308, 317, 324, 327–31, 333, 335, *383*, *385* (also Noldorin *Silevril*, see *Pennas*); (other names *Ilumírë* 361, *Noldomírë, Mirion, Mîr in Geleidh, Goldamir, Golo(ð)vir, 373, 377*)

Silmaril(s) (X) 19, 48, 94–7, 100, 104, 107–10, 112, 122, 125, 132, 137, 144, 182, 187–93, 198–200, (268), 274–6, 280, 282, 287, 291, 293–7, 319, 340, 371–2, 390, 402; *Silmarilli* 94. See *(The) Jewels*.

Silmaril(s) (XI) 36, 38, 41, 62–6, 68–9, 130–2, 177, 247, 345–51, 353, 355. See *(The) Jewel(s)*.

Silmaril(s) (XII) 256, 337, 348, 357, 369; *Silmarillë* 363, *Silmarilli* 30. See *Jewels*.

Silmaril, The (VII) 100–2, 104–5; *Silmarils* 256

Silmaril, The (VIII) (of Eärendel) 193, 203

Silmarilli (I) The Silmarils. 58, 128. See *Silubrilthin*.

Silmarillion, The (I) 23, 26, 49–51, 60–3, 79–80, 82, 87–92, 110–12, 131–8, 156–61, 171–3, 198–202, 222–5, 227, 231, 236, 241–5

Silmarillion, The (II) 50, 52–9, 61–6, 68, 119–21, 123–31, 134–5, 137, 139–42, 145, 204, 206–14, 216–17, 245, 247–9, 251, 257–9, 261–2, 264–5, 292, 300, 305, 324, 328

Silmarillion, The (III) 21, 23, 25–6, 50–3, 55, 81, 87–93, 103–4, 125,

127, 136, 138–9, 149, 169–71, 183, 196, 198, 209–10, 222–4, 235, 244, 246–8, 257–9, 271, 274, 283–4, 293, 305–6, 309–10, 312–14, 349–51, 353. The 1930 version (*Quenta Noldorinwa*) 25, 28–9, 53, 80–1, 93, 104, 137, 139, 152–4, 170, 219, 293; references to the work in general sense 83, 85, 103, 183, 209; earliest 'Silmarillion' map 87–9, 103, 160, 244; later map 350

Silmarillion, The (IV) (other than references to the published work) 3, 9, 11, 42, 50, 76, 174, 254, 259, 284, 291–2, 314; O.E. *Eorclanstána gewyrd* (284), 291

Silmarillion, The (VI) 105, 108, 122, 187, 214, 433; *Quenta Silmarillion* 11, 68, 71, 121, 182, 186–8, 329, 412–13, 432, 437, 466

Silmarillion, The (VII) 95, 138, 144, 146, 239, 260, 263, 313, 345. See *Maps, Quenta.*

Silmarillion, The (VIII) 169, 222

Silmarillion, The (IXa) 13, 45, 58–9. See *(The) Quenta, Quenta Silmarillion.*

Silmarillion, The (IXb) 308, 312, 376, 405, 411–12; (published work) 340, 353, 393, 411. See *Quenta Silmarillion.*

Silmarillion, The (X) (general references) 5–6, 43, 63, 75, 88, 141–4, 149, 152, 156–7, 181, 192, 197, 200, 205, 283, 290–1, 300, 303, 329, 337, 342, 349, 359, 369–71, 373, 394, 406–7, 414, 422; (references to the published work) 40, 64, 123, 126, 136, 151, 157, 165, 170–1, 179, 182, 200–4, 267, 271, 283, 306, 357, 360, 387, 408

Silmarillion, The (XI) (1) =*Quenta Silmarillion*. 120, 129, 179, 196, 199, 207–8, 213, 244–5, 247, 297–8, 317. (2) 'The Silmarillion tradition' 106, 113, 132–3. (3) The published *Silmarillion*. 4, 115–16, 123, 126, 129–32, 135–6, 138, 140, 144, 148–9, 151, 156, 165, 168–70, 175–6, 180, 186, 191, 210, 212–13, 215, 226–8, 236, 238, 240–3, 298, 302, 310, 314, 317–19, 321–3, 325, 333, 338, 340–1, 350, 354–6, 419; and see *Maps* (3).

Silmarillion, The (XII) (1) Author's references. 14, 190, 295, 309, 335, 343, 346, 357, 379–81, 383, 388–90; origin of the work 357. (2) The published work. 82, 140, 142–3, 153, 183, 294, 318, 331, 349, 351–2, 358, 364, 366, 372, 390, 404, 420. See *Quenta Silmarillion.*

Silmarils (I) 128, 138, 145, 149, 152, 156–7, 159, 162, 169, 238, 240

Silmarils (VI) 122, 183–4, 187

Silmerossë (V) A Quenya name of the White Tree of Valinor (Gnomish *Silivros*). 210–11, 384–5

Silmerossë (IXa) The White Tree of Valinor. 58

Silmo (I) The guardian of the tree Silpion. 73–4, 88, 116, 178, 189, 192, 202

Silmo (IV) Guardian of Silpion. 49, 171

Silpion (I) The silver tree of Valinor. 73–4, 76, 88–9, 113, 116–17, 122, 125–9, 133, 135, 142–4, 146, 152–3, 160, 176–9, 181, 189–91, 193, 200–2. See *Rose of Silpion*.

Silpion (II) The silver tree of Valinor. 33, 215, 285

Silpion (IV) The White Tree of Valinor. 12, 20, 43, 49–50, 74, 80, 82–3, 92, 97, 167, 171, 237, 255, 269, 281, 283; *Rose of Silpion* 49; O.E. *Glisglóm* 281, 283. See *Telperion*.

Silpion (V) The White Tree of Valinor. 111, 118, 209–12, 231, 240–2, *385*

Silpion (VI) The White Tree of Valinor. 122, 187–8

Silpion (IXa) The White Tree of Valinor. 58

Silpion (X) The former common name of the White Tree of Valinor, later *Telperion*. 54, 90, 155, 157, 193, 198

Silpion (XII) 130. See *Eldest Tree*.

Silubrilthin (I) Gnomish name of the Silmarils. 128, 130

Silvan (X) (language) 182

Silvan Elves (VII) 244; *silvan folk* 226. See *Wood-elves*.

Silvan Elves (XII) 223, 329; *Silvan* 66, 221; *woodland race*, ~ *tongue* 79

Silver Bowl (IV) Falls in the Taiglin. 31, 61, 129–31, 185–6, 222, 313, 325. See *Celebrindon, Celebros*.

Silver Bowl, Fall of the (II) 101, 105–6, 110–11, 115, 130, 132–5, 140

Silver Wherry (III) The Moon. 74, 93, 128

Silver-bowl (XI) See *Celebros*.

Silverhorn (VII) See *Silvertine*.

Silverlode, River (VI) 433, 462. See *Redway*.

Silverlode, River (VII) (1) Earlier name of Blackroot, q.v. 177, 187, 241, 298, 306, 310–11. (2) Celebrant. 173–5, 190, 213, 235–6, 238, 240–1, 279–80, 288, 291, 296, 306, 355–6, 368

Silverlode, River (XII) 279, 286. See *Celebrant*; *Kibil-nâla, Zigil-nâd*.

Silvern Elves (X) A name of the Sindar. 164

Silvertine (VII) Celebdil. 174, 288. Earlier name *Silverhorn* 174, 431–2

Silvertine (XII) 279. See *Zirak-zigil*.

simbelmynë (VIII) The flower 'Evermind' (q.v.). 423–4

Sindar (IV) 167; *Sindarin* 174, 255, 261

Sindar (V) 181, 190, 198; *Sindarin* 190, 219, 345–6. See *Grey-elves*.

Sindar (X) 86, 91, 93, 103, 146, 149, 154–5, 164, 170–1, 202, 349; language of the Sindar 86, 144, 201–2; first occurrence of the name 170. See *Grey-elves*.

Sindar (XI) 5, 9, 12–14, 19–21, 23–8, 35–6, 38, 40, 42–7, 104, 107, 109, 113, 116, 120, 126, 175, 179, 186, 189, 192, 195, 197, 219, 240, 326–8, 338, 344, 365, 369, 372–3, 375–89, 400, 403, 409–10, 420; origin of the name 9, 384, 410–11. See *Eglath*, *Grey-elves*, *Sindel*.

Sindar (XII) (and singular *Sinda*) 62, 78, 223, 297, 312, 318–19, 328–9, 345–6, 358, 360, 379, 385–6, 389, 392, 401, 404; *Northern Sindar* 372. See *Grey-elves*.

Sindarin (I) 51, 132

Sindarin (II) 50

Sindarin (III) 87, 160

Sindarin (VI) 466

Sindarin (VII) 174, 291

Sindarin (VIII) 20, 161

Sindarin (IXa) 58, 128–9

Sindarin (IXb) 304, 379; Sindarin words cited 302, 306

Sindarin (X) 76, 91, 126, 155, 165, 180, 182, 217, 349–50, 373, 387–8

Sindarin (XI) (of language) 20–8, 44, 104, 116, 189, 197, 201, 219, 223, 240, 318–20, 337, 359, 362–72, 376–9, 383, 385, 387–91, 394, 396, 400, 402–4, 407, 410–16, 419; *North Sindarin* 400 (see *Mithrim*); (with other reference) 4, 25, 28, 104, 126, 192, 378, 380, 385, 396

Sindarin (XII) (of language) 61–2, 65–6, 78–9, 125, 136, 138, 143, 146, 189, 210, 260, 305–6, 308, 315–16, 318–21, 324, 329–32, 337, 340–50, 352, 358–72, 374, 376, 379, 385, 392, 395, 400–1, 404–5; *North Sindarin* 342, 344, 369–70, 372; verb '*Sindarize*' 318, 343, 345–6, 360, 366, 368. See *Grey-elven*, *Lemberin*, *Noldorin*.

Sindarin (XII) (with other reference) 79, 298, 328, 348, 350, 379, 381, 388

Sindel (XI), plural *Sindeldi* (Quenya) Sindar. 384, 410

Sindicollo (X) 217, 385. See *Elwë* (2), *Greymantle*.

Sindicollo (X) See *Singollo*.

Sindikollo (XI) 'Greycloak', Thingol. 410. See *Greymantle*, *Singollo*.

Sindikollo, Sindicollo (XII) Elwë (Thingol). 357; *Þindikollo* 337, 357; *Greycloak* 78, 392

Sindingul (IV) Thingol. 264, 270. (Replaced by *Tindingol*.)

Sindingul (V) Thingol. 187. (Replaced by *Tindingol*.)

Sindo (V) 'The Grey', Thingol. 119, 168, 174, 186–7, 215, 218, 392 (also Telerian *Findo*, Ilkorin *Thind*)

Sindo (X) 'The Grey', Thingol. 88, 169. See *Elwë* (2).

Singers of the Shore (X) A name of the Teleri. 164

Singers Unseen (X) A name of the Nandor of Ossiriand. 164

Singoldo (II) Replaced *Tinwë Linto*. 41, 51. Later form *Singollo* 50

Singoldo (V) 'Elvish' name of Thingol in the *Lost Tales*. 187

Singollo (I) See *Elwë*.

Singollo (V) 'Greymantle'; *Elwë Singollo*, Thingol, 217

Singollo (X) 'Greymantle'. 82, 84, 86, 88, 91, 104, 163, 169–70, 172–3

Singollo (XI) 'Greymantle', Thingol. 7, 9. See *Elwë*.

Sir Orfeo (III) Middle English lay. 248

Sirannon (VI) The Gate-stream of Moria. 445–6. See *Caradras dilthen*.

Sirannon (VII) 187. See *Gate-stream*.

Siriombar (V) Sirion's Haven. 407. See *Sirion*.

Sirion (I) 238, 240–2, 244; *Pass of Sirion* 244

Sirion (II) 41, 47, 53, 62, 77, 81, 91, 123, 137, 141, 153–7, 161–2, 165, 195–6, 198, 201, 207–9, 211, 214, 217, 242, 249, 252 *Doriath beyond Sirion* 249. References to the Mouth(s) of Sirion and the dwellings there (*Sirion* often ='the dwellings at the Mouth of Sirion') 196, 205–6, 209, 214–15, 217, 252–6, 258–63, 265, 276, 279; *Isle(s) of Sirion* 254, 262

Sirion (III) 23, 59–61, 87–9, 129, 142–3, 148, 160, 213–14, 222–3, 227, 233–4, 237, 254–5, 257, 259–60, 278, 309, 312, 314; *Sirion's vale* 276, 284, 357; *Pass of Sirion* 284; *Sirion's Isle, the isle in Sirion* 260, 278, 357; *Sirion's Well* 59, 87

Sirion (V) 22, 128–30, 132–4, 137, 139–40, 144, 153, 221, 253, 257, 260–3, 267–8, 272, 274, 285, 287–8, 311, 315, 320, 329, 336, 385, 404, 406, 412–13; length of the river 260, 272, 406–7

Sirion (V) *Sources of Sirion* 283, 407; *Sirion's Well*, see *Eithel Sirion*. *Pass of Sirion* 128, 136–7, 145, 254, 257, 260, 264, 272, 311, 314–15, 406; *West(ern) Pass* 283–4, 287, 307, 314, *West passes* 133. *Vale of Sirion* 126, 130, 132–3, 142, 259–60, 284, 287, 310, 317. *Isle of Sirion* 284. *Falls of Sirion* 262, 272; *Gates of Sirion* 262, 268

Sirion (V) *Mouth(s), delta of Sirion* 126, 128, 133, 140, 142, 175, 177, 260–1, 272, 287–8, 406–7 (see *Eges-Sirion*); *Sirion's Haven* 142, 187, 190, 201, 203, 407 (see *Siriombar*); *Sirion* used for *Sirion's Haven* 143, 407

Sirion (VII) 95, 239, 292; *Havens of Sirion* 102; *Sirion's mouth* 454–5. *New Sirion*, see *Sirvinya*.

Sirion, River (IV) 34–5, 37, 60, 65–6, 118, 127, 136–9, 141–2, 147, 157, 161, 185, 191, 193, 195, 210–11, 214, 221–7, 230, 258–9, 299–301, 305, 309, 326, 330–1, 334; O.E. *Fléot, Scírwendel* 211; island in the river 103, 106, 296, 316, 330 (see *Tol Sirion, Tol-na-Gaurhoth*). *Pass of Sirion* 301, 321, 324, 374 (*West Pass* 120, 321); *Gorge of Sirion* (137), 144; *Vale of Sirion* (139), 192, 296–8, 308, 316, 318, 320, 328, O.E. *Sirigeones dene* 339; *Sirion's fall and passage underground* 226; *Marshes, Fens of Sirion* 106, 225–6; *lands, plain of Sirion* 24, 54, 103, 153

Sirion, River (IV) *Mouth(s), delta of Sirion* (often with reference to the Havens) 33–8, 66, 68–70, 74, 134, 136, 141–2, 145, 149, 192, 195–6, 296, 299, 305, 307–8, 319, 324, 327, 329–31, 335, O.E. *Sirigeones múþas* 339; *Waters of Sirion* (land at the mouth) 37–8, 69, 146, 226; *Havens of Sirion, Sirion's Haven* 69, 149, 152–3, 155, 190, 263, 274, 308, O.E. *Siriones Hýþ* 281, 284, 290; *Sirion* used for *Havens of Sirion* 39, 148, 151–2, 308; folk of Sirion 149–52, 196, 308, 326; haven of Gondolin at the mouth 138–40, 192

Sirion, River (VI) 432

Sirion, River (X) 174; *Vale of Sirion* 83

Sirion, River (XI) 5–6, 15, 38, 49, 53, 56–7, 72–3, 76, 81, 84–5, 90–1, 104–6, 113, 127, 150, 178, 181, *183–4, 191, 193–5, 197–9, 215, 219, 228, 261, 265, 267, 278, 301, 303, 408; length of the river 193; its source, see *Eithel Sirion*.

Sirion, River (XI) *Pass of Sirion* 38, 59, 76–7, 89, 125, 133–4, 157, 193, 299; *west(ward) pass* 54, 125; *Passes of Sirion* 52, 71–2, 75, 85, 92, 141; see *Narrow Land*. *Vale of Sirion* 6, 36, 44, 49, 53, 90, 113, 127, 178, 241; *Vales of Sirion* 17, 54, 261, *north vales* 85, 142. *Falls, Fens, Gates of Sirion* *184

Sirion, River (XI) *Mouths of Sirion* 5, 7, 23, 38, 54, 80, 89–90, 136–7, 146, 345–6, 348, *Sirion's Mouth* 397; *Waters of Sirion* *184. *Delta of Sirion* 193

Sirion, River (XI) *Havens (of Sirion)* 298, 311–13, 348–9, 35 1–3; *Sirion's Haven* 244; *the New Havens* 351; *Sirion* 351

Sirion, River (XII) 396; *Mouth(s) of Sirion* 350, 369, 381, 387–8

Sirion's Well (IV) 222, 300, 311, 315, 320, 330. See *Eithel Sirion*.

Siriondil (XII) (1) Eleventh King of Gondor. 197. (2) Father of Eärnil II, King of Gondor. 201, 216

Sirith, River (VII) In Gondor. 312, 322

Sirith, River (VIII) In Gondor. 436

Sirius (I) 200. See *Helluin, Nielluin*.

Sirius (II) 282. See *Bee of Azure, Nielluin*.

Sirius (IV) 75

Sirnúmen (I) The dale in Valinor where the Noldoli dwelt after their banishment from Kôr. (142), 144, 146 (*Sirnúmen of the Plain*), 147, 149, 153, 155, 157–9, 163–4, 192. (Replaced *Numessir*.)

Sirvinya (VII) 'New Sirion'. See *Anduin*.

Six Years' War (IXb) 157–8, 190, 225, 234, 283; *Second German War* 283; *War of 1939* 284

Sketch of the Mythology (III) The original 'Silmarillion' (1926). 3, 5, 28, 52, 84–6, 93, 137–9, 147, 153–4, 170, 220–2, 244, 293

Sketch of the Mythology (VII) 95–6

Sketch of the Mythology (XII) 374–5

Skidbladnir (IXb) 174, 214

Skilled of Hand, The (V) A name of the Noldor. 215

Skilled of Hand, The (X) A name of the Noldor. 164

Skinbark (VII) Ent. 412. See *Fladrif*.

Slag-mounds (VIII) Before the Morannon. 118–20, 140–2, 291; *Slag-heaps* 136; *Slag-hills* 430–2

Slavonic (IXb) 418

Sleeper in the Tower of Pearl (I) See *Tower of Pearl*.

Sleeper in the Tower of Pearl (II) 254, 256, 263, 274, 276. See *Tower of Pearl*.

Sleeper in the Tower of Pearl (IV) 69

Slieve League (IXb) On the coast of Donegal. 267, 293

Slocum (VI) Hobbit family name. 31

Slumbrous Dale (I) See *Murmenalda*.

Smallburrow, Robin (IXa) Also *Smallburrows* (80, 104). Hobbit, one of the Shirriffs. 80–1, 95, 104, 106

Smaug (VI) 256. See *Dragon(s)*.

Smaug (XII) (including references to *the Dragon*) 35, 39, 54, 57, 72, 237, 239, 276–7, 281–3

Smeagol (VII) Gollum. 23–4, 27–8, 118, 148

Sméagol (XII) 38–9, 53, 57, 81, 166, 225, 233, 239, 251. See *Gollum*.

Smeagol Gollum. (VIII) 97–8, 105, 109–12, 115–16, 124, 129, 196, 203 223

Smial (VIII) 45

Smial(s) (XII) 11, 14, 39, 53, 58, 81, 111; *Great Smials* 106, 108, 235

Smials (IXa) 105, 107; *(Great) Smials* at Tuckborough 105; earlier *Long Smial* 87, 105, 107, *(Old) Smiles* 99. 105, 107

Smith, A. H. (VI) 144

Smygrave, Tobias (VIII) First grower of pipeweed in the Shire. 37; *Smygraves* 37; the name 45. See *Elias Tobiasson, Hornblower*.

Snaga (VII) Orc scout. 410. (See LR Appendix F, 111.409.)

Snaga (IXa) Orc of the Tower of Kirith Ungol. 26, 30

Snaga (XI) Name of lesser kinds of Orc. 390, 419

Snorra Edda (I) The 'Prose Edda' by Snorri Sturluson. 245

Snorri Sturluson (V) Icelandic historian, author of the *Prose Edda*. 96

Snorri Sturluson (IXb) Icelandic historian, author of the *Prose Edda* (*Snorra Edda*) 214, 307–8, 410

Snowbourn, River (VIII) In Harrowdale. 238, 240–1, 245, 257, 259, 264 296, 313, 316, 318, 343, 348; spelt *Snowborn* 235–7, 264

Snowfax (VI) 'Snow-mane', suggested name for Gandalf's horse. 351

Snowmane (VII) Théoden's horse. 450

Snowmane (VIII) Théoden's horse. 9, 15, 17, 246, 317–19, 365, 369

Snowmen of Forochel (XII) See *Forochel*.

Snow-white! Snow-white! O Lady clear! (VI) 59, 68, 280

Solar System (IXb) 167, 204, 213, 219; another Solar System 207. See *Planet(s)*, *Low Worlds*; *En*.

Solar System (XI) 419

Solar System, The (X) 337, (338, 342), 349, 358, 374–5, 383–5, 403

Soloneldi (IV) The Sea-elves. 86. (Replaced *Solosimpi*.)

Soloneldi (V) A name of the Teleri. 214, 379, 387 (Quenya *Solonyeldi*), 403–4; 'Musicians of the Shore' 215, 403

Soloneldi (X) A name of the Teleri of Valinor. 163. (Replaced by *Falmari*.)

Solosimpi (I) The third kindred of the Elves (afterwards called Teleri). 16, 19, 22, 48–50, 58, 61–2, 94, 119–21, 123–9, 132–7, 141, 143, 155, 157, 163–5, 169, 171, 176, 178, 199, 208, 210, 219, 223, 231; earlier *Solosimpë* 22, 61. See Shoreland Pipers, *Teleri* (2).

Solosimpi (II) 8, 42, 50, 253, 255, 258, 278, 281, 303; *Solosimpë* 261. See *Shoreland Pipers*.

Solosimpi (III) The Third Kindred of the Elves, later called the Teleri. 140

Solosimpi (IV) The Sea-elves. 9, 13, 44–6, 68, 85–6; *Shoreland Pipers* 13, 44, *pipers of the shores* 85–6. (Replaced by *Soloneldi*.)

Solwë Name transitional between *Elwë* (1) and *Olwë*. 169

Sômar (XI) 'Wisdom' (Felagund), name replaced by *Nóm*. 226. See *Samûri*; *Vidri*.

Somerset (V) 80–1, 83

Somerset (IXb) 268, 270, 278–9, 293; *Somersets* 'men of Somerset' 269, 293

Song of Ælfwine, The (V) (poem) 100–4, 203

Song of Eriol, The (II) (poem) 298–300

Song of Frodo and Sam (VII) Lament for Gandalf. 264, 266

Song of the Banished Shadow (VII) See *(The) Shadow*.

Song of the Ent and the Entwife (VII) See *Ents*.

Songs for the Philologists (VI) 142–5

Songs of the Philologists (VII) 66

Sons of Elrond (VIII) 274, 289, 297, 301, 305, 307, 389, 394, 415, 438 *the brethren* 410. See *Elbereth*, *Elboron*; *Elrohir*, *Elladan*.

Sons of Elrond (IXa) See *Elrond*.

Sons of Fëanor (I) See *Fëanor*.

Sons of Fëanor (II) 44, 65, 220, 241–2, 245, 248, 250–1, 259

Son(s) of Fëanor (III) 6, 32, 50, 65, 84, 86–7, 96, 98, 102, 131, 134–6, 138, 159, 171, 182, 192, 210–11, 216–17, 221–2, 227, 236, 241, 244, 260–1, 265, 287, 313, 353, 359

Sons of Fëanor (IV) 6–9, 15–16, 18–19, 21–2, 24–5, 27, 33, 35, 38–9, 41, 46–7, 51, 56–7, 64, 69, 71, 74, 88, 91–2, 94, 96, 100–1, 103, 106, 109, 111–16, 118–19, 121, 133–5, 137–8, 140, 145, 147, 149–52, 158, 161, 172, 180–2, 201, 212, 220, 222, 233, 266–8, 280, 282, 295–8, 300, 302, 307, 316, 318, 326, 328, 330, 332–3, 335, 338. See *Brósingas*. *Dispossessed*, *Fëanorians*.

Son(s) of Fëanor (V) 115–19, 125–8, 130, 132, 137, 142–3, 145–6, 149–50, 177, 189, 223, 225, 229, 232, 234–5, 237–8, 248–50, 252, 260–1, 263–5, 274, 279, 282–4, 286, 290, 306–8, 310–12, 330, 336; speech of 177, 189

Sons of Fëanor (VIII) See *Fëanor*.

Sons of Fëanor (X) 96, 112–14, 119–21, 123, 126, 128, 177, 179, 181–2, 188–9, 210, 272, 276–7, 279, 287, 292–3, 311

Sons of Fëanor, The (XI) 18–19, 26, 29, 31, 33–4, 39, 41–3, 53, 62, (66), 70, 72, 74–5, 77, 113–15, 122, 165, 167, 176, *185, 188,

194, 255, 311, 313, 318, 323, 325–30, 335, 345, 348–9, 351, 379; *Five Sons of Fëanor* 327, 329. See *Fëanorians*.

Sons of Fëanor (XII) 294, 317, 331, 336, 339, 345, 352–5, 357–8, 360, 366–9, 372

Sons of God (IXb) See *Eruhildi*.

Sons of the Gods, of the Valar (XI) See *Gods, Valar*.

Sons of the Valar (IV) 37, 39, 68, 72, 75, 149, 154, 157–8, 160, 163–4, 195, 313; *Sons of the Gods* 166, 205, 309, 313. See *Children of the Valar*.

Sons of the Valar (V) 326, 332–3; *Sons of the Gods* 14, 25–6, 74, 79, 143–4, 176, 328, 330. See *Children of the Valar*.

Sons of the Valar (X) See *Children of the Valar*.

Sons of the Valar (XII) 163, 172, 375. See *Children of the Valar*.

Sorcerer King, The (VIII) See *(The) Wizard King*.

Sorcerer, The (XII) Sauron. 193, 234–5, 237, 239, 252, 276–7.

Sorcerer-king, The (XII) 209–10, 215–17. See *Witch-king*.

Sornontur (II) The house of Tuor at the Mouth of Sirion. 201

Sorontar (X) King of Eagles. 410. See *Thorondor*.

Sorontar (XI) King of Eagles. 272. See *Thorondor*.

Sorontur (I) King of Eagles. 73, 89, 148–9, 158, 176, 178, 198. (Replaced *Ramandur*.) See *Thorndor*.

Sorontur (II) King of Eagles. 192, 203. (Replaced *Ramandur*.) See *Thorndor*.

Sorontur (IV) King of Eagles. 10, 44, 47, 52–3, 67. See *Thorndor*.

Sorontur (V) King of Eagles. 75, *389*, 392 (*Sorontar*). See *Thorondor*.

Soronúmë (X) Name of a constellation. 160

Sorrowful City, The (II) (poem) 295, 298

South Beleriand (V) 283

South Downs (VII) 79

Southfarthing (VIII) 36–7, 45, 58

Southfarthing (IXa) 95, 117, 126; *Southfarthing post* 117, 126

South Haven (VII) 301, 423. See *Harlond*.

South Kingdom (VIII) Gondor. (72), 154, 371

South Kingdom (XII) Gondor. 170, 177, 230–2, 330; *the Kingdom* 311, 316

South Lane (IXa) Lane leading from the Bywater Road to the Cottons' farm. 84, (87), 96, 98

South Mountains (VI) Range south of the Misty Mountains. 397, 399, 409, 411, 440. See *Black Mountains, Blue Mountains*.

South Road (IXa) 103

South, The (IXa) 62, 83, 89

South, The (IXb) 334, 344, 362, 366, 383

South, The (X) 7, 17, 32, 93, 97–8, 104–5, 109, 123, 284, 299, 377

South, The (XI) 12, 15, 29, 53, 90, 95, 109–11, 239, 377

South, The (XII) 149, 152–3, 194, 229, 240, 242, 328; Men of the South 187, 302

Southern Line (XII) The Heirs of Anárion. 188, 190, 196, 210–11, 217–18, 222, 255

Southern men (VIII) 127, *men of the South* 137; *the Southerner at Bree* 52. See *Barangils, Haradwaith, Haradrim, Swertings*.

Southern Star (XII) A variety of pipeweed. 6

Southerner (at Bree) (VII) 42, 45, 71. Men from the South at Bree 71, 74

Southerner (VI) The 'squint-eyed Southerner' at Bree. 142, 176, 334, 336, 342, 354

Southfarthing (VI) 241, 284, 298, 313; *South Shire* 241, 278

Southland (IV) 239, *249–51; southern land* 238; called *Dark Land* *250–1

Southland (VIII) Harad. 237

Southrons (VIII) 136, 140–1, 182, 260, 263, 289, 425; *Southron men* 135, 340; *fleets of Southrons, Southron fleets* (VIII) 259–60, 263

Southrons (IXa) 50

Sóval Phárë (XII) See *Common Speech*.

Sow (I) River in Staffordshire. 196

Sow, River (V) In Staffordshire. 413

Space (IXb) (including references to Space-ships, Space-travel) 146, 151, 163–4, 166–71, 173–6, 178–9, 195, 198, 201, 205–6, 209, 213, 215, 220. See *Deep Heaven*.

Spear-elves (V) A name of the Lindar. 215

Spear-elves (X) A name of the Vanyar. 164

Speght, Thomas (III) Editor of Chaucer. 144

Spell of Bottomless Dread (I) The spell laid by Melko on his slaves. 239, 241–2

Spell of Bottomless Dread (II) See *Melko*.

Spider of Night (I) 153. See *Gwerlum, Móru, Ungoliant, Ungweliantë, Wirilómë*.

Spiders (VIII) In the earlier story of Kirith Ungol. (VIII) 104, 113, 125, 184–5, 187–94, 199, 220, 222. *Spider Glen*, see *Kirith Ungol*.

Spiders of Kirith Ungol (VII) 209, 213–14, 330–1, (335), 347

Spring (IXa) 117, 119, 128; Sindarin *Ethuil* 129

Spring of Arda (X) (18), 27, (32), 53, 67, 70, 75, 384

Square of the Folkwell (II) In Gondolin. 181; *Place of the Well* 179, 182

Square of the Palace (II) In Gondolin; also called *Square of the King, King's Square, Place of the King.* 160, 179, 182–6, 212, 216 The king's hall(s), house, or palace 160, 183–7, 199–200, 207; the king's tower 160, 180, 185–7, 200, 207–8, 212; the king's fountain 162, 176, 182–4, 189, 215

Staddle (VI) Village of the Bree-land. 132, 140, 332, 344, 354

Staddle (VII) In the Bree-land. 41, 56

Staff-elves (X) A name of the Nandor. 171. (Replaced *Axe-elves* (1).)

Stafford, Staffordshire (I) 25, 91, 108, 196

Staffordshire (II) 292, 328

Staffordshire (IXb) 294

Stainer, Ranulph (IXb) Member of the Notion Club. 151, 160, 211, 223, 233–4, 238–40, 245–6, 253–5, 260–1, 277, 302, 305

Stair Falls (VII) Falls in the Gate-stream of Moria. 178

Stair-falls (VI) Falls in the Gate-stream below the West Gate of Moria. 446–8

Standelf (VI) Village in Buckland. 298–9, 304

Standing Silence (IXa) Before meals in Gondor. 50

Standing Stone (VII) On the Barrow-downs. 41

Staniland (VII) Ondor. 318

Stanrock, The (VIII) Earlier name of the Hornrock. 10–11, 13, 16–19

Stanshelf (VIII) Earlier name of Helm's Dike. 13, 23; Old English form *Stanscylf* 13, 23

Stapledon Magazine (II) 273

Stapledon, Olaf (IXb) 214; *The Last Men in London* 175, 214

Star of the Dúnedain (VIII) (299), 309; *star(s) of Elendil* 370, 395, 411; *of the North Kingdom* 395. Other references to the star(s) as device 338, 370, 389, 395, 397; 'stars of Sun and Moon' 359, 363, 399, 422

Star of the North (IXa) 55–6; star on Arangorn's brow 56; star(s) on his standard 15–16, 56

Star-folk (X) See Eldar.

Star-folk (XI) Elves (for the original linguistic elements and the development of meaning see 360, 362–3, 374). 360, 374, 418, 423

Starkhorn (VIII) Mountain at the head of Harrowdale. 242, 257, 259 267, 301, 308, 312–13; *Lap of Starkhorn* 245–6, 259. Earlier name *Dunharrow*, q.v.

Starkhorn (XII) Mountain above Dunharrow. 53

Star-kindler (X) Varda. 388. See *Tintallë*.

Star-making (X) 20, 34, 38–9, 54, 61, 71, 156, 159–60, 166, 374, 376, 388

Starmoon (VII) 187. See *Ithildin*.

Stars (I) 64–5, 67, 69, 71, 73–4, 99, 111, 113–16, 127, 133, 135, 154, 171, 175, 178, 181–2, 186, 188, 192–3, 195, 200–2, 216, 221, 227, 231, 233; *Fountains of the Stars* 216. The star-making of Varda 69, 113–4, 133, 181

Stars (II) Selected references: 274–5, 281, 317

Stars (IV) Selected references. The Star-making 43, 45, 82, 84, 168, 264, 270, 272, 276, 281, 286, 289; pursuit of the stars by Tilion 97, 171; courses of the stars 236, 241, 253 (see *Elenarda, Tinwë-mallë*).

Stars (V) Selected references. The Star-making. 111, 121, 212, 216; moveless stars 177, 189; few stars in the skies of the South 175, 187; meteors 241–2

Stars (VI) *Ages of the Stars* 122. *Lady of the Stars* (Varda) 364. Red star in the South seen from Rivendell 409, 415

Stars (VII) On West Door of Moria 180–1 (cf. 404); *Star of the House of Fëanor* 180

Stars (IXb) 199, 207, 237, 301, 427

Stars (X) 12–13, 16, 20, 28–9, 34, 38, 54, 61, 70–3, 76–7, 79, (81), 82–3, 86, 95, 106, 111, 130–3, 135–6, 145, 148, 153, 156, 159–61, (162), 166, 172, 175–6, 178, 346–7, (370), 372, 374–8, 382–4, 386–9; stars in the Dome of Varda (*tinwi*) 286, 292–3, 386–8; shooting stars 136; *the significant Star* 385. See *Great Stars; Eldar*.

Star of Eärendil (Azrubêl), The (IXb) (278), 301, 308, 343, 360, 371, 376, 378, 399, 402; *Land of the Star* 368, 390. *The Star* (in *The Death of St. Brendan*) 261, 263–4, 296, 298

Stars, The (XI) (including references to *starlight*) 6–7, 9, 14, 30, 47, 105–6, 108, 110–11, 113, 176, 360, 373, 410, 417, 421–4; *the great stars* 5; Elvish words for 'star' 360, 362–3; '*Star-lore*' 414

Stars, The (XII) 123, 127, 130. For 'Stars' day' see 123–4, 130. *The Star* (of Eärendil) 144

Starwards (IXb) See *Gimlad*.

Statute of Finwë and Míriel (X) (including references to *the Statute*) 208–9, 233, 236, 239, 243, 246–8, 251–2, 254–5, 258, 263–5, 270; *Doom of ~* 226; *Namna Finwë Míriello* 258

St. Brendan (IXb) See *Brendan*.

Steepholme (V) Island in the mouth of the river Severn. 80–1

Steward of Gondor (IXa) See *Faramir*.

Steward's Reckoning (XII) 128, 132–4, 138; *Stewards' ~* 132

Stewards of Gondor (VIII) 153, 168, 337, 374, 378; *House of the Stewards*: their line 335, 388; in Rath Dinen 380, 391. *The Steward* 282, 292, 324, 374–5, 379, 385, 389–90, 400–1; *the Stewardship* 360, 363, 375, 377, 379. See *(The) Closed Door*.

Stewards of Gondor (XII) 43, 128, 132, 188, 202–7, 217–18, 220, 222, 225–6, 234, 245. *Roll of, House of, the Stewards* (records) 191, 253, and see *Book of the Kings*; *Tomb of the ~* 207

Stiffbeards (XII) One of the kindreds of the Dwarves. 301, 322

Sting (VI) Bilbo's sword. 223, 246, 262, 315, 371, 397, 443–4

Sting (VII) 10, 16, (115), 137, 162, 192–3, 229, 240, 331–2, 335, 337, 355, 371

Sting (VIII) 92, 185, 187–91, 193–4, 197–8, 205–7, 209–12, 222, 230

Sting (IXa) 5–6, 23–5, (29), 32, 50, 52, (64), 72, 86, 92, 94, 105–6

Sting (XII) 11

Stirring (IXa) The season before Spring. 128; Sindarin *Echuir* 129

Stock (VI) Village in the Marish. 66, 105, 107–8, 286, 289, 295–6, 298, 325, 387

Stock (IXa) Village in the Marish. 107

Stock (XII) Village of the Marish. 98

Stock-brook (VI) 287

Stone Hills (VII) 233, 250, 267, 269, 287, 325, 374

Stone of the Hapless, Standing Stone (XI) See *Talbor*.

Stoneait (VII) See *Tolondren*.

Stonefoots (XII) One of the kindreds of the Dwarves. 301, 322

Stone-giants (VII) 411. See *Trolls*.

Stonehouses (VIII) Ghân-buri-Ghân's name for Minas Tirith. 351.

Stonehouses (IXa) Ghân-buri-Ghân's name for Minas Tirith. 67

Stone-land (VI) Gondor. 379. See *City of Stone, Ond*.

Stone-Men (VI) Men of Ond. 379–80, 382

Stones, The (VIII) See *Seeing Stones*.

Stones, The (XII) See *Seven Stones*.

Stone-trolls (X) 412. See *Trolls*.

Stonewain Valley (VIII) In Anórien. 353

Stoningland (VIII) Gondor. 371

Stony Ford (II) 236–8, 250. See *Sarnathrod*.

Stony Ford (IV) (33), 62–3, 190, 209, 223–4; *Ford of Stones* 133. See
     Sarn Athra(d).

Stony Road (VIII) See *Monoliths, Road of*.

Stonydelph, Warwickshire (VI) 304

Stoors (VI) 124, 294

Stoors (XII) 10–11, 15, 37–8, 54, 56–7, 66–7, 81, 227, 229–31, 233,
     248, 250, 311, 328; *Stoorish* 56–7; the name *Stoor* 39, 53

Storm, The (IXb) See *Great Storm*.

St. Peter and St. Paul, Feast of (IXb) 211

Strachey, Barbara (VI) *Journeys of Frodo*. 202, 205, 298, 305, 367,
     440

Straight Path (IV) *246–7

Straight Road, The (V) 17, 28, 43, 47, 56, 76–8, 80, 82, 86, 97–8,
     103; *Straight Path* 12–13, 18, 21, 78

Straight Road, The or *A* (IXb) (into the Ancient West) 247, 279–80,
     310, 312, 338, 393, 395, 404; *Straight Way* 243, 259, 394, 396,
     409; *Straight Path* 339; O.E. *riht weg, reht weg* 243, 258; *the old
     road* 264–5, 298, 392, 394–5; *the ancient way* 392

Straight Road, The (X) 5

Straits of Ice (IV) *249, 258. See *Bridge(s) of Ice, Grinding Ice, Helk-
     araksë*.

Straits of the World (IV) *250–1, 259

Straits of the World (V) (260–1), 267

Strangers (X) An Elvish name for Men. 21, 37

Strangers, The (V) An Elvish name for Men. 245

Strawheads (VIII) See *Forgoil*.

Street of the Lampwrights (VIII) See *Rath a Chelerdain*.

Stricken Anvil, The (II) Emblem of the people of the Hammer of Wrath
     in Gondolin. 174, 179

Strider (VI) 126, 160, 186, 190, 192–3, 199–200, 204, 210, 336, 359–
     60, 430

Strider (VII) 56, 64, 163

Strider (IXa) 78, 121, 128. See *Telcontar*.

Strider (X) 216. See *Telcontar*.

Strider (XII) 189

Stybba (VIII) Merry's pony of Rohan. 301, 319, 348

Súlimë (III) Quenya name of the third month. 88

Súlimo (I) Name of Manwë. 52, 56, 58–9, 62, 65, 79, 93, 100, 115,
     117, 122, 142, 146, 151, 179–80, 183, 209, 218; *Súlimo Lord of
     the Airs* 212

Súlimo (II) See *Manwë*.

Súlimo (V) Name of Manwë. 162, *393*

Súlimo (X) Name of Manwë. 19, 114, 148; *Manwë of the Winds* 377

Sumharrowland (VII) See *Harrowland*.

Summer-days (XII) See *Seasons*.

Summons of Mandos (X) 219, 223–4, 232, 236, 339, 364–5

Sun, The (I) 36, 39, 43, 60, 64, 68, 83, 85, 88, 118–19, 125, 139, 151, 174–5, 182, 186–91, 193–203, 207–8, 212, 214–21, 226–8, 230–1, 236–7, 242; in many passages called *the Sunship*, also *galleon, bark, of the Sun*; *Ship of the Heavens* 186; *Ship of (the) Morn(ing)* 188, 190, 194, 198. See *Haven of the Sun*; and for other names of the Sun see 186–8, 196.

Sun, The (II) Selected references. First rising of 9–10, 20, 65–6, 116, 208; accounts of sunset 261, 320, 325; ship of 281–2, 286; haven(s) of 266, 268–9; recall of 285–6; imprisonment of 286; Melko's attack on 281, 286; dwelling of 255, 276; Sun-dwellers 261; beyond the Sun 162, West of the Sun 271–2; an emblem of the King's Housë in Gondolin 172. See *Magic Sun, Urwendi*.

Sun, The (IV) Selected references. Making of 20, 49, 97, 269; ship of 20, 49, 97, 252; Sun-maiden 49, 170; course of 20, 49, 97–8, 165, 170, 236–7, 241, 252–4 first Sunrise 20, 22, 52, 99, 102, 172, 269, 272, 295; *Years of the Sun* 171, 270, 273, 277–8, etc.; prophecies concerning 50, 73–4, 98, 165, 205; 'magic Sun' 20, 49, 98; the Sun and Eärendel 38, 41, 71, 150, 164, 197, 203–4; *Song of the Sun and Moon* 97, 170. See *Land of the Sun, Walls of the Sun*; *Sári, Ûr*.

Sun, The (V) 12, 20, 31–2, 41, 56, 63–4, 68, 72, 79, 99, 101, 109, 118, 120, 123, 125, 168, 171, 177, 184, 187, 189, 238–45, 250, 252, 259, 325, 331, 333, 335; the Sun and Men 64, 72, 118, 240; *Elder Sun, Magic Sun* (the Golden Tree) 242, 244; *Song of the Sun and Moon* 240; *Sun-years, Years of the Sun* 109–10, 118–19, 122–3, 125, 176–7, 179, 190, 194, 224, 252, 256, 274. See *Anar, Anor, Ûr, Úrin*.

Sun, The (VI) 57, 121–2, 329; *the Sunless Year* 59, 68

Sun, The (VII) 37, 93–4, 98, 101, 170–1, 232, 248, 257, 263, 265, 284, 363, 429, 439

Sun, The (VIII) 167, 174, 359, 363, 399, 422

Sun, The (IXb) 195, 198–9, 205, 219, 302, 306, 400, 410, 413, 426; *suns* 199; another sun 205, 207. See *Anar, Arbol*.

Sun, The (X) (not including references to *Sun Years, Years of the Sun*)

3, 10, 12, 30, 40, 42–4, 50–1, 58–60, 89, 94, 127, 129–30, 132, 134–7, 149, 163, 173, 196, 198–9, 299–300, 327, 346–7, 357, 370–86 *passim*, 389–90, 423, 426, 430; *the Fruit of Noon* 371; *the Sunship* 371; *the Elder Sun* (the Golden Tree) 198, 372; *the Unmarred Sun* 390. See *Anar* (2), *Âs*, *Naira*, *Úr*, *Úrin*, *Vása*; and *Reckoning of Time* in entry *Time*.

Sun, The (XI) 20–1, 24, 26, 30–1, 47, 110, 113–14, 175, 177, 196, 341, 373, 417–18, 423; *the Daystar* 30; *Years of the Sun* (8, 16), 20, 22, 24, 27, 30, 206, 419. See *Anar*.

Sun, The (XII) 123, 127, 130, 374, 401–2, 423; sun-rounds *(coranári)*, years, 120, 126–8, 131. For 'Sun's day' see 123, 130, 137

Sundering Sea(s) (VI) 182, 215

Sundering Seas (II) 264

Sundering Seas (III) 126

Sundering Seas (IV) 154, 156, 197

Sundering Seas (V) 115, 327

Sundering Seas (X) 115

Sunlands (VII) 313, 439

Sûr (V) Sauron. 9, 15–16, 27, 30, 75

Súruli (I) Spirits of the winds, attendant on Manwë and Varda. 66, 144, 181, 192, 195, 200

Súruli (III) Spirits of the winds. 137, 306

Súruli (IV) Spirits of the winds. 49

Sussex (IXb) 234, 284

Sutherland (VII) 306, 313, 389. See *Haradwaith*.

Swabians, Swabes (V) Germanic tribe. 91; Old English *Swæfe*, Latin *Suevi*, 91

Swabians (IXb) 276

Swallow, The (II) Name of one of the kindreds of the Gondothlim. 173, 176, 178–83, 193. See *Duilin* (2).

Swan (II) As emblem of Tuor and of his men in Gondolin (swanwings on helm and shield). 152, 164, 172, 193, 205, 210, 276; *house of the Swan* 160. See *Alqarámë*, *Swanwing*, *Wing*.

Swan fleet, River (IXa) 70, (72). See *Glanduin*.

Swan, House of the (IV) 5

Swanhaven (I) See *Haven of the Swanships*.

Swanhaven (II) 258; *Haven of the Swans* 11, 65. See *Cópas Alqalunten*, *Kópas*.

Swanhaven (III) 104; *Swans' Haven* 70, 118; *Swanships' Haven* 17. See *Alqalondë*, *Cópas Alqalunten*.

Swanhaven (V) See *Alqualondë, Havens.*

Swanhaven (X) 87. See *Alqualondë, Haven of the Swans.*

Swanhaven, Haven of the Swans (IV) 14, 18–20, 37, 48, 68, 88, 95–6, 98–9, 149, 154, 170, 265, 276, 283, 341; the curse of Swanhaven 18–19, 21, 23, 49, 95–6, 99, 107, 116, 159, 162, 267, 278. See *Alqualondë, Kinslaying.*

Swanherds (X) A name of the Teleri. 164

Swann, Donald (VII) 85, 107

Swanwing (II) Tuor's ship. 253–5, 260, 263, 265. See *Alqarámë.*

Swanwing (IV) See *Alqarámë.*

Swart Men (VIII) 105

Swarthy Men (IV) 120–1, 300 (described), 320; *Swart Men* 118, 320. See *Easterlings, Incomers.*

Swarthy Men (V) 134 (described), 192 (speech), 268–7, 291, 307. See *Easterlings, Rómenildi.*

Swarthy Men (XI) 60 (described), 61, 64, 74, 127. See *Easterlings, Eastrons.*

Swedes (V) 91, 97; *Sweden* 96

Swedes (IXb) 276

Swertings (VIII) Men of the South. 127, 136–7, 144, 243, 252–4. See *Southrons.*

Swertings Men of the South. (VII) 313, 439

Swift, The (X) A name of the Teleri. 164

Sword that was Broken, the Broken Sword (VII) 77–8, 80, 116, 120–2, 125, 128–9, 137, 146–7, 393, 402. See *Elendil.*

Swordmen (IXb) 276

Sword-elves (V) A name of the Noldor. 215

Sword-elves (X) A name of the Noldor. 164

Table Mountain (IXb) (Cape Town) 179

Tacitus (V) 97

Tad-dail (XI) Petty-dwarves. See *Levain tad-dail.*

Taiglin, River (IV) 127, 129, 185, 219, 222, 224–6, 305, 324, 330

Taiglin, River (V) 128, 130, 134, 139, 260–1, 320, *369*, 413

Taiglin, River (VII) (1) In Beleriand. 238. (2) Earliest name of Nimrodel. 222, 238–9

Taiglin, River (XI) 49, 57, 66, 88–9, 92, 97–8, 100, 103, 139, 147, 151, 153, 156–8, (159), 160, 164, *182, 193, 254, 265, 267, 271. Later forms *Teiglin* 147, 223, 228, 234–5, 310; *Taeglin* 257, 265,

267, 273, 296, 307, 309, *Taeglind* (and etymology) 309. On the forms of the name see 309–10.

Taiglin, River (XI) *Crossings of Taiglin (Teiglin, Taeglin)*, also *the Crossings*, 92–3, 95, 99, 101, 14l, 147–8, 157, 159, 161, *182, 186, 223, 256, 264–5, 267, 270–1, 273, 302, 307; *Ford of Taeglin* 274

Taimonto (II) =*Telimektar*. 281, 328; *Taimondo* 328

Taingwethil (IV) Gnomish name of Taniquetil. 43, 80; *Tengwethil* 12, 43

Tain-Gwethil, Taingwethil (III) Gnomish name of Taniquetil. 17, 31, 49–50, 79, 118, 123, 127, 135–6. See *Tengwethil, Danigwethil*.

talan (VII) Flet, platform in mallorn-tree. 227–8

Talath Dirnen (I) The Guarded Plain of Nargothrond. 240

Talath Dirnen (II) The Guarded Plain of Nargothrond. 61

Talath Dirnen (V) See *Dalath Dirnen*.

Talath Dirnen (XI) 85, 140, *182, 186, 225, 228; earlier form *Dalath Dirnen* 140, 186, 223, 225, 228. See *Guarded Plain*.

Talath Rhúnen (XI) Name replacing *Radhrost* (Thargelion). 197–8

Talbor (XI) The stone of Túrin and Nienor at Cabed Naeramarth. 257, 300, 309. *The Standing Stone* 257, 274, 290, 295, 298, 309; *Stone of the Hapless* 295–6; other references to the Stone 103, 251, 258–9, 273–4, 294–6, 298. See *Tol Morwen*.

Talceleb (II) See *Idril*.

Tale of Years (II) 208

Tale of Years (VI) 85, 160

Tale of Years, The (X) (title) 49, 56–7

Tale, The; Tale of Arda (X) See *(The) Great Tale*.

Tale-fire (I) In Mar Vanwa Tyaliéva. 17, 46, 48, 65, 107, 174–5, 229, 241; *Room of the Tale-fire* 140, 229; *Room of the Log Fire* 15 *Room of Logs* 17

Tale-fire (II) In Mar Vanwa Tyaliéva. 144–5, 197, 221, 252. See *Room of Logs, Tôn a Gwedrin*.

Tal-elmar (XII) 422–4, 426–38

Taliska (V) Original language of the Fathers of Men. 179, 191–2, 196, 279; *Taliskan* (V) 194, 196

Taliska (VII) Language of the Fathers of Men. 455; *Taliskan* 455

Talkamarda, i·Talka Marda (I) 'Smith of the World', Aulë. 180, 186

Talkative Planet, The (IXb) Earth. 127, 148–9, 153, 205. See *Thulcandra*.

Talking Trees (VIII) 47, 50, 55; *trees with voices* 55. See *Galbedirs, Lamorni, Ornómi*.

Talmar Ambaren (IV) The roots of the Earth. 241. See *Earth roots, Martalmar*.

Taltelepta (II) See *Irildë*.

Tamar (XI) Precursor of Brandir in the *Tale of Turambar*. 160

Tamar Lamefoot (II) Son of Bethos of the Woodmen. 101, 103, 106, 108–11, 130, 132–4, 215. (Replaced by *Brandir*.)

Tamar the Lame (IV) 31, 185. (Replaced by *Brandir*.)

Tamil (IXb) Language of S.E. India and Ceylon. 300

Tamworth (IXb) In Staffordshire. 273, 294

Taniquetil (I) 21, 58, 62, 68, 70, 73, 77, 82–3, 85, 88–9, 91, 93, 100, 103–4, 113, 115, 125, 133, 144–6, 148, 154, 158–9, 180, 186, 188–9, 191, 194–5, 210–12, 219; *Mountain of the World* 214

Taniquetil (II) 77, 141, 161, 163, 171, 202, 257, 262, 265, 271–2; *Mountain of the World* 77

Taniquetil (III) 22, 50, 127, 139, 222

Taniquetil (IV) 12, 70, (73), 80–1, 92, 167, 170–1, 211, *249–51, 257, 260, 266; O.E. *Tindbrenting* (see this entry); *the holy mountain* 94, *the Holy Mount* 97. See *Amon Uilas, Elerrína, Ialassë, Taingwethil, Tinwenairin*.

Taniquetil (V) 15, 17, 27, 115, 162, 209, 225, 230–2, 235, 251, 325, 378, 389 (also Noldorin *Nimdildor*), 393. See *Amon Uilos, Elerína, Ialassë, Oiolossë, Tinwerína; Holy Mount, Manwë*.

Taniquetil (VII) 95

Taniquetil (IXb) 336, 338, 391; *the Mountain of Amân* (Manwë) 391; *the White Mountain* 393, 396

Taniquetil (X) 19, 24–5, 29, 54, 67, 71–2, 74, 77, 98–100, 105, 108, 115, 135, 154, 159, 161, 167, 179, 190, 285–7, 289, 294, 384; *the Mountain* 262, 287. See *Holy Mountain, Mountain of Manwë, Oiolossë*

Taniquetil (XI) 'High-Snow-Peak', properly the highest peak of the mountain Oiolossë. 399, 403, 416–17 (origin of the name). See *Arfanyarassë, Ras-Arphain*.

Taniquetil (XII) 157

Tanyasalpë (I) 'Bowl of Fire.' 187. See *Faskala-númen*.

Tanyasalpë (II) 'Bowl of Fire'. 138. See *Fauri, Faskalan, Fôs'Almir*.

Tar (VII) See *Keleborn*.

Tar Kalimos (XII) Earlier name of Armenelos. 145–6

Taragaer (V) Earlier name of Caradras. 345, 391

Taragaer (VI) Early name for Caradhras. 419, 421–2, 433, 438, 440

Tarakil (VIII) The name *Trotter* in Quenya. 390, 395; *Tarakon* 395; *Tarantar* 395; *Telkontar, Telcontar* 395

Tar-Aldarion, Aldarion (XII) Sixth Ruler of Númenor, 'the Mariner'. 155, 329

Tar-Ankalimë (XII) Daughter of Tar-Aldarion and Erendis; seventh Ruler of Númenor. 155

Tar-Ankalimon (-Ancalimon) (XII) Fourteenth Ruler of Númenor, son of Atanamir. 150–2, 186.

Tarannon (XII) Twelfth King of Gondor (see *Falastur*). 197, 213

Tarantar Trotter. (IXa) 121

Taras, Mount (V) 259, 267

Taras, Mount (XI) 44, *182, 192, 197, 256, 379

Tar-Atanamir (IXb) Thirteenth King of Númenor. 382

Tar-Atanamir, Atanamir (XII) Seventh and later thirteenth Ruler of Númenor. 149–53, 164, 170–1, 177, 180, 184, 186

Tar-Atanamir, Tar-Ciryatan (V) Rulers of Númenor. 21, 77

Tar-Calion (IXb) See *Tarkalion*.

Tareg the Ilkorin (I) 237, 240

Tareldar (X) High-elves 349, 360

Tar-Elendil (XII) Fourth Ruler of Númenor. 154–5, 257

Tar-Ellion (V) 'Queen of the Stars', Varda (*Elentári*). 200

Targlîn (XI) Rejected name of (1) Maeglin, 323; (2) the metal of Eöl, 322 (see *Galvorn*).

Targon (VIII) Keeper of the storehouse of Berithil's company of the Guard. 288. Earlier names *Duilas* 283, *Garathon* 283

Tári (I) 'Mistress, Lady', applied to Varda, Vána, and Fui Nienna. 66–7. See *Qalmë-Tári, Tári-Laisi, Tinwetári*.

Tári-Laisi (I) 'Mistress of Life', Vána. 67

Tar-Ilien (V) Wife of Tar-Kalion. 27, (69); *Ilien* 27. (Replaced *Istar*).

Tar-Ilien (IXb) Earlier name of *Tar-Míriel*. 335, 351, 387; *Ilien* 316–17, 336; O.E. *Iligen* 316–17. See *Ar-Zimrahil*.

Tark (IXa) Man of Gondor (Orc-name derived from *Tarkil*). 26, 30

Tar Kalimos (IXb) Elvish name of Arminalêth. 381

Tar-kalion (IXb) (also *Tarcalion, Tar-Calion*, and including references to *the King*) 246, 248, 257–8, 290, 310–11, 313–17, 334–7, 339–40, 345–8, 350, 352–3, 355, 381, 401, 404, 408–9; O.E. *Tarcaligeon* 316–17; called *the Golden* 316, 336, 381, 404. See *Ar-Pharazôn*.

Tar-Kalion (-Calion) (XII) Quenya name of Ar-Pharazôn. 151, 153, 155, 164, 169–72, 175

Tar-Kalion (V) Ruler of Númenor; called 'the Golden' (27). 9, 26–7, 31, 47, 56, 60, 66–9, 76. (Replaced Angor.)

Tarkil (VII) Númenórean. 8, 83–4, 106, 113, 116, 120, 137, 147, 163 (of Aragorn); 393 (of Arathorn).

Tarkil (VIII) Númenórean, Dúnadan. 310

Tarkil (XII) Sixth King of Arnor. 192

Tarkil Númenórean. (IXa) 30

Tarkilion (XII) Rejected name of Annúminas. 167. See *Dunhirion*.

Tarkilmar (VII) Earliest name of Annúminas. 144–5, 157, 304. See *Torfirion, Westermanton.*

Tarkiryan (XII) Brother of Tarannon (Falastur), King of Gondor. 197, 213

Tar-Kiryatan (-Ciryatan) (XII) Eighth and later twelfth Ruler of Númenor, 'the Shipbuilder'; also *Kiryatan, Ar- ~.* 150–2, 171, 180. See *Ar-Balkumagan.*

Tarlang's Neck (VIII) Pass between the White Mountains and an outlying spur, west of Kiril. 411, 419, 424–5, 437

Tar-Melian (III) Melian. 349–50. See *Ar-Melian.*

Tarmenel (VII) 'High Heaven'. 97, 99–100, 104, 108

Tar-menel (X) The firmament. 388. See *Nur-menel.*

Tar-Meneldur, Meneldur (XII) Fifth Ruler of Númenor, father of Aldarion. 155, 351

Tar-Minastir (XII) Eleventh Ruler of Númenor. 153; *King Minastir* 164

Tar-Minyatur (IV) See *Elros.*

Tar-Minyatur (XII) Elros. 257, 348 ('high first-ruler').

Tar-Míriel (IXb) Queen of Tarkalion (Ar-Zimraphel). 387. See *Tar-Ilien.*

Tar-Míriel, Míriel (XII) Daughter of Tar-Palantir, queen of Ar-Pharazôn. 154–5, 157, 159–61, 165, 181. See *Ar-Zimraphel.*

Tarn Aeluin (V) Lake on Dorthonion where Barahir made his lair. (134), 298

Tarn Aeluin, Aeluin (III) Lake on Dorthonion where Barahir and his companions made their lair. 171, 335–6, 339–41, 345, 350

Tarn Felin (VII) See *Sarn Gebir* (1).

Tarn Fui (I) 'The Door of Night'. 215, 222; *Tarna Fui* 222. See *Door of Night, Moritarnon.*

Tarnin Austa (II) 172. See *Gates of Summer.*

Tarnost (VIII) In South Gondor (south-east of the crossing of Ringlo). 437

Tarnost, Hills of (IXa) In South Gondor. 15, 17

Tarondor (XII) (1) Seventh King of Arnor. 192. (2) Twenty-seventh King of Gondor. 198, 200, 215, 231

Tarostar (XII) Eighth King of Gondor (see *Rómendakil I*). 197, 228

Tar-Palantir (IXb) Twenty-fourth King of Númenor. 381–2

Tar-Palantir (XII) Twenty-fourth Ruler of Númenor; Adûnaic *Inzila-dan*. 154, 159–62, 164, 181

Tarqendi (V) 'High-elves', a name of the Lindar. *389*, 403–4. See *High-elves*.

Tarquesta (V) 'High-speech', Quenya. 56, 172, 184, *389*

Taruithorn, Taruktarna (II) Gnomish and Eldarissa names of Oxford. 292–3

Tarumbar (X) 'Lord of the Earth' (Morgoth). 121

Tasarinan (III) The Land of Willows. 89. See *Nan-Tathrin*. *Taur-en-Faroth* See *Hills of the Hunters*.

Tasarinan (VII) Land of Willows, *Nan Tathren*. 417

Tasarinan The (II) Land of Willows. 140, 225, 248, 278; *the Battle of Tasarinan* (II) 70, 140, 154, 219–20, 278–9. See *Land of Willows, Nan-tathren*.

Tata (XI) 'Two', the second of the Fathers of the Elves. 380, 418, 420–2; *Companions of Tata* 423. See *Tatyar*.

Tathrobel (V) See *Tavrobel*.

Tatië (XI) Spouse of Tata. 421

Tatyar (XI) Elves of the Second Clan. 380–1, 420

TaurDanin (IV) See *Taur-na-Danion*; *Taur Fuin*, see *Taur-na-Fuin*.

Taur-en-Faroth (XI) The highlands west of Narog. 197; earlier form *Taur-na-Faroth* 116, *184, 189–90, 197. See *High Faroth, Hills of the Hunters*.

Taurfuin (II) The Forest of Night. 34–5, 47, 62, 78. Later form *Taur-nu-Fuin* 62, 123. See *Forest of Night*.

Taur-im-Duinath (XI) 'Forest between the Rivers' (Sirion and Gelion). 191, 193, 195, 197, 239. See next entries.

Taur-i-Melegyrn (XI) 'Forest of the Great Trees', a name of *Taur-im-Duinath*. *185, 193

Taur-na-Chardhîn (XI) 'Forest of the Southern Silence', a name of *Taur-im-Duinath*. *185, 193

Taur-na-Danion (IV) 'Forest of Pines' (330). 211, 296, 299, 315–16, 318–19, 330, 332, 334, 336; *Lords of Taur-na-Danion*, the

brothers of Felagund, 330; O.E. *Furhweald* 211. Earlier form *Taur Danin* 107, 173, 211, 316; later form *Taur-na-Donion* 211. (Replaced by *Dorthonion*.)

Taur-na-Danion (V) 'Forest of Pines' (127). 127–8, 130–3, 145, 147, 150–1, 404–5; *Taur-na-Thanion, -Thonion, -Donion* 145, (*392*). See *Dorthonion*.

Taur-na-Faroth (V) The Hills of the Hunters. 262, 268, 299, *387* (*Taur-na-Faras*); later form *Taur-en-Faroth* 299

Taur-na-Foen (XI) See *Foen*.

Taur-na-Fuin (III) 34, 36, 40–1, 53, 55, 63, 89, 146–8, 155, 160, 170, 227, 234–5, 255, 257, 263, 271–3, 276, 282–3, 297, 311, 348; earlier form *Taur Fuin* 55, 146, 160; later form *Taur-nu-Fuin* 171, 282, 284, 332, 348. Ancient Orc-road through the forest 39, 53. See *Deadly Nightshade, Dorthonion*.

Taur-na-Fuin (IV) 'Forest of Night'(26). 26, 28, 34, 59, 65, 103, 111, 118, 124, 136, 138, 140, 173–4, 183, 192–3, 199, 211, 221, 223, 259, 299, 302, 318, 321; O.E. *Nihtsceadwesweald*, etc. 211; Orc-road through 29, 103, 124, *Orcs' road of haste* 222. Earlier form *Taur Fuin* 223. See *Deadly Nightshade*.

Taur-na-Fuin (V) 'Forest of Night' (133). 133–6, 139, 144, 153, 282 (translated 'Mirkwood'), 289, 300, 310, 315, 336, *382* (also Quenya *Taurë Huinéva*), *391–2*, 405–6; with reference to Greenwood the Great 289; later form *Taur-nu-Fuin* 289, 300. See *Deldúwath, Fuin Daidelos, Gwathfuin-Daidelos*.

Taur-na-Fuin (VII) 124, 145, 175; *Taur-nu-Fuin* 138. See *Tol Fuin*.

Taur-nu-Fuin (XI) (also earlier *Taur-na-Fuin*) 'The Forest under Nightshade' (56), 'Mirkwood' (239), later name of Dorthonion. 56, 67–8, 82, 121–2, 126, 133, 140, 143, *183, 239–40. See *Fuin (Mountains of)*.

Tauron (X) 'Lord of the Forests', name of Oromë. 146, 149, 202; earlier form *Tauros* 111, 124, 146, 151. See *Aldaron*.

Tauron (XII) Oromë; *(Aran) Tauron* 'the (king) forester'. 358

Tauros (III) Name of Oromë. 195, 282, 356. (Replaced *Tavros*.)

Tauros (IV) 'Lord of Forests' (79), name of Oromë. 79, 167, 207–8; earlier form *Tavros* 79, 167. See *Aldaron*.

Tauros (V) Name of Oromë. 206, *359, 391*

Taurossë, Tavaros(së) (II) Eldarissa forms for *Tavrobel*. 292

Taurost (VIII) Name given to the 'High City' (Citadel) of Minas Tirith. 260

Taur-rimmon (VIII) See *Rimmon (Forest)*.

Tavari (I) Fays of the woods. 66

Tavrobel (I) A place in Tol Eressëa. 25, 175, 196, 230; *Bridge of Tavrobel* 175, 196; *Tower of Tavrobel* 174; *Gilfanon a·Davrobel, Gilfanon of Tavrobel* 174, 195–6, 203, 229

Tavrobel (II) 145, 283–4, 287–9, 292–3, 307, 310, 323, 326; *Tavrobel the Old* 310, the *New* 310; tower of 287; bridge and joining rivers at 288–9; *Golden Book of* 285, 310; *Tales of* 290. See *Gilfanon, Great Haywood, Pine of Belaurin*.

Tavrobel (IV) 10, 263, 274, 281–2, 284, 288, 290–1 (in O.E. texts also *Taprobel*); *Golden Book of Tavrobel* 76

Tavrobel (V) 201, 203, *380, 390*, 412–13; *Tathrobel* 203, 412

Tavrobel (VII) 173

Tavrobel (IXb) In Tol Eressëa. 280

Tavrobel (XI) In the Forest of Brethil. 148, 157, 186

Tavros (III) Name of Oromë. 186–7, 195, 198, 235–6, 243, 245, 276, 282, 356. (Replaced by *Tauros*.) See *Ormaid*.

Tavros (IV) See *Tauros*.

Tavrost (II) =*Tavrobel*. 292

Teeth of Mordor (VIII) Towers of either side of the Morannon. 113, 122, 362; *Towers of The Teeth* 123, 131, 431. See *Naglath Morn, Nelig Myrn*.

Teiglin (II) 130, 132, 135, 140, 249; *Crossings of Teiglin* 127, 130, 132; ravines of 132–4

Teiglin, River (XI) See *Taiglin*.

Teiglin, Taiglin, River (XII) 326

Tekel-Mirim (IXb) [Ramer] 207–211, 222; earlier name *Tekel-Ishtar* 222

Telchar (II) Dwarf smith of Nogrod. 58, 129

Telchar (III) Dwarf smith of Nogrod. 115, 126

Telchar (IV) Dwarf smith of Belegost. 118, 182; originally of Nogrod, 182

Telchar (V) Dwarf smith of Belegost, or of Nogrod. 303, 319, 322. [The statement in the Index to Vol. IV that Telchar was 'originally of Nogrod' is an error; see IV.182.]

Telchar (XI) Dwarf smith of Nogrod (formerly of Belegost). 12, 109

Telcontar (IXa) Strider. 121, 128

Telcontar (X) 'Strider'. 216

Telcontar, Telkontar (VIII) See *Tarakil*.

Teld Quing Ilon (II) 'Rainbow Roof', earlier name for *(Cris) Ilbranteloth*. 202

Telelli (I) Name of certain Elves (see Appendix, p. 267). 19, 22; earlier *Telellë* 22

Telemnar (XII) Twenty-sixth King of Gondor. 200, 203, 215, 231, 254

Teleporno (XII) See *Celeborn* (2).

Teleri (I) (1) The first kindred of the Elves (afterwards called Vanyar). 48–50, 52, 59, 62, 115, 118–19, 121–4, 126, 132, 134, 143, 163, 169, 175–6, 210, 220, 231, 234. (2) In later sense, =Solosimpi of the *Lost Tales*. 50, 62, 132–8, 157, 171, 198, 223

Teleri (II) The first kindred of the Elves (afterwards called Vanyar). 4, 253, 255, 278, 307

Teleri (III) (1) The First Kindred of the Elves (afterwards called Vanyar). 28, 139. (2) In later sense, = Solosimpi of the *Lost Tales*. 140

Teleri (IV) (1) In *the Lost Tales*, the First Kindred of the Elves. 44. (2) The Third Kindred. 13–15, 17–18, 37, 40, 44–6, 48, 68, 72, 85–8, 90, 94–5, 149, 153–4, 59, 162, 168, 195–6, 198, 202, 227, 264–7, 272, 276–7, 293, 309, 326; adjective *Telerian* 295, 328; O.E. *Telere* and *Teleri*, sing. *Teler*, adjective *Telerisc*, 281–2, 286–7, 338 separation of the language of the Teleri 87, 277. See *Third Kindred*.

Teleri (V) 112–13, 115–16, 119, 122, 143, 161, 168–71, 173–4, 178, 180–4, 186, 193, 197, 200, 214–15, 218, 221–6, 231, 233, 235–6, 239, 242, 256, 266, 324, 326, 332, 334, 344, *391* (also *Mirimor 373, Fallinelli, Falanyeldi 379, 381*), 403; language of the Teleri 171, 173–4, 180, 184, 222, 224, 226; meaning of the name 168, 183, 214, 218, *391–2*; in old sense, the First Kindred, 165, 182; other names 215, 403

Teleri (X) 20, 24–5, 35, 82–91, 93, 99–100, 115–16, 120, 125, 128, 133, 163–4, 169, 173–5, 177–9, 183, 199, 217, 274, 283, 287, 289, 340, 349, 360

Teleri (XI) 6–8, 13, 16, 20, 25, 28, 104, 109, 112, 177, 322, 329, 344, 371, 374–5, 378–84, 400, 405, 408, 418, 423; singular *Teler* 371; origin of the name 382, 411. See *Lindar*.

Teleri (XII) (and singular *Teler*) 30, 73, 76, 82, 305, 318–19, 324, 329, 332, 337–8, 340–1, 344, 347, 354, 357–8, 385–7, 391, 401; Sindarin *Telir, Telerrim* 385

Telerian (V) (of language) 175, 181, 184, 187; (with other reference) 125, 148, 169, 176, 182, 187, 194, 218–19, 253, 256, 261, 326

Telerian (XI) 19, 22–3, 179, 195

Telerian (XII) (of language) 30, 36, 65, 73–4, 392; (with other reference) 174, 366

Telerin (V) Language of the Teleri. 172, 188–9, 193–5, 347; adjective to *Teleri* 347

Telerin (VII) (language) 453

Telerin (X) (not of language) 169–70

Telerin (XI) (of language) 21, 359, 362–5, 367, 369–73, 375–6, 380, 382–3, 392, 394, 403, 407, 409, 411; *Common Telerin* 375, 410, 412; (with other reference) 115, 375–6, 384, 410

Telerin (XII) (of language) 318, 340–1, 345–7, 356–7, 359–63, 365, 368; (with other reference) 337, 364, 385

Telimektar (I) Son of Tulkas. 101, 154, 182, 200. See *Telumehtar*.

Telimektar (II) Son of Tulkas; Orion. 281–2; *Telumektar* 302, *Telumaith* 302. See *Taimonto*.

Telimektar (IV) Son of Tulkas, Orion. 68, 75

Telimpë (I) The cauldron of silver light in Valinor; name varying with *Silindrin*. 79, 113–14, 127, 129–30, 178, 181, 189, 192, 196, 202

Telperion (I) 88, 133, 135, 201

Telperion (IV) 171. See *Silpion*.

Telperion (V) A name of the White Tree of Valinor. 209, 211, 244

Telperion (IXa) The White Tree of Valinor. 58

Telperion (X) 50, 55–6, 59, 62, 71, 85, 90, 98, 130–1, (154), 155, 157, 159, 176, 180, 193, 197–8, 261, 372, 386; *the White Tree* 176. See *Silpion*.

Telperion (XI) 401

Telperion (XII) 147–8, 337, 404. See *Eldest Tree*.

Telumehtar (I) Orion. 200. See *Telimektar*.

Telumehtar (XI) 'Warrior of the Sky', Orion. 411. See *Menelmakil*, and also I.268.

Telumehtar (XII) Twenty-eighth King of Gondor (see *Umbardakil*). 200, 215.

Telumendil (X) Name of a constellation. 160

Temple (IXb) The temple of Morgoth in Númenor. (1) On the Pillar of Heaven. 289, 315, 335, 339, 356, 384, 401. (2) In the City of the Númenóreans. 250, 258, 335, 339, 347, 350, 353, 356–7, 367, 371, 374–5, 384, 390. O.E. *alh* 257, *ealh* 314. The temple described 347, 367, 384, 390

Tengwar (VI) 384

Tengwar (VII) 188

tengwar (IXb) 148, 292, 313–14, 317–27

tengwar (X) 30, 103, (350). See *letters*.

Tengwethil (III) Gnomish name of Taniquetil. 22, 58, 79, 123, 135–6, 139, 259; *Tengwethiel* 49. See *Tain-Gwethil*.

Tengwethil (IV) See *Taingwethil*.

Tents of Murmuring (I) Dwelling of the Noldoli by the Helkaraksë. 168, 173

Terch Ungol (VIII) 'The Spider's Lair'. 202. See *Torech Ungol*.

Terendul (V) 'Slender and dark', derisive name given to Herendil son of Elendil. 59, 70, *355*, *376*, *392*

Terrible Battle (IV) 39, 309, *Battle Terrible* 157, 160, 164. See *Last Battle* (1).

Terrible Battle (V) See *Great Battle*.

Tevildo Prince of Cats (I) 47, 52

Tevildo Prince of Cats (II) 15–17, 21–33, 35, 45, 49, 51, 53–6, 58, 281; *Tevildo Vardo Meoita* 15 *Meoita* 54. See *Tiberth, Tifil*.

Tevildo Prince of Cats (III) 220–1, 257–8, 270, 272

Thain (of the Shire) (XII) 6, 11, 14–15, 107–8, 116, 118, 232, 235–7, 250, 268–9; *Shire-thain* 232; earlier *Elder* 11, *Thane* 11, 14, 87. See *Shirking*.

Thain of the Shire (VI) 31

Thain of the Shire (IXa) 90, 101, 103. See *Took, Paladin*.

Thaliodrin (III) Name of Túrin, 'son of Thalion'. 9, 22, 49, 79

Thalion (III) 'Steadfast'. (1) Name of Húrin; also *the Thalion*. 4, 6–9, 11–14, 21–2, 37, 71, 92, 96–7, 100–2, 111, 114. (2) Name of Túrin. 32–3, 48–9, 51, 60, 66, 72

Thalion (VIII) (1) Name of Húrin of Dor-lómin. 293. (2) Man of Minas Tirith, father of Gwinhir. (284), 285, 293

Thalion (XI) Name of Húrin, 'Steadfast'. 231, 234, 272, 275, 277, 281, 286–7, 298

Thalos, River (IV) 135, 189, 230, 232, 234

Thalos, River (V) 128, 263, *388*

Thalos, River (XI) In Ossiriand. 13, *185*, 216

Thames (II) 295, 297

Thames, River (IXb) (210); *Thames Valley* 211

Thanador (VI) See *Rohan*.

Thangorodrim (I) 26, 158, 243

Thangorodrim (III) 8, 24, 33, 37, 39–40, 49, 55, 59, 87, 101, 212, 222, 227, 275, 281–3, 309–10; the triple peaks 40, 55

Thangorodrim (IV) 22, 27, 29, 66, 101, 119, 124, 137, 139, 157, 160, 172, 191–2, 194, 203, 212, 220, 223, *250–1*, 259–60, 269, 274,

295, 298, 303, 309, 314, 328, 333, 338; see especially 220, 260, and see *Black Mountains*.

Thangorodrim (V) 117–18, 125, 132, 137, 144, 249–51, 254, 257, 259, 264, 266, 271, 279–80, 283, 290, 310, 313, 329, 336, *388*, *412*; see especially *259, 271*

Thangorodrim (VI) 182, 187; *the black mountain* 182; *the Mountain of Thunder* 187

Thangorodrim (VII) 110, 142, 198, 247, 262–3

Thangorodrim (IXa) 44–5

Thangorodrim (IXb) 332

Thangorodrim (X) 67, 109, 138, 297–8, 402, 404, 419; *the Mountains of Oppression* 298

Thangorodrim (XI) 15, 18, 29–30, 52, 68, 73, 78, 111–14, 135, 166, 168, 181, 246–7, 252, 321, 329; *the Tyrannous Towers, Mountains of Oppression* 111

Thangorodrim (XII) 143, 163, 172, 233, 380

Tharbad (VII) 79, 164, 172, 282, 292, 299

Tharbad (IXa) 72, 103

Tharbad (XII) 11, 38, 66, 330 (great bridge of Tharbad).

Thargelion (IV) Caranthir's land, east of Gelion and north of Ascar. 174, 335, 337

Thargelion (V) The land of Cranthir, 'Beyond Gelion'. 262, 265, 268–9, 273, 277, 283, *392*; earlier form *Targelion* 268. See *Dor Granthir, Radhrost*.

Thargelion (VI) 466

Thargelion (XI) The country beyond Gelion's upper waters. 121, *183, 194, 197, 201, 203, 225, 227, 236, 320, 337; *Thargelian* 320, *331, 337. See *Thorewilan*.

Tharkûn (VIII) Gandalf's name among the Dwarves ('Staff-man', *Unfinished Tales* p.397). 153. Earlier form *Sharkûn* 153

The world was young, the mountains green (VII) 183–4

Themes (of the Music of the Ainur) Roads (X) *The Three Themes* 23, 408; *the Second Theme* (10), 14, 40, 275, 282, 358; *the Third Theme* 10–11, 22, 282, 358; *Themes of the Children* 336, 342, 358; *a new theme* 379; *two Themes, those of Eru and Melkor*, 406, 408. See especially 358, and *Great Theme*.

Thengel (VII) Father of Théoden. 399, 402, 441, 451; called *Master* (i.e. of Rohan) 402

Thengel (VIII) Sixteenth King of the Mark, father of Théoden. 355, 366, 372, 408. *Thengling*, son of Thengel, 371

Thengel (IXa) Father of Théoden. 62

Thengel (XII) Sixteenth King of Rohan. 239, 270, 272, 296, 316

Théoden (III) King of Rohan. 145

Théoden (VII) 390, 399–402, 405, 430, 432–5; 437, 440–51. *Father and Master of the Riddermark* 393, *First Master* 400; first named as *King* 444

Théoden (VIII) (including many references to *the King*) 3–31 *passim*, 36–51 *passim*, 55–8, 62–3, 67–74, 77–9, 95, 100–1, 103, 119–20, 129, 140–1, 146, 155, 182, 219, 226, 231, 235–67 *passim*, 272–6, 289, 296, 298–322 *passim*, 343–60 *passim*, 365–9, 371–2, 380, 384–6, 389, 395–6, 404, 406–8. Legend of Théoden's Howe 385, 389, 393

   Théoden (VIII) *The King's Guard* (VIII) 9, 14–16, 265, 316–19, 343, 345, 347–51, 353, 355–6, 372, *knights* 352, 368–9, *household-men* 357

Théoden (IXa) 36, 52, 57, 61, 62, (67), 68, 72–3; *king of the grassland* 63. Lament for Théoden 72

Théoden (XII) Seventeenth King of Rohan. 7, 21, 26, (49), 53, 59–60, 69, 81, 83, 239–40, 242, 244, 270–4, 296, 316; called *Edníwe*, *Ednew* 'Renewed' 274

Théodred (VII) In LR Théoden's son; see 437, 451.

Théodred (VIII) Son of Théoden; Second Marshal of the Mask. 8, 22, 59

Theostercloh (VIII) See *Heorulf's Clough*.

Théodred (XII) Son of Théoden. 242, 274

Théodwyn (VII) Théoden's sister. 451

Théodwyn (XII) Sister of Théoden. 240, 271

Thilevril (VII) See *Ithildin, Mithril*.

Thimbalt (IV) Fortress of Morgoth (?). 223

Thingódhel (XI) Late proposed substitution for *Pengolodh*. 417

Thingol (I) 107, 238, 243; *Elu Thingol* 132. See *Tinwë Linto, Tinwelint*.

Thingol (II) 42–3, 45–6, 50–2, 63, 65, 69, 127–9, 245–6, 251; *Elu Thingol* 50; *Thingol of the Woods* 43, 251. (Replaced *Tinwelint*.)

Thingol (III) 9–14, 16–17, 19–20, 24–8, 30, 32–4, 43, 50–2, 61, 98, 104–5, 107, 111–15, 117–18, 124, 127, 138; *passim* in *Lay of Leithian* and commentaries. *Elu Thingol* (III) 347; *Robber Thingol* 229, cf. 16, 117; *the Grey King* 352; *King of Doriath* 12, 17–18, 112–13, 117; his wealth 26, 160–1. See *Tinwelint*.

Thingol (IV) 5, 13, 23–30, 32, 44, 57, 59, 61–2, 72, 85, 103, 105–6,

424

109–11, 113–14, 116–17, 119–23, 125–6, 128, 131–3, 162, 168, 173, 176, 179, 182, 184, 188–9, 264, 271, 276, 278, 281, 286, 288, 296, 299, 301, 304, 306–7, 311, 320, 325, 327–9, 334, 336, 339; *Thingol's Heir* (Dior) 134, 140. See *Sindingul, Tindingol, Tinwelint*.

Thingol (V) 112–14, 119, 125–6, 134–5, 138, 141–2, 148, 168, 174–6, 181, 186–7, 189–90, 194, 215, 217, 220–1, 225, 253, 261–3, 266, 281, 287, 292, 295, 298–300, 308, 316–22, 326, 332, *362*, *389, 392–3* (also *Tor Thingol*; *Tor Tinduma* 'King of Twilight', Noldorin *Aran Dinnu*); *the hidden king* 266; *Thingol's Heir*, see *Dior*.

Thingol (VI) 182–3, 216; *Thingol's Heir* 68

Thingol (VII) 110, 454–5

Thingol (VIII) King of Doriath. 297

Thingol (X) 86, 88–91, 93, 104, 106, 164, 168, 170–1, 173–4, 217, 228, 340. For *Elu Thingol* see *Elwë* (2).

Thingol (XI) 4, 9–16, 19, 21–3, 25–7, 32–5, 39, 41–4, 49–50, 57, 59, 61–7, 69–72, 79–82, 85, 89, 93, 95, 108–12, 114–16, 119, 123, 126–7, 129–30, 132–3, 136, 138, 148–9, (158), 162–3, 177, 195, 223–4, 228, 231, 244, 252, 255, 258–9, 297–8, 310, 312, 321–2, 333, 345–7, 350–5, 379–80, 409–10, 418, 420; his high-kingship, overlordship 19, 21, 23, 25–6, 115, 380, 410, 418; his ban on Noldorin 23, 25–7, 43. For *Elu Thingol* see *Elwë*, and see *Greymantle, Sindikollo, Singollo; Tinwelint; Dior*.

Thingol (XII) 76, 78, 301, 328, 360, 365, 369, 372, 387; *Elu* ~ 337, 348, 357, *Elu* 369, 372. See *Elwë, Sindikollo*.

Third Age (II) 216, 327

Third Age (III) 145

Third Age (IV) 327

Third Age (VII) 9, 146, 450

Third Age, The (IXb) 408–9

Third Age (X) 5, 341, 414, 418–19, 423

Third Age (XI) 390

Third Age (XII) 12, 25–7, 29, 33, 37, 65–6, 73, 75, 79, 140, 166–71, 173, 177–8, 192, 195–6, 201–2, 208, 211, 223, 225–7, 233–4, 236, 243, 246–7, 265, 275, 285, 293, 296–8, 301, 304, 311, 314–15, 320–1, 323–4, 327–9, 332, 360, 378, 380–1, 383, 385, 392, 419

Third Age, The (IXa) 45, 52, 68, 110, (124); *Guardian of the Third Age* (Gandalf) 132. In different sense 68

Third Battle (X) See *Battles of the Gods.*

Third Battle of Beleriand (IV) The Battle of Unnumbered Tears. 301. Later the Battle of Sudden Flame became the Third Battle, 108, 115, 173, 179, 333, 336

Third Battle of Beleriand (V) The Battle of Sudden Fire. 130, 280. See *Dagor Húrbreged, Dagor Vregedúr.*

Third Battle of Beleriand (XI) 21, 25–6, 36–7, 179. See *Glorious Battle* (formerly the Second Battle).

Third Host (X) The Teleri. 168, 349

Third House of the Noldor (XI) The House of Finarfin (=Finrod (1)). 115

Third Kindred (III) 140, 235

Third Kindred (of the Elves) (IV) 44, 46, 212; *Third Host* 257, 277 O.E. names 212. See *Foam riders, Sea-elves, Soloneldi, Solosimpi, Teleri.*

Third Kindred (of the Elves) (V) 182, 217; *Third host* 217. See *Teleri.*

Third Theme (X) See *Themes.*

Thirsty Plain (III) Dor-na-Fauglith. 39, 55, 213, 222

Thirsty Plain (IV) Dor-na-Fauglith. 107, 117, 121, 124, 181, 220, 223

Thompson, Francis (I) 29

Thompson, Francis (II) 329

Thompson, Francis (X) 157–8

Thor (VII) 106

Thor (IXb) 301, 307–8

Thorewilan (XI) =Thargelion; see 336.

Thorin (Oakenshield) (VII) 142–3, 154–5, 159–60, 185

Thorin (Oakenshield) (VIII) 357

Thorin (Oakenshield) (XI) 207–8

Thorin I Son of Thráin I (XII). 275–7

Thorin II (Oakenshield) (XII) 35, (53, 81), 237–9, 249–50, 276–7, 279–89

Thorin III (Stonehelm) (XII) 277–9

Thorin Oakenshield (VI) 85, 209, 217, 391, 399, 403

Thorin Oakenshield (IXa) 78

Thórin son of Thrór (VIII) 357–8

Thorn Sir (II) Falling stream below Christhorn. 192–4; *Eagle-stream* 194

Thorndor (I) Gnomish name of Sorontur, King of Eagles. 89; later form *Thorondor* 158

Thorndor (II) Gnomish name of Sorontur King of Eagles. 192–4, 202. Later form *Thorondor* 251

Thorndor (III) Gnomish name of Sorontur, King of Eagles. 286, 292; later form *Thorondor* 292, 309–10, 314

Thorndor (IV) King of Eagles. 23, 34, 37, 52, 66, 102, 106–7, 115, 137, 139–40, 145–6, 173, 177–8, 190–2, 299, 308, 328; later form *Thorondor* 66, 140, 146, 192. See *Sorontur*.

Thornhoth (II) 'People of the Eagles'. 192–3

Thornsir (III) Falling stream below Cristhorn in the Encircling Mountains about Gondolin. 142; *stream of Eagles* 143

Thorondir (XII) Twenty-second Ruling Steward. 206

Thorondor (V) King of Eagles. 145, 251–2, 256, 285, 288, 290, 298, 301, 303, 329, 336, 392 (also *Thorntor, Torthurnion*), 405; earlier *Thorndor* 126, 132–3, 142, 145, 256, 290–1, 303. See *Sorontur*.

Thorondor (IXa) King of Eagles in the Elder Days 13, 44–5; earlier form *Thorndor* 13, 44

Thorondor King of Eagles. (X) 412. See *Sorontar*.

Thorondor King of Eagles. (XI) 32, 53, 55, 57–8, 63, 68, 123, 175, 198, 239–40, 302; earlier *Thorndor* 175, 349. See *Sorontar*.

Thorongil (VII) Aragorn's name in Gondor. 157

Thorongil (VIII) Aragorn's name in Gondor. 309

Thorongil (XII) Name taken by Aragorn II in Gondor. 258

Þórr (II) 290. See *Þunor*.

Thousand Caves (II) 245, 248. See *Menegroth*.

Thousand Caves (III) 9, 12, 20, 28, 34, 50, 53, 76, 98, 105, 113, 127, 156, 160, 194–6, 312, 314; *Thousand Caverns* 186, 332. See *Menegroth*.

Thousand Caves (IV) 13, 23, 28, 32, 59, 61–2, 85, 123, 132–3, 185, 189, 221, 223–4, 278, 299, 307, 325, 336 O.E. *Þúsende Þéostru* 288. See *Menegroth*.

Thousand Caves (V) 114, 141, 187, 220. See *Menegroth*.

Thousand Caves (X) 173. See *Menegroth*.

Thousand Caves (XI) 11, 108, 111, 138, *183, 334, 352, 355, 415. See *Menegroth*.

Thráin (VI) Son of Thrór (but said to be his father, 403). 85, 398–9, 403, 414, 429

Thráin (VII) (1) Thráin the Old, Thráin I. 160. (2) Son (or father) of Thrór (see 159–60). 136, 142–3, 154–5, 158–60, 178

Thráin (IXa) 9

Thráin I (XII) Son of Náin I. 252, 275–7, 286, 288

Thráin II (XII) Son of Thrór. 237–8, 249–50, 252, 276–81, 283–4, 286–8

Thranduil (VII) King of the Elves of Mirkwood. 163, 257

Thranduil (XII) King of the Elves of Mirkwood. 36, 79, 82, 174, 239, 242, 244, 329

Three Clans (XI) (of the Elves) 360, 380, 420

Three Houses (of Men) (XI) 50, 77, 128, 224, 377–8, 386; *Three Kindreds* 219

Three Houses (V) (of the Fathers of Men or of the Elf-friends). 19, 24, 64, 131, 276, 286–7, 310, 328, 336–7

Three Houses (IXb) (of the Men of Beleriand) 331–2; *the Faithful Houses, three kindreds* 402

Three Houses (XII) (of Men, of the Fathers of Men, of the Edain) 31–2, 55, 62–4, 146; *Three Peoples* 324

Three Houses of Men (VIII) 157, 159–60, 162, 169; *of the Elf-friends* 161

Three Houses of Men, of the Elf-friends (IV) 297, 317; genealogical table 315

Three Kindreds (I) 51

Three Kindreds (III) 8, 100, 132, 138

Three Kindreds (of the Elves) (V) 112, 168, 171, 181, 183, 197, 214, 218, 227

Three Kindreds (X) See *Kindreds*.

Three Kindreds (XII) (of the Elves) 23, 77

Three Rings (of the Elves) (VII) 112, 149, 155–6, 159, 254–6, 259–60, 286; *Elf-rings* 237, 265; Galadriel's Ring, see *Ring of Earth*.

Three Rings (of the Elves) (IXa) (52), 57, 111, 132; *the Great Rings* 109. See *Narya, Nenya, Vilya*.

Three Rings (VI) See *Rings of the Elves*. Three Rings of Men 78, 269

Three Rings (XII) See *Rings of Power*.

Three Rings of the Elves (VIII) 98

Three-Farthing Stone (IXa) 81

Thrihyrne (VII) The three peaks above Helm's Deep. 320. Earlier name *Tindtorras* 320

Thrihyrne (VIII) The three peaks above Helm's Deep. 12, 22. See *Tindtorras*.

Throne of Gondor (VII) 395–6, 404

Thrór (VI) Father of Thráin (but said to be his son, and the father of Thorin Oakenshield, 403). 403, 414, 429

Thrór (VII) Father (or son) of Thráin (see 159–60). 136, 142–3, 154–7, 159–60, 178; Thrór's Map, see *Maps*.

Thrór (IXa) 9

Thrór (XII) 236–8, 249–50, 252, 275–8, 280–1, 284–6; Thrór's Map 284, 286

Thrór 357; Thrór's map 357

Thû (II) The Necromancer. 54

Thû (III) 16, 27–8, 117, 146–8, 153, 170, 220, 227–8, 230–8, 240–1, 244–6, 249, 251–4, 256–60, 276, 279, 284, 288, 290, 293–4, 297, 306, 311, 313; called *necromancer* 228, 234. (Replaced by *Gorthû*.)

Thû (IV) 25 ('the hunter'), 26, 40, 73, 75, 106, 110–12, 114, 116, 120, 164, 178, 205, 299–300; Lord of Wolves 25–6, 106

Thû (V) 11–13, 15, 18, 22–3, 29, 33, 78–9, 133–5, 338, 393 (also *Morthu*); called *the Wizard* 133; *Tol Thû* 407. See *Gorthû, Sauron, Sûr*.

Thû (VI) 131, 216, 218. See *Morthu*.

Thû (XI) *182. See *Gorthaur*.

Thulcandra (IXb) [Lewis] The Silent Planet, Earth. 213

Þunor (II) Old English name of the Germanic god in Old Norsë called *Þorr*; by Eriol identified with Tulkas. 290

Thurin (XI) 'The Secret', Finduilas' name for Túrin. 299

Thuringud (XI) 'The Hidden Foe', Túrin's name for himself in Nargothrond. 256, 299

Thuringwethil (II) Bat-messenger of Sauron from Tol-in-Gaurhoth. 57

Thuringwethil (III) (1) Name given to herself by Lúthien before Morgoth. 297, 304, 306. (2) The bat-messenger of Sauron 283–4.

Thuringwethil (IV) Name given to herself by Lúthien before Morgoth. 178

Thuringwethil (XI) The bat-messenger of Sauron. 68, 131

Thurisind (V) King of the Lombards. 37, 53–4

Thurismod (V) Son of Thurisind. 37, 53–4

Tibba (VII) Precursor of Tídwald (Tída) in *The Homecoming of Beorhtnoth*. 106–7

Tiberth (II) Gnomish name of Tevildo Prince of Cats. (Replaced *Tifil*.) 45, 47–9, 51; *Tiberth Bridhon Miaugion* 451 *Miaugion* 54

Tides, The (IV) (poem) 214

Tídwald (V) In *The Homecoming of Beorhtnoth*. 55

Tifanto (II) Earlier name for Dairon. 49–50, 59. (Replaced *Kapalen*.)

Tifil (II) Gnomish name of Tevildo Prince of Cats. (Replaced by *Tiberth*.) 15, 45, 51; *Tifil Bridhon Miaugion* 15

Tighfield (VIII) Village in the Shire. 95

Tighfield (XII) Village of the Shire. 112, 114–16

Tilion (I) Steersman of the Moon. 88, 202, 222

Tilion (IV) Steersman of the Moon. 97–8, 170–1, 254. See *Ilinsor*.

Tilion (V) Steersman of the Moon. 240–2, 244, 393

Tilion (X) Steersman of the Moon. 130–4, 136–7, 198, 376–7, 383–5; called a Vala 376, 384; Old English name *Hyrned* 130, 136, 198

Tilion (XI) 'Guardian of the Moon'. 30, 114

Tilkal (I) Metal devised by Aulë for the chaining of Melko. 100, 104, 111, 114

Timbrenting (III) Old English name of Taniquetil. 133–6, 139, 211, 222, 250, 259; alternative form *Tindbrenting* 123, 127, 139. On the name see 127, 139.

Timbrenting (IV) See *Tindbrenting*.

Timbridhil (III) (1) Name of Varda. 139, 170. (2) Name of the Great Bear. 169–70

Tim-Bridhil (IV) Gnomish name of Varda. 82. See *Bridhil, Tinwetári*.

Time (I) See especially 218–19, 227–8

Time (IV) See especially 99, 171–2, 263, 270, 295, 328, 338

Time (V) See 110, 119, 156, 160, 177, 184, 189, 245

Time (X) 14, 21, 28, 37, 40, 50–1, 56, 58, 99, 144, 219, 242, 245, 251–2, 292, 318, 326–7, 331, 333–5, 366, 376, 382, 403–5, 408, 424–6, 430, and see *Deeps of Time*; *circles of time* 40. Reckoning of Time 49–51, 56–62, 72, 82, 131–2, 155, 183, 425–6, 430–1

Time, Reckoning of (XI) 16, 20, 24, 174, 343

Time, Time-travel (IXb) 151, 159, 164, 169, 175–6, 178–9, 182, 195, 198–9, 201, 209, 215, 218, 220

Timeless Halls (X) 14, 42; *Timeless Void* 407

Timon of Athens (X) 157–8

Timpinen (I) Name of Tinfang in the tongue of the Eldar. 94–5, 107

Timpinen (II) Name of Tinfang in Eldarissa. 4, 59

Tindbrenting (III) See *Timbrenting*.

Tindbrenting (IV) Old English name of Taniquetil. 12, 43, 80–1, 94–5, 98, 102, 155, 211 (*Tinbrenting* 153, 155); variant form *Timbrenting* 12, 16–17, 19, 21, 23, 43

Tindbrenting (V) Old English name of Taniquetil. 209

Tindbrenting (X) Old English name of Taniquetil. 157

Tindingol (IV) Thingol. 270. (Replaced *Sindingul*.)

Tindingol (V) Thingol. 112, 119, 187. (Replaced *Sindingul*, replaced by *Sindo*.)

Tindobel, Tower of (IV) On the cape west of Eldorest (> Eglorest). 229, 331, 335. See *Barad Nimras*.

Tindobel, Tower of (V) On the cape west of Eglorest. 129, 265, 270, 380, 394; *Tindabel* 270

Tindobel, Tower of (XI) Of the cape west of Eglarest. 118, 196–7; *Tindabel* 118, 190, 198. See *Ingildon*, *Barad Nimras*.

Tindriel (I) Early name of Melian. 106–7, 131–2. (Replaced by *Wendelin*.)

Tindriel (II) Earliest name of Melian. 50, 244

Tindrock, The (VII) Tol Brandir. 285, 288, 356, 359–60; high seat upon, 360

Tindtorras (VII) See *Thrihyrne*.

Tindtorras (VIII) Earlier name of *Thrihyrne*. 8–10, 12, 22, 95

Tinfang (I) Gnomish name of Timpinen the piper; called *Tinfang Warble* (see the Appendix, p. 268). 94–5, 107–10; poems *Tinfang Warble*, *Over Old Hills and Far Away* 107–10

Tinfang (II) Gnomish name of Timpinen; called *Tinfang Warble* (Gnomish *Gwarbilin* (II) 'Birdward', I.268). 10, 59

Tinfang (III) Gnomish name of Timpinen the piper. *Tinfang Warble* 181–2; later *Tinfang Gelion* 174, 181–2

Tinfang Gelion (IV) Gnomish name of Timpinen the piper. 115, 179; earlier *Tinfang Warble* 113, 115, 179

Tintallë (V) 'Star-kindler', Varda. 200, 212, 216, 344–5, 394

Tintallë (VII) 'The Kindler', Varda. 285

Tintallë (X) 'The Kindler', Varda. 159, 166, 384, 388–9

Tintanië (V) 'Star-maker', Varda. 345, 390, 394

Tinthellon (II) Earlier (Gnomish) name of Tinwelint. 51, 69, 116, 118–19

Tinto Ellu (II) Earlier (Eldarissa) name of Tinwë Linto. 50–1, 69

Tinto Ellu (IV) See *Tinwelint*.

Tinto'ellon (II) See *Tinthellon*. 50–1

Tintoglin (I) Earlier name of Tinwelint. 131–2

Tintoglin (II) Earlier (Gnomish) name of Tinwelint. 69, 71, 116–19, 136–7

Tinúviel (I) Daughter of Tinwelint (afterwards Lúthien (Tinúviel) daughter of Thingol). 27, 107, 115, 132; the *Tale of Tinúviel* 27, 51–2, 203–4, 231, 233, 238–9, 241. See *Lúthien*.

Tinúviel (II) 8, 10–14, 17–38, 40–3, 45–9, 51–63, 66, 68, 72, 116,

123, 139–40, 215, 223, 233–4, 238–40, 243, 246–7, 249–50, 252, 259, 302, 330. See *Lúthien* (4).

Tinúviel (III) 9, 22, 87, 89, 104, 107–9, 120, 122, 124–5, 153, 159, 180–4, 193, 197–9, 203, 209, 215, 244, 257–9, 261, 270, 272, 277, 282–3, 291, 297, 305, 307, 309, 312, 314, 354, 357, 360; *Tinwiel* 22. On the meaning of the name see 124, 182.

Tinúviel (IV) 24, 56, 63, 109, 191, 311

Tinúviel (V) 134, 292, 306, 323–4, *385, 393* (also *Tindúmhiell, Tindómerel*); *the Fountain of Tinúviel*, see *Eithel Nínui*.

Tinúviel (VI) 179–82, 184; as name of the song *Light as Leaf on Linden tree* 412

Tinúviel (X) 288; *Narn e·Dinúviel* 373. See *Lúthien.*

Tinúviel (XI) 'Nightingale' (Lúthien). 62, 65, 69, 231, 327

Tinwë (Linto) (II) Name of Tinwelint in Eldarissa. 8, 50–1, 63, 116. (Replaced by *Singoldo*.)

Tinwë Linto, Tinwë (I) Lord of the Solosimpi, who was lost on the Great Journey and became Lord of the Elves of Hisilómë afterwards *Thingol*. 115–16, 120, 130–3. (Replaced *Linwë Tinto*.)

Tinwelint (I) Gnomish name of Tinwë Linto (afterwards Thingol). 115, 131–2, 238, 240, 243–4. (Replaced *Tintoglin*.)

Tinwelint (II) King of Artanor (later Thingol); called 'the hidden king'. 8–10, 12–14, 17–20, 26, 32, 35–41, 50–3, 56, 59, 61, 63–5, 69, 72–4, 76–7, 79, 91–5, 102–3, 113–17, 119, 121, 127–9, 132, 135–7, 140–1, 144, 221–34, 236–9, 243, 245, 249–51, 259. Other Gnomish names: *Ellon, Tinthellon, Tinto'ellon, Tintoglin*.

Tinwelint (III) King of Artanor (later Thingol of Doriath). 26, 124, 148, 160–1, 305; *Tinwë Linto* 124

Tinwelint (IV) Name of Thingol in the *Lost Tales*. 44, 51, 57, 59, 62, 168, 188–9; other early forms *Tinto Ellu, Ellu*, 44; *Linwë* 59

Tinwelint (V) Name of Thingol in the *Lost Tales*. 217; *Tinwë Linto* 186

Tinwelint (XI) Precursor of Thingol in *The Book of Lost Tales*. 355

Tinwë-mallë (IV) Star-street', name of Ilmen. 241, *243, 253. See *Elenarda*.

Tinwë-mallë (X) 'Star-street', the path of the stars, Ilmen. 29

Tinwenairin (IV) 'Crowned with Stars', Taniquetil. 81, 167. See *Elerrína*.

Tinwenairin (V) 'Crowned with Stars', Taniquetil. 210. (Replaced by *Tinwerína*.)

Tinwerína (V) 'Crowned with Stars', Taniquetil. 200, 210, 216, *383*. (Replaced by *Elerína*.)

Tinwerína (X) 'Crowned with stars', Taniquetil. 387. See *Elerrína*.

Tinwerontar (V) 'Queen of Stars', Varda. 200, 216, 344–5, *389*, *393*. (Replaced by *Elentári*.)

Tinwerontar (X) 'Queen of Stars', Varda. 389

Tinwetar (V) 'Queen of Stars', Varda. 345, *389* (also *Tinwetári*), *393*

Tinwetári (I) 'Queen of Stars', name of Varda. 100

Tinwetári (III) 'Queen of Stars', Varda. 170

Tinwetári (IV) 'Queen of Stars', name of Varda. 82, 281, 283, 286; O.E. *Steorrena Hlæfdíge* 281, *Tungolcwén* 286

Tinwiel (III) Transient form for *Tinúviel*. 22

Tirannë (II) Earliest name of Mavwin (Morwen). 138–9

Tirin (II) 'Tower'; *Ingil's Tirin* 5–6

Tirion (I) 26, 49, 135, 159–60, 198, 222–3

Tirion (II) 207–8, 246, 257, 265, 292

Tirion (IV) Later name of the city of the Elves (Tûn) in Valinor. 169, 198, 292

Tirion (V) City of the Elves in Valinor. 185; the Tree of Tirion 211

Tirion (VII) 92–3, 95, 97–8, 100–2, 284, 292. See *Tûn*.

Tirion (IXa) City of the Elves in Aman. 58

Tirion (IXb) City of the Elves in Valinor. 403, 412–13

Tirion (X) 8, 84–5, 87, 90, 92, 96, 103, 106, 110, 113–15, 125, 137, 176, 178, 180, 185, 191, 193–4, 205, 256, 282, 290; *the Court of the King* 110–11; called *the Hallowed* 84, 90, *the Watchful City* 84, 176. See *Túna*.

Tirion (XI) 35, 41, 178–9, 199–200, 246, 398, 406; *the Tree of Tirion* 178. See *Kôr, Tûn, Túna*.

Tirion (XII) 147, 361. See *Túna*.

Tirmindon (VII) See *Amon Hen*.

Tir-nan-Og (V) 'Land of Youth' in Irish legend. 77, 81, 98–9

Tiron (III) 93, 149

Titmass, J. R. (IXb) Historian of Oxford. 156, 158; earlier name *Titmouse* 149

Titus, Timothy (VI) Landlord of the inn at Bree (replaced by *Barnabas Butterbur*). 130, 140–1, 162, 173

Tíw (II) Old English name of the Germanic god in old Norse called *Týr*. 290

Tíw (IXb) (O.E.) Germanic god equated with Mars; Old Norse *Tír*. 286. Plural *Tíwas, Tívar*, see *Gods*.

Tol Brandir (VII) 287–8, 318, 323, 344, 355, 359, 361, 366–71, 373, 381, 393–4, 396–7, 426; high seat upon, 359. For earlier names see *Tolondren*; also *Brandor* 285, 323; *Tol Brandor* 285, 323, 355, 359. See *(The) Tindrock*.

Tol Eressëa (I) 13, 21–7, 32, 47–50, 52, 83, 85, 90, 97–8, 107, 120–1, 123–6, 129–30, 134–7, 165, 196, 224–5, 235. See *Lonely Island*.

Tol Eressëa (II) 4–5, 7–8,42, 215, 217, 253, 255, 258–9, 263–4, 278, 280–1, 283–6, 289–94, 300–12, 323–4, 326–8, 330, 333–4. See *Lonely Isle*.

Tol Eressëa (III) 148, 183

Tol Eressëa (IV) 41, 45–6, 50, 69, 72, 75, 78, 87, 155, 165, 172, 197–8, 200, 202, 2o6, *249, 257–9, 263–5, 272, 274, 276, 281, 283–4, 287, 290, 337; *Eressëa* *246–7; O.E. *Ánetíg (Ánetég)* 281, 283–4, 287, 290. See *Lonely Isle*.

Tol Eressëa (VIII) See *Eressëa*.

Tol Eressëa (IXa) The Lonely Isle. 58; *Eressëa* 132

Tol Eressëa (IXb) See *Eressëa*.

Tol Eressëa (XII) See *Eressëa*.

Tol Eressëa and *Eressëa* (X) 5, 8, 22, 30, 74, 84–5, 91, 109, 123–4, 134, 155, 175–6, 178–9, 183, 341, 365, 408; the White Tree of Eressëa, see *Celeborn* (1). See *Lonely Isle*.

Tol Eressëa and *Eressëa* (XI) 21–3, 36, 106–7, 117, 192, 311, 313, 343, 393, 396–7

Tol Fuin (IV) Island in the Great Sea. 199

Tol Fuin (VII) Island off the North-west coast, once Taur-na-Fuin. 124, 138, 301

Tol Galen (VII) (1) The Green Isle in Ossiriand. 271. (2) See *Tolondren*.

Tol Galen (XI) 'The Green Isle' in the River Adurant. *185, 191, 195, 350

Tol Morwen (IV) Island in the Great Sea. 199

Tol Morwen (XI) Island in the sea after the drowning of Beleriand on which stood the Stone of the Hapless. 296

Tol Sirion (II) 55, 123

Tol Sirion (IV) 173, 192, 221, 296, 299–300, 302, 311, 316, 319, 330; other references 103, 206, 110–11, 116, 120

Tol Sirion (V) 128, 133, 136, 150, (264), 266, 269, 290, 293; *Isle of Sirion* 284

Tol Sirion (XI) (38), 54, 66–7, 77, 125, 131, 135, *182

Tol Thû (V) =*Tol-na-Gaurhoth*. 407

Tol Varad (VIII) See *Cair Andros*.

Tol-eressëa (V) See *Eressëa*.

Tolfalas (VIII) Island in the Bay of Belfalas. 268

Tolfalas (XII) Island in the Bay of Belfalas. 183, 187

Tolfalas (XII) Island in the Bay of Belfalas. 298, 435, 439

Tol-galen (V) 'The Green Isle' in the river Adurant. 268, 305–6, 313, (362)

Tolharn, Tollernen (VII) See *Tolondren*.

Tol-in-Gaurhoth (II) 'Isle of Werewolves'. 53–4, 56–7

Tol-in-Gaurhoth (III) The Isle of Werewolves in Sirion. 306, 313, 350; *Gaurhoth Isle* 337. See *Wizard's Isle*.

Tol-in-Gaurhoth (X) 'Isle of Werewolves'. 408

Tol-in-Gaurhoth (XI) 'Isle of Werewolves'. 54, 62, 66, 68, 125, 131, 239; earlier *Tol-na-Gaurhoth* 125, 239. See *Sauron's Isle* in entry *Sauron*.

Tolkien, Arthur (IXb) 308 (see *Arthurson, John*).

Tolkien, C. R. (VI) 44, 106–8, 142, 200, 297, 299, 304–5, 323, 441

Tolkien, C. R. (IXb) In *The Notion Club Papers*. 219

Tolkien, Edith (IXb) 286

Tolkien, J. R. R. (III) Works: *The Hobbit* 26, 152; *The Lord of the Rings* 81, 152, 330, 356–7, 360; *The Fellowship of the Ring* 124, 127, 158, 269; *Unfinished Tales* 5, 26, 53, 83, 89, 91, 94, 145, 357 (see also *Narn i Hîn Húrin*); *Pictures by J. R. R. Tolkien* 53, 88, 90, 223, 234; *Sir Gawain and the Green Knight, Pearl, and Sir Orfeo*, translations, 248; *The Monsters and the Critics and Other Essays* 23, 140. *The Silmarillion* is referenced separately.

Tolkien, J. R. R. (IV) Works: *Sigelwara land* 209; *The Hobbit* 44, 257; *The Lord of the Rings* 70, 199, 210, 255, 257, 262, 294, 341; *Guide to Names in* 211, 283; *Pictures by J. R. R. Tolkien* 192, 221; *Unfinished Tales* 66, 73, 182, 187, 193, 195, 230, 324; see also *Lost Tales, Narn i Hîn Húrin*.

Tolkien, J. R. R. (V) *The Hobbit* 23, 199, 277, 338; *The Homecoming of Beorhtnoth* 55; *The Lays of Beleriand* 211, 268; *Letters of J. R. R. Tolkien* 7, 23, 55, 57, 199, 336, 341; *The Monsters and the Critics and Other Essays* 341; *The Notion Club Papers* 81–3, 85–6, 90–1, 98, 100; *Unfinished Tales* 19, 21, 70–1, 75, 77, 149, 111, 187, 289, 316, 322, 324. *The Lord of the Rings* and *The Book of Lost Tales* are entered separately, and *The Silmarillion* is not referenced.

Tolkien, J. R. R. (VI) *Letters*: 11, 17, 31, 40, 43–4, 84, 108–10, 115,

173, 198, 200, 202, 305, 309, 370, 382, 384, 461. (Works are indexed separately.)

Tolkien, J. R. R. (IXb) In *The Notion Club Papers*. 150, (216), 219–22, 308–9; and see *Arthurson, John*. Referred to by C. S. Lewis 309. The name *Tolkien* translated *Rashbold* 151, 291

Tolkien, J. R. R. (IXb) *On Fairy-Stories* 216–17, 221. See *Letters*, *(The) Lord of the Rings*, *Unfinished Tales*.

Tolkien, M. H. R. (IXb) 284

Tol-na-Gaurhoth (IV) 311, 319. See *Isle of (the) Werewolves*, *Wizard's Isle*, *Tol Sirion*.

Tol-na-Gaurhoth (V) 'Isle of Werewolves' (133). 133–4, 284, 300, (377), 407; later form *Tol-in-Gaurhoth* 300

Tolondren (VII) Early name for Tol Brandir (also *Tol Ondren*, *Tollondren*; original forms *Toll-ondu*, *Toll-onnui*, 268). 267–71, 282, 285, 287, 315–16, 323, 325, 345, 367. Other early names: *Tol Galen* 271; *Tolharn* 324, 345; *Tollernen* 324, 345, 350; *Stoneait* 324, 345; and see *Carrock*, *Emris*, *Eregon*, *Tol Brandir*.

Tom Bombadil (VI) (including references to *Tom* and *Bombadil*) 42–3, 106, 109–31 *passim*, 134–5, 152, 159–60, 164, 194, 196, 198, 213–14, 297, 303, 327–9, 334, 336, 338, 340–1, 351, 397, 401–2, 413–14; 'Aborigine' 117, 121, 329; 'Eldest' 121. *The Adventures of Tom Bombadil* 116, 123, 296, 412; *Bombadil Goes Boating* 116; *Ho! Tom Bombadil/Whither are you going* 11–16. On Gandalf and Bombadil see 126, 213–14, 397, 401, 413

Tom Bombadil (VII) (including references to *Tom* and *Bombadil*) 7, 10–13, 16, 36–7, 41–2, 56, 64, 69, 72–3, 80, 111–12, 125, 130, 136, 139, 15 1–3, 158, 161, 416, 419–20; 'Ab-Origine' 36. Other names: *Eldest* 125; *Erion* 125, 152, 158; *Porn* 125, 138, 152, 158; *Frumbarn* 158; *Iaur* 125, *Yárë* 125, 158; *Orald, Oreald, Orold* 158. *The Adventures of Tom Bombadil* 85, 90, 95–6, 107

Tom Bombadil (VIII) 98, 209, 219

Tom Bombadil (IXa) 53, 77, 79, 109

Tombo (I) The 'Gong of the Children' in Mar Vanwa Tyaliéva. 15. See *Gong of the Children, Littleheart*.

Tôn a Gwedrin (II) The Tale-fire in Mar Vanwa Tyaliéva. 145, 197. See *Tale-fire*.

Tongue, The (VII) (in Lothlórien) (268), 280–1, 285, 287–8, 291, 324, 330, 350. Other names: *Calendil, Calennel* 268, 288; *Green Spit* 268, 287–8; *Green-tine* 268, 288; *Lamben* 280; *Angle, Naith* used in this sense 268, 280, 287–8, also *Nelen* 268, 288

Took family, *Tooks* (VI) 13–16, 22–5, 29, 31, 33, 37, 39, 94, 100, 106, 135, 141, 221–2, 224, 234, 236, 245, 251, 267, 284, 291, 313, 316–17 (genealogical table), 319, 324, 334, 385–6, 392; *Tookish(ness)* 16, 18, 33; *Hole of Took* (clan-name) 251

Took, Adelard (VI) 247. (Replaced *Uffo Took*.)

Took (VI) ~ *Amanda* (VI) 32, 36. (Replaced *Arabella Took*.)

Took (VI) ~ *Arabella* (VI) 32, 36. (Replaced *Melba Took*.)

Took (VI) ~ *Bandobras, the Bullroarer* (VI) 311, 316–17, 329–30

Took (VI) ~ *Belladonna* (VI) Married Bungo Baggins; Bilbo's mother. 25, 35, 249, 317

Took (VI) ~ *Caramella* (VI) A relative of Bilbo's. 15, 17, 32, 35–6, 38, 315. (See *Caramella Bolger*.)

Took (VI) ~ *Donnamira* (VI) Married Hugo Boffin; grandmother of Peregrin Boffin (Trotter). 316–17, 385–6

Took (VI) ~ *Drogo* (VI) See 41, 45–6.

Took (VI) ~ *Esmeralda* (VI) Married Saradoc Brandybuck; Meriadoc's mother. 106, 267. (Replaced *Yolanda Took*.)

Took (VI) ~ *Everard* (VI) 315. (Replaced *Prospero Took*.)

Took (VI) ~ *Faramond* (VI) (1) Grandfather of Folco Took (2) and Merry Brandybuck. 317. (2) Replaced Folco Took (2) as Frodo's friend and companion of his journey. 406–7, 409–10, 419, 421, 423, 427, 436, 440, 447, 456

Took (VI) ~ *Ferumbras* (VI) Grandfather of the Old Took. 316–17

Took (VI) ~ *Flambard* (VI) Son of the Old Took. 316–17

Took (VI) ~ *Folcard* (VI) Father of Folco Took (2). 316–17

Took (VI) ~ *Folco* (VI) (1) Father of Frodo Took (2). 94, 100, 251, 267, 290, 309

Took (VI) ~ *Folco* (VI) (2) Replaced Frodo Took (2) (Bingo's friend and companion of his journey) when Bingo became Frodo (Baggins). 309, 314, 316–18, 323–30, 332, 334, 341, 343, 352–3, 355–8, 360, 366–8, 374–5, 392, 395–8, 409; see especially 323–4. (Replaced by *Faramond Took* (2).)

Took (VI) ~ *Fortinbras* (VI) Father of the Old Took. 316–17

Took (VI) ~ *Fosco* (VI) (1) Bilbo's first cousin, a candidate for 'Trotter' in his earlier life. 223–4, 373, 387. (2) Bilbo's uncle, son of the Old Took. 317

Took (VI) ~ *Frodo* (VI) (1), *Frodo the First* The Old Took. 19, 30, 37–9, 240, 245, 249, 251, 267–8, 316. (Replaced by *Gerontius Took*.)

Took (VI) ~ *Frodo* (VI) (2), *Frodo the Second* Bingo's friend and companion of his journey; replaced by Folco Took (2). 41–71 *passim*, 74, 83–4, 88–106 *passim*, 109, 112–15, 118–19, 124–5, 127–8, 130, 136–7, 139, 141, 148, 154, 156, 159–60, 169, 171–2, 177, 179, 185, 193, 221–2, 250–3, 267–8, 273, 275–80, 284–302 *passim*, 305, 309; references after *Frodo* > *Folco* 316, 323–5, 327–8, 330, 366, 375. See especially 70, 299–300, 323–4.

Took (VI) ~ *Gerontius* (VI) The Old Took. 267, 316–17, 385–6. (Replaced *Frodo Took* (1).)

Took (VI) ~ *Hildigrim* (VI) Son of the Old Took. 222

Took (VI) ~ *Isambard* (VI) Son of the Old Took. 316–17

Took (VI) ~ *Isengrim the First* (VI) Earliest recorded Took in the old genealogy (in LR *Isengrim II*, 316). 311, 316–17

Took (VI) ~ *Isengrim the Second* (VI) Son of the Old Took (in LR *Isengrim III*). 316–17

Took (VI) ~ *Isumbras* (VI) Son of Isengrim the First (in LR *Isumbras III*, 316). 316–17

Took (VI) ~ *Melba* (VI) 24, 32, 36. (Replaced by *Arabella Took*.)

Took (VI) ~ *Mirabella* (VI) Married Gorboduc Brandybuck. 37–8, 249, 317–18, 385

Took (VI) ~ *Mungo* (VI) 15, 17–18, 32, 36, 247. (Replaced by *Uffo Took*.)

Took (VI) ~ *Odo* (VI) See *Bolger, Odo.*

Took (VI) ~ *Paladin* (VI) Father of Peregrin (Pippin). 267, 386

Took (VI) ~ *Peregrin* (VI) (including references to *Pippin*) 70, 112, 119, 128, 140, 267–8, 277, 286–7, 297, 300, 324–5, 328, 330, 358–9, 365–6, 386, 441; see especially 267, 324

Took (VI) ~ *Prospero* (VI) 38, 106, 315. (Replaced *Prospero Brandybuck*, replaced by *Everard Took*.)

Took (VI) ~ *Thamanda* (VI) Married Olo Bolger (2); Odo's mother. 317

Took (VI) ~ *the Old* (VI) See *Took, Frodo I* and *Took, Gerontius.*

Took (VI) ~ *Uffo* (VI) 247. (Replaced *Mungo Took*, replaced by *Adelard Took*.)

Took (VI) ~ *Vigo* (VI) Odo's grandfather. 317.

Took (VI) ~ *Volanda* (VI) Married Caradoc Brandybuck; mother of (Marmaduke >) Meriadoc. 120, 251, 267, 316–17. (Replaced by *Esmeralda Took*.)

Took (VI) ~ *Young* (VI) 222, 316

Took(s) (VIII) 45, 54

Took, (IXa) *Bandobras* 107, 115, 119; *the Bullroarer* 119

Took, Adelard (VII) 20. See *Uffo Took.*

Took, Faramond (VII) 6, 8, 15, 21, 30–2, 39, 112, 115, 166; nicknamed *Far* 8. See especially 30–2.

Took, Folco (VII) 6–9, 15–16, 21, 30–2, 35–6, 41, 47, 50–2, 56–8, 62, 64, 172. See especially 30–2.

Took, Frodo (VII) 31–2, 39

Took, Gerontius (the Old Took) (IXa) 71, 114, 121; *'Ronshus'* 62, 71

Took, Isengrim the First (VIII) 38, 45; in LR *Isengrim* 11, 45

Took, Odo (VII) See *Bolger, Odo.*

Took, Paladin (VIII) Father of Peregrin. 26, 41, 323, 334–5

Took, Paladin (IXa) Thain of the Shire, father of Peregrin. 99

Took, Peregrin (Pippin) (XII) 11, 15, 43, 51, 59, 69, 83, 85, 87, 90–2, 107–8, 110–11, 115–16, 118, 157, 255, 261, 268–9, 421; true Hobbit name 51, 59

Took, Peregrin (VII) (also *Pippin*) 30–2, 35–6, 41, 47, 50–2, 56–8, 64, 76, 78, 82, 112, 115, 162, 164, 166–7, 170–1, 175, 179, 183, 193, 210–11, 214, 216, 226, 228, 230, 232, 235, 243, 250, 253, 264–5, 271–2, 274–5, 279, 285–6, 328–30, 339, 344, 346–9, 352, 375–8, 385–6, 397–8, 401, 404, 408–9, 411–17, 419–20, 423, 426–7, 429, 434, 436–7

Took, Peregrin (VIII) (also *Pippin*) 3–4, 6, 26, 36, 39, 41, 48–50, 53, 55, 57–60, 66–8, 72–81, 119–20, 130, 140–3, 229, 231–3, 241, 246, 249, 255, 259–60, 262–4, 270–301 *passim,* 306, 322–7, 329–31, 334–42, 362, 367, 374–5, 378, 380–92 *passim,* 399, 403, 405, 407, 410, 415–17, 419, 421, 423, 427, 430. His age 283–5, 292–4; his sword 49, 59, 277, 292, 294; his brooch of Lothlórien 49

Took, Peregrin or *Pippin* (IXa) 7, 18, 22, 26, 47–9, 51–2, 63–4, 70, 77, (79), 81, 83–8, 92–3, 95–6, 98–102, 105, 107–11, 115–16, 122, 135. *Knight of Gondor* 83

Took, Uffo (VII) 20. (Replaced by *Adelard Took.*)

Took-house (IXa) See *Tooks.*

Tookland (VI) 50, 95, 278, 284, 294–5, 3 12–13

Tookland (XII) 115

Tookland, The (IXa) 100–1, 105; *Tooklanders* 87–8

Tooks (VII) 7, 31; *the Hole of Took* (clan-name) 39

Tooks (IXa) 92, 99–101, 105, 108; *Took* 79, 87, 92; *Great Place of*

the Tooks 105; *the Took-house* 87, 105, *Tookus* 105. See *(The) Tookland.*

Took-Took, Obo (VI) Bilbo's great-uncle. 15, 18, 32, 36. (Replaced by *Rollo Took-Took.*)

Took-Took, Rollo (VI) 32, 36, 38. (Replaced *Obo Took-Took*, replaced by *Fosco Bolger.*)

Topless Forest, The (VII) See *Fangorn.*

Torbarth (XI) Companion of Túrin in the attack on Glaurung (replaced by *Hunthor*). 97–8, 152, 156–7, 164, 238, 267, 299

Tor-dilluin, Mount (VIII) Original name of Mindolluin. 77, 80

Torech Ungol (VIII) 'The Spider's Hole', Shelob's Lair. 202; earlier form *Terch Ungol* 202

Torfir Trotter. (VII) 61

Torfirion (VII) Early name for Annúminas; replaced *Tarkilmar.* 144–5, 296, 304. See *Westermanton.*

Torhir Ifant (XI) Maker of the work *Dorgannas Iaur.* 192

Torhthelm (V) In *The Homecoming of Beorhtnoth.* 55

Tórin (I) See *Daurin.*

Tormen (IV) North. *244–5, *248–9, 254–5. (Replaced by *Formen.*)

Tower Hills (VI) 280. See *Emyn Beraid.*

Tower Hills (VII) 34, 304. See *Emyn Beraid, White Towers.*

Tower Hills (XII) 17, 112, 176, 186, 313–14; *the Towers* 112, *Elf-towers* 17. See *Emyn Beraid.*

Tower of Doom (IXb) In *The Death of St. Brendan.* 262, 292

Tower of Guard (VII) See *Minas Tirith.*

Tower of Guard (VIII) Minas Tirith. 138, 153, 325

Tower of Pearl (I) Tower on one of the Twilit Isles. 68, 125, 221; *the Sleeper in the Tower of Pearl* 15, 27, 215, 221

Tower of Pearl (II) 256, 260, 263, 273–5. See *Sleeper in the Tower of Pearl.*

Tower of Seabirds (IV) See *Isle of Seabirds.*

Tower of Snow (II) Name of one of the kindreds of the Gondothlim. 173, 179. See *Penlod.*

Towers of Darkness (VI) 300

Towers of Mist (X) See *Misty Mountains.*

Towers of the Teeth (VIII) See *Teeth of Mordor.*

Towers of the Teeth (IXa) 20, 23, 28. See *Carchost, Narchost, Nargos.*

Towers, The (VI) 254, 280, 380, 402. See *Elf-towers, West Towers.*

Towers, The (IXa) The White Towers on the Tower Hills. 53, 109

Town of Dreams, The (II) (poem) 295–6, 298 (*The Town of Dead Days* 298).

Townlands (VIII) See *Pelennor*.

Tramorie (III) Unknown. 122

Trandóran (VII) See *Sarn Gebir* (1).

Tree, The (II) Name of one of the kindreds of the Gondothlim. 173, 176, 182, 189, 215, 217. See *Galdor, Nos Galdon*.

Tree, The (IXa) On Aragon's standard. 15, 56

Tree, The (IXb) In *The Death of St. Brendan*. 261, 263, 265, 296–8; the White-tree Strand 263, 298. *The White Tree of Númenor*, see *Nimloth. The Blessed Trees* [Ramer] 194; see *Drama of the Silver Tree*.

Treebeard (II) 140

Treebeard (VI) (in most references called *Giant Treebeard*) 363, 367, 381–2, 384, 397, 399, 410–1l, 440

Treebeard (VII) 6–7, 9, 71–2, 81, 130, 210–11, 214, 216, 250, 330, 339, 344, 389, 405, 409, 411–20, 425, 427–9, 436–7, 448. References to Treebeard as a *giant* 9, 71–2, 81, 210, 330, 405, 411; *and his Three Giants*, 210. *King of the Treebeards* 428; *oldest living thing* 429. Treebeard's song 417, 420. See *Fangorn*.

Treebeard (VIII) 3, 6, 25–6, 30, 39–40, 43, 47–55, 57, 66–8, 76, 79, 266, 282, 343–6, 361, 364; Treebeard in Anórien 343–6, 364

Treebeard (IXa) 63–4, 68–9, 71–3, 116, 123

Treebeard (XII) 36–7, 55

Tree-folk (VII) See *Ents; Galadrim*.

Tree-giants (VI) 410–1l. *Tree-men* 254, 319, 386

Tree-giants (VIII) See *Ents*.

Tree-men (II) 254, 261

Trees of Gondolin (II) See *Gondolin*.

Trees of Gondolin (IV) 167

Trees of Kôr (I) See *Kôr*.

Trees of Valinor (I) See *Two Trees*.

Trees, The (X) See *(The) Two Trees*.

Trees, The (XI) 6, 8–9, 14, 16, 20, 22, 24, 30, 40, 175, 196, 200, 247, 401, 403; *Years of the Trees* 30. The Trees of Gondolin 200

Trent, River (I) 196

Trent, River (V) 413

Tréowine (IXb) Friend and companion of Ælfwine the Mariner. 268–71, 273, 276–80, 293–4; Céolwulf's son 269, 273. See *Jeremy, Wilfrid Trewin*.

Troll Song (VI) 142–4, 194, 222, 360, 412

Troll-country (VI) 192, 360; *Troll-lands* 205

Trolls (II) 283

Trolls (VI) References to the three Trolls of *The Hobbit* (also *Troll Stones, Stone Trolls*) 126, 144, 162, 192–4, 203–4, 212, 360, 365, 444, 454. Other references 178, 192, 253, 272, 318, 443–4

Trolls (VII) 10, 14, 59–61, 193–4, 197–9, 201, 205, 211, 411, 413; *Troll-ridge* 14, *Troll-lands* 250, *Troll-fells* 306, 439; *cave-troll* 201; *Troll Song* 59–61, 66, 3.33. *Stone-gaints* 411

Trolls (VIII) 30; 223 (in *The Hobbit*); *half-trolls of Far Harad* 369

Trolls (X) 251, 409, 412, 414; *Stone-trolls* 412. See *Olog-hai.*

Trolls (XII) 35–6, 75, 79–80, 82, 196, 235, 238, 263; *Stone-trolls* 80. See *Olog-hai.*

Trollshaw(s) (VI) 162–3, 170, 200–2, 355, 412; *Troll-wood* 162, *Trolls-wood* 195

Trollshaws (XII) 208

Trotter (VI) 133, 138–41, 148–79 *passim*, 182, 184–98, 204, 207–14, 216–17, 223–4, 226, 269, 332, 336–9, 341–3, 350–63, 365–8, 371, 373–4, 376, 379, 386–7, 392–403 *passim*, 406, 408–10, 413–27 *passim*, 430–1, 434–8, 445–7, 449, 451–3, 462–5. On the history of Trotter see 214, 223–4, 332, 371, 373–4, 376, 384–6, 392–3, 414, 430–1; and see *Boffin, Peregrin.*

Trotter (VII) 6–10, 13–15, 19, 21, 31–7, 39, 42, 44–6, 48–52, 56–9, 61–5, 70–84 *passim*, 105, 111–14, 116, 118, 120–2, 146, 161, 163, 165, 167–9, 171–2, 175–6, 178, 192–4, 197–8, 203–5, 218–21, 236, 272–3, 275–8, 280, 290–1, 293, 327–9, 347, 350–63, 365–6, 370–1, 375–95 *passim*, 407, 409, 411–13

Trotter (VIII) 38, 49, 100, 246, 390, 417

Trotter (IXa) 76, 78, 121. See *Tarantar.*

Trotter (IXb) 340

Trough, The (IXa) See *Morgai.*

True West, The (V) 17, 25, 31, 33

True West, The (IXb) 309, 333, 336, 338, 386, 395, 409; *the Ancient West* 393, 395, 409

Trui (II) Troy. 196, 203; *Troy* 203

Trumbold (VIII) Precursor of Erkenbrand. 8–9, 23. (Replaced by *Heorulf.*)

Tû (I) The wizard or fay who became King of the Dark Elves. 232–4, 237, 244; *Lord of Gloaming* 232. (Replaced *Túvo.*)

Tuatha-de-Danaan (V) A people in Irish legend. 77–8, 82–3

Tuckborough (VI) Chief place of the Tookland. 294, 312

Tuckborough (VIII) Chief place of the Tookland. 26, 284

Tuckborough (IXa) 87, 99–101, 105, 107, 115

Tuckborough (XII) Chief place of the Tookland. 11, 110–11. *Great Writ of* ~ 40, 123, 137, *Yearbook of* ~ 67, 137; see *Yellowskin.*

Tuilérë (I) Name of Vána. 67

Tuivána (I) Name of Vána. 67, 99, 116–8, 180

Tulkas (I) 66–7, 70, 73, 75, 78–80, 89, 101–5, 111, 115, 140, 145, 147–9, 152, 154, 158, 176–7, 179, 182, 184–6, 198, 200–1, 209–10, 218, 224. See *Astaldo, Poldórëa.*

Tulkas (II) 19, 46, 68, 138, 195, 201, 220, 278–83, 290

Tulkas (III) 127, 137

Tulkas (IV) 68, 71, 79, 84, 90–2, 98, 157, 165, 168, 195, 198, 205, 207–8, 253, 263, 265, 275, 277–8, 285, 287, 291–3; *Tulcas* 17–16, 37, 149, 291; O.E. *Afoðfréa* 208 (*Tulkas, Tulcas* in the texts).

Tulkas (V) 110, 113, 120, 122, 205–8, 213, 228, 230–1, 233, 242, 333, 395 (named *Ender, Enner* ('bridegroom') 375, 395), 407. See *Poldórëa.*

Tulkas (VI) 122

Tulkas (X) 17, 25, 27, 31, 38, 41, 48–9, 52–4, 59–60, 62–3, 65–7, 69, 71, 75–6, 94, 96–7, 101, 107, 112, 144, 146, 151, 153, 159, 161, 166, 168, 186, 189–90, 192, 202, 204, 273, 279–80, 283, 289, 364, 376, 380–1, 392–3, *Tulcas* 382. Latecomer to Arda 17, 27, 41, 52, and cf. 380; suggested origin as Vala of the Sun 376 (see *Auron*).

Tulkas (XI) 77, 399 (origin of the name), 404

Tulkas (XII) 375

Tulkassë (I) Earlier name of Tulkastor. 22. (Replaced *Turenbor*.)

Tulkastor (I) Father of Vairë wife of Lindo. 16, 22. (Replaced *Tulkassë*.)

Tum Dincelon (VI) Dimrill-dale in the original application (north of Rivendell). 432

Tumbled Lands (I) 240, 244; in another sense 214

Tumhalad (II) Battle in which the host of Nargothrond was defeated. 135

Tum-halad (V) Site of the battle (between Narog and Taiglin) before the sack of Nargothrond. 139, 152

Tumhalad (XI) The site (see 139–40) of the battle before the fall of

Nargothrond. 85, 89, 139–40, 142, 144, 147, 149, *182, 186, 238, 256, 299

Tumladen (XI) The vale of Gondolin. 57, 118, 179, 198; *Tumladin* 53

Tumladen, Vale of (VIII) In South Gondor, west of Minas Tirith. 283, 289

Tumladin (II) 'Valley of smoothness' (163), the plain or vale of Gondolin. 163–4, 167–8, 171–2, 174, 179, 194–5, 200, 211, 214, 217

Tumladin (III) The plain of Gondolin. 142; later form *Tumladen* 83

Tumladin (IV) The plain of Gondolin. 147–8; later form *Tumladen* 148. See *Guarded Plain* (1).

Tumladin (V) The vale of Gondolin. 142, 287, 368, 394

Tumultuous Winds, Cavern of the (II) Where the river Sirion went underground. 195, 217

Tumunzahar (V) Dwarvish name of Nogrod. 278. (Replaced Khazad-dûm in this sense.)

Tumunzahar (XI) Dwarvish name translated as *Nogrod (Novrod)*. 10, 108, 206, 209, 389

Tûn (I) Name that replaced Kôr (as the name of the city). 222

Tûn (II) Later name of Kôr (see 292). 202, 262, 292; *Hill of Tûn* 313, 330

Tûn (III) 17, 21, 29, 36, 49, 53, 73, 81–2, 93, 123, 132, 192, 210, 217, 219. See *Côr, Corthûn*.

Tûn (IV) City of the Elves in Valinor. 9, 14, 16–19, 38, 40, 45, 47–8, 72, 74, 87–91, 4–5, 147, 149–50, 152–4, 159, 169, 196, 200, 202, *249–51, 257, 260–1, 264, 266, 279, 281, 286; O.E. *séo hwíta Elfaburg* 286; *the Hill of Tûn* 6, 200. See *Côr, Tirion*.

Tûn (V) 112, 114–15, 119, 156, 167, (170), 173, (181), 185, 192–3, 195, 218, 222, 225–6, 229–31, 233–5, 250, 252, 264, (269), 325, 395. See *Eldamar, Eledûn*.

Tûn (X) Old name of Tirion. 8, 193–4

Tûn (XI) Name replacing Kôr. 22, 116, 175, 177, 246. See *Túna*.

Tûn, Túna (VII) 95; *Rúmil of Túna* 453; *Túnian letters* 453. See *Tirion*.

Túna (III) 149

Túna (I) 26, 82, 135, 222

Túna (II) 208, 292

Túna (V) 119, 173, 185, 218, 222–6, 395; 'the Hill-city' 222. On *Tûn* beside *Túna* see 225–6

Túna (IXb) City of the Elves in Valinor (see *Tirion*). 316, 336, 403, 412–13; *Tûn* 280

Túna (X) The hill on which Tirion was built, but also often used of the city itself (see 8, 90, 193, 282), and not in all cases distinguishable. 8, 30, 84, 90, 92, 96–7, 99, 110, 114–15, 118, 133, 135, 137, 151, 155, 157, 175–6, 178–80, 183–5, 188–90, 193–4, 196–7, 238, 252, 256, 261–2, 276–7, 279–80, 282–3, 287, 291; the White Tree of Túna (Tirion), see *Galathilion* (2).

Túna (XI) Name replacing *Tûn*. 175, 177, 179; subsequently the hill on which the city (Tirion) was built, 35, 179, 199, 246, but still used also of the city, 323

Túna (XII) 147–9, 352. See *Tirion*.

Tunglin (IV) Folk of the Harp. 4–5

Tunnelly (VI) Hobbit family name. 137

Tunnelly, Tom (VI) Original name of the Hobbiton miller's son. 269

Tuor (I) 48, 52, 238. For the tale of *Tuor and the Exiles of Gondolin* ('The Fall of Gondolin') see *Gondolin*.

Tuor (II) 88, 123, 130, 144, 148–72, 174–8, 180–210, 212–21, 240, 252–7, 259–66, 276, 278–9, 325. See *Tûr*.

   Tuor (II) 'The later *Tuor*', in *Unfinished Tales*, 203–7, 211, 217, 219

Tuor (III) 83, 89–90, 143–4, 145, 148–9; variant form *Tûr* 142–3

Tuor (IV) 5, 35–7, 50, 65–70, 104, 141–9, 15 1–2, 155, 160, 191–6, 214–15, 229–30, 274, 298, 303–8, 312–13, 315, 317–18, 322, 324–5, 327; numbered among the Noldoli 155; song of Tuor for Eärendel 142, 213–14 (see *Horns of Ylmir*). See *Fengel, Tûr, Turgon* (1), *Turlin*.

Tuor (V) 59, 64, 70–1, 131, 137–8, 140–3, 151, 179, 191, 275, 311, 316, 324, 326, 329, 359, 394, 407

Tuor (VII) 15, 261

Tuor (IXa) 44

Tuor (IXb) 290, 340

Tuor (X) 359, 407; *the Tale of Tuor* 3, 142, 298

Tuor (XI) (45), 52, 79, 81–2, 88–91, (120), 124, 135–7, 146–7, 176, 224, 231, 234–5, 256, 258, 299–302, 344–8, 351–2, 354; called *the Blessed* 52, 124; and see *Eladar, Ulmondil*.

   Tuor (XI) The later *Tale of Tuor* 176, 179, 181, 186, 192, 200, 228, 244, 299–300, 302, 316–17, 323, 344, 354

Tuor (XII) 348, 364, 380, 387, 390

Tuor 155

Tûr (II) Form of Tuor's name. 148, 198, 202, 260–1

Tûr Haretha (XI) The burial-mound of the Lady Haleth. 225, 228;

earlier *Tûr Daretha* 223, 225, 228; *the Ladybarrow* 223. See *Haudh-en-Arwen*.

Tûr (IV) Tuor. 5

Turamarth (V) Noldorin form =Quenya *Turambar*. 294, 321, 372, 395; earlier *Turumarth* 321

Turambar (III) 29

Turambar (I) See *Túrin*.

Turambar (II) 'Conqueror of Fate' (86–7). 41, 70, 86–91, 99–112, 116–19, 125, 129–35, 137–8, 140, 142, 282. See *Turumart*, *Túrin*.

Turambar (IV) 'Conqueror of Fate', Túrin. 30–1, 60–1, 73, 127, 129–30, 165, 183, 186–7, 196, 205, 223, 226, 294, 305–6, 323. See *Turumarth*.

Turambar (V) 'Master of Fate' (147). 140, 333, 372, 395

Turambar (XI) 'Master of Doom' (154), name of Túrin in Brethil. 92, 95–103, 148, 150–7, 160, 163–4, 231, 234, 247, 257, 315. See *Turumarth*.

Turambar (XII) Ninth King of Gondor. 197, 228. See also *Túrin* (*Turambar*).

Turenbor (I) Earlier name of Tulkastor. 22. (Replaced by *Tulkassë*.)

Turgon (I) 115, 132, 170–3, 238–42, 244–5. See *Turondo*.

Turgon (II) 43–4, 65, 70, 73, 77, 83, 120, 160–2, 164–5, 167–8, 170–1, 173, 175, 177, 180, 182–7, 199–200, 204–5, 207–12, 216–18, 251, 257, 263, 266. See *Turondo*, *Square of the Palace*, *King's House*.

Turgon (III) 6–7, 21, 23–4, 96–100, 103, 137–8, 146–7, 149, 222

Turgon (IV) (1) Transiently used =Tuor. 3–5. (2) King of Gondolin. 5, 8, 15, 24, 27, 34–6, 46, 49–50, 56–8, 65–7, 88, 109, 116–21, 136–48, 167, 174, 181–2, 191–3, 213, 219–20, 296–9, 301–3, 305–7, 316, 318–19, 321, 329–30, 334, 339–40; *the hidden king* 301; *Mountains of Turgon* 66; O.E. *Finstán* 213, but *Turgon* in the text 339–40

Turgon (V) 22, 64, 126–8, 132, 135–7, 139–42, 145, 148, 150, 177, 210–11, 223, 226, 238, 253–4, 257–9, 264, 269, 285, 287–8, 291, 301, 307–15, 326, 362; *the hidden King* 135

Turgon (VIII) Man of Minas Tirith, father of Beren (2). 282

Turgon (IXb) 316

Turgon (X) 106, 112, 118, 121, 125, 128, 155, 177, 182, 188, 196; Turgon's wife (died in the Helkaraxë) 128

Turgon (XI) 26, 28, 35, 38, 40, 44–5, 47–8, 53–4, 57–8, 70, 72–6,

77–8, 80, 84, 91, 116, 118, 120–2, 125–7, 133–7, 146, 166–70, 177–9, *182, 192–3, 195, 198–201, 243, 245, 254–5, 258, 260–1, 272, 301, 317–19, 323, 325, 327–9, 345–6, 348–9, 351, 409; his wife 323

Turgon (XII) (1) King of Gondolin. 317, 344–5, 348, 352, 361–3, 370, 374–5, 379–81, 388–90; Turukáno 345, 362, 370, 379

Turgon (XII) (2) Twenty-fourth Ruling Steward. 206, 220, 248

Turgon, Mountains of (IXa) 45. See Encircling Mountains.

Túrin (I) 244 the Tale of Turambar 27, 158, 229–31, 233, 239, 244

Túrin (II) 21, 41, 47, 62, 70–7, 79–86, 91–5, 98, 110, 112, 115–31, 134–5, 137–8, 140–2, 144, 205, 222, 252. See Turambar.

Túrin (III) (including references to him as son of Húrin, etc.) 6, 9–14, 16–20, 22–8, 30–3, 37, 40, 43–60, 62–7, 70–9, 82–3, 86–94, 96–7, 104–7, 110, 112–18, 121, 124, 126–7, 148, 215, 217, 259. His age 14, 25, 115, 127; his character 14, 27, 115–16; his stature 44. See Thaliodrin, Thalion.

Túrin (IV) 28–32, 35, 37, 40–1, 58–60, 73, 104–5, 122–32, 165, 172, 182–5, 187, 193, 196, 205, 220, 222, 224, 294, 301, 303–6, 3 11–12, 315, 317, 322–4, 327; dates of his life 322–3; his destiny 40, 73, 165, 205

Túrin (Turambar) (X) 71, 76, 166, 373–4; his black sword 76 (see Mormacil).

Túrin (V) 124, 131, 135, 137–41, 149, 151–2, 187, 256, 275–6, 293–5, 314–24, 361, 395 (also Quenya Turindo), 412; in the Second Prophecy of Mandos 333

Túrin (VI) 180

Túrin (VII) 6, 15

Túrin (VIII) 155, 159, 218; Túrinssaga 372

Túrin (IXb) 340

Túrin (XI) 4, 51, (60)-1, 63–4, (78), 79–93, 96, 99–103, 124, 129–31, 135–48, 152, 156, 160–4, 180, *182, 187, 224, 231, 234, 238, 241, 244–5, 247, 253–9, (261), 263–4, 266–8, 270, 290–1, (294–7), 298–300, (301), 304–5, 308–14, 344, 352, 354, 409, 420; 'Túrins Saga'. 'Saga of Túrin' 244, 314, 321, 352. See Turambar, Turumarth; Agarwaen, Iarwaeth, Mormegil, Thurin, Thuringud, Wildman of the Woods.

Túrin (XII) (1) Turambar 309, 372, 374–5, 404; Tale of Turambar 374

Túrin (XII) (2) Túrin I. Sixth Ruling Steward. 204, 219. (3) Túrin II. Twenty-third Ruling Steward. 206, 220, 238, 250

Turinqi (I) See *Meril-i-Turinqi.*

Turinqi (II) See *Meril-i-Turinqi.*

Turkildi (IXb) (IXb) 'Lordly Men' (Númenóreans). 246, 248, 286, 3 10–11, 399. See *Fréafíras.*

Turlin (IV) Transient name for Tuor. 3, 5

Turondo (I) Son of Finwë Nólemë, called in Gnomish Turgon. 115, 132, 167, 170–1, 245

Turondo (II) Name of Turgon in Eldarissa. 70–1

Turosto (XI) (Quenya) Belegost. 389

Turuhalmë (I) The 'Logdrawing', bringing in of wood to Mar Vanwa Tyaliéva. 229–30, 244. (Other forms *Duruchalm* and *Halmad-hurwion.*)

Turuhalmë (II) The 'Logdrawing', bringing in of wood to Mar Vanwa Tyaliéva. 69

Turukáno (XII) See *Turgon* (1).

Turumart (II) Gnomish form for *Turambar.* 70, 86, 89, 119. See *Turambar.*

Turumart (III) Gnomish form for *Turambar.* 29

Turumarth (IV) Gnomish form for *Turambar.* 127, 131, 305, 325, *Turumart* 313, 325; earlier form *Turmarth* 30, later form *Turam-arth* 131, 325

Turumarth (XI) Sindarin form of *Turambar.* 311, 315; *Turamarth* 135, 315; original form *Turumart* 315

Túvo (I) Earlier name of Tû. 234–6, 238, 243

Twelve Rings of Men (VI) 269

Twilight Meres (III) 214, 222. See *Pools of Twilight, Umboth-Muilin.*

Twilight Meres (V) See *Meres of Twilight.*

Twilight Meres (XI) 35, 194; *Twilit Meres* 149. See *Aelin-uial, Umboth Muilin.*

Twilit Isles (I) Islands in the Shadowy Seas, west of Tol Eressëa. 15, 68–9, 82, 85 (*Tolli Kimpelëar*), 120–1, 123, 125, 134, 224

Twilit Isles (II) 256, 273, 275, 324–5; *Twilit Isle* 254

Twilit Isles (IV) 42, 69, 257

Twilit Meres, Twilight Meres (IV) 185, 226. See *Umboth-muilin.*

Two Captains (III) Beleg and Túrin in the Land of Dor-Cúarthol. 51

Two Kindreds (IV) 74, 196, 198, 204, 306, 326; *two races* 154 > *two kindreds* 156, cf. 309

Two Kindreds (V) Elves and Men. 18, 29, (213), 294, 302, 304, 325–6; *star of the Two Kindreds*, Eärendel, 141

Two Kindreds (VI) Elves and Men. 184

Two Kindreds (IXb) Elves and Men. 402

Two Kindreds (X) See *Kindreds.*

Two Kindreds (XI) Elves and Men. 50, 63, 130, (219)

Two Towers, The (IXb) 145

Two Towers, The (X) (title) 192

Two Trees (I) (including references to *the Trees*) 82, 85 (*i aldas*), 88, 100, 105, 107, 110, 114, 121–2, 125, 128, 134–5, 141, 143–7, 152–4, 157–60, 164–5, 169, 171, 174, 176–80, 182–4, 187, 190–1, 194, 196, 199–202, 207, 209, 213, 227, 234

Two Trees (II) (including references to the *Trees*) 3, 9, 64, 160, 207, 216, 271–2, 275–6, 281, 286–7, 307–8; *Tree of Gold* 33. *Trees of Gondolin,* see *Gondolin.*

Two Trees (III) 93, 350; *Trees of Light* 132; *the Trees* 139, 210

Two Trees (IV) 3, 6–7, 9, 12, 14, 16–17, 20, 33, 37, 40, 42, 47, 49–50, 52, 73–4, 80–2, 85, 87–8, 92, 94, 97–8, 149, 151, 165, 167, 172, *250–1, 257, 259, 263, 265, 269, 273, 278, 283, 295, 328; O.E. *Þá (Twégen) Béamas* 281–2, 285, 287–8, 338; *Years of the Trees* 171, 269, 273; the Trees described 12, 80–1; the periods of the Trees 12, 43, 80–3, 167

Two Trees (V) (including references to *the Trees*) 109, 111–14, 118, 125, 171–2, 180, 185, 197, 209–11, 214–15, 222, 224, 227, 231–3, 240–2, 244–5, 333; names of the Trees 209–11; *Years of the Trees* 118

Two Trees (VI) 68, 122, 187–8

Two Trees (XII) 123, 130, 147, 337, 356, 375. See *Eldest Tree*; and for 'Tree day', 'Tree's day' see 123, 125, 130.

Two Trees, The (X) (including references to *the Trees*) 22, 43, 47–8, 50–1, 55–62, 70, 77–8, 81, 85–6, 90, 95, 97, 99–100, 104–5, 107–8, 120, 122, 125, 129–32, 135, 137, 152, 154–5, 157, 162–3, 173, 175–6, 178, 180, 186–7, 190, 197–8, 201, 238, 247, 261, 268, 274, 283, 287–8, 291–3, 298, 300, 326, 371–2, 375, 377, 385–6, 389–90, 429–30; *the Elder Sun and Moon* 198, 372

Twofoot, Mr. (VI) Hobbit of Bagshot Row, Hobbiton 244

Tynwfiel (II) Original spelling of *Tinúviel* in the typescript text of the *Tale of Tinúviel.* 41, 51

Týr (II) 290. See *Tíw.*

Tyrn Goerthaid (XII) The Barrow-downs. 194

Udul (XII) Village in the tale of Tal-elmar. 433–4, 438

Udûn (VII) Between the Morannon and the Isenmouthe. 213

Udûn (IXa) Vale between the Morannon and the Isenmouthe. 34, 51. Earlier name *the Narch*.

Udûn (X) Utumno.382

Udushinbar (VII) See *Bundu-Shathûr*.

Ufedhin (II) A Gnome, allied with the Dwarves, ensnarer of Tinwelint. 223–30, 232–6, 239, 243, 245–8

Ufedhin (III) A Gnome allied with the Dwarves, ensnarer of Tinwelint. 52

Ufedhin (IV) The renegade Noldo in the *Tale of the Nauglafring*. 61–2, 188–9

Ufthak (VIII) Orc of the Tower of Kirith Ungol. 225. *Uftak Zaglûn*, see *Zaglûn*.

Uglúk (VII) (1) In the rôle of Grishnâkh. (2) Leader of the Isengarders in the Orc-raid. 408–9

Uglúk (XII) 83

Uin (I) The great whale. 85, 118–20

Uin (II) The great whale. 283, 286, 328

Uinen (I) 63,79, 121, 130,172, 192, 220; *Oinen* 211, 220; *the Lady of the Sea* 211. (Replaced *Ónen*.)

Uinen (II) 20, 51; *Oinen* 324; *Ónen* 51

Uinen (III) Lady of the Sea. 205

Uinen (IV) Lady of the Sea. 14, 46, 48, 78, 169, 207, 263, 275, 285; O.E. *merehlæfdige* 207, *merecwén* 285. See *Óin*.

Uinen (V) Lady of the Sea. 110, 161, 205, 208, 236, 239, *376, 396*

Uinen (X) 'Lady of the sea(s)'. 20, 35, 49, 69, 84, 116, 145, 151, 201–2, 204, 286

Uinen (XI) 7, 404

Úlairi Ringwraiths. (XII) 153, 175, 177–8, 193, 200–1, 208, 215–17, 233–4, 241; *Chief, Lord of the Úlairi* 193, 217

Ulband (IV) See *Ulfand*.

Ulbandi (I) Mother of Melko's son Kosomot. 93

Ulbandi (II) Mother of Kosomot (Gothmog). 216. See *Fluithuin*.

Uldor the Accursed (IV) 118, 121, 146, 300, 302, 320–1

Uldor the Accursed (V) Eldest son of Ulfang. 134, 136–7, 179, 287, 293, 309, 311, 314, 329, *396*, 402

Uldor the Accursed (XI) Son of Ulfang. 61, 64, 72, 74–5, 82, 133–4, 167–8; *Folk of Uldor* *183

Ulfand (IV) Easterling. (House of, sons of) 300, 303, 311–12, 320; earlier form *Ulband* 311–12, 320; later form *Ulfang* 121, 180, 320, 337

Ulfang (IV) See *Ulfand*.

Ulfang (V) Easterling; called 'the Black'. 147, 192, 287, 291, 307–11, 387, 396. Earlier form *Ulfand* ('the Swart') 134–5, 137–8, 147, 402

Ulfang (XI) Easterling; called 'the Swart'. 61, 64, 70, 74, 127

Ulfast (IV) Son of Ulfand (Ulfang). 180, 300, 302, 320–1.

Ulfast (V) Second son of Ulfang. 134, 137, 287, 311, 314, *381, 396*, 402

Ulfast (XI) Son of Ulfang. 61, 64, 74

Ulmo (I) 26, 56, 58–63, 66–8, 70–1, 74, 79–80, 83, 85–7, 89, 100–2, 104–6, 114, 117–26, 132, 134–5, 137, 144, 153–4, 171, 177–8, 190–1, 198–9, 209–11, 213–18, 220, 223–6; *Lord of Vai* 190, 214. See *Linqil, Vailimo*.

Ulmo (II) Called 'Lord of Waters' (150, 205), 'Lord of the Sea' (316, 319). 7, 77, 125, 150, 152–7, 159–62, 164–5, 167, 184, 195–8, 204–5, 208–9, 217–19, 253–4, 256–7, 260, 263–4, 269, 279, 283, 308, 311, 316, 319, 328, 331; described 154–5. See *Man of the Sea, Neorth*.

Ulmo (III) 5, 79, 87, 89, 93–4, 137, 183, 347; *Dweller in the Deep* 61, 93; *Lord of Ocean* 130

Ulmo (IV) 3–5, 13, 45–6, 50, 65–9, 74, 78, 86–8, 90, 97–9, 103, 136–42, 145–9, 151, 153, 160, 166, 182, 191, 193–6, 202, 207–8, 214–15, 229, 236–7, 252, 254–5, 263–4, 270–1, 275, 277, 285, 287, 291–2, 299, 305, 308, 318, 326, 329, 334, 339. See *Garsecg, Lord of Waters, Ylmir; Men*.

Ulmo (V) Lord of Waters. 20, 97, 110, 112, 114, 122, 126, 132, 140, 142–3, 145, 159–61, 164–5, 174, 187, 205, 221–2, 224–5, 228, 236, 241–2, 244–6, 253–4, 257, 262–4, 283, 287–8, 326, 328, 396 (Noldorin *Ulu;* also *Núron* 378, *Guiar, Uiar* 396–7, Quenya *Vaiaro* 397); the conches of Ulmo 161, 165 (*hyalma, 389*)

Ulmo (IXb) 412

Ulmo (X) 12–15, 20, 24–6, 29, 34–5, 40, 48–9, 65, 84–6, 88–91, 93, 115, 120, 132, 137–8, 144–5, 147, 151, 161, 168, 174–5, 178–9, 183, 186, 199, 201, 204, 240–2, 245, 253, 273, 286, 361, 393, 401, 406–7

Ulmo (XI) 7–8, 35, 40–1, 44–5, 53, 57, 77, 80, 89–91, 120, 135, 141, 146, 178, 192, 198–9, 235, 256, 301, 346–8, 352, 379, 400 (etymology); *Lord of Waters* 53, 301

Ulmo (XII) 348, 364, 387, 390

Ulmonan (I) Ulmo's halls in the Outer Ocean. 61–2, 68, 83, 85–6, 214

Ulmonan (II) Ulmo's halls in the Outer Ocean. 154

Ulmondil (XI) Name of Tuor. 235

Ulthanador (VI) See *Rohan*.

Ulumúri (X) The horns of Ulmo. 202. (Replaced *Falarombar*.)

Ulwar (IV) Son of Ulfand (Ulfang). 300, 302, 320–1; later form *Ulwarth* 180, 320–1

Ulwarth (IV) See *Ulwar*.

Ulwarth (V) Third son of Ulfang. 147, 287, 291, 311, 314, *396–7*. Earlier form *Ulwar* 134, 137, 147, 354, 402

Ulwarth (XI) Son of Ulfang. 61, 64, 74

Úmaiar (X) Evil spirits that followed Melkor. 79, 165, 203

Úmaneldi (XI) =Úmanyar. 373

Úmanyar (I) Elves 'not of Aman'. 196, 241

Úmanyar (II) Eldar 'not of Aman'. 64

Úmanyar (V) Elves 'not of Aman'. 198

Úmanyar (X) Later name of the *Alamanyar*. 163–4, 170–1, 173

Úmanyar (XI) (Eldar) not of Aman. 373; *Úmanyar* 371, 373

Úmarth (III) 'Ill-fate', fictitious name for Húrin given by Túrin in Nargothrond. 92

Umbar (IXa) *fleet of Umbar* 18; *the black fleet* 22

Umbar (XII) 151, 153, 155–6, 175, 178, 182–3, 186, 197–200, 205, 213–14, 218, 220, 222, 231, 236, 242, 262. See *Corsairs of Umbar*.

Umbar (XIII) 255, 265, 276, 296, 388, 392, 426, 439; *Haven(s) of Umbar* 265, 268, *Haven(s) of the Corsairs* 388, 392; *Corsairs of Umbar, Corsairs* 283, 293–4, 372, 388, 390–1, 393, 413, 420; *Shipmen of Umbar* 412, *fleets of Umbar* 413, 420; *Shipfoes* 425

Umbar, Havens of (IXb) 389

Umbardakil (XII) Name taken by Telumehtar, twenty-eighth King of Gondor. 200

Umbarto (XII) See *Amrod*.

Umbor (VIII) Passing form for *Umbar*. 243–4, 265; *Havens of Umbor* 243

Umboth Muilin (V) 128, 262, 268, 372, 374. See *Aelin-uial, Hithliniath, Meres of Twilight*.

Umboth Muilin (XI) *185, 194. See *Aelin-uial, Twilight Meres*.

Umboth-muilin (II) The Pools of Twilight. 225, 248. See *Pools of Twilight, Silent Pools; Aelin-uial*

Umboth-Muilin (III) 56, 214, 222. See *Pools of Twilight, Twilight Meres*.

Umboth-muilin (IV) 223, 226, 330. See *Twilit Meres*.

Umuiyan (II) Tevildo's doorkeeper. 24–5. See *Gumniow*.

Umuiyan (III) Tevildo's doorkeeper. 257

Unbodied, The (X) (Elves) See *(The) Unliving*.

Undead (VIII) 368

Undeeps, The (VII) In Anduin. 318, 320

Underharrow (VIII) Village in Harrowdale. 318

Underhill (VI) 149. See *Bag End*.

Underhill, Mr. (VI) Assumed name of Frodo at Bree (in LR). 140, 336. See *Hill, Mr.*

Underhill, Mr. (VII) Frodo's assumed name at Bree. 28, 48, 77. See *Green, Hill of Faraway. The Underhills of Staddle* 41

Undolaurë (II) Name of Glorund in Eldarissa. 84. See *Laurundo,*

Undómiel (IXa) 59, 66. See *Arwen*.

Undúna (XII) See *Common Speech*.

Undúnië (IXb) See *Andúnië*.

Undying Lands. (V) 20. Cf. *Deathless Lands*.

Undying Lands (IXb) 380. See *Deathless Land*.

Undying Lands (XII) 147

Unfinished Tales (I) 158, 244

Unfinished Tales (II) 119, 123, 146, 203, 207, 329. See *Narn i Hîn Húrin, Tuor*.

Unfinished Tales (VI) 295

Unfinished Tales (VII) 79, 137, 278, 292, 299, 301, 307, 318, 322, 399, 403, 422

Unfinished Tales (VIII) 79, 154, 180, 309, 340, 352, 357

Unfinished Tales (IXa) 44, 72, 133

Unfinished Tales (IXb) 286, 290, 316, 378–9, 381–2, 387, 406

Unfinished Tales (X) 3, 128, 182, 298–9, 374, 407

Unfinished Tales (XI) 103–4, 110, 112, 116, 137, 140–5, 148–9, 151, 157, 159–60, 165, 169, 176–7, 180–1, 186–7, 189, 192, 200, 228, 232, 235, 238, 298–300, 302, 304–5, 307, 311, 313–15, 317, 321, 323, 349–50, 352, 354, 420

Unfinished Tales (XII) 141, 144, 151, 154–5, 159, 163–5, 184, 186, 208, 210, 222–3, 282, 287–8, 293–5, 309, 314, 317, 319, 321, 326–31, 349, 351, 356–7, 364, 372, 384–5, 390

Unwin, Sir Stanley (XII) 7, 15, 18; *Unwin, Rayner* 80, 190, 246

Ungol (VIII) See *Kirith Ungol*.

Ungoliant (I) Form of the name of the great Spider in *The Silmarillion*.

157, 160–1, 201. Ungoliont, her Gnomish name in the *Lost Tales* 152, 156, 160–1, 214. (Replaced *Gungliont*.)

Ungoliant (III) 132, 141. See *Gloomweaver*.

Ungoliant (IV) 16–17, 38, 47, 69, 74, 91–3, 98, 149, 152–3, 155, 169; *Ungoliantë* 155, 265, 288; *Ungweliantë* 69. See *Gloomweaver*, *Wirilómë*.

Ungoliant (VI) 122; *Ungoliantë* 188

Ungoliant (VII) 93, 95, 99

Ungoliant(e) (VIII) Earlier name of Shelob (q.v.).

Ungoliantë (V) 114, 147, 152, 230–3, 242, 290, 299, 325, *386*, *396* (also *Ungweliantë*); *Ungoliant* 299; *Ungweliant* 187; 'Gloom-weaver' 230. (The Noldorin name was *Delduthling*, *354–5*, *386*.)

Ungoliantë (X) 98–101, 105, 108–9, 119, 123, 132, 190, (193), 194, 283–6, 288–9, 291–3, 298, 386; *Ungoliant* 295–6, 298–9, 423; *the Cloud of Ungoliantë* 101, 289, (294), 295–8; her origin 98, 105, 190, 284, and fate 109, 123, 297, 299

Ungoliantë (XI) 14–15, 110–11, 194, 404; *Ungoliant* 333

Ungweliant(ë) (II) 11, 254, 256, 261, 286; the *Spider* 261. See *Gloom-weaver*, *Wirilómë*.

Ungwelianti (I) The great Spider. 188, 209, 220; *Ungwë Lianti* 152; *Ungwë* 152, 154; *Ungweliant* 182, 200, 223. See *Gwerlum*, *Móru*, *Wirilómë*.

Union of Maidros (III) 274. See *Marching Forth*.

Union of Maidros (IV) (26), 56–7, 116–17, 188, 301, 320; *the Marching Forth* 181

Union of Maidros (V) 135, 305–8, 313

Union of Maidros (XI) 69, 236

Universe, The (IXb) 163, 166, 169, 183, 185, 196, 208, 401

Universe, The (X) 7, 38–9, 63, 330, 337–8, 350, 374, 387

University College, London (VI) 142, 144

Unlight (X) 194, 285, 288–9

Unliving, The (X) (Elves) 232. *The Unbodied* 224, 232

Unmarred (X) See *(The) Marring of Arda*.

Unnamed, The (VIII) Sauron. 154

Unnumbered Tears (III) See *Battle of Unnumbered Tears*.

Unwin, Rayner (VI) 40, 43, 108

Unwin, Rayner (VII) 89

Unwin, Stanley (VI) 11, 40, 43–4, 108, 173, 189, 370, 461

Uolë Kúvion (I) The Elf known as the Man in the Moon. 193, 198, 202, 206, 215. (Replaced *Uolë Mikúmi*.)

Uolë Mikúmi (I) Earlier name of Uolë Kúvion. 198, 202

Upbourn (VIII) Village in Harrowdale. 318

Upon the hearth the fire is red (VI) 48, 57, 66–7

Uppsala (V) 97

Ûr (I) Name of the Sun. 85, 187, 196

Ûr (IV) Name of the Sun given by the Gods. 97, 170

Ûr (V) Name of the Sun. 243; *Úr-anar* 72. See *Úrin*.

Úr (X) The Sun. 377. *Úrin* 136, 198

Ûrî (IXb) The Sun. 306, 426; *Uir*, *Ȳr* 306

Úrien (IV) The Sun-maiden. 97–9, 170–1. (Replaced *Urwen*, *Urwendi*; replaced by *Árien*.)

Úrien (V) Name of the Sun-maiden. 243. (Replaced by *Arien*.)

Úrin (I) Form of *Húrin* in the *Lost Tales*. 240–1; *Children, Sons, folk, of Úrin* 239, 241–2, 244

Úrin (II) Father of Túrin and Nienóri; called 'the Steadfast'. 44–5, 52, 70–4, 79, 82, 86–7, 89–91, 93–6, 102, 109–16, 118–20, 128, 135–9, 141, 144, 221–2, 226, 230, 242, 245–6, 250; *Úrin of the Woods* 112. (Replaced by *Húrin*.)

Úrin (III) See *Húrin*.

Úrin (IV) See *Húrin*.

Úrin (V) 'The Fiery', name of the Sun. 56, 240, 243, 396

Úrion (V) See *Fionwë*.

Urko, plural *Urqui* (XI) (Quenya) Orc(s). 390–1. For Quenya *Orko* see *Orcs*.

Urthel (III) One of the twelve companions of Barahir on Dorthonion. 335, 349

Urthel (V) Companion of Barahir. 282

Urthel (XI) Companion of Barahir. 56

Uruk (XI) (Black Speech) Orc. 390; *Uruk-hai* 419

Uruk-hai (VII) 409; *Uruks* 205

Uruk-hai (VIII) 22

Uruk-hai (IXa) 34; *Uruks* 34. See also 436.

Uruks (VI) 462

Uruktharbun (VI) Dwarvish name, probably of Dimrill-dale, preceding *Azanulbizâr*. 458, 465

Urulókë (XI) 'Fire-serpent', dragon. 85, 141 (referring to Glaurung); plural *Urulóki* 46, 121

Urundil (XII) Father of Nerdanel, Fëanor's wife. 366. Other names *Sarmo*, *Mahtan* 366; unnamed 353–4, 368

Urwen (I) Earlier name of Urwendi. 73, 76, 88, 154, 196

Urwen (XI) Túrin's sister who died in childhood, called also *Lalaeth*. *Urwen Lalaeth* 234–5, *Lalaeth* 314. See *Nen Lalaith*.

Urwen, Urwendi (IV) Original names of the Sun-maiden. 73, 170–1. (Replaced by *Úrien*.)

Urwendi (I) Guardian of Laurelin and mistress of the Sun. 178, 187–90, 192, 194, 196–7, 202, 207, 215–16, 219, 222; *Urwandi* 197. (Replaced *Urwen*.)

Urwendi (II) Mistress of the Sun. 116, 281–2, 286

Urwendi (X) Original name of the Sun-maiden. 136

Urwendi (XII) The Sun-maiden. 374

Usurpers, The (V) An Elvish name for Men. 247

Útgársecg (IV) (Old English) Vaiya, the Outer Sea. 207–8, 210, *250–1, 261, 285, 289

Uthwit, The old (VII) Saruman. 409

Utumna (I) The first fortress of Melko. 69, 82, 99, 101–4, 106, 111, 176, 198, 209; *Fortress of the North* 237; later form *Utumno* 82, 87, 110, 112, 198, 223

Utumna (IV) The first fortress of Melko in Middle-earth. 44, 235, 240, *249, 257, 259–60, 313; later form *Utumno* 44, 239–40, 257, 260–1. On relation to Angband see 257, 259–60.

Utumno (V) 33, 208, 210, 213, 233, 238, 259, *394* (also *Udun, Uduvon, Utum*). Earlier form *Utumna* 108, 111, 121, 210, 238

Utumno (IXb) 383

Utumno (X) 'The Deep-hidden' (67, 69). 18–19, 25, 27, 33, 35, 38, 53, 61, 67, 69–71, 73–6, 78–9, 81, 99, 110, 130, 156, 161, 165, 167, 197, 284, 288, 291–2, 297–8, 377–8, 382, 390–1, 393, 407–8, 410, 431. See *Udûn*.

Utumno (XI) 105, 111, 196, 344; *the War of Utumno* 104

Úvalear (I) Name of the Shadow Folk of Hisilómë. 237

Úvanimor (I) 'Monsters, giants, and ogres' bred by Melko. 75, 236–7

Úvanimor (II) See 136, 247

Úvanimor (IV) Creatures bred by Morgoth. 293

Úvanimor (V) Creatures of Morgoth. 216, *351, 359, 396*

Úvanimor (X) Evil creatures bred by Morgoth. 79. See *Vaninor*.

Úvanwaith (VII) The Nomenlands. 281, 283, 320

Vai (I) The Outer Sea. 59, 61–2, 83, 85–7, 154, 190, 196, 214–15, 226. See especially 85–6, and see *Outer Sea(s)*.

Vai (II) The Outer Ocean. 273

Vai (IV) In the original cosmology, the Outer Sea. 214, 252

Vailimo (I) Name of Ulmo, Ruler of Vai. 101, 114, 214–15

Vainóni (II) Earliest name of Nienor(i). 138–9

Vairë (I) (1) Elf of Tol Eressëa, wife of Lindo. 14–18, 20, 22, 31, 45, 65, 80, 90, 94–5, 129, 140, 195, 207, 212–13, 219, 221, 225, 227, 229–31. (2) 'The Weaver', wife of Mandos. 90

Vairë (II) Wife of Lindo. 8, 144, 257, 286, 290, 302

Vairë (IV) Spouse of Mandos. 270, 275, 285, 289

Vairë (V) 'The Weaver', spouse of Mandos. 110, 205, 207, *398* (also Noldorin *Gwîr*).

Vairë (X) 'The Weaver', wife of Mandos. 49, 65, 69, 145, 148, 151, 201, 244–5, 248–50, 253, 260, 263–4; *the house of Vairë* 206–7, 237, 250, 253, 258, 261, 263–5

Vairë (XII) 'The Weaver', wife of Mandos. 359

Vaitya (I) The outermost of the three airs. 65, 67, 83, 85–6, 181, 226

Vaitya (IV) In the original cosmology, the outermost of the three airs. 252–3

Vaiya (I) 'The Enfolding Ocean'. 86, 227

Vaiya (IV) The Outer Sea. 236–8, 241, *242–3, *245, *247, *249, 254; *Encircling Ocean* 241, ~ *Sea* 254; *Enfolding Ocean* 236, 241. See *Outer Sea(s)*, *Útgársecg*.

Vaiya (V) 55, 165, 207–9, 241, *335*, *358*, *397* (also Noldorin *Gui*, *Ui*). See *Encircling Sea*, *Outer Sea(s)*.

Vaiya (X) The Outer Sea. 28, 136, 154, 156. See *Ekkaia*.

Valacirca (I) 'The Sickle of the Valar'. 133; *the Silver Sickle* 133

Valacirca (III) The Sickle of the Valar. 170. See *Great Bear*, *Sickle of the Gods*.

Valahíru (I) Title of Manwë, 'Lord of the Valar'. 180

Valakar (XII) Twentieth King of Gondor. 198–9, 213–14, 230–1, 260–1; *Valacar* 259

Valai (IXb) Valar. 404

Valakirka (X) The Sickle of the Gods. 71, 160, 166, 378, *Valacirca* 388. See *Great Bear*, *(The) Plough*, *Burning Briar*.

Valandil (V) (1) Father of Elendil. 34, 60, (66), 69, 71; 'God-friend' 60. (2) Brother of Elendil. 33–4, 71. (3) In later applications, 71

Valandil (VI) (1) Elendil's father in *The Lost Road*. 175. (2) Elendil's brother in *The Fall of Númenor*. 175. (3) Preceding or varying with Elendil. 169, 175, 270, 320, 355. See *Orendil*.

Valandil (VII) (1) Brother of Elendil. 123–4. (2) Son of Elendil. 121. (3) Son of Isildur. 121–3, 128–9, 147, 359–62, 366

Valandil (IXb) Named as father of Elendil. 401. *Valandili* 'Lovers of the Powers', name given to certain Númenóreans. 400

Valandil (XII) (1) First Lord of Andúnië. 160, 164. (2) Earlier name of Amandil, father of Elendil. 156, 163, 175, 186, 189, 191. (3) Youngest son of Isildur; third King of Arnor. 186, 191–2, 207–8, 227–8

Valandur (VII) Son of Isildur (?). 120, 122

Valandur (XII) Eighth King of Arnor. 193

Valaquenta (I) 79, 82

Valaquenta (IV) 76, 166–7

Valaquenta (V) 207

Valaquenta (XII) (title) 143, 390

Valar (I) *Passim*; see *Gods*. (Singular *Vala*; plural also *Vali* 18, 61, 65, 104, 107, 114, 148, 154, 178, 180, 186, and *Valur and Valir* 61.) See *Children of the Valar*.

Valar (II) (also *Vali*, 243). Selected references (including *Gods*). Passages concerning the relations of the Valar (Gods, Ainur) to Elves and Men: 5, 7, 15, 19, 35, 37, 44–5, 47, 68, 72–3, 76, 79, 101, 111, 115–16, 141, 151–2, 161, 188, 198, 200, 204, 219, 280, 282, 295. Warfare of the Gods 312, 323; *Wrack of the Gods* 285; withdrawal from the affairs of Men 283, 285; reverence for (in Gondolin) 165, 174, 218. *Vala of the Western Isles* 95, 141. Túrin and Nienóri 'as shining Valar' 116. See *Great Folk of the West, Lords of the West, Children of the Gods*.

Valar (III) 26, 54, 127, 136–7, 173, 192, 243; *the Nine Valar* 133, 137; *Vali* 137, 306

Valar (IV) 5, 12–13, 17, 21–2, 36–7, 39–40, 42–3, 45–6, 50, 52, 57, 65, 68, 72, 75, 78–9, 82, 84, 86, 89–90, 94, 99–100, 104, 106, 108, 138–9, 142, 149, 151–2, 155, 162, 164, 166, 169–70, 191, 195–6, 198–9, 202–5, 208, 211, 238–9, 252–3, 255–6, 263, 265–7, 271, 275, 278–9, 285, 288, 291–3, 335; O.E. *Brega* 211, but in texts always *Valar (Ualar, Falar)*, 206, 281, 283, 285–7, 291; *the Nine Valar* 11, 42, 78, 166, 206, 263, 275, 285, 291. On the interrelations of the Valar see 275; and see *Children of Sons of the Valar, Gods, Powers*.

Valar (V) 7, 20, 25, 64, 72, 97, 104, 110–11, 113–16, 120–3, 125, 161–5, 168, 172–3, 175, 179–80, 185–7, 191, 193, 204–47

passim, 273, 283–4, 328, 330, 332, 335, 338, *350* (also Noldorin
Balan, plural *Belein, Belen*), 407. *Land of the Valar* 125, 241, 244.
See *Ban of the Valar; Gods, Lords of the West, Powers; Children
of, Sons of, the Valar.*

Valar (VI) 122

Valar (VIII) 136; *Battle of the Valar* 353; *those who dwell beyond the
West* 401; *the Powers* 157. See *God(s).*

Valar (IXb) 241–2, 246, 252, 286, 292, 305, 310, 332–3, 340, 355,
376–7, 394, 396, 400–2, 404–6, 409–10, 412; *Chief of the Valar*
(Manwë) 402, 406; *Children of the Valar* 332, 377. See *Gods,
Powers; Children of the Gods.*

Valar (X) (and singular *Vala*) 4, 8, 14–43 *passim*, 48–62, 65–75, 77–
82, 84, 86, 88, 90–1, 93–101, 105, 107–8, 110–20, 125, 128–
33, 135–8, 144–7, 149, 152–4, 157, 159–62, 166–8, 172, 174–
6, 178, 183, 185–91, 194, 196, 198–204, 211, 218–20, 223, 226,
235, 238–9, 241, 243–4, 246–7, 250–1, 253–5, 258–61, 268–
93 *passim*, 295, 297, 311, 313, 318–19, 321–2, 327, 330–1, 334–
41, 350–1, 355, 357, 362–4, 372, 374–82, 384, 386–94, 396–
407, 410–12, 415–16, 424–30.

Valar (X) The number of the Valar: nine 48, 69, 144, 147, 201,
204, seven 69, 201, 204, (and see *(The) Great Ones); Queens of
the Valar* 49, 52, 58, 65–6, 69, 145–7, 201, 244 (see *Valier).* Their
appearance, 'shapes', 4, 15, 69, 99, 105, 131, 144, 151, 218, 272,
284, 286, 289, 412; their 'errors' 162, 166, 168, 394, 401, 405,
407; 'fading' or impotence 401, 405; the Debate of the Valar 208–
9, 239–46, 254, 258, 263–4, 269, 271, 326–7, 339, 361. *Land
of the Valar* 15, 108, 132, 156, 202, 288, 291. See *Aratar, (The)
Deathless, Gods, (The) Great Ones, (The) Mighty, (The) Powers,
(The) Rulers of Arda; Children of the Valar.*

Valar (XI) (and singular *Vala*) 5–7, 11–12, 14, 18–19, 30, 36–7, 41–
2, 54–5, 104–6, 111, 119, 173, 175, 196, 203, 206, 239–40,
246, 296, 340–1, 345–6, 360, 372–3, 386, 397–407, 413, 418;
etymology 403; *language of the Valar* 118, 359, 397, 419, ~ *and
Maiar* 397, 416, and see *Valarin.*

Valar (XII) (and singular *Vala*) 123, 130, 143, 145, 150, 152, 154,
158–9, 174–5, 180–1, 305, 312, 321, 323, 333–8, 343, 348, 354,
357–8, 360–1, 363–6, 368, 370–1, 374, 378–81, 383–6, 388,
390–1, 396, 400–1, 403–4; *People of the Valar* (Maiar) 364. *Ban
of the Valar* (on the Númenóreans) 149, 175, (on the Exiled

Noldor) 370, 376, 380, 390. See *Children, Sons of the Valar; Guardians, Powers.*

Valaraukar (X) Balrogs. 165, 203

Valarauko (XI) 'Demon of Might' (Balrog). 415

Valarin (V) The speech of the Valar. 174, 180, 185–7, 192–5. See *Valian, Valya.*

Valarin (X) 88

Valarin (XI) 359, 398–406, 411, 419, and see *Valar; lambë Valarinwa* 397; Valarin words and names 399–402, 411, 417; the language described 398, 402

Valarin (XII) (language) 356–7, 363

Valarindi (IV) Lesser spirits of Valarin race. 263–4, 275, 285–6, 293. See *Vanimor.*

Valarindi (V) 110, 121, 186 (language of), 404; see especially 120–1, and see *Children of, Sons of, the Valar.*

Valarindi (X) 'Offspring of the Valar'. 49, 59, 66, 69, 152. See *Children of the Valar.*

Valaróma (X) The horn of Oromë. 7, 35, 39, 101, 105, 149, 151, 203, 289. (Replaced *Rombaras.*)

Valaróma (XI) The horn of Oromë. 14, 400

Valatar (VII) Father of Eldamir (Elfstone). 362, 404

Valaturu (I) =*Valahíru.* 180, 190

Vale (Valley) of Weeping Waters (I) 239–40, 244. See *Gorfalon(g).*

Vale of Dread (VIII) 327. See *Minas Morghul.*

Vale of Sleep (I) See *Murmenalda.*

Vale of Weeping Waters (IV) 5

Vale of Willows (V) See *Land of Willows.*

Valhalla (IXb) 242

Valian (V) (1) Valian tongue. 168, 174, 178, 185, 190. (2) *Valian Years, Year(s) of the Valar.* 109–18, 121–3, 171, 175–6, 189–90, 193, 224 (*years of Valinor*); (*ennin*, a Valian Year, 400, *randa, anrand*, a hundred Valian Years, 382).

Valian Age, Valian Year (IV) See 263, 269, 273

Valian Age, Valian Years (X) See *Years of the Valar.*

Valiant, The (V) A name of the Noldor. 215

Valiant, The (X) A name of the Noldor. 164

Valier (X) The Queens of the Valar. 201, 203–4. See *Valar.*

Valier (XI) The Queens of the Valar; singular *Valië* 383

Valimar (VII) City of the Valar in Valinor. 285

Valimar (IXb) 409

Valimar (X) See *Valmar*.

Valinor (I) 'Land of the Gods' (70); *Valinórë* 182. *Passim*; 'vale' or 'plain' of Valinor 68, 70–3, 75, 77 (Valinor 'upon the plain'), etc.; beechwoods 99; glades 126–7; sand of gold 126; Valinor nearer to the Wall of Things than the shores of the East 238, 253; *Hiding of Valinor* 27, 137, 195, 207, 209, 213, 220, 222–4; *Darkening of Valinor* 169, 203. See *Mountains of Valinor*.

Valinor (II) 3, 9–10, 15, 34, 40, 42, 55, 58, 60–1, 65, 77–8, 82, 87, 114, 125, 129, 140, 160–2, 207–9, 215–16, 218, 222–3, 228, 232–3, 239–40, 246, 249–50, 253, 255–8, 260, 262–5, 271–2, 278–83, 285–7, 289, 292, 302–3, 307–8, 316, 325–6, 328; *God-home* 316, 325. See *Mountains of Valinor, Hiding of Valinor*.

Valinor (III) 28, 37, 92, 94, 104, 127, 136, 139, 142, 147, 149, 182, 210-l1, 231, 235, 247, 253, 259–60, 274, 276, 284, 288, 291, 331, 346, 348, 350; *Mountains of Valinor* 172, 346, *Mountains of the West* 74; wine of Valinor 111, 127. See *Aman, Blessed Realm, Land of Light, Lands of Ease*.

Valinor (IV) *Passim*; on *Ambarkanta* maps *246–7, *249–51. *Darkening of Valinor* 82, 92, 269; *Hiding of Valinor* 50, 98, 198; tongue of Valinor 174; effect of Ilmen not Vista in Valinor 236; called the *Guarded Realm* 158, 161; O.E. *Breguland* 211, *Godéðel* all (and frequently in the texts, used interchangeably with *Valinor*), *Ésaeard* 283, *Valaríce* 286. See *Outer Lands* (2), *Western Land(s)* (1); *Mountains of Valinor*; *Gods*.

Valinor (V) 11–15, 20–1, 24–7, 29–32, 64–5, 73, 75–6, 97, 110–29 *passim*, 133, 142–4, 153, 161–2, 168–253 *passim*, 263–6, 269, 273, 288, 290–1, 298, 303–4, 312, 319, 322–8, 330–5, 338, 350 (also Noldorin *Balannor*), 376; *Land of the Gods, of the Valar* in entries *Gods, Valar. Darkening of Valinor* 118, 171, 176, 184, 193, 210, 232; *Hiding of Valinor* 22, 114, 243. See *Mountains of Valinor*.

Valinor (VI) 122, 182–4, 188, 285

Valinor (VII) 256, 263, 265, 453–4; *Bay of* 97, 100; *Mountains of Valinor* 95, *Mountains of the West* 263, *the Mountains* 248, 257, 263, 265; *Hiding of* 263; *Valinonian letters* 453

Valinor (VIII) 158, 164, 168; *Valinorian, Valinorean* 394

Valinor (IXa) 58

Valinor (IXb) 284, 286, 292, 316–17, 332–4, 336, 354–5, 379–80, 386, 388, 394, 396, 409–10, 412–13; *Land of the Gods*, see *Gods*;

461

O.E. *Ósgeard* 316–17, *Ésa-eard*, *Godépe1* 316, and see *Regeneard.*
Annals of Valinor 280, 291, 316, 377

Valinor (X) 7, 16, 18–21, 24–5, 27–8, 33–5, 37–8, 43, 48, 50–1, 54–
6, 61–2, 67–8, 70–4, 76–8, 80–1, 83, 85, 87, 89, 91–101, 105,
108–11, 113, 115, 117–18, 126–7, 129–34, 136–7, 144–6, 149,
152–6, 160–3, 166–7, 170, 172–9, 181–90, 192, 196, 198, 201–
2, 204, 238, 240, 247, 250, 253–4, 256, 258, 261, 265–9, 276–
7, 279–8 1, 283, 285–9, 292, 294–5, 297, 312, 371–2, 375, 377–
8, 385–6, 388, 390, 392–4, 402, 407. See *Land of the Gods, ~
Valar* (in entries *Gods, Valar*); *Aman, (The) Blessed Realm, (The)
Guarded Realm; Mountains of Aman.*

Valinor (X) *The Darkening of Valinor* 128, 155, 248; *the Hiding
of Valinor* 129, 133–4, 137, 142, 401, 406–7; *the Noontide of
Valinor* 185, 273

Valinor (XI) 5–11, 14, 16, 19–25, 29–30, 32, 38, 40, 47, 54, 62–3,
66–7, 77, 105, 108–9, 116–17, 119, 122, 130, 135, 174, 177,
189, 196, 203, 210–11, 219, 239–40, 243, 246–7, 318, 323, 343–
8, 350–1, 353, 373, 398–9, 402–3, 409, 413; *Valinórë, Valandor*
413; *Mountains of Valinor* 417 (see *Aman, Pelóri*); *Valinórean* 342

Valinor (XII) 30–1, 123, 130, 144, 146–8, 173, 175–6, 183, 305, 325,
331–3, 336–9, 341, 350, 354–6, 358, 360, 363, 368, 375–6, 378–
83, 385–7, 389, 392, 401; *Host of ~* 163, *Darkening of* 335

Valinórean, Valinorian (XII) 30, 331

Valinórelúmien (IV) Annals of Valinor. 284, 290–1; O.E. *Godéðles
géargetæl* 284, 290

Valinórelúmien (V) The Annals of Valinor. 202, (370).

Valinorian (V) (language) 168, 190, 192–5, 346

Valinorian (X) 91, 141, 388

Valkyrie (IV) 208; O.E. *wælcyriga (Nefantur Mandos)* 207–8

Valkyries (IXb) 242

Valley of the Dead Awaiting (III) 20, 28. *Land of Waiting* 309; *Land
of the Lost* 308. See *Gurthrond.*

Valley of the Fountains, Vale of Fountains (I) 239–40, 244. See *Gor-
falon(g).*

Valley of the Wraiths (VIII) 180. See *Minas Morghul.*

Valmar (I) 73–5, 77–8, 82, 89, 100, 103–4, 113–14, 116, 120, 123,
126–7, 140, 142–4, 146–9, 153, 155, 158, 177, 184, 193, 213,
217, 230

Valmar (II) 60, 253, 257; *Valimar* 257

Valmar (III) 198, 236, 279

Valmar (IV) City of the Gods, called 'the Blessed' (80–1). 12, 14, 80–1, 85, 88, (89–90), 92, 98, 154, 163–5, 167, 169, 198, 205, *249–51, 257, 263–4, 278, 285, 289; O.E. *Bregubold* 211, *Godaburg* 211, 285–6, 289

Valmar (V) City of the Gods, called 'the Blessed' (209). 111, 117, 193, 206, 209, 213–14, 217, 220, 224, 227, 230–2, 236, 242, 325, 332

Valmar (X) City of the Gods, called 'the Blessed'. 55, 61, 81, 94, 97–100, 113, 116, 146, 154, 160–2, 166–7, 172, 178, 186, 241, 278–80, 283, 286–9, 291, 386; *Valimar* 68; *the plains of Valmar* 133. See *Gods*.

Valmar, Dome of (XII) 371. See *Varda*.

Valwë (I) Father of Vairë wife of Lindo. 16, 22, 26. (*Manwë* for *Valwë* 22.)

Valwë (II) Father of Lindo. 219, 278–9. [Note. The definition of Valwë as *Father of Vairë wife of Lindo* in the Index to Part I is an error. Vairë's father was Tulkastor. Similarly I.22 *Vairë's father* should read *Lindo's father*.]

Valya (V) The speech of the Valar. 174, 180, 185. See *Valarin, Valian*.

Vána (I) 67, 71–3, 75–6, 79–80, 88–9, 93, 105, 117, 154, 177–80, 183–7, 190, 199, 202, 209–10, 212; *the Lamp of Vána*, the Sun, 197. See *Tári-Laisi, Tuilérë, Tuivána, Vána-Laisi*.

Vána (II) 218, 240

Vana (V) 110, 206, 240, *351* (also Noldorin *Banwen*).

Vana (Vána) (IV) 49, 79, 97, 99, 167, 171, 207, 263, 275, 285; *Queen of Flowers* 79

Vána (X) (also *Vana*) 49, 53, 59, 61, 65, 67, 69, 131, 146, 149, 151, 201

Vána (XI) 383

Vána-Laisi (I) Name of Vána. 180

Vanë Hansto (I) See *Hanstovánen*.

Vanimor (IV) 'The Fair', lesser spirits of Valarin racc. 293. See *Valarindi*.

Vanimor (V) 'The Beautiful' (see 121). 110–11, 121, 216, 351, 396, 403–4. Also as a name of the Lindar, 403 (see *Irimor*).

Vanimor (X) 'The Beautiful'; precursors of the Maiar. 56, 59, 79. See *Úvanimor*.

Vanished Isles (III) 142–3

Vansamírin (I) Road of the ceremonial procession of the Feast of

Double Mirth. 207, 222 (description of the road 143). See *Samírien*.

Vanyar ((XI) and singular *Vanya*) 6–7, 28, 44, 106, 130, 243, 246, 323, 374–5, 380, 382–3, 393, 399, 405, 411, 417–18, 423; meaning of the name 382–3. Telerin *Vaniai* 383. See *Lindar*; *First Clan*.

Vanyar (I) 26, 44, 50, 62, 132, 134–5, 159, 169, 220, 223, 234. See *Teleri* (1).

Vanyar (II) 305

Vanyar (III) 139. See *Teleri* (1).

Vanyar (IV) Final name of the First Kindred of the Elves. 44, 72, 196. (Replaced *Lindar*.)

Vanyar (V) The First Kindred of the Elves. 198, (351). (Replaced *Lindar*.)

Vanyar (VI) The First Kindred of the Elves. 188

Vanyar (X) 34, 57, 82–5, 87–90, 94, 99–101, 103, 110, 129–30, 133, 162, 164, 168, 171, 174–6, 178–81, 184, 186, 193, 198, 205, 207, 237, 249, 261–2, 268, 274, 287–8

Vanyar (XII) (and singular *Vanya*) 62, 77, 82, 318, 332, 336–8, 340, 343, 349, 386, 402; *Banyai* 402. *Vanyarin* 77

Vanyarin (X) 136, 166

Vanyarin (XI) (of language) 361, 363, 417

Varda (I) 58, 62, 65, 69–71, 73–4, 79, 88, 99–100, 111, 113–17, 127, 133, 144, 148, 154, 176, 178, 180–3, 185–6, 189, 192, 194–6, 199–201, 208–9, 212, 216, 223, 227; *Varda of the Stars* 126, 192, *Lady of the Stars* 178, *Queen of the Stars* 58, 62, 180, *the starfashioner* 183; *the Wells of Varda* 160. See *Tinwetári*.

Varda (II) 281

Varda (III) 139, 170, 211, 219, 230, 233, 251, 259, 301, 306, 349; called the *Holy* 211, 219. See *Bridhil, Timbridhil, Tinwetári*.

Varda (IV) 5, 43, 45, 78–82, 84–5, 87–8, 92, 94, 97, 167–8, 206–7, 236, 263–4, 270, 272, 275–6, z81, 283, 285–6, 291; O.E. *uprodera cwén, tunglawyrhte* 206–7. See *Bridhil, Tim-Bridhil, Tinwetári*.

Varda (V) 110–1l, 121, 162, 205–7, 209, 212, 214, 216, 223, 227, 231, 234, 240–1, 243–4, 330, 344–5, *351* (also *Breðil, Berethil, Elbereth*). See *Elbereth, Elentári, Tar-Ellion, Tintallë, Tintanië, Tinwerontar, Tinwetar*.

Varda (VI) 68. See *Elbereth, Gilthoniel*.

Varda (VII) 285

Varda (VIII) 174

Varda (X) 15, 20, 24–5, 32, 34, 38–9, 49, 52, 54–5, 59, 61, 67, 69,

71, 95, 100, 106, 112, 130–2, (135), 144–52, 153–6, 159–60, 163, 166, 176, 180, 187, 193, 198, 201–2, 204, 211, 223, 244, 275, 285–8, 293, 313, 372, 374, 376–7, 379–82, 384–90, 406

Varda (X) *Queen of the Valar* 15, 20, 145, *Queen of Arda* 387; *Queen of the Stars*, see *Elbereth, Elentári, Tinwerontar. The Vats or Wells of Varda* 61, 100, 106, 193, 288, other references 55, 68–9, 155, 157, 159. See *Dome of Varda, Star-making, Tintallë.*

Varda (XI) 5, 105, 369, 399, 402–3; *Varda Aratarya* 369; *'the Sublime'* 402; *the Dome of Varda* 399

Varda (XII) 334, 358, 363(-4); *Airë Tári* 363–4; *Dome of Varda* 376. See *Elbereth.*

Variags (VIII) The people of Khand. 369

Variags (XII) The people of Khand. 79

Vása (X) 'The Consumer', the Sun. 130, 136, 198

Vastuman (X) Name replacing *Arvalin* and replaced by *Avathar.* 291

Vê (I) Name of Vefántur (Mandos) given to his hall. 76–7, 89–90, 146, 150. See *Mandos.*

Vê (III) The hall of Véfantur Mandos. 28

Vê (IV) Name of Vefantur Mandos given to his hall. 166

Vê (X) Original true name of Mandos; also *Vefántur.* 150

Vëandur (XII) Third son of Isildur. 191, 208. (Replaced by *Ciryon.*)

Veaneldar (V) 'Sea-elves', a name of the Teleri. 403. See *Sea-elves.*

Vëannë (II) A child of Mar Vanwa Tyaliéva, teller of the *Tale of Tinúviel.* 4–8, 40–2, 50–1, 53, 66, 68, 294, 300–1. See *Melinir.*

Vëantur (XII) Númenórean navigator. 329

Vefántur (I) 'Fantur of Death', the Vala Mandos. 66, 76, 82, 89–90, 100, 106, 144, 167, 172. See *Fantur, Mandos.*

Vefántur (II) 'Fantur of Death', the Vala Mandos. 115

Vefántur (IV) Mandos. 166. (Replaced by *Nefantur.*)

Vefántur (V) Name of Mandos in the *Lost Tales.* 207. (Later *Nefantur, Nurufantur.*)

Vefántur (XII) Mandos. 374

Veins of the World (IV) 236, 255

Venus (II) 266

Venus (IXb) (the planet) 168, 204, 212–13, 220. See *Perelandra, Zingil.*

Verona (V) 54

Vettar (II) Wood-rangers(?). 101

Vidri (XI) 'Wisdom' (Felagund), name replaced by *Sômar* (itself replacing the original word *Widris*, V.275). 202

Vidugavia (XII) King of Rhovanion. 198, 259–60, 262; rejected name *Vinitharya* 262

Vidumavi (XII) Daughter of Vidugavia; wife of Valakar. (198, 213–14, 259), 260. See *Galadwen*.

Vikings (II) 322–3, 330–1, 333. See *Forodwaith, Gwasgonin, Winged Helms*.

Vikings (V) 80, 84–5

Vikings (IXb) 295. See *(The) Heathen*.

Vilna (I) The innermost of the three airs. 62, 67, 83, 85–6, 181, 187, 199

Vilna (IV) In the original cosmology, the innermost of the three airs. 253

Vilvarin (X) See *Wilwarin*.

Vilya (IXa) The mightiest of the Three Rings of the Elves, borne by Elrond. 111; *the Blue Ring* 132; *the Ring* (i.e. of Rivendell) 115

Vingalótë (IXb) 'Foam-flower', the ship of Eärendil. 356, 360, 377, 388; *Wingalótë* (IXb) 342, 356, 377, 388; *Vingelot* 292, 356; *Wingelot* 356. See *Rôthinzil*.

Vingelot (II) See *Wingilot*.

Vingelot (IV) See *Wingelot*.

Vingelot (V) Eärendel's ship. 325, 327, 329, 335; *Wingelot* 22, 143, 335, *370, 398* (also Noldorin *Gwing(e)loth*); 'Flower of the Foam' 143

Vingelot, Vingilot (XI) Eärendil's ship. 246

Vingilot (XII) 'Foamflower', Eärendil's ship. 143, 163, 387, *Vingilótë* 365, 367, 392; *Wingelot, Wingelótë* 371, *Wingalótë* 370–1; Sindarin *Gwingloth* 370. See *Eälótë, Rothinzil; Guingelot*.

Vinitharya (XII) Name in the language of the Northmen of Eldakar, King of Gondor. 199, 260–2; *Vinthanarya* 214

Vinland (V) Old Norse name for America. 77

Vinya (V) 'The Young', 'the New Land', Númenor. 19, 25, 64, 70

Vinya (IXb) 'The Young', 'The New Land', Númenor. 315, 332

Vinyamar (I) Turgon's house in Nevrast. 52

Vinyamar (II) Turgon's dwelling in Nevrast. 204–5, 217

Vinyamar (IV) Turgon's dwelling in Nevrast. 65, 316, 318, 334

Vinyamar (IXb) (1) Númenor. 315, (2) The house of Turgon in Nevrast. 316

Vinyamar (X) Turgon's dwelling in Nevrast. 407

Vinyamar (XI) Turgon's dwelling in Nevrast. 44, 120, 146, 178, *182, 192, 199

Vinyamar (XII) The house of Turgon in Nevrast (Nivrost). 364, 390

Vinyarion (XII) Twenty-fourth King of Gondor (see *Hyarmendakil II*). 199, 214

Virgin Mary, The (X) 357

Vírin (I) Substance devised by Aulë for the vessel of the Moon. 192–3

Vision, The (X) (shown by Ilúvatar to the Ainur) 11–15, 24–6, 28, 31, 38, 40, 68, 144, 149, 159(-60), 318–19, 327, 336, 351, 388, 425

Vista (IV) The inner air, in which are Fanyamar and Aiwenórë. 236, 240–1, *242–7, 253–4, 261. See *Wilwa*.

Vista (V) The inner or lower air. 13, 78, 165, 399. See *Wilwa*.

Voice (of Eru), The (X) See *Eru*.

Voice of Goth (II) Gothmog. 67

Voice, The (XI) (of Ilúvatar) 211

Void, The (IV) 80, 164, 203, 237, 252–3. See *Ava-kúma, Kúma, Outer Dark*.

Void, The (V) 24, 64–5, 73, 157, 159, 204, 209, 303, 335; *the voids* 327, *the Timeless Void* 332–3. See *Ava-kúma, Outer Darkness*.

Void, The (VI) 122

Void, The (IXb) 332, 401, 404

Void, The (X) 9, 11, 13, 27–9, 38–9, 53, 58, 63–4, 144, 154, 157, 375–6, 380, 388, 403, 407; *the voids of Eä* 53, 62–4, 67, 76. See especially 403, and see *Outer Darkness* (X) (in entry *Dark*), *Kúma*.

Volcano (IXb) See *(The) Pillar of Heaven*.

Völsung legend (IV) 187

Völuspá (I) Poem of the Old Norse *Edda*. 245

Völuspá (VII) See *Elder Edda*.

Völuspá (XII) Poem of the Old Norse *Edda*. 71, 278

Vorondil (VIII) Father of Mardil the Steward. 288, 292. See *Faragon, Orondil*.

Vorondil (XII) Son of Pelendur; Steward to King Eärnil II. 204, 218–19

Voronwë (I) =Gnomish *Bronweg*. 48, 52

Voronwë (II) Form of Bronweg's name in Eldarissa. Called 'the faithful' (156). 145, 149, 156–60, 162, 166, 178, 186–8, 195, 198, 200, 203, 205–7, 209, 214–15, 254–6, 258, 260, 263–5, 286. See *Bronweg*.

Voronwë (III) 90. See *Bronweg*.

Voronwë (IV) 67, 69–70, 74, 191, 324. See *Bronweg*.

Voronwë (IXa) Elf of Gondolin. 44

Voronwë (IXb) ('Steadfast, Faithful'). (1) Elf of Gondolin. 290. (2) Companion of Elendil; identified with Tréowine; Jeremy so named by Lowdham. 278–9, 290, 293.

Voronwë (XI) Companion of Tuor. 80, 91, 136, 146, 256, 299, 352, 354. See *Bronwë*.

Voronwë (XII) See *Mardil*.

Vorotemnar (I) The manacles set on Melko's wrists. 101, 104

Voyage to Arcturus, A (IXb) See *Lindsay, David*.

Vultures (VII) Steeds of the Winged Nazgûl. 208–9, 213, 338, 341, 343–4, 353–4

Vultures (IXa) Steeds of the Winged Nazgûl. 3–4

Wade (XII) 371 (see III.142–4).

Wade of the Helsings (III) 142–4; *Wada* 143–4; *Gado* 144

Wæfre (II) See *Ottor Wæfre*.

Wainriders (XII) 195, 200–1, 215–16, 218, 232, 254–5

Waking Water (III) See *Cuiviénen*.

Walda (VIII) Twelfth King of the Mark. 408

Walda (XII) Twelfth King of Rohan. 274

Wales (V) 81, 92; *South Wales* 80. See *Wealas*, *Welsh*.

Wales (IXb) 272; *South Wales* 267; *West Wales* (Cornwall) 279

Wales (XII) 50

Walker (VI) Name assumed by the hobbits at Bree. 141

Wall of Things (I) 214–15, 221, 226–7; *Eastern Wall* 216, 221–2, 226

Wall of Things (II) 259; *the Wall* 317, 325; *Western Walls* 320, 325; *Wall of Space* 274

Wall(s) of the World (IV) 40, 72, 80–1, 91, 164, 235–8, 241, 252–4 (see *Eärambar, Ilurambar*); *the final Wall* 12; *Wall of Things* 252 (*Eastern Wall* 252); *Walls of Night* 253

Walls (of the World) (X) 26, 28–9, 62–3, 95, 107, 135, 146, 154, 157, 190, 193, 407; *Walls of Arda* (X) 64. See *Eärambar, Ilurambar*.

Walls of (the) Night (X) 53–4, 58, 62–4, 67, 136–7

Walls of Night (V) The Walls of the World. 12

Walls of the Sun (IV) Mountain range in the far East. 236–7, 239, *249–51, 253, 255; *Mountains of the Sun* *249

Walls of the Sun (V) Mountain-range in the far East. 303

Walls of the World (I) See *Ilurambar*.

Walls of the World (V) 15, 21, 161, 206–9, 230, 302–3, 332–3, 335, 338. See *Ilurambar*.

Walls of the World (VI) 122

Wanderers, The (V) A name of the Teleri (cf. 169). 215

Wanderers, The (X) A name of the Nandor. 164

Wandering Companies (VI) (of Elves) 65 cf. 60, 72

Wangs (VII) 178–9, (215)

Waning of the Elves (X) See *Elves.*

War of the Dwarves and Orcs (XII) 205, 220, 237, 249–50, 276–8, 301, 319, 323

War of the Elves and Sauron (XII) 168–9, 172, 174, 177–8, 180

War of the Gods (IV) See *Battle of the Gods; War of Wrath,* see *Battle of Wrath and Thunder.*

War of the Gods (V) See *Battle of the Gods.*

War of the Great Jewels (VIII) 161

War of the Jewels (X) See *(The) Jewels.*

War of the Jewels (XII) See *Jewels.*

War of the Ring (V) 211

War of the Ring (VIII) 71, 162

War of the Ring (IXa) 111; *the War* 100

War of the Ring (XII) 25, 137, 173, 196, 242, 244–5, 253, 255, 257, 261–3, 265–9, 282, 309, 411

War of Wrath (V) 328, 336. See *Great Battle.*

War(s), The (XI) Also *the Wars of Beleriand.* 14–15, 17, 22, 24, 27, 36–7, 112, 116, 133, 343, 377, 386, 396–7, 409, 411

Warden of the City, of the Keys (VIII) See *Húrin* (2).

Wards of Melian (X) A name of the Sindar. 164–5

Wargs (IV) 209

Wargs (VI) 416, 445

Warwick (I) 25–6, 32; *Warwickshire* 25

Warwick (II) 292–3, 295, 300, 308, 310, 328; *Warwickshire* 324; poem *The Town of Dreams* 295–6, 298

Watcher in the Water, The (VII) 179, (181), 191, 201

Watchers, The (VIII) See *(The) Silent Watchers.*

Watchers, The (IXa) At the gate of the Tower of Kirith Ungol. 23, 25–6

Watchet (V) In Somerset. 80–1; Old English *Wæced* 80

Watchet (IXb) In Somerset. 269–70, 293

Watchful Peace (XII) 234–5, 249

Water, The (VI) 22, 37, 46, 50, 56, 72, 106

Water, The (VII) 39

Water, The (XII) 117

Water(s) of Awakening (IV) 12, 44, 84, 168, 276. See *Cuiviénen.*

Waters of Awakening (I) 50, 85, 115, 131, 231–2, 234. See *Cuiviénen*, *Koivië-néni*.

Waters of Awakening (II) 64, 197, 285

Waters of Awakening (III) See *Cuiviénen*.

Waters of Awakening (V) See *Kuiviénen*.

Waters of Awakening (X) See *Kuiviénen*.

Waters of Awakening (XI) See *Cuiviénen*.

Waters of Sirion (IV) See *Sirion*.

Way of Dreams (II) 8, 42, 48. See *Olórë Mallë*, *Path of Dreams*.

Way of Escape (II) 158, 163, 166–7, 177, 189, 195, 210, 213–14. See especially 206–7, and see *Bad Uthwen*.

Way of Escape (IV) The tunnel beneath the Encircling Mountains of Gondolin. 37, 66, 139, 144, 194, 221; other references 34, 36, 137, 142, 147; *the hidden door* 142, 146–7, 194, 222

Way of Escape (XI) The tunnel beneath the mountains encircling Gondolin. 271, 302

Way of Running Waters (II) In Gondolin. 186

waybread (VIII) See *lembas*.

Waymoot (IXa) Village in the Westfarthing where the roads from Sarn Ford and Little Delving joined the East Road. 92, 100, 106; *Waymeet* 106

Wéalas (II) (Old English) The Welsh. 290; adjective *Wíelisc* 292

Wealas, *Walas* (V) (Old English) The Celts of Britain. 80–1, 91; the Romans 92

Weaponless, The (X) A name of the Nandor of Ossiriand. 164

Weather Hills (VI) 175; unnamed 167–9, 174, 177–8, 355

Weather Hills (XII) 189, 193–4, 209, 313

Weathertop (Hill) (VI) 126, 133, 154, 158, 161–79 *passim*, 184, 186, 189–93, 195, 198–202, 206, 208, 216, 219, 223–4, 325, 353–6, 359–60, 365, 367–8, 375, 396

Weathertop (III) 124, 126

Weathertop (VII) 7, 10–15, 31, 44, 52, 56–7, 61–2, 64–5, 69–70, 72, 76, 78–9, 135, 152, 157–8, 439

Weathertop (VIII) 17

Weathertop (IXa) 6, 75–6, 78, 109, 112

Weathertop (XI) 130

Weathertop (XII) 56, 189, 229. See *Amon Sûl*.

Weaving of the Days and Months and Years (I) 217, 221, 227

Wellinghall (VII) Treebeard's house. 417. Earlier names *Fonthill*, *Funtial* 417, 420; *Wellandhouse* 417

Wellinghall (VIII) Treebeard's house. 3

Wells of Varda (X) See *Varda*.

Wells, H. G. (IXb) 165–6, 212. *The Time Machine* 165; *The First Men in the Moon* (IXb) 165, 212

Welsh (V) 39, 83–4; =Roman 91–2; *Welsh Mountains*, the Alps, 92

Welsh (IXb) 269, 273, 293; (language) 192, 270, 417; =Roman 276 (see V.91); *West Welsh*, the people of Cornwall, 270, 293

Welsh (XII) 50, 81

Wendelin (I) Early name of Melian. 106–7, 115, 120, 131–2. (Replaced *Tindriel*.)

Wendelin (II) Early name of Melian. 8, 48–51, 63, 244

Wendelin (IV) Early name of Melian. 289

Wendelin (V) Name of Melian in the *Lost Tales*. 186

Wendelsæ (II) (Old English) The Mediterranean Sea. 294

Werewolves (XI) 17, 54, 62, 66–7. Cf. *Tol-in-Gaurhoth*.

Wessex (II) 301–2

Wessex (V) 80, 83

Wessex (IXb) Kingdom of the West Saxons. 269, 273; *West Saxon* (dialect) 291

West Beleriand (IV) 299

West Beleriand (V) 261, 272 (its extent).

Westfarthing (VIII) 284

West Gate(s) of Moria (VI) (including references to *the gate(s)*) 430–1, 443–9, 451–2, 454–5, 461, 463–4; 'two secret gates on the western side' 429; *West-doors* 454; 437. The design on the Gate 450, 463

West Midlands (IXb) (of England) 291; *West-midland* (dialect) 257, 291; *West-midlander* 291. See *Mercia*.

West Pass (IV) See *Sirion (Pass of Sirion)*.

West Towers (VI) 155, 159, 269. See *Elf-towers, Towers*.

West Towers 39. (VII) See *White Towers*.

West Wind (II) 261

West, The (VI) 60, 71, 187, 215, 225, 260, 364, 396, 402; the *Far West* 182, 212; *the Far West Island*, Númenor, 215; the West of Middle-earth 182. See *Men*.

West, The (VII) In various applications (West over Sea, Númenor, the West of Middle-earth, of the Shire). 110, 123 *(the True West)*, 127, 152–3, 249, 255, 259, 263, 277–8, 286–7, 331, 392. *Host of the West* 142, 263; *Lords of the West* 422; for *Men of the West* see *Númenórean(s)*.

West, The (VIII) (in various applications) 41, 45, 153, 155, 157, 162, 184, 187, 219, 271, 324, 400–1, 403, 410, 418; *Host(s) (army, forces) of the West* 229, 256, 359, 399, 415–16, 430–2; *Captains of the West* 373; *the western world* 159, 162. See *Window of the Sunset*.

West, The (IXa) 67, 83, 132; *island of the West* 53; *King of the West* 74; *the True West* 110. See *Captains of, Men of, the West*.

West, The (IXb) 152, 251, 265, 280, 332, 334, 336–8, 341, 345, 349–52, 354–7, 359–60, 364–5, 369–72, 374–5, 378, 381, 383, 394–6, 399–402, 404, 407–9, 412–14. *Dwellers in the West* (O.E. *Westware*), *Westfarers* (O.E. *Westfaran*) =Númenóreans, 257–8, 313–16; *West Land* (Valinor) 401; *West of the World* (O.E. *Westwegas*) 244, 280; *Men of the West* 271, 398–400. See *Lords of the West, True West*.

West, The (X) 19, 25, 73, 75, 79, 81–2, 117, 127, 130–1, 134–5, 146, 156, 160–4, 167, 174–5, 370, 377–8; (of Middle-earth) 309, 349, 419; *the uttermost West* 18, 27, 33, 153, 163; *the hosts of the West* 74, 203. See *Great Sea, Lords of the West*.

West, The (XI) (across the Great Sea) 5–6, (8), 17, 19, 21–2, 27, 32, 39–41, 44, 54, 80, 146, 196, 217, 227, 345, 352, 354, and see *Lords of the West*; (the West of Middle-earth) 48, 72–3, 76, 118, 206, 220, 225, 227, 232, 242, (293), 334, 378, 382, 386, *the Westlands* 13, 219, 410

West, The (XII) (the lands beyond the Great Sea, *ancient West, Far Uttermost* ~ , and the West of Middle-earth (cf. *Westlands*), or in more general sense) 16, 20, 30, 32–3, 55, 72, 149, 164, 173, 176, 183, 211, 228–9, 235, 242–3, 252, 257, 264, 266, 271, 294, 297–8, 300–1, 305, 312–15, 317, 324, 328, 363, 385–6, 388, 399, 401; and see *Lords of the West. Men of the West* 21, 64, 189, 324, 437, *Western Men* 62

Westemnet (VIII) 28

Westerland (II) 267–8

Westermanton (VII) Annúminas. 144–5, 157, 296, 304. Also *Aldemanton* 157; and see *Tankilmar, Torfirion*.

Western Elves (XII) 70, 73, 78

Western Havens (IV) 271, 296, 314, 329, 341; O.E. *of þám Westhýþum* 339, 341. See *Falas*.

Western Isles (II), *Western Islands* 5, 332; *Islands of the West* 331; *Vala of the Western Isles* 95, 141

Western Havens (V) See *Havens*.

Western Isles (IV) 159, 162, (174), 199

Western Isles (V) 332

Western Land (V) Valinor (with Eruman and Arvalin). 236, 242; *West-world* 116

Western Land(s) (IV) (1) Valinor, with Eruman and Arvalin. 21, 45, 52, 170, 198, 233, 239, 254–5, 258, 260, 267; *Westland or Westerness* *249. (2) The West of Middle-earth. 159, 161, 264

Western Men (V) See *Men of the West. Western Pass*, see *Sirion*.

Western Men (X) 7

Western Sea (III) 224; *Western Shore* 268

West(ern) Sea(s) (IV) 29, 34–5, 100, 115, 125, 132, 134, 136, 141, 159, 162, 188, 199, 238–9, *249, 256–8, 270, 283, 325, 331, 335; O.E. *Westsǽ* 210, 285. See *Belegar, Great Sea*.

Western Sea (V) (1) The Great Sea of the West. 11, 23, 33, 36, 39, 79, 86, 98, 119, 129, 221, 224, 248, 265–6, 272, 305, 331, 337; *Western Ocean* 63, 81. See *Belegar, Garsecg, Great Sea*. (2) The Outer Sea, Vaiya. 247–8

Western Sea (VII) See *Great Sea(s). Western Shore* 264, 266

Western Sea (X) 26, 78, 175, 178, 365. See *(The) Sea*.

Western Sea (XI) 64, 175, 203; *Western Ocean* 136

Western Sea(s) (II) 5–7, 294, 299–300, 311, 315, 320, 330. See *Great Sea*.

Western Seas (VI) 59, 68. See *Great Sea, (the) Sea*.

Western Shore (V) 112, 128. See *Falas*.

Western Tower (VII) The tower in which Gandalf was besieged. (Including references to *The Tower*) 9, 11–12, 33, 35, 44, 72, 130, 139; *White Tower* 12. See *Dream of the Tower, White Towers*.

Western Water (I) See *Great Sea*.

Westerness (IV) See *Western Land(s)*.

Westernesse (V) Númenor. 14, 19, 25, 33

Westernesse (VI) Númenor. 215, 320

Westernesse (VII) (1) Númenor. *Men of, race of, Westernesse* 84, 106, 119, 123, 127, 137, 144–6, 400, 440. (2) The West Lands (see the map in IV.249). The *Flammifer of Westernesse* 94–5, 98, 102, 105

Westernesse (VIII) Númenor. 76, 155, 281, 368, 396

Westernesse (IXa) Númenor. 49

Westernesse (IXb) Númenor. 240, 305, 311, 332, 343–4, 361, 378, 400, 409, 426. See *Anadûnê*.

Westernesse (X) Númenor. 192

Westernesse (XII) Númenor. 21, 31, 64, 74, 79, 152, 173, 181

Westfarers (IXb) See *(The) West*.

Westfarthing. (VI) 298, 312–13

Westfold (VII) 320 (in the Misty Mountains); *Westfold Vale* 320 *Westemnet* 318, 401, 404, 434

Westfold (VIII) (1) Valleys in the west of the Misty Mountains (see *Dunland*). 8, 21–3, 41; *Westfolder* 21–2; *tongue of Westfold* 21. (2) In Rohan (see *Westmarch*). 10, 22, 40, 51–2, 59–60, 238, 245, 250–1, 256, 259, 276, 371; *Westfold Vale* 12, 21, 70; *Lord of Westfold* 24; *tongue of Westfold* 159

Westfold (IXb) In Rohan. 309

Westfold (XII) 65

Westfolde (IXb) (O.E.) Númenor. 303, 309, 313, 3 15–16

Westland (X) Aman. 118, 132, 194; *western land* 194. *West-lands of Middle-earth* 82–3

Westlands (IXa) 117, 128. See *Aragorn*.

West-lands (VI) (of Middle-earth) 182

Westlands (XII) (of Middle-earth) 12, 32, 35–6, 39, 55, 61, 78, 119, 125, 133, 146, 172–3, 176, 179, 191, 196, 204, 228, 240, 242, 244–5, 255, 267, 287, 424

westmansweed (VIII) pipeweed. 396

Westmarch (VIII) Earlier name of Westfold (2). 17, 21; *Westmarch Vale* 21; *Westmarcher(s)* (VIII) 8, 11, 19, 21, *Marcher* 10

Westmarch (IXa) See *Red Book of Westmarch*.

Westmarch (XII) 17, 25, 112; and see *Red Book*.

Westnish (XII) Term preceding *Westron*. 55, 57, 64; *Western language* 72

Westron (VI) 466

Westron (VII) 244, 288

Westron (VIII) 161

Westron (IXa) 30

Westron (XII) 17, 28, 32–9, 44, 55, 57–8, 64–5, 68–9, 72, 76, 78, 81–3, 316. See *Common Speech*.

Westrons (XI) Men of the West. 252

Wetwang (IV) 341

Wetwang (VII) 268–9, 281, 283, 287, 313, 315–16, 320–1, 328. See *Nindalf*.

Wetwang (VIII) 112. See *Nindalf*.

When winter first begins to bite (VII) 163

Where now the horse and the rider? (VII) 443, 449

Whitburn and Thoms (IXb) Oxford publishing house and bookseller. 149, 153; *Whitburn* 303. See *Blackwell*.

White army (IXa) 8

White Council (VI) 319

White Council (VII) 22-3, 38, 132, 138, 147, 149, 233, 248, 257

White Council (VIII) 77 *(the Council)*.

White Council (XII) (also *the Council*) 204, 226, 235, 237-9, 241, 248-9, 251, 283

White Crown (VIII) On Aragorn's standard. 399; *the Crown* 359, 363, 389, 395; *the Crown of the North Kingdom* 395

White Crown (IXa) 55-6; on Aragorn's standard 15, 56

White Downs (VI) 278, 295, 312

White Downs (IXa) 92-3, 109

White Downs (XII) 6, 112, 115

White Elves (X) A name of the Vanyar. 164

White Eye (VIII) The Moon. 109, 116; *White Face* 116, 180

White Fire (VII) Gandalf's fire opposed to the Red Fire of the Balrog. 198, 203; *White Flame* 203

White Hand (VII) Emblem of Saruman. 382, 409

White Hand (VIII) Emblem of Saruman. 20, 31

White Horse (VI) Original name of the inn at Bree. 129, 131

White Lady (VIII) Galadriel. 163

White Lady of the Noldor (X) 102, 106, 177, 182. See *Isfin, Írith*.

White Mountain (IXb) See *Taniquetil*.

White Mountains (VI) Ered Nimrais. 399

White Mountains (VII) Later name of the Black Mountains. 124, 177, 239, 320-1, 357, 395, 433

White Mountains (VIII) (including many references to *the mountains*) 137, 141, 155-6, 167, 232, 235, 237, 244, 251, 253, 260, 262-3, 265, 268, 273, 277-8, 283, 288-9, 293, 296, 315-16, 321-2, 354, 397, 405-7, 410-11, 417, 421, 433, 438. Change of the name from *Black Mountains* 137. See *Ered Nimrais*.

White Mountains (IXa) 119, 122; *the mountains* 15, 116; *the Dales* 15. See *Ered Nimrais*.

White Mountains (XI) 13, 110. See *Eryd Nimrais*.

White Mountains (XII) 34, 205, 235-6, 244, 267, 272, 274, 309, 313, (415)

White Rider (VIII) See *Gandalf*.

White Rider, The (VII) See *Gandalf*.

White Ship (IXa) The ship that bore the Ringbearers from the Grey

Havens. 120, 123, 132; other references to the ship 109–10, 133

White Tower (of Minas Tirith) (VIII) (including references to *the Tower*) 139, 253, 256–7, 260, 263, 276, 279, 281, 288–9, 292, 294, 330, 334, 336, 338, 340, 375–6, 378, 380–1, 394, and see *Denethor, Ecthelion* (2). *The Tower Hall*, see *Minas Tirith*.

White Tower (V) (of Elwing) 327, 335–6. *White Towers* (on Emyn Beraid) (28), 30

White Tower (IXa) See *Minas Tirith*.

White Tower (XII) (in Minas Tirith) 200, 205–6, 215, 232, 236, 238. See *Ecthelion I.*

White Towers (VII) 304, 423; *the Towers* 154; *West Towers* 39; *Elf-towers* 34, 39, 130. See *Western Tower.*

White Tree (IV) 43. See *Silpion, Telperion.*

White Tree (V) of Númenor (*Nimloth*) 211; of Tol-eressëa (*Celeborn*) 211

White Tree (X) Of Valinor, see *Telperion*; of Tuna, see *Galathilion* (2); of Eressëa, see *Celeborn* (1); of Númenor, see *Nimloth.*

White Tree (XII) (1) of Tirion/Túna. 147–9; *Galathilion the Less* 147–8. (2) of Eressëa. 147–8, 176, 191; *Nimloth* 147–8, *Galathilion* 147–8, *Celeborn* 148. (3) of Númenor. 130, 147–8; *Nimloth* 147–8. (4) of Minas Ithil. 176, 191–2. (5) Of Minas Anor, Minas Tirith. 163, 170, 177, 192, 200, 204, 206, 217, 220, 231, 234, 238, 243

White Tree of Gondor (VII) 396, 404; *Silver Tree* 395

White Tree of Gondor (VIII) The dead Tree in Minas Tirith. 276, 281, 336; as device, and in the Rhyme of Lore, 65, 267, 279, 281, 325, 363

White Tree of Númenor (IXa) Nimloth. 58. (The sapling found on Mount Mindolluin 57–8.)

White Tree of Númenor (IXb) See *Nimloth.*

White Tree of Valinor (I) 88. See *Silpion, Telperion.*

White Wizard (VII) 212, 330, 389, 422, 436

White Wizards (VI) 218

White-elves (V) A name of the Lindar. 215, 403. See *Ninqendi.*

Whitelock (VII) See *Arod.*

Whitfoot, Will (IXa) Mayor of the Shire. 81, 108, 110; called *Flourdumpling* 81

Whitfurrows (VI) Village in the Eastfarthing. 387

Whitfurrows (IXa) Village in the Eastfarthing (replaced *Bamfurlong*). 107

Whitfurrows (XII) Village in the East Farthing. 98, 117

Whitwell (VIII) Village in the Shire near Tuckborough. 284

Wide World, The (VI) 63–4

Wídfara (VIII) Rider of Rohan. 353

Wídlást (V) 'Far-travelled'; see *Ælfwine*.

Widris (V) Word meaning 'Wisdom' (Gnome) in the speech of the People of Bëor. 275, 279

Widsith (III) Old English poem. 143

Widsith (V) Old English poem. 54, 91–3

Wíelisc (II) See *Wéalas*.

Wihawinia (IXb) See 242, 287

Wild Elves (VIII) The Avari. 157

Wild Elves (X) Dark-elves. 375

Wild Hobbits (VI) See *Rangers*.

Wild Men (V) 11, 14, 25–6, 68, 74

Wild Men (VIII) 155, 157 (in Faramir's distinctions). Men of the western vales of the Misty Mountains (see *Westfold* (1)) 9–10, 16, 18–19, 21, *(wild) hill-men* 8, 20–1; the Druedain of Anórien 344–6, 350–2; of the East 105, 243–4, 340; of the South 340; *wild peoples* 400, 403

Wild Men, Wild Man (IXa) (of Druadan Forest) 22, 61, 68; *Wild Men of the Woods* 57; *Ghân of the Wild Woods* 56, 67

Wild Men (IXb) (of Middle-earth) 334, 374, *men of the wild* 352

Wild Men (XII) (of Drúadan Forest) 65, 309, 316, 324; (out of the East) 197, 205, 272, 413, 422, 426

Wild Men out of the East (VI) 398, 409; *Eastern Men* 398

Wilderland (VI) Lands east of the Misty Mountains. 81, 261, 263–4, 321, 416–17; *the Wild* 43, 208. Map of Wilderland in *The Hobbit* 204–5, 218, 432, 438, 440

Wilderland (VII) 119, 144, 264, 266, 352, 354, 360, 365. Map of Wilderland, see *Maps*.

Wilderland (XII) 38, 56, 66–7, 214, 230, 250, 323, 437; map of ~ 323. See *Rhovan(n)ion*.

Wildman of the Woods (XI) Name taken by Túrin in Brethil. 92, 148

William (VI) One of the Trolls turned to stone. 193, 212, 360

William of Malmesbury (V) Mediaeval English historian. 55, 92

Williams, Charles (VII) 419

Williams, Charles (VIII) 104, 107, 144, 171, 183–4

Williams, Charles (IXb) 219; *Carolus* 200, 216

Willow-man (VI) 42–3, 109, 111–12, 115, 117, 120, 302; *Old Man*

Willow 113, 115–16, 120, 123, 327 *the Old Man* 111; *the Willow* 112–13; *the Great Willow* 116

Wilwa (IV) Earlier form for *Vista*. 240, *242, *244, *246–7, 261

Wilwa (V) The inner or lower air. 12–13, 78, *398*; 'the heavy air(s)' 16–17, 21. See *Vista*.

Wilwarin (X) Name of a constellation. 160, 166; *Vilvarin* 166

Winchester (XII) 44

Windbeam (VII) See *Elendil*.

Windbeam (IXa) The horn of Elendil. 4

Windmane (VII) See *Hasofel*.

Window of the Sunset (VIII) Henneth Annûn. 164. *Window of the West* 164, 271; ~ *on the West* 132

Wing, The (II) Emblem of Tuor, see *Swan*; *White Wing* 172; *men, folk, guard, of the Wing* in Gondolin 174, 176–8, 180, 182, 190, 192

Wingalótë, Wingelot (IXb) See *Vingalótë*.

Winged Crown of Gondor (VII) 396, 404

Winged Helms (II) The Forodwaith. 330, 334. See *Gwasgonin*.

Wingelot (III) Eärendel's ship. 144

Wingelot (IV) Eärendel's ship. 37–8, (45), 69–70, 74, 149–50, 152–5, 164, 166, 195–6, 201, 203–4; *Wingilot* 155; *Vingelot* 155–6, 166; 'Foam-flower' 149, 152

Wingelot (V) See *Vingelot*.

Wingelot (XII) See *Vingilot*.

Wingildi (I) Spirits of the sea-foam. 66

Wingildi (II) Spirits of the sea-foam. 276

Wingilot (I) Eärendel's ship. 15, 21; *Wingelot* 21

Wingilot (II) 'Foam-flower', Eärendel's ship. 145, 253–4, 256, 260–1, 263; *Wingelot* (II) 260, 262, 272; *Vingelot* 262, 272

Winseld (VII) The Golden Hall in Eodoras. 402, 429, 433, 437, 441–2, 447. Earlier names *Meduarn, Meodarn* 402

Winseld (VIII) Earlier name of *Meduseld*. 321

Winter Comes to Nargothrond (III) (poem, also called *Storm over Narog*) 128–9

Wirilómë (I) The great Spider, 'Gloomweaver'. 152–3. See *Gwerlum, Móru, Ungoliant, Ungweliantë*.

Wirilómë (II) 'Gloomweaver'. 260–1. See *Ungweliant(ë)*.

Wirilómë (IV) Gloomweaver', Ungoliant. 69

Wiruin (I) A great whirlpool near Helkaraksë. 167

Wisdom (IV) 'Gnome', name of Felagund among Men. 105, 108, 175

Wisdom (XI) Name of Felagund among Beor's people. 217, 226. See *Nóm, Sómar, Vidri.*

Wise, The (V) The Noldor. 215, 403

Wise, The (VI) 212, 262, 364

Wise, The (VII) 82

Wise, The (VIII) 335

Wise, The (IXa) 111

Wise, The (X) 381, 383, 419–20; the Wise of Eressëa 17, 74, 124, 408–9; among Men 305–6, 308–11, 313–15, 318, 352–3; the Wise of Númenor 374. A name of the Noldor, 164

Wise, The (XI) (in Valinor) 108, 203; name of the Noldor 217, 226

Wise, The (XII) 229, 234, 238, 249, 264–5

Wise-elves (VI) Noldor. 60, 71, 93; the Elvenwise 212, 217, 364

Wise-women (X) (among Men) 305, 307; *Wise-woman* (of Adanel and Andreth) 304–7, 323

Wise-women (XI) (of the Edain) 233

Witan (X) (Old English) The Gnomes. 163, 168

Witch-king (XII) (of Angmar) 193–5, 201, 209–10, 230, 232–3, 241–2, 248, 256, 258, 378. See *Sorcerer-king.*

Withered Dale (II) Where Tevildo encountered Huan. 48, 56

Withered Heath (II) Heath near Tavrobel, after the Battle of the Heath of the Sky-roof. 284, 287

Withered Heath (V) 413

Withered Wold (VII) The Brown Lands. 351, 356

Withywindle (IV) 211

Withywindle, River (VI) 110, 112–17, 119, 127, 327–8

Withywindle, River (VII) 36

Wizard King, The (VIII) 326, 331, 359, 361–4, 367, 430; the Sorcerer King 336, 368. See *Angmar, Black Captain, Nazgûl.*

Wizard's Isle (III) The Isle of Werewolves (Tol-in-Gaurhoth). 228, 248, 251, 258, 271, 273, 279, 283, 293, 306. Other references to the isle 227, 234, 241, 260, 270–1, 276, 278, 284, 288; the isle described 227, 234

Wizard's Isle (IV) 177. See *Isle of (the) Werewolves, Tol-na-Gaurhoth, Tol Sirion.*

Wizard's Tower (III) The tower of Thû on the Isle of Werewolves. (258), 270–1, 293

Wizard's Vale, The (VIII) 4–6, 29, 79; the Valley of Saruman 7. See *Nan Gurunír.*

Wizard(s) (VII) (not including references expressly to Gandalf) 22–3,

72, 136, 326, 411, 418, 422, 436; referring to the King of the Ringwraiths 9, 132, *the Wizard King* 116

Wizard(s) (VIII) (other than references expressly to Gandalf and Saruman) 36–8, 47, 53, 60, 282, 285, 332, and see *(The) Wizard King*; *the Five Wizards* 64, 67; the order of Wizards (63), 326, 331

Wizards (VI) References to wizards other than Gandalf: 211, 260, 270, 364; *White Wizards* 318

Wizards (IXa) (not referring expressly to Gandalf or Saruman) 26, 77. *The Wizard King* 6–7; *the Wizard's Vale* 136 (see *Nan Gurunír*).

Wizards (XII) 228, 245, 311, 360, 392; *the Five Wizards* 384–5; *the Two Wizards (Blue Wizards)* 384–5; *Wise Men* 228. See *Istari*.

Wóden (I) 23

Wóden (II) Old English name of the Germanic god in Old Norsë called *Óðinn*; by Eriol identified with Manwë. 290

Wold of Rohan (VII) 318, 400, 404

Wold of Rohan (VIII) 244, 256, 259, 262, 274, 343–5, 348, 361, 363, 404

Wold (of Rohan) (IXa) 63, 71

Wolf (VI) One of Farmer Maggot's dogs. 290, 293

Wolfdale (VII) See *Entish Land(s)*.

Wolfriders (II) See *Orcs*.

Wolfriders (III) 10, 40, 110, (278)

Wolfriders (VII) 412

Wolfriders (VIII) 9–10, 29, 51, 54

Wolf-Sauron (II) 55

Wood Eaton (VI) Earliest name of Buckland (as village). 35, 105. (Replaced by *Bury Underwood*.)

Wood-elven (XI) (speech) 410

Wood-elves (IV) 296, 329; *Woodland Elves* (of Doriath) 13, 85, 188

Wood-elves (VI) (of Mirkwood) 264–5, 320, 392; *King of the Wood-elves* 395, 400

Wood-elves (VII) (both of Mirkwood and of Lothlórien) 28, 118, 137, 148, 157, 218, 221–2, 239, 244, 296; woodland folk 167, 229; language 223, 227, 239–40, 251. See *Silvan Elves*.

Wood-elves (VIII) 96; *Elves of the Woods* 157 (see *Lembi*).

Wood-elves (X) A name of the Nandor. 164

Woodhall (VI) Village in the Eastfarthing. 61, 66, 72, 89–90, 96, 100–1, 105, 107–8, 200, 291, 298

Woodhall (VII) 11

Woodhall (XII) Village in the East Farthing. 93, 95, 118

Woodland Elves (II) Elves of Artanor. Also *Woodelves*, *Elves of the wood(land)*, *of the forest*, etc. 11, 13, 18, 34–5, 37, 43, 45, 52, 63, 65–6, 69, 73–4, 78, 92, 142, 222–3, 228, 242–3, 245–6; *wood(land) fairies* 23, 35, 63; *hidden Elves* 10; *secret Elves* 11, 73, 123

Woodland Elves (III) The Elves of Doriath. 24, 159–60; *Wood-Elves* 239, 312; *folk of the wood* 9, 16, 29, 105, 116, *of the caves* 20. See *Hidden People*.

Woodland Elves, *Elves of the Woods* (XII) (in various applications) 20, 22, 26, 75–6, 185; *Wood-elves* 70

Woodmen (II) (later *Woodmen of Brethil*) Also *woodfolk*, *wood(land)-rangers*. 91, 100–8, 112–13, 125, 127, 130–5, 138, 141–2. See *Vettar*.

Woodmen of Brethil (III) 50, 93

Woodmen (of Brethil) (V) 131, 140, 413. See *Brethil*.

Woodmen (VII) (of Western Mirkwood) 296, 390

Woodmen (XI) (of Brethil) 51, 72, 92, 95–7, 147–8, 150–2, (166), 236, 280, *Wood-folk* 97, and see *Brethil*; (of the woods south of Taiglin) 306–8

Woodmen of Mirkwood (VIII) See *Mirkwood*.

Woodmen of Mirkwood (XII) 34, 71

Woodmen of Wilderland (VI) 264

Woodmen, *Woodfolk* (IV) Túrin's people in the woods about Taiglin. 31–2, 60, 127–30, 184–6, 223, 226, 305–6, 322; *Men of the Wood(s)* 30, 127, 302, 321

Woody End (VI) 50, 52, 56, 58, 72, 278, 280, 284, 304, 324–5; earliest form *Wood-end* 47

Woody End (VII) 11, 33, 215, 365

Woody End (IXa) 52, 101, 109, 112

Woody End (XII) 93, 118

World Made Round (V) 11–12, 21–2, 78, 98, 153–4

World, The (I) Used in the sense of 'the Great Lands' 16, 26, 49, 70, 82, 129, 146, 155, 159, 169, 176–7, 196, 199, 208, 220; *the inner world* 168, *the world without* 174, 180–1, 207, 223, *the world beyond* 208

World, The (IV) As used explicitly =lands east of the Great Sea, 15, 21, 39, 87, 99, 149, 152; cf. 101 and note 3, and see Earth. *Edge of the World* 156

World, The (VIII) Middle-earth. 410

World, The (IXb) (Passages bearing on the conception of The World Made Round at the Downfall of Númenor) 264–5, 278–9, 298, 331, 336–9, 345, 347, 352, 355, 364, 366–7, 381, 383, 386, 392–6, 400–1, 404, 408–12; and see *(The) Cataclysm, (The) Straight Road.*

World, The (IXb) *The New World* 338–9, 392–3, 395; *the Old World* 338–9, 387, 408–9, 414; and see *New Lands, Old Lands. The circle(s) of the world* 372, 409

World, The (X) 7–8, 11–44 *passim,* 48–50, 54, 56, 58-9, 62–3, 66–8, 72, 76, 80, 95, 98, 106, 108–9, 118, 131, 144–50, 152–4, 160–3, 165, 176, 179, 186, 189–90, 203–4, 214, 223–4, 232, 244–5, 249, 251, 255, 259–60, 266–7, 270, 273, 275, 277, 284–5, 293–5, 299, 308–11, 314, 318–24, 329–30, 335, 337, 342, 345–7, 351, 355–6, 358–9, 364–6, 372–3, 376, 378–81, 387, 395–7, 399, 405, 407, 410, 428; and see *(The) End.*

World, The (X) *The Little World* (X) 17, 27, 31, 40–1, 44, *Little Kingdom* 31; *Lord of the (this) World* 296, 312–13, 320. See *Change of the World, Circles (of the World), Walls (of the World).*

World, The (XI) 10, 15, 22, 30–1, 41, 50, 63, 70, 111, 173, 177, 198, 212, 220, 224–5, 227, 242–3, 247, 297, 397, 402 *(=Arda),* 424; *the ancient world* 258–9; *the Change of the World* (at the end of the Elder Days) 105; *the World made Round* 105; and see *Circles of the World, (The) End.*

World, The (XII) References to the change of the world. 156, 176, 244, 257, 266, 270, 275, 314, 359, 381, 401. See *Circles of the World, (The) End.*

World's End (VII) 94, 98–9, 101; *margin of the world* 286

World-Ship (I) See *Ship of the World.*

Worm of Greed (III) See *Glórund.*

Wormald, W. W. (IXb) Oxford scholar interested in *The Notion Club Papers.* 156–8

Wormtongue (VII) 214, 401, 430, 437, 443–6, 450. See *Frána.*

Wormtongue (VIII) 3, 6, 9, 11, 26, 55, 58, 60, 63–6, 75, 78, 80, 355, 372. See *Frána, Gríma.*

Wormtongue (IXa) 64–5, 73, 100. See *Frána, Gríma.*

Woses (VIII) 344, 352. See *Druedain, Wild Men.*

Wraiths (VI) See *Elf-wraiths, Men-wraiths, Ring-wraiths.*

Wraiths (VII) See *Ringwraiths.*

Wraiths (VIII) 107, 364; *Valley of the Wraiths* 180; *Wraith-road* 195, 222. See *Ringwraith(s).*

Wulf (XII) (of Rohan) 271

Wychwood (IXb) 291 (see *Hwiccian*).

Yagûl (VIII) (1) Orc of the Tower of Kirith Ungol. 225 (replaced by *Shagrat*). (2) Orc of Minas Morghul. 216–18, 225–6 (replaced by *Gorbag*). Spelt *Yagool* 217

Yagûl (IXa) Orc of Minas Morghul. 13. (Replaced by *Gorbag*.)

Yale, The (VI) Region of the Eastfarthing. 66, 387

Yale, The (XII) Region of the Shire. 88, 97–8, 100–1

Yandúnë (XII) See *Common Speech*.

Yárë (VII) See *Tom Bombadil*.

Yare, River (I) 205–6

Yarmouth (I) 205–6

Yavanna (I) 66, 79–80, 88, 98–100, 110–11, 114, 116–118, 123, 127–8, 131, 135, 159, 177, 179–80, 183–5, 187, 190, 199, 209, 214. See *Earth-lady, Kémi, Palúrien*.

Yavanna (II) 286. See *Belaurin, Palúrien*.

Yavanna (III) 248. See *Palúrien*.

Yavanna (IV) 12, 43, 78, 80–2, 97, 99, 165, 167, 205, 263–4, 270, 275, 280, 289, 291, 293; in O.E. texts variously spelt, *Iauanna, Geauanna*, etc. 207, 285–6, 289, 291, 293. See *Belaurin, Bladorwen, Palúrien*.

Yavanna (V) 14, 19, 24, 110–11, 120–1, 205–6, 209, 212, 220, 240, 246, 333, 348, 399 (also Noldorin *Ivann*). See especially 120, and see *Palúrien*.

Yavanna (IXa) 58

Yavanna (IXb) 332

Yavanna (X) 15, 19, 24–5, 32–5, 38, 49, 52, 55–6, 59, 62, 65, 67, 69–71, 75, 79–80, 85, 90, 98–9, 106–9, 120, 122, 129–31, 135, 145–54, 157, 159, 166, 172, 175–6, 180, 185, 197, 201–3, 241, 244, 257, 269, 286, 293, 295, 297, 372, 377, 384, 395. See *Palúrien, Kementári*.

Yavanna (XI) 106, 247, 340–1; *the Sleep of Yavanna* 6, 9, 20, 24, 28, 30, 105–7

Yavanna (XII) 147–8, 403–5; *Sleep of Yavanna* 398; *Ivann* 405

Yavannildi (XII) 'Maidens of Yavanna' 404; Sindarin *Ivonwin* 404–5

Year of Dread (XII) 382

Year of Lamentation (II) 120

Year of Lamentation (XI) The year of the Battle of Unnumbered Tears. 71, 200

Year of Sorrow (IV) 301

Year of Sorrow (V) 136. *Years of Darkness* 118. For *Years of the Sun, Years of the Valar* see *Sun, Valian.*

Years of Darkness (IV) The Darkening of Valinor. 269

Years of Double Mirth (I) See *Double Mirth.*

Years of the Sun, Sun Years (IV) See *Sun; Years of the Trees,* see *Two Trees.*

Years of the Valar (Valian Years) (X) For references to the nature and computation of the Ages, Years and Days before the Sun see *Reckoning of Time* in entry *Time;* for the later conception see 425–6, 430–1

Years of the Valar, Valian Years 6, 8, 16, 20, 24, 28, 105, 108–9, 344, 419; *War of the Valar and Melkor* 373; *Children of the Valar* 246, *Sons* ~ 14, 246, *host* ~ 246, 345–6. See *Gods.*

Yearsday, Yearsend (XII) See *New Year, Old Year.*

Yellow Eye (VIII) The Sun. 116; *Yellow Face* 116, 180

Yellow Mountains (IV) 239, *249, 255–6

Yellowskin (XII) 40, 67. See *Tuckborough.*

Yénië Valinóren (V) The Annals of Valinor. 202, (400). See *Nyarna Valinóren.*

Yénië Valinóren (X) 'Annals of Valinor'. 57, 200

Yénonótie (X) The treatise of Quenna Onótimo. 51, 57

Ylmir (III) Gnomish form for *Ulmo.* 5, 59, 61–2, 79, 87, 93. See *Gulma.*

Ylmir (IV) Gnomish form for *Ulmo.* 13–15, 20, 34–8, 46, 49, 65–6, 68–9, 169, 215–17, 229; *Ylmir's Way* (35), 229–30, (305). See *Horns of Ylmir.*

Yoreth (VIII) Woman of Gondor serving in the Houses of Healing (in LR spelt *Ioreth*). 386–7, 390–3, 396

Yoreth (IXa) See *Ioreth.*

Yorkshire (VI) 246; *Yorkshire Poetry* 145

You and Me and the Cottage of Lost Play (I) (poem) 27–30, 32, 136

Younger Children (XI) See *Children of Eru.*

Younger Days (VII) 150

Younger Days (IXa) 68

Yôzâyan (IXb) The Land of Gift. 241, 247, 286, 312, 375, 388–9, 391, 396–7. For earlier names see *Land of Gift.*

Yrch (VII) See *Orcs.*

Yrch (XI) See *Orcs.*

Yssion (XI) Sindarin name of Ossë. 400. See *Gaerys.*

Ythlings (II) 'Children of the Waves'. 319–20, 322, 325, 331–2, 334; *Ythlingas* 331; described, 318. See *Eneathrim, Shipmen of the West.*

Yule (X) 307

Yule (XI) 351

Yule (XII) 121, 127; *Yuletide* 129; *Yuleday(s)* 121, 124, 128–9, 131–2, 138

Yule-days (VII) 368; *Foreyule* 368

Zaglûn (VIII) Orc of Minas Morghul. 212–13, 225; *Uftak Zaglûn,* see 225. (Replaced in succession by *Shagrat, Yagûl, Gorbag.*)

Zealand (V) 97

Zen'nabâr (IXb) The Land of Gift. 378, 380, 385, 388; earlier *Zenn'abâr* 378. (Replaced by *Abarzâyan.*)

Zen'namân (IXb) The Blessed Realm. 380, 385

Zeus (IXb) 221, 289

Zigil-nâd (XII) Silverlode. 279, 286. See *Kibil-nâla.*

Zigûr (IXb) Sauron. 231, 247, 250–1, 257–8, 284, 290, 311, 345, 353, 356, 363, 366–8, 371–2, 374–5, 380, 383–4, 389(-90), 392, 394 (and see 437).

Zimrahil (XII) See *Ar-Zimraphel.*

Zimrahin (XI) Wife of Malach Aradan. 234. See *Meldis.*

Zingil (IXb) [Ramer] The planet Venus. 205, 220

Zirak the Old (V) The teacher of Telchar the Smith. 319, 322

Zirakzigil (VII) One of the Mountains of Moria (Silvertine). 174–5, 432; *Zirak* 174 (and *Zirik*). Earlier name *Zirakinbar* 431–2

Zirakzigil (IXa) One of the Mountains of Moria (Silvertine). 45. Earlier name *Zirakinbar* (IXa) 45

Zirak-zigil (XII) Silvertine. 279